A LOVE FOR ALL TIME

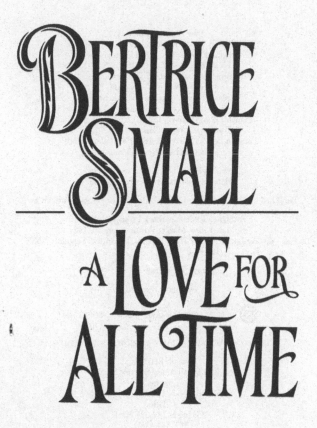

BERTRICE SMALL

A LOVE FOR ALL TIME

NEW AMERICAN LIBRARY

New American Library
Published by New American Library, a division of
Penguin Putnam Inc., 375 Hudson Street,
New York, New York 10014, U.S.A.
Penguin Books Ltd, 27 Wrights Lane,
London W8 5TZ, England
Penguin Books Australia Ltd, Ringwood,
Victoria, Australia
Penguin Books Canada Ltd, 10 Alcorn Avenue,
Toronto, Ontario, Canada M4V 3B2
Penguin Books (N.Z.) Ltd, 182–190 Wairau Road,
Auckland 10, New Zealand

Penguin Books Ltd, Registered Offices:
Harmondsworth, Middlesex, England

Published by New American Library, a division of Penguin Putnam Inc.

First Signet Trade Paperback Printing, July 1986
First Signet Mass Market Printing, January 1987
First New American Library Trade Paperback Printing, September 2001
10 9 8 7 6 5 4 3 2 1

 REGISTERED TRADEMARK—MARCA REGISTRADA

LIBRARY OF CONGRESS CATALOGING-IN-PUBLICATION DATA:

Small, Bertrice.
A love for all time / Bertrice Small.
p. cm.
ISBN 0-451-20474-3 (alk. paper)
I. Title.
PS3569.M28 L677 2001
813'.54—dc21
2001030887

Set in Goudy Regular
Designed by Leonard Telesca

Printed in the United States of America

PUBLISHER'S NOTE
This is a work of fiction. Names, characters, places, and incidents either are the product of the author's imagination or are used fictitiously, and any resemblance to actual persons, living or dead, business establishments, events, or locales is entirely coincidental.

BOOKS ARE AVAILABLE AT QUANTITY DISCOUNTS WHEN USED TO PROMOTE PRODUCTS OR SERVICES. FOR INFORMATION PLEASE WRITE TO PREMIUM MARKETING DIVISION, PENGUIN PUTNAM INC., 375 HUDSON STREET, NEW YORK, NEW YORK 10014.

A Love for All Time *is dedicated to my past, to the future, and to my here and now*

To Snoggy with love until we meet again—and we will,

And for her legacy to us, our son, Thomas Small,

And for my husband, George, who knows and loves us all,

For what would any of us be without love?

THE PLAYERS

IN ENGLAND

Aidan St. Michael—The heiress of *Pearroc Royal*

Payton St. Michael—Her father, the third Lord Bliss

Conn O'Malley, later *Conn St. Michael, Lord Bliss*—The youngest brother of Skye O'Malley, and a favorite of the queen

Elizabeth Tudor—Queen of England, 1558 to 1603

William Cecil, Lord Burghley—The queen's Secretary of State, and her greatest confidant

Elizabeth Clinton—Aidan's cousin, the Countess of Lincoln

Edward Clinton—Her husband, the queen's Lord Admiral

Robert Southwood—The Earl of Lynmouth, a son of Lady de Marisco, the queen's favorite page

Robert Dudley—The Earl of Leicester, the queen's favorite

Lettice Knollys—The queen's cousin

Skye O'Malley de Marisco—Conn's famous elder sister

Adam de Marisco—Her husband

Sir Robert Small—Their business partner in a trading house

Dame Cecily—His elder sister

Mag Feeney and Cluny—The servants of Aidan and Conn

Wenda and Nan—Nurse maids

Lady Glytha Holden—A lady of the court

Grace and Faith—Her twin daughters

Master Norton—The queen's chief dungeon master

Peter—His assistant

Miguel de Guaras—A Spanish agent

The Players

~~~

IN IRELAND

Brian, Shane & Shamus O'Malley—Conn's elder brothers, buccaneer
   captains
Rogan FitzGerald—Aidan's grandfather
Cavan FitzGerald—His bastard nephew
Eamon FitzGerald—His son and heir
Henry Sturminster—Lord Glin of Glinshannon

IN THE EAST

Murad III—The Turkish sultan
Nur-U-Banu—His mother, the sultan valideh
Safiye Kadin—His first wife, the mother of his heir
Ilban Bey—The agha kislar
Osman Bey—A famed Algerian astrologer
The Dey of Algiers—The sultan's governor in Algiers
William Harborne—First English ambassador to the Sublime Porte
Prince Javid Khan—The Crimean ambassador to the Sublime Porte
Esther Kira—The head of the House of Kira, a family of bankers and
   merchants
Jinji—Aidan's eunuch
Marta—Aidan's waiting woman
Iris & Fern—Her daughters
Sadira—English favorite of the dey
Zora—An ikbal of the sultan
Rosamund & Pipere—Captive English sisters
Tulip—Aidan's cat

Prologue

AUGUST

1577

*L*ord Bliss was dying. It had been a slow though painless process, but now as the summer was waning in a burst of apple-scented air and Michaelmas daisies he knew he had not much time left. If he had any regrets at all it was that he was leaving behind but one descendant, his daughter, Aidan. Even now she sat by his bedside, her fingers busy with her needle, his dear and dutiful daughter, a silent reproach to the selfishness of his deep love for her, for Aidan should have been married long ago. He, however, had been unable to part with her, the child he loved above all people.

He had waited so long for her birth. She had been everything that he could have hoped for in a child, and more. It was easy to forgive Aidan her female gender for her mother would give him other children, strong sons to match the healthy daughter. When she did not, it didn't matter, for he had already given that part of his heart that wasn't his wife's to his daughter. Now she would be alone, and what would become of her? he fretted to himself.

Would the queen to whom he was entrusting the wardship of his precious child really see to Aidan's happiness? When he had been able to clearly face his fate he had written to the sovereign placing Aidan's keeping in her charge, asking that Elizabeth Tudor see his daughter safely married to a good man of at least equal rank. He had only recently received a reply that impersonally agreed to his dying requests. Nonetheless, he had been enormously relieved.

He was leaving his daughter an heiress of great wealth both in lands and in monies. That wealth, however, had not been able to overcome the stigma of his less-than-noble name. Most good matches were made in the cradle, and he found to his regret that great names married great names. Then there was his daughter herself. Aidan was no great beauty. Oh, she was pretty enough when she worked at it, but most of the time her hair flew about in a hoydenish manner, and more often than not her face was dirty. When he remonstrated with her about it she always laughed, and replied, "I cannot oversee these vast tracts of lands that you and my grandfather persisted in amassing without riding about them, and riding is a dusty business, father."

He protested more often than not. "Leave it to the bailiff, my child. It is his duty to see to such things, and his family was on these lands before we were."

"The bailiff," replied Lord Bliss' daughter wisely, "responds best to a light rein, father, but nonetheless he must feel that rein. Besides, it does our people good to see me riding about. I know them all. Their names, their children, their problems, their aches and pains." She smiled at him. "They can only be loyal to the master they see, father."

When she smiled it was as if the sun had come from behind a cloud. Aidan was not the true and pure beauty that her mother had been, but beneath the tangles and smudges the prettiness *was* there. His own mouth formed itself into a little smile as he remembered his second wife, Bevin FitzGerald.

He never set eyes upon her until the day that she arrived from Ireland to wed with him. She had only been sixteen, and she was alone but for her servant, a suspicious creature named Mag. Most young women would have been frightened crossing the wild seas to another land and marrying a stranger, but Bevin had not been. She was as curious as a magpie, and as brave as the brace of wolfhounds that she had brought with her as her wedding gift to him.

A distant cousin of Elizabeth FitzGerald Clinton, the Countess of Lincoln, Bevin had, like her elegant kinswoman, a tall, and graceful carriage. She also had masses of warm reddish-chestnut hair, and light blue eyes that reminded him of the pale skies at dawn. Her expression was so incredibly sweet, her manner so pleasing that he was, to his surprise, very anxious to make her happy. When he had undressed her on their wedding night her skin had seemed wondrously fair to his experienced and jaded eyes. She had stood proudly before him in the flickering golden candlelight, confident in her youthful nudity, totally unashamed of her magnificent body. He had marveled that he had been so lucky as to have obtained such a great prize for his bride.

Lord Bliss' family, the St. Michaels, had been London merchants of wealth and good reputation. They had gained their titles and lands when Lord Bliss' grandfather had rescued Henry VII's eldest son, Prince Arthur, from serious financial difficulties with several less-than-reputable goldsmiths. It was only by chance that he had learned of the prince's misfortunes, and had cleverly bought the royal offspring's notes from the goldsmiths who were not wise enough to see the advantage in holding them as did Cedric St. Michael. Once in possession of the prince's notes, the clever merchant had generously forgiven him the debt.

The king, a miserly man in his old age, had been grateful. Not grateful enough to offer a royal appointment to the St. Michaels' trading houses which Cedric St. Michael had been hoping for, but grateful enough to bestow upon the merchant a small, somewhat run-down, royal estate in Worcestershire, and confer upon him the hereditary title of Baron Bliss. Lord Bliss' grandfather had graciously accepted the royal token which had cost the king not a copper pennypiece. Then he had quietly rebuilt his family's fortune.

Over the years as the lands bordering on the estate, which was known as *Pearroc Royal*, had become available due to the death or foolishness of their owners, the St. Michael family had bought them up. In this present generation what had once been a small estate was an enormous one, but despite their nobility each succeeding heir had learned his father's trade for sloth was as foreign to the St. Michaels as would have been a red Indian from the New World had they chanced to come across one.

The St. Michaels seemed to thrive almost magically, their ventures prospering far more than their fellows'. They never forgot their origins, but in the midst of all this good fortune they had one lack. Sons. There had been but one per generation until now when all that was left of the family was one daughter who seemed doomed to spinsterhood unless the queen kept her promise and found Aidan St. Michael a worthy husband.

The dying Lord Bliss had been wed twice. His first wife, the youngest daughter of a north country baron, had lived to celebrate thirty-four anniversaries with him. For twenty-five of those years she had struggled in vain to produce an heir for her patient and kindly husband. There had been miscarriages, and stillbirths, and even three children, a frail boy, and two little girls who had lived anywhere from several months to almost two years. Finally there were no more babies, and no hope of any. The first Lady Bliss fell into a melancholy that lasted nine years until her merciful release to death. Lord Bliss had felt some guilt at his relief that she had died while he still had the opportunity to remarry and sire children, but he understood King Harry's desperation at last.

He had been fifty-two years of age when his first wife died, and he dutifully mourned her for a full year for she had been a good woman. It was at the end of that time that he had had the very good fortune to be of financial assistance to Lord Edward Clinton and his wife who had been in need of additional monies to keep up with the court. Like many of the nobility, their credit was not particularly good. Lord Bliss had loaned them the amount requested, waiving any interest in a gesture of goodwill, though why he had done that he could never remember, except that he still grieved for his wife, and was not thinking clearly.

Lord and Lady Clinton were surprisingly grateful, and Lady Clinton in a burst of generosity said, "If there ever be anything that we might do for ye, m'lord, ye need not hesitate to ask it of us."

Suddenly Lord Bliss heard himself say, "I am a widower, madame, and I seek a wife. Would ye know of a suitable and healthy young woman not previously contracted?"

"It is just possible that I may be able to help ye, m'lord," came the reply. "Give me but a few days to think upon it," said Elizabeth FitzGerald Clinton graciously.

Afterward Lord Clinton had said gruffly to his wife, "What cheek the man has. His merchant antecedents yet show. I am glad that ye put him off, Beth."

"Nay," his spouse replied thoughtfully. "I do have someone in mind for Lord Bliss, Ned. My cousin Rogan FitzGerald in Munster has a young daughter, and no dowry for her. Not even a convent will have the girl without a dowry of some sort, but I will wager that Lord Bliss would be delighted to wed with the cousin of the Lord Admiral's wife."

"And becoming a family connection would not press us for repayment of the loan!" said her husband slapping his knee. "By God, Beth, yer a smart woman. I'm glad I married ye!"

Elizabeth Clinton smiled at her husband. "We are both well served in this," she said. "Lord Bliss' reputation is that of a decent man, and despite his origins he has certainly shown himself to be a gentleman. Having us as a connection will give his family greater legitimacy. My cousin Rogan's daughter is a big, healthy girl who will undoubtedly give her husband many children, and that is, after all, why Lord Bliss seeks to remarry."

The Lord Admiral's wife had been quite honest with Lord Bliss about her cousin's daughter. There was no dowry for the girl, for these Fitz-Geralds had no wealth. Bevin FitzGerald would come to her husband with no more than the clothes upon her back, but she was young, and she was healthy, and she was of good and noble stock. The inference was plain, and Lord Bliss was not a stupid man. Lady Clinton did not have to outline the advantages of this marriage point by point. He knew that his loan was now no more than a down payment on a noble young wife; but the match was made nonetheless for Lord Bliss was a practical man. Along with the marriage contracts sent to Rogan FitzGerald in Ireland went a purse heavy with gold for the bride to outfit herself with the finest materials for gowns and cloaks. Bevin FitzGerald, however, arrived with a small wardrobe for her father knew that the bridegroom would not begrudge such a beautiful bride anything, and, besides, Bevin's family had a greater need for the bridal gold than to waste it on clothing.

In the end it had turned out to be a love match, for Bevin FitzGerald St. Michael was a caring, sweet-natured young woman, and Lord Bliss was a gentle, lonely man, quite ready to love and be loved. Aidan had been born in the first year of their marriage. Her father was fifty-four, and her mother seventeen. She had been a big, strong, healthy baby from the beginning to her father's great delight. Her mother's easy confinement and birth pangs gave favorable portent of more children to come.

Lady Bliss spent the next few years of her short life gamely attempting to give her husband the desperately sought-for son and heir. The best she had been able to do was to produce but a set of healthy twin girls who had died with their mother in a spring epidemic when they were just past three, and Aidan was ten years of age. After that Lord Bliss had no one but his beloved only child. He might have married again as many men of his class did, but he did not believe he would ever again find the happiness he had found with Bevin, and he had reached an age where he could settle for no less. Aidan became her father's heiress, and her continued good health only convinced him that it was God's will he have but a daughter.

The years had passed too quickly, and now to his surprise, for he had always been robust, he found himself close to death; and Aidan was no longer a child. She was a young woman of twenty-three years. Bent over her embroidery frame she was totally unaware that her father was studying her with great concern. She had not her mother's looks, he thought regretfully as he had thought so many times before. Where Bevin's hair had been a full, luxuriant mass of tumbling chestnut curls, Aidan's hair was an odd reddish color, a mixture, he supposed, of his once blond hair and his wife's reddish-chestnut. It was also long and poker straight. Bevin had had eyes the soft blue of an April dawn, but Aidan's eyes were plain gray. He sighed softly. Why had Aidan not gotten her mother's perfect heart-shaped face instead of the common oval that was hers? In only two ways did their daughter resemble her mother, thought Lord Bliss. She had Bevin's lovely fair and creamy skin, and she was big and tall for a woman, as her mother had been.

Quietly he sighed again. He had done his best by his child. While Bevin had lived she had seen to it that their daughter learned all the housewifely arts such as the salting of meats and fish; the preserving of game; the making of jams and jellies and conserves; the varied and many duties of the brewhouse and the stillroom; baking; sewing; mending; cookery; care of both the herb and the kitchen gardens; the making of salves and ointments; smoking and curing; candle and soap and perfume making; the knowledge of how to lay in stores for the winter, or an emergency; the overseeing of the maids.

When Bevin and the twins had died Lord Bliss had taken upon himself the formal education of his surviving child as an antidote to his sorrow. To his total amazement, Aidan turned out to be a brilliant pupil, so much so that he had hired a retired scholar from Oxford to tutor her. She had learned languages, both modern and ancient, and was able to converse as easily in Greek and Latin as she could speak in English or French. She was taught mathematics and how to keep accounts; reading and writing; and histories both ancient and current. She had an ear for music and performed well upon the virginals, and upon the lute. The dancing master came to instruct her four times each week.

Far more important to Lord Bliss was her wit which was uncommonly sharp, and Aidan could repartee most cleverly with the quickest mind. He only wished she had entered society as other girls of her station did, but Aidan appeared not to be interested in such things. She constantly reminded him that she far preferred remaining home at *Pearroc Royal* with him, and it had pleased him to hear her words.

Lord Clinton had become the Earl of Lincoln in 1569, and Lord Bliss now realized that he might have pressed the connection between them for his daughter's sake, but he had been too selfish not wanting to lose her. Besides, he was a proud man, and after his marriage to Bevin Fitz-Gerald he had seen precious little of Clinton and his wife, famed now thanks to the poetry of the Earl of Surrey, as *The Fair Geraldine*.

Knowing that he was dying, he had left the wardship of his daughter not with the Clintons to whom she was related, for he knew that the powerful Earl of Lincoln would have simply absorbed Aidan into his household where she would have been lost; but rather with the queen herself. Hopefully she would find Aidan a place at court where she might be seen by eligible gentlemen, and sought after for her good character, as well as her wealth. The Tudors had advanced men of less-than-noble families than his, and they had been accepted by the old nobility. Perhaps his daughter would have her chance at happiness once she was at court. It was the best that he could do now.

"Father?" Her voice cut into his thoughts. "Would ye like some soup?" Aidan had risen from her embroidery frame and was looking questioningly down at him.

Suddenly he was terribly exhausted, and he felt every day of his seventy-six years. "Nay, my dear," he said weakly.

"Father?"

He saw the look upon her face. A look that told him she was torn by her concern for him, and by what she felt she must say.

He was unable to resist the wan smile that creased his face, and his voice when he spoke was warm with his love for her, and faintly teasing. "Say what ye must, Aidan. I can tell that ye will have no peace unless ye do."

"Father!" The words came in a rush. "I wish ye would reconsider yer plans for me. I am far too old to be placed in wardship! I will be sent to court, and I will hate it! I am not a social animal by nature, father. I will be pursued for my wealth, and eventually the queen will marry me off to suit her purposes alone. There will be no thought for my happiness. Please do not do this to me!"

"A woman must be wed," he said stubbornly. "She is not capable of managing her wealth without the help of a man. Yer an intelligent lass, Aidan, but a husband is a necessity for every decent woman of good breeding. Ye must accept my decision in this matter. I know yer reluctance to leave *Pearroc Royal*, but these are maiden fears. In yer whole life, my daughter, ye have never been anywhere past Worcester. This is my fault, but ye've trusted me before, and have I not always done the right thing for ye? The court is an exciting place, Aidan, and as the queen's ward the best of it will be open to ye. Yer no simpering maid to be gulled by the insincerity of a fortune hunter. Yer a survivor, Aidan. Ye always have been."

She sighed deeply. There was no arguing with him now. She would have to try again tomorrow. "Yes, father," she said obediently, and he smiled weakly up at her, exhausted with the effort their argument had cost him, and knowing she had not really accepted his will in this matter even if she was willing to let it rest for tonight.

"Yer a good girl, Aidan," he whispered huskily. He was so tired now. So very, very tired.

She stood up, kissing him gently upon the forehead, rearranged his coverlet so that it was once again smooth, and wrinkle-free. "It is late, father, and I am weary. We made both lavender and rose potpourri today after the linens were washed. The laundress has two new girls, and they need constant overseeing, as they are not yet skilled enough." She gave him a small smile that pierced his heart. "I will see ye in the morning, father. God grant ye a peaceful night."

"And ye also, my daughter," came the loving reply, and he had watched her as she left the room, tears for some unknown reason springing to his tired eyes.

When Aidan went to wake her father in the morning, Payton St. Michael, Lord Bliss, had gone to his maker, and his daughter, to her great dismay, found herself an undisputed, if unwilling, ward of the crown.

Part One

The Queen's Ward

1577–1578

Chapter 1

❦

"*I*ncompetents!" shouted the queen, and she threw her workbasket across the room. "I am surrounded by incompetents!" A movement by the corner of her eye caught her attention, and she turned to see her favorite page, the thirteen-year-old Earl of Lynmouth, waiting patiently for the royal storm to subside. "What is it, Robin?" she demanded in harsh tones, but young Robin Southwood knew that she was not angry at him, and so he gave her a dazzling smile.

"The newest royal ward has just arrived from the country, madame," he said.

"God's foot! Another one? Well, tell me, lad! Is my newest charge male or female? Yet in nappies, or out of them? Give me a name. Some hint or clue as to this latest in my long line of royal responsibilities." Her lips were now twitching with amusement seeing the laughter in the boy's lime-green eyes.

"It is a young lady, madame. She is Aidan St. Michael, the heiress and only living child of Payton St. Michael, Baron Bliss. Her home is near Worcester. The baron's estates border on my mother's home."

The queen thought a moment, and then nodded. "Lord Bliss' family is originally of good London stock," she said. "The family has always supported the ruling monarch, and stayed free of court entanglements to my knowledge. Well, Robin Southwood, fetch her in to me. I would see this orphaned heiress."

The boy bowed himself from her presence, and Elizabeth Tudor smiled to herself watching him go. He grew more like his late father every day, although he had greater warmth than Geoffrey had had at that age. That was due to his mother, that Irish vixen, Skye O'Malley, now married to Adam de Marisco, and exiled from court with her husband to the royal estate of *Queen's Malvern*.

I miss her, thought the queen. Our whole relationship has been difficult, and yet I miss the excitement that always surrounds dear Skye. Her glance took in the other women in the room, and she snorted softly to herself. With few exceptions they were a bunch of silly cows who giggled and minced their way through her court seeking husbands. Most of them had the barest of educations, and could converse on nothing but men and fashions, and the latest gossip. She knew that behind her back they mocked her, and made fun of her despite her sovereignty over them. They did not dare to do it to her face, for even they understood her power, the power of life and death that she held over them all. Still, she had few real friends among her women. They but served her to advance either themselves or their families.

The door to the queen's dayroom opened to re-admit young Robin, and two other women, one young, one in her late middle years. The younger woman was attired in a high-necked black velvet gown of dated design, but excellent quality. Upon her head was a white linen cap edged in lace. Immediately the queen's women ceased their chatter, and looked bright-eyed at the visitors.

"Madame, this is Mistress St. Michael," Robin said.

Aidan curtsied prettily as did her companion. The older woman, however, was obviously stiff in her joints, and needed her mistress' help to arise. This caused the queen's ladies to giggle, and Aidan's cheeks flushed, embarrassed.

The queen shot the women an angry look for she disliked such unkindness. "You are welcome to court, Mistress St. Michael," she said. "I did not know yer father, but yer family's good reputation precedes ye."

"Yer majesty is most gracious," Aidan replied.

"Now," said the queen, "the question is what are we do to with ye."

"If I might serve yer majesty," Aidan said sincerely, "I should count myself content."

There was a sharp giggle at Aidan's words which caused her to flush once more, and eyes narrowing the queen sought out the culprit, a dainty girl with a rosebud mouth and sunshine-yellow hair. "Ye find Mistress St. Michael's desire to serve me amusing, Mistress Tailleboys?" the queen purred, and the Countess of Lincoln, who was the queen's close friend, suddenly looked up and across the room at the newcomer.

Now it was Mistress Tailleboys who reddened, and stammering she attempted to excuse her rude behavior. "N-nay, madame, 'twas just that her gown is so old-fashioned."

"Fashion," said the queen archly, "is something I will admit to yer knowing. Fashion and loose behavior, Mistress Tailleboys."

Now the miscreant paled. Did the queen know about her recent assignations with Lord Bolton? How could she know? It was not possible, and yet sometimes it seemed as if the queen knew everything. She bit her lower lip in vexation. What could she say to her mistress?

Seeing the fourteen-year-old maid of honor hesitate, the queen knew she had hit upon something. So the wench is lifting her skirts behind my back, is she? Elizabeth hated it when her women played the wanton, and far too many of them did these days. "Are ye not responsible for my workbasket, Mistress Tailleboys?" she demanded.

"A-aye, yer majesty," came the nervous reply.

"And yet just minutes ago I sought to find something within that very basket, and it was a jumble with nothing in its proper place. It would appear, Mistress Tailleboys, that yer interests lay in other directions than serving yer queen. Since that is so, ye are dismissed from my service, and ye will return home immediately, this very day."

With a shriek of dismay Althea Tailleboys flung herself across the queen's dayroom, and at the queen's feet. "Oh, please, yer majesty," she cried, "do not send me home in disgrace! What will my parents say? How can I explain to them?"

"Ye will not need to," came the terrifying reply. "I will send a letter along with ye explaining my reasons for yer dismissal; expressing my displeasure at yer lack of manners, yer unkind heart, and yer lewd behavior with a member of my court who shall remain nameless."

Mistress Tailleboys swooned at the queen's feet with a sound that was somewhere between a cry and a moan.

"Remove that baggage!" snapped Elizabeth to the other maids of honor who had watched wide-eyed as one of their privileged number was lashed by the queen's sharp tongue. Each of the others was grateful that it was not she who was the queen's victim, and in unison they hurried to do their mistress' bidding, lest they incure her further wrath, lifting the dainty Althea Tailleboys between them, and stumbling from the room with her prone form.

"Mistress St. Michael," said the queen, her voice more kindly now. "Ye will take Mistress Tailleboys' place amongst my maids of honor, and my workbasket is now in yer charge."

"They will not like me for it," Aidan heard herself saying.

The queen chuckled. "No," she replied, "they will not, but they will tolerate ye because I have favored ye."

The Countess of Lincoln now moved forward. "Forgive me, madame," she said, "but I believe I am related to Mistress St. Michael. Are ye not the daughter of Payton St. Michael, and Bevin FitzGerald, my girl?"

"Aye, m'lady, I am," Aidan replied.

The countess turned her attention to the queen. "Bevin FitzGerald was my cousin, madame. It was I who arranged her marriage to Lord Bliss many years ago." She looked again at Aidan. "*Both* yer parents are dead?"

"Aye, m'lady. My mother and twin sisters when I was ten. My father just a month ago."

"Are ye impoverished?" came the next question as the Countess of Lincoln wondered whether the queen would make the Clintons financially responsible for the girl. She was relieved when Aidan said,

"Nay, m'lady. I am not impoverished."

Interesting, thought the queen. She does not wish to discuss her financial status with her relative. "All but Mistress St. Michael, and Robin are to leave me now," she said, and the Countess of Lincoln, and the two other ladies in the room curtsied themselves out of her presence. "Bring us some wine and biscuits, Robin," the queen commanded. "Ye may be seated, Mistress St. Michael. Take that high-backed stool there. I want to know about ye.

"Now," said Elizabeth Tudor, "who is this lady who guards ye?"

"She is Mag, my tiring woman. She came from Ireland with my mother, and served her until she died."

"And why were ye so reluctant to tell Lady Clinton of yer finances?" Aidan looked to Robin, but the queen said, "He has heard far more sensitive information than ye will divulge to me, my dear, and has always been most discreet. He will say nothing of what passes between us."

"Lady Clinton knows little about my family other than the fact she arranged my parents' marriage, madame. She did it in gratitude for a loan my father made to her husband many years ago. A loan arranged at no interest to Lord Clinton. My father had been widowed after many years of marriage, and no surviving children. When Lady Clinton offered him a favor in return for his favor he asked her if she knew of a woman he might wed. My mother was the daughter of Lady Clinton's cousin, and had no dowry to offer either a husband or a convent. Lady Clinton knew my father would be pleased to be related to her family despite my mother's dowryless condition, and so the match was made. Afterwards, however, we never saw them.

"I am, yer majesty, a very rich woman, but I do not want the knowledge of my wealth bruited about yer court. My father has asked that ye find me a husband, and indeed I hope that eventually ye will; but I have never been away from my home, and although I admit to having resisted my father's will in this matter, he was indeed correct when he promised me I should enjoy traveling, and the many new experiences I should find with ye. Still, I have never been courted by a man before. I have no experience in matters of the heart, and I am fearful of being taken advantage of by the sophisticated gentlemen of yer court.

"If my wealth were known, I should undoubtedly be overwhelmed by suitors seeking my gold rather than my heart. My lack of knowledge would make me prey to the guileful. If, however, my wealth is not known, then any who seek my company will do so out of a genuine caring for my person, and *not* my purse. For now, however, I am more than satisfied to serve my queen as best I can."

Elizabeth Tudor nodded slowly. The girl has a brain! She was not to be burdened with some flibbertigibbet of a wench this time. Was it possible she might even be educated as well? It was too much to hope for, but the queen asked anyway. "Have ye studied at all, Mistress St. Michael?"

"Aye, yer majesty. I speak Greek, and Latin, as well as French; and a bit of German, Spanish, and Italian. I can also read and write in these languages as well as our own."

"Mathematics?"

"Simple, as well as accounts," was the answer.

"Ye've studied history?"

"All that the old master from Oxford that my father employed could teach me. I can also compose poetry, dance, sing, and play upon two instruments."

"They are?"

"The lute, and the virginals, madame."

"Praise God!" the queen said. "Yer an educated female which means ye'll have something to talk about other than clothing and men."

"I'm not very knowledgeable about fashions, madame."

"Yer father has asked that I find ye a husband?" The queen smiled at Aidan.

"Aye, madame."

"And ye wish it so?"

"I would be like yer majesty, my own mistress, but I know that cannot be. I must eventually wed. I only ask that ye give me a little bit of time, madame. Besides, as my father was the final male of his line, he requested in his last testament that my husband take our family name, that his baronetcy not die out as did his life."

"Such a request is not unusual," said the queen, "and in deference to yer family's loyalty to my family I will honor that request. Now, Robin Southwood will show ye where ye are to stay here at Greenwich. Return with him as soon as ye have settled yerself. My workbasket is a shambles, Mistress Aidan St. Michael, and 'tis now yer duty to see it neat."

Aidan stood up, and curtsying to the queen departed the room with

Mag. Outside the queen's dayroom they found the Countess of Lincoln awaiting them. The young earl made the lady an elegant leg.

"Where are ye taking my young cousin, my lord?" demanded Elizabeth Clinton.

"I do not know yet, m'lady. I must find the master of the household, and see where we may squeeze Mistress St. Michael in. The palace, as ye well know, is full to bursting."

"There is an extra room in the attics assigned to us that we rarely use," said the countess. "Do ye know the one of which I speak?"

Robin, whose duty it was to know such things, nodded. "I do," he said.

"Where is yer luggage, cousin?" asked the countess.

"In the courtyard with my coach," Aidan replied. "My livery is blue and green, and my family's crest has a ship, a tree, and a red saltaire upon it."

Robin gave her a quick smile. "I will find it, mistress, and see it gets safely to ye," and with another smile and a brief bow he was off.

"Come along," said the Countess of Lincoln to her kinswoman, "and I will show ye the place ye'll be calling home. It will seem strange at first, my dear, but I came to court when I was just nine, the Orphan of Kildare I was called, and frightened though I was, I managed to survive as ye will too."

"I have not had time yet to be frightened," said Aidan honestly. "It is all so very exciting, and so very different from *Pearroc Royal.*"

"*Pearroc Royal?*"

"My home just west of Worcester."

"Well," said Elizabeth Clinton, "this will be no *Pearroc Royal*, my dear Aidan. I may call ye Aidan, mayn't I? And ye will call me Beth?" Without waiting for an answer she continued on. "The court is always overcrowded with those who belong here, those visiting, those trying to belong, and all their servants. Ned, my husband, as the Lord Admiral, has apartments wherever the queen goes, but usually the maids of honor must live their lives entirely in the Maidens' Chamber unless they have family or friends who can offer them space. The lack of privacy is terrible. I am very happy to be able to offer ye this little room, and it is little, Aidan. Nonetheless I am sure that ye and yer servant will manage. Are ye betrothed?"

"No, Beth. I preferred staying with my father. He was old, and he needed me. His dying request of the queen was that she find me a suitable husband. For now, however, I am satisfied to do what I can to serve the queen."

"Yer very wise, my dear," hummed the countess with approval. "Still, we mustn't allow our lady to forget her promise to yer father, and she might easily do that. The queen doesn't like her ladies leaving her for

18

marriage. I suppose it is because she isn't married herself. Whether her attitude stems from jealousy, or merely thoughtlessness, I do not know. How old are ye?"

"Twenty-three this past August nineteenth, Beth."

"Lord bless me, cousin! Yer a bit long in the tooth, ain't ye? We had best not tarry too long in finding ye a husband. I will speak to my husband, and we will see what eligible gentlemen are available. Ye'll probably have to wed with a widower, but then both my first husband, and Ned were widowers when I wed them."

As she had chattered on, the Countess of Lincoln had led Aidan and Mag up one flight of stairs, and then another, and another, and through a maze of corridors so winding that Aidan despaired of ever finding her way through them again. Finally they stood before a small plain oak door.

"Well, here we are, my dear. Go in, and make yerself comfortable. Young Robin will be along shortly with yer baggage, and he will lead ye back to her majesty," said Elizabeth Clinton. She gave Aidan a peck on each cheek, and was gone around the corner before the girl might say a word.

The more practical Mag threw open the door to the offered chamber, and gasped in shock. "God bless me, Mistress Aidan! 'Tis so small ye couldn't swing a cat in here."

Aidan peered in dismay, and her heart sank. Mag had not exaggerated one whit. There was but one little window, a tiny corner fireplace, and a bedstead which took up most of the floor space. She shook her head. "If my kinswoman says that it is all that is available, I must believe her, Mag, and be grateful that we have it. The bed will sleep two, never fear. We'll need each other's warmth in the night for I fear Greenwich is a damp palace."

They entered the room, and as they stood awaiting the baggage Mag looked about her with sharp eyes, and sniffed. "This place is filthy. I doubt it's been cleaned in months, and that mattress has got to go, Mistress Aidan. I've not a doubt it's filled with bedbugs and fleas, nasty diseased creatures!"

Aidan nodded, silently agreeing with her servant. "When the men come with the baggage, Mag, we'll have them remove the old mattress, and bring water for cleaning. I don't want my possessions set about until the chamber is clean."

They stood staring about them for what seemed a very long time, and then suddenly Robin Southwood was standing in the doorway, a smile upon his handsome young face. "Here we are, Mistress St. Michael, yer baggage."

Mag bustled forward. "Tell yer men to hold off, m'lord," she said. "I'll not have my mistress sleeping on yon moldy mattress. I want it removed, and water for the scrubbing down of this room. I've no doubt the place is alive with vermin!"

Robin grinned at her. She reminded him very much of his mother's tiring woman, Daisy, but she was certainly right. His mother had a passion for cleanliness that he had inherited although many of their contemporaries were less than fastidious about their persons and surroundings. Turning he ordered the footmen who had accompanied him to put the baggage down. Then he set them to work removing the old mattress, and dismantling the carved bedstead, and bringing water so that Mag might clean the chamber. "Leave yer cloak with yer woman," he said to Aidan. "I'll take ye to the Maidens' Chamber where ye can wash the dust of yer travels off, and then return ye to the queen. Yer woman will be safe, and I'll see that a serving wench is sent up to help her." He turned to a sturdy serving man. "You! Fetch a goodly supply of firewood for Mistress St. Michael's room, and remain to help her woman."

"Yes, m'lord," said the man, and he hurried off to do the young earl's bidding.

"Ye give orders well," Aidan observed.

"I am Southwood of Lynmouth," he said proudly as if that explained everything, and Aidan realized how very much she had to learn. "I have been at court since I was six."

"I must go back now with the earl," Aidan said to Mag, who barely nodded, and waved her along. Meekly Aidan followed the boy back through the confusing corridors and down the several flights of stairs.

"It must seem very strange compared to yer home," remarked Robin, "but never fear, Mistress St. Michael, ye'll soon find yer way about Greenwich as if ye'd been doing it all yer life."

"I'm not certain of all the turns yet," Aidan said, "but at least I know to go up three flights of stairs."

"I'll help ye for I well remember my first days here. If one of the other pages hadn't been kind, I would have been lost."

He ushered her into a room he identified as the Maidens' Chamber, and signaling to a serving woman told her to bring warm water that Mistress St. Michael might bathe. To Aidan's embarrassment Althea Tailleboys and another girl were also in the room, but strangely the deposed girl seemed not to hold any grudge against Aidan.

"Well," she said, "ye'll soon envy me safe at home, Mistress St. Michael. Serving the royal bitch isn't as easy as I expect you imagine."

"Althea!" chided the other girl. "Do not speak so of the queen."

Mistress Tailleboys shrugged. "Ye'll not repeat my words, any of ye," she said, "and what more can she do to me? I'm ruined! Coming to court was my chance to make a good match. Now my father is sure to marry me off to old Lord Charlton. The dirty lecher has had his eye on me for the last five years." She shuddered. "Always putting his hands up my skirts when he thought no one was looking. Well, at least I've cheated the lustful, old satyr of my virginity. That belongs to Henry Bolton!" she finished on a triumphant note.

"Althea!"

Mistress Tailleboys laughed harshly. "Oh, don't look so shocked, Linnet Talbot! Ye've all lifted yer skirts at one time or another."

"Well, I certainly haven't!" said Mistress Talbot, but Althea Tailleboys snorted at her friend's denial.

"I'm sorry ye lost yer place," Aidan said quietly. "It was not, however, my doing."

"I know that," came the reply. "If you'll take my advice, Mistress St. Michael, ye'll stay on the good side of the old dragon. She's as vain as can be, and has a cruel streak, but then ye'll find that out soon enough."

There was nothing more to be said, Aidan realized, and so she quickly washed her hands and face in the basin of perfumed water that the serving woman had brought her, and then looking into the mirror the woman held up Aidan sighed. Her hair was a disgrace! Doing the best that she could she tucked the wisps and strands carefully beneath her cap, and looking at herself again shook her head. From the few people she had already seen here at court it was painfully obvious that Mistress Tailleboys' observation had been correct. Her gown was, if not old-fashioned, dull. The black velvet of the fabric did nothing for her skin, and the high neckline was positively prim compared to what the other women were wearing.

"We must hurry," Robin said to her gently. "Don't worry about how ye look. I'll give ye the name of my mother's dressmaker."

She flashed him a quick grin, and Robin thought surprised that Mistress St. Michael wasn't quite the plain Jane he first thought her to be. With the proper clothing, the right hairdo, and jewels, she would be more than passable. He brought her back to the queen.

"Ahh, my country mouse is back." Elizabeth, who was now in a good humor, smiled. "Are ye settled?"

"Yes, madame, thank ye. My kinswoman, Lady Clinton, has most kindly given me a tiny room belonging to her husband for my servant and me."

"Very good," came the queen's reply, and then she handed Aidan her elegant workbasket.

Opening it Aidan frowned. " 'Tis a disgrace, madame. Yer box has not been neatened in weeks. 'Twill take me several days to sort it all out."

"I will want to work on my embroidery after supper," the queen said testily.

"Show me the piece, madame, and I shall gather the threads ye'll need," Aidan answered calmly.

Across the room Elizabeth Clinton smiled softly to herself. Mistress St. Michael was obviously going to be a credit to the family, and she could not have been more pleased. She must speak to her husband about the possibility of making a good match for the girl. One that would aid their family, and make it more powerful. She cudgeled her brain to remember what she could about the St. Michaels. There had to be money for it was rich merchant stock. There were certainly lands, and as she remembered both the late Lord Bliss and his father had had a mania for adding to the original grant. She couldn't be certain—after all it had been twenty-four years since they had had any contact with Lord Bliss and his family—but it was very possible that Aidan was an heiress of considerable wealth. She hadn't been quick to volunteer any information about herself, but thought the Countess of Lincoln, there was plenty of time to learn what she needed to know. In the meantime she must speak to Ned.

When it was time for the evening meal to be served Robin signaled discreetly to Aidan, and took her into the dining hall, showing her where to sit with the other maids. "Ye stay with the queen until she dismisses ye," he said. "I'll be there to lead ye back to yer room later."

"Thank ye, Robin. I may call ye Robin? Yer most kind."

"Of course ye must call me Robin. All my friends do, and I know already that I can count ye among my friends, Aidan St. Michael."

Suddenly at the end of the hall there was a disturbance of sorts. Two young men were quarreling noisily, and one of them made to draw his sword. "Not in the queen's presence!" hissed the other loudly. "I will apologize before I will allow you to ruin yerself that way, man!"

Looking at the man who spoke Aidan found herself unable to turn away. He was without a doubt the handsomest, most beautiful man she had ever seen in her whole life. Dark, dark hair. A tall, perfect form. The face with its high cheekbones, and dimpled chin. *What color were his eyes?* She was desperate to know, but stood too far from him to be able to see. "Who is *that* man?" she demanded of Robin.

"Who?" he said not particularly interested in a silly quarrel.

"Over there!" Aidan tried not to be too obvious as she pointed. "The taller of the two. The one who would apologize rather than fight in the queen's presence."

Robin glanced to where she indicated, and then he laughed. " 'Tis my uncle Conn O'Malley."

"Yer uncle?! He doesn't look a thing like you!" she protested.

"He's my mother's youngest half-brother, and I look exactly like my late father, Geoffrey Southwood," came the answer.

"I never saw such an attractive man in my entire life," Aidan almost whispered.

"He's called the Handsomest Man at Court," Robin said dryly. "All the ladies make fools of themselves over him. The queen calls him Adonis."

"It suits him," Aidan said softly.

Robin snorted. "Ye should have seen him when he first came to England. He was in truth a wild man with a black beard, and hair to his shoulders. He wore woolen trews and a plaid, and couldn't speak decent English, and when he did speak our tongue his brogue was thicker than a Devon fog. My mother sheared him like a sheep, taught him civilized manners, and brought him to court. Within a day ye'd have thought he'd been brought up here. Uncle Conn took to court like a gentleman to the manor born. He's one of the queen's favorites. She appointed him to her guard, the Gentlemen Pensioners. He has not done bad for a man who was born his father's last child."

Aidan laughed. "I thought," she said, "that the queen commended yer discretion. Yer gossip is better than a goodwife's on market day."

"I only told ye so ye'd be warned, Aidan," replied Robin, his voice sounding a trifle offended.

"Warned about what?"

"My uncle is the biggest rake this court has ever seen. I have already said women make fools of themselves over him, and they do. There hasn't been a night since he came to court that his bachelor's bed hasn't been warmed by some pretty chit. He can charm a duck from the water and onto a spit," said Robin with just the barest hint of admiration in his voice.

"How kind ye are to care about me," Aidan said to the young earl, "but I doubt yer uncle will ever look in my direction, Robin. I am not nor will I ever be one of this court's great beauties. It is said, however, that a cat may look at a king, and he really is gorgeous!"

Her words, and gentle manner somewhat mollified the boy Earl of Lynmouth. Looking up into Aidan's face he chuckled at the merriment in her eyes. " 'Tis a terrible word to use to describe a man," he said, but his mouth turned up in a grin.

"But 'tis true, Robin Southwood!"

Robin laughed. "I suppose it is," he said. Then finding the other maids of honor he said, "I'll fetch ye when the queen dismisses the court later," and he was gone to stand behind the queen's chair which was his own special post at meals.

For a moment Aidan stood not quite certain what to do, but then the girl she had seen earlier, the one called Linnet Talbot, made room for her on the bench, and she squeezed in amongst the others.

"Thank you," Aidan said. "I am sorry about your friend."

"It wasn't yer fault," said Linnet. "Sooner or later Althea was going to be sent home for one misbehavior or another. She had no sense."

"Have ye been friends long?"

"Only since she came here four months ago. Her family is from York. Where are ye from?"

"My estates are near Worcester," said Aidan.

"I come from Kent," said Linnet. "My family are distant relations of the Earl of Shrewsbury's family. Let me introduce ye to the others. This is Mary Warburton, Dorothy Saxon, Jane Anne Bowen, and Catherine Baldwin. The others aren't at this table, but then most of them are from the high-and-mighty families, and we're not. We're here because our families have connections that have allowed us the opportunity to serve the queen, and better ourselves. We all expect to find husbands while we're here. Do ye?"

"I am a royal ward," said Aidan, "and the queen promised my father that she would marry me off to a good man so I suppose I, too, expect to find a husband at court like the rest of ye."

"Yer older than we are," remarked Linnet.

"I'm twenty-three," Aidan answered the girl honestly.

"*Twenty-three!*" Linnet said the word as if Aidan had said one hundred and twenty-three. "We're all sixteen but for Cathy. She is fourteen. Why are ye not already wed? Did yer betrothed die? Have ye no respectable dowry?"

Aidan reached for the loaf of bread upon the table, and tore off a chunk. "My mother died when I was ten. I had been born to my father when he was virtually an old man, and he needed me particularly after mama was gone. I am, ye see, his only living child. How could I marry, and leave my father to suffer loneliness?" She helped herself to a wing of capon as a servant offered a platter with the neatly carved bird upon it.

The other girls nodded their agreement, and their sympathy of her plight. They fully understood the obligations of family. No decent girl would leave an aged parent. Curiosity satisfied they settled down to eat, much to Aidan's relief. What a bunch of cackling little hens, she thought amused, and then turned her attention to her own meal. She hadn't eaten since morning, and she was starving. She wondered if poor Mag knew where to eat, and decided to take her a capon leg, and some bread, and a pear in her napkin afterwards. Then conscience quieted she filled her own plate high with prawns broiled with herbs; a small individual game pie which was still hot, steam coming through the vents in its crust; a slab of juicy beef; and an artichoke that had been braised in white wine. Her first pangs relieved she refilled her now empty plate with a piece of Dover sole, a slice of pink ham, more bread, and a wedge of sharp cheddar cheese. Amazingly she yet had room for a large slice of apple tart that was served up with thick clotted Devon cream. She drank sparingly, however, as she had never had much of a head for wines.

Her young companions had watched as she had devoured the three platefuls of food without so much as a belch. Their eyes were wide with amazement at her appetite for they had been taught that a lady takes a little, and then eats only sparingly of her portion.

"Ye don't get fat?" Cathy Baldwin finally asked, unable to contain herself.

"Nay," said Aidan. "I'm a big girl, and I need my food. Yer but a little bit of a thing. Ye all are."

They nodded. It was perfectly true. They were all just over five feet in height, Dorothy being the tallest at five feet three inches. Aidan St. Michael had to stand at least five feet ten inches in her stockinged feet. She was fully as tall as many a man. Each had the same thought in her head. Poor Mistress St. Michael. What man would wed with such a big lummox of a woman? Her family was unimportant, and obviously she had no decent fortune else her father would not have commended her care to the queen. At least she would not be competition.

"We must all be friends," said Linnet Talbot speaking for the five of them, and feeling in her heart that she was doing the charitable thing.

"How kind ye are," replied Aidan. "I should indeed appreciate yer friendship for I am woefully ignorant of the court, and all its customs. I would not want to bring shame upon my family by being socially inept."

The five younger girls murmured sympathetically. "Do not fear," Linnet said. "We will guide ye through the maze of customs, and in just a few weeks ye will feel as if ye had been here all yer life. Everything else will pale in comparison to the life here at court. This is probably the most exciting place in the entire world to live! We are all so very, very lucky, aren't we?" She looked to the others for approval, and all nodded.

After the meal which ended with plates of paper-thin sugar wafers, and tiny glasses of Malmsey wine, there was dancing. The queen adored dancing, and any gentleman who hoped to catch her favor was wise to be light on his feet. Shyly Aidan watched from the sidelines as the evening progressed. She noted that Conn O'Malley danced with no one before he danced with the queen; but once he had satisfied honor, he never danced with the same lady twice. At one point two beautiful young women got into a scratching, screaming match over whose turn it was to dance with the handsome man. Aidan never knew what it was Conn said to the two to stop them, but suddenly both were sunny-smiled, and one waited patiently on the sidelines while the other danced with the tall Irishman.

No one asked Aidan to dance although her five pretty companions were most active. It didn't matter to her, however, as she was extremely weary from her trip. She far preferred watching for she was discovering that the court was a fascinating place, and she expected that once she was up on all the current gossip, and knew the faces that matched the great names it would be even more interesting. As intriguing as it all was she was relieved when the queen called an end to the evening, and she trekked out with all the other maids of honor to accompany her majesty back to her apartments. There Elizabeth Tudor dismissed her maids, and Aidan found Robin at her side ready to lead her back to her own little room in the attics of Greenwich Palace.

"The queen never found time for her embroidery tonight," remarked Robin mischievously.

"Nay, she did not," replied Aidan, "but had she, the threads she needed were ready, my lord Southwood."

He chuckled. "Yer going to do just fine here, Aidan. My sister, Willow, the Countess of Alcester, will be returning to court for the Christmas revels, and I shall introduce ye to her. She is a bit younger than ye, but yer much alike. I think ye'll find her a very good friend to have."

"Perhaps a lady of such exalted rank will not want to be friends with one of lesser rank."

"Willow married rank," Robin remarked, "although she has behaved her entire life as if she were royalty. She was plain Mistress Willow Small until she was fortunate enough to trap Alcester in her little net."

"She is older than ye then?"

"Willow will be seventeen in the spring. She met Alcester here when she was a maid of honor."

Aidan was curious. "How is it," she asked, "that yer family name is Southwood, and hers Small? Has yer mother been married twice?"

"My mother has had six husbands," said Robin calmly, "and children by all but the fifth one."

"How many children?" Aidan was fascinated.

"Eight. Seven of whom are alive today. My father, and my younger brother, John, died of the whitethroat. I have two elder brothers named O'Flaherty, one of whom is on his estates in Ireland, and the other at sea for he would one day captain his own ship. Both are wed. Willow is my older sister, but I have two younger sisters, Lady Dierdre Burke, and Velvet de Marisco, as well as a younger brother, Lord Padraic Burke. Padraic is a page with the Earl of Lincoln's household."

"Where does yer mother live, Robin? In Ireland?"

"My mother lives on the estate of *Queen's Malvern* which borders yer own *Pearroc Royal*."

"They are the family that moved in last year?"

"Aye."

"I never had time to pay them a call, and welcome them to the district as I should have. My father was ill then, and we could not entertain."

"I am sure," said Robin, "that my mother knew that, and understood."

At this point they had arrived back at Aidan's chamber. Robin bowed to her politely saying, "You will be expected to accompany the queen to chapel in the morning. I will come to fetch you. Good night, Aidan."

"Good night, my lord." She opened the door to the room and stepped inside. "Ohhh," she said softly as looking about she viewed the amazing metamorphosis the little chamber had undergone. A bright orange fire burned merrily in the corner fireplace, and next to it on her high-backed stool Mag sat nodding. The stone mantel above the fireplace held her silver candlesticks, and her small jeweled clock that even now ticked reassuringly. The floor beneath her feet was plush with her Turkey carpet, and both the single window, and the bed were now hung with dark velvet curtains. Aidan could see that the bed's old mattress was gone, and her own plump one was now in its place; the bed freshly made with her own lavender-scented fine linen sheets, a fluffy down coverlet, and pillows. Beneath the window was one of her trunks, but what had happened to the rest of her luggage she knew not. Still in all the improvement in her quarters was amazing.

"Mag." Gently Aidan shook her tiring woman who from habit awoke instantly.

"Yer back, my chick. Was it an exciting evening then?"

"Interesting," was the reply. "I have brought you something to eat, Mag." Aidan brought forth the chicken leg, the bread, and the pear from her dress pocket.

"Thank ye, dearie, but the serving wench the little lordling sent to help me showed me the servants' dining hall, and I have already eaten."

"Then I shall eat it," said Aidan. "I find that I'm hungry again despite the good supper I ate this evening. Oh, Mag! What wonders ye've wrought with this little nest of ours. I cannot believe it is the same room! Thank you! Thank you!" She sat down upon the bed, and began to devour the food she had brought with her.

" 'Twasn't easy, dearie, but once the bed was gone, and I could see what we had, I knew what to do. We scrubbed the flooring down good before I would allow yer precious carpet to be laid. I found a cabinet built right into the walls, and would ye believe there was a nest of mice in it? Well, they're gone now I can tell ye! After the carpet was put down I had them reassemble the bed against this wall rather than centering it in the room. It allowed me the room for a trunk by the window, and the stool by the fire. I've hung yer gowns in the cabinet, yer shoes are there, and the necessaries I've repacked in the trunk. Everything else I've sent back to *Pearroc Royal* with the coachman. We simply have no room, dearie."

"I know," said Aidan. "I'll probably have to have new gowns made, Mag, for the ones I've brought with me are out of fashion. The young earl has promised to introduce me to his mother's dressmaker."

"Ye'll not be wearing those shameless dresses that all but allow yer titties to hang out? What would yer father say!"

"If I wish to blend in with the others, Mag, I cannot look different now, can I? Do not fear. I can be fashionable without being immodest." She had finished the chicken, and taking the bone from her Mag opened the window and threw it out.

"I'll have no more mice in this room," she announced. "Next they'll be eating yer shoes!"

Aidan chuckled. "I hope not for I've not a pair to spare!"

Mag bustled about now preparing her mistress for bed. To Aidan's surprise there was a basin of warm water to wash her face and hands, and when Aidan had bathed the window was opened, and the water followed the chicken bone. "It ain't like our home," the tiring woman said wryly, "but we have to get rid of it somewheres. I hope we don't have to stay here too long." She helped her mistress into her white silk nightgown and matching nightcap with its pretty pink ribbons. Then she tucked her into the bed.

Feeling the soft mattress beneath her, warm and dry beneath the coverlet, the scent of lavender in her nostrils Aidan watched sleepily as Mag put away her clothing. She didn't think this was the time to explain to her servant that the queen had honored her greatly by appointing her a maid of honor. It was very unlikely that they would be going home in the near future, but Mag would learn to cope she knew. As soon as the older woman got her bearings, and found a place for herself amongst the others of her own kind she would feel better. Everybody needed someone. She yawned, her eyes drooping heavily. I wonder who my someone is, she thought as she slid off into sleep.

Chapter 2

T he golden-red flames from the great fireplace cast their wild shadows all about the chamber in Greenwood House. Upon the great bed two nude figures were entwined in passionate combat. The big man towered over the woman beneath him, imprisoning her neatly between his muscled thighs, thrusting into his partner's soft flesh over and over again with increasing rapidity until she suddenly shrieked a high-pitched wailing sound, and a moment later both figures collapsed, the man falling away from the woman.

For a long moment only the crackle of the fire could be heard in the room, and then a husky female voice purred, "Jesu, Conn! Yer the best lover I have ever had! I would venture yer the best lover in the entire world. What a pity this will be our last time together."

Conn O'Malley was surprised. Usually it was he who ended his affairs, and Lettice Knollys wasn't even really his mistress. She had never been, but they had been attracted to each other ever since he had come to court two years ago. In that time they had engaged in sweet combat any number of times although it had been done secretly, and discreetly for neither Conn O'Malley nor Lettice Knollys had any intention of endangering their hard-won positions in Elizabeth Tudor's exciting court. Lettice was the queen's cousin; a far prettier version of Elizabeth, and the queen had always been jealous of her. As for Conn he owed his place in the Gentlemen Pensioners to her majesty who greatly favored him. Elizabeth enjoyed her Adonis, as she had nicknamed Conn, not only for his physical beauty, but his quick tongue as well. No one could pass as pretty a compliment, nor spin as delightful a tale as Conn O'Malley.

"Ye devastate me, Lettice," he said in reply to her remark. "Have I done something to offend ye, sweetheart?"

Lettice Knollys propped herself up upon an elbow, and looked down on her lover through narrowed amber-gold eyes. "Don't tell me ye care, Conn?" she murmured.

He chuckled. "I'm curious. In one breath ye tell me I'm the world's greatest lover, and in the next ye say ye'll not see me again. 'Tis puzzling, sweetheart, wouldn't ye say?"

"So 'tis yer curiosity I've pricked, Conn, and not yer vanity. What a man ye are! I envy the lady who'll be yer wife one day."

He laughed. "I've no intention of marrying soon, Lettice. Women are like sweets, and I'm afraid I've got a terrible sweet tooth. I'll not settle down until I've sampled all the tasties I can. Now, tell me why ye'll not be seeing me again?"

"Because I am getting married," said Lettice Knollys.

"*Married?* I had not heard."

" 'Tis a secret, and ye must swear to me that ye'll not tell anyone."

"By anyone ye mean the queen. Don't ye need her permission to wed, Lettice? Yer family."

"I am a widow, Conn, not some maid in the first blush of youth. Neither I nor my children will ever be any threat to my cousin's throne, but ye know how she is, Conn. She'll refuse me permission just to be spiteful."

"True," replied Conn who had no illusions about the queen, although personally he liked her.

"Promise me ye'll say nothing," Lettice persisted, and bending down she bit at the lobe of his ear.

Reaching up he crushed one of her white breasts in his big hand. "Tell me who the lucky bridegroom is first."

"Not until ye promise me yer silence," Lettice said.

"Lettice, what are ye up to?" Conn O'Malley had a sudden premonition of disaster.

"*Swear first!*"

"I am not certain now I either should or want to know," Conn said.

Her pretty face stared down into his, her red hair tumbling about her shoulders. "Conn, please! Yer not just a good fuck, yer a friend, and frankly the only friend I would trust with this information. *I need to tell someone!*" she finished desperately.

He sighed. He had always had a tendency to be softhearted, and her plea touched him. Nay, it flattered him, if he were to be totally honest with himself. "All right, Lettice, I swear I will not reveal either yer plans or the bridegroom's identity; but I warn ye that if the queen learns of what ye've done, and asks me, I shall deny ye ever told me!"

"Fair enough, Conn." She paused, and then announced dramatically, "I am marrying Robert Dudley!"

"Jesu Christus!" Pushing her away he sat bolt upright in the bed. "I did not hear ye, woman! D'ye understand? I do not hear ye! God in his heaven, Lettice, are ye totally mad? The Earl of Leicester? The queen's very own beloved? Do ye have a death wish then? Bess will not bring a swordsman in from France to sever yer head from yer shoulders, she'll wield the bloody ax herself!"

"I love him!" Lettice cried dramatically.

"If ye love him then why are ye here in *my* bed? *Love Dudley?* Only Bess can see anything lovable in that snake! Whether ye'll admit to it or not, Lettice, yer marrying the queen's passion in order to spite her!"

"He wants children!"

"Then he'd have been wise not to murder his first wife, but poor Amy Robstart had to be disposed of in order that Dudley might marry the queen. Fortunately for England the man lacks finesse, and caused such a scandal with the deed that even Bess didn't dare defy the world to wed with him."

"It was never proven that Robert killed his first wife!" said Lettice Knollys angrily. "He wasn't even at their home that day, and hadn't seen her for weeks. She was dying of a canker in the breast, and killed herself rather than suffer any longer."

"Whatever the truth of the matter is, Lettice, Robert Dudley is Elizabeth Tudor's personal and private property. If ye marry him ye risk both of yer lives. Bess may not be able to wed him herself, but she doesn't want him to wed with anyone else either."

"We're being married tomorrow, Conn. Robert wants an heir. An heir I am already carrying!"

"He's got two by Lady Douglas Sheffield if he'd but acknowledge their marriage which she claims took place several years ago."

"Robert doesn't love Douglas Sheffield," Lettice Knollys said smugly. "He loves me! Loves me enough to defy that dragon on the throne to wed with me! Besides, he swears to me that he did not wed Douglas Sheffield."

"He's hardly defying Bess if she doesn't know about it," Conn observed wryly, "but then Dudley was never one for doing anything straight out in the open."

"Yer opinion is formed by yer sister Skye," said Lettice. "She never forgave Robert for casting her aside."

"Lettice, if ye believe that then yer a bigger fool than I think ye are for even considering to marry the Earl of Leicester. Yer husband-to-be raped my sister while she yet mourned her third husband. The queen knew it, and allowed him to get away with it in order to keep him happy because she yet believed then that she might wed with him herself."

32

"I'll not stay here and hear my betrothed insulted, ye upstart of an Irishman!" Lettice shouted at him indignantly.

"Nay," said Conn with a wicked smile upon his face, "but ye'll stay because no one, ye ginger-haired vixen, makes love to ye like I can, and yer right! This is the last night we'll spend together unless yer widowed quickly. I'll not fuck Dudley's leavings, but it delights me that he'll never know he'll be fucking mine!"

"Whoreson!" Lettice screamed, and hit him across the face as hard as she could.

He smacked her back, and grabbing at her they wrestled violently across the great bed. "Bitch!" he hissed at her. "Yer nothing more than a bitch in heat, Lettice!"

"And ye, Conn O'Malley, are a bastard with an unquenchable itch! I hope ye never find a woman to satisfy that itch!" She clawed down his broad back.

She was right, he thought, and damn her for it! He adored women, adored making love to them, adored giving them pleasure, and although he never failed to gain a physical release in his lovemaking, he had never yet met a woman who really satisfied him. He had never yet met a woman he could love. Angrily he jammed his knee between her soft, white thighs forcing them to part for him. Brutally he drove himself into her pushing himself as deeply as he could go, ramming into her over and over and over again; wanting to hurt her as her astute knowledge of him had pained him.

Instead Lettice urged him on with moans of white-hot desire. "Ahhh, God's cock, Conn! Yes! Yes! Yessssss!" She writhed lewdly beneath him encouraging him to give totally of himself. "Fill me full, my wild Irish lover! Stuff me till I burst! Ahhh! God, Conn! 'Tis not enough! Don't stop! *Don't!*" She thrust her hips up at him in a rapid rhythm, never ceasing her lustful litany. "Do it to me, Conn. Use me! Ahhhhh! Ohhhhh! Yes! Yes! Yessssssss!" This last word moaned in a pitch that rose in intensity until it was almost a scream, and then Lettice stiffened for a brief second, and he felt her passion break as his own poured into her hot body in fierce staccato bursts that left him momentarily defeated.

Then suddenly Lettice said, "God, I'm going to miss ye, ye randy bastard! Dudley fancies himself a great lover, but Conn, he doesn't know the half of it!" She laughed throatily down into his face and unable to help himself Conn laughed, too.

"What a hot bitch ye are, Lettice," he gasped. "Thank God 'tis Elizabeth Tudor who's queen and not ye!" Rolling off her he slid off the bed, and walking across the bedchamber to a sideboard poured them each a goblet of dark, sweet red wine. He returned to the bed, and handed her one of the two goblets.

"What time is the wedding?" he demanded.

"Just before dawn in my family's chapel," she said.

He laughed again. "Yer going from my bed to yer wedding with another man? Have ye no conscience, woman?"

"Of course I do," she said indignantly, "but what I do before my marriage to Robert is not his business, Conn."

"I hope ye have reliable witnesses," he remarked. "Don't forget that Douglas Sheffield claimed marriage to Dudley, yet the priest could not be found when she sought to have her first child legitimatized."

"My father, the Earl of Warwick, the Earl of Lincoln, and Lord North are witnessing the marriage which will be performed by our own family chaplain," Lettice Knollys said smugly. "They are all sworn to secrecy. There will be no doubt as to the honesty of *my* marriage lines, or the legitimacy of *my* children, Conn."

"I should not have underestimated yer determination, sweetheart," he answered her.

"What I am determined to, Conn darling, is to have ye at least half a dozen times this night," she murmured seductively placing her goblet upon the bedside table, and lying back against the pillows.

"Ahh, Lettice love, ye've always been overgreedy for the finer things that life has to offer, haven't ye? I'm not sure we have all that time as much as it saddens me to disillusion a lady." His finger teasingly encircled one of her nipples.

" 'Tis just past midnight," she said, "and it is not necessary that I leave ye till five." Then she pulled his head down so she might kiss him.

He chuckled deep in his throat. "Lettice, I can but try. It would grieve me deeply to disappoint such a worthy opponent," and then he gave himself up to her greedy lips.

One minute blended into another as the night progressed, and Conn didn't even remember falling asleep, but suddenly he found himself waking with a start, and he was alone. The place where she had lain next to him was still faintly warm so she was not long gone. He pulled the coverlet up, and over his big frame, and snuggled down into the warmth. Good Fortune, Lettice, he thought sleepily. Yer going to need it, especially when Bess learns of what ye have done. She'll not hold her precious Lord Robert responsible, my pet, but rather 'tis ye who will bear the entire blame of this episode. Then he fell back asleep.

When he opened his eyes again Cluny, his body servant, was drawing back the draperies of the bedchamber. "Good morning, m'lord Conn.

God grant ye had a good night, and from the looks of ye, ye did." Cluny's brown eyes twinkled in his wrinkled face. He had the look of the little people about him.

"How many times have I told ye that I'm no milord, Cluny?"

"Well, ye will be in time, I'm certain." Cluny always had the same answer for Conn, and Conn usually laughed.

This morning, however, he didn't feel like laughing. His mouth was dry. His whole body in fact had been wrung dry by his greedy partner of the night before. "Get me some wine," he groaned. "That vixen nigh killed me."

Cluny cackled knowingly, and did his master's bidding, but as he handed him the goblet he gently scolded him. "Ye can't go on like this forever, wasting yer youth, exhausting yerself on white English thighs, m'lord. 'Tis past time ye were married. Look at yer brothers. They're all married."

"*Cluny!*" The sharpness of his own voice made him wince. "Dammit, man, don't be holding up the fine example of Brian, Shane, and Shamus to me. Have ye looked at their women? None of them are much past twenty, and already they're worn out and faded. Thank ye, no!"

"Life isna easy on Innisfana," Cluny reminded him.

"No, it isn't, and that's why I came to England. I had no mind to go pirating with my brothers, and what else was there for me? Here in England I have a position of respect as a member of the queen's personal guard. My investments with my sister's trading company have made me a rich man. I'm content for now."

"A rich man needs a wife to give him sons. Ye have gold, but no land to call yer own. Even this house in which ye live belongs to yer sister, and were she not barred from the queen's court ye'd not have even that, m'lord."

"Yer beginning to sound like my mother," grumbled Conn.

"Yer mother is a good woman, and yer father, may God assoil his soul, Dubhdara O'Malley, him of sainted memory, married young so he might breed up a fine crop of sons."

"And didn't stop until he killed one wife with his excesses, and given my mother four sons in as many years. Had he not died when he did my own mother might not be alive today. Dammit, Cluny, have not my three brothers given the O'Malleys enough heirs for the next generation?" Then he chuckled. "I could almost wish my father were alive to see it. Five sons he finally bred. One a priest, three no better than he, pirates all with randy cocks, and me! The Handsomest Man at Court!" He burst out laughing.

Cluny, however, did not laugh with his master this time. Rather his face was disapproving, and finally, he said, "Yer not like yer brothers, m'lord. Yer like yer sister, Lady Skye. She is nothing like her sisters. You two are the rare birds in Dubhdara O'Malley's nest."

"What of Father Michael and Sister Eibhlin, Cluny? Surely yer not putting them with the others; the three pirates and the four disapproving goodwives our father sired?"

Cluny shook his head. "They went to the church, m'lord," he said as if that explained everything. "Church people are always different. What I mean was that ye and yer sister, Lady de Marisco, are the ones with the ambition. Look how far she's gone, and her just a mere woman."

The admiration in Cluny's voice for Skye bordered on the worshipful, thought Conn, but he couldn't blame his man. He, too, adored his older sister. She was intelligent and wise and loving. The damnedest, and the most incredible woman God had ever created. She met life head-on which was something he had to admit to himself that he didn't. He was more cautious, looking for his opportunities, taking them quickly when they appeared. He wasn't a stupid man, he knew, but he relied a great deal upon his appearance and his charm to carry him through life. Perhaps he relied on those things a little too much, he thought suddenly. As quickly, however, he shook his guilt off, and said easily, "I shall try to reform, Cluny, but not today. Today I am going to sleep off the excesses of the last few nights. I am not due at court until tomorrow, but when I return there, I had best be in very good form. The queen does not like a dullard, and our fortunes are, after all, tied to those of our Gloriana."

Cluny nodded. He, too, was no fool, and he knew that his master spoke the truth. Still he wished that Conn would marry and settle down. He was apt to burn himself out if he continued on his self-destructive path much longer. He owed a great deal to Conn O'Malley. Conn had taken him into service when a ship's mast had fallen on him in the drydock where he had worked as a carpenter. His arm had been crippled in the accident, and he was unable to continue on with his craft. He might have starved to death, and his mother with him, but for Conn O'Malley. Conn had assured him a weakened arm would not hinder him in his work as the young O'Malley's valet, and had taken him on. His elderly mother had died soon afterward, but her death had been a peaceful and a comfortable one thanks to Conn O'Malley, and Cluny had felt no distress in leaving Ireland and following his young master to England when Conn had come with his sister several years ago.

Cluny had grown up on Innisfana Island where Dubhdara O'Malley's family had their stronghold. They were *his* family. He was *their* man. Like

Conn he was a man who took opportunity when it presented itself, and service with Conn O'Malley in England offered him a world such as he had never seen before. England itself had been a revelation with its fertile, well-watered valleys and its great city of London. He went to court with his master, and knew all the great names that went with the noble faces. He was on speaking terms, and in some instances drinking terms, with servants of the oldest and greatest names in England. His was a position to be envied. If he regretted anything it was that he could not write all these wonders to his friends back home, but then had he been able to, they could not have read his letters. Cluny would have liked to tell them how this year at the Feast of All Hallows her majesty had appointed his master the Lord of Misrule for the entire holiday season which began that very night of October 31, and would run until Candlemas on February 2.

The court could not remember a more fun loving Lord of Misrule than Conn O'Malley. He was constantly inventing wonderfully funny games and penalties which he imposed upon the court. Having been duly "crowned" by her majesty he then picked a bodyguard of twenty-five young gentlemen of the court, and dressed them at his own expense in liveries of grass green and scarlet, gold ribbons tied about their arms, and tinkling brass bells about their legs. They were equipped with gaily painted hobbyhorses, or dragons; and wherever Conn went, he and his followers were followed by a group of musicians hired for the season by the Lord of Misrule.

One Sunday morning Conn and his followers accompanied by their musicians playing upon drums and pipes burst into the queen's chapel during services. Crowned with a tinsel crown Conn was borne in upon a litter while about him his attendants capered and danced down the nave, and up the chancel halting to demand "proper obeisance" from not only the royal chaplain, but her majesty as well.

"Conn O'Malley!" scolded Elizabeth Tudor, "do ye dare make a mockery of our Lord God?"

Conn slid from his litter, and towering above the queen looked down at her saying, "Nay, Gloriana. I am merely making a joyful noise as the Bible says!"

About them the congregation tittered, the solemnity of the service having been destroyed. Even Elizabeth smiled in spite of herself, and rapped him sharply upon the arm with a small jeweled mirror that hung from her waist upon a gold chain. "Yer a disrespectful rogue, Conn!"

"Nay, Gloriana, 'tis ye who have shown disrespect to the Lord of Misrule, and as a forfeit I claim a kiss of ye." Then before the queen could protest Conn bent down, and engaged her lips in a most ardent, and drawn-out kiss.

Elizabeth was riveted to the spot for a long minute while about her there were gasps of surprise and shock. She did not, however, pull away from him; and when finally the kiss ended she was rosy in color, turning an even deeper hue when Conn whispered in her ear so only she might hear, "Isn't it nice to know yer still alive, Bess?"

The queen burst out laughing, but Robert Dudley, the Earl of Leicester, snarled, "Ye go too far, O'Malley! Perhaps a visit to the Tower would help to cool yer heels."

"Since ye'll never be king, Dudley, 'tis not yer decision to make, is it? At least in me Bess finds an honest man."

"Gentlemen, enough!" The queen's voice was sharp. She was annoyed at Leicester for having broken the spell. Conn O'Malley was a virile and handsome young man, and she had enjoyed his daring kiss; a kiss he would have never given her were he not protected by his office. "It is the season of joy and goodwill, gentlemen, and I will have no squabbling about me. Rob, yer too quick to take offense where there is none. As for ye, Conn O'Malley, yer much too bold."

"And ye would have me no other way!" Conn quickly riposted falling back onto his litter; and quickly he signaled his bearers, and was borne off out of the royal chapel while behind him the queen laughed heartily at his antics.

The eleventh of November was St. Martin's Day, and as the venerated saint had ordered slain a noisy goose who had interrupted his sermon, it was goose that was served in all the best households. Conn found offense in almost every great name at court that day, and gathering them all up he had his assistants herd them along, the noblemen forced to waddle like geese, and cackle, too. The rest of the court was convulsed with laughter, and most of Conn's victims were, too, when their tempers cooled.

The twenty-fifth of November brought the Feast of St. Catherine which was usually the time of the apple harvests, and so was celebrated with apple dishes and cider. There was dancing, and bear baiting, and Conn terrified the ladies of the court by dressing up in a bear's skin, and rushing amongst them growling fiercely which caused them to run shrieking and screaming while he chased after them, and catching them kissed and tickled them.

December brought St. Nicholas' Feast on the sixth, St. Lucy's on the eleventh, and St. Thomas' on the twenty-first. Conn oversaw all the feasting and hilarity of the season with as good a will as anyone had ever known in a Lord of Misrule. It was up to him to plan and see executed all the masques, and mummeries and entertainments of the holidays. Greenwich was decorated with garlands of greenery fashioned from ivy, bay, and laurel leaves which were interspersed with red berries. Enormous candles of the purest beeswax were placed upon mantels and sideboards; slender columns of creamy wax were set in the silver candlesticks and candelabra.

Elizabeth couldn't remember ever having laughed so hard as she did the day the Yule log was dragged into the hall, Conn dressed in scarlet silks and cloth of gold, perched upon it singing loudly a popular song of the season:

> Wash yer hands or else the fire
> Will not tend to yer desire:
> Unwash'd hands, ye maidens know,
> Dead the fire though ye blow!

Everyone rushed to help with the log, lord and lady alike, as well as the servants for it was considered good luck for the coming year to aid in bringing in the Yule log. Although Elizabeth usually preferred Christmas festivities in which others participated while she watched, Conn's wild revelry reminded her of her childhood in her father's court with all its unbridled gaiety, and she was frankly enjoying it. He was an exciting man, her wild Irishman, and far less complex than his elder sister, her enemy and her friend.

Christmas Day began with the entire court attending services in the queen's chapel. Most had been up all the night, helping to ring in Christ's birth as midnight had come, and bells all over England pealed joyously. Afterward there had been a great deal of drinking, and too soon it was time to attend chapel. The queen had had the good sense to get a few hours' sleep as did some of her women.

St. Stephen's Day followed Christmas, and then St. John's Day, The Feast of the Holy Innocents, New Year's Eve and New Year's Day, and finally the Feast of Twelfth Night. Each evening saw dancing, and feasting, and masking, and games as the court cavorted happily. On New Year's Day Conn O'Malley, the Royal Lord of Misrule, presented the queen with a brooch so magnificent that it was talked about for several days. The design was that of a crowing cock that had been carved from a solid ruby. The bird's wing and chest feathers were outlined in gold. He had a bright diamond eye, and was crowned with a golden coxcomb that was tipped with diamonds. The cock was then placed upon a round golden sunburst whose rays were studded with tiny diamonds. The brooch had been presented in a carved ivory box that had been enclosed in a cloth-of-silver bag.

Elizabeth was visibly astounded, and delighted by the magnanimity of his gift. The queen was in a particularly good humor today. For several months she had borne a painful ulcer upon her leg which, as suddenly as it came, now healed. For a moment she could not find her voice, and when she did she said, "Yer a rogue, Conn, but yer a rogue with exquisite taste."

He smiled. "The ruby came off a Portuguese galleon that my brothers took. They thought I should enjoy the stone, and so they sent it to me. I, however, thought of the design, and had my jeweler execute it. I am the cock, but ye, my Gloriana, are the sun without whom I could not crow. Remember me whenever ye wear the brooch."

The queen nodded thinking as she did that she couldn't ever remember amongst all the flattering tongues that spoke to her one that spoke with such sincerity. There was nothing hidden in Conn's nature, and she found it a relief.

When Twelfth Night came Conn was wise enough not to try to surpass his New Year's gift. He gave the queen a simple chain of gold and diamonds to which her brooch might be attached thus serving a double purpose for the jewel. It might be either pin or pendant. The queen was delighted, and the other men of her court envious of the current influence held by Master O'Malley.

"Ye'd think he was to the manor born instead of a bog-trotting, ignorant Irishman," sneered the Earl of Leicester to Lord Burghley.

William Cecil smiled a frosty smile at Robert Dudley. "I find Master O'Malley quite harmless both politically and dynastically. He pleases the queen with his antics, and asks nothing in return. It is a refreshing attitude on the part of a gentleman of this court, and an unusual one. What is there to dislike in the man, my lord?"

"He is a commoner! He has no right to be here at court rubbing elbows with his betters, even making mock of them in his exalted position."

"Yer jealous," observed Lord Burghley, "but lest that jealousy overcome yer memory, remember who created ye Earl of Leicester, Robert Dudley. It is the queen who is all-powerful here, and who says who may come, and who may stay, and who may be an earl. She could just as easily create yon handsome Irishman a duke." Then with a smile William Cecil looked out upon the wild game of Blind Man's Bluff currently being played in the queen's presence.

Conn O'Malley, blindfolded, was stumbling with outstretched arms amongst the queen's maids of honor who scampered shrieking all about him. He stopped for a moment, listening, attempting to determine a near victim. Then suddenly he swung completely about, and reaching out his hands closed about a supple waist. Without even waiting to draw the blindfold off his eyes he pulled the girl toward him, and found her lips with his own. To his very great surprise, the generous mouth beneath his was stiff with inexperience, but his prisoner made no attempt to escape him. She had to be one of the youngest girls serving the queen, but yet she could not be for she was tall against him. Expertly he molded both his body and his mouth against the girl, and then felt her lips soften beneath his while at the same time she trembled; a reaction which immediately brought out a protective instinct in him. *Who was this wench?*

He loosened his grip upon her just slightly, and murmured against her lips, "Don't be frightened, sweetheart," and reaching up he removed his blindfold to see the girl. He didn't recognize her at all, and as his green eyes met her gray ones she blushed scarlet, and with a little cry fled to the queen's side. The other girls were now giggling, and he asked one of them, "Who was that?"

"Mistress St. Michael, the queen's latest ward. The queen made her a maid of honor when she dismissed Althea Tailleboys, and sent her home."

He looked to the girl who now sat on a stool by the queen's chair, her slender fingers now busily, almost too busily, untangling the rainbow-colored threads from the queen's embroidery basket. He couldn't ever remember having seen her before, but then there was nothing about her to distinguish her. She had never been kissed before, of that he was certain. Yet he could see she was not the very young girl that most of the queen's maids were. How did it happen that a girl of her age hadn't been kissed before? Her lips had been incredibly sweet. It was her innocence, he supposed, though he thought her rather old to be so innocent. Then with a shrug he replaced the blindfold, and began anew to play Blind Man's Bluff amid the giggling girls of the queen's inner circle.

He didn't think about Mistress St. Michael until later, and then only briefly as Lady Glytha Holden kissed him with such a passionate expertise he was almost left breathless. How different, he thought, as he loosened his mistress' laces so he might fondle her breasts, how very different Glytha's kisses are from the little wench I kissed earlier.

Glytha stirred in his arms. "What are you thinking of?" she demanded of him.

"I'm thinking that you have the most beautiful tits," he returned, bending to kiss each nipple of the firm breasts she presented him. She really was a lovely woman; small-boned, and not too tall, with fine white skin, and gold hair that held just a hint of red; eyes as blue as a lake. She had a pious Puritan husband who having gotten a son and heir as well as twin daughters upon her preferred being on his knees in prayer to being on his wife's body in passion. Though her daughters were of marriageable age and Glytha herself was past thirty, she was still filled with lustful fires. Conn was not the first of her lovers, nor would he be the last. Even now they were becoming bored with each other, and Conn had only recently noticed what delicious and ripe miniatures of their mother Grace and Faith Holden were.

"Yer a liar," Glytha said petulantly. "Yer thinking of another woman, aren't ye?"

"What woman?" he countered.

Glytha sniffed. "I don't know what woman, but not me, Conn. Every bitch at court is sniffing at yer tail. How can I hope to keep yer interest when all the others buzz about ye like bees about a particularly sweet flower?"

It was the perfect opening, and he took it. "Are ye saying that yer leaving me, Glytha?"

"I think it's best, Conn."

They made love that night, and in the morning parted amicably. Glytha Holden, however, would have been furious to learn that her twin daughters, learning quickly that their mother had discarded yet another lover, began to stalk the handsome Irishman. The twins looked like angels, but they had lost their virtue at thirteen to cousins who were delighted to discover how lusty and eager for passionate play Mistress Grace and Mistress Faith were.

Reared in the country because their father feared their contamination by the wicked world the twins and their brother had been left to the haphazard care of servants while their parents followed the court. Lord Edwin Holden, Baron Marston, was a financial wizard whose expertise was necessary to Elizabeth Tudor. When his son, Edward, had been seven, and the twins five, the boy had been fostered out to another noble family to begin his education. His sisters, however, had remained home in the Kent countryside until one day two years ago their mother had realized that unless they came to court it would be hard to find them suitable husbands as there were no young men of ranking families near their Kent manor.

Grace and Faith had taken to court easily. They had been trained all their lives for this, and they joined in with little difficulty or discomfort. The young gentlemen of the court found them particularly adept at naughty games although clever, they did not give a great deal lest they spoil their chances of a good match. Conn O'Malley, however, was another matter. He was not a man that their father would consider for ei-

ther of them being Irish and Catholic to boot. The ladies loved to talk
about him, but they had never heard it said that Conn talked about his
conquests. They knew that they might have their little fling with him,
and no one the wiser. It had been two years since they had indulged in
carnal play with their cousins. Both twins were adept at giving each other
pleasure, but it was not, they both agreed, like having a man inside you.
They decided that the direct approach was best, and Conn arriving home
after being on duty for three days, in addition to his duties as Lord of Misrule, found two naked nymphs in his bed.

"Jesu!" he swore softly, his green eyes glittering with anticipation, his
weariness suddenly evaporating. "Cluny, go to bed!"

The manservant cackled, and without a word disappeared from the
bedchamber, closing the door to the room firmly behind him as he went.

Conn felt a grin splitting his face. "Mistress Grace and Mistress Faith,"
he said. "How nice of ye both to come and visit. I wonder, however, if yer
mama and yer papa know of yer whereabouts."

The twins giggled, and then Grace said, "We're neither of us virgins,
and since we've come to court we haven't fucked."

"We don't dare for fear papa will find out if we do, and then we'll not
be given fine husbands," chimed in Faith. "Ye won't tell on us, will ye?"

"Nay, sweeting," said Conn pulling off his clothes so he might join
them in the bed. "I'm rather flattered that ye think me man enough to
satisfy ye both."

"Oh, we know how to keep a man's cock good and stiff," said Grace
matter-of-factly. "Our cousins taught us, and we practiced enough on
them before we came to court. There'll be enough of ye for both of us."

He was somewhat nonplussed by her, but then he sandwiched himself
between the two girls, and pulling Faith to him he kissed her hungrily, his
tongue plunging into her mouth while Grace took him into a warm
mouth, and tugging upon his manhood sent darts of purest desire shoot-
ing into it. His hands found themselves filled with soft, warm flesh, but
Faith was pulling away from him to rub her pink-tipped breasts over his
face. He groaned and captured a nipple to suck upon. Then Grace was
mounting him, and plunging down to encase him within her hot sheath
while Faith straddled his head offering him her hidden flesh to feast upon.

The twins had not lied when they claimed proficiency in the arts of
love. Each time he believed himself close to release they seemed to sense
it, and they would pull back, switching places to begin anew with him
until he thought that he was going to burst so fierce was his passion. He
realized that he was not in control of the situation, and he found it an uncomfortable position to be in for it was Grace and Faith who were ma-

nipulating his condition. Only when they deemed it permissible was he allowed release.

Once roused they were wild women finding nothing too strange, or daring to do. Conn was, at first, enchanted with his good fortune, but then as the night wore on he began to realize they would kill him with their loving if he did not regain a mastery of their circumstances. He began by pushing Grace away from him as she sought to mount him once again.

"No! I'll do my own fucking, sweeting," he told her, and when she protested he sat up, and pulling her across his lap spanked her across her plump bottom, and pushed her from the bed onto the floor. Surprised Grace began to weep, but Conn paid little attention to her instead yanking the more compliant Faith beneath him, he mounted her, and thrusting himself into her, moved furiously upon her until he was at last able to spill his seed in a glorious wild burst that left him exhausted and drained. "Get me some wine, Grace," he commanded, and she rushed to do his bidding. Within minutes he had been revived, and he gave to Grace that which he had given her twin sister. Then firmly sending both girls home, he fell asleep.

In the morning Conn vowed that never again would he entertain Mistress Grace and Mistress Faith Holden. He felt as if he had been battered, and his lean and long body was covered with bite and scratch marks. After he had bathed in a hot tub that Cluny prepared he stood nude before the pier glass examining himself with shock. He had not felt them marking him. His handsome face was unmarked, and as he stared into the glass his green eyes stared back from beneath heavy black brows. *The Handsomest Man at Court*, he thought, looking at himself closely as if he expected to find something different or unusual. He knew that he was a handsome man for he was neither a fool, nor coy. He was clean-shaven, the better to show off his chiseled, somewhat squared jaw with its dimple. He had a long, straight nose in perfect proportion with his size for he stood six feet four inches tall in his stocking feet. His cheekbones were high, and sculpted giving him a look of vulnerability that was borne out in the high forehead, and his mouth which was almost too delicate for such a big man, being thin-lipped rather than wide. He was very fair-skinned for a man which only made his dark hair seem all the darker, particularly as one errant lock of hair persisted in tumbling over his brow, giving him a boyish look he deplored. Long legs, long torso, broad chest and shoulders that needed no padding—he looked magnificent in his clothing. His brother-in-law Adam de Marisco had said when he had first seen Conn in decent clothing, "By God, the women will be throwing themselves at his feet," a statement quickly borne out for truth. He had also said that they would end up in altercations with many of the gentle-men at court due to Conn's handsomeness.

Conn, however, had managed to avoid fighting with possibly outraged husbands and fathers by his utmost discretion in matters of the heart. He was wise enough to realize that brawling, particularly public brawling, would lose him royal favor, and he knew that gold could get him only just so far. He owed his position to Elizabeth Tudor, but that which Bess gave so freely she could take away as easily. He had come to England to find his fortune as had many Irishmen before him. As the youngest son in his family there was nothing for him in Ireland, particularly an Ireland ruled by England. He knew his fate was here, and he had no intention of en-dangering his future. Consequently the Holden twins would have to be forgotten. Instinctively he knew that passionate pair held an element of danger for him, particularly since he had only recently courted their mother. He would seek a less flamboyant arrangement for the court was full of lovely and willing ladies.

Ladies like Signora Eudora Maria di Carlo, the wife of the ambassador from San Lorenzo. A most toothsome wench who had spent the weeks since her recent arrival in England staring at him with her marvelously expressive amber eyes, and brushing against him as they passed. The am-bassador's wife was tiny and plump, and he doubted not, a delicious arm-ful. The thought of the chase ahead sent a tingle of anticipation down his spine. Last night had given him a distaste for bold and forward women. He far preferred sweet surrender and melting charms to the demands of Baron Marston's daughters. He intended avoiding them if at all possible, but then perhaps it would not be possible, and he certainly could not cause a scandal. It was a difficult situation, but he had cleverly avoided worse in his lifetime.

Chapter 3

❧

"There is no help for it now," said Lord Burghley to the queen. "The scandal has been caused, and by not acting to punish Master O'-Malley ye make it appear as if ye condone his actions. Yer apt to be tarred with the same brush that tars him. Remember the Dudley scandal. Ye cannot afford it, madame."

The queen sighed deeply. "I know yer right, my dear friend. Ye have always had only my interests at heart, but I cannot help but be saddened. I like Master O'Malley!"

"I know that, madame, and I would tell ye that I like him also. There is really no malice in him at all, and the fact that he has been caught in this situation is unfortunate for there are those here at court who do worse daily, but are never found out. Conn O'Malley is a good-hearted young man, but he has not learned, forgive my bluntness, madame, to keep his cock confined to his codpiece, and it is that sin that has brought us to this moment. The ambassador from San Lorenzo is outraged as he has every right to be. There is no doubt he has been insulted, which means his tiny, but valuable to England, country has been insulted. We cannot have him return to his master, madame, and break off relations with us."

"What am I to do then?" Elizabeth Tudor fretted. "I have had Conn confined to the Tower, but I cannot keep him there indefinitely simply because he was caught kissing the ambassador's wife in a hidden corner."

That, of course, was not quite the matter, thought William Cecil, and the queen knew it. Conn had been found wrapped in a torrid embrace with Eudora Maria di Carlo, whose ample bosom was bared to his caresses, whilst the lady had ardently fondled the Irishman. It was in fact the ambassador's wife's delighted little cries of pleasure that had drawn attention to their dark corner in the first place. A knock upon the door to the queen's private closet brought one of her secretaries into the chamber.

"Madame, Baron Marston, and his family are without. The baron says it is urgent that he speak with ye. It pertains, he says, to the Conn O'Malley matter."

Lord Burghley raised an eyebrow. What was this? Was there going to be more difficulty relating to young O'Malley?

"Let Lord Holden and his family come in," the queen said, and she turned to Cecil. "I do not think this augurs well, William." She seated herself in a comfortable highbacked chair for Lord Holden was known to be long-winded. Garbed in a white velvet gown with a wide gold lace neck wisk, the bodice of the gown bejeweled and embroidered with heavy gold threads in the pattern of grape vines, the sleeves slashed to show gold tissues beneath, Elizabeth was a regal figure. Upon her head was a red-gold wig for her own hair was thinning, and fading. Still she was a hand-some woman. She wore about her slender neck the chain with the pendant Conn had given her, and in her ears were fat round pearls.

Lord Holden entered the room quickly as if he were being pursued by all the fires of hell. Behind him came his wife, looking rather somber for once, and his pretty twin daughters whose almost identical faces bore signs of recent weeping. All three of the women were garbed in plain black velvet gowns with simple white lace ruffs, a departure, the queen thought, from their usual gaudy garb. Lord Holden, a portly gentleman, was also garbed severely in black. All four made their obeisance to the queen.

She nodded back, her mouth quirking itself into a small frown. "Say on, my lord! Ye said ye wished to speak to me in the O'Malley matter."

"It distresses me, madame, to grieve ye in any way for I know how fond ye are of the Irishman, still I must report this to ye even though in doing so I expose myself and my own honor to shame." He paused to glower at his wife and his daughters. "When the scandal of Ambassador di Carlo's wife was made known, my own wife could no longer hide her own dis-honor. She confessed to me that Master O'Malley had seduced her. Since it was necessary as an object lesson to our own dear impressionable daughters that she admit her guilt before them, ye can well imagine our surprise and horror to learn that the same Master O'Malley had also de-bauched our innocent girls as well! I demand that ye punish this deflow-erer of virtuous wives and maidens! I would prefer not to make public my humiliation and mortification in this matter, but I shall if ye do not chas-tise this reprobate. I will hold my own wife up to ridicule, my precious daughters to the fate of spinsterhood, but I will see Conn O'Malley chas-tened!"

"God's foot!" The queen's face bespoke her outrage, but whether that outrage stemmed from Conn's behavior, or Lord Holden's tone, Lord Burghley was not certain. "He shall be banished from court!" Elizabeth pronounced loftily. "I will not have such a man about me! As for you, my lord, it would be best if ye removed yer wife and daughters to Kent for the rest of the winter. They are invited to return at Whitsuntide, but until then it is best they return to the country to meditate upon their many female weaknesses. Prayer and fasting will help them to turn from the path of wickedness. We will help ye to make *suitable* marriages for the twins, and the sooner, I would think, the better."

Lord Holden fell to his knees, and taking the hem of the queen's gown kissed it reverently. "Madame," he said, "ye are all that is wise and good! I thank ye most heartily for this fair judgment. We will leave immediately this day for Marston Manor, but I will return as quickly in order to be of aid to ye."

Elizabeth smiled. "Stay with yer ladies, my lord, until the month of March begins. I feel they will need yer guidance if they are to be properly repentant. Be sure to beat them well to start them off along the right path, and then return to me." She held out her hand so he might kiss her ring.

Lord Holden's face glowed with his admiration of the queen. Kissing the proffered hand, he scrambled to his feet, and roughly herded his women from the room, the door closing firmly behind him.

For a moment the room was silent, and then the queen swore. "Damn him! Damn him! Damn him! I shall not be able to ask him back to court for at least a year, William, and it will be unutterably dull without him. How could he? Lady Holden *and* her daughters? It really is quite unforgivable!"

"Lady Holden," said Lord Burghley in an effort to soothe his mistress' feelings, "has a reputation for taking lovers, madame. She is discreet, but I cannot believe that even her husband is unaware of her conduct. As for her daughters, they are said to be a pair of teasing drabs, and though the father might be fooled, neither came innocent to court or young O'Malley, I am certain. He is a rogue, and filled to the brim with mischief, but he is no wanton taker of innocence, madame."

"Bring me my embroidery frame, Aidan," said the queen to the maid of honor who had been seated quietly, and unobserved on a stool in a corner by the fire.

Quickly Aidan St. Michael hurried to obey the queen, and then pulling her stool next to Elizabeth Tudor, she sat down, and prepared to hand the queen her threads as she needed them.

"Nonetheless some devil in hell has encouraged both Lady Holden, and her offspring to confess their misdemeanors with Conn, placing, of course, the entire burden of guilt upon him. I doubt not 'twas jealousy on the part of all three. Lord Holden had no other choice than to come to me in light of the episode with the ambassador's wife," continued the queen. "I had intended to banish Conn from court for a few weeks, perhaps through the Lenten season. Now I must keep him away for a goodly time, and where to send him? It cannot be Ireland. That is too far, and what would poor Conn do? I will wager although I have never met them, that he is nothing like his elder buccaneer brothers. I had thought to send him to the de Mariscos, but will they be able to tolerate him for an entire year?"

"He must be married, madame," said William Cecil quietly.

"Married? Conn? No!"

"There is no other solution, madame," Lord Burghley replied patiently. "He will come back to court when his period of punishment is over filled to the brim with even more mischief. Who knows what scandals he will cause then? Ye must marry him to a respectable woman before he even leaves court, and then send him off to his estates for at least a year. Let him beget a legitimate heir on his bride while he cools his very hot heels."

"He has no property to which I may banish him," the queen said.

"He has gold, madame, and comes of a good Irish family. He is a member of your own guard. He is a most eligible young man. Find him a wife with property."

"That is not as easy as ye make it sound, William. It cannot be a great name for his blood is not blue enough for a great name. It cannot be a nobody for he is too good for just some anonymous wench. It cannot be a Protestant lord's child for he was raised a Roman Catholic, although I have not known him to seek a priest while in England. He seems content to follow the Church of England, but one cannot be certain. Each one of these things narrows our field of search, and I cannot think of one girl who would be suitable as a wife for Conn O'Malley," finished the queen.

"I can."

For a moment both the queen and Lord Burghley thought that they had imagined the voice that spoke those words, and then their eyes swung to the figure seated by the queen's knee.

"Was it ye who spoke, Aidan St. Michael?" demanded Elizabeth.

"Yes, madame."

"Who is this young woman, madame?" asked Lord Burghley, his eyes interested and bright.

"She is the daughter of the late Lord Bliss, and one of my royal wards," said the queen looking hard at Aidan.

Aidan flushed, and her heart hammered fiercely within her chest, but her gaze never wavered.

"Tell us then, Mistress St. Michael, who in your opinion is suitable to be wife to Conn O'Malley?"

"I am, madame." *There!* She had said it. Nothing could change the words whatever the queen said or did.

"You?!" The queen looked surprised.

"Tell me, Mistress St. Michael," said Lord Burghley in a kindly tone, "what makes ye think that ye are an eligible *partie* for Master O'Malley? Do ye know him? Are ye perhaps in love with him?"

"I am of a good family, my lord, but my lineage is not that of a great line. It was my great-grandfather who was ennobled by her majesty's own grandfather. My mother was Irish, a cousin of the Countess of Lincoln, and so that makes me half-Irish. Although I was born a member of the Holy Mother Church, after my mother's death my father and I found we preferred the new church. I am an heiress of considerable fortune, and my lands border those of Master O'Malley's sister, Lady de Marisco. It would appear to me that I possess all the qualities necessary to be Master O'Malley's wife, and although I enjoy the court I long to go home. I am indeed as her majesty terms me, a country mouse."

Lord Burghley looked to the queen. "The maiden is correct, madame. She is a perfect choice!"

"I do not know," hedged the queen. "Do ye really want to leave me, Aidan St. Michael? I believed ye happy here."

"How could I not be happy in yer presence, madame? Ye have been to me as a wise elder sister."

Lord Burghley hid a small smile. Elizabeth Tudor was more than old enough to be the girl's mother. He could see the girl was determined to have her way, however, and her reasons interested him greatly.

"Nonetheless," Aidan continued, "I am uncomfortable amid the sophistication of yer court. I am a simple girl, madame. Besides my people need me. A bailiff is not fit substitute for the mistress or the master of the land. Then, too, ye will remember that ye promised my father that ye would find a husband for me. Can ye think of another man ye might wed me to, madame? It is true that I do not know Master O'Malley, but he seems to me a kindly man."

"I cannot deny that," Elizabeth said.

"Then I could be content, perhaps even happy with him. Oh, madame! Forgive my boldness, but ye have seen many arranged marriages in yer lifetime, some happy, some not. With Master O'Malley I have the chance of a good marriage, but if ye can name another man ye would prefer to give me to, I will accept yer judgment in this matter."

Clever, thought Lord Burghley! She has reminded the queen of her promise to a dead man, and no one has greater honor than the queen. The queen is boxed in for she must find a bride for O'Malley, and she cannot, I am certain, think of another bridegroom for Mistress St. Michael.

The queen was silent for a long few minutes during which time Aidan scarcely drew a breath. She had fallen in love with Conn O'Malley on Twelfth Night when he had kissed her. It distressed her because the truth was that the kiss had meant nothing to him, and she knew it. She did not really know him, and he had shown no indication of wanting to know her. In a sense she was throwing herself at him, and yet when Lord Burghley had said that Conn O' Malley must have a wife, Aidan had known she could not bear it if another woman were to wed with the big Irishman. The queen's voice made her start.

"What do you think, my lord Burghley? Shall I wed Master O'Malley to Mistress St. Michael? Is this the answer to my problem? He will gain a great deal by such a match."

"Besides a pretty wife, madame, what else is there?" Lord Burghley's gaze as he looked at Aidan was almost a fatherly one.

"He will gain a large estate, half of the fortune her father left, and that in itself is considerable. Then, too, there is a last request that Payton St. Michael made of me which I granted. The late Lord Bliss, may God assoil him, was the last of his line. He asked that any gentleman wed to his daughter be required to take his name, and be permitted to continue the title of Lord Bliss. By the marriage Conn O'Malley becomes Conn St. Michael, Lord Bliss."

William Cecil, Lord Burghley, nodded, and after a moment's consideration said, "And, as an English nobleman, one less Irish rebel to consider, madame. It will bind his sister, Lady de Marisco, even closer to yer realm."

"Then so be it, Aidan St. Michael. I will keep my promise to yer father, and ye'll have Conn O'Malley for yer husband. Ye understand, however, that there can be no fuss or fanfare about yer wedding? Due to the nature of Master O'Malley's offense ye must be quickly wed, and sent immediately from court. What is today's date, my lord?"

"February the twelfth, madame."

A smile spread over the queen's face. "It is pure providence!" she said. "Perhaps this is indeed a marriage made in heaven. Ye shall be wed two days hence on the fourteenth, St. Valentine's Day, Aidan St. Michael. The ceremony will be a private one in my chapel, and 'twill be attended only by myself and Lord Burghley. Is it agreed?"

"I would also have my tiring woman, and young Lord Southwood, madame. I do not object to privacy, but I would have more witnesses."

"Very wise, Mistress St. Michael," said William Cecil. "Particularly yer choice of the young earl." He turned to the queen. "Master O'Malley's nephew is an ideal witness, madame. He will, of course, bring word of the marriage to his mother and stepfather for I hope ye will allow him to travel with the newly wedded couple as far as *Queen's Malvern*. He will carry a personal message from yer majesty herself to the de Mariscos which will explain the situation. Lady de Marisco should be quite pleased with the way ye've treated her brother."

"Excellent!" exclaimed Elizabeth Tudor, and then she turned to Aidan. "Go now, child, and do yer packing. Ye will be wed early in the morning on St. Valentine's Day so that ye will have the whole day for travel. It will take ye several long days to reach yer home. Ye may tell yer companions here that I am allowing ye to return to *Pearroc Royal* for a visit. No other explanation will be necessary at this time."

"My marriage is to be a secret, madame?"

"Not from Master O'Malley's family, Aidan, but it would be wise if the court were kept in the dark for the present. It would be somewhat difficult for me to explain to San Lorenzo's ambassador and to Lord Holden that I am punishing Conn O'Malley by marrying him off to an heiress, and creating him Lord Bliss." The queen chuckled, and even Lord Burghley smiled slightly.

"May I ask one favor of ye, madame?" said Aidan.

"Of course, child!"

"Please, madame, please do not tell Master O'Malley that it was I who suggested he be my husband. I do not know him except by sight, and he does not know me, but I would be most mortified if he believed me to be like the other silly women who chase after him. I know that ye will understand that, madame."

The queen nodded her head. "Aye, Aidan St. Michael. There is no need for Conn O'Malley to believe he has any more advantage over ye than any husband has over his wife. Ye may put yer mind at rest that what has happened here between us today will remain our secret. Ye have my word on the matter."

Aidan curtsied to her majesty, and then almost ran from the royal chamber. She couldn't believe it! She was to be married in less than two days' time! She was to be married to Conn O'Malley, the Handsomest Man at Court! She was going home to *Pearroc Royal*! Then suddenly she stopped, and her hand flew to her mouth. *What had she done?* She didn't even know Conn O'Malley except by his rather colorful and scandalous reputation. What if he didn't like her? She had boldly planned her future with a man she didn't know, and all based upon one kiss! Had she lost what few wits she had? She was, after all, no better than those foolish women who were always attempting to gain Master O'Malley's attention. Suddenly shocked by her own daring actions she stumbled in her flight, and bumped into someone.

"Aidan? Aidan St. Michael, are ye all right?" The young Earl of Lynmouth was taking her by the hand.

Slowly her eyes focused upon his boyish face. "I am to be married, Robin," she whispered. "The queen is marrying me to yer uncle Conn, and it is to be a secret."

"*What?*" he said astounded. "What is this ye say to me?"

"Go to the queen," Aidan said pulling away from him, and hurrying off down the hallway.

Robin followed her advice, and was admitted to the queen's presence. He bowed, and then quickly coming to the point said, "I have just seen Aidan St. Michael in the hallway. Is what she says true, madame? Is she indeed to be married to my uncle?"

"Conn O'Malley has caused a scandal of possible international implications to this court unless I can remove him from our presence, Lord Southwood," said the queen formally. "My lord Burghley has suggested that a wife might curb your uncle's high spirits. I agree. Mistress St. Michael's late father requested of me on his deathbed that I find a good husband for his daughter. Aidan is an excellent match for Conn. He will take her family name for his own according to another last request by Payton St. Michael, and thereby become Lord Bliss of *Pearroc Royal*. He is banished for at least a year from court for his somewhat outrageous behavior not only with Eudora di Carlo, but also with Lady Glytha Holden, *and* her twin daughters. Baron Marston has already been to see me with his complaints. Do ye now understand the seriousness of this matter, Robin?"

"Aye, madame, but why Aidan? Aidan is special. She is gentle and loving, and I do not know if my uncle is worthy of her."

Lord Burghley turned away so that young Lord Southwood would not see his smile. The boy was obviously in the throes of puppy love for Mistress St. Michael. William Cecil tried to remember back that far in his own life, and suddenly recalled an older female cousin with whom he had shared the pangs of growing up. For a moment he fought back the prickling sensation of tears that threatened to push forward. His cousin had married at seventeen, and died in childbirth at twenty when he had been but fourteen.

"Perhaps ye are right, my Robin," said Elizabeth Tudor. "Perhaps Conn O'Malley is not worthy of Aidan St. Michael at this time, but he will be one day; and Aidan will help him to grow into the fine man that I see beneath the surface veneer of the gay rogue he so loves to play. Aidan will not suffer by the marriage, believe me. Now, my lad, I have other news. Ye are to be a witness at this wedding which will be celebrated early on the morning of the fourteenth, two days hence. Then I want ye to travel with Aidan and Conn as far as *Queen's Malvern* to personally bring yer mother and stepfather word of the nuptials. Visit with yer family for a few weeks, my Robin, and then come back to court."

The decision had been made, and Robin Southwood, the fourteen-year-old Earl of Lynmouth, was too skilled a courtier to argue with, or question further his sovereign. Instead he made a most elegant bow, and said, "Your majesty could not make an incorrect decision, and I shall be delighted to welcome Aidan into our family as my aunt."

The queen appreciated the boy's manners. How like his father he is, she thought remembering Geoffrey Southwood, the Angel Earl, as he had been called. "Now, Robin," she said briskly lest sentiment overtake her, "I will send ye with a message to the warden of the Tower, and he will release yer uncle to ye. Bring Conn O'Malley back to me with all possible haste. It is only fair he be prepared for his fate," and she chuckled. "I cannot wait to hear what he will say to my clever proposal."

"No!" said Conn O'Malley. "No, Bess! And no again! Marry some wench I don't even know?"

"I did not ask ye *if* ye wished to marry, Master O'Malley," snapped the queen. "I am telling ye that yer to be wed on the fourteenth to Mistress Aidan St. Michael, and then ye and yer bride will depart for her estates. Ye've caused a terrible scandal, Conn!"

"For Christ's sake, Bess, all I did was kiss and fondle the woman. We were not caught *in flagrante delicto*!"

"Only because there was not enough time!" the queen shouted. "Tell me about Lady Glytha Holden, *and* her twin daughters, Grace and Faith, I believe they are called! Did ye take the sisters together, ye bloody lecher? Ohh, I know all about yer conduct with those three drabs! Baron Marston was here earlier today with his list of complaints regarding your *seductions* of his wife and daughters!"

"Seduced! Those three? Nay, Bess, there was no seduction."

"But ye'll not deny yer involvement with them, Conn, will ye?"

He flushed and mumbled, "Nay."

"I could have left ye in the Tower, Conn. Left ye there until hell froze over, but instead I am supplying ye with an heiress for a wife, a fat dowry, a rich estate, *and* a title. There are those who would say I was less than harsh with ye."

"A title?" Conn was suddenly intrigued, and Lord Burghley was unable to refrain from chuckling at the big Irishman.

"Payton St. Michael was the last of his line. His family had only been ennobled in my grandfather's time, and although they prospered in many ways there was one place where they lacked. There was but one son in each generation until this present generation when the only St. Michael born to survive was a daughter. It was Lord Bliss' dying request of me that the man I chose for his daughter take his family name, and with it the family title."

"Change my name?" Conn looked outraged. "I'm an O'Malley!"

"Ye've got four elder brothers, three of whom are fathers of how many sons, Conn?"

"Eleven," he answered her honestly.

"I think judging from that number, my Adonis, that there will always be plenty of O'Malleys upon this earth. Think on it, Conn. Yer the youngest child of yer father who was to all intents and purposes a pirate," said the queen. "Ye've one brother who is a priest, but the others are privateers who will probably not live to grow old. Why did ye come to England if not to seek yer fortune? Ye've grown rich with yer sister's trading company, and ye have my favor and friendship. Now I seek to take ye a step farther in yer climb up the social ladder. Why are ye fighting me?"

"Dammit, Bess, what will I do in the country? Ye tell me that Mistress St. Michael is the possessor of much land. I know nothing of how to manage a great estate. I'm a courtier by nature, and by inclination."

"If yer to marry a woman with lands then ye had best learn how to manage them lest ye lose those lands for yer son," said the queen quietly.

"*My son?*" he said softly.

"Aye, Conn, yer son. It is to be hoped that during yer period of exile in the country that ye will sire an heir upon yer wife. Is that not what all men want?"

"I had not intended to wed for many years to come, Bess. I planned to choose my own wife."

He was a strong opponent, thought Lord Burghley. Every bit as tough as his beautiful sister had been when dealing with Elizabeth Tudor. He would, however, capitulate to the queen as his sister had been forced to do.

"Ye could not, my Adonis, find a more suitable wife than Aidan St. Michael. Her mother was a FitzGerald, a cousin of the Countess of Lincoln. She is wealthy, educated, and what's more, she has wit and a clever tongue. She will be a far more interesting wife than any ye might choose. Yer taste, I have noted, runs to the bovine, or the obvious."

Conn chuckled. He could not help it. What was worse, the queen was correct. He had never seriously looked at a woman, his main concern being how quickly he might get them on their backs. Hardly a fit attitude when wife-hunting. He sighed. "Yer determined that I marry this girl then, Bess?"

"I am," replied the queen sternly, but he thought that he detected a faint smile for a brief moment.

"Well, then, Bess, I will obey ye in this matter for ye've yet to do me a bad turn, but if I had the choice, I'd tell ye nay."

"But ye have not the choice, Conn O'Malley. It is my wish that on the morning of the fourteenth of February fifteen hundred and seventy-eight, ye take to wife Aidan St. Michael. Now pour us some wine, my Adonis, and we will toast yer happiness, and that of yer bride."

Walking to the sideboard where the delicate crystal goblets, and the decanters of wine were set, Conn chose a fruity golden vintage, and poured three goblets which he then distributed to the queen and Lord Burghley.

"To yer future, my Adonis," said the queen raising her goblet.

"To prosperity and many sons," said Lord Burghley raising his.

"To the bride," said Conn. "God help us both," and he drank his wine down in three quick gulps. "Now, Bess, with yer permission I shall withdraw from yer presence in order that I may meet with my betrothed. Will ye tell me where I may find her?"

"Robin is waiting outside," said Elizabeth Tudor. "He will take ye to Aidan, and ye have our permission to retire."

Placing his goblet back upon the sideboard Conn bowed to the queen, and walked from the room with the air of a man condemned while behind him both William Cecil and Elizabeth smiled conspiratorially at one another. Outside the queen's private closet Robin Southwood stood talking with Mistress Talbot, but seeing his uncle he quickly excused himself, and hurried up to him.

"Bess says ye'll take me to Mistress St. Michael," said Conn.

"Keep yer voice down, uncle," Robin chided him. "This matter is a private one. Follow me."

"Ye don't sound very happy, Robin," said Conn O'Malley as he followed his nephew. "Do ye then agree with me that this marriage is foolish?"

Robin said nothing at first, but once they had gained the outside corridor, and he saw that there was no one about he turned on his uncle. In anger, he said fiercely, "She is the most wonderful girl I have ever met, Uncle Conn! Hurt her, and ye will have me to answer to! Do ye understand?"

Conn's first urge was to laugh, but then he saw that his nephew was in deadly earnest with his threat, and so swallowing his mirth he said quietly, "She must be a fine girl, Robin, to have so won ye over. I am counting upon ye to help us both bridge the gap of awkwardness that is certain to be between us in the beginning. Will ye help me?"

"Aye," the boy said, "but be warned that I am Aidan's knight first and foremost."

Conn nodded seriously, asking, "Where the hell are ye taking me, lad? I've not been this way before."

"Aidan's room is one the Countess of Lincoln was able to spare, but it is in the attics. At least she has had her privacy which is more than most of the girls have." Having reached Aidan's door at this point Robin rapped sharply upon it, and it was opened almost instantaneously by Mag.

"Good day, yer lordship."

"Good day, Mag. Is Mistress St. Michael here? I have brought my uncle Conn O' Malley to meet her."

"Aye," said the tiring woman, "he looks like an O'Malley. Skirt-chasing pirates every one of them, I've heard!"

Conn gently pushed Robin aside, and stood before the open doorway looking down on the small, plump woman who glowered up at him with snapping brown eyes, her hands balled into fists and set upon her ample hips. "Indeed," he said, "and where does yer knowledge stem from, little woman?"

" 'Tis common gossip in Ballycoille, and am I not Mag Feeney of Ballycoille?"

Conn laughed. "Well, Mag Feeney of Ballycoille, I'll not say yer wrong for there are many O'Malleys who seek their living from the sea, and there are just as many who enjoy a pretty girl, but I've one brother who's a priest, and not as likely soon to be a bishop, and a sister who's a holy nun known for her skill at doctoring, and four other sisters who disapprove of me just as much as ye seem to, and one magnificent sister who's one of the wealthiest women in England. We're hardly an ordinary lot. Now be a good soul, and tell yer mistress that I've come calling."

Mag shut the door firmly, and Conn and Robin waited. Finally the door opened again, and stepping aside Mag said, "Ye may come in, *Master* O'Malley," and then she gave a little shriek as passing her by he reached down, and gave her bottom a small pat. "Ohh, 'tis a bold one ye are!" she scolded him. "Yer mother has, I've not a doubt, wept bitter tears over ye!"

"My mother loves me," he replied, "and ye will, too, Mag, when ye get to know me."

"That, *Master* O'Malley, remains to be seen," she replied.

"Mag," said Robin, "come and have a tankard of ale with me," and before the tiring woman might protest he drew her out the open door, and pulled it shut so the betrothed pair might be alone.

Conn stepped past the bed that took most of the room's floor space into the little bit of open room. Before him, her back to the tiny window, stood a girl. She was far taller than most women, and bigger boned than his sister Skye. Her face was oval, her chin dimpled as was his. He could not tell the color of her eyes, or her hair which was hidden beneath her cap, but he noted that she had pretty hands that plucked nervously at the amber velvet of her gown. She was no beauty, this bride the queen had picked for him, but he thought she might be pretty if she would only smile. Still in all it wasn't as bad as he had thought it might be. She could have been pockmarked. He looked closely at the girl again. There was something familiar about her. Where had he seen her before?

"Twelfth Night," said Aidan recognizing his predicament.

The sound startled him, but he decided, he liked her voice. It was moderate in tone, and sweet. "Twelfth Night?" he questioned.

"Ye played Blind Man's Bluff with us, and ye caught me."

"Of course!" Now he remembered! "I kissed ye, and ye trembled. Ye don't know how to kiss. I thought to myself that ye'd never been kissed before, and 'twas strange for yer not a very young lass like the others."

Aidan laughed, and it was a somewhat rueful sound. "Nay, I'm not as young as the others," she agreed. "I will be twenty-four on the nineteenth of August next."

"I will be twenty-three on the twenty-third of June," he answered.

They were silent again neither one of them sure where to take this awkward conversation from there. Then Conn said, "Yer very pretty when ye smile, Mistress St. Michael."

"I think ye had best call me Aidan, Conn O'Malley, as we will very shortly be man and wife." She was surprised by her daring speech.

"Do ye know what it means in the Gaelic?" he asked her.

"I do not know Gaelic."

"It means 'Fiery One.' Are ye fiery, Aidan?" His eyes were studying her, noting suddenly the slender waist, the full bosom, her straight carriage.

"I do not believe so, Conn O'Malley," she answered, and she blushed at his scrutiny.

He was suddenly very curious to see the color of her hair. "Take off yer cap, Aidan," he said, and when she hesitated, shy, of his request, Conn stepped forward, and gently pulled the small linen cap that was heart-shaped in the front, but draped baglike in the back to conceal her hair, from her head. Then his hands moved expertly to undo the gold and tortoise hairpins that held her hair so neatly in place. To his surprise the hair suddenly came undone, falling in a silken swath to just below her hips. "God's nightshirt!" he swore softly, "ye have hair like pale molten copper, lass! 'Tis lovely. Why do ye conceal it beneath that damned cap?" His hands slid through the perfumed tangle of it.

"M-my father said my hair was a funny color. He preferred my mother's hair, and so after she died I kept my hair beneath a cap so as not to annoy him." She felt rooted to the floor as his fingers gently caressed her long tresses.

He had never seen hair like this, Conn thought. It was the most beautiful color, and so wonderfully soft to his touch, yet it had texture. For some reason he could not fathom her hair aroused him in the most incredible way. "I think," he said softly, his own voice sounding thick in his ears, "I think it is time, Aidan St. Michael, that we seal this betrothal the queen has made between us with a kiss," and without waiting for her answer he cupped her head with one hand, and found her lips.

For a moment she felt as if all the blood had drained from her veins to be swiftly replaced by boiling, thick, and sweet, hot honey. She couldn't move. She didn't want to move. The pressure of his lips on hers roused in her mind that most lascivious of thoughts. She wanted to tear the clothes from her body, *and from his*. She wanted to lie with him, and touch him, and have him touch her. She felt his other arm slip about her waist, and to her mortification she found herself falling back against that arm while his lips trailed down her arched throat leaving a path of burning kisses. She felt a hand move to cup her breast, heard his voice, heavy with passion groan her name, "Ahh, Aidan," and in that moment sanity returned to her. She was as bad as those silly women who were forever chasing him. She was as bad as any damned drab who so easily lifted her skirts here at court. She didn't know this man, and yet here she was locked in passionate embrace with him, allowing him to fondle her! Why in another minute or two he'd have her on the bed, and what was left of her virtue would be gone! He'd be bored with her before the wedding!

With a grim burst of determination Aidan stamped down hard on Conn's booted foot, and using all her strength pulled herself from his delicious embrace. "Master O'Malley!" she tried to make her voice sound stern and scandalized. "Master O'Malley! We are not wed yet, sir!"

His head was spinning, and he felt like a schoolboy. What bewitchment was this that she had ensnared him with? One look at her coppery hair, and he had desired her. It was unbelievable, and even he was surprised by his own actions. What was worse he wasn't certain what he could say to her. "Aidan . . ." God's foot! Where were the proper words?

Aidan's head was beginning to clear, and with several swift motions she had her hair pinned up, albeit untidily, and was replacing her linen cap upon her head again. She drew a deep breath, and said in what she hoped sounded like a no-nonsense tone of voice, "Master O'Malley, I think it is best that we not see each other again until the wedding lest we cause gossip. It could draw attention to our match which is not what the queen desires at this time."

He was finally able to find his voice, and he almost stammered his agreement, feeling like a bumbling fool as he did so. Hastily making her a leg, he hurried from the little room. What the hell was the matter with him? he frantically questioned himself. He had never behaved like such a lackwit with a pretty female in his entire life. She was simply a girl!

As the door closed behind him Aidan sank to the bed, finding to her great surprise that she was shaking. What was the matter with her? He was only a man! She was suddenly terribly aware of how little she actually knew about the more intimate relationship between a wife and her husband. What was worse there was no one she could ask, and she felt like a total fool. She wanted to be his wife, but she suddenly knew that until they had grown to know one another better their marriage could be one in name only. She didn't dare allow him any more intimacies lest she be tempted into further wanton behavior. His kisses, his embraces, were like heady sweet wine, and she wanted to drink until she was blind drunk. It shocked her to face that truth, but what surprised her more was the realization that she, Aidan St. Michael, wanted her husband, Conn O'Malley, to love her; to *really* love her!

He was not, she knew, impressed by her monetary wealth for he had wealth of his own. He gained lands, and of course, her father's title by their marriage, but it was not a marriage he had sought; and he was far too honest, she hoped, to court her unless he actually cared for her. She wondered what would happen if he ever learned that it was she who had suggested their marriage. He must never know! The clock on the mantel chimed four o'clock of this February afternoon, and a log dissolved into a shower of red-gold sparks in the fireplace grate.

Aidan stood up, and turning to look into the small mirror that Mag had hung near the fireplace she stared into it. Did she look any different now that she had been well and truly kissed? She didn't think so, and she smiled at her foolishness as she was sure Linnet Talbot would have smiled if she but knew; but then perhaps not. Was it not Linnet who had insisted that they follow the strict conditions for St. Agnes Eve just this last month? She smiled again at the memory, amused now that she had allowed the younger girl to bully her into so silly a superstition, and yet she had.

St. Agnes Eve fell on the night of January 20–21. It had been a snowy, cold night, Aidan recalled. It was the night that a maiden, if she followed a strict set of rules dreamt of her future husband. None of them had been on duty with the queen that night, and it was this coincidence of scheduling that had given Linnet the idea that they must all celebrate according to tradition. Each had gone separately to the chapel. First Cathy, who was the youngest, and then Dorothy, Jane Anne, Linnet, Mary, and finally Aidan. She wondered if the others had prayed as hard as she had. After all, they were so very young, and she was facing her twenty-fourth birthday. Leaving the chapel, looking neither to the left nor to the right, and most certainly not behind her, each girl had gone supperless to her bed, never speaking to a soul. That part had been the easiest for Aidan with her little chamber, and Mag, warned in advance, had humored her mistress. Once asleep the maiden was supposed to dream of the man she would marry. Aidan had dreamt of Conn O'Malley to her intense discomfort for she was, or so she thought, a practical girl, and Conn O'Malley was not a practical dream. He had never paid her the least attention, and other than his kiss on Twelfth Night he had had nothing to do with her.

"Who did ye dream of? Who?" each girl demanded of the others in the morning, but Aidan had lied, and said she had dreamt of no one, and must therefore be condemned to spinsterhood. The others had sympathized, but she had seen the knowing looks that passed between them. Poor Aidan, the looks had plainly said. If she were meant to marry it would have happened long since.

Aidan's smile suddenly broadened. "I wonder," she said softly to herself, "I wonder what ye will all think when ye learn that I have married the Handsomest Man at Court! Aidan St. Michael, Lady Bliss! Mistress of *Pearroc Royal*!" and then she laughed. It was such a wonderful joke, and she had no friend with whom to share the humor. It would be so wonderful if her husband became that friend.

The next day she was excused from her duties, and she and Mag worked very hard to pack all of their possessions. They would be making the journey in the young Earl of Lynmouth's traveling coach, he had informed them when he had come with his liveried footmen to take away her trunks. The other girls had come to bid her farewell for they had already been told she would go early.

"This is sudden," pried Linnet Talbot. "If ye were anyone else I would say ye were with child."

"Linnet! Where is yer modesty," shrieked Cathy, but the other girls laughed.

"It was not meant that I remain at court," said Aidan quietly. "I really only came so the queen could get a good look at me. Being allowed to serve her majesty was a privilege and a treat for me, but I cannot remain off my lands for too much longer. I had actually hoped to be home by Twelfth Night."

"Is there a man involved? I mean back at yer *Pearroc Royal?*" demanded Linnet.

Aidan laughed. "If there were, Linnet, I should have been home long since! Now come, ye silly child, and kiss me good-bye!"

Each girl had stepped forward and pecked Aidan upon her cheeks, and then without further ado they trooped out of the room. As the door closed behind them Aidan felt a funny sort of sadness. They had not really been her friends for they were far too young, and much too feather-headed, but they had all been companions in the queen's service, and they had been kind to her. She must remember in the spring to send each of them a dress length for none came of wealth, and they would appreci-ate her practical thought.

"I want a bath," she said to Mag. "Go and bribe some of the footmen to bring enough hot water to fill my little tub before it must be packed. I will be so glad to get home where I may bathe again each day."

The footmen who had served this part of Greenwich Palace thought Mistress St. Michael's concern with her own personal cleanliness a great eccentricity, but they liked the piece of silver her tiring woman tipped them each time to bring up the hot water. They were sorry to learn that this would be the last time the silver would be theirs. After the tub was filled Mag shooed them out, and poured a goodly dollop of bath oil into the steaming water. Instantly the room was perfumed with the scent of lavender, and Aidan smiled.

"It may not be as elegant a fragrance as some I've smelt here, Mag, but it reminds me of home, and it makes me happy," she said.

"Aye," said the tiring woman helping her to disrobe, and sit down in the little tub, "and glad I'll be to see *Pearroc Royal* again, m'lady."

"M'lady?"

"Well, ye will be in a few short hours!" Mag pinned Aidan's long hair atop her head. "And high time ye were getting married! Ye should have been wed years ago but neither ye nor yer father could see it. It's a mercy he went when he did lest ye end up an old maid like the queen! I've saved two buckets of water for yer hair. I'll not have ye louse-ridden like so many of these *fine* ladies!"

She was bathed, and her hair was washed, and then as she dried it by the fire Mag went to the kitchens to fetch her a bit of supper, but she found her normally good appetite gone, and when she went to bed she could not sleep although Mag snored comfortably next to her. She finally slipped into a restless doze only to have Mag shaking her awake. Already a bright fire burnt in the grate, but the room was chill with winter, and she dressed in her undergarments and stockings while still beneath her down coverlet. Mag had thoughtfully warmed them before the fire, but once out of bed it didn't help.

"Brrrr," she shivered.

"Ye'll be warmer when ye put yer dress on," Mag promised, and she helped her mistress into the gown. "I'd always hoped to see ye wed in yer mother's satin wedding finery, but there was no time to send for it. I'm not certain I approve of this kiss-me-quick ceremony the queen has planned for ye."

"Master O'Malley must leave court, Mag. Don't deny that ye know the scandal he has caused."

Mag chuckled lewdly. "What a rare devil he is, m'lady Aidan! The mother *and* the daughters both! Then the ambassador's wife! Hee! Hee! Hee!"

"I would have thought ye'd be shocked," Aidan said puzzled.

"If ye'd been wed to him then I would have been, but a bachelor is entitled to his little adventures, and since time began there have always been women who were willing. Besides it attests to his virility, m'lady. Ye'll be with child quick enough, and that will be good for *Pearroc Royal*."

Aidan barely heard her for she was staring at herself in the pier glass. I am pretty, she thought. In this dress I am really pretty! It was a gown that had been made by the dressmaker who sewed for Robin's mother, and it was the most beautiful thing she had ever owned. It had been finished in time for the holidays, but Aidan had been shy of wearing such an exquisite gown, afraid of drawing attention to the richness of her dress which would have possibly meant explanations of her worth. The dress had been left to hang in the cabinet. It was the only gown she owned, however, that was lovely enough to serve as a wedding dress.

The overskirt and the bodice were of a heavy, soft velvet in a wonderful shade of peacock's-tail blue. The underskirt was a rich cream-colored satin embroidered in a gold thread pattern of windflowers, small hearts, and darting butterflies. The sleeves of the dress were leg-of-mutton and held by small gold silk ribbons, the embroidered wristband turned back to form a cuff. The fan-shaped neck-wisk was made of a creamy old lace.

Aidan scarcely dared to breathe for the neckline of the dress was shockingly low. She remembered protesting when the gown had been fitted, but the dressmaker had brushed her protests aside proclaiming, "It is the fashion, madame!" Now, however, that she saw herself in the finished dress Aidan worried for only the lace edging in her chemise prevented her nipples from bursting over the rim of the neckline.

"Ye'll be wearing yer mother's pearls," said Mag, handing Aidan a long rope of pink-tinged beads, and as her mistress looped the strand once about her neck, allowing the rest of the pearls to fall over her bosom, the tiring woman fastened the large matching earbobs into Aidan's ears.

Aidan was pale with her lack of sleep, and the sudden realization of what was happening. "How shall I wear my hair?" she asked Mag.

"Loose, of course, as befits a maiden on her wedding day, m'lady. I'll dress it with the rest of the pearls. Sit down."

Mag parted Aidan's hair in the center, and brushed it free of its sleep tangles. Then she pinned several loops of pearls on either side of the girl's head. "There, now, yer ready, but for yer shoes, m'lady," and the tiring woman knelt to fit them to Aidan's feet.

The clock on the mantel struck five o'clock of the morning as Mag stood up. " 'Tis time," said Aidan, and there was a knock upon the door.

Mag handed her mistress a lovely round muff of ermine tails, and opening the door said, "Good morning, Lord Southwood. The bride is ready."

"Good morning, Aidan," said Robin, and she managed a small smile for him thinking how handsome he looked in his red velvet suit that dripped elegant lace.

Mag picked up their cloaks, and together the three hurried through the darkened, cold corridors of Greenwich Palace to the royal chapel where the queen, her chaplain, and Conn O'Malley awaited them. As they reached the chapel a footman came up to Aidan, and handed her a wreath of gilded rosemary and bay leaves saying, "Her majesty wished ye to have this for yer head, m'lady." Mag took the wreath, and placed it upon her mistress' head as a second footman stepped forward and proffered a small bouquet of white violets and green leaves saying, "These are from Master O'Malley."

Aidan took the little bouquet thinking that it was kind of Conn to remember such a thing. In her mind it somehow augured well, this small thoughtfulness.

At the door of the chapel Mag left her mistress, and entered alone. She was dressed in her best gown of black velvet with a fine lawn collar and cuffs. Quietly she made to the front of the chapel to stand behind the queen, but Elizabeth turning drew the tiring woman forward.

"Come, Mistress Mag, for she is your child, and ye will want a good view."

Mag was overwhelmed, and tears sprang to her eyes. "Thank ye, yer majesty," she whispered.

"Let the ceremony begin," the queen commanded, and Conn entered the chapel from a side door with the priest. Escorted by Robin Aidan was brought to the altar to take her place on Conn's left side.

Aidan peeped at her bridegroom from beneath her sandy lashes. His beauty almost took her breath away. He was garbed in black velvet, his doublet encrusted magnificently in pearls, and tiny diamonds sewn with silver thread. His short trunk hose were made of black velvet and cloth of silver in wide stripes, and his stockings were black with silver thread clocks embroidered upon them. His shoes were black leather with rounded toes, cut high over the instep, each adorned with a silver rosette. His short Spanish cape with its half-erect collar was black velvet lined in cloth of silver. He wore no cap, his dark hair brushed simply, its tempting forelock falling over his forehead.

The queen's chaplain raised his prayer book, and began.

"Dearly beloved, we are gathered here in the sight of God, and in the face of this company, to join together this Man and this Woman in Holy Matrimony; which is an honorable estate, instituted by God in the time of man's innocency, signifying unto us this mystical union that is betwixt God and His Church."

The words seemed to burn themselves into Aidan's brain. Marriage was a sacrament. Should she be partaking of such a sacrament with a man she barely knew? Bridal nerves, said her more practical side. Many brides are married to men they don't know. There is nothing unusual in that. Her eyes swept the altar with its lace-edged linen cloth, the tall and shapely beeswax candles that burned in the graceful gold candleholders. There was a lovely peace within the chapel. The candles flickered on the stained-glass arches. It was still dark outside.

The queen's chaplain now questioned whether "any man could show just cause" why this couple should not be "lawfully joined together, let him now speak, or else hereafter forever hold his peace." He paused for a long minute during which time there was not a sound within the royal chapel but for Mag's gentle sniffling. The chaplain turned to Conn.

"Wilt thou have this Woman to live with . . . after God's ordinance in the holy estate of Matrimony . . . to love her, comfort her, honor and keep her in sickness and in health forsaking all others for so long as ye both shall live?"

"I will," said Conn O'Malley, and Aidan's heart skipped a beat.

The priest then repeated the same question to Aidan. "Wilt thou have this Man to live with after God's ordinance in the holy estate of Matrimony . . . to obey and serve him, love, honor, and keep him in sickness and in health, forsaking all others for him so long as ye both shall live?"

"I will," whispered Aidan, and then Robin gave her over to the queen's chaplain, who placed her ungloved right hand in the right palm of Conn O'Malley who repeated after the priest the words:

"I take thee to be my wedded Wife, to have and to hold from this day forward, for better and for worse, for richer and for poorer, in sickness and in health, to love and to cherish, till death do us part, according to God's ordinance; and thereto I plight thee my troth."

His hand firmly clasping hers was warm and strong. She felt a small sense of loss as he loosed her hand so she might reverse the procedure, and taking his hand in hers she spoke her vows to him. Next came the exchanging of rings, and the queen's chaplain took them sprinkling them with holy water, and blessing them then accepted a symbolic bag of gold and silver from the groom. He then gave the bride's ring to the groom who took it with his thumb and his first two fingers, and said in a strong voice, "With this ring I thee wed, and this gold and silver I thee give, and with my body I thee worship, and with all my worldly chattels I thee endow, in the name of the Father," he held the ring over the thumb of her left hand, "and of the Son," then over the end of the first finger, "and of the Holy Ghost," over the tip of the second finger, "Amen!" and he pressed the ring down on her third finger.

The queen's chaplain offered the benediction: "May ye be blessed by the Lord, who made the Universe out of nothing!" Then concluding the ceremony with a recital of the Lord's Prayer, and several other prayers, the priest said as he united Conn and Aidan's hands, "Those whom God hath joined together, let no man put asunder." Then he declared them Man and Wife, and giving the benediction finally concluded the service by blessing the refreshments of wine and cake that the queen had prepared. "Bless, O Lord, this bread and this drink and this cup, even as thou blessed the five loaves in the desert, and the six water pots at Cana of Galilee, that they who taste of them may be sane, sober, and spotless: Savior of the world, who lives and reigns with God the Father in the unity of the Holy Ghost."

The bridecup with a sprig of rosemary was passed about, and the queen's chaplain gave Conn the benediction kiss which he then gave to Aidan who blushed becomingly. The few guests smiled at this, and the queen raising her goblet toasted the newly wedded couple.

"Happiness, long life, and healthy children, Lord and Lady Bliss."

Conn took the queen's hand, and kissed it. "My thanks, Bess. I suspect it is not too harsh a punishment ye have visited upon me."

The toast was drunk, and then the queen said, "It is time for ye to leave now lest ye be seen. It is almost dawn." Then to Aidan's surprise Elizabeth Tudor kissed her on both cheeks. "I shall miss ye, my country mouse, but I know ye will be happy. We will look forward to welcoming ye both back to court in another year."

Aidan curtsied, and kissed the queen's hand. "I shall never forget yer kindness, madame," she said.

"Be good to her, Conn St. Michael, or ye shall answer to me," said the queen, and then she turned and left the chapel.

Mag had already donned her cloak, and now she placed her mistress' cape about her, drawing the hood up so that Aidan's identity might be protected. Then she handed her gloves which were lined in warm fur.

Robin drew from his doublet several black velvet masks which he passed to Conn, Aidan, and Mag. " 'Twill doubly protect us," he said.

Masked they hurried from the royal chapel, and through the palace out into the gardens down to the quay where a barge awaited them. The tide was with them, and they swept down the river to Greenwood House where they might change into more comfortable traveling clothes before beginning their journey north to *Pearroc Royal*. It was damp and bitter cold upon the river, and Aidan shivered, snuggling down into her cloak. The sky was beginning to lighten, but the dawn was gray, and there was the slap of the wavelets against the barge.

Finally Robin said in an effort to break the tension, "Ye'll find my coach quite comfortable, and warm, Aidan. 'Twill make the journey bearable."

"I thank ye, Robin, for it would have been impossible for my coach to come from *Pearroc Royal*. Have ye sent men ahead along our route of travel to book us rooms at respectable inns?"

"Aye. Whenever we stop there will be comfortable accommodations for us all. Mag will ride in the baggage coach with Uncle Conn's man, Cluny, and will be as comfortable as we are. I want to ride a ways today so I hope ye will excuse my company."

Conn was quite impressed by his young nephew's command of the situation, and amused at his attempt to give himself and Aidan some privacy. He had not known Robin's father, but if the stories were true then Robin was certainly becoming as his father had been before him, a perfect courtier. Conn was amazed to realize that he could learn much from the boy.

The barge arrived at Greenwood, and Robin leapt lightly to the stone dock. Reaching down he aided Mag in clambering out. Conn followed, and turning back reached out to draw Aidan up.

"Good morning, Lady Bliss," he said softly.

"Good morning, my lord," she answered, her face grave and her eyes serious.

"Ye wore yer hair down," he said.

" 'Tis tradition, my lord, for a maiden to leave her hair unbound."

"Ye looked beautiful, Aidan."

"All brides are beautiful."

"I have arranged," he said as he escorted her up to the house, "that we break our fast before we begin our journey. Then ye will want to change into more comfortable clothing for traveling. We will eat together, alone."

"Alone?" She eyed him nervously.

"We are married, Aidan. Yet we know little of one another. I have not come willingly to this wedding for I wanted to choose my own wife, according to my own tastes. Instead I find that for my indiscretions I am punished by being given a wife not of my own choice. My views of marriage are varied, and most not pleasant. I barely remember my father who died when I was still in nappies, and long skirts. My mother never remarried. I have six half-sisters. One is a nun. Four are sour-faced, disapproving women made old before their time by the harshness of life in Ireland. Perhaps that is why I did not want to stay there. I cannot remember in my entire lifetime ever seeing my sisters laugh with their husbands, or share an intimate moment or touch with them. My brothers are not much better with their wives. Until I came to England I did not know that a marriage could be a good thing. I learned this from my sister Skye. Ye will meet her in a few days, and I want ye to like her, Aidan. She is the most incredibly loving and magnificent woman I have ever known."

"And ye wanted a wife like her," said Aidan in a small, tight voice.

"I don't know what I want in a wife exactly, Aidan, but surely Skye and Adam cannot be the only married couple in the entire world who share everything, and respect one another's individuality. That is what I have always wanted when the time came for me to marry. I still want it."

"Those things come," said Aidan, "from knowing, and loving one another. My parents loved each other dearly, and were always kind and thoughtful of one another. That is what I seek, Conn, so it seems, we are not too different in our goals for a married life."

They entered Greenwood House, and Aidan looked about her with interest. It was a lovely house, small yet spacious. A maidservant came to take her cloak, and Conn led her up the stairs, and down a wide corridor into a cheerful and warm apartment.

"Greenwood," said Conn, "belongs to my sister Skye, but she is banned from court, and so does not come to London. She was kind enough to put the house at my disposal."

"And now ye are banned from court," chuckled Aidan. "Is it a family tradition, Conn? Is this perhaps something that ye should tell me about?"

He laughed a deep, warm laugh, enjoying her teasing as much as the humor in the situation. "My sister, and the queen are very much alike, and as a consequence often clash. Unfortunately for Skye, it is Elizabeth Tudor who holds the supreme power, and so my sister finds herself living at *Queen's Malvern*." A young maid came forward, and Conn said, "Perhaps ye would like to refresh yerself, Aidan. We will eat very shortly."

When she had washed her face and hands in a silver basin in the bedchamber of the apartment, she began to tidy her hair, pinning it up, but Conn seeing it from the doorway said, "Nay, Aidan, leave yer hair down," and so pulling the pins from her head, she brushed it, and returned to join him.

The servants had set up a lovely table in the main room of Conn's apartment. It was laid with a fine linen cloth, and silver, and her little wedding bouquet had been made into a centerpiece. After Greenwich Palace she found this room warm and toasty. Through the windows she could see that dawn had finally broken, but true to the earlier sky the day was overcast and gray.

Conn held out her chair for her remarking as he did so, "If ye'd worn gowns like that at court, Aidan, I certainly would have noticed ye, and so would every other man with eyes in his head."

"I wanted to be liked for me, and not for my face and figure, or for the fact that I am an heiress." She laughed. "Without something to recommend me, however, no one noticed the queen's country mouse. I was as anonymous as bread pudding even considering my size."

"When we return to court next year I want ye to wear only the most beautiful clothes, my funny wife, for I shall very much enjoy being the envy of the gentlemen of the court, none of whom could see the jewel beneath stone."

"Hah, Conn St. Michael! Even ye did not see the jewel until the queen stuffed it in yer pocket!"

He laughed again. " 'Tis a truth, Aidan." Then he grew somber. "Conn St. Michael," he said. "*Conn St. Michael*. Well, it has a good ring to it."

"Is it hard, exchanging yer name for mine?"

"Perhaps not so much as strange. As the queen pointed out to me, there are plenty of O'Malleys, but without me, there will be no more St. Michaels. Do ye realize, lass, that we are the founders of a new family, a new dynasty? Shall we have many fine sons and daughters, Aidan, my wife? How many of each do ye desire?"

"Oh, I should think half a dozen of each, my lord. At least! But could we first eat breakfast? I am starving!"

He grinned delighted at finding to his immense surprise that he liked her. The queen had been correct in saying his bride had wit. Other than Elizabeth Tudor who was a law unto herself, he had never considered wit a virtue in a woman, but he was rethinking his position.

The servants offered beautifully cooked and prepared dishes of eggs poached in heavy cream and malmsey, thick slices of sweet, pink ham, and a bowl of stewed pears and apples. There was a fresh loaf of bread, still warm from the oven, a crock of sweet butter, a small cheese, and a choice of wine or ale. Conn was amused to find that Aidan had a hearty appetite, that she ate with a good will, and refused nothing. He was careful in his table manners for hers were delicately refined, and he was not used to sharing his meal with a woman.

When they had finished she sat back in her chair, and declared, "That is the best meal I have had since I left *Pearroc Royal*! The queen's cooks are fine, but they tend to oversauce, and their food is not always the freshest. I could taste it beneath the spices. Did ye like those eggs? I will ask the chef for the recipe before we leave today."

"Those things interest ye?"

"Everything that has to do with the running of a house and estate interests me. It is what my father raised me to do. How were ye raised, Conn? I know as little about ye, as ye do about me."

"How was I raised?" He thought a moment, and then he said, "I was the youngest of my father's sons. His first wife had produced six daughters before my eldest brother, Michael, was born. Michael is the priest. His mother died birthing him, and my father quickly remarried, this time choosing a young, healthy girl although I've no doubt his first wife was healthy enough before all her confinements. She bore ten children, losing three sons in infancy, before her own death.

"My mother quickly proved a fertile breeder to my father's delight, I am told. He doted upon her, they say. She bore him four healthy sons in as many years. He died when I was three, and I remember little of him but for a big, black-bearded man with a deep laugh and a voice like thunder. My mother is a sweet woman, but without Dubhdara O'Malley she was lost. My brothers and I ran roughshod over her. Only Michael, our half-brother, respected and honored her properly. When she could our half-

70

sister Skye tried to tame us, even sending my two eldest brothers off to learn the sea as our father had before us. Then my third brother wanted to go, and finally myself."

"Did ye like the sea?" Aidan questioned him.

"I hated it! I was always getting sick at the least sign of rocky weather, and how Brian, Shane, and Shamus teased me for it. When Skye found out, however, she brought me home, and sent me off to St. Brendan's where my brother Michael was in school. Michael, of course, was studying for the priesthood, but Skye simply wanted me educated enough to handle the trading company she had formed in the name of the O'Malleys in an effort to make our family more respectable. Our father was little more than an elegant pirate who lured treasure ships to their doom along our rocky coast, and then helped himself to the salvage.

"I didn't take to school any better than I had taken to the sea, and I stayed just long enough to learn how to read, and write. The good monks were happy to see me go," he chuckled. "I returned home where my mother spent the next several years spoiling me. I outgrew my seasickness, and eventually went off to sea for a time with my brothers, but it wasn't what I wanted."

"How did ye come to England?" Aidan queried him. She was absolutely fascinated with his small history which was so unlike her own.

"Several years ago my brothers joined with a distant cousin in privateering ventures against English ships. Her name is Grace O'Malley, and she is called the Pirate Queen of Connaught. Her fleet was made considerably stronger by the addition of our ships. The queen wished it stopped, and so she kidnapped my infant niece Velvet de Marisco in order that my sister Skye, who was then the head of our family, help her.

"Skye suggested that the queen give my brothers letters of marque to sail for England rather than with Grace against it. When she came home to Ireland to persuade them, I returned with her afterward to England, and that is how I arrived at court. Bess liked me from the start."

"Robin says ye were bearded, and wore trews and a plaid when ye came. He says ye could barely speak English."

"He's right," chuckled Conn. "I was a true Irish savage as that fancy little milord, my nephew, has noted."

"He admires ye," said Aidan not wishing to cause a breach between the two.

"He's in love with ye," said Conn mischievously.

"What?" said Aidan, very surprised.

" 'Tis puppy love to be sure, but I've been warned to be good to ye else I face young Lord Southwood's wrath."

Aidan smiled a soft smile. "He was so good to me when I first came to court five months ago. Without him I should have been totally miserable."

"They say he is like his father, and Skye certainly loved Geoffrey Southwood. He was a child born of love."

"All children should be born of love. I know I was."

"Did yer parents know each other long before they married?"

Aidan laughed. "They never laid eyes upon one another until the day my mother arrived from Ireland, and the wedding was almost immediately. My mother was a wonderful woman. I never heard a harsh word from her. She always seemed to be gay, and even in the bad times when she would lose her babies she was convinced that the next time would be different. She and my twin sisters died when I was ten. My father never really recovered from her death. He devoted himself to me, and I to him."

There was a knock upon the door, and Walters, the majordomo of Greenwood House, entered the room. "My lord, the coach is ready for ye anytime ye wish to leave, and may I say that we shall miss yer lordship, and are sorry to see ye go."

"Thank ye, Walters, but I shall be returning in another year with Lady Bliss. My wife must change her clothing for she does not wish to travel in her wedding gown. We will not be long."

"Very good, my lord. Please convey the staff's good wishes to Lord and Lady de Marisco," said Walters, and then he discreetly withdrew.

"I shall need Mag, and one of my trunks," said Aidan standing up.

"There is no need," replied Conn. "I shall maid ye myself. I have a surprise for ye in the bedchamber. Come along, wife!" and standing up he took her hand and drew her into the next room.

There upon the bed was a beautiful, high-necked gown of a rich, brown velvet, trimmed in gold. Next to it were several flannel petticoats, and a pretty pair of knitted woolen stockings in a natural color. On the other side of the dress was a matching full-length cloak with gold frog closures, a corner of which had been turned back to show its furred lining. Next to the cape was a pair of Florentine leather gloves, soft, cream-colored leather embroidered in tiny pearls.

Aidan's mouth formed itself into an O of surprise much to her new husband's pleasure. "Where . . . ?" she began. "How . . . ?"

"Yer wedding gown came from my sister's dressmaker. Robin had told me that. After we spoke two days ago I went to her, and requested she make several gowns for ye that would flatter yer coppery hair. I dislike all the black ye wear. I realize that yer mourning yer father, but now I would like to see ye in colors that complement yer hair, and yer skin. Yer father obviously had old-fashioned ideas about dressing ye."

"My father—" began Aidan hotly, but Conn interrupted her.

"Yer father looked at ye as a daughter. I, however, am looking at ye like a husband, and a lover. Now turn around, Aidan, so I may unlace ye!" and he spun her about so he might undo her gown.

"Ohhh!" Aidan was outraged. She was also suddenly very aware that she was alone with this man, and he was undoing her gown. Her first instinct was to protest, and the words of outrage were already forming upon her lips. Then she remembered who this man was. He was her husband, and every law known, both England's and God's, gave him the power of life and death over her. Aidan stood very still as Conn pushed her long hair aside, and undid her gown.

"There, lass, now I'll leave ye to change out of my own finery. When ye need me to redo yer new gown, I'll come."

Aidan whirled about. "Conn!" He stopped, and turned back to her. "The gown, it's lovely! It all is!"

"There's more coming from the dressmaker, but 'twill be sent to *Pearroc Royal*. I convinced Madame to hurry one gown so ye'd have it for traveling."

"Thank ye."

He flashed her a grin, and then left her.

Aidan stepped from her wedding dress, eager to try on the lovely brown velvet gown. The color had almost a faint golden tone to it, or was it the gold embroidery upon the bodice, and the creamy antiqued color of the collar that made it appear that way? She kicked her silken petticoats aside, and gratefully slipped into the flannel ones he had provided. She appreciated again Conn's thoughtfulness which had first been evidenced in the fragrant white violets he had given her for a wedding bouquet. She rolled her elegant silk stockings from her long legs, and put on the gossamer fine woolen ones. How had he guessed the proper length? She was certain that the dressmaker did not have those measurements, and yet the stockings fit her perfectly. Then she saw by the side of the bed a pair of beautifully made brown leather boots that were lined in rabbit fur. She didn't even have to try them on to know that they would fit, she thought as sitting upon the bed she pulled the boots onto her feet. Standing up again she was finally ready to put on the velvet gown, and when she had slipped it on she twirled before the long pier glass at her reflection in the mirror. Never before had she noticed the faint rosy shade of her cheeks, or the rich color of her copper hair. It was amazing, and yet Conn had known what this color would do for her.

"Here," he said coming up behind her, and startling her, "let me fasten yer gown for ye, Aidan." When he had finished he whirled her about, and looking at her critically finally smiled saying, "I knew it! It's a perfect color for ye!" He, too, had changed into warmer, more practical clothing of less spectacular elegance. Gone was his splendid jewel-encrusted doublet, and in its place was a plain dark green velvet one to match his trunk hose. He wore leather boots to his knee, and a wide belt from which dangled a rapier and a short dagger. "Are ye ready now?" he asked her.

Aidan bit her lip. "There is one thing I must do, my lord, and then I shall be ready."

"What?"

She blushed. "I must make a trip to the necessary, my lord."

Now it was Conn's turn to flush, and then he laughed softly at himself. "I can see having a wife will involve getting used to many things. No woman has ever spoken to me of the necessary before."

Aidan began to see the humor in their situation. "I think this will not be the last time I mention it to ye on our long journey. Though I strive for delicacy of speech, my lord, I know not how else to word it."

"I, too, shall strive for delicacy of manner, my lady. I shall await ye in the dayroom," and giving her a bow and a mischievous wink he withdrew.

When Aidan entered the dayroom several minutes later she had bound her hair up into two thick braids which she had wound about her head.

"But I like yer hair loose," he protested.

"I will wear it loose in the privacy of our home, but I cannot travel with it that way, or wear it so in public. It is not seemly now that I am a matron."

"Do ye always behave according to convention, Aidan?"

"Yes, my lord, I do."

Moving to face her he locked her eyes with his, and pulled the pins from her hair in a slow and deliberate manner. "I do not behave according to convention, *wife*," he said, and his look dared her to challenge him as he ran his fingers through her tresses to loosen the braids.

The green eyes staring into her face mesmerized her, and as had happened the other day Aidan found herself forgetting to breathe again. The touch of his fingers was sending little shivers through her. Why, her numbed brain demanded, why could he have this effect upon her? Then she grew dizzy, and gasping gulped several breaths of air into her lungs.

If Conn noticed her peculiar behavior he said nothing. Instead he fastened the gold frog closings upon her cape, and drew her hood up over her hair. "There, no one will know of yer wanton behavior in leaving yer hair unbound, and I shall be able to enjoy the sight of it as we ride along.

Do ye have yer gloves, madame? The dampness in the air makes it even colder than it is today." Reaching down he took her bouquet from the table and handed it to her. Then taking her arm when she nodded, still speechless, he led her from the room and downstairs to where the coach awaited them.

The staff of Greenwood House had lined up to bid Conn a fond farewell for he had been living there since his arrival at court over two years ago. He had been an easy master to serve; a courteous man who always remembered to acknowledge a kindness, or a service well done. Although their lives would be simplified by his going, they would miss him, and Walters said as much. It was unfortunate that Master . . . rather Lord Bliss, was leaving them especially now that he had a wife. She was no beauty like Lady de Marisco, but they could see she was a modest and sweet-natured lady, just the sort of wife he should have.

Conn and Aidan were settled into Robin's large, comfortable traveling coach. Bricks warmed and wrapped in flannel were placed at their feet, a fur lap robe was tucked about them, a small brass brazier of lit charcoals was placed upon the floor of the carriage. The coach was upholstered both on its seats and walls in padded dark green velvet. It even had glass in its windows, and small interior carriage lamps that could be lit if it grew dark while they were still traveling.

Walters stuck his head in a final time to be assured that they were well settled. "The back of the front seat pulls down, my lord. Behind it ye will find a hamper should ye grow hungry before ye reach yer destination. God go with ye!" Then pulling his head back he slammed the door to the coach shut, and ordered the driver forward.

Because of the time of year it had been decided that they would travel the entire day, each day, stopping only to change horses, the earl's carriage animals having been taken ahead by his grooms to the various posting places. February weather could be treacherous, and under the best of conditions it was several days' journey from London to *Pearroc Royal*. Then, too, it being winter, the days were short. The hamper, which could be replenished each day, would serve to feed them until they stopped each night. The coachman and his assistant up upon the box had also been supplied with a filled hamper for not only themselves, but the dozen outriders who accompanied them to protect them from highwaymen. The smaller baggage coach that followed them was equally provisioned. The servants would eat as the horses were being changed, but the lord and lady who traveled in such style could eat whenever they chose.

The journey would take them five days for *Pearroc Royal* was outside the town of Worcester several miles to the west toward the Welsh border.

Being deepest winter the landscape was somewhat dull, the bare-limbed trees, black and spare, reaching out to the slate sky. It was very cold, and although the Thames was open to traffic, there were sheets of ice floating upon it, and the ponds and lakes they passed were for the most part frozen. As the day progressed they saw little sign of life except for smoke which came from the chimneys of the farms and other homes they passed, or perhaps a dog which would run yapping from some farmyard to chase snapping after the wheels of the coach as it passed by.

It wasn't until late morning that having traveled a distance of ten miles they stopped to change horses at a large inn. Robin was already there ahead of them, and had ordered hot mulled wine. Aidan was delighted to have the opportunity to alight from the coach, and move about. In the few minutes that they allowed themselves one of the servants from the inn reheated their bricks in the fire and rewrapped them as well as putting fresh, burning charcoals in the brazier.

Climbing back into the coach she found that the wine had made her sleepy, and the motion of the carriage lulled her. Her eyes grew heavy, and she never remembered dropping off. When she awoke it was growing dark with late afternoon, and she found herself nestled against Conn, their heads touching against one another as he, too, dozed lightly. The coach was cold, and her feet were chilled, but where his arm was about her she felt warm, and contented, and so she stayed quiet. The light was fading, and the inky darkness that was fast descending hinted of snow. Then up ahead she could see the lights of a village, or an inn, and feeling the horses slowing she knew that they were approaching their lodging. She felt just the tiniest bit of disappointment for it had been pleasant lying here in the gloom against him.

Conn had been awake, and he had also been aware of when she had awakened, but realizing she thought him asleep he had stayed still for he was frankly enjoying their closeness. He knew that if he spoke she would feel bound to break the contact. Sleeping had relaxed Aidan, and he had had ample opportunity to study her features. She had lovely skin, and her features were pretty, but her forehead was high, and her nose just a shade too short. She had thick, stubby eyelashes of a sandy hue, and thin brows that arched over her eyes, the color of which he was still not yet able to determine. The dimple in her chin was not deep, but he detected a strong hint of firmness about that chin. He liked her mouth best of all her features. It was a generous mouth, wide, the lips full without being ugly, and it seemed to him, infinitely kissable.

He would kiss that mouth tonight, but remembering the last time he had done so he amended his thought. He would teach her how to kiss him tonight, and he smiled to himself. He somehow thought he would enjoy playing the schoolmaster. She didn't dislike his kisses. Both on Twelfth Night, and two nights ago when they had met formally she had melted into his embrace. Then a thought occurred to him. Had she truly enjoyed his kisses, or had it simply been her inexperience, and she was indeed very inexperienced. He couldn't imagine a girl reaching his wife's age, and never having been kissed, or cuddled, but Aidan's behavior convinced him that she was telling him the truth.

Tonight. Tonight was their wedding night. For the first time in his life he had the legal right to bed a woman, and he didn't know whether he should or not. Lack of familiarity or knowledge of his bedmate had certainly never prevented him from enjoying a woman before; but this was his wife. He was going to have to live with this woman until death parted them. It was a sobering thought. What did she know of marital relations? Surely her mother had instructed her, but then he remembered that her mother had died when she was still a child, and he doubted her father had gone into such matters with her. He had never had a maid before, not even his own first time when full of whiskey and randier than a young billygoat he had caught a milkmaid and tumbled her beneath a hedge. To his surprise she wasn't the least bit shy, and had helped him to find his way egging him on with small cries of delight. Encouraged Conn had gone on to other women, and found that where lovemaking was concerned he had a definite talent.

On the mainland across from his island home of Innisfana he had caught the eye of an older woman, the widow of a nobleman, whose name was Peggy Brady. Peggy had taught him patience, and how a woman's pleasure could only increase his own. She had shown him caresses and kisses that were daring and exciting, and when she had decided he had learned all she might teach him, she had dismissed him as if he were a schoolboy. He would always be grateful to Peggy, and particularly now. Another man might demand his rights from his bride, but Conn had already decided that he wanted Aidan to know him better, to feel comfortable with him, to perhaps even like him a little. Tonight he would tell her that; tell her that she need have no fears on his account.

Ahead he could see the lights of the inn where they would be staying tonight. Yawning, he stretched, and sitting up said, "Are ye awake, Aidan? We'll be at the King's Head in a few minutes."

"I'm awake, my lord. I see that ye slept as little as I did last night. I am still tired."

"Ye'll feel better after a hot meal, lass," he said.

"We never ate the food the Greenwood staff packed for us."

"No matter," he said. "It's so cold it will keep until tomorrow."

The coach drew into the inn yard of the King's Head, and no sooner had it stopped than the innkeeper hurried out to open the door. "Welcome, m'lord, m'lady! We've kept yer rooms and a hot supper waiting!"

Conn sprang from the vehicle, and then turning he reached into the carriage and lifted Aidan down. Following the innkeeper inside they found they had been given two pleasant rooms, both with fireplaces, on the ground floor of the building. Mag and Cluny hurried in behind them, each anxious to help their master and mistress.

"Take the capes!" snapped Mag to Conn's man.

"And who are ye to be giving me orders, Mrs. Mag?"

"Capes is the man's job where there is a man for the job," she answered him. "Boots is a man's job too. 'Tis obvious ye don't know yer duties."

"Not know me duties?" Cluny was totally outraged. "I'll have ye know, Mrs. Mag, that I've served his lordship for these last six years, and never a complaint from him!"

"How could he complain? He obviously knows no more than ye do."

"Mag!" Aidan's voice was slightly reproving, and she even surprised herself for Mag had raised her, and she had never found it necessary to seriously scold her tiring woman. "I do not want ye and Cluny quarreling. As body servants to my husband and myself ye must set an example for the rest of the servants at *Pearroc Royal*. When we arrive home I will set ye each yer duties, but in the meantime ye must settle it between ye." Mag looked properly chastened, and she was suddenly aware that the child she had raised lovingly was now a woman. Aidan turned to Cluny. "There was no time for us to be introduced, Cluny, but judging from my husband's elegant clothing ye must take fine care of him. Will ye take our capes, please. They are heavy, and Mag so little that they will weigh her down."

Cluny shot Mag a look that plainly said, well at least yer lady has manners, and then bowing neatly he took first Aidan's cloak and then Conn's. "Thank ye, m'lady."

"Put out my night things, Mag, and then go have some dinner."

"Will ye be wanting a bath, m'lady?"

"Nay, not tonight."

Mag curtsied, and went to do her mistress' bidding while Cluny having hung the cloaks in the cabinet was also placing his master's things out for the night. Neither servant would leave until the other was ready, and when they had left both Conn and Aidan looked at each other and burst out laughing.

"Do ye think they'll ever like each other?" Conn asked. "Yer Mag is a scrappy little terrier of a woman."

.   "I don't think yer Cluny is about to be bullied by her. She's simply very protective of her duties and of me. She'll get used to ye both soon enough."

The innkeeper's wife hurried in with two maidservants to lay the table, and begin serving the supper. Upon the sideboard a row of covered dishes and platters were set, and all exuded fragrant odors to various degrees. There were two decanters of wine, and two frosty pitchers, one filled with nut-brown ale, and the other with cider.

"We will serve ourselves," Conn told the innkeeper's wife, and the goodwife beamed and nodded as she backed from the room.

"Ye've quite enchanted her," said Aidan. "She was quite speechless."

"A strange effect I seem to have on some women," he admitted. "Are ye hungry?"

"Aye! I'm always hungry, and Mag declares that I eat as much as a day laborer working in the fields which she tells me is not at all ladylike. I hope my appetite will not shock ye. I never seem to grow heavier despite my great lust for good food."

"I don't like a woman who picks at her plate," he said. "Eat hearty for Robin will not be joining us tonight," said Conn.

"Why not?"

"I believe he is making an attempt to be discreet. It is, after all, our wedding night."

"Yes," she said, and lifting the cover from one of the dishes exclaimed, "Quail! Oh, I do love quail!" and she helped herself to one of the small birds that had been roasted to a turn.

Conn smiled softly. She *was* nervous. "Serve me one of those quail, too, madame," he answered her.

Aidan heaped her husband's plate high with quail, and a thick slab of beef, a piece of rabbit pie, a spoonful of tiny white onions that had been braised in milk and butter and were topped with ground peppercorns, and a second spoonful of carrots. In a separate dish she served him a generous helping of mussels that had been steamed in white wine, and topped with a Dijon mustard sauce. "What will ye have to drink, my lord?"

"Ale."

She poured him a gobletful, and then setting his supper upon the table she offered him his napkin. Sitting opposite her he could see that her plate was as full as his, and neither of them spoke as they ate hungrily. She tore off a piece of bread from the round cottage loaf, and handed it to him, then took a piece herself and sopped up the juices on her plate with it. She drank white wine, perhaps a bit too much, he thought as she re-filled her goblet a third time during their meal.

Finally she sat back, a satisfied look of contentment upon her face, and said, "I can eat no more!"

"There's a gooseberry tart on the sideboard," he said.

She looked regretful, but shook her head. "I couldn't. Not now. I am tired for I was up early this morning, and did not sleep a great deal last night. I want to go to bed now."

"Go, and prepare yerself then, madame," he said. "Let me help ye with yer gown." He turned her about, and undid her dress for her.

Aidan never even looked back at him. She walked to the bedchamber, and entering the room closed the door behind her. There was a key in the lock. She turned it softly. He was not coming into this room tonight. She had made that decision two nights ago when they had met formally for the first time. Her own mother had come from Ireland to wed and bed a stranger, but that had been different. Bevin had been raised to expect such a thing. She had not. She had always assumed that when the time came for her to marry she would know her betrothed husband.

Ye picked him, the small voice in her head said. Why did ye pick him if ye didn't want him? "I do want him!" she whispered, "but not until we know one another better. I will not be like all the other jades he has known."

Removing her gown she spread it carefully over a chair, adding her petticoats, chemise, and stockings to the pile. Mag had laid a white silk nightgown upon the bed, and Aidan slipped it over her head. It had a high neck with pink ribbons which she tied together, and full sleeves that were edged in lace. Methodically Aidan washed her face, and hands, and teeth in the basin of water that had been left to warm on the hearth. Then she brushed her hair, and finally putting on her little lawn night-cap, and tying their matching pink ribbons, she climbed into the comfortable bed opposite the fireplace. She was just dozing off when his voice called through the door, "Aidan, may I come in now?" She tensed, and debated whether or not to answer him. Finally she decided it was better to pretend she was asleep.

He knocked upon the door. "Aidan! Are ye all right? Answer me!" He sounded worried, and she felt guilty.

"I have retired, my lord," she said faintly.

"I, too, would like to retire, Aidan. Open this door!"

"Ye will sleep in the parlor, my lord."

"*Will I?*" His voice sounded faintly ominous.

"Ye cannot expect me to welcome a stranger into my bed, my lord. I am not some lightskirt like the women ye knew at court!"

"I am hardly a stranger, Aidan. I am yer husband."

"But I don't know ye!" she wailed, and then gave a little shriek as the door to the bedchamber was kicked open.

He stood silhouetted in the entryway for a moment, and he looked so big that she was suddenly frightened. "Madame! There will be no locked doors between us, *ever*! Do ye understand me?" He advanced into the room, and he seemed to increase in size as he neared the bed. "Do ye understand me?" he repeated.

"If ye come any nearer," she shot back at him, "I shall scream the inn down!" She clutched the bedclothes to her breasts, her knuckles white in the firelight that lit the room.

"And having screamed the inn down what will ye tell those who come, Aidan? What is there to be fearful of?"

Her oval face stared up defiantly at him. "I will scream," she reiterated her threat.

He sat down upon the edge of the bed, and she gasped, but he threatened menacingly, "If ye scream, I shall beat ye!" Startled, her lips clamped shut. "That is better," he said. "Now listen to me, Aidan, *my wife*, ye do not have to fear me this night, or any other night. I have already realized that yer far more innocent than most girls of sixteen, let alone twenty-three. I have never needed to resort to rape, and because yer legally mine has not changed my thoughts in that direction. I am going to get undressed, and I am getting into this bed, but there will be nothing between us, Aidan, until ye feel yer ready. Do ye understand me?"

She nodded, but then said, "Why must ye sleep in this bed?"

"Because there is no other, and it is damnably cold. When we arrive at *Pearroc Royal* we may have separate bedchambers."

"There is only one master's chamber at *Pearroc Royal*. It is not the largest house in the world, my lord."

"Then we will continue with this arrangement, Aidan, but I will never force ye." He got up from the bed, and began to undress before the firelight.

She had never seen a man's body, and half-curious, half-fearful she spied on him through partly closed eyes. He was so big. Clothes frequently added to a man's girth, but in Conn's case it was not so. His long slender legs soared into tight buttocks which flared into a slim waist and broadened into a wide back and shoulders. When he turned about to wash in the basin that Cluny had left him, Aidan squeezed her eyes tightly shut. She was not quite ready to know everything! She felt the bed sag with his weight, and immediately she tensed.

"Are ye asleep yet?" he asked in a gentle voice.

"N-nay."

"Come here to me then," he said softly, and drew her into the curve of his arm, her head upon his shoulder.

"There! Is that not cozy, Aidan? Will ye give me a kiss good night?"

"If y-ye wish i-it, my lord." Damn! She felt like such a fool! He was being so reasonable, so thoughtful of her sensibilities. Was this the man whose reputation was that of a lecher, and a rake? Why was he being so kind?

Conn raised himself up on one elbow so he might look down upon her. "Tell me the truth, Aidan. Until Twelfth Night when I took my forfeit in our game of Blind Man's Bluff, had ye ever been kissed before? Ever played courting games that men and maids are apt to play?"

"Nay," she said softly.

"Ye've never been courted by any man?"

"Nay."

"Then ye must be courted, sweetheart, for I would not rob ye of that joy which every lass must taste." He bent, and touched her lips with his own.

Aidan felt a thrill race through her as he touched her, and her mouth softened. She was beginning to understand why so many ladies succumbed to Conn. He was a very persuasive and romantic man.

"That's it, sweetheart," he murmured against her lips. "Let me love ye just a little. I'll not hurt ye."

His kisses trailed down her throat, and around to a spot beneath her ear that was incredibly sensitive. She actually quivered when his mouth buried itself there. "Ohhh!" She blushed at having revealed herself so, but it seemed to please him. His fingers slid into the tangle of her hair to cup her head, and he kissed her ear, murmuring soft sounds into it as he did so. She could feel her own senses reeling, and she thought, *if I knew what he wanted to do I would let him. I want something, but I don't know what it is I want! Should a wife be so bold? Oh, God, I wish I knew! And yet I don't want him to believe he has made another easy conquest lest he be quickly bored with me as he has been bored with all the others.*

She was sweet! Dear heaven, this delightfully innocent bride of his was so very sweet. It came to him as something of a shock to realize that Aidan was the one woman he had been seeking all his life! He did not understand how he knew this fact, but know it he did. At this very moment his desire to possess her was growing fast. He wanted to make love to this girl he had only met briefly but two days ago. He wanted to tear her prim little nightshift from her body, and bury himself in her softness. The warm sweet scent of her body, faintly perfumed with lavender, taunted him, but it was up to him as the more experienced of the two to treat her with courtesy and gentleness. Whatever transpired between them tonight would set the tone for their whole marriage. He regretted they were such strangers.

"Do ye like being kissed, sweetheart?" he said gently.

She opened her eyes and looked up at him, slightly bemused, and for the first time he was able to place their color. Her eyes were gray, a silvery gray with tiny flecks of gold in them that reminded him of bits of leaves in an October pond. Her gaze was shy, but unwavering. "Aye, my lord," she said in a low tone. "I like yer kisses, but then," and suddenly the eyes twinkled at him, "I have naught to compare them with so perhaps my judgment is not the very best."

Conn laughed softly although at the same time he was perhaps a trifle put out. She was certainly honest to a fault. "Since I don't intend to have ye making comparisons, sweetheart, I am glad that I please ye. Now go to sleep, Aidan, my wife. We must make an early start tomorrow for I do not like the looks of the weather at all, and we have many miles to travel. I suspect a winter storm is brewing, and I can only hope that we reach *Pearroc Royal* before it breaks."

Aidan smiled up at him, and then turning on her side tried to sleep. Turning against her Conn slipped an arm about her to draw her back against him in spoon fashion. Aidan's heart skipped a quick beat as he lightly kissed the sensitive back of her neck, but then he settled down, and was soon snoring lightly, his breath coming in little puffs against her nape, and tickling it lightly. Lying there in his embrace she found that she enjoyed this conjugal closeness. It pervaded her entire body like warm honey, relaxing her so that she sighed deeply, and when she did his embrace tightened slightly. With a small smile of happiness upon her lips, she at last fell asleep.

Chapter 4

To her blushing surprise Aidan found herself awakened by a quick teasing kiss the following morning. Conn was up, and dressed, and it was yet dark outside. A fire already burnt in the room grate to Aidan's relief for despite the warmth from the fireplace the floors were icy cold.

"Good morrow, sweetheart! Ye look so pretty and peaceful sleeping there that I hated to wake ye, but 'tis past four, and we must be on the road by five at the latest. There's a small breakfast laid in the parlor, nothing special, just a little oat stirabout, bread, honey, and wine, but 'twill serve, and the innkeeper's wife is packing up a large basket for the coach."

His efficiency amazed her. She hadn't thought about Conn as efficient, but then realized that her only knowledge of him stemmed from her brief contact with him, his nephew's admiring tales, and the royal court's gossip, which swirled mistily about her husband, *the Handsomest Man at Court*. Conn was the stuff of which admiring men and women made legends about, but very little of these stories revealed the whole man; a man she was only beginning to see. It was becoming very obvious to her that beneath the elegant, beautiful, and polished courtier there was an extremely capable man.

"Thank ye, my lord. How thoughtful of ye to think of a hot breakfast. I am ravenous!" She slid from the bed, wincing at the cold floor.

They departed the inn shortly before five o'clock of the morning. It was almost two hours before sunrise, but the waning moon slipping in and out of the lowering clouds offered them occasional light along the road. The weather threatened for the next few days, but it wasn't until the chimneys of *Pearroc Royal* came into view that the snow finally began to fall.

Conn was enchanted by his first view of *Pearroc Royal*. It was a very old gray stone house caught in the tender embrace of dark green ivy that climbed up its four walls. Constructed in the year 1460 by a nobleman who, seeking to gain favor with his king, had raised upon his own lands a small hunting lodge, simple in its design. It was not particularly large, having never been meant to contain more than a few men out for sport. Whether or not its patron had received any largesse from the monarch he gifted was not known by the St. Michaels, but the records showed that royalty had only visited *Pearroc Royal* twice.

The first Lord Bliss had found that although the house was basically sound, it needed a good deal of work to make it habitable for a family. He had rebuilt *Pearroc Royal*, adding great windows and several brick chimneys that soared above the peaked and snow-clad roofs of Cotswold slates. He had left the main floor of the house practically as he found it, but on the upper floor he had done much construction according to Aidan. She told her husband that where there had once been only a Great Chamber, there were now several bedchambers off a central hallway.

The original grant had also included a two hundred acre deer park from which the estate had taken its name, *Pearroc Royal* being the old English for *Park Royal*. Deer, however, brought in no revenues with which to fatten the parsimonious king's purse, and so it had been relatively easy for Henry VII to give away the small estate to Aidan's great-grandfather in exchange for his generosity to Prince Arthur.

The coach rumbled up the driveway, and came to a stop before the front entry. At once the arched oaken door swung open, and several servants hurried out to aid the vehicle's occupants. The door to the carriage was opened, its steps pulled down, and a hand was thrust in to help Aidan descend.

"Welcome home, Mistress Aidan!" said the white-haired butler.

"Thank ye, Beal, but 'tis Lady Bliss now, and this gentleman is the new Lord Bliss." She waved her hand at Conn who had descended the coach behind her. "Let us go inside. Are all the servants assembled? I shall explain everything." They hurried into the building entering through a covered porch that opened into a long hallway. Aidan led the way into the Great Hall which was on the left, and separated from the corridor by two beautifully carved screens that sat on either side of the entry to the Great Hall.

In the Great Hall there were over twenty people milling about, but at their first sight of Aidan all chatter ceased, and their faces were, to a man, wreathed in smiles. "Welcome home, Mistress Aidan," they chorused.

Aidan smiled happily back at the household staff. "Thank ye," she said. "I have missed ye all, but I have come home because I have a happy surprise for ye. When my father gave my custody to her majesty he requested two things of our queen. That she find me a good husband, and that he take our family name so that there would be another generation of St. Michaels. This gentleman is my husband, Conn St. Michael, Lord Bliss. He is yer new master, and I hope ye will all serve him as loyally as ye have served my beloved father, and as ye have served me."

Beal, who was the butler and head of the staff, stepped forward. He was an older man, of average height, but with a stately bearing that was increased by his snow-white hair. "Welcome home, my lord," he said. "If ye will allow I will present the staff."

Conn nodded.

"Mistress Beal, my spouse, is the housekeeper," he began, and then went on to introduce Erwina the cook, Leoma the laundress, Rankin the gardener, Haig the head groom, Martin the coachman, and Tom his assistant. Then came the four footmen, the four housemaids, the two kitchen maids, the potboy, the knife sharpener, the two assistant laundresses, the four men who helped in the garden, and two of the four stablemen, the other two currently stabling the young Earl of Lynmouth's coach and horses.

To each servant Conn nodded his acknowledgment, smiling winningly at all the ladies who were immediately enchanted by him. "I thank ye for yer kind welcome," he said. "I hope ye will welcome as kindly my personal servant, Cluny, to yer midst."

"We traveled from Greenwich," said Aidan, "in the Earl of Lynmouth's coach. His lordship left us at Worcester to travel by horseback on to his mother's estate at *Queen's Malvern*, but with the storm his coach and coachman will remain until after the storm. Please see that he is made comfortable."

"Of course, m'lady," said Beal, and then he dismissed the staff.

"If there is nothing else, m'lady," said the butler, and with a nod Aidan dismissed him.

"This is a fine hall," said Conn looking about curiously now that the servants had gone, and they were alone.

"Isn't it?" Aidan agreed. She was very proud of her home, and it pleased her that he was apparently appreciative of the aesthetics of the manor house. "My father put the wooden floors in. Beneath them are the original stone floors which were fine when we used rushes, but my father preferred fine carpets from the East."

"So do I," said Conn. "For one thing it is cleaner and warmer. There is no temptation to throw the bones upon the floor when ye've carpets."

The hall was a good-sized almost square room, and on one wall there was a large fireplace with a fine carved stone mantel, its great crowned lions seated, holding up the mantelshelf upon their heads. The frontal panel of the mantelshelf had a frieze of vines and fruits carved into it. Upon the mantelshelf were a pair of heavy silver candelabra that burned fine beeswax candles. On the far side of the fireplace was an oriel window facing west that allowed the hall to be flooded with bright sunlight even on a winter's day, and on the other side of the room was a matching window facing east. The east window was not actually a part of the Great Hall, but rather it belonged to a corridor outside the Great Hall that housed the staircase to the upper floor. There was no door, however, between the staircase corridor and the Great Hall, and so light could flow from the east window unimpeded unto the room.

Behind the Great Hall there were two rooms, one small, and one of medium size. The smaller of the two was used as the estate office, and was entered via the staircase corridor. The larger of the rooms was the family parlor, and entered from the office. This room had a fine fireplace, and windows facing west, whereas the office had but one little window. The rest of the ground floor of the house was given over to the buttery, the kitchens, the pantry, and the family chapel, which was a small room located in the front of the house just off the porch. It was a pretty room with two tall arched windows of fine stained glass, a testament to the wealth of the St. Michaels. In the cellars below the ground floor was a laundry room with stone tubs, and a hearth for heating the water, a brew room, a wine cellar, and the servants' quarters.

Conn liked the look of the house which was furnished in sturdy oak pieces, pleasantly mellowed with time. The ceiling in the Great Hall was paneled in heavily carved sections of dark oak that contrasted with the white plaster walls which were hung with three well-worked tapestries. The rooms were well lighted with wall brackets made of iron that held candles, and tall candlesticks of the pricket type stood upon their three legs in various parts of the chambers.

Aidan led her husband upstairs, and upon the second floor of the manor house there were five bedchambers, the master chamber running the width of the building at the south end; the other four rooms were set lengthwise along the west wall, their entry gained from a windowed corridor. The master chamber was spacious, the other bedchambers comfortably large, and each room had the supreme luxury of its own fireplace. In the attics above were additional servants' rooms.

Conn stood in the center of their bedchamber which had a thick Turkey carpet upon its wide board floors. The fireplace was lit with a good fire, and the air was sweet with the fragrance of potpourri. "This is a fine house, Aidan," he said quietly. "More than a house it is a home. We can be very happy here, my wife."

"It has always been a happy house, Conn," she answered him. "It is not a grand place, but it is a good house for a family."

"A *family?*" he gently teased her. "And how, madame, do ye intend to manage that?"

Aidan blushed. "We have been wed only five days, sir," she protested. "Ye promised me that ye would be patient."

"And so I shall, Aidan, but until we come together as man and wife there will be no children. We are wed, and there can be no changing that. The longer ye demur, the harder it will be to give yerself to me." He put his arm about her. "Come, lass, we like each other, and that is a good start, better than many have."

She shook him off. "Must ye have every woman ye meet fall into yer bed immediately, sir? I may lack experience in matters between men and women, but I will not behave like all those highborn drabs who have warmed your backside these two years past!"

Conn burst out laughing. "Is that what is bothering ye, Aidan, my fiery wife? Ye would not have me lump ye in with all those delicious ladies who were so kind to a young Irishman, far from his home? Sweetheart, yer my wife! There is a difference between a wife, and a mistress."

"What difference?" Her voice was filled with suspicion. He was making her feel silly, and she didn't like it.

"A wife is not like other women."

"*Oh?*" She folded her arms across her chest, one foot tapping, and pierced him with a fierce gaze.

Suddenly Conn was most uncomfortable. Aidan's look bore into him, and he began to stutter and stumble over his words. "A wife . . . a w-w-wife is t-to be . . . respected! Cherished!" he finished triumphantly.

"And a mistress is not? The poor woman gives ye her good reputation, and is scorned for it? That is unfair!"

"Aidan, God's foot! That's not what I meant!"

"Then what did ye mean? I am eager to understand, Conn! When ye have sorted it all out I hope that ye will tell me!" Then with a swish of her skirts she departed the room leaving him standing openmouthed.

How the hell had she done it? One minute he was trying to ease her into normal marital relations, and the next she was confusing him totally by demanding to know what made her different from other women. Suddenly Conn laughed, for he realized that the joke was on him. She was a damnably clever wench! It was going to take a great deal to outsmart her. Following her back downstairs to the Great Hall he saw her giving Beal orders for their supper.

Then suddenly upon the door came a great knocking, and Beal hurried to answer the pounding. Aidan was close behind him, for she was curious as to who was out in such a snowstorm with night upon them. Beal opened the heavy oaken door, and in with a gust of wind and snowflakes two caped figures came. One was a tall man, taller than Conn, with an elegantly barbered black beard, and deep blue eyes. His companion threw back the furred-edge hood of her cloak, and Aidan found herself face to face with the most beautiful woman she had ever seen. The face was a perfect heart, the eyes a wonderful blue-green, the hair a mass of dark curls. She knew at once that this was Conn's sister, and her heart sank. How could she expect to compete with such a woman?

"Skye!" Conn dashed forward, and embraced his elder sister. "How the hell . . . I mean, what brings ye out on such a night?"

"*What brings me out?*" The voice was musical. "Robin comes home unexpectedly, and tells me that ye've been banned from court, and are at *Pearroc Royal*, less than a mile away across the fields, and then laughs uproariously saying ye've a surprise for me. What have ye done, ye young scrapegrace? I thought ye had that Tudor bitch wrapped about yer little finger! Why are ye banned? For how long? Why are ye here?"

While she pummeled him with her barrage of questions, her companion turned to Aidan.

"I am Adam de Marisco," he said quietly.

"I am Aidan St. Michael," she answered him.

"The young heiress? Of course! We came to call after yer father had passed on, but yer servants told ye were gone to court."

"It was my father's wish that the queen find me a husband, my lord."

"A husband?" Then suddenly Adam's eyes began to twinkle, and looking to Conn he then looked questioningly at Aidan.

"Yes, my lord," she confirmed, and when her mouth turned up into an impish smile he saw how pretty she actually was, and he began to laugh.

Diverted, Skye turned from her brother. "What is so amusing, Adam?" she demanded.

"Will ye tell her, Conn, or shall I?" chuckled Adam.

"I am married, Skye." Conn took Aidan's hand, and drew her into his sister's line of vision. "This is my wife, Aidan St. Michael. Aidan, my sister, Lady de Marisco."

"Bess banned ye for marrying! Of course! 'Tis just like her, dried-up old maid she is!"

"No, no!" Conn began to laugh. His sister and the queen had always been at loggerheads. "I was brought kicking and protesting all the way to the altar, my dear sister."

"*What?*" Skye looked somewhat surprised, and then her eyes narrowed, and she hit her brother a hard blow upon the arm. "Did ye seduce this poor lass?" she demanded, outraged.

"Nay, madame," said Aidan beginning to see the humor of the whole affair, and the only one able to explain, as both Conn and Adam were doubled over with mirth.

"Nay?" said Skye. "Then why are ye married if he did not seduce ye, or ye did not elope?"

"Conn is, I am afraid, rather high-spirited," Aidan said with great understatement. "If he could learn to confine himself to one lady at a time, but alas for him, he could not. He was caught in a rather delicate situation with an ambassador's wife, and then while the entire court was laughing about that, it came to light that yer brother, my husband, had been involved not only with Lady Glytha Holden, *but* her two comely daughters, Grace and Faith, as well! The queen had no choice with not only the ambassador crying for Conn's head, but Lord Holden as well, than to send Conn from court in disgrace."

"With an heiress for a wife?" said Skye. "Ye have yet to tell me how that all came about."

"Come into the hall," said Aidan graciously. "I am a bad hostess to keep ye both here in the corridor. Beal, fetch some mulled wine. Lord and Lady de Marisco must be chilled to the bone."

"Conn, ye young devil," said Adam de Marisco, "yer a lucky man! She's a bonnie lass!"

His compliment warmed Aidan, and gave her the courage she needed to continue on with this beautiful and commanding woman who was her sister-in-law. Settling her guests before the blazing fire she continued. "Marrying Conn was actually Lord Burghley's idea. He felt a good wife would settle Conn so that when he came back to court he would not cause any more scandals. I was a royal ward and as my estates are near to yers both the queen and Lord Burghley thought a marriage between yer brother and myself the ideal arrangement."

"I do not like arranged marriages," said Lady de Marisco. "I have had six husbands, and of the six, two were arranged marriages. They were appalling mismatches. I detested both men, and neither were kind to me."

"This is different," cut in Conn.

"How?" demanded Skye.

"Although Aidan and I were somewhat surprised to find ourselves man and wife, we like each other. Dammit, Skye, most marriages are arranged by others, and not the people involved. Ye know that! Ye've lived differently because ye are an unusual woman."

Skye turned to really look at her new sister-in-law. She was no beauty, thought Lady de Marisco, but she seemed a good young woman. "Are ye happy about this marriage, Mistress O'Malley?" she asked.

Aidan smiled. "Aye, madame, I am, but 'tis not Mistress O'Malley. When my father died he requested two things of the queen, both of which she agreed to grant. The first was that she find me a good husband, and the second was that my husband take our family's name of St. Michael since my father was the last of his line. When Conn married me five days ago he become Conn St. Michael, Lord Bliss."

Surprised, Skye looked at her youngest brother. "Ye would give up yer name?"

"Da left four other sons, and three of them have between them eleven boys for the next generation. The O'Malleys of Innisfana don't need my offspring, but the St. Michaels of *Pearroc Royal* do. Besides, 'twas not my choice, but rather Bess's decision."

"Well, that's settled," said Adam de Marisco turning to his wife. "Now, little girl, can we go home?"

"Oh, no!" Aidan cried. "Night has fallen, and the storm is fierce. Listen! Hear the wind? Ye must stay with us at least until morning, and longer if the snow has not stopped! Beal!"

"M'lady?"

"Tell Mrs. Beal to prepare the best of the guest chambers for my lord's sister and her husband, and tell Erwina that we have guests at our table."

"Yes, m'lady," said the white-haired butler, and he backed from the hall.

"There!" said Aidan, and they all laughed.

"Well at least Elizabeth Tudor has found my brother a wife who I can see will stand up to him, not some milk-and-water miss who is impressed by his beauty," said Skye matter-of-factly.

"He was called the Handsomest Man at Court," said Aidan softly, "but then I heard it said that ye were the most beautiful woman at court when ye were there. I think Conn looks like ye."

"Nay," teased Adam, "Conn is prettier!"

"May I remind ye, my lord," said Skye sweetly, "that 'tis a cold night, and if ye expect to share my bed ye had best be kind to me."

Lord de Marisco's blue eyes smoldered, and leaning forward in his chair he pierced his wife with a passionate look. "And when, little girl, have I not been kind to ye?"

Aidan blushed at the sight of such raw passion between these two people. They were obviously very much in love, and she was a little jealous. Would Conn ever look at her like that? Would he ever love her like that? A small ache began in her chest. She could not bear to sit here a moment longer, and watch them. Standing she said briskly, "I must see that Erwina has her kitchens under control. It is our first night home, and they had no notice of our coming."

"Oh, let me come with ye," said Skye. "I am curious to see the house."

"But ye have not had yer wine," replied Aidan, remembering it now as Beal entered the Great Hall with a tray.

"Let the men sit and drink," said Skye. "I have admired this house ever since we arrived at *Queen's Malvern*."

"*Queen's Malvern* is much larger than *Pearroc Royal*," Aidan noted. "Like this estate, it was a royal possession."

"The queen gave it to my husband since she took his own holding from him."

"Why on earth did she do that?" Aidan was surprised.

"Because, my pretty sister-in-law," said Adam who had been able to overhear them, "I am married to this rebellious Irishwoman who persists in offending the queen. The truth of the matter is that I got the better of the bargain."

"Elizabeth Tudor was simply afraid that ye would rebuild Lundy Castle when ye married me, and she wasn't going to let ye," snapped Skye.

"Go and see the house with Aidan, Skye. 'Tis too cold a winter's night to argue the matter. Besides we are here, and here I intend to stay. Lundy was a place for me to hide from hurt. I no longer hurt, little girl."

The two women left the Great Hall, and went to the kitchens, but Erwina, the fat cook, chased them out. "Go on now, m'lady, ye'll spoil the surprise!" she scolded waving her wooden spoon. Laughing, Aidan and Skye ran from the warmth and good smells, and back into the main corridor.

"Come and see the chapel," said Aidan, and she proudly showed this treasured room to Skye.

"Are ye of the Mother Church?" asked Skye.

"I was raised in England's church," came the quiet reply, "and 'twas in that church that Conn and I were wed."

"It matters not," said Skye. "Our dear Uncle Shamus was the Bishop of Mid-Connaught, and our brother Michael a priest. We have a sister, Eibhlin, who is a nun. Ye must have her come to ye when yer going to give birth. There is no one like Eibhlin for doctoring! Do ye know what the queen once said to me? There is but one Lord Jesus Christ. The rest is all trifles. 'Tis the one thing on which Elizabeth Tudor and I agree although we worship in different churches."

They reentered the Great Hall, but the men before the fire paid them no heed, and Aidan led Skye to the second floor of the house to show her the bedchambers. There were two maids in the largest of the guest chambers airing the bed, and remaking it with herb-scented sheets. Already a fire had been laid in the fireplace. Secretly Skye was delighted by the house, and pleased that her brother had married so well thanks to the queen. Wordlessly she followed Aidan to the very end of the upstairs hallway, and into another room.

"This is the master chamber," said Aidan.

Skye clapped her hands in pleasure. "What a charming room!" she exclaimed, her eyes taking in the blazing fire, the fine big bed with its linenfold-paneled headboard, the green velvet draperies and bed hangings. " 'Tis a wonderful room to make love in, to bear yer babes." Then she saw Aidan's face. "God's foot! What is the matter? Has Conn been unkind or rough with ye? I'll soon set him straight!"

"Nay, 'tis not that," said Aidan hastily.

"Then what is it, Aidan? Ye looked distressed when I mentioned lovemaking and babes."

"Conn and I . . ." began Aidan, and she blushed to the roots of her copper-colored hair. "Conn and I haven't . . ."

"Why not?" demanded Skye knowing precisely what it was her sister-in-law wasn't saying.

"I . . . I can't!"

"Are ye afraid?" Skye was distressed for Aidan.

"A little, but that is natural, I imagine."

"Yer a virgin?"

"Of course!" This said indignantly.

"Tell me," said Skye gently. "Yer married to my little brother, and I want ye both to be happy. As happy as Adam and I are!"

"There are several reasons, Lady de Marisco," said Aidan.

"My name is Skye, Aidan."

"I do not really know Conn, Skye. When I went to court I asked the queen not to reveal that I was an heiress lest I be falsely courted by men seeking only my wealth and my lands. I had never been away from *Pearroc Royal* in my entire life, but to go to Worcester. My father and I lived quietly after my mother and sisters died. I had no suitors. I am no beauty like ye are, and feared to fall prey to an unscrupulous man. So the queen honored my request, and no one knew of my wealth. I was virtually ignored, but I did not really mind for it gave me opportunity to observe everything and everyone about me."

"Did you like the court?"

"It is an exciting place, but I far prefer living here in my own home. The court can often be like a dark and dangerous forest. Ye never know where the danger is coming from there."

"Aye," said Skye. Then she smiled at Aidan. "I like ye better with every word ye utter, sister! Tell me the rest."

Aidan smiled back. How nice Conn's sister was! Not at all as she had expected the famed beauty to be. "On Twelfth Night Conn was playing a game of Blind Man's Bluff with the maids of honor. He was 'it,' and we were all avoiding him quite successfully. Then one of my companions pushed me into his path as he swung about. Naturally he caught me, and before he even removed his blindfold he claimed a kiss as a forfeit. It was a wonderful kiss, and I . . . I'd never been kissed before.

"Several weeks later when the scandal surrounding Conn broke it was I who was with the queen. She was at her embroidery frame, and 'twas my job to keep her workbox neat, and to hand her the threads as she needed them. When Lord Burghley had come into her private closet she had dismissed all the girls but me, and so I was privy to all that was said. When Lord Burghley said that Conn must be wed to curb his exuberance the queen demurred at first. She said she could not think of any suitable bride for him." Aidan stopped in the middle of her tale, and drew a deep breath. "Skye," she continued, "what I am about to tell ye ye must promise me ye will not reveal to Conn. Will ye promise me?"

Skye looked into the girl's face. There was nothing in her eyes that would lead Lady de Marisco to believe she was a dishonest person. What secret was it that she was keeping? It was too fascinating. "I promise!" she agreed.

The tension eased on Aidan's face. "When the queen said she could think of no suitable bride for Conn, I said I could. I said that I was a suitable bride for him, that the queen had promised my father she would find me a good husband, and now the queen needed a wife for Conn. I am half-Irish. I have monies and lands, and there was my father's title. Conn is a wealthy man, and so the solution was a natural one.

"At first the queen was not certain, but Lord Burghley thought the idea an excellent one, and 'twas he who convinced her. The marriage was set for less than two days hence on the fourteenth."

"Then ye wanted to wed with my brother?"

"Oh, yes! But he must not know 'twas I who suggested it! He believes me as much a victim of the royal will as he is."

"Do ye love him?" Skye looked closely at Aidan as she answered.

"I don't know! I think I do, but I've never been in love before! He is so handsome, and so very kind, and I like him very much. I would die, however, if he knew what I had done! Look at me, Skye; I am not like ye. Yer the most beautiful woman I have ever seen. I am not. Sometimes I am pretty, but other times I am not. What chance would I have had with

Conn had not the queen agreed to see us wed? If it had been known that I was an heiress I would have been overwhelmed with suitors, but how could I have been certain that they sought me as a wife, and were not simply interested in my wealth? And I could not live with that doubt. In the entire time I was at court, and I was there five months, not one gentleman spoke to me freely. When I was spoken to by anyone it was in the line of my duties for the queen. I have never been more lonely in my entire life. Had not my tiring woman, Mag, been with me, there would have been no one in whom I might confide.

"By choosing Conn, I was certain of a husband who does not seek my wealth, and who perhaps in time will learn to care for me. I know he likes me, but we are virtually strangers. How can I allow myself to be like all the women Conn has known by eagerly joining in his bedsport? Besides, the truth of the matter is that I know nothing of matters between men and women. My mother died when I was young, and my father certainly never spoke to me of such things."

"Then I must," said Skye firmly. "Aidan, ye cannot deny yerself to yer husband, and expect yer marriage to be successful. The truth of the matter is that men are charming but weak creatures who due to their natures need regular loving contact with women. If it is not their wives, then it will be other women. Another woman is not a good thing for a marriage. Conn has sown enough wild oats in his youth, but now he is a husband. If ye keep him happy, then he will never stray."

"Did any of yer husbands ever stray?" Aidan asked candidly.

"My first, but he was a pig, and I was glad when he strayed from my side. Glad? I was relieved!"

"I know nothing of womanly arts," Aidan repeated.

"I do." Skye smiled, and then she laughed. "My brother is a good man, if perhaps a trifle dull-wilted. Now tell me, have ye seen a man's body?"

"Only the back," said Aidan.

"Why only the back?" Skye was curious.

"Because I close my eyes tightly when Conn turns about," came the answer.

Skye muffled a laugh. "The front is the more interesting part," she said. "Do ye know what a manroot is?" and when Aidan nodded, Skye said, " 'Tis in the front, and 'tis that part of a man that pierces a woman in a spot between her thighs. The first contact can be painful, but afterward it can be pure delight."

"Are the man and woman naked during this?" asked Aidan.

" 'Tis better when they are, but 'tis not always possible."

"What else is there to making love, Skye?"

"Kissing with the mouth, and the tongue. Caressing of each other's bodies. I have always believed that as long as pleasure is both given and received, there is no wrong thing lovers can do."

"It is still mysterious," said Aidan.

"And it will continue to be unless ye allow yer husband to make love to ye, Aidan. Yer fear stems from the unknown. How old are ye?"

"Twenty-four come summer."

"I have just had my thirty-sixth birthday this December past, and I have been making love since I was fifteen. Do I look any the worse for the wear?"

Aidan giggled. "No. On the contrary ye have a wonderful glow such as I have never seen in a woman."

"That," declared Skye, "is because I am very well loved by my Adam. Tonight we will snuggle beneath the down coverlet in yer guest chamber, and make delicious and passionate love. 'Tis a fine activity for a stormy winter's night. Ye should do the same with Conn."

"But if I yield so easily to him will he not think me as brazen as the women who constantly chase after him?" Aidan was definitely in a quandary.

Skye chuckled. "Even wives should occasionally be bold, my sister. You will soon learn to join in the bedsport, and tell Conn what it is that pleases you; ask what it is that pleases him. Most women have a tendency to lie in their beds like sodden lumps accepting only what is offered. Some, I have been told, even recite their rosaries silently to themselves as their husbands labor over them. No wonder men seek other women! My brother is *very* knowledgeable about lovemaking, Aidan, and knows more of passion's pathways than I suspect even he is willing to admit. Ye've been very sheltered, and cannot possibly learn unless he teaches ye. Ask him!" Her gorgeous eyes twinkled. "Oh, what delights await ye!"

"I do not think I could be so bold as ye are, Skye," Aidan admitted. "Could I not ask ye the things I need to know about men, and about lovemaking? I should be very embarrassed right now to speak with Conn of such things."

Poor girl, thought Skye sympathetically, and my poor brother who is used to loving the ladies as the mood suits him. If I do not aid her, heaven only knows how long it will take her to rouse up her courage. Conn will not wait forever, and I suspect with the right start they will be very happy. "Of course ye may come to me to answer yer questions, Aidan," Skye said, "but ye must promise me that tonight ye will encourage Conn to consummate yer marriage."

Aidan sighed. "I feel like such a ninny," she said. "I am competent to run an estate, and I am educated far beyond most women, yet any of my milkmaids knows more of love than I do. I haven't the faintest idea even of how to begin."

"It's really very simple," answered Skye. "When ye retire tonight, simply tell Conn that though yer innocent, and haven't the faintest idea of what to do, ye want to make love with him. Don't tell me he hasn't kissed and cuddled ye a little bit since yer wedding."

Aidan blushed pinkly, and Skye was relieved to know her brother wasn't so put off by his bride's innocence that he hadn't at least kissed her. "It would seem odd to the servants if we didn't share a bed," she noted.

Skye laughed. "Have ye found it unpleasant?"

Aidan's mouth turned up in amusement. "Nay, I've not found it unpleasant at all," she admitted, "and I will admit to being curious about what comes after the kissing and the cuddling."

"Ye can find out tonight," Skye teased her gently, and then she said, "I imagine the gentlemen will be wondering what is keeping us. Let us return to the hall."

Together the two women left the master bedchamber, and descended to the main floor of the house. If Conn and Adam had missed their wives they gave no indication of it for they were engaged in deep conversation as Skye and Aidan returned to them. As Skye drew near to her husband's chair, however, Adam reached up wordlessly, and drew her down into his lap, never pausing once in his conversation. How marvelous, thought Aidan. He is so attuned to her, and she to him.

Conn looked up at his wife. "Will the supper be ready soon, sweetheart? I am ravenous with all our traveling."

"Erwina chased us from her kitchens, my lord, but from the delicious smells coming from that direction I would venture to guess that the meal will soon be served. If ye would care to wash the travel from yer person I shall take ye to our chamber while Skye leads Adam to theirs."

"Why, lass, then the supper may never get eaten," laughed Adam de Marisco leering at his wife wickedly.

"Then, sirrah, ye must wash in the courtyard with the snowflakes blowing about ye!" Aidan said pertly.

"With the other rutting beasts," added Skye as she bounced off his lap. "Well, my lord, what is it to be? Will ye behave yerself, or shall we set ye outside to cool yer spirits?"

The laughter rumbled deeply up from Adam's big chest. "Should I tender ye my apologies, madame, for desiring my own wife? Ahh, Skye, yer a hard woman." He rose to his full height. "Very well, Lady de Marisco, lead me to our chamber, and I shall promise to behave myself."

"And what of ye, my Lord Bliss?" Aidan demanded coquettishly.

Conn was a trifle surprised, but not altogether displeased by this sudden flirtatiousness of his bride's. "Why, sweetheart," he said standing, "I shall promise most faithfully to behave myself."

"What a pity," said his sister mischievously, and to Conn's delight Aidan burst out laughing, then catching his hand led him off up the stairs. Once in their chamber she served him herself, pouring out warm water from a silver pitcher by the fireplace into a matching silver basin, presenting him with a cake of hard-milled soap with which to wash. It smelled of her lavender fragrance. When he had finally finished she offered him a fresh linen towel.

"So this is to be our bedchamber," he said as he tossed the towel aside. " 'Tis a lovely room, warm and comfortable, I can see."

"Will ye mind sharing a chamber with me?" she asked. "This is not a great house like *Queen's Malvern*, or Greenwood. We have no room for separate bedchambers, and when the children come I am not certain we will even have room for guests."

"We can always add on to the house to make it larger. Are ye anticipating a large family, madame?" He was curious for the truth was that he knew so very little about her. He wasn't even certain that she liked children.

"I never had a large family," replied Aidan, "but I always thought it would be wonderful to have several sisters and brothers. Yes, my lord, I do believe I should like a big family. Then none of my children should ever find themselves alone as I did when my father died last summer. It is a terrible thing to be that alone."

He was touched by her admission, and reaching out he gently pulled her into his arms, and her copper head rested against his chest. "Ye'll never be lonely with me, Aidan," he promised her quietly, and he felt her sigh, and thought that she snuggled herself for just a moment against him. It came to him suddenly as he held her so lightly within his embrace that he was falling in love with her. There was something about Aidan, a serenity, a steadfastness, a permanence, that reached out to him to ensnare him. He wondered if Elizabeth Tudor had been aware of the real favor she had done him by marrying him to Aidan for Aidan was the kind of woman with whom a man could found a dynasty. Tipping her face to his he brushed her mouth softly with his own.

Skye is right, Aidan thought, as she had nestled against Conn. This man is my husband until death parts us. I chose him freely, but I cannot continue playing the coy virgin any longer. It is ridiculous. My own mother didn't know my father, and yet she wed him and bedded him in the same day. If I lose Conn to another woman I shall have no one but myself to blame. Then his lips found hers, and Aidan knew that whatever scruples she had were now gone. She wanted to be Conn's wife in every sense of the word.

"Will ye make love to me tonight?" she heard herself ask him. "Here in our own bed, in our own home?" She felt her cheeks growing warm with the boldness of her own words.

Instinctively his arms tightened about her. "Are ye ready to be my wife now?"

"Yes," came her answer, so low in tone that he had to bend his head to be certain he had heard her. "I am a little frightened of what is to come, but I am not afraid of you, Conn. Does that make any sense to you?"

"Aye, sweetheart, but don't be frightened. I'll love ye so sweetly, so gently that afterward ye'll realize how foolish yer fears all were." His hand stroked her head.

Suddenly upon their bedchamber door came a loud knocking, and Adam de Marisco's voice called, "Come now, ye two! If I am forbidden from taking my pleasure with my wife at this time, then so should my host and hostess be forbidden!" and he pounded upon the door.

"Adam!" Skye's voice admonished her husband, but they could hear the laughter in her tone.

Loosing Aidan Conn grinned down at her. "He has a rather wry sense of humor, our brother-in-law."

"I am being a rather bad hostess," Aidan said.

"Nonsense! We are supposed to be on our honeymoon."

Aidan hurried to open the door, and as it swung wide she scolded Adam mischievously. "My lord, what a noisy fellow ye are! The way ye bray and bellow I am not certain that I should not house ye in the stables! Come along now, sir, for Erwina does not like to be kept waiting when she is ready to serve the supper," and she swept by him with a twitch of her skirts.

"What, madame!" Adam chased after her. "Are you calling me an ass or a bull that ye suggest I bellow and bray?"

"Perhaps, my lord, a little of both," said Aidan with a laugh.

Both Skye and Conn joined in the laughter as the four of them returned to the Great Hall. "My dear little brother," Skye said, "I am so glad that Bess Tudor had the good sense to add this quick-wilted lass to our family."

"So am I," replied Conn, and putting an arm about his wife he drew her close.

"And I also," added Adam. He grinned at Aidan. "I'm afraid ye've got to be a scrapper, and able to hold yer own in this pack. I think the quietest members in this entire family are Skye's daughters-in-law, Gwyneth and Joan."

"Nay," Skye corrected her husband. "Gwyn has shown admirable backbone since Ewan took her to his estates in Ireland. She marshaled the housemaids the last time old Black Hugh Kenneally and his sons came raiding. Ewan was away for the night, and they knew it. Gwyn was with child, but gathering the women together she held off that old reprobate and his robber band by pouring the contents of the household slop jars upon them from the upper windows of the house."

"Erwina is ready to serve dinner, my lady," said Beal coming to Aidan's side.

Aidan wiped the tears of mirth from her eyes, and led her husband and their guests to the high board where four places had been set. She and Conn, as lord and lady of the house, sat in the center two seats while Adam sat to her right, and Skye to Conn's left. The oak table had been laid with a white linen cloth of exceptional quality, and despite its many years of use it had a shimmering, silken look to it. There were twisted silver candelabra with good beeswax candles in them, and place settings consisting not only of silver spoons, but forks and knives with horn handles as well. At each place there was a heavy silver goblet carved around with vines and grapes that were obviously of Italian design. A young footman now poured a dark red wine into each of the footed goblets. The plates, too, were silver, with the letters *St. M.* engraved upon each. It was, Skye noted, a nicely set table.

The servants began to arrive from the kitchens bearing bowls, and platters, and plates. Skye was totally amazed to be offered oysters, cold and raw and very, very fresh.

"Where on earth did yer cook find oysters so far from the sea?" she asked, unable to prevent her curiosity.

Aidan shrugged. "Erwina's sources have always been a mystery. My father always said 'twas better not to inquire lest we offend her. He said as long as the sheriff didn't object to Erwina's actions, then neither could he."

"I'm sorry we didn't know yer father," said Skye.

Aidan nodded. "I understand, and besides he was already ill when ye arrived at *Queen's Malvern*. He would have liked ye though. He always liked the Irish, and enjoyed a beautiful woman better than most."

"Ye loved him very much, didn't ye?"

"Aye, I did," she admitted, "and he was so lonely after my mother died. We only had each other."

"Then that is why ye never married?"

"I never wed because my father never made a match for me. There always seemed time, and then suddenly one day there wasn't any time left at all. Oh, how distressed I was when I learned that he planned to put me in the queen's charge, that he had asked her to find me a husband! I have never felt so helpless in my entire life. I suddenly realized that I was to be put in the care of a stranger. That someone other than my father was to be master over me. Father had never appeared to me in that light. He only partly calmed my fears by telling me that half of his wealth would be mine and mine alone so that I would have a certain measure of freedom from my husband. That was an unusual thing for my father to do for he was an old-fashioned man. I think because he could not choose my husband himself he worried." She smiled at Conn. "He need not have feared. The queen chose me a good lord."

"She chose me a good wife," Conn replied gallantly, and when their eyes met there was something there that had not been before. Each saw it. Each felt the funny, little tug upon their heartstrings.

Skye felt the sting of tears in her eyes. They're falling in love, she thought. Before our very eyes, mine and Adam's, it is happening; and she was relieved and happy not just for her brother, but for Aidan, too.

The meal continued on, the footmen coming to each place to present each offering. There was a platter with small trout that had been broiled and were now settled upon individual beds of watercress; and cod that had been creamed and flavored with sherry. There was a lovely plump capon, roasted golden, and stuffed with apples, bread, and chestnuts; a duck, its skin crisp and black, and sauced with plums and cherries; a small leg of baby lamb with tiny roasted onions set about it; three ribs of rare beef that had been packed in rock salt and then roasted to seal in the juices; a large rabbit pie, its pastry flaky and brown oozing fragrant steam from the carefully decorative vents in its top crust. There was a bowl of new lettuce braised in white wine, and another of carrots. Newly baked bread with egg-glazed crust was set upon the board along with sweet butter.

"Your Erwina is an amazing lady to have produced such a fine supper with such short notice," Skye noted.

"The larder is always well stocked," said Aidan. "We did not entertain greatly during the last year of my father's life, but before then one never knew who would arrive upon our doorstep. It might be some of father's relations from London, or traveling merchants who did business with my family's firm. Father's hospitality was famous. He and my mother both loved company. Erwina has been the cook in this house all my life, and before her there was her mother. We do not change our ways easily here at *Pearroc Royal*."

They had all eaten heartily, the ladies perhaps a little less than the gentlemen, although both Skye and Aidan enjoyed good food. Now suddenly into the hall came Erwina herself bearing a silver tray upon which rested an exquisitely decorated little wedding cake complete with a spun sugar bride and groom. The fat cook was beaming from ear to ear with her own pleasure at this feat. Boldly she strode up to the high board, and plunked her offering down before Conn and Aidan.

"Mag tells me, my lord and my lady, that ye had no time for a proper wedding feast or the cake because of the hurried nature of yer nuptials. We love ye, my lady, and we would have ye remember yer marriage celebration even if it is a few days after the fact." Then she curtsied, the look upon Aidan's face telling her that she had made her lady very happy.

But it was Conn who spoke first. "Yer a fine woman, Mrs. Erwina, and one of great sensitivity. The court is a fabulous place, but there could be no real celebration for my lady and myself until we came home to *Pear-roc Royal*, and her people who are our family. Thank ye all!"

"Oh, yes, Erwina! Thank ye from the bottom of our hearts," Aidan managed to say for she was still overcome with the thoughtfulness of the cook.

Conn saw that most of the servants had crowded into the hall now, and he called to Beal. "Wine for everyone, Beal. We should appreciate everyone's good wishes."

Beal had anticipated his lord's request, and in short order everyone within the Great Hall had been given a draft. On the butler's command they raised their cups and cried out, "Long life, prosperity, and many children to ye!"

When the toast had been drunk Aidan and Conn sliced into the wedding cake, and everyone in the hall was given a little bit of Erwina's wonderful confection. The unmarried maidservants kept part of their portions, for they intended to sleep with it beneath their pillows this very night, and dream of their true loves. Everyone else, however, enjoyed the treat with much lip smacking before returning to their duties. When the hall had emptied save for the two couples, and those serving them, Aidan arose from her place.

"We have been several days on the road from Greenwich," she said, "and I should very much like to bathe before I retire. Will ye excuse me?" Then with a pretty curtsy she departed up the stairs. Gaining her chamber she discovered to her delight that Mag had already anticipated her desire. To one side of the fireplace which was merrily burning with scented apple logs the large oak tub had been brought and filled. Warm steam, redolent with lavender, perfumed the room.

"Oh, Mag, bless ye!"

"Do I not know ye?" huffed the older woman affectionately. "Not that I approve of all that bathing ye do but it's harmless enough, I suppose. Here! Let me help ye with those laces, my lady." She kept up a steady line of chatter as she worked to undress her mistress, taking the clothing into Aidan's dressing room which was adjacent to the bedchamber, and putting it away but for the underclothing which she would take to the laundress. In very short order Aidan was settled in her tub, seated upon a small wooden stool, her hair pinned atop her head. The fragrant water was just the right temperature, and felt wonderful after several days on the road, and nothing but little basins in which she could only wash her face and her hands.

"This is heaven, Mag."

Mag chuckled. "Yer just happy to be home, my lady."

"That too, but how I missed bathing in this marvelous tub when we were at court! That little thing we carried with us was barely big enough to contain me, and my knees were always sticking up out of the water, and getting cold."

"And the good silver we had to bribe them uppity footmen of the queen's with in order to get some hot water," said Mag. "I hope yer not going to be of a mind to travel again soon. The inconveniences are not to be borne, my lady."

"Nay, Mag. I don't ever want to leave *Pearroc Royal* again! Why should we? I do not think my lord is of a mind to either. I know he will love it here when he sees the estate, and gets to know everybody."

Mag nodded. "He seems a sensible sort for all he's an Irishman. The Blessed Mother only knows that we come from a land of dreamers, poets, and fools, yet my lord seems a good man, and I like his lady sister, and her husband. They have welcomed ye nicely, my chick, and the gossip in the servants' hall is that they are good people. Yer dear lord father, may God assoil his soul, would have approved this match ye've made." She gathered up Aidan's stockings and undergarments from the pile in which she'd placed them. "Ye sit quietly and soak now, my lady. I'll just take these things to Leoma for washing. Ye know how she dislikes having the laundry pile up." The door clicked closed behind Mag.

Aidan settled herself deep into the oily water. She could have sworn that she felt her winter-dry skin soaking it up. The fire crackled cheerily in the grate while outside the windows the wind moaned softly, but steadily as the tempo of the storm increased. In the deep silence she could almost hear the snowflakes falling, and she sensed that the weather would not break for at least another day, but it mattered not. They were snug and safe at last. They were home. With a deep sigh she closed her eyes and relaxed, enjoying the wonderful feeling of contentment that she had not felt in months.

There had been no contentment for her at Elizabeth Tudor's court. As one of the queen's women she had been at her majesty's command virtually twenty-four hours a day, seven days a week. Her place in the queen's service had been relatively unimportant, but Elizabeth had liked Aidan, giving her a status of sorts. Then, too, as an orphan she had had no family obligations to distract her, and when she had a little free time she usually spent it taking the place of one of the other girls who needed, or simply desired, to get away.

For the first time in her life Aidan had been lonely. She lived amid a sea of people, and yet she was lonely. She had not pursued her connection to the Earl and Countess of Lincoln, afraid they might learn of her vast wealth, and claim of the queen the privilege of marrying her off to one of their own thereby usurping her fortune for themselves. The earl stood high in Elizabeth's favor.

Fortunately the Clintons had not considered Aidan's case a particularly pressing matter assuming her at court for the duration, and therefore at their disposal. Elizabeth Clinton was one of the queen's favorite people, and she was really a kindly woman, but her husband's interests came first. She had made certain that the other women who served the queen knew of her relationship to Aidan, and because of that Aidan was not abused by those ladies as was often the case with one who was seemingly unprotected by a powerful family, and lacking in wealth and influence.

Still Aidan had felt isolated from everything around her for the very habits she cultivated in order to give her time to acclimate herself to this strange and hurly-burly world she was now part of, had in reality served to blend her into the colorful background of the court. Her simplicity of dress, and lack of ornamentation had accentuated her plainness. But rarely did she sprout fine feathers, and then no one recognized her as anyone they knew. Her education and intellect separated her from the other girls, and put off many of the older women who had lacked her advantages. Only with the queen did she dare to be herself for with the women who were her equal she dared not put herself forward lest she be considered bold, and make enemies.

So Aidan was modest and diffident to others. A quiet, apparently colorless girl whom almost no one ever noticed, and as a consequence she was lonely. There were times when days went by without anyone at all speaking to her except in relation to her duties. Had it not been for her faithful Mag, who each night regaled her mistress with all the latest court gossip, Aidan would have been totally alone. She was not unhappy, however. She had no time to be, or to feel sorry for herself for the court was far too fascinating a place, and so very different from anything she had ever known. Then, too, the court had brought her her husband.

Conn. She shifted restlessly in her tub. Conn, who she was suddenly realizing was a great deal more than his reputation for pranks, and debauchery, and fair face would warrant. He had taken control of their journey quite capably, and he had treated her with respect and gentleness. There was nothing of the boy in him despite the fact she was his senior by almost a full year; and he was certainly unlike anyone she had ever known before. Aidan was beginning to realize that although she had chosen the most beautiful stallion in the herd, he might possibly be the hardest of all to tame. Conn wasn't like other men.

"Is the water still warm, sweetheart?"

Aidan started, her heart leaping at the sound of his voice. She moved her hands to shield her breasts only afterward realizing that the water covered her.

"Is the water yet warm?" Conn repeated. His eyes were surveying her with sudden interest although he could see nothing but her shoulders, neck and a surprised face.

"A-aye, the water is quite pleasant, my lord," she managed to stammer.

"Good! Then I'll join ye. That fine old oak tub was made for two people." Calmly he began stripping off his clothes, and Aidan squeezed her eyes tightly closed.

Then as suddenly she opened them up again. The front, Skye had said, was the more interesting for 'twas there the manroot lodged, and as she had already decided that tonight she would give her husband her virginity, she might just as well look her fate in the eye in a manner of speaking. She giggled, and he looked curiously at her.

"What amuses ye? Make no jokes about my legs, madame, I warn ye. They are overlong, I warrant, but I do not look like a heron as some have dared to suggest!"

" 'Twas not yer legs I was contemplating, sir," she answered him pertly, and then blushed at her own words.

Conn roared with laughter and he flung his shirt aside. His green eyes twinkled with delight, and he wondered once again about this wise yet shy girl he found himself married to. "What is it then, madame, about my person that interests ye?" he teased her cocking his head, and arching one very black eyebrow.

"What is between yer legs," she answered him bluntly. "I've closed my eyes each night when ye've undressed, but Skye says 'tis the front of a man that's more interesting. I was just thinking about it . . ." Her voice trailed off, and she blushed again.

He chuckled softly, pleased to see her exhibit a natural curiosity of his body. Too many lasses were falsely modest when it came to their men. His older sisters back in Ireland were proof of that. Tight-lipped and sour women who disapproved of Skye and her passion for life; who clucked their sharp tongues at their sister Eibhlin, the doctoring nun, whom they believed should have remained cloistered in her convent on her knees instead of roaming the countryside healing the sick, rich and poor alike; and who had on his only visit home since he had come to England with Skye, scolded him roundly about his gaiety and lustful behavior. Even his own pretty mother had never remarried, though he knew that she had had chances enough. Once he asked her why she hadn't remarried.

"No one," said Anne O'Malley, "could take yer father's place," but then he had overheard her speaking with her tiring woman about a persistent suitor. "I have obeyed the teachings of the holy church, Bridget, and I gave my husband children. Four sons in all, but I'll never be victim to a man's passions again. I've just never enjoyed it. If only one could be married to a man and just be friends."

"Aye," agreed Bridget, "but 'tis not the nature of a man, m'lady. They always want to be dipping their wicks into one honeypot or another, and a poor wife has no choice but to submit."

Conn pulled off his boots, and then peeled his trunk hose off his muscled form. Standing straight he looked directly at his wide-eyed wife saying, "Well, madame, do I meet, pass, or fall short of yer expectations?"

Aidan's serious gray eyes took him in from the top of his night-dark hair to his toes. He was as handsome without his clothing as he was with his clothing. There was a thick mat of tight curly hair spread across his broad chest that narrowed into a thin line between his rib cage down over his pelvis, and ending in a lavish black bush between his long, shapely legs. There, she noted, was lodged what appeared to be a small white sausage, slightly and delicately curved, and lying amongst the dark curls. "It isn't very big," she said without thinking.

"Ye've not yet attracted its interest," he answered her, and mounting the steps to the tub, he lowered himself into the water which came up to his waist. He sniffed. "Lavender? I'm going to smell like an herb garden!"

Aidan had been seated upon a stool within her tub. Now she slipped from her perch to stand facing him. "I did not invite ye to share my tub, my lord. 'Twas of yer own free will ye entered it." Her heart was beating wildly, and she was very amazed by her own boldness. It suddenly dawned upon her that she was standing stark naked in her tub with a man who was equally unclothed.

He saw the play of emotions across her face, and correctly guessed her thoughts. "Aye, lass," he drawled softly, "there can be no going back now." Then he pulled her into his arms, and lowering his head to hers began to slowly kiss her long, sweet, lingering kisses. Her fragrant wet body, surprised by his quickness, relaxed against him to his pleasure, and he felt his desire begin to awaken and stir.

The hair upon his chest tickled and irritated her nipples. She squirmed uneasily against him, but her head was whirling and she felt dizzy with the heat of the bath and his embrace. Nervously she placed her palms flat against his chest as if to hold him off. Conn kissed the corners of her mouth with his tongue sending a small flash of weakness through her.

"Aidan," he breathed against her lips. "Aidan, my sweet, prim little wife." One arm about her waist he allowed his other hand to move upward to cup a breast.

She stiffened, a little shocked. No one had ever touched her breasts. *No one.* "Conn!" Her voice sounded squeaky, and perhaps a little frightened.

"It's all right, sweetheart," he soothed. "Touching is very much a part of making love, and a woman's breasts were made to caress as well as nourish." He fondled her gently and lovingly.

She shivered, but she was neither cold nor fearful any longer. His hands made her feel strange, not quite herself.

Conn could see she was skittish, and so he did not press his advantage over his wife. It would be better to continue this game after they had left the bath. Later when Aidan was surer of herself, and of what making love could involve, he would reintroduce water sports. "Yer a very tempting creature, Lady Bliss," he said, and then he kissed her mouth firmly. "Do ye also scrub backs?"

Aidan colored becomingly, but with his hands gone from her body she was able to regain control of herself. "Aye," she answered him. "Turn about, my lord husband," and she set to work to wash him.

Her hands were firm, but soft, and Conn closed his eyes a moment. To his surprise he found that she was arousing him with her seemingly innocent touch which first smoothed down his back and then up again. Plunging her hands back into the water she soaped his buttocks beneath the water, and then requested that he turn about so she might wash his chest. He looked down at her, and smiled. Her face was very serious as she worked the fragrant lather over him. He could feel his blood beginning to boil. God's bones! The witch was beginning to really excite him! Unable to help himself he yanked her against him wrapping his arms tightly about her, and taking her lips in a fierce kiss.

He had a perverse longing to discompose her seeming quiescence, and in this he succeeded. He coerced her lips apart; plunging his tongue into her mouth to make his first penetration of her. She initially stiffened with shock, and then she tried to fight him, tearing her head away from his passionate embrace.

"No! Oh, Conn, no!"

He gritted his teeth. "Aidan, dammit, yer my wife! I've been patient, I'm trying to be patient, I want to be patient; but God's nightshirt, woman! I'm only a flesh-and-blood man! Ye excite the devil out of me, and I want to make love to ye!" He didn't let go of her.

Startled by his words she looked up at him. "I . . . I arouse ye?" she whispered.

"Aye."

Her eyes filled with tears that threatened to spill over, and run down her cheeks. "Oh, Conn, I feel such a fool! To be such an ignorant creature at my age is embarrassing, but I just don't know what to expect, or what to do with regards to this lovemaking. I am afraid, and I am not. I want to, and I don't. I don't know what to do or think!" She looked helplessly up at him.

Conn looked down into Aidan's face, and then his hand came up to gently caress her cheek with his fingers. "Ye said earlier that ye wanted me to make love to ye tonight; that ye were ready to be my wife. Is it still so, sweetheart?"

This was her chance! This was her opportunity to change her mind, but somehow she knew that if she did she would endanger the yet young and fragile relationship that they were building. She had quickly realized that he was a good man, and certainly he was a patient one as well, but as he had said, he was only flesh and blood. A mortal. Not some perfect being, or a saint. Besides, that wasn't the kind of man she wanted.

"Aidan? Have ye changed yer mind?"

Mutely she shook her head in the negative, and could almost see the relief wash over him.

Hoisting himself from the tub he reached back down, and drew her out of the water. Then taking a towel he began to rub her down with it. "I couldn't possibly catch ye in that tub with all that lavender oil, sweetheart. Why yer as slippery as an eel."

Wordlessly Aidan took a second towel from the warming rack, and began to dry her husband in return. He was going to catch a chill, she thought, and somehow the idea of cuddling with him, and whatever came after that appealed to her far more than nursing him through a winter sickness. Suddenly both were quite dry, and it dawned upon Conn to look at his bride of almost a week. He had never seen her without her clothing. Gently he set her back a bit from him, and slowly his eyes began to travel the long length of her body, widening in total and delighted surprise as they went. A long sigh hissed from between his lips.

"God's great cock!" he said, and then he began to chuckle. "What a wonderful joke, Aidan! What an absolutely wonderful jest!"

"*What?*" She was blushing again, and feeling horribly mortified by his words, and his laughter. What was wrong with her now? She reached for the sodden towel to cover herself, but he snatched it away with a mild oath.

"Damnation, sweetheart! Don't cover yerself. Yer the most beautiful woman I have ever seen, and if I live to be one hundred I don't think that I could get my fill of looking at ye."

Her face crumbled, and she began to weep. "Oh, monster! Oh, beast to taunt me so! I believed ye a kind man, Conn, but yer not!" She hit out at him with her fist. "Yer not!"

Surprised he reached out to draw her into his arms and comfort her. "Aidan, what is this? How have I hurt ye?"

"Ye say that I am beautiful, and we both know that I am just barely short of being quite plain," she sobbed.

"Of face, aye, my sweet wife," he agreed, "but Aidan, the Creator has played a delicious prank for though ye be plain of face, ye have without a doubt the most beautiful and flawless body I have ever seen on any woman, and ye must believe me when I tell ye I have seen many a lovely form."

"*What?*" she gasped. "What is this ye say?"

In reply he practically dragged her across the room to place her before the pier glass. "Look, sweetheart! Yer beautiful!"

She stared at the naked figure in the mirror. She had never before seen herself naked, but the sight meeting her eye was certainly not an unpleasant one, just a little shocking to her senses. Unconsciously she straightened her shoulders, and gazed hard at the nude figure in the pier glass. Her arms and legs were pleasingly shapely, and long. Her torso was also long, the narrow waist flowing into invitingly contoured hips, the bones wide-spaced and nicely fleshed. There was just the hint of a little rounded belly, or was it the shadow of the dancing firelight that made it seem so, the flesh swelling just slightly above her plump Venus mound. Slowly Aidan's gray eyes moved to her breasts. They were neither too large, nor too small, but rather soft, perfect globes of warm flesh with sweetly formed pink nipples that now stood erect in the chill of the room.

She looked questioningly at him standing in the glass behind her. "Are ye telling me, Conn, that ye have never seen a more beautiful female form than mine? This is the truth? Not just a bridegroom eager to please his wife, eager to bed her?"

"Aye, my sweetheart, I swear it!" he answered. "I have never seen *any- one* with a more beautiful form." Then he chuckled once again. "If ye prove to be wanton, my wife, I shall never ask the Creator for anything else ever again. I vow it on the Blessed Mother!"

Laughter bubbled up in her throat, and spilled over into the quiet room. "Oh, Conn!" she said, spacing her words between her mirth, "there is still a great deal of the boy in ye after all."

"But more than enough man for ye, Aidan, I promise ye!" he murmured, his arms slipping about her waist for a moment as he bent to kiss her shoulder.

She felt her breath catch in her throat as his lips grazed her skin. It was as if his mouth were burning her, leaving a fiery imprint upon her flesh.

His hands slid upward to cup her round breasts, his warm strong fingers kneading the flesh gently, teasing at her nipples. "Sweet," he whispered against her ear. "Oh, my Aidan, how very sweet ye are!"

His touch no longer shocked or terrified her even as with curious eyes she watched his actions in the mirror. Indeed his touch seemed to release her final inhibitions. Closing her eyes she sighed deeply allowing the honeyed feelings his hands seemed to encourage to sweep over her, to catch her up in budding passion. "Conn," she breathed softly turning, and slipping her arms about his neck as she felt her legs weakening under her.

He stopped just long enough to lift her up, his lips taking hers once more in a tender kiss, and then cradling her in his arms he walked across the bedchamber floor to gently deposit her in their bed. "Aidan?" he questioned her softly, a final time.

"Did ye not say, my lord, that there can be no turning back now," she murmured up at him, and reaching up drew him down to her.

With a pained groan he fell to the bed, rolling over and drawing her with him. He couldn't believe how quickly his own desire had risen, and now a voice within his head cautioned further patience. How he initiated her into the art of Venus would determine the future happiness of their bedsport. He could hear in his brain an echo of the voice of Peggy Brady who had taught him so well how sweet passion could be.

Slowly, Conn, my darling. Remember that a woman is like a fine lute. If ye would get the best tune from it, ye must play oh so gently, and skillfully upon its delicate strings.

He could feel the swellings of her breasts against his hard chest. Opening his eyes he found her looking at him, her gaze a mixture of shyness and curiosity. He reached up, and undid her hair which had been pinned atop her head for the bath. The coppery tresses tumbled free, and he ran a hand through the silkiness of them, singling out one lock which he took between two fingers, and kissed. A faint aroma of lavender clung to the curl.

Aidan shivered with delight both from his kiss, and from the sensation of feeling her hip-length hair upon her skin. A second shiver rippled through her as a long finger traced the line of cheekbone, and down her jaw. Turning her from her side onto her back he bent and began to press feathery kisses onto her breasts. A soft, surprised, "Ohhh," escaped her. His mouth closed over a tempting nipple, and began to draw upon it. She had never felt anything like the sensation that suddenly raced through her tingling her from the soles of her feet to the top of her head. "Mmm-mmmmm," she murmured. His hand smoothed across her belly. "Ahh-hhh," she sighed, and squirmed with pleasure.

Conn was somewhat surprised for he had expected protests long before this. Instead she was almost purring as his touch aroused her innocence. His fingers moved lower, seeking the very source of her femininity, and as he found it he heard her intake of breath, her tiny gasp. It was reassuring for although he had no doubts as to her virginity, her easy acceptance of his exploration had somewhat unnerved him.

"Conn," she whispered, a small nervous note to her voice. She had enjoyed the stroking, and his attentions to her breasts, but this was too intimate a touch. Her hands moved to prevent further liberties.

"Nay, sweetheart," he reassured her pushing her hands away. "This is all part of it. I swear."

"I've never even touched myself there," she said.

"I'll not hurt ye, Aidan. It helps to prepare ye for yer first time. Will ye trust me?" God's nightshirt! He was burning for her!

"Aye, my lord," she said low. "I will trust ye."

He kissed her softly, and then continued in his explorations of her.

She tried very hard to remain still as he toyed with her, but the tiny jewel of her womanhood proved extremely sensitive, and a low moan escaped from between her lips. Her hips began to move almost of their own volition as his delicate tickling caused a sensation of little thrills to sweep over her. She was beginning to understand why both men and women succumbed to the lure of lust, and she was unable to prevent herself from saying, "Oh, Conn! 'Tis so delicious! Tell me that there is even more!"

His first instinct was to be shocked, but then he chuckled, relieved that she was enjoying herself. It was all to the good, and he really didn't want a woman like his elder half-sisters, or his mother. "There is more, sweet-heart!" he answered her.

"I . . . I want it now, Conn! I want it all now! I can bear no more of yer trifling! Love me!"

"Aidan, sweet . . ." he began. He *must* go slowly.

"Now!" she pleaded with him. "Oh, please now!" A fine sheen of per-spiration had suddenly surfaced on her body, and she squirmed restlessly.

He covered her body with his, his weight almost crushing her for a mo-ment until he had readjusted their positions. She flung her arms about him, pressing herself fiercely against him, loving the feel of his body upon hers. Passionately he kissed her, their tongues fencing sweetly, and then he whispered to her, "Open yer legs for me, Aidan." She shivered in-tensely, but there was no hesitation in her compliance. She had been quick to arouse, and now he found her young body moist and ready for him. Gently he positioned himself, trying with utmost care to breach her maiden defenses, but to his surprise she whispered in his ear.

"Nay, Conn! I know there is pain the first time. Ye do me no kindness to dally. Thrust home hard, my husband! Let us have done with this trou-blesome virginity of mine so we may attain the sweet portion!" and she pushed her hips up hard at him.

Instinctively he pressed back, driving into her in one powerful stroke, absorbing her cry of pain into his own mouth, pinioning her beneath him in passionate thrall.

Aidan had known that there would be pain, but she had not been quite prepared for the fiery burst that spread into her loins with a throbbing smarting ache. She had cried out, but he had muffled her sob, stroking her face and her hair tenderly in a soothing gesture. She felt the tears upon her cheeks, but he kissed them away as he lay still for a moment atop her. As the pain began to subside she suddenly became aware of a fullness within her, a throbbing fullness. It was then that he began to move against her.

No one had prepared her for what happened next, but then in the af-terward she wondered if anyone could have explained it. As her hand-some husband moved upon her, thrusting slowly at first with deep measured strokes until she moaned uncontrollably; then thrusting with increasing speed until she knew for certain that she would die in this maelstrom of desire; Aidan began to lose control of her own mind, and body and soul. She felt as if she were climbing a high hill, climbing, and climbing toward a top that never seemed to materialize; and then sud-denly it did, and she was hurled down with wild speed into a kaleidoscope of rainbow colors, and that was all that she could remember until she heard Conn's dear voice calling to her, almost pleading with her to speak to him. Slowly, and with great difficulty she opened her eyes, but it was hard to keep them open for her eyelids felt so heavy.

"Aidan! Aidan, sweetheart! Ah, my little wife, ye were so damned brave, and I love ye for it!" He was relieved when she smiled up at him, and then her eyes closed, and she fell into a natural sleep.

He drew the coverlet over them both, and with a murmur of contentment Aidan turned onto her left side, her sleep deepening as each minute went by. Lying back, his hands beneath his head, Conn smiled broadly to himself. He was astonished by her, dazzled that despite the fact she was a virgin she had attained total and complete satisfaction her first time. Not only that, she had given him incredible pleasure as well. He remembered his careless words of so short a time ago that should she prove a wanton he should consider himself blest. A small chuckle escaped him. Wanton was not a word he would apply to Aidan, but she had certainly been most eager for his loving, and not once had she drawn back in fear, or demurred in false modesty. Indeed she had encouraged him onward, and despite the pain he had seen in her eyes she had not reproached him his part in her deflowering. More and more he realized his good fortune. A title, an estate, a fortune, a charming and eager wife. He must beware of becoming smug. His eyelids grew heavy, and he dozed.

She slept perhaps an hour or two, and then Aidan awoke fully, clear-headed and acutely aware. She rolled onto her back, stretching lazily, a faint smile turning up the corners of her lips. Propping herself upon an elbow she gazed down on Conn. He lay sleeping upon his back, sprawled somewhat like a child, his right arm across his eyes, his left leg bent. Gently she drew back the coverlet, and looked upon his manroot. She was amazed that something that small and soft could have given her such delight. Reaching out she boldly took it in her hand and began to caress it. To her great surprise the little creature within her hand suddenly gained life of its own and began to stretch and grow within her grasp. Fascinated she continued her ministrations to the awakening beast, watching with widening eyes as it lengthened and thickened, a growing awareness that she had taken its bigness within her own body.

Conn had been sleeping lightly, and then he felt the cold air of the room on his naked body as she drew the coverlet back. He watched her from beneath the shelter of his arm as she stared down at him, wondering what thoughts went through her mind, tingling with delight as she began with gentle, and innocently skillful fingers to caress him. He was stunned to find how quickly she could arouse him, and when he could finally bear no more of her teasing he said softly, "Now, my Aidan, ye must pay a forfeit for awakening yer husband on this winter's night." Reaching up he pulled her down on him, tangling his hands in her coppery hair, brushing her lips with his own.

"Do ye remember earlier, sweetheart, that ye thought my manhood small, and I told ye ye had not yet aroused its interest? Well, *now* ye've aroused its interest!" He rolled her beneath him, and his mouth fastened upon one of her breasts sending darts of delight through her. She murmured her approval of his actions, and he chuckled, "Ahh, wench, ye like that, do ye?"

"Aye, my lord, but this time I hope ye will not neglect its sister as ye did before."

He raised his head grinning. "Nay, sweetheart, now that I know yer not fearful there is a great deal more I can teach ye," and his head dipped to her other breast to initiate it into passion.

She stroked his dark head as he did so, feeling the silky strands slip through her fingers. The back of his neck, she noted seemed particularly sensitive to her touch, the hair at the nape becoming bristly as it rose up.

His mouth moved down her long torso to her belly, pressing warm kisses upon the delicate skin, causing her to shudder with surprise. He wanted to go lower, but he feared shocking her, and spoiling what had become a very pleasant wedding night for them both. Her skin was so sweetly fragrant with lavender, so soft and so tender. Unable to help himself, he licked the flesh of her belly, and she cried out his name.

"Ohh, Conn! Conn! 'Tis too sweet!"

"Nay, sweeting, there is much, *much* more!" he promised her, and pulling himself up he found her lips again. She had the most wonderful mouth, he thought as he pressed kiss after kiss upon her lips. They parted, her moist little tongue seeking out his, frolicking with his, teasing him gently. Her loveplay kindled his ardor until he could no longer refrain from plunging deep into her warmth, and to his delight she urged him onward, all traces of maidenly modesty gone.

"Ohh, Conn, yes! Yes! Yes!" she sobbed as he drove hungrily within her sheath. Dear heaven! It was going to happen again! she thought. That incredible wild and wonderful fusing of their bodies that led to a dissolving of her entire being. She cried out her pleasure, and unable to contain his passion Conn poured himself into her, shuddering uncontrollably until he finally fell to one side of her, pulling her into his embrace.

"Aidan, Aidan," he murmured into her hair, "what is this witchery ye surround me with?"

She laughed weakly. "I was going to ask ye something of a similar nature, my lord. Oh, Conn! I didn't know! *I didn't know!*"

He hugged her gently. "Of course ye didn't know, Aidan, my sweeting. How could ye?"

"Will it always be like this, Conn?" she asked him artlessly.

"God's nightshirt, my love, I hope so!" he answered her fervently. Then he drew the coverlet over them again. "Now go to sleep, sweeting."

"Will we not do it again, my lord?"

Now it was his turn to laugh. "Yer a greedy wench, Aidan," he teasingly scolded her. "I'll need a bit of rest before we love again, sweetheart, and so will ye. We have our whole lives before us. We have forever!"

My love. He had called her "my love"! Of course, she reasoned with herself, he hadn't really meant it. It was simply a term men used she supposed when in an intimate situation. Still, how sweet the words had sounded to her. He seemed pleased with her, with their coupling; and Lord help her she had certainly enjoyed his lovemaking. As sleepy as she now found herself she felt her cheeks grow warm with the memory of her own boldness in encouraging him onward. Yet he had not seemed displeased or shocked by her actions. She would have to ask Skye come morning for her beautiful sister-in-law certainly seemed to be knowledgeable when it came to the amatory arts. Aidan's eyes closed. She felt warm and safe, and eminently satisfied with her lot in life.

Part Two

LORD BLISS' BRIDE

Chapter 5

✦

*R*ogan FitzGerald stood several inches over six feet in height, but he was, in spite of his seventy-eight years, as straight as a young man, lacking the hunch of old age. He was clearheaded, too, despite the great deal he had drunk that night. It was as if he hadn't touched a drop. Comfortably sprawled in the tapestry-chair at the head of the high board he watched the familiar activity about him. The women clustered together gossiping; the men by the fire dicing and drinking; the children scampering about the hall at some game or other.

Outside the tall stone round tower that was his home he could hear the howl of the spring storm that lashed the land this late April night. In the massive fireplace the flames leapt and blew wildly as the wind swept down the chimney with a mournful swoosh. He could almost imagine the keening of the banshee in that wind. His time on this earth was fast drawing to a close, and he knew it, but it mattered not a whit to him. There was nothing left, and his Ceara was already gone on before him.

The door to the hall flew open, and two heavily muffled men entered the room. Since the hour was late, and the weather outside so terrible, it was considered unusual that anyone would be out in it and abroad. A silence fell upon the hall, and its occupants looked up curiously.

Rogan waved the visitors forward while shouting to the others, "Get out, now, all of ye! Get out! 'Tis still my house, and I'll have some privacy in it, I will!"

No one argued with him for the old man had an evil temper when aroused, and had never been loath to use his fists on relatives or retainers alike. All but the two chosen hurried from the hall while a servant quickly took their sodden capes and quietly exited lest he incur his master's wrath. The old man waved his guests toward the high board.

"Help yerselves to wine, and sit down," he invited.

"Yer looking well, uncle," said the younger of the two men.

119

"I'll live to see the dawn, Cavan, me boy. Is this the Spaniard?"

"Aye. May I present to ye Señor Miguel de Guaras, uncle."

"Ye may! Welcome to Ireland! 'Tis a brave man ye are disembarking in weather like this."

"There was no choice, my lord," the Spaniard replied. "The English are very vigilant about the coast, even in this weather. It was necessary that I leave my ship today as I did, or return to Spain and disappoint my master, the king. As my brother, Antonio, has already done that by managing to get himself arrested by the English, I must now uphold the family honor." Miguel de Guaras lifted the goblet to his lips, and drank, putting it down with a grimace, a fact noted by his host who smiled grimly.

When the two men had seated themselves Rogan FitzGerald looked directly at the Spaniard, and said, "All right, what does yer King Philip want with me? I'm mystified as to how he even knows about me. I'm no grand lordling, just the master of Ballycoille, a town of no importance at all. What are we to Spain's might?"

"Has it not been said, my lord, that the least shall be first?" Señor de Guaras replied, but when Rogan looked blankly at him he quickly continued, "Ye have a granddaughter, my lord."

"I have several granddaughters, and a few great-granddaughters, too, if I recall correctly."

"This would be yer daughter's child."

"Bevin's lass?" His eyes misted over as he remembered the daughter he hadn't seen since he had sent her to wed the rich English milord, a man his own age, back twenty-five years ago. She had been so very beautiful, his youngest child, and but for the fact he had nothing with which to dower her, and the Englishman had been willing to take her that way, he should have never allowed it. Still in all she had been happy. She had written him each Michaelmas telling him of life with her husband and children until the year she had died. Only one of those children had reached adulthood. A girl. A girl named Aidan!

"I have a granddaughter named Aidan, aye," he said.

"She is an heiress of considerable wealth," said the Spaniard. "Her father died last summer leaving her a ward of the crown, and she was married off this St. Valentine's Day past to Master Conn O'Malley. Do ye know the O'Malleys of Innisfana Island, my lord?"

"By reputation only," was the reply. "They're great mariners, I'm told, as was their father before them."

"They are traitors to Ireland, and the Holy Mother Church," said Señor de Guaras vehemently. "They sail under the protection of the heretic bastard who rules England, usurping the rightful place of its true queen, Mary of Scotland, who even as we speak languishes in cruel captivity despite the righteous protests of my master, Philip of Spain."

"And how does that concern me, and mine?" snapped Rogan. "The lass was raised to be an Englishwoman, and regrettable as I find it, she is her father's daughter as it should be. If I remember correctly her husband is the youngest of Dubhdara O'Malley's children which would mean he had nothing. The girl is a good match for him, and he at least is no pirate. What does all this matter to Spain, Señor de Guaras, and give me no more blather about the Holy Mother Church. It is a game of power yer master King Philip plays for all his piety." Rogan took a deep draft of his goblet, and looked straight at the Spanish agent.

Miguel de Guaras did not flinch under the flinty gaze of the Irishman. Instead he picked up his own goblet, and managed to swallow down some of the disgusting brew within without shuddering. Drawing a breath he said, "For many years the O'Malleys of Innisfana have been a thorn in Spain's side, my lord. Their ships have successfully pillaged Spain's merchant fleet in the New World for the last several years, robbing us of much gold. Their sister, one Lady de Marisco, along with her business partner, Sir Robert Small, has built a trading network that interferes with Spain's business, but worse is of value to Elizabeth Tudor. My master has vowed to bring these pirates to their knees once and for all; to take from the usurper the wealth the O'Malleys supply her with; to sow dissent between England and the O'Malleys; and to totally destroy them. My master, Spain, needs your help to do this, my lord."

"I have no quarrel with the O'Malleys of Innisfana," said Rogan FitzGerald.

"They are rich, my lord, and you are poor. By marrying your granddaughter to the least of them they have siphoned off her wealth for themselves when you might have had it by wedding the girl to your nephew, Cavan.

"Conn O'Malley, or Lord Bliss as he is now known, is an Anglicized Irishman who licks the slipper of the English queen as no true patriot would do."

Rogan FitzGerald's face darkened with outrage as the Spaniard had fully intended.

"Help us, my lord! We intend to make it appear as if Conn O'Malley is involved in a plot against Elizabeth Tudor to bring Mary of Scotland to the English throne. He will, of course, be caught, imprisoned, and eventually executed. His entire family will then come under suspicion of disloyalty as a consequence. The queen is certain to revoke the letters of marque the O'Malley brothers now carry, and England will be robbed of needed revenues. The brothers, hotheads all, will, of course, then turn on their former masters causing great chaos. Their sister's trading company will be ruined by royal displeasure, and your granddaughter will be a widow ripe for the plucking.

"Cavan will make her an excellent second husband, and once in control of her wealth those monies can be used to fund a successful uprising against the English. You will have Spain's aid in this, my lord, I vow it. We will supply you with weapons, and horses. All ye need do is use your granddaughter's wealth to pay yer soldiers, and that wealth will buy many mercenaries.

"There is already an actual plot afoot, engineered and funded by the French, to free Mary of Scotland, and place her upon England's throne. Think of it, my lord! England will be under siege from the north! The French will land on both their south and east coasts. Ireland will be in revolt to the west! They cannot possibly direct their attentions to it all, and will first seek to defend their homeland which will, of course, be their main concern. It is Ireland's best chance to be free, to finally rid itself of foreign shackles."

Rogan FitzGerald felt the blood hammering in his veins with new vigor. Ireland to be free! Free of the hated English! Was it as simple as the Spaniard said, or was Spain again using Ireland to stir up England? Then, too, there was his granddaughter, Bevin's child. What matter, he quickly decided. He didn't know the girl, and she was an Englishwoman besides. Besides no true patriot, and he considered himself as loyal an Irishman as any, would allow even blood to stand between Ireland and her freedom. She might grieve her O'Malley husband, but one husband was very much alike as another, and he would give her Cavan to assuage her. Her estates in England could be sold to raise further monies, and she and Cavan would come home to a free Ireland. The more he thought on it the better he liked the idea.

Both the Spanish agent, and Cavan FitzGerald watched Rogan curiously, and waited, each wrapped within their own thoughts. The Spaniard considered his brother, a valuable agent for Spain, now rotting in London's Tower because he had been careless, or had he been? Antonio had been in England for seven years before he was caught. Were the English growing more vigilant? More clever? It was up to him to redeem the family's honor, and this plot of King Philip's was very dear to his majesty's heart. The king was an incredible ruler, Miguel de Guaras thought admiringly. He knew things of which most monarchs were not even aware, and little details fascinated him the most. Having been given all the details that could be gathered about their family, the King had conceived this plot against the O'Malleys. And it was he who had given Miguel de Guaras the opportunity to remove the stain from his own family's honor by carrying out this mission.

Cavan FitzGerald cared nothing for Spain's politics. He was far more interested in the prospect of a rich wife, and respectability. Each was equally important to him having been born on the wrong side of the FitzGerald blanket. His father had been Rogan's youngest brother, a priest. His mother had been Father Barra's heartmate, and she had died shortly after his birth. Cavan's father was a good man in his own way. He might have given the infant away to an orphanage, leaving it anonymously by the convent's door, but instead he had acknowledged his paternity, and asked his elder brother's wife to raise the baby. Ceara FitzGerald, mother of twelve, had agreed for her youngest, Bevin, was ten at the time.

Bevin filled Cavan's earliest memories; a beautiful smiling lass with luxuriant hair, and a gentle manner about her. If her daughter was anything like her he would be quite happy, but it was the girl's wealth that actually meant more to him. All his life he had been forced to meekly accept the taunts and sly innuendos of his cousins. They did not dare to tease him before his uncle, whose favorite he was, but he had taken his share of unkindness. It wasn't until he was grown, and had beaten senseless each of his male cousins that Cavan was grudgingly accepted, but even now he felt a stranger amongst them. He was thirty years old, but since all in Ballycoille knew of his birth, and he had nothing other than a handsome face and his uncle's tenuous favor to recommend him, there had been no match made for him. Now if he played his part right in this Spanish plot he would have a wife at long last, and although Rogan could think what he might, the girl's wealth would not go down a rabbit hole to fund the old man's foolish dreams. It would stay in his hands, and he would be powerful at last for Cavan FitzGerald knew one certainty. Money was power.

"Tell me," said Rogan FitzGerald, "tell me how ye intend to entrap my granddaughter's husband. I assume that Cavan will be involved."

"Aye, my lord," said Miguel de Guaras. "Although your nephew looks nothing like Conn O'Malley he is of the same height and build. It is he who will deal with the English, but he will be masked, and heavily muffled so that they will not see his face. All they will know is that they do business with a tall man, with the sound of Ireland in his speech who calls himself Conn O'Malley. You need know nothing else of this business."

"I need to know if my nephew will be safe! He is most dear to me."

"He will be safe," was the reply.

"Ye've given me a new lease on life, Señor de Guaras," said Rogan

FitzGerald. "I believed myself close to death, but now I shall live at least long enough to see blessed Ireland free! I shall die happy then!" Reaching out he splashed wine from the decanter upon the table into the three goblets, and picking his up toasted, "Ireland! God bless her!"

His companions raised their goblets in reply, though neither said a word before they drank down their wine. But Rogan FitzGerald did not notice for his head was filled with an old man's dreams of glory.

Just before dawn the lord and lady of *Pearroc Royal* exited their home where a tousle-headed, sleepy-eyed stableboy stood holding their mounts. Cupping his hand Conn bent, and boosted his wife into her saddle. When he stood to see her safe her gray eyes met his green ones, and he knew for certain what he had not dared admit to himself these last few weeks. He was in love with her. He wanted to tell her so, but despite her passion in their bedchamber, she still held herself somewhat distant from him. To admit his love when she did not feel the same was to play the fool, and he could not do it.

He broke off their gaze, and as she gathered her reins into her hands he mounted his own horse. "Go back to yer bed, lad," he said in a kindly voice to the stableboy. "The sun's not yet up, and when we return we'll stable our own beasts."

Together they walked their animals from the stableyard, and then breaking into a gentle canter headed out across the open fields to the hills beyond. The air was very still and clear; the sky a flat blue-gray that told them nothing of the day to come.

"Yer a madwoman, Lady Bliss," he told her teasingly. "Who else but a madwoman would come out to see the sunrise?"

" 'Tis May madness," she laughed at him. "Ever since I can remember I have arisen on May Day to see the sunrise. When I was a little girl I would come with my parents, and then we brought my sisters. When they were gone Papa and I came every year until he was too ill to ride, and I came alone. 'Tis tradition with me, Conn. My luck! Do ye understand?"

"Aye, sweetheart, I understand. Luck is something the Irish are very superstitious about. Where did this custom come from?"

"My mother brought it with her from Ireland, but other than that I don't know. She used to say ye'd have good luck for a full twelve months if ye but rose to see the sunrise on May Day. This year past has certainly brought me good luck, my lord. Although my father died, I went to court, and fetched me back a fine husband!"

Conn laughed so loudly that not only did the horses' ears lie back, and their mounts dance skittishly; but he startled a game bird off her nest, and she flew fluttering into the dawn sky with an indignant squawk. That set Aidan to laughing, and they both laughed until they were weak with their mirth.

The sky had suddenly begun to glow, a deep rose pink sweeping up from the horizon, and spreading outward across the vast roof of the heavens with thick fingers of color. They hurried their horses in order to arrive at the crest of the hill that Aidan had promised would offer them the best view. Reaching it they could see a wide band of gold, edged in deep purple rolling up behind the pink. Above them the flat sky was now a bright blue, and there was just the faintest hint of a breeze. Drawing their horses to a stop they watched silently as the rich colors poured across the horizon, and then, heralded by a burst of red orange the round ball of the sun arose in a fiery blaze.

How many sunrises had he seen, and yet he had never really seen one, Conn thought. Instinctively he reached out for her hand, and took it in his, squeezing it gently. She squeezed back.

"I knew ye would understand," she said to him softly. "Now we will both have luck this year."

Loosing her hand he swung off his mount, and lifted her down. Then hand in hand they walked quietly to the top of the hill just a little distance, leaving their animals to graze amid the new grass. Spreading his cloak upon the dewy ground Conn turned back to his wife, and drew her into his arms. Slowly he bent his head, and kissed her deeply and passionately. Her arms slipped up around his neck, and she molded herself to him, pressing herself hungrily against him. As if a signal had been given they slipped to their knees, facing one another. With gentle fingers he undid the ties to her cape, and let it fall to the ground. His seeking fingers unbuttoned the little pearl buttons that held her white silk shirt together, unlaced her lawn chemise, pushed the fabrics off her shoulders to bare her lovely breasts. Aidan lay back, and for a long moment Conn simply gazed upon her beautiful body. Then his fingers reached out to lovingly tease her nipples into prominence, and when they thrust boldly toward the dawn sky Conn began to fondle her breasts with his hands. She murmured and sighed beneath his touch arousing him so unbearably that he loosened his own clothes, and raised up her deep green velvet riding skirt above her silken thighs.

Aidan felt the cool morning air touch her skin, felt his hands removing themselves from her breasts, and sliding up her legs, her thighs, her hips. She adored the mystical power he seemed to have over her that made her desire him so desperately. He slid between her legs, and she opened her arms to him welcomingly, eager to have him penetrate her as he quickly did. Oh Conn, she thought, I love ye so very much! If only I dared to tell ye. If ye would only love me back!

He groaned as he pushed himself into her tightness, thrusting as deeply as he could go, and finding himself yet unsatisfied. It wasn't enough to simply possess her willing body. He wanted more! He wanted her to love him, and unable to help himself he half-sobbed, half-cried out, "Ahh, Aidan, sweeting! Love me as I love ye, my darling! Love me!"

Lost as she was in her own passion Aidan heard him. Or did she? She shuddered with her first release, and then he said again, "I love ye, Aidan. Can ye not love me, too?" She tumbled from her mountain, her gray eyes flying open. "Ye love me? Ye *really* love me?"

He looked down into her face, and suddenly she could see the truth in his wonderful green eyes. *He loved her!* He really loved her! The tears slipped unbidden from her eyes, and coursed down her face. His face fell. "Ye don't love me," he said tonelessly.

"Don't love ye?" she gasped. "I have loved ye from the first moment I laid eyes on ye, ye mad Irishman! From the very first day I came to court. Of course I love ye!"

Happiness ran riot in his heart and mind. "Ye love me? Then why didn't ye tell me, Aidan?"

"Because ye didn't love me when we were first married. Because I didn't want to be like all those silly women who made such fools of themselves over ye at court!"

He was astounded by her confession for she had kept her secret well. Never had he even suspected she might love him. Never had it occurred to him that she might harbor the same feelings that he himself nurtured.

Aidan pulled his head down to her and kissed him, whispering against his mouth as she did so, "My lord! Will ye not finish what ye began?"

"Nay, sweeting," he said withdrawing from her. "Not here. I want to take ye home, and into our bedchamber where I may keep ye for the next fortnight, upon yer back, and hot for me." Readjusting his own clothes he pulled her skirts down.

"But I'm already hot for ye, Conn!" she wailed.

With a chuckle Conn drew his wife onto her feet, and lifted her into her saddle. "I am pleased to hear it, madame, but a short ride will make ye even more eager."

"Yer a bastard, my lord!" she hissed at him, suddenly furious. This was just what she had feared. He was certain of her now, and would take advantage. Yanking her horse about she kicked it into a trot, and headed off down the hill. Reaching the bottom she encouraged her mount to a gallop, outdistancing her husband whom she had caught unawares.

"Aidan! Aidan, dammit, wait!" What the hell was the matter with the woman? he thought. Had he not admitted he loved her, was completely within her power? He urged his horse after her as they both raced for home.

The friction of the saddle was driving her mad. She wanted to kill him for doing this to her! She was going to lock herself in their bedchamber, and not come out for a month! Then he might know how she felt, for she knew he would not dare to amuse himself with the maidservants. Gaining the stableyard she rode directly into the stable with her horse, and slipping off its back she led the beast into its stall, and quickly unsaddled it.

"*Aidan!*" His stallion filled the doorway.

"Go to hell!" she spat at him.

"What in God's name has gotten into ye, woman? I love ye, and ye love me. We're going to go to our own chamber, and make sweet love for the rest of the day, sweeting."

"Ye were making love to me, Conn! Making love to me beneath the dawn sky upon my favorite hill, and then just because I admitted my folly in loving ye ye stop, yank me up, and say we'll go home to make love! I am not one of yer creatures to be used! I am yer wife, Conn, and if ye ever do that to me again, I'll cut yer ears off, I swear it!"

Conn slid easily from his horse, and closing the stable door behind him led his animal to its own stall. "So, madame, ye don't care where I take ye as long as I finish what I start? Is that it?"

"Aye!" She glared at him furiously.

"Come here!"

"What?"

"Come here!" he repeated.

In the dimness of the stable she could see his eyes glittering in what she thought was a rather dangerous fashion. She moved closer to her horse as if for protection, and he laughed softly. "Open the door," she said nervously.

"And let the entire household see me making love to my wife? I think not, Aidan, sweeting."

"Ye would make love to me in a stable?"

Reaching into the stall he pulled her out, and picking her up dumped her most unceremoniously into a pile of hay. "I understand that yer in a hurry, sweeting, and thinking back I realize that yer perfectly right. I'm a damned fool to have ceased so sweet an activity simply to be more comfortable." His hands slipped into her shirt. "We never did button ye up, did we?" He caressed her passionately, his fingers kneading at her flesh until she thought she would scream. He pushed the fabric back, tearing the silk in his impatience, and then his head was lowered and he took a nipple between his lips to suck upon it hungrily. Daintily he nibbled upon it with tiny sharp bites of his teeth, and she moaned with surprise for he had never been rough with her, yet what he did was pleasant for he was not cruel.

"My sweet wife with her outrageously beautiful body," he murmured against her. "I want to bury myself within ye, Aidan! I want to spend a lifetime making love to ye. I adore ye, wench! Do ye understand that? I love ye!" He raised his head and looked into her eyes. "I've never said that to a woman before, Aidan. I've never told any woman until ye that I loved her. Love is too precious a commodity to make light of, my darling." He reached out, and caressed her again.

"Damn ye, Conn," she said weakly, and with not a great deal of conviction. "I will be treated with respect. I am not one of yer light o' loves, my lord, but God help me I love ye, too." She pulled his head back down to her so they could kiss again, and as their lips touched in a sweetly searing caress he entered her, filling her with his passion. For a moment he rested upon her thighs enjoying the embrace, and then he began to move upon her, slowly at first, then faster in tempo. His heart was pounding with his excitement, and he thought that if he died in that very moment he should count himself fortunate.

How could he do this to her? Aidan's mind blurrily questioned. How could this marvelous man to whom she was married make her feel so incredibly wonderful? Her feelings were a jumble of confusion. She wanted him to go on forever, and yet at the same time the passion he aroused in her made her want to bite and claw him. She ran her nails lightly down his long, hard back, and he growled with pleasure in her ear, "Sweet! Sweet!"

She could feel herself losing control as she was swept away into a sea of blinding desire. She soared higher and higher like a hawk riding the whorls of the wind. Deeper and deeper he thrust into her, and all she felt was the rapture he offered her, not the rough straws that mottled her bottom with little scratch marks. Then came the explosion, and she could feel her body letting down its libation of sweetness, crowning the throbbing ruby head of his great manhood, and drawing from it an answering tribute. The horses in the stable shifted nervously as both Conn and Aidan cried out their pleasure, and he fell slowly upon her breasts with a final groan.

They lay that way upon the pile of hay for several delicious minutes, and then Aidan said, "Conn, get off me! 'Tis well past dawn now, and the stablemen will be coming from the kitchens to attend to their duties ere long. Would ye have them see their master playing the rutting stallion to their mistress' mare in season?"

He chuckled with a contented sound. "Nay, sweeting. 'Tis difficult to keep order amongst the servants if they suspect yer as human as they themselves." He rolled off her, and pulled her skirts down, next seeing to his own dishabille. "Is that how ye see yerself, Aidan? A mare in season?"

She sat up, and relacing her chemise, buttoned her shirt back up. "I must be," she answered, "for I am certainly shamelessly hot to be possessed by ye, my husband."

He reached over, and pulled several wisps of straw from her glorious hair. Then leaning down he picked up her green silk riband which had come undone in their tussle, and handed it to her. "I find, madame, that I am equally hot to possess ye," he said with a smile, and then standing he drew her up with him. Turning her to face him he kissed her slowly and lingeringly, his mouth working gently and carefully across the sensuousness of her lips.

With a soft sigh she slid her arms about his neck. The tip of her velvety tongue insinuated itself into his mouth, seeking out his tongue. Finding it she stroked it with her own, sending a stab of desire through him once again. Something wonderful had happened, he thought. By the admission of their love for one another all barriers had fallen between them. He had never known her so wonderfully compliant although she had never denied him. Still, it was different now, and he liked it. Their kisses became deeper, more passionate, and suddenly by a supreme effort Conn broke off the embrace.

Aidan pouted. "My lord!" she protested.

"I hear the stablemen," he said with a groan, "but did I not, Aidan, my wife, I should tumble ye right back in that pile of hay again."

"Rather ye should think to the sight of yer condition, my lord," she teased him and reaching out stroked the bulge beneath his trunk hose which despite the contours of his clothing was most visible.

"Damn!" he grumbled, and she giggled as she slipped back into her horse's stall, and pretended she was brushing down the animal as the stable doors opened, and several stablemen noisily entered.

"M'lady!" They stopped.

"Good morning, Haig," Aidan said to the head stableman, and she nodded pleasantly to the others. "My lord and I have just come in, and finding no one about unsaddled our mounts ourselves. We'll leave the animals to ye now. I wish them given a ration of oats in honor of May Day." Then with a gracious smile Aidan took her husband's arm, and swept from the stables.

They were halfway across the stableyard when a giggle escaped her, and Conn began to laugh himself. "What a courtier ye would make, sweeting."

"I intend to go back to court," she surprised him.

"Ye do?"

"At least once," she said mischievously, "when I am first with child so I may preen and lord it over all those females who so delighted in chasing ye. Would ye mind?"

"Nay." He grinned at her. "I will enjoy showing ye off in proper court clothing, with yer pretty titties showing, just daring enough to make the gentlemen realize what they lost by losing ye."

"Hah! Ye never noticed me yerself, Conn St. Michael," she huffed.

"Ah, but I did, sweeting. On Twelfth Night when I kissed ye that first time, and yer lips were so incredibly sweet. For a moment I couldn't imagine what a girl like ye was doing at court."

"But in the next minute yer mind strayed to one of those jades ye were forever prodding with yer lance," she accused.

"True," he admitted blandly, and ducked the blow she aimed at him with a laugh. "Yer jealous!" he exulted.

"Of every woman ye've ever known," she admitted ruefully.

They had reached the house, but before they entered he caught her to him, and hugged her. "I'll never stray from yer side, sweeting. That I promise ye. Ours, I believe, is a love for all time." Then he kissed her softly. "Now, sweeting, I'm ravenous for food first, and then yer sweet self once again! Shall we spend the day abed?"

But when Conn and Aidan reached the house, they discovered a visitor waiting. Beal hurried forward to greet them. "There's a gentleman waiting in the Great Hall, m'lord," he said. "He claims to be m'lady's cousin."

Aidan looked confused. "I don't have any cousins," she said. "My father was an only child."

"But yer mother wasn't," said Conn.

"A cousin from Ireland? But I don't even know my mother's family."

"The gentleman does have the lilt of Ireland in his voice, m'lady," Beal volunteered.

They hurried into the house, and seeing them coming toward him Cavan FitzGerald arose from his seat by the fireplace, but before he might speak Conn said, "I am Lord Bliss, and ye are?" Conn's eyes swept over the man who was as tall as he but a trifle thicker set. He did not like the look of him though he knew not why. Perhaps it was his light blue eyes that never quite met his gaze.

"Cavan FitzGerald, my lord," came the reply, and then Cavan swiftly turned to Aidan. "And ye'll be little Aidan, my darling Bevin's child. I bring ye greetings from yer grandfather, Rogan FitzGerald, Aidan."

"Is my grandsire still alive?" she replied. "We heard nothing after my mother's death."

"The old man cannot write," said Cavan. "He used to have my father do it for him, and then when he died he recruited the new priest."

"Ye will forgive me, Master FitzGerald, but I know little of my mother's family, and I cannot place ye at all."

Cavan FitzGerald smiled broadly but the smile did not light his eyes, Conn noted. "Of course, yer confused, little Aidan, and I don't blame ye. Doubtless yer English father preferred ye forget yer Irish relations."

"Not at all, sir," said Aidan frostily. " 'Twas rather a case of my Irish relations not seeming to want anything to do with my mother once she wed with my father. They were happy enough to have him take a dowryless girl, but in all the years my parents were wed though my mother wrote her father faithfully, he wrote her but twice, and both times to ask for money."

Cavan recovered his error in judgment quickly. "Aye, little Aidan, they can be hard people, the FitzGeralds, but Ireland is a harsh land. Ye ask my place within the family, and so I shall tell ye. Yer grandfather had a brother many years his junior. His name was Barra, and he was a priest. I am his bastard, the child of his hearthmate who died shortly after my birth. I was raised by yer grandmother, Ceara, of the sainted memory. I grew up in my uncle's house, and have spent all of my life there."

"What brings ye to England then?" demanded Conn.

"Uncle Rogan's steward is soon to be retired to his cottage. He's almost as old as Rogan FitzGerald himself. I am to replace him. I have been trained all my life to take his place, but my uncle fears if he dies before I can, his eldest son, my cousin Eamon, will not give me my living. I've come to England to see how yer estates are run here. Perhaps, my lord, ye'd be so kind as to allow yer own steward to show me about."

"Of course," said Conn coolly.

"And he should see *Queen's Malvern*, too," chimed in Aidan, "and perhaps he can go down to Devon and see Robin's home also. We could arrange that, couldn't we, Conn?"

"I wouldn't want to be an imposition, my lord," Cavan said quickly seeing Conn about to refuse, and cleverly preventing it.

"I would never consider any member of Aidan's mother's family an imposition," Conn replied dryly, "but do ye want to go as far south as Devon, Master FitzGerald?"

"Anything I can learn that will help me to aid and modernize my Uncle Rogan's estates will be all to the good. I owe him a great debt for taking me in, and raising me. All Irishmen are not as lucky as ye are, my lord."

"Aye," said Aidan innocently, "Conn has marvelous luck," then seeing her husband's frown she continued, "but how I prattle on, cousin. I must see Erwina about feeding ye for I've not a doubt yer hungry. Ye must see the rest of *Pearroc Royal*, and then in a few days we'll visit Conn's sister's home."

"She lives nearby?" Cavan FitzGerald asked.

"Just a few miles across the fields. 'Tis called *Queen's Malvern*, and 'tis Lady de Marisco's son, the Earl of Lynmouth's estate that ye'll visit in Devon."

"Lady de Marisco?"

"Conn's sister."

"She has a son who is an English earl?"

"Oh yes! Robin's family stands very high with her majesty. His father was a great favorite of the queen, and young Robin is her favorite page, although he will soon be going to France to the university. That is something he wants very much, and his older brothers have both gone. They are a very close family."

Cavan FitzGerald digested this piece of information with interest. He didn't like the idea of Aidan being so attached to Conn's family. He was beginning to realize that although he might be able to carry out part of the Spanish plot, he might not be able to succeed completely. If, however, he was to gain Aidan's riches for himself, he would have to destroy Conn, and his O'Malley brothers. The sister with her highly placed English son might not be so easy, and was, he decided, not worth the trouble. She would be unable to save her brothers for she certainly would have no influence being a woman, and there would be no one to take revenge upon Cavan FitzGerald, or indeed even uncover the plot. Little Aidan was pretty enough although he had seen prettier, and Bevin had certainly been a great beauty; but in the dark a warm cunt was a warm cunt no matter the face.

He smiled at the woman he intended to make his wife. "Ye remind me of yer mother," he said warmly.

"I do? How strange as I favor my father," she said.

She was no fool, he quickly realized. He would have to be far more subtle with her. "Not in features," he quickly amended, "but rather in yer mannerisms, the way ye use yer hands, the tilt of yer pretty red head. I was barely breeked when Bevin sailed across the seas to marry the Englishman."

"How old were ye?"

"Just six, but she had been around me all my life. She was like a sister to me, and I cried for days after she left for it was all so quick, the betrothal and the wedding coming within a month. There was barely time for the banns to be posted in Ballycoille so the marriage might be celebrated by proxy in Ireland allowing her family to see her marry."

"She was married here in England when she arrived," said Aidan. "The Earl and Countess of Lincoln, she is Elizabeth FitzGerald, our distant cousin, arranged the match, and they came, I am told, to the wedding, the earl giving the bride away himself. It was a great honor."

"Aidan, Erwina will need time to prepare a meal for our guest," Conn reminded his wife, and then as she gave the two men a quick smile and hurried from the room, Conn turned to speak to their guest. "The FitzGeralds live in the south to my memory. Where did ye sail from that brings ye here to the middle of England?"

"I had estate business in Dublin, my lord, and so I sailed from there to Liverpool. I bought a horse there, and since yer on my way to London, I promised my dear uncle I would stop and see little Aidan. He remembers her with great fondness."

"He never laid eyes on her," Conn remarked.

"But the letters his daughter sent to him were so vivid that it was as if he had," was the smooth reply.

"And how are things in Ireland?" Conn asked.

"The same. The English continue to plantation the land with their own people thus displacing us. Nothing has changed."

"There are no plantations in Connaught," said Conn.

"Nay," agreed Cavan FitzGerald. "Yer people have learned how to cooperate with the English. Mine prefer to remain free."

Conn shrugged the insult aside. "One Ireland needs one king, not a hundred, and as long as there are a hundred kings Ireland will remain enslaved. Ye don't understand that, however, do ye? Ye think I'm a traitor to my country because I live here, but in Ireland I was Dubhdara O'Malley's youngest child, landless and worthless. My existence was an aimless one. Here in England I am useful. I have made my fortune."

"By marrying my cousin," said Cavan FitzGerald.

"Nay! I was a rich man before I ever met Aidan, but that is not yer business. I welcome ye to *Pearroc Royal* as family. See that ye do not abuse the privileges of yer status, Master FitzGerald. If ye do, ye'll have me to settle with. I'm still a Celtic warrior for all the veneer of the English gentleman ye see. Be warned."

Cavan FitzGerald was no fool. What had seemed an easy task when he had first been approached by the Spanish did not seem so simple now.

During the next few days as he wandered about the vast estate he was amazed by Conn's knowledge as Lord Bliss discussed with him rotation of crops, the details involved in the sale of garden produce, the breeding of stock, the replenishment of the gardens, the household accounts, all of which Aidan had turned over to her husband when they had married. Conn had obviously learned quickly enough so that he had already appointed himself an assistant, young Beal, the butler and the housekeeper's eldest son, to be his steward. Young Beal was a man in his late thirties, and he had in turn appointed his younger brother, Harry, as gamekeeper.

All the servants were very loyal to their master and their mistress, and the more Cavan FitzGerald saw, the more he realized that like Conn, he would prefer living here in England, in the lap of luxury. Why should he return to Ireland? His uncle wouldn't live much longer, and once his cousins came into their inheritance they would toss him from his precarious perch. His grudging acceptance into the family was only good as long as Rogan FitzGerald lived. Cavan realized now that he was going to have to make his own way in this world.

He would aid the Spanish in the quest to destroy the O'Malleys, or at least the O'Malley brothers. Then he would, after a suitable time, court the grieving widow for he could see that Aidan would mourn greatly. There was no doubt in Cavan FitzGerald's mind that Aidan and Conn were lovers in every sense of the word; but he would make her like him while he remained with them, and then she would be ripe fruit for the plucking when he was ready. He already knew that Conn disliked him, was suspicious of him and of what he was doing in England. Only the fact that he had actually told the truth when he said he had been trained as a steward had saved him.

He was in no great hurry to travel on to London to meet with Miguel de Guaras who was already there, smuggled into England on the deserted Cornish coast. De Guaras' mother had been French, and he would pass himself off as a Frenchman. Cavan, however, bided his time with Conn and Aidan, attempting to win over his cousin with a mixture of Irish charm and wit. Aidan, delighted to have a blood relative of her own at long last, blossomed with his attentions. She might be a happily married woman, but she was not impervious, she found, to a handsome man, and Cavan FitzGerald was attractive. Not as beautiful as her husband, she thought with pride, but still a handsome fellow with his light blue eyes, and hair which was not coppery like hers, but russet.

She and Conn took him to *Queen's Malvern*.

"This is my cousin, Master Cavan FitzGerald," Aidan said proudly as she presented him to Conn's family. "And this, cousin, is my sister-in-law,

Skye, and her husband, Adam de Marisco." Aidan had her arm through Cavan's and she was obviously pleased to have a relation to present to them.

Skye and Adam had the same reaction to Cavan FitzGerald as had Conn. Instinctively they did not trust him, but they kept silent knowing how important this *cousin* was to sweet Aidan.

Alone with Skye later that day Aidan had confided to her, "I barely remember my sisters for it has been so long since they died, and they were only babies, after all. Mama's family was never real to me until Cavan came. He tells me stories of all my relations, both living and dead, past and present. I can actually see my mother as a little girl through his eyes! Mama died so long ago, and but for my father I never really had a family. I'm not certain I like my Irish relations for they have never bothered with me, but at least I know them now through Cavan. It's as if I really do have a family thanks to him. I know Conn doesn't like him, but he is so kind to me, and patient that I can't help but be grateful to him. Surely ye understand that, Skye?"

Lady de Marisco nodded, and hugged Aidan reassuringly. "Of course I do, my dear sister, and your cousin is most welcome to bide with us too should he desire."

The smile Aidan gave Skye in return for her generous words touched the older woman. She knew her instincts regarding Cavan FitzGerald were correct, but although she disliked the smooth-talking Irishman, she did not believe he could harm sweet Aidan, and so she held her peace for her sister-in-law's sake.

Cavan spent several days with the de Marisco's steward and realized how rich a country England was just in her land alone. He would be happy here, he decided, and if he could get a son on Aidan quick enough he might even match him with the little de Marisco heiress, and then all of this estate and Aidan's would belong to the FitzGeralds. *His family.* The dynasty he intended founding!

June came, and Cavan FitzGerald knew he could no longer delay his departure to London. To his surprise Conn and Aidan said they would travel with him, for they had written to Lord Burghley their desire to see the queen, and had only just received permission to come to London. Cavan had suspected long since that Conn eagerly awaited his going, but the timing was perfect. It meant that Conn would be in London as he went about the business of impersonating him. There would be no way in which Lord Bliss could avoid the trap about to be sprung upon him.

"Having ye with me as I travel will make the trip all the more pleasant," he said smiling broadly.

"Ye must stay with us in London, too," said Aidan generously. "We don't have our own home there, but we stay at Skye's house, Greenwood, at Chiswick, on the river just outside the city itself."

Before Conn might protest, however, Caven FitzGerald was declining graciously. "Nay, little Aidan, 'tis most generous of ye to offer, but my plans are already made, and since it is likely to be the only time in me life I ever get to see yer Londontown, I should prefer to stay in its very heart at some bustling inn. I know ye understand, cousin."

Conn almost groaned aloud when Aidan pressed Cavan. "Yer sure, Cavan? I hate to think of ye in some uncomfortable place when ye could be so wonderfully comfortable with us."

"Aidan, staying with ye has been a rare treat for me for although yer grandsire is landed, his home, most of the homes in Ireland, have nothing like the comforts I've seen here at *Pearroc Royal*, and *Queen's Malvern*. 'Tis been a rare treat, but the sooner I get back to reality, the better." He laughed lightly. "Yer grandsire will not believe the half of it, little Aidan, and all these years he fretted that he had sent his Bevin into a cold exile."

"I understand just what Cavan is saying," added Conn. "Don't forget, sweeting, that ye've never been to Ireland, and like yer cousin, I grew up there."

"I've never been anywhere until last year when I went to court," chuckled Aidan. "The queen liked to call me her country mouse."

"Ye know the queen?" Cavan said. This was a subject that hadn't come up before, and it did not bode well, he thought.

"Of course I know the queen," replied Aidan. "I was one of her maids of honor. She personally arranged my match with Conn for he was a great favorite of hers."

Now that, thought Cavan, was better. Conn's seeming involvement in a plot against Elizabeth Tudor would seem doubly worse by virtue of the fact he had been in her favor.

"When," Aidan continued with a grin, "Conn's natural exuberance got him sent down from court the queen made his punishment more palatable by marrying him to me. She told him that there were those who would hardly think her too harsh marrying him to an heiress."

Conn laughed. "Ye've heard of the reluctant bride, Cavan? Well, I was a reluctant bridegroom." He slipped his arm about Aidan. "What a fool I was, but then how was I to know I should fall in love with this witch?"

Aidan looked up tenderly at her husband. "I wouldn't have it any other way, my lord," she said softly.

"Why were ye sent from court?" asked Cavan, wondering if the information might aid him in his plot.

"For getting caught with too many ladies at once," said Aidan mischievously. "A mother, her two daughters, and an ambassador's wife!"

"*All at once?*" Cavan was stunned and admiring all in the same breath.

As much as Conn would have loved to let the misunderstanding on Cavan's part remain, he knew he couldn't. "Within the period of several days," he said, and Aidan giggled.

Cavan chuckled back at the two of them, but in his mind he was already formulating a scenario. Conn, angry at Elizabeth Tudor for sending him from court, and forcing him into marriage; Conn, raised in the Holy Mother Church, and his eyes suddenly open to the royal bastard; Conn seeking revenge for himself while at the same time helping to place England's rightful Catholic queen, Mary of Scotland, upon the throne. It was perfect, and it was all he could do not to show his exultation. With that background, the Spanish plot could not help but succeed.

London was several days' traveling from *Pearroc Royal*, and once again Cavan FitzGerald was impressed by all he saw. The countryside was green and fertile, the towns appeared prosperous. They stayed at clean, comfortable inns along their route, and Lord and Lady Bliss and their party were welcomed graciously; the accommodations given them spacious and cheerful, the food served them the best of what England had to offer. There was peace and contentment here, Cavan realized. It was something he could never remember feeling in his entire life, and he suddenly realized that he was jealous of Conn. Why should all this good luck go to an O'Malley, and not a FitzGerald? Why should Aidan not be his wife? Her wealth, his wealth?

Suddenly he knew for certain that he did not want to return to Ireland. He didn't want to have to lick the boots of his cousin, Eamon, in order to ensure his very survival. He wanted a wife and a family, things long denied him. He didn't want to have to depend upon others for his very existence. He wanted to be his own man, and having Aidan for his wife would ensure that. He had never had any real feelings where the politics of Ireland were concerned. He was too busy surviving to have time to waste on patriotic emotions. He didn't give a damn what happened to Ireland or the FitzGeralds. He just wanted to be a man of property with a cozy wife.

Conn and Aidan bid Cavan FitzGerald farewell at Greenwood, and sent him on his way with a wave and good wishes. Then as their coach turned into the drive of the house Conn heaved a mighty sigh.

"Thank God he's gone!" he said with deep feeling.

"Conn! He's my cousin!"

"He's the bastard get of yer great-uncle, and I don't like him, Aidan.

Oh, he was pleasant enough, but I don't believe for one minute that he's in England on 'estate' business for yer grandsire. Ye can't even be certain the old man is still alive, sweeting. All ye have is *cousin* Cavan's word on it. If he is, and yer cousin is in his favor, then why didn't the old man send a personal message written by the priest for ye?"

"Then why did Cavan bother to come see us?" she demanded irritably.

"Who knows! Perhaps to cadge a few weeks' lodging and food off us at the least. At the worst, I don't know."

"Yer a suspicious man, Conn, and I never knew it," Aidan said.

"In Ireland ye learn to be suspicious for yesterday's friend can easily turn out to be today's foe. Remember until just four years ago my whole life was spent in Ireland. I've an instinct for troublemakers, and Master Cavan FitzGerald is a troublemaker." Leaning over he gave her a quick kiss. "Don't fret, sweeting. We've come to London to see if the queen has forgiven me, and so ye may lord it over all the other lassies. 'Tis a pity ye can't claim a babe, but it cannot be long now, I suspect."

"But I am with child," Aidan said calmly.

"What?" He shifted himself from her side into the coach seat opposite her, and looked into her face. "Yer going to have a baby? Yer certain?" His eyes were alight with his happiness, and somewhat damp with emotion.

"I wasn't sure at first, and I wanted to wait until I could be sure. I am now. I believe I conceived on May Day. The baby will be born next winter, Conn."

"We're going to turn right around and go home immediately," Conn declared. "London in the summer can be terrible, and I would never forgive myself if the plague broke out, and ye caught it."

Aidan laughed merrily. "Don't be silly, Conn! It is too early for plague, and the June weather is cool yet. This is a wonderful opportunity to regain the queen's favor. If she will see us, and I know she will, we will tell her of our gratitude to her, our happiness, our coming child. She will love being the first to know, and we will ask her to be our baby's godmother! Even if she is still somewhat piqued at ye, she will forgive ye at our news. We will also tell her we plan returning to *Pearroc Royal* immediately, and that we just came to London to share our news with her. The queen is really a very sentimental woman, Conn. Ye know that."

"Aye," he agreed. "Bess's heart has been known to soften on occasion." He caught her two gloved hands and raised them to his lips, kissing them passionately. "A son," he said. "We'll have a son!"

Aidan's laughter rang out. "Or a daughter, my lord," she said. "Babies have been known to be daughters."

"But we'll have a son!" he insisted with a grin.

"I shall do my best to please ye, my lord," she said softly, a smile upon her lips. She had never felt happier in her entire life!

The coach had drawn up before Greenwood, and the servants hurried from the house to greet Lord and Lady Bliss. Cluny and Mag had come on ahead that morning to be certain that everything was in readiness for their master and mistress. They squabbled constantly, each trying to gain superiority over the other in the service hierarchy of the household. Now as the coach door was opened, the steps pulled down so the occupants might descend, Mag was heard to say, "The capes, Master Cluny, the capes! When will ye ever learn they are yer job?"

"Perhaps," snapped Cluny "if ye'd but give me a chance to do me job without all yer interference I could, old woman."

"*Old woman?*" Mag was mortally offended. "If I'm an old woman, then yer an old man, Master Cluny!"

Conn and Aidan alighted from the coach laughing, hearing their servants scolding at each other again. Since neither of the pair would give over they provided a constant source of amusement to Lord and Lady Bliss. Quarrel as they might amongst themselves, they would, however, defend each other from anyone else.

"Cluny!" Conn's voice was sharp. "Did ye dispatch a footman to Lord Burghley with our message?"

Cluny, free of Mag's carping, hurried forward. "Aye, m'lord! First thing we got here, and I told him just what ye told me to, that he was to wait for a reply. He ain't back yet."

Conn nodded, and escorted his wife into the house and up to their apartments. "We'll have to stay here at Greenwood until William Cecil decides to reply to our message. Neither of us can be seen at court until we are invited. I hope we'll not be kept waiting. I don't want ye in the city any longer than is necessary."

"Conn, I am not invalided," protested Aidan.

"The city is not a healthy place with all the damned garbage in the streets, and open sewers. If I'd known last week what I do now we'd not have come to London at all."

"I wasn't sure last week," replied Aidan sweetly.

"My sister always knew," said Conn suspiciously.

"Each woman is different, my lord, and I doubt that Skye would allow anyone to prevent her doing what she chose to do, certainly not a husband. Ye cannot deny that!"

The arrival of the returning footman brought the conversation to an end. Now they would know if they were welcome at court, or if they had made the trip in vain. The note from William Cecil, Lord Burghley, however, was gracious. He was certain that her majesty would welcome Lord and Lady Bliss back, if only for a short time, and he therefore bid them come to Greenwich in two days' time before the queen left on her summer progress to present their compliments to Elizabeth.

"I have nothing to wear!" Aidan announced dramatically.

"How could ye have nothing to wear?" her husband demanded. "Ye knew we were coming to London for the express purpose of seeing the queen."

"Our decision to come was so hurried I really didn't have time to pack properly," said Aidan with very feminine logic. "I will have to send to yer sister's dressmaker, the one who made my wedding-journey traveling dress for ye, and have a decent court costume made for the occasion. Would ye have me looking like a country drab so that all yer admirers will feel sorry for ye?"

She was doing it again, he chuckled to himself. Turning a situation about so that in the end it was he who was responsible for the entire thing. There had been more than enough time to prepare herself. "Ye want a new gown?" he accused.

"Of course," she answered him blandly. "I want the most outrageously fashionable gown that can be made! I want every woman at court that ignored me when I was there fearfully jealous, not only of my handsome husband, but my gorgeous clothing as well!"

"Then there is nothing for it but that I send for the dressmaker," said Conn laughing. "May I help ye choose?"

"No! I want to surprise ye, too!"

"Minx!" he grumbled, and pulling her against him began to unfasten her gown, kissing her shoulder as he bared it.

Aidan squirmed away scolding, "No, no, my lord! First send for the dressmaker! We have but two days' time before we are expected at Greenwich." She drew her gown back up over the shoulder.

He laughed. She was full of surprises, his darling wife. "Very well, madame. I'll send for the dressmaker first," he said, reaching over to yank at the bellpull.

Madame came, and with her three assistants, each heavily laden with bolts of fabric. "My lord Bliss," she said smiling broadly, for Conn paid in honest coin for her work, "welcome back to London. Will ye and yer good lady be with us long?"

" 'Tis a short visit, madame, but we are called to court in two days' time, and my lady was so pleased with the gowns ye sent to *Pearroc Royal* that nothing would do but ye make her a gown to visit the queen in."

"The most magnificent and fashionable gown in all of London, madame!" said Aidan, and the dressmaker smiled at Lady Bliss' ingenuousness.

"Then we must begin at once!" she said. "Will ye be helping m'lady to choose, my lord?"

"Nay, my wife says it is to be a surprise, and so I will take my leave of ye now," Conn said with a smile, and blowing a kiss at the assembled females he departed the room.

One of Madame's assistants, a very young girl not more than twelve, almost swooned at Conn's leaving, but the sharp voice of her mistress, punctuated with a small slap, quickly brought her around. Aidan settled herself in a high-back chair, and waited expectantly for a show of fabrics.

"I have brought along many bolts, m'lady Bliss," said Madame, "but seeing ye now in person, I have one which I know will be utterly perfect for it is a color that not every woman could wear. Certainly Lady de Marisco could not, but ye can! Susan! The gold-bronze silk!"

The girl named Susan lifted from the pile of fabrics a bolt which she then unrolled across the floor in Aidan's direction. It was a wonderful, rich bronze-colored silk with dull gold overtones. Aidan adored it instantly, but Madame said, "Think of it with the bodice and the skirt panel sewn over with olive-green peridots and pearls. This color will highlight yer beautiful hair to perfection! I have just received it from France. It is *very* sophisticated, and," she added slyly, "ye will be the envy of every woman at Greenwich! I swear it!"

"Then I must have it, of course," laughed Aidan, "for that is just the effect I wish to inspire. Pea-green envy!"

Her tone was so positively gleeful that the dressmaker had to laugh, and so did her three assistants although in a more restrained fashion lest they offend the lady. At Madame's instruction they set at work to measure Aidan, Madame setting the figures upon a small piece of parchment as she was the only one who could read and write. It was silently noted that Aidan had not increased with girth since the last gowns had been made, and yet Madame would have sworn that Lady Bliss was with child. There was something in the eyes of a woman when she was in that condition. The dressmaker shrugged to herself.

The day they were to go to Greenwich dawned fair and cool. Aidan was beside herself with excitement for her gown had been delivered in the early hours of the morning, just before the dawn, and it was everything that she had hoped it would be. Conn had been chased from their apartments with Cluny to be dressed elsewhere while Mag aided by two young maidservants belonging to the house readied her mistress.

Aidan's glorious coppery hair had been washed first, and then she herself had bathed. Dried, her silken undergarments had been handed her one by one; knitted stockings of palest gold with pretty matching ribbon garters with their saucy rosettes sporting pearl centers, gossamer silk chemise of a creamy hue shot through with gold threads in the sleeves which would show through the slashes in Aidan's dress sleeves only as a glittering, a verdingale over which several petticoats were added, but Madame disdained hipbolsters which she considered clumsy, and Aidan was much too lithe for a corset. The underskirt of the gown was put on, its center panel embroidered with sparkling green peridots and tiny seed pearls in a field of wheat pattern upon the faintly greenish silk. Next came the overskirt, and the bodice of the gown, sewn from the wonderful golden-bronze fabric that Madame had shown Aidan just two days before. The skirt of the gown was bell-shaped, the bodice very low-necked, so low-necked that Mag drew in her breath with sharp disapproval, and Aidan's eyes widened to see her swelling breasts exposed almost to the nipple.

"Whatever was that dressmaker thinking of, m'lady? Ye can't be seen publicly like that!"

" 'Tis the fashion, Mistress Mag," said one of the other maidservants. "All the fine ladies dress like that now."

"M'lord won't let ye go out looking like that!" said Mag severely.

"M'lord won't see me until we reach Greenwich," chuckled Aidan. "I'll have my cloak on, and by then 'twill be too late."

"Milady, ye wouldn't!" Mag was scandalized. "To show yer titties to virtual strangers, 'tis a scandal!"

"Nay, Mag, 'tis the fashion," laughed Aidan, looking at herself in the mirror, and extremely pleased with what she saw. The gown was simply wonderful! Not only the deliciously low neckline but the sleeves too were perfect. The leg-o'-mutton sleeves were slashed on the upper arm allowing her beautiful chemise sleeves beneath to show to their best advantage. Below her elbows the sleeves were molded to her arms, and dotted with gold ribbons that had been embroidered with the crystallike green peridots. "Is there a neck wisk?" she asked.

"Aye, milady," said Jane, and handed the item to Mag who fastened the wired golden-green, fan-shaped upright collar in its place.

Jane next handed the tiring woman a flat case which Mag opened to reveal a magnificent necklace of olive-green peridots. "And where did these come from?" she demanded.

"My lord asked what jewelry I should like while we were here in London, and I told him these. Mary," Aidan spoke to the younger serving maid. "There should be another box with earbobs."

" 'Tis here, m'lady," said Mary, offering the box to Aidan.

While Mag fastened the glittering necklace of peridots about her lady's neck, Aidan calmly put the green stones in her ears. They hung twinkling from large baroque pearls. Aidan surveyed the effect critically, and decided that she had never looked better. "Now, Mag," she said pleased, "do my hair, and I shall be ready to see the queen."

"More than likely the queen is going to see ye," grumbled Mag, "but whether she'll like what she sees, I don't know." She shot a quelling look at Jane and Mary who giggled behind their hands at her words. Then setting to work she parted Aidan's thick long hair in the middle, and affixed it into a very elegant chignon that rested at the base of her mistress' neck in heavy coils. Lady de Marisco's tiring woman, Daisy, had taught her the style. Standing back she surveyed her work a moment, and satisfied she fastened the hair securely with gold and diamond pins. "Well, yer as done as yer going to be, my pet! You! Useless giggling Mary! Fetch m'lady's cloak at once!" She had no words for Jane who already knelt dutifully at Aidan's feet putting on her mistress' pretty matching silk slippers with their high heels, which were narrow-toed, and decorated with pearls.

Aidan stood up, and the cloak was placed over her shoulders. It was long and loose-fitting, the same bronze silk as her gown, and lined in cloth of gold. A gauzy gold veil was handed to her which she placed over her head to protect her hair upon the river from its breezes. A small, elaborate muff decorated with lace and jewels completed her costume. Within the muff she carried a lace-edged handkerchief and a pomander ball studded with precious cloves. As an afterthought she added several rings to her fingers, the better to flaunt her wealth.

For a moment she studied herself in the mirror thinking that fine feathers did indeed make a difference. Her clothing had never been either this magnificent or elegant, nor had the woman who stared back at her been quite so pretty. She wondered how much of it had to do with her clothing, and how much of it had to do with her own personal happiness. Whatever the reasons she had never felt more confident, or more lovely in her entire life, and she was definitely ready to take on the court, but this time upon her own terms.

Conn, awaiting below, smiled as she came down the stairs. "Ye've put yer cloak on," he said disappointed. "Do I not get to see the wonderful gown?"

"We are almost late as it is," she said, her tone worried. "Ye'll see it when we get to Greenwich. It will not do for us to be late, Conn. Ye know how her majesty prizes punctuality."

"Yer absolutely right," he agreed, not in the least suspicious as he escorted his wife down to Greenwood's stone quay for the voyage downriver to Greenwich in their barge.

Their boat, by good fortune, had caught the tide, and was quickly sped down the Thames River to the royal residence at Greenwich. There it joined a line of other barges, both privately owned like theirs, and public conveyances hired for the trip to court, that waited in a somewhat ragged line to land at the watergate of the palace. Several persons in the other boats recognized Conn immediately, and called out to him. Elegant in the black velvet suit his wife had requested he wear, he bowed right and left.

"Why is it," Aidan teased her husband, "that there are more ladies than gentlemen addressing ye, m'lord?"

"I made many friends while I served Bess in the Gentlemen Pensioners," Conn said dryly with a mischievous wink at his wife.

"Indeed ye seem to have, but should any of those jades attempt to renew old acquaintances, I shall claw them to ribbons!"

Leaning over he kissed her ear sending a ripple of pleasure down her spine. "Ye can't deny me the looking, sweeting, for there's only one who has my heart in her gentle keeping, and 'tis ye."

"Yer a rogue," she muttered at him.

"Aye, but a rogue who loves only his wife, Aidan. Believe that. I'm a courtier by nature, but I'll never play ye false though I flirt with relish."

"Then ye'll not mind if I flirt also?" she asked.

"Nay, sweeting, for as I am true to ye, I know ye'll be true to me. Just be careful, Aidan, for yer not practiced in such arts, and ye could mislead a man easily which I know ye wouldn't want to do. Still, sweeting, have yer fun as long as yer careful."

"I wonder," she mused smiling, "how many other husbands give their wives leave to flirt?"

"Not many. They cannot trust their spouses as I can trust ye."

Their barge's turn now came to make a landing, and they quickly, with the help of royal footmen, stepped from their boat onto the little stone quay, and hurried up the staircase and into the palace of Greenwich. There waiting servants took their cloaks from them, and Conn got his first look at his wife's new gown. His surprised expression was so comical that Aidan began to giggle.

"Jesu!" he hissed. "Ye leave little to the imagination, do ye, sweeting?"

" 'Tis the height of fashion, m'lord."

"Says who?" He dragged her into a corner where none could overhear them, or see her.

"Madame," said Aidan calmly. "She made my gown to yer sister's specifications, her exact specifications. I carried them from home, and gave them to Madame when she came two days ago. Madame says that Skye is a perfect authority on fashion, and I am wise to take her advice."

"That gown is positively indecent! If ye breathe deep once ye'll be out of it! Yer going home to change, Aidan! I'll not have every man at court ogling yer tits!" He grasped her by the arm, but she pulled away angrily.

"This gown is totally in fashion. Look about ye, Conn! Every woman here is wearing as low a neckline if not lower! The queen is expecting us now, and besides I have nothing back at Greenwood I could wear. That is why I had this gown made in the first place. I believe ye are jealous, m'lord. How wonderful!"

He gritted his teeth in frustration. She was perfectly correct in everything she said, and the truth of the matter was that he was jealous. Then seeing the delight upon her face at the fact he was jealous he saw the humor in the situation, and laughed softly. He was totally prepared to be liberal in his attitude toward his plain little wife, but she was no longer quite so plain in her magnificent court dress, with two of her best points more than apparent. His liberality had vanished with his realization that if he found his wife attractive then so would others. "Dammit, Aidan, couldn't ye have put a little bit of lace there?" he asked, trailing his fingers along the tops of her breasts.

"No," she said with a finality in her voice that ended the matter. Then, "We will be late, my lord," she gently reminded him.

Bested he took her arm, and escorted her down the broad corridor to the receiving room where the queen would come to greet all of her guests. As they moved along amid the other courtiers several ladies called out, their tones dulcet with promise, "Conn O'Malley! Welcome!" Conn nodded noncommittally. "Conn, darling! 'Tis good to see ye!" "Oh, Conn! We've missed ye!"

"More than likely they've missed yer fine cock," teased Aidan, and he laughed at her irreverence for the court beauties.

"My dear child, welcome back to court. Please introduce me to yer husband for I know him only by sight." Elizabeth Clinton stood before them.

Aidan curtsied politely, and Conn bowed gallantly to the Countess of Lincoln. "My lord," Aidan said formally, "may I present her ladyship, the Countess of Lincoln, to whom I am fortunate enough to be related through my mother's family. Madame, my husband, Conn St. Michael, Lord Bliss."

"I am sorry," said the countess, "that we did not get to meet before ye left court, my lord. Will ye be joining us on the summer progress? We leave in a few days' time for Long Medford."

"Alas, no, madame," said Conn politely. "We have only come to court to share with her majesty some happy news, and to thank her for wedding us. Then we must return to *Pearroc Royal*, my wife's health being delicate now."

"Ahh." Elizabeth Clinton smiled, understanding without being told what the happy news would be, and obviously very happy to see her young relative had made a love match in the end. Young O'Malley had a wild reputation that she doubted not, but he was also obviously a man of principle, and with his marriage had settled down. She knew it was what the queen had hoped for after last winter's scandal.

"I am happy for ye both," she said, "and I know that her majesty will be too. She is anxious to see what her matchmaking has wrought, and I think she will be pleased with the results." Then the Countess of Lincoln gave Aidan a motherly hug, kissing her upon both cheeks, and even gave Conn a maternal buss. "Good fortune to ye both," she said, and then she moved away.

"Aidan! Uncle Conn!" The young Earl of Lynmouth hurried up to them.

"God's blood, youngster," said Conn. "Ye've grown another foot, I vow! How do ye manage it with all the running ye do here?"

Robin Southwood grinned. "I've learned how to eat and sleep on the run," he said offhandedly. Then he looked closely at Aidan. "Yer happy," he noted.

"Very happy," she answered. "Yer uncle has taken yer good advice, and treated me quite well. Why the man even admits to loving me." She smiled at the blushing Earl of Lynmouth.

"I hope he knows ye love him, and were positively cow-eyed over him from the first night ye came to court."

"Oh ho, what's this?" Conn suddenly looked fascinated.

Now it was Aidan's turn to blush, and Robin realized his error. "Yer uncle," said Aidan in an attempt to regain control of the situation, "is well aware that I love him, Robin."

"But I want to hear about the cow-eyed part," teased Conn.

"Sir!" She shook her little muff at him. "Will ye leave me no secrets?"

He slipped his arm about her, and quickly kissed her cheek. "Nay, sweeting. There'll be no secrets between us ever. 'Tis not healthy for a marriage."

"My lord, I ask you nothing of what went on in yer life with regard to other ladies before we wed. Ye, in return, must not ask me about my cow-eyed state before we wed."

He chuckled. "Very well, madame. In the interest of discretion I am forced to agree."

"I was sent to bring ye to the queen's private closet," said Robin. "We must hurry for she'll wonder where we are."

Lord and Lady Bliss followed the young earl from the receiving room, and down a corridor, and up a flight of stairs to the queen's apartments which overlooked the river. Entering she and Conn were warmly greeted by the girls who had been her companions just several months back.

"Aidan!" Linnet Talbot squealed. "Ye look positively gorgeous! That gown must have cost a fortune!"

"It did," said Aidan with a laugh. "How are ye, Linnet?" She smiled at the girl, and her smile took in the other young ladies she had known during her stay at court. "Mary, Dorothy, Jane Anne, Cathy," she named them. "And who is this young lady? My replacement, I presume."

"Yes," said Linnet. "This is Bess Throckmorton, the sister of Sir Nicholas."

"Mistress Throckmorton." Aidan smiled at the serious young girl who couldn't have been more than fifteen.

Mistress Throckmorton curtsied politely.

"I'll tell the queen yer here," said Robin, and he hurried off.

Aidan smiled again. "I don't believe any of ye have ever been formally introduced to my husband, Lord Bliss," she said.

The queen's six maids of honor curtsied to Conn who bowed in return to them. Then Linnet, ever bold, said, "Sweet Mary! He's as gorgeous close up as he is at a distance. No wonder ye retired to the country. I wouldn't want to share him either!"

"Linnet!" Mistress Throckmorton looked shocked, but Aidan laughed.

"He's even better without his clothes," she teased Linnet, and casting quick looks at Lord Bliss, the queen's maids of honor burst into laughter, even Bess Throckmorton.

"Ye've changed," remarked Linnet Talbot, "and I think it's for the better."

" 'Tis all due to me," Conn said mischievously. "I've made my lass bloom."

"Well," said Linnet matter-of-factly, "yer marriage made her the envy of every lady at court who ever coveted ye, my lord. Have ye come back to join us this summer?"

"Nay," said Conn to the girl, but before she might question him further Robin returned to bring them into the queen's private closet.

The queen was seated in a comfortable chair, clad in a pale blue chamber robe embroidered with pearls. Behind her one of her women was brushing her fading reddish locks. Both Conn and Aidan made a deep obeisance to Elizabeth Tudor, and as they slowly rose she gave them one of her rare smiles.

"How happy ye both look," she said with just a hint of sadness in her own voice. "Come and sit by me, my dears, and tell me yer news."

147

It was a special invitation for the queen did not invite everyone to sit by her. One of the Ladies of the Bedchamber brought forth two stools, and set them before the queen. Conn and Aidan sat.

"We wanted to come personally to thank ye, yer majesty, for our happiness," said Aidan. "Had it not been for ye we should have never found each other."

Elizabeth's eyes misted. She conveniently forgot the embarrassing circumstances that had forced her to find a wife for Conn, and she seemed to have forgotten that it was Aidan who had boldly put herself forth as a candidate, in fact the only logical candidate, for Conn's hand. She reached out to take Aidan's hand. "Dear child, I am so happy that in keeping my word to yer dying father, I have also been able to make ye happy, too. Is this wicked rogue good to ye?"

Aidan smiled a smile of such genuine happiness that even before she assented, "Aye, he is," the queen knew the answer.

"And ye, Conn O'Malley! Yer pardon, Conn St. Michael, my lord Bliss. Are ye happy also?"

"Aye, Bess. As always ye knew better than I what was right for me."

The queen preened beneath his honest flattery. "I want ye both to join us on this summer's progress," she said. "Marriage seems to agree with ye, Conn. I can see in yer eyes that ye've settled down."

"Bess, 'tis a gracious invitation, graciously given, but I would beg yer permission to decline it. We have happy news that we came to share with ye, and 'twas our main reason for coming back to court." He put his hand over the queen's and Aidan's. "My wife," he said, "is with child. The babe is due next winter."

"We would be so honored," said Aidan, "if ye would agree to be our child's godmother, madame."

This was the kind of thing that Elizabeth Tudor loved. Her own single state had often made her bitter toward those who found marital happiness, and had children of their own; but in the case of her involvement in a romance she could be all graciousness. Thus it was with Conn and Aidan. She had been responsible for their marriage, and it worked out well. She was delighted to accept the credit for it all, for did it not show her own foresight and her wisdom? Now there was to be a fruit of that marriage, and once again she was to be included, indeed play a major role in the drama.

Conn and Aidan had actually come upon the queen at a rather fortunate time. A French marriage was once again being discussed, this time with Catherine de'Medici's youngest son, François, Duc d'Alençon. Elizabeth was in a particularly good humor. She had spent the month of May at Wanstead House, which belonged to her favorite of favorites, Robert

Dudley, the Earl of Leicester. It had been an idyllic time for her among people she loved, and who loved her. She had had another portrait painted, this time in the gardens at Wanstead standing upon an Oriental rug, wearing a white gown embroidered with sprays of flowers and leaves, colored in their natural colors.

She had returned for only a short time to Greenwich, and would in less than a week be off on her summer progress which would this year take her into the county of Norfolk, ending at the city of Norwich in East Anglia. She was to meet with the Duc d'Alençon's agents, Monsieur de Boc-queville and Monsieur de Quincy, at Long Medford, and she was very ex-cited. Not by the thought of marriage for Elizabeth had no intention of marrying, particularly a young prince but half her age; but she did look forward to the negotiations, and the wooing that would be involved. It had been suggested that Monsieur, as the Duc d'Alençon was called, might come to England. This would be a first in all the marriage negoti-ations that Elizabeth had lived through, and the idea frankly appealed to her. It was just one more springtime fling before her old age set in, for at forty-five, the queen of England was hardly in her prime.

"Will ye, madame?" Aidan was looking anxiously at her. "Will ye be our child's godmother?"

"Of course, my dearest country mouse," said the queen in her best ma-ternal fashion. "It is I who shall be honored to be your heir's godmother. I am touched that ye would even think to ask me."

"Whom else should we ask but the one responsible for all our happi-ness," replied Aidan with deep sincerity, and Conn once again felt total admiration for his wife.

"Madame," said one of the queen's women, "it is time to prepare ye."

"Of course," said the queen, and she stood. "Go now, my dears, and have a wonderful time with us for the next few days. I shall regret the loss of yer company this summer, but I realize how delicate a woman's health may be with her first child, and how very much it will mean to Aidan to be safely in her home at *Pearroc Royal*. I shall come there next winter for my godchild's christening."

Lord and Lady Bliss arose, and bowing to the queen a final time backed from her private closet, and out into the antechamber.

Chapter 6

❦

They had stayed in London only four days, and then Conn had insisted that they return home to *Pearroc Royal*. They had attended two masques, and gone to the bear gardens but for once that particular sport sickened Aidan greatly. She had begun to be ill in the mornings to her discomfort, but Conn considered it a wonderful sign, a sign of a healthy son.

"If," she said to him acidly their final morning in London, and having just lost her breakfast into a basin, "ye felt as wretched as I do, ye would not be so full of glee about sons!" She rinsed her mouth with lukewarm minted water, and spit it into the basin.

Picking her up Conn settled her gently back into their bed. "Don't fret, sweeting. In a few weeks ye'll feel better, I'm bound."

Aidan eyed him with a slightly jaundiced look, and curling onto her side went back to sleep as Conn tiptoed, a huge grin upon his face, from the room. He was, however, concerned that she travel in comfort, and so he decided to send their coaches, both personal and baggage, on ahead of them while he and Aidan traveled by barge upon the river. Aidan was delighted with the idea, and strangely felt much better as they glided along the water than she did upon the land.

The weather was perfect for such a venture, the skies were bright, clear blue, and totally cloudless; the sun warm and bright. There was just the faintest hint of a breeze, so light in fact that it did not even ruffle the surface of the upper river. Greenwood's staff of bargemen were delighted for the opportunity to get out of London. Since Lord and Lady de Marisco were banished to *Queen's Malvern*, and young Lord Bliss and his wife were living out of London, too, there was little for them to do. Indeed they considered themselves fortunate to be employed at all with no one living permanently at Greenwood. Sometimes guests of their master and mistress used the house, and then they kept busy; or perhaps the young Earl

150

of Lynmouth needed their services; but in general the last few months had been quiet. They rowed smoothly along, enjoying the weather every bit as much as their passengers.

Aidan found the barge enormously comfortable for she was able to stretch out and doze far more easily than she was in the coach. They glided along passing all other sorts of river traffic, barges filled with freight, fishing vessels, ferries, and other private conveyances. The countryside was in lush full bloom, and there was so much to see that she grew tired with the variety. Along the banks of the river they passed cottages and great houses, children splashing in the heat of the midafternoon, washerwomen busily scrubbing, the clean linens spread over the nearby bushes drying in the hot sun, fishermen hauling in their catch.

Conn had taken off his doublet, and unbuttoned his shirt in the warmth, an idea Aidan had followed, removing her bodice, and opening the neck of her silk chemise. Although there was a helmsman at the stern of the barge he had no view of their open-sided cabin, the roof of it blocking him; and as for the oarsmen, their backs were to their passengers. It allowed them a goodly measure of privacy. Sprawling next to his wife Conn could not help but be aroused by her tempting state. The waistband of her skirt was loosened for her comfort and he unlaced her chemise to her navel as she dozed. For a long while he watched her, fascinated, intrigued by her perfection of form. Then as he began to fondle one breast, he bent his dark head to encircle the other nipple with his tongue.

"Ummmm," she murmured sleepily, as heavy-lidded she opened her eyes for a moment. Then she closed them again, and her fingers began to caress his neck. He nipped gently at the nipple, and then he sucked upon it, setting her blood aboil for her nipples were more sensitive now than she had ever known them to be. "Conn," she whispered frantically, "don't! Ye make me want ye!" In answer he drew her hand down to where he throbbed, already hard and long.

"I want ye to want me, sweeting," he whispered back, and then without even taking his mouth from her breasts he reached over to draw the drapes about their enclosure.

Her cheeks flamed at his daring, and she could still not believe that he meant to take her here, in their barge, with just thin velvet curtains separating them from the entire world. He fondled both her plump treasures noticing for the first time that Aidan's pink nipples were now more of a deep rose in color. His hands were making her feel totally shameless, and she squirmed beneath his delicious touch.

"Roll onto yer side, Aidan," he murmured in her ear sending a prickle of shivers down her spine.

When she had complied she could feel him raising her skirts and bunching them about her waist. Then he was pulling her back against him, and to her great surprise she felt his manhood seek and finding her passage, fill it with his warm, pulsing length. "Ohhh," the breath was forced from her, and he laughed softly.

"There is a lot I can teach ye, sweeting," he murmured against her cheek, kissing her softly. "This saves ye from having to bear my weight against yer thighs right now. I don't want to injure the babe."

That was a revelation for she had wondered what they would do when she grew big; but right now all she knew was that he was moving inside her, and it was wonderful. She pushed against him, and catching her rhythm he was able to remove his hands from her hips, and occupy them more profitably with her breasts again. As the feelings of passion began to mount within her Aidan bit hard on her lower lip to keep from shrieking aloud. He excited her unbearably, the situation which they were in excited her, and her breath came in fierce little pants as their fulfillment approached. Then with exquisite timing, and at the precise moment of their mutual passion, Conn swiftly covered her mouth with one hand, grunting with surprise as her teeth sank into the lower heel of his palm. For several long moments they shuddered with their meeting, and then he removed his hand which she quickly caught back, and kissed where her teeth had marked him. Gently he drew her skirts down, and opening the draperies upon one side of the barge allowed the faint breeze within.

She was feeling wonderful, Aidan thought. Her whole body was relaxed, the breeze drying the light sheen of wetness that covered her breasts. "What a learned man ye are, my husband," she said with total understatement. "I hope ye have more such lessons, and surprises in store for me." She rolled over onto her back, and looked up at him.

Damn, he thought, how pretty she's become. Is it me, or is it the babe, or perhaps a little of both? In either case he felt humbled. He smiled down on her. "Oh, Aidan, my love," he said, "I have the world to show ye, and we've a long and lovely lifetime in which to enjoy it!" Then he kissed her, feeling her lips part to take his tongue in her mouth. How sweetly eager she was still, and he adored her for it. Her eyes grew heavy again, and he watched her as she dozed thinking again as he had each day over the last few months, how very lucky he was to have found her.

The Greenwood House barge traveled slightly north of the city of Oxford where Lord and Lady Bliss once again took passage in their coach. They were almost halfway home at that point, and so those last miles didn't seem so terrible as the carriage bounced along the summer-dusty roads.

They arrived at *Pearroc Royal* to find that little Velvet de Marisco's betrothal would be taking place the following week. Conn's youngest niece was to be married when she reached sixteen years of age to the heir of the Earl of BrocCairn, young Alexander Gordon. He and his father, Angus, would be arriving in a few days from their home, Dun Broc, in the highlands to the west of Aberdeen.

Angus Gordon was an old friend of Adam de Marisco. The two had been boys together in France where the earl had gone both to study, and to serve for a time his half-sister, the little Queen of Scots, who was married to the young and frail French king. As boys they had spoken of one day uniting their families by marriage, and now the dream was to become fact with the official betrothal of Adam's five-year-old daughter, Velvet, and Angus' fifteen-year-old son, Alex.

Skye had not been happy with the possibility of an arranged marriage. Her first marriage had been such, and it had been a disaster from the beginning. She wanted her daughters to marry well, but she also wanted them to marry for love. She had attained this wish with her eldest daughter, Willow, who was married to James Edwardes, the personable young Earl of Alcester. She wanted the same good fortune for her other two daughters, Dierdre Burke and Velvet de Marisco. Still in all she disliked going against her husband, and so she had agreed to the match on the proviso that if when Velvet grew up she was unhappy with her parents' arrangement, she need not abide by it, but rather seek her own heart's desire.

Although her house would be full, it was a large house, and so Skye had insisted that Conn and Aidan remain overnight during the festivities, particularly when she learned of Aidan's condition.

"I'm so happy for ye," she said hugging her sister-in-law. "It seems to be a year for babies. Willow is due next month, and yer babe will come in the winter. Both my eldest sons were born in winter. We'll ask my sister Eibhlin to come from Ireland if she can, to look after ye. Has Conn told ye of Eibhlin?"

"The doctoring nun? Aye, and I'm truly anxious to meet her for I've never heard of a woman doctor."

"She's quite amazing," Skye said. "Our Da had eleven living children, and there are four of us considered not right by our siblings. Me, of course, for I dared to accept the responsibility of the entire family when my father died. My elder sisters, but Eibhlin, never forgave me it. Eibhlin herself who chose to become a nun, and then refused to be cloistered, but instead runs about the countryside caring for the sick. Michael who became a priest when he might have gone off to sea, and become a freebooter like our Da, and of course, Conn, who chose to find a future in England instead of fighting the English!" She laughed. " 'Tis quite a family ye've married into, Aidan."

Queen's Malvern began to fill up with Skye's children. From Ireland came her eldest son, Ewan O'Flaherty, his wife, Gwen, and their children. Ewan's brother, Murrough, arrived home from a voyage, and stopping in Devon to collect his wife, Joan, who was Gwen's sister, brought her and their children. Willow, enormous with her first pregnancy, but blooming with pride and happiness, came with her husband. From court came the two half-brothers, Robin Southwood, the Earl of Lynmouth, and Lord Padraic Burke. Padraic's elder sister, Deirdre, might also have gone to court, but Deirdre had no desire to do so, preferring to remain by her mother's side instead. Now they all assembled for the betrothal of their youngest sister, and the boys teased Deirdre that their little sister would be wed long before she would.

Usually quiet Deirdre looked to the Earl of BrocCairn, and his son, and said with foresight, "I would not be happy marrying a man like Alexander Gordon. He is too fierce for me. I want a quiet man, a gentle man."

Aidan put her arm about her young niece. "I think ye speak with much wisdom for such a little lass," she said looking at young Alexander Gordon.

He was an arrogant-looking boy, tall and lanky with a shock of dark hair, and amber-gold eyes. He spoke English carefully, with measured tones, but a distinct Scots accent. He was educated, attending the university of Aberdeen, but he had never been out of Scotland before although his father did mention something about future schooling in France as he had had.

The betrothal was celebrated just within the immediate family including Sir Robert Small and his sister, Dame Cecily. The Mass was currently forbidden, but none of the servants at *Queen's Malvern*, most of whom were old church, would have informed on the de Mariscos, or their priest, a young French relation who was much beloved in the district. The tiny bride-to-be was adorable in a pale rose silk gown, a wreath of wild pink roses in her auburn hair. She was very proud that even given her youth she was able to sign her own name to the legal document right next to that of her bridegroom.

Aidan watched the couple with some amusement, and thought how glad she was that her father hadn't betrothed her young. Alex was embarrassed by the display of affection being made over him, and the little girl who would be his wife someday. Looking at her he could not imagine her grown, a state he believed he had already attained. In an effort to be friendly he had offered the little maid some sweetmeat. She had taken it from him, lisping her thanks, and then with a strangely adult glance at him from beneath her lashes she had hurried back to the protection of her mother's lap.

It had been a short affair, lasting only a day for Angus Gordon's only daughter was being married in a few weeks' time, and he had left both her, and his wife behind in Scotland during troubled times in order to quickly come south to see the betrothal of his heir. It was also not particularly wise to leave his holding without its lord. The morning after the betrothal saw the Earl of BrocCairn and his son ride north, but not before an exciting end to the previous day when Skye's daughter Willow went into early labor and delivered her first baby, a healthy, squalling boy, who because of the unusual circumstances of his birth, was baptized immediately with the newly betrothed couple standing as godparents.

As they rode back across the fields to their own home the following afternoon Aidan was still laughing over all the excitement that young Willow had caused, and how her sister-in-law, usually totally in control, had been visibly shaken by her daughter's ordeal.

"I can't believe it," said Conn for what seemed the hundredth time. "I never thought to see Skye get so upset. She's had enough babies of her own."

"But this was *her* baby having a baby," replied Aidan. "It's one thing to suffer yer own pain, but to see yer child suffering is a completely different matter. I am only to be a mother, but already I understand these things."

He reached over and took her hand as their two mounts plodded placidly along. "I love ye," he said quietly. "I love ye very much."

They rode across a field of yellow yarrow, and up a very gently sloping hillock. Stopping a moment upon its crest they gazed down upon *Pearroc Royal*, peaceful in the late-afternoon sunlight. The camomile lawn was neatly cropped, and looked like a piece of pale green velvet spread out about the house. The gardens were a riot of bright color, and upon the estate lake waterfowl swam serenely upon the untroubled waters. On one side of the lake there remained the small forest that was home to the deer of *Pearroc Royal*, and as they watched a doe with her twin fawns came out of the woods to drink in the lake. No words passed between Conn and his wife. None were necessary. They simply sat quietly smiling at each other, then looking back down upon their unruffled little world. Finally the horses began to stir restlessly beneath them and they began the easy descent to the manor house.

As they arrived a stableboy came forth to take their horses, and Beal hurried from the building. "My lord, there are some gentlemen awaiting ye."

"Thank ye, Beal," said Conn, and hurried into the house with Aidan.

There in the hallway were some half-dozen men, dressed in the uniform of the queen's Gentlemen Pensioners. Conn strode forward.

"Welcome to *Pearroc Royal*, gentlemen. I hope Beal has offered ye refreshment." He didn't recognize any of the men, but then men were always retiring as he himself had done, and it was a great honor to serve in the queen's own personal bodyguard. "How may I be of service to ye?"

The captain of the unit stepped forward. "Ye are Conn St. Michael, born an O'Malley of Innisfana Island, now known as Lord Bliss?"

"I am, sir."

"Then it is my painful duty to inform ye, my lord, that ye are under arrest in the queen's name."

"*What?*" Conn looked totally stunned.

"We are come, my lord, to escort ye to London where ye will be lodged in the Tower at her majesty's discretion."

"*No!*" Aidan had gone white with her terror. "*No!*" she repeated. "There is some mistake! There has to be!"

Conn put his arm about his wife. "It's all right, sweeting. I have done nothing wrong. This is simply a mistake."

"They have come to take ye to the Tower!" she cried. "I shall never see ye again!" Then she burst into tears.

He held her close, vainly attempting to comfort her. "My wife," he said to the distinctly uncomfortable captain of the guard, "is but newly with child." Then he tipped her tearstained face up to him. "I trust Bess, Aidan. Now get a hold of yerself, my love, and listen to me. I am going with these gentlemen. Ye are to send to *Queen's Malvern* for Adam, and tell him what has happened. He will know what to do. Do ye understand me, Aidan?"

"A-aye," she sniffled.

"Beal!" Conn called.

The butler was immediately there. "My lord?"

"Fetch my sword, immediately!"

They stood for what seemed an eternity in the main hall of the manor while Beal brought Conn's weapon. Aidan clung to her husband, unable to control her fear. Conn held her tightly against him, his own heart pounding nervously. He could not imagine what had happened to bring him to this. Could his elder brothers be acting up again, but if that was the case why hadn't the queen spoken of it while they were in London? The queen's own men shifted their feet restlessly as they waited. They knew nothing themselves except that they had been sent to arrest this man. Who knew what he had done? It could be anything from a serious offense like treason, to something totally silly like the seduction of an important man's wife or daughter. He had a reputation for such playful antics.

"Yer sword, my lord." Beal handed Conn the blade.

Conn nodded his thanks, and then releasing Aidan from his grasp, turned to the captain of the guard, and offered his weapon. "My sword," he said quietly.

The captain took it, and said, "May we have yer word, my lord, that ye'll not try to escape?"

"Ye have it," Conn answered with more calm than he was feeling.

"Thank ye, my lord, then we are ready to depart."

"No," Aidan cried, "surely not now, sir! It is late in the day. Wait until morning!"

"My lady, I have my orders to bring yer husband to London with all possible haste. We have at least six hours of light left, and we can be many miles on the road to London by the time it is dark." He looked to Conn. "Have ye ever been in the Tower, sir?"

"Aye," said Conn.

"Then ye know ye'd best bring a good purse with ye, my lord. The kind of lodging ye receive will depend upon yer ability to pay. Those who can't pay usually end up in the cells beneath the river, but those with silver can arrange for decent housing, and food, and on cold days even wood and wine to warm them. Everything costs in the Tower."

Aidan was beginning to calm down, and think. "Wait!" she said sternly. "Since ye yerself have said ye've plenty of daylight left to this day ye can bide but part of an hour while my husband changes his clothing, and I gather certain things for him. He cannot go as he is, and without funds."

"Agreed, my lady," said the captain. "I have no objections, but do not dally in an effort to prevent our departure, madame."

Aidan drew herself up to her full height, and stepped away from her husband. She was, the captain of the guard found to his great discomfort, as tall as he himself was. "Sir, ye have my husband's parole, and now I offer ye mine. We will not be long." Then she moved toward the Great Hall. "Come in, gentlemen, and wait here. The stairs to our chamber lead up from here."

Alone in their bedroom Aidan turned a white face to Conn, but her voice was calm. "Do ye know what this is all about?"

"Nay, unless my brothers have been up to some mischief again. Bess usually holds Skye responsible for them. She's done her time in the Tower, and come out safe."

"Skye was in the Tower?" Aidan was amazed.

"Aye, Deirdre was born there. Skye and the queen have been at odds for many years, sweetheart. They are much alike, ye see. Two strong women, each of whom has always fought to control her own destiny despite her sex. In the beginning when Skye first came to England, and was wed to Geoffrey Southwood she and the queen were friends. Then Southwood died along with their younger son. In his will he left Skye completely in charge, but the queen ignored the earl's last testament, and placed Lord Dudley in charge of Robin. Bess knew that Dudley lusted after Skye, and because she herself was unable to wed with him she sought to please him in other ways. She knew that Skye disliked Dudley, and so she felt my sister would be no threat to her own relationship with the man. Robert Dudley raped Skye, and when she complained to the queen, Bess admitted to her that she knew what Dudley wanted of Skye, but that she would turn a blind eye because she wanted to make him happy.

"From that moment on the relationship between the queen and my sister turned. English merchant ships began being pirated off Ireland, and in the waters between England and Ireland. The queen lost a great deal of revenue. She blamed Skye for the piracies."

"Was she indeed responsible?" Aidan was wide-eyed at these new revelations about her beautiful sister-in-law.

Conn chuckled. "The queen could never prove it," he answered his wife, but his merry countenance even as he spoke told Aidan what she wanted to know. Conn continued. "Skye married again. This time to Niall Burke. She was not yet, however, finished with the queen. Bess, however, set a trap for Skye which my sister skillfully evaded. Furious, the queen ordered her arrest, and lodged her in the Tower for some weeks. That is how Deirdre came to be born there.

"Finally with the help of Adam and Lord Burghley, Skye was released, and she and Niall returned first to Devon, and then to Niall's home in Ireland where Padraic was born. After Niall's death Skye needed Bess's help in holding the Burke lands for Padraic was only an infant of less than a year. The queen agreed provided that Skye would make a political marriage for England which she did, but she was quickly widowed again, and when she and Adam married in France without the queen's permission Bess stole the Burke lands and gave them to an Englishman.

"Again peace was made between them, and then the queen took Velvet from Skye and Adam because once again she needed their help. Of course when she got it she returned my niece to her parents, gave them the use of *Queen's Malvern*, gave Padraic lands in England, and banished my sister from court, and from London. She pretends it is because she fears Skye near the sea can cause her danger. She made my sister pass on her authority as *The O'Malley* to our brother Michael, the bishop of Mid-Connaught, so that the tale does not hold water to my mind. Actually I think she is jealous of Skye as much as she secretly admires her. As for Skye she actually likes Bess though she would never admit it aloud." He smiled reassuringly at his wife. "Ye see, sweeting, it's really not terrible my going to the Tower. Many good people have come and gone into it, the queen included, and come out safe."

"And many have gone in alive only to exit without their heads," she answered.

"Aidan, I have done nothing wrong. Whatever this is about will be quickly straightened out. Now help me change, and then fetch me a fat purse. I'm unhappy enough at having to return to London in the summer. At least I'll be comfortable in the damned place."

She laughed. It was almost a relief to see him cranky instead of so elegantly polite as he was with the captain of the queen's guard. "I'll pack some clean linen for ye, my darling, and alert Cluny. I want him to go with ye." Now calm Aidan went about her tasks quickly, making a small bundle for her husband to take with him that contained clean stockings, and other personal items, brushes for his hair and teeth, and his dice that he might have something to amuse him. Then she hurried off to find Cluny.

Cluny, however, had already been alerted by Beal of the rather startling developments that had occurred. When Aidan returned to the Great Hall he was already booted and waiting for his master. She called him to her side.

"Ye know?"

"Aye, and I'd be interested to know what it's all about, too, m'lady. I'll get word to ye as soon as possible. Servants get to come and go in the Tower as they please." He hesitated a moment, and then said, "Keep an eye on Mistress Mag for me, but for mercy sakes, m'lady, don't tell her I asked. I'll ne'er hear the end of it if ye do. That old woman of yers is bad enough as it is."

Aidan hid her smile. She knew that Mag was fonder of Cluny than she would admit, but it pleased her to know that Conn's man returned the sentiment. "Yer a good man, Cluny," she said quietly. "Watch over my lord, and see he comes to no harm."

"I will, m'lady."

Aidan then hurried into the estate office to fetch a purse for her husband from the strongbox. She filled it with silver, but also added ten gold pieces. Then as an afterthought she added a smaller purse to give to

Cluny for an emergency, and so instructed him when she once again regained the hall.

Conn was awaiting her now, and she handed him the purse which he put within his doublet. He was now dressed for travel, in high sturdy boots, an embroidered brown velvet doublet which was unbuttoned several buttons as was his silk shirt unlaced beneath for comfort, and he carried a long cloak.

"Where are yer riding gloves?" she asked. "Ye can't ride all the way to London without them, Conn."

"I have them, Aidan," he said softly, and he held them up.

"How long?" she whispered.

"I don't know, but whatever it is, it can't be serious. Not long, I think."

"I love ye," she said low.

"I love ye," he said, and then pulling her to him he kissed her passionately, his lips tracing hers as if he were memorizing them. "Take care of the baby," he instructed her, and then loosing her he strode from the hall.

"Conn!"

He stopped and turned. "Stay here, Aidan," he ordered her. "I don't want my last glimpse of home to be ye waving me off. Rather I would prefer my first sight of home to be of ye waiting for me in the door."

She nodded, understanding him totally. "Godspeed, my lord," she called, "and bring ye safely home to me."

Blowing her a lighthearted kiss he turned and hurried from the house. He was damned near close to tears, and he certainly didn't want her to see them. They mounted their horses.

"Ye'll ride next to me, my lord," said the captain of the guard. "My name is William Standish."

Conn nodded. "Thank ye, Captain Standish."

They had not yet come to the end of the drive when two figures came galloping across the fields halloing to them to stop.

"'Tis my sister, and her husband, Lord and Lady de Marisco," said Conn.

"By God, my lord," said Will Standish with a smile, "news travels faster here in the country than it does at court."

"One of the servants probably set off the second we knew yer mission," said Conn. "We're a close family."

Skye and Adam drew abreast of Conn and his escort, and Skye demanded, "What is this, Conn? Is it true that ye've been arrested? Why? I thought ye said yer trip to London was successful, and that ye were back in *her* good graces once again."

Captain Standish was openmouthed at the beauty of the woman before him. He had heard stories of Skye O'Malley, and he had never expected the legend to outstrip its reputation, but she did.

"Skye, as God is my witness, I do not know what is going on. I have no idea why I have been arrested, and don't bully this poor captain here because he doesn't know either."

"Doesn't know, or won't tell," she snapped. "Will that woman never leave our family alone? I'm going to London with ye!"

"Ye can't, Skye. Yer forbidden London and the court. Adam, reason with her! Yer her husband."

Adam de Marisco chuckled a deep, rumbling sound. "I very much appreciate yer confidence in my ability to deal with yer sister, Conn, but ye know better. However in this particular instance I am going to try." He looked straight at her. "Listen to me, little girl, yer brother is right to worry. The queen has sent ye here out of her sight. If she wanted to see ye in this matter she would request yer presence, and she may yet. If she does then ye may go to London, but for now, ye'll stay home and watch over yer two daughters both of whom need ye a great deal more than Conn. I will escort Robin and Padraic back to their respective posts, *and* see what I can learn."

"But . . ."

"There are no buts, Skye! Do ye think ye can aid yer brother by offending the queen?"

"Skye, please look after Aidan. She's very frightened. Her whole life has been a quiet one, and I'm afraid for both her and the baby," Conn pleaded with his sister.

"Do ye have monies?" she demanded of him. "It costs a fortune to survive in the damned Tower."

He nodded, giving her a smile.

How alike they are, thought Captain Standish seeing her return the smile.

"Then God speed ye, little brother, and if *that* woman should harm a hair on yer head, I'll . . ."

"Skye!" cautioned Adam, and with a little moue of her mouth she ceased speaking, and turning her horse about galloped off. "Don't worry, Conn. She'll ride off her bad temper, and her fears for ye before she gets home. She'll watch over Aidan, and I'll be in London by week's end, my lad." He held out his big hand, and Conn grasped it with an equally large paw.

"Thank ye, Adam. See what Robin can ferret out."

"I will." Adam backed his horse up a bit, and addressed Captain Standish. "Ye'll see that my brother-in-law arrives safely?"

"Ye need have no fears on that account, my lord de Marisco," was the reply. "We are ordered to deliver Lord Bliss to the Tower, and that is precisely what we will do."

Adam nodded. "Then I'll wish ye a Godspeed, too," he said, and with a wave to Conn he followed his wife's trail back across the fields again.

Conn and his escort rode until past ten that night, only stopping when the twilight grew too thick and dark for them to continue on their way. They sheltered in the large barn of a prosperous farm whose goodwife offered them nut-brown ale, fresh bread and a tasty hard cheese the following morning to break their fast. Conn's easy manners, and good looks brought him a great deal of attention from the farmer's two buxom daughters. As they were preparing to leave he gave them each a kiss, and dropped a silver penny down their bodices to the accompaniment of high-pitched giggles.

"We've done naught fer yer generosity, me lord," said one of the girls.

"But if yer not in too much of a hurry," said the other, "we'd be happy to take ye to the loft."

"Ahh, lassies, I do regret refusing such a kind offer," Conn said, "but 'tis the queen's business we're about, and it cannot wait."

They rode off, and the Gentlemen Pensioners accompanying Conn voiced their admiration amongst themselves while Cluny grinned like an idiot, as Conn quickly told him, and thought that it was just like the old days.

"Ye've quite caught the attention of my men," Captain Standish said, smiling.

"They're young," noted Conn dryly, "and youth is easily impressed."

Each day they rode from dawn until dusk, stopping only to rest their mounts, eat, drink, and relieve themselves. Reaching the city Conn was escorted to the Tower, and admitted as a prisoner. His silver bought him a fairly decent-sized room with both a fireplace, and a small window that looked out upon the river. The room was empty, but for a pile of moldy straw and a slop bucket, and more silver was required to acquire pallets for them both, a table, and two chairs. When a guard came to inform Conn that he was wanted for questioning Cluny said, "I'll be going out, m'lord, to buy us some things we're going to need."

Conn nodded to his servant, and followed the guard from his cell through the corridor, and down three flights of stairs to a dark, windowless room. It took a moment for his eyes to grow used to the dimness, but when they did he realized that the room was indeed lit though not particularly brightly. He also saw William Cecil, Lord Burghley, and another man he didn't recognize sitting before the table. He was brought to stand before them.

"My lord Burghley?"

"Lord Bliss," came the reply.

"My lord, why am I here?"

"Come now, Lord Bliss, let us not be coy with one another. Ye are caught in yer treason. Tell me all, and we will see what can be done to aid ye."

"*Treason!*" Conn's jaw dropped. "I know naught of treason! All I know is that several days ago I was arrested without explanation, and brought from my home to London. My wife is frantic with worry. She is expecting our first child. Who accuses me of treason? Against whom? Against what?"

"Come now, Lord Bliss," said Lord Burghley in a fatherly tone. "Will ye deny that ye are yet a member of the old faith?"

"Nay, though God knows it matters not to me."

"And will ye deny that with others of yer persuasion ye have plotted to assassinate the queen, and place Mary of Scotland upon the throne?"

"*What?*" Conn shouted outraged. "*Kill Bess?* Nay! Never! Replace her with that poor misguided Scots whore? Nay! A thousand times nay!"

Lord Burghley looked a trifle perplexed for a moment. His information was usually reliable although he, himself, had to admit that this particular tale had disturbed him for he would have never considered Conn a man to involve himself in treason. Still in all one had to be careful, and his usually reliable informant had claimed that Spain was involved once again in a plot against Elizabeth Tudor.

It would not be the first time Spain and its ambassador entangled themselves in this sort of business. There had been five ambassadors from Spain during the queen's reign to date. The first, Count Feria, a holdover from Mary Tudor's reign had been married to Jane Dormer, an English gentlewoman. He had departed England in 1559 to Elizabeth's great relief for she had not liked the pompous count at all.

Alvarez De Quadra, the Bishop of Aquila, had come next, and served his king four years before dying of plague in London. The queen enjoyed outwitting him which she always did since the bishop lacked a sense of humor. He was followed by the only ambassador from Spain that the queen had liked.

Diego Guzman de Silva, Bishop of Toledo, had remained for six years. A naturally elegant, cultured sophisticate he was well liked by the entire court. He, in turn, liked Elizabeth for though he was loyal to Spain, he was clearheaded, and not fanatical as had been his two predecessors. But the bishop grew so homesick for Spain, that he requested his release of King Philip, and was granted it.

In choosing his successor, Spain did a complete turnabout, and sent

England Guerau de Spes, an unpleasant little man whose outrageous manners, thoughtless remarks, and genuine capacity for troublemaking made him highly unpopular. Involved in the Ridolfi plot he was expelled from England in late December 1571.

For the next six years there was no ambassador from Spain to England, and then just last year Bernadino de Mendoza had arrived. The queen was highly dissatisfied with him for he was an ignorant, pompous, and vengeful man. Already there was indication that he was as his predecessor had involving himself in plots to remove the queen. Just several months ago, Antonio de Guaras, a Spanish agent in England since 1570, had been imprisoned for his involvement and dealings with the captive Queen of Scots.

Now another plot, code name: *Deliverance*, was being unraveled by Lord Burghley's secret agents, and everything pointed to Conn St. Michael, Lord Bliss, as being hip-deep within it. Still Conn was denying it. Of course he denied it, William Cecil chided himself. They never admitted anything except under torture. He turned to the man by his side.

"It appears, Master Norton, as if we shall have to interrogate my lord Bliss a little more strongly."

"Aye, me lord," came the reply, and the man called Norton smiled showing several blackened stumps of teeth.

Norton! The name slammed into Conn's brain, and he felt sick to his stomach. Norton, the Tower's infamous dungeon master! Norton, who had perfected the art of torture so well that he could drive a man to the brink of insanity without even breaking a bone. What in God's name was happening? How had he become involved in something so serious? Feeling himself beginning to panic he took a deep breath, and spoke.

"My lord, ye accuse me of involvement in a plot to kill the queen, and replace her with Mary of Scotland, and yet ye offer me not one shred of evidence of my culpability. Have I been accused? By whom? Let them say it to my face, my lord! Is this English justice?"

Again Lord Burghley found himself rattled, and somewhat nonplussed. He liked young Lord Bliss. He had never known him to be either a plotter, or a fanatic. This whole thing was most disturbing, and when the queen learned of it she was going to be very distressed. Still there was evidence, and Elizabeth Tudor's safety was paramount. Already three people had been rounded up, betrayed by one of Lord Burghley's double agents, and each one had implicated Conn St. Michael, Lord Bliss, as the ringleader in this plot. He shook himself.

"Ye've been accused by three men in this plot," said Lord Burghley. "Tell me, my lord, if yer as innocent as ye claim, then why would three men implicate ye in such a plot? Nay, we shall have Master Norton interrogate ye for a bit, and then we shall see what ye have to say."

Before he might struggle Conn's arms were pinned to his sides, and he was dragged across the room to where upon the wall he could see a large wheel rack which was now lowered so he might be hoisted upon it. His doublet was expertly removed, his boots roughly yanked from his feet, his shirt pulled open to his waist, and then he was spread-eagled upon the rack which was raised up again some six feet off the floor.

Horrified, and yet fascinated in spite of himself, Conn watched as below him the infamous Mr. Norton checked the ropes and levers that operated the rack. Why hadn't he struggled against his captors? he wondered, but he knew. He couldn't actually believe that the whole thing was serious, and now as he felt the ropes securing him begin to tighten, drawing his arms and legs into a painful stretch he suddenly realized just how very serious this whole thing really was.

With seemingly great care Mr. Norton tightened one of his screws, and Conn, unable to help himself, screamed as a sharp pain tore through his shoulder; and screamed again as his opposite leg was loosened within its hip socket. The pain continued to pour through him, now filling his entire body with such incredible agony that Conn began to pour sweat. The dungeon master looked up at him, smiling his unpleasant smile.

"Do ye have anything ye want to say to my lord Burghley, Lord Bliss?" he inquired solicitously.

Conn groaned. "I know of no plot," he gasped. "I am not in-involved in a-any damned plot. Arrrrrugh!" he cried out as his other leg was pulled out at an unnatural angle, and the people below him began to fade before his eyes. His head slumped upon his chest as he began to lose consciousness.

"Water!" snapped Norton, and one of the guards climbed up upon a ladder to slosh a pail of brackish, cold river water in Conn's face.

He sputtered back to reality, and to pain as the ropes were tightened upon his other arm, and he cried out again, but this time it was a particularly foul oath, and it was aimed at William Cecil.

"He don't have a particularly high threshold for pain, m'lord," noted Norton. "I've gone easy with him so far, and I ain't never had a man pass out on me this quick."

"Then he is experiencing severe pain?"

"I'm a mite surprised, but it would appear so," said the dungeon master. "He's a big fellow, m'lord, but I thinks it's because his bones is delicate like."

"Can ye inflict just a bit more pain on him without injuring him, Master Norton?" asked William Cecil.

"Aye," he said, and then he turned to his assistant. "Peter, ye handle the arms, but mind remember, we want no broken bones. I'll put ye up there meself if ye break anything."

Peter nodded, his eyes alight at the thought of actually aiding his master in this important interrogation. What a tale he'd have to tell his mother tonight, and that little serving wench in the tavern he'd been trying to impress might even lift her skirts at long last once she heard of his new stature.

Together the two men moved in unison as they tightened and fussed with the levers connecting the ropes attached to their prisoner's limbs. It was subtle at first for Conn was already in such pain that he could not feel their new efforts, but then the agony slammed into him, forcing all the breath from his lungs, leaving him gasping for air he could not seem to find as fiery fingers of pure, undiluted pain ran swiftly up and down his entire form. His big, straining body poured water, the muscles in his neck bulged, as did his torment-filled eyes, and his mouth opened wide as he howled in an unhuman-sounding, animal-like anguish. There was a roaring sound in his ears, but through the mist he could hear Lord Burghley saying, indeed almost pleading with him,

"My lord, my lord, spare yerself further torture. Ye have only to tell me the details of yer plot, and the pain will be stopped."

With incredible effort Conn managed to find his voice. "I know of no plot, Burghley! *No plot!* Ye've the wrong man!" and then he fainted.

William Cecil was not a man easily fooled. Lord Bliss was suffering greatly, and still he denied involvement in *Deliverance*. Could it possibly be that he was telling the truth? And if he was who was using his name, and why? "Release him, Master Norton, and revive him. It is my opinion that he is not lying."

"I'd have to agree with ye, m'lord, if ye'll forgive my boldness," said the dungeon master. "Some of 'em can take far worse than I gives this gentleman before they even passed out. This man ain't good with pain so what we did to 'im really made 'im suffer. A man don't lie to me when I makes 'im suffer. I ain't so old yet that I can't do me job."

The wheel rack was lowered, and more cold river water was casually sloshed over Conn by Peter. As his eyes began to flutter open, a cracked earthenware cup of wine was forced through his lips, and down his throat. It burned as it hit the pit of his stomach like a hot rock, and Conn retched half of it back up, but managed to keep the rest of it down. His eyes began to focus, William Cecil coming first into view.

"Ye bastard!" he managed to croak.

"I am delighted to see that yer recovering so quickly," said Lord Burghley dryly. He didn't blame Lord Bliss' anger, but then his first loyalty was to his queen, and her safety. He had known her since she was a child. In his private moments he thought of her as he did his own daughters, and he would do anything to see her safe from all harm. Now, however, he needed time to sort out this puzzle. Something was very amiss. Was there a plot against the queen, or not? "Escort Lord Bliss back to his quarters," he ordered the guards, and as they aided Conn to stand he said, "We will talk again, my lord."

"Ye better have some answers for me," snarled Conn. "If ye want to know who is responsible for this, then so do I!"

Lord Burghley nodded in agreement. "In that thought we concur, my lord."

"Jesus God!" Cluny cried as his master was helped back into their cell. "What did they do to ye, m'lord? Are ye all right? Put him down gentle, ye great oafs!"

"We'll treat 'im just like a babe in arms," said a grinning guard, and they unceremoniously dumped Conn upon the nearest pallet.

As they stamped out laughing Cluny shook his fist at them, and muttered an oath. "English scum," he muttered, but fortunately they didn't hear him.

Conn couldn't help grinning up at his body servant even through his pain. "I'm alive, Cluny," he said, "though just barely."

"What the hell did they do to ye, m'lord?"

"The rack," came the grim reply.

"The rack?" Cluny's face registered his deep distress. "Why the rack? What the hell did ye do, m'lord?"

"I did nothing, but Lord Burghley believes, or at least he thought he believed that I was involved in a plot against Bess Tudor."

"Ye ain't involved in any plot," said Cluny loyally. "Why, hell, m'lord, if ye were then I would be, too. Ye wouldn't go off and get into trouble without yer faithful Cluny."

Conn managed another weak grin. "No, Cluny, I wouldn't get into trouble without ye. Yer a good man to have at one's back, but ye see, someone has somehow managed to involve me though I know not how. Let's hope William Cecil manages to find out before he takes it into his head to talk with me again."

Lord Burghley was indeed seeking answers, but he was getting nowhere in his search. He carefully went over the reports that had been written on the matter from the statements given the other prisoners involved in this matter. They had all been most eager to talk, and little persuasion had been needed at all to encourage them. Reading over the reports on the matter he could find nothing, and yet he was absolutely certain now of

Lord Bliss' innocence. He wanted to speak with the other plotters himself, but no sooner had he given the order for their presence than Adam de Marisco was brought in to him.

"My lord Burghley," he said by way of greeting. "I think ye know why I am here."

William Cecil nodded sourly. What had he expected? "I suppose that yer wife is here also," he replied.

"My wife is at home at *Queen's Malvern* with our children. Ye will remember she is forbidden London and the court."

"I forget nothing, my lord, and I am relieved that Lady de Marisco is finally of an age to show discretion."

Adam slapped his thigh, and chuckled. "She was ready to come," he admitted, "but both Conn and I prevailed upon her not to for Aidan needs extra courage now. Please, my lord, what is this all about?"

"Yer brother-in-law has been involved in a plot to assassinate the queen, and put Mary of Scotland upon the throne," said Lord Burghley.

"Impossible!" said Adam de Marisco.

"I am beginning to agree with ye," admitted Lord Burghley.

"Beginning to agree? God's nightshirt, man! 'Tis not Conn's style at all, and ye know it! There's no secrecy in the man at all. He's an open book which is one reason the queen always liked him."

"I cannot, ye will understand, my lord, be too careful of her majesty's safety," said William Cecil. "Both Spain and France have done nothing else since Elizabeth Tudor took the throne of England but intrigue to pull her off it. This is not the first plot that has come to light that sought to murder her. I trust no one, my lord de Marisco, no one."

Adam nodded. He fully understood Lord Burghley's position. "What made ye believe Conn involved?" he asked.

"The three men we caught in the plot all accused him of being the mastermind behind it. Each named him by name, but there is something in the reports I have that disturbs me, and I cannot put a finger on it. Sit down, my lord, for I have asked to have those three prisoners brought to me now. Yer brother-in-law under torture protested his innocence quite convincingly, even going so far as to slander my parentage in the process."

Adam was horrified. "Ye tortured him? How?"

"The rack," was the flat reply. "All men protest their innocence until persuaded otherwise. Lord Bliss would not implicate himself despite Master Norton's best efforts. Do not look so troubled, my lord. No bones were broken. It seems yer brother-in-law has a low threshold for pain, and Norton is a master of his craft. Even he was convinced of his subject's purity.

Now, however, I must unravel the mystery of whether there actually is a plot, and why these men implicated Lord Bliss."

They had been seated in a chamber on an upper level, part of the apartment of the governor of the Tower. William Cecil arose, and said, "Will ye come with me, my lord? I must go below while Master Norton interrogates the other three. I am certain ye'll want to be there."

"Aye," replied Adam grimly. "I do."

The two men descended into the bowels of the Tower of London to the realm of Master Norton. There in the dungeon master's workshop stood three men shackled to the wall. Two were young, one no more than sixteen, the other probably twenty. The third man was somewhat older, and was Adam realized looking at him related to the boys.

"A father and his two misguided sons," said Burghley dryly, and then. "Which one first, Master Norton?"

"The young 'un. He's the most fearful. See how he sweats, my lords? Peter, the boy!"

The silent Peter unlocked the shackles binding the lad, and pulled him forward across the room to refasten him within a high-backed wooden chair. A heavy leather strap held him about the midsection, leg irons held his ankles immobile, and his arms were bound at the wrists to the wooden arms of the chair. Peter then affixed a contraption to the boy's hand that Adam immediately recognized as a thumbscrew. Slowly he began to tighten it, and within a short order the boy began to shriek out his pain, screaming for mercy, crying for his mother, and to the Blessed Virgin Mother as well. At a signal from Master Norton his assistant ceased tightening the screw, and William Cecil said to the two men still hanging from the wall, "Well, sirs, will ye stand by idle while the lad suffers? Ye have but to tell me what I want to know, and he will be released, but refuse to answer, and I will see to it that both yer sons are hung without delay, Master Trent."

The man called Trent looked ill, his color slightly green, and slightly white about the lips. "My lord," he pleaded. "We have told ye everything we know. I swear it! Do ye think I want my sons dead? Not for any cause!"

"Who caused this plot to be made?"

"We have told ye. Conn St. Michael, Lord Bliss. He came to my shop one evening as I was about to close, and said he knew that we were members of the true faith. He had, he said, been empowered by the church to grant us everlasting salvation if we would aid him in killing the queen, and helping Mary of Scotland, an honest Roman Catholic ruler, to gain her rightful throne. England would bless us, he said. What man wouldn't take the chance of eternal salvation in God's heaven, my lord? We agreed to help him, my sons and I."

"A man offers ye eternal salvation, and ye merely accept it. The word of a stranger? Come now, Master Trent! What is this tale ye seek to have me believe?"

"He had a paper, my lord! I can read, at least a little! It was signed by the pope hisself with all sorts of pretty seals, and a ribbon. I never saw such an official-looking document. That was good enough for me!"

"Probably forged," said William Cecil, "but official-looking enough to fool a simple man." He looked at Master Trent again. "Are ye not happy and prosperous under the queen's rule?"

"Aye," replied the man, "but her can't give us eternal salvation."

"A butcher's logic," remarked Cecil. "That's what he is, ye know. A butcher. Is it not fitting? He's been an outspoken religious for years, but never considered a threat. That's how we were able to catch him so quickly. He was eager to brag of his about-to-be good fortune, and word of it came to us so we arrested him."

"Ask him about Conn's involvement," said Adam de Marisco.

William Cecil nodded. "Tell me of Lord Bliss, Master Trent. How did ye come to meet him?"

"Him came to us," was the reply. "Said he had heard we were the type of men who might aid him, and if not, keep our mouths shut."

" 'Tis the same story as he told before," said Lord Burghley wearily.

"What did Lord Bliss look like?" demanded Adam. "Describe him to us."

"Him were a big, tall man who spoke with an Irish accent," came the reply.

"Be more detailed!" Adam's voice said sharply.

"I can't, m'lord."

"Why not? What color eyes did he have? Was his nose long or short? What color was his hair? Did he have any marks upon his face that ye recall."

"I can't tell ye, m'lord. He was masked, and well muffled by his cloak."

"Had ye ever met Conn St. Michael before this encounter? Ever seen him at all?"

"No, m'lord."

"Then how did ye know who he was?"

"Because he told us, m'lord," said Master Trent to Adam in a tone that implied that perhaps Adam was not too bright.

"Of course," said Lord Burghley slowly. "That's what has been bothering me about these reports. Nowhere is there a description of Lord Bliss."

"Aye," said Adam, "because it wasn't Conn. Whoever it was wanted this poor fool to believe it was, but he dared not show his face for it was meant that ye discover this alleged plot, and that Conn be arrested."

"I believe yer right, my lord de Marisco, but first I would be satisfied on one thing." He signaled to Master Norton, and the dungeon master hurried from the room.

They sat in grim silence for several minutes, and then Norton returned, and with him was a masked, and heavily cloaked figure. Lord Burghley turned back to Master Trent.

"Is this man Lord Bliss?" he demanded.

"Nay," the butcher said quickly.

"How can ye be sure?"

"Lord Bliss weren't quite so tall although nearly so, and he was heavier set than this man."

"Tell them yer name," said Lord Burghley to the masked and cloaked man.

"I am Conn St. Michael, Lord Bliss," came the reply.

"Nah, ye ain't! Ye can't fool me, m'lord. Lord Bliss had a real Irish accent. This poor fellow has but the hint of Ireland in his voice. I should know. My mother came from Ireland."

"Take them away," said Lord Burghley, and the guards released the three, and hustled them from the room.

"Are ye all right?" Adam asked Conn anxiously.

"I'll live," said Conn somewhat wryly, "despite Master Norton's gentle ministrations, and the insult that Englishman just dealt me saying I didn't sound like an Irishman. Of course I sound like an Irishman though granted my accent has softened during my years here in England. I noticed it when Aidan's cousin was here recently. Next to him I sounded positively civilized."

"Could Cavan FitzGerald have anything to do with this?" Adam mused aloud.

"What the hell would he have to gain by concocting such a plot?" Conn asked.

"I don't know," said Adam, "unless he hopes to get ye killed, and marry yer wife himself."

" 'Twould seem a trifle elaborate a plot to simply dispose of a rival," said Lord Burghley. "There is always the chance that if Conn were convicted of treason his estates could be confiscated. If this fellow were after Lady Bliss it would be her wealth that attracted him. He wouldn't chance losing it. It would have been far simpler to have Lord Bliss murdered."

"But," Adam mused, "what if the fellow were actually part of a plot, and Aidan and her wealth were to be his reward, and therefore it became necessary to use Conn as a scapegoat? The official-looking paper Master Trent claimed to have seen smacks of something more sophisticated than just a man seeking a rich wife."

"Who is this FitzGerald fellow?" asked Lord Burghley.

"He arrived on our doorstep May first," answered Conn. "He claims to have come from Aidan's grandfather, Rogan FitzGerald. Says he's the son of the old man's younger brother who was a priest, and that Aidan's grandmother raised him."

"Indeed," remarked William Cecil, "and what was his reason for being in England?"

"He said he'd been raised to take over the duties of steward on FitzGerald's estate, and now that the old steward was retiring the family thought it would be a fine idea if Master Cavan FitzGerald came to England to see how prosperous estates were run here, and bring back more modern ideas to Ireland."

The three men had now departed the torture chamber of the Tower, and were once again in the governor's apartments. Lord Burghley called for a messenger to be brought to him, and sat down at a table to personally write a message. When he had finished he said to Conn and Adam, "I am sending this to the Countess of Lincoln. She would best know the situation of her family in Ireland, and I am assuming that this Rogan FitzGerald is related to her."

"A distant cousin, I believe," said Conn.

"Indeed," came the reply. "Lady Clinton is with the queen on her progress right now, but she will reply quickly for I have said this information is of the utmost importance to me. Let us learn if your Cavan FitzGerald is actually who he says he is, and if he came to England for the reasons he claims. I am convinced, however, Lord Bliss, that yer not involved in any plotting against her majesty."

"Then I may go home?"

"Not yet, my lord. There is, I am certain, a plot of some sort, and yer apparent guilt has been given to us to throw us off the real scent. If I release ye now then those involved escape me, and live to plan another plot against the queen. Help me ferret them out, and I promise ye will be rewarded."

Conn shook his head. "I'll help ye, my lord, but speak not to me of rewards. What I do I do for Bess. She had given me everything that means anything to me, but if Cavan FitzGerald turns out to be involved in this, let me have the privilege of beating him senseless!"

Lord Burghley smiled his faint wintry smile. Lord Bliss' attitude smacked of his elder sister, and he nodded. "I am going to ask ye to remain here in the Tower for just a short while, my lord. Just enough time to clear this matter up. Yer incarceration will make it appear to the plotters that all goes as they have planned. In the meantime our agents will be seeking to find out who they are, and what they are actually up to in this matter. Ye have, I am told, arranged for comfortable living quarters, and have yer servant with ye."

"Aye," said Conn. "I can manage, but I don't want my wife worried needlessly in her condition."

"Young Lady Bliss appeared to me to be a young woman of strong moral fiber," said Lord Burghley. "I understand yer concern, but if I allow ye to communicate with her then her fears will be eased, and who knows who is watching her. She must continue to appear worried lest we be given away. Lord de Marisco, what think ye? Can yer sister-in-law survive the worry these next few weeks?"

"Aidan is tougher than ye think, Conn," said Adam. "It's unfortunate to fret her so, but there is no help for it. She will be all right, and so will the babe."

Conn sighed. "So be it then," he said, but they could hear the reluctance in his voice. "One thing, however, my lord Burghley. If plague breaks out in London ye must move me at once. Is it agreed?"

"Of course, my lord. It was not even necessary to ask," came the reply.

Conn smiled a wry smile. "I apologize if I've offended ye, sir, but my experience with the Tower is little."

William Cecil actually chuckled, and then made a small joke. "My experience with the Tower, however, is great," he said. Then, "I think it is time ye be returned to yer quarters, my lord, lest anyone grow suspicious. The guards have a tendency to tavern talk, especially when in their cups." He yanked at the bellpull which was immediately answered. "Take Lord Bliss back to his cell," he commanded.

"Farewell, Conn," said Adam. "I will tell yer sister that I have seen ye, and of what transpired here today."

"Give her my love," said Conn, "and look after my wife."

Adam nodded. "Never fear," he said quietly. "She will be safe under our care."

"We will speak again," said Lord Burghley, his voice heavy with implied meaning.

"My lords," said Conn, and then he departed the room, but not before turning a moment when the guard's back was to him, to wink broadly at the two other men.

When he had gone Adam said to William Cecil, "Will ye need my help, my lord? I will do whatever I can to aid ye in getting to the bottom of this riddle."

"Go home, my lord de Marisco," said Lord Burghley. "I know from experience that yer wife is not a patient woman, and her outraged presence could complicate matters for us greatly. Tell her the truth of things, and tell her that I require her silence for now. With luck we will have this puzzle unraveled in a matter of a few weeks, and for now yer brother-in-law is comfortable, and safe. I will issue an arrest warrant for Master FitzGerald so we may question him also in this matter. From what you have said, my lord de Marisco, it is highly possible that this FitzGerald will be able to shed some light on this affair."

Adam agreed with William Cecil, Lord Burghley, in his assessment of the matter, and so after spending the night at Greenwood House he rode off on the northwest road that led from London to *Queen's Malvern*, in the fertile Midlands of England, a journey of several days. He made the trip in record time for he had been eager to leave the city, and return to the beautiful home that he shared with his beautiful wife. It was a peaceful place, and never more so than at this time of year. Turning off the highway and onto the graveled road that led up to his house he was filled with contentment at the perfect day, the warm breeze, the flower-scented air. A stableboy hurried to take his horse as he arrived at the front door which flew open to reveal his wife hurrying out. He would have sworn that Skye had grown more beautiful in the ten days since he had last seen her. She wore a wine silk dress trimmed with ecru-colored lace, and her beautiful hair was unbound, and deliciously disheveled.

"Skye, my darling!" he cried to her, sliding from his horse, and holding out his arms.

"Oh, Adam," she said, going gratefully into his embrace. "Aidan is gone!"

Chapter 7

Aidan St. Michael had lived in an agony of suspense since her husband, Conn, had ridden off with his escort of Gentlemen Pensioners. For several days she alternated between despair and hope. Skye had come by each day to reassure her that whatever the problem was it would be straightened out quickly for Conn was well-liked by all. Aidan tried to content herself with that, but it just wasn't enough. Finally she ordered Mag to pack their things, and called for her traveling coach.

"We are going to London," she said. "We are going today."

"Ye can't go off just like that, m'lady," protested Mag. "Ye could injure the baby with all that jouncing along the road."

"I've never been of a delicate constitution, Mag," came the reply. "Both the child and I will be fine, but I must be near to Conn! I can get no news here."

"What of Lord de Marisco? Wait until he gets back, m'lady!" Mag pleaded.

"Who knows when that will be," said Aidan. "We leave today."

"At least ask Lady de Marisco to go along with ye."

"Skye is barred from London and the court, Mag. Besides I don't need her, and her children do. Pack only a few things, Mag. With luck we'll be home quickly."

Martin, the coachman, bore stoically the lecture from Mag on how to drive, but both he and his assistant, Tom, eased their big awkward vehicle carefully along the London road for the next few days. The trip took an extra day, but Aidan was content as long as her destination was London. She was even content to rest a full day once they had gained the safety of Greenwood House. The servants were amazed to see her for Lord de Marisco, who had left just two days before, had said nothing of Lady Bliss' coming. The morning after her arrival, however, she began to consider how to go about the task of gaining information about her husband.

"The queen is away," she said to Mag, "as is the court, and so I have no recourse there. I do not think I can simply go to the Tower, and demand information of my husband."

"Nay, m'lady, I don't believe it's done that way," answered Mag who actually knew no more about it than did Aidan. "I think ye should send a man."

"What man? I can't send a footman. A footman has no authority."

"What about yer cousin, Master Cavan?" said Mag. "He still might be here in London. What was the name of that inn he said he was staying at in the city?"

Aidan thought a long moment. "The Swan," she said, "but he would have long since gone down to Devon."

"Not necessarily," Mag reasoned. " 'Tis his first trip to London, and he would have wanted to stay awhile, and enjoy its pleasures, I'm sure. He's a young man, m'lady, and when will the likes of him ever see this city again? Once he's back in Ireland he'll be on yer grandfather's lands for the rest of his days. This is his only chance, most likely, to sport himself."

"Send a footman, Mag, to the Swan, and if my cousin is there have our man bring him back!" said Aidan excitedly.

The quickly dispatched footman found Cavan FitzGerald at the Swan as Mag had predicted.

"Go back to my cousin, and say I will attend her directly," Cavan told the serving man. Then he hurried back into the taproom where Miguel de Guaras was awaiting him. "My cousin has come back up to London, and wants to see me," he said to the Spaniard.

"What does she want?"

"The footman didn't say. All he said was that she urgently requested my presence."

"Lord Bliss is in the Tower, and has already been racked once," said de Guaras with a smile. "Old Lord Burghley himself has been in charge of his interrogation my informant tells me. The Trents, father and sons, have also been tortured."

"But what if Conn O'Malley admits nothing despite the torture?" asked Cavan.

"It will not matter. The butcher and his sons are convinced that they dealt with Conn St. Michael, Lord Bliss, and they will not change their story whatever your cousin's husband may say. The seeds of distrust will be sown, and my mission to destroy the O'Malleys will succeed. The king will be pleased. Go to your cousin, and see what it is she wants. Undoubtedly it is comfort, and ye will be only too pleased to supply that, Master FitzGerald, won't ye?"

176

Cavan FitzGerald smiled. "Her face," he said, "may be only pretty, but she has nice plump tits. She'll keep me warm on long winter nights."

"I wonder how much of her wealth will go to aid Ireland," murmured the Spanish agent smoothly.

Cavan FitzGerald laughed. "Let Ireland aid herself," he said, and then with a wolfish smile he was gone from the taproom. He hurried down the riverbank, and hailed a passing werryman. "Take me to Chiswick-on-the-Strand, Greenwood House," he said, climbing into the small vessel, and settling back to enjoy the ride.

Luck, he thought. All his life he had had luck. Born a bastard he might have been left on a hillside to die, but instead he had been raised by the gentry. He had met Miguel de Guaras by chance in Cobh last year where he had gone to check on a consignment of Spanish wines his uncle ordered. They had spent an evening drinking, talking, and wenching, and he had known instinctively that the Spaniard wasn't the wine merchant he claimed to be. A fact borne out several months ago when de Guaras had contacted him again to meet him in Cobh where he had made his extraordinary offer. It had been easy to convince his uncle to join the plot. Rogan FitzGerald saw himself as the savior of Ireland, even in his old age, leading his country to freedom over the English oppressors. Cavan FitzGerald smiled. All he could see was the possibility of wealth, and a respectable wife, and freedom over his FitzGerald cousins who had always delighted in reminding him that he wasn't as good as they due to the circumstances of his birth. He would have his revenge on them though. He would marry Aidan St. Michael, and have real wealth. Not just lands, but lands and chattels and good, honest gold to back it all.

He let his mind drift along with the river to all he had seen since he had come to this England. Ireland was beautiful. England was not only beautiful, but prosperous as well. He was going to be very happy here with Aidan, and the children they would have. It would be good to have his own family about him. His mind played with these thoughts going back and forth over them again in infinite combination while the werryman rowed down the river to Greenwood House.

"We're here, sir," said the boatman interrupting his passenger's daydreams.

Cavan stood up, and tossed the man a rather generous piece of silver, more than enough to compensate him for his trip back up the river. The man gaped, and then finding his voice said, "Shall I wait, me lord?"

Cavan smiled. *My lord*. He liked the sound of that. "Nay," he said graciously. "I may be staying the night." Then he hurried up through the gardens to the house.

Mag saw him coming from an upper window. Well, she thought, he came quick enough, didn't he? I thought he'd still be in London. He didn't appear to me to be too anxious to go about his business, if indeed he's really got any business here. I wonder where he gets his money. I don't recall Rogan FitzGerald having a great deal, or being too generous with what he had. The tiring woman shook her head. Times could change, she concluded, and then said to Aidan, "Yer cousin has come, m'lady. I'll go and fetch him to ye."

When she returned Cavan preceded her through the door of Aidan's apartments. "Dearest little Aidan, I have heard," he said. "I am so sorry about Conn. What can I do to aid ye?"

"Ye heard?" She was surprised. "How on earth did ye hear?"

Cavan shrugged delicately. "A plot against the queen is a serious thing, my dear."

Aidan looked stunned. "What plot against the queen?" she said.

"Oh, my dear," he said, looking distressed. "I thought ye knew. Yer husband has been charged with plotting to assassinate the English queen."

Aidan was staggered, and shocked by his words. "Conn never plotted to kill her majesty," she cried. " 'Tis a mistake!"

"Then he will be found innocent," Cavan FitzGerald said comfortingly, and put an arm around her as if for support. God's nightshirt, he thought, his eyes plunging down her cleavage, they are sweet fruits, and soon they will be mine! She put her head back against his shoulder, and he kissed her forehead in a brotherly fashion. "Come, little Aidan, let us sit down. Ye must not fret," and he led her to the nearby settle.

"Oh, Cavan," she cried to him, "I am so frightened for Conn! Ye must go to the Tower, and see what information ye can gather. Ye must find out if I may see my husband."

"Of course, I will go," he promised her. "I shall go first thing tomorrow, and seek word for ye."

"And ye'll stay the night, Cavan? I need yer company. Ye can use the Greenwood barge tomorrow."

"My dear, do ye think it wise? I do not. Yer husband is not here, and there could be talk for people's tongues are cruel. I will accept yer offer of the barge to take me back into the city today, but I shall go on my own tomorrow, and then come back to ye."

Aidan was about to protest, but Mag broke in, "Listen to Master FitzGerald, m'lady. He shows more sense then ye do."

"Perhaps yer right," Aidan allowed.

"Of course she is," Cavan agreed thinking that as soon as he was wed to Aidan that busybody of a tiring woman of hers was going to go. When he was master at *Pearroc Royal* it would be done his way alone, and the servants would answer to him only. Those who didn't would soon find themselves on the roads.

He bade Aidan a tender farewell, and returned back up the river in supreme comfort, enjoying every minute of his ride in the luxurious barge. Wealth was indeed a marvelous thing, and he knew that he could quickly become used to its privileges. It was with regret that he left the comfortable vessel at a place on the river near the Swan. Late the following afternoon he returned to Greenwood House to bring Aidan his news.

Taking his cousin in his arms he hugged her lovingly. She looked up into his face, and he said, "The news is not good, my dear little Aidan. Yer husband's accomplices have all implicated him. He is guilty without any doubt, and I fear for him. The queen will not easily forgive one she trusted. Ye must be brave, cousin."

Aidan began to cry softly, burying her face into Cavan FitzGerald's shoulder with her sorrow. "It cannot be," she protested. "How could Conn have been involved in a plot, and I not know of it? How could it be? He rarely left my side. When did he have time to plot?" She looked to Cavan for answers.

"My dear," he said in his soothing Irish voice, "the plot could have been formed months ago while yer husband was a bachelor, and at court. Ye don't know. How could ye? He has been accused by three reliable witnesses, and charged with treason. Aidan, I must be honest with ye. There is every chance that Conn will lose his handsome head."

"I want to see him!" she cried.

"I made the request for ye," he answered, "but they will allow him no visitors at this time."

"I will go to the queen! Surely she will show me the same kindness she has shown in the past!"

"Take my advice, Aidan, and don't go to the queen yet. If ye offend the governor of the Tower he will find subtle ways of making Conn's last days difficult. Surely ye don't want to do that, do ye? What if the queen refuses ye? Then ye have no other recourse. Wait until the last possible moment to plead with the queen." He held her close, enjoying the fresh lavender fragrance of her body, and her clothing. Then he felt Mag's eyes upon him, and seeing her hard stare loosed Aidan from his embrace. Damned old busybody, he thought. She didn't like him, he had already surmised. Good thing she didn't know that he had not been to the Tower of London at all, but had spent the day quite profitably dicing, and winning at the bear garden. The story he told Aidan, knowing she would accept it without question, was one that he and Miguel de Guaras had invented the previous evening as they enjoyed themselves in a London Bridge brothel.

"What am I do to?" Aidan said softly. "How can I help Conn?"

"Wait a day or two," said Cavan FitzGerald, "and I will see what further information I can gather, little Aidan," he promised, and then he took his leave of her once again.

For several hours after he had left her Aidan was sunk into the deepest despair. How could Conn have deceived her so totally? she asked herself over and over again. Then she decided that he had not deceived her at all. Conn would never involve himself in a plot to kill Elizabeth Tudor. That sort of perfidy was simply not a part of the man. Her experience with men might be scant, but she was not a stupid girl. Conn was an honorable man, and there was no deception in him.

Why then had he been accused by three men of this foul thing? Conn might be charming, she reasoned, but he was not without enemies at court. How many men had he bested in love including the two angry gentlemen whose protests against his behavior had led to his expulsion from court, and their marriage? Had the queen herself not said there were those who would hardly consider her actions in marrying him to an heiress as just punishment? What if these unknown persons had banded together to revenge themselves upon Conn? How was she going to find out?

Was Conn's situation really as dire as Cavan FitzGerald had said? How could he be certain that his informant was correct, and it was simply not some embroidered gossip? Despite what he had said to her Aidan knew that she would have to go to the Tower herself, and speak to the governor. Perhaps if she begged him he would allow her to see her husband so she might be reassured. Could he really be so heartless as to refuse a woman expecting her first child? Having learned a little about the nature of men Aidan did not think so, and she imparted as much to Mag.

To her great surprise Mag agreed. "I'll go with ye," she said. "It wouldn't do for ye to go about London without a chaperon. I think it far better ye seek yer own information than trusting to that *cousin* of yers."

"Ye don't like him, do ye, Mag?" Aidan had seen the black looks her tiring woman cast at Cavan FitzGerald.

"No, I don't," Mag said honestly. "There's something about him I don't trust, and ye shouldn't trust him either. Yer grandda had lands right enough, but he never had gold the way Master Cavan implies. I don't know what his game is, m'lady, but I'd thank him for his time, and have nothing further to do with him!"

Aidan dressed in the very best gown she had brought with her, a black silk dress with a delicately embroidered underskirt done in a simple gold thread design. The neckline on the gown was more than modest and heavily trimmed in lace as were the wrists of the garment. The dark color against Aidan's fair skin gave her a fragile appearance, particularly as her lovely hair was partly hidden beneath a delicately sheer lawn cap. She was every inch the helpless gentlewoman.

The Greenwood barge returned from carrying her cousin into the city, and now the bargemen rowed their mistress back up the river to where the Tower of London stood soaring forbiddingly against the early-evening sky. She was landed at the Water Gate, her vessel to await her return. Aidan and Mag climbed the stairs leading into the Tower, following behind a somber-faced guardsman. To her complete surprise, for Cavan had given the impression that he was a most inaccessible man, the governor of the Tower was more than happy to grant her an interview, even at this late hour.

"But I had been given to understand that ye lived near Worcester, Lady Bliss," he said by way of greeting.

"Under the circumstances, Sir John, I thought it best I come to London, even though I am with child," she replied softly.

"My dear madame," the governor said distressed, "please to be seated," and he ushered her himself to a chair. "Ye want to see yer husband, of course?"

"Yes," she said.

"That will be no problem at all, my lady, but first will ye take a glass of wine with me? Ye must be exhausted from yer travels."

Aidan nodded politely. There was no necessity to tell the governor that she had been here for three days already. "I would be most grateful for the refreshment," she said sweetly, her heart beating joyously at the knowledge that she could see Conn.

The governor's serving man offered her a goblet, and she sipped delicately at the delicious liquid while Sir John reassured her, much to her surprise, and to her relief, that he was certain her husband's incarceration was but a temporary thing, and that she would soon have him home again. Then she realized that the kindly man was but making a clumsy attempt to comfort her which she thought rather dear of him. Finally she was able to take her leave of Sir John, and she and Mag were led up a winding flight of stairs and down a corridor to a door which the warder on guard unlocked, and opened wide.

"Conn!" She flew into the room and into his surprised arms.

"Aidan!" His arms locked about her, and he kissed her with a gentle passion. "Sweeting, what are ye doing here?"

"How could I remain at *Pearroc Royal* without ye, Conn? It was too far, and I feared for ye! Yer birthday was yesterday. I had hoped for a better day for ye." She lowered her voice. "I have been in touch with my cousin Cavan, and 'twas he who told me of yer plight, and how grave the situation is. I wanted to go to the queen, but he advised against it. He also advised against my petitioning Sir John, but after he left I took the barge and came to the Tower, and Sir John was ever so nice."

"He is a decent man considering his job," said Conn quietly, but his mind was busily digesting what she had said about her cousin. "How is it, sweeting, that ye spoke to Cavan?"

"I sent to the Swan for Mag said she was certain he hadn't left London yet."

"And he hadn't, had he?" mused Conn. "Interesting." Then coming to himself he said, "Just what did Cavan tell ye, Aidan?"

"That three men had accused ye of being involved in a plot to kill the queen, but I told him such a thing was impossible!" she said.

He hugged her hard. "Thank ye for yer trust, my love. Now try to re-member what else Cavan said to ye."

"He said ye could have become involved in the plot while ye were still at court. He said . . . he s-said that ye could l-lose yer h-head! Oh, Conn! Tell me that it cannot happen!" She clung to him trembling.

Damnation! he thought. Wasn't Cavan FitzGerald the busy and in-formed one? Conn considered the delightful possibility of beating him senseless when this was all over. For now, however, he had to reassure his pregnant wife. Gently he set her back from him, and tipping her face up-ward looked down into her eyes. "Aidan, I want ye to believe me when I tell ye that I am in no danger whatsoever of losing my head. More than that I cannot say to ye now. Do ye understand me?"

She gained strength from his very presence, and now as his words pen-etrated her brain she realized exactly what he was telling her.

"It is possible," he continued on confirming her thoughts, "that yer cousin Cavan is involved in this scheme. Ask me no more, however, sweeting. I cannot tell ye."

"But how will they catch him?" she persisted.

He put his hand over her mouth. "Aidan!" he said warningly, and when she nodded resigned he removed it. "Now listen, my love, I don't want ye to see Cavan again if ye can help it. I want ye to go back to Greenwood, and tomorrow morning yer to go home. Do ye understand me? Yer to go home! I don't think I've ever given ye an order in all the time we've been married, but this is an order. Go home!"

Her heart felt much lighter at the secret knowledge that he was going to be safe, and she smiled relieved at him saying meekly, "Yes, my lord."

"Indeed, madame, and I have never heard ye sound so biddable before," he teased her, kissing her again quickly upon the mouth. "Oh, my sweet wife, how very much I want ye, and how very much I have missed ye!"

"I thought," she answered him, "that I was lonely before, but only since we have been parted, my darling Conn, have I really learned what loneliness is all about. I don't ever want to be separated from ye again!"

His strong arms enfolded her once again. "We won't be, sweeting. I promise ye!" He kissed her tenderly this time, and then putting her from him said, "Now leave me, Aidan, take care of our child, and remember what I have told ye."

"I'm not afraid any longer, Conn," she said. "Mag and I will leave for *Pearroc Royal* in the morning, I promise."

And while Aidan and Conn had been having their small reunion Mag and Cluny had squabbled happily in a corner, delighted to see one another though neither would have admitted it. Now as Aidan called to her tiring woman Cluny said impulsively, "Ye be careful, Mistress Mag, for when we gets home I'll need ye to quarrel with."

Mag flushed, but recovering snapped at him, "Yer an old fool, Master Cluny, but take care of yerself. Ye need watching over far more than I do."

Conn smiled at the two, and addressed Mag quietly. "I've told Aidan that she is to avoid seeing FitzGerald again, and that yer to both return home tomorrow morning. Ye'll see to it?"

"Aye, my lord, I will, and that is good news. M'lady will not listen to me."

"But she will listen to me, won't ye, Aidan?"

"Yes, my lord," came the dutiful reply, and Aidan curtsied to her husband.

He laughed. "Then be off with ye both, and a safe journey home!"

The two women followed the guardsman back to the governor's apartment for Aidan wanted to thank Sir John for his kindness. Arriving she was surprised to find William Cecil, Lord Burghley. He arose from his chair, and ushered her to a comfortable seat before sitting back down again himself.

"Ye have seen yer husband, madame?"

"Thanks to Sir John," said Aidan smiling at the governor of the Tower. "Thank ye, sir. My mind is much eased having seen Conn."

Lord Burghley nodded. "Would ye like to help yer husband, Lady Bliss?"

"Of course!" Aidan cried.

William Cecil nodded. "We do not," he said, "believe for a moment that yer husband is part of a plot to assassinate her majesty, but someone has gone to the trouble of making it appear so. It is a clumsy effort at best, madame, but there ye have it. It is very possible that the man who calls himself Cavan FitzGerald may be involved, and that his motive is to see ye widowed so he may marry ye. That is the simplest of it. It may be, however, that there is more. We need to flush out any accomplices should Master FitzGerald have them, and in that we need yer help."

"How?" said Aidan.

"If Master FitzGerald is after yer wealth then the news ye will have nothing should yer husband be convicted of this alleged crime will send him on his way quick enough. If there is more, then he will linger on in London. Knowing which way the wind is blowing will enable us to decide the true seriousness of this business.

"I want ye to go to yer cousin tonight, and tell him ye have just been informed that yer estates and all the wealth that they entail are about to be confiscated by the crown. Perhaps ye should even ask him to intercede with yer grandfather for ye. Tell him that ye received yer information from the Countess of Lincoln, but that she said she can be of no more help to ye under the circumstances. If it is yer gold that Master FitzGerald is after, then he'll be gone before the morning's light."

"And ye will release my husband then?"

"Aye."

"But what if it is not, my lord?"

"Then Lord Bliss must remain here until we can find out just who is actually behind this plot. I'm sure ye understand, Lady Bliss."

Aidan nodded. "Aye, I do, and of course I will aid ye, my lord. I am more than anxious to prove our loyalty to the queen. I shall go directly to the Swan from here."

Mag coughed discreetly from her place by the door.

Aidan smiled. "What is it, Mag?" she asked.

"Forgive me, m'lady, but ye did promise my lord that ye would have nothing further to do with Master FitzGerald, and that ye would go home tomorrow. Yer not forgetting that now, are ye?"

"No, Mag, and we will go home tomorrow, but this is such a very little thing to do, and perhaps it will clear this matter up so that when we go home tomorrow, my lord and Cluny will be with us. Ye would like that too, wouldn't ye?"

"But ye promised my lord ye wouldn't bother with that man, m'lady!" Mag insisted.

"Conn didn't say I couldn't see Cavan FitzGerald, Mag. He simply said to avoid him until we left if possible," Aidan reasoned. "Ye've heard Lord Burghley, Mag. This whole thing may have been concocted by my cousin merely for the purpose of gaining my wealth. What a terrible man he must be! He would sacrifice Conn's life merely to gain my riches! Would ye have him go unpunished?"

Mag sighed. "Of course not," she said, "but if he is so lacking in scruples that he would allow my lord to be killed, what might he not do to ye, my chick?"

William Cecil nodded slightly. The servant was very wise. "I would not send yer mistress into any danger, Mrs. Mag," he said. "She need only in feminine fashion go weeping to her relative to confide this new disaster, and to seek his comfort. Confiscating a traitor's wealth is often done. It will not seem unusual or suspicious to Master FitzGerald, but if all he is after is yer lady's riches, he will bolt fast enough, and the mystery will be solved."

"And if he does will ye let him away with it?" demanded the tiring woman boldly.

"No," said Lord Burghley, "we will not. He will be quickly caught, and imprisoned for fraud, and attempted murder. He'll not see his homeland soon again, I promise ye."

"Ye go home, and pack for us, Mag," Aidan instructed the servant. "I will go by coach to the Swan, and be home before ye even miss me."

"What coach?" demanded Mag. "We came by barge. Ye'll not hire a public coach, m'lady!"

"I will send her in my own coach," said Lord Burghley. "It is a plain vehicle for I do not like to be recognized in the streets. It will wait for yer mistress, and then conduct her home safely. Sir John will give me the loan of his barge for my own trip home."

Satisfied by those arrangements Mag left her mistress, and Lord Burghley conducted young Lady Bliss to his coach where he bid her farewell.

"Do not," he warned her, "attempt to elicit any information from Master FitzGerald whatsoever. Simply play yer part, and then depart, Lady Bliss. If the man is not a fool, then he is dangerous, and I would not like anything to happen to ye."

"I am not a fool," said Aidan quietly. "I will take great care not to arouse his suspicions, m'lord. I have far more to lose. I am with child, ye know?"

"I did not," came the reply, "and now I fear perhaps I should not have asked ye to do this."

"Nonsense, my lord! 'Tis no great thing." Aidan smiled, and then climbing into the coach she waved him good-bye as it moved from the Tower courtyard, and out into the evening streets. Aidan chuckled to herself at Mag's boldness in questioning Lord Burghley so fiercely, but he had not been in the least offended by the servant. Instead he had calmed her fears, and answered her questions without fuss. He was a consummate politician, thought Aidan, and she understood why the queen valued him so highly. He had understood Mag's concern for her because of his own concern for his mistress, Elizabeth Tudor. Loyalty was something Lord Burghley both understood and valued highly.

They arrived at the Swan, a large comfortable commercial inn located on a respectable street near the river, and alighting the coach without a backward glance, Aidan entered into the building. She was immediately greeted by the landlord for it was the dinner hour, and the Swan's dining room was well known.

"May I help ye, madame?"

"I am Lady Bliss," said Aidan. "I seek my cousin, Master FitzGerald."

"Of course, m'lady. Yer cousin, and his friend, Monsieur Michel, have rooms here on the main floor, in the rear." He reached out to grab at a boy hurrying by. "Bob! Take Lady Bliss to her cousin's rooms. That'll be Master FitzGerald, the Irishman."

"Aye, Da!" Bob gave Aidan a friendly grin. "Right this way, m'lady," and he led her back down to the end of a hallway to a door. Knocking sharply he barely awaited for the permission to enter before he was throwing open the door to permit Aidan passage.

Cavan FitzGerald, and another man had been sitting before the small fireplace drinking. Both men were casually dressed, without doublets, their shirts open. They leapt to their feet as Aidan came into the room.

"Ohh, Cavan!" she cried, and throwing herself at him she began to sob. " 'Tis terrible, Cavan! Oh, 'tis just terrible!" and her shoulders shook with the force of her weeping.

With a surprised wiggle of his eyebrows Bob pulled the door closed behind him, and Cavan FitzGerald put his arms about Aidan saying, "Dearest little Aidan, what is it? What has distressed ye so?"

"Wine," she sobbed convincingly. "I must have some wine!"

Cavan nodded to Miguel de Guaras who filled a small goblet, and handed it to him. "Here, Aidan, my sweet," Cavan said soothingly as he seated her in a chair. "Now tell me what is troubling ye."

Aidan sipped slowly at the ruby liquid, half-closing her eyes as she quickly surveyed the room. It wasn't very big, but along with the fireplace was a window that looked out on the back courtyard of the inn. Besides the door to the hallway there was another door through which she could see a bedchamber. There was only a table, two chairs, and a wooden settle by the fireplace in this room. The wine was not the best vintage, and it slid down her throat, burning slightly, and causing her to cough. She caught her breath, and looked up at the two men through her wet eyelashes. "Ohhhh, Cavan!" she cried again.

"Is it Conn?" he said trying to keep the eagerness from his voice.

"Partly," she allowed. "Ohhh, Cavan!"

"What is it, Aidan? What is troubling ye?" he demanded, trying to keep the impatience from his voice.

"I had a message from my cousin the Countess of Lincoln," Aidan said dramatically, and then she began to sob again.

"And?" he coaxed her.

"Because of what Conn has done our estates and our wealth are to be forfeit to the crown! I will be penniless, Cavan! Penniless!"

He looked stunned.

"Ye must help me," she continued. She had seen his face, and knew then that Lord Burghley had been correct.

Ye bastard, she thought angrily, but then she spoke again. "Ye must help me, Cavan. I will have nothing. Where can I go? What shall I do? Will ye speak to my grandfather for me? Perhaps he will allow me to live with him in Ireland." Then she put her face in her hands, and began to cry again.

"What of yer husband?" It was the other man who spoke.

Curious, thought Aidan, but she answered nonetheless, "He will be condemned to be hung, drawn, and quartered unless the queen shows him mercy, and allows him to be beheaded. My cousin the countess says, however, that the queen is very angry. My cousin says she can no longer help me because of Conn. Oh, Cavan! What am I to do? Ye'll help me, won't ye?"

But Cavan wasn't even looking at her at this point. He turned to Miguel de Guaras. "Did ye anticipate this, de Guaras? When ye offered me my cousin's wealth to help ye, did ye anticipate that that wealth would be forfeit to England's rapacious ruler? Did ye?"

Aidan sat very still, suddenly very aware that there was more involved here, and just a little frightened that she had perhaps stumbled into something far more serious than she realized. She had to get out of this place before more was said. Before they became aware that she even suspected anything.

"Oh, Cavan," she said, "I am so unhappy! Will ye escort me back to Greenwood? My coach is waiting outside."

He whirled on her, and for the first time she saw that he was jowly, and that his mouth was narrow to the point of meanness. "Shut up, Aidan!" he snapped at her.

"Ye cannot talk to me like that," she cried, leaping to her feet. "I shall go home this minute! I was mad to come to ye for help!"

"Sit down, madonna," said Miguel de Guaras. "I do not think it wise that ye go anywhere at this time."

Aidan drew herself up to her full height, and the Spaniard's eyes flicked over her admiringly. "How dare ye?" she said coldly. "Stand aside, sir, and let me pass or I shall scream this inn down!" Her fear was growing with every breath she took, but she hid it well.

"*Sit down!*" Cavan snarled, and he shoved her none too gently back into the chair. Then he turned to de Guaras. "Tell me what is in this for me, de Guaras? If Aidan's estates and monies are confiscated then why should I marry her? She has nothing to give me. I didn't aid Spain out of the charity of my heart, or because I believe that the Holy Mother Church should be restored to England. I don't give a damn one way or another. I helped ye to gain this woman and her wealth. Now I find she is to have no wealth! What good is she to me? Tell me that?"

"Be calm, amigo," said Miguel de Guaras. "Our plot has been successful. Lord Bliss faces execution and his brothers will be next. Retribution will fall upon his sister Lady de Marisco. The O'Malley thorns will be removed from the paw of Spain, and King Philip will show ye his gratitude, I promise ye. There was always the possibility that this could happen. It is not uncommon for convicted traitors to have their properties confiscated."

"I don't recall ye mentioning it though," said Cavan bitterly.

Miguel de Guaras shrugged. "An oversight, but ye need have no fears. We will leave tonight for Spain, amigo, and once there my king will reward ye suitably."

"With what?"

"A small estate," said Miguel de Guaras smoothly. "Surely that will make up for the loss of this woman's puny lands."

"*Puny lands!*" Cavan's face grew mottled with his anger. "Have ye any idea the size of her estates, ye fool? Several thousand acres is what ye've lost me! And the heiress next door for my future son! An heiress with an equally large holding! I was going to build a dynasty, de Guaras, and now ye offer me in exchange a *small estate* in some godforsaken village of Spain? And what of her wealth? Her gold? Will yer damned king make up for that as well?"

"King Philip's generosity extends only to giving ye lands, FitzGerald, and ye should be grateful to him. As for gold, well, my innocent Irish fool, ye have a prime opportunity to gain a small fortune if ye would but open yer eyes."

"What the hell do ye mean?" demanded Cavan angrily.

"What do ye intend to do about yer cousin? Ye can't let her go now, can ye?"

"What do I care about her," said Cavan FitzGerald meanly. "Strangle the bitch for all I care! She's no use to me now."

"She's gold in yer pocket, amigo!"

"What?"

"London is an international port, man. How do ye think we're getting out of here tonight? We're going down to the river, amigo, and hiring a werryman to row us into the London pool to the ship of an old friend of mine; Rashid al Mansur."

"A Moor?"

"No, a Spaniard who decided the crescent was far more profitable than the Cross. In Spain they call him a renegade, but it has never detracted from our friendship. Rashid brings little luxuries to England. Oranges and morocco leather goods. He returns with tin, and English wool, and more often than not a delectable girl for the slave markets of Algiers. Fair-skinned, light-eyed women are highly prized.

"Look at yer cousin, amigo. Fair-skinned, light-eyed, and hair like polished copper. She's no great beauty, but she's pretty enough, and she'll bring ye a fortune. That's better than killing her, isn't it? Killing her will gain ye nothing. Selling her will bring ye wealth."

"Cavan, ye can't!" Aidan cried. She was suddenly terrified but not just for herself, for her baby. "Cavan, I am with child!"

"That is even better!" said Miguel de Guaras. "A fiery-haired woman with fair skin and a big belly. The Turks and the Arabs love a fertile woman! Ye'll get double the price!"

"And how the hell am I to arrange for that? Do I go to Algiers with her?"

"No, no, amigo, it is not necessary. My brother, Antonio, he who is now imprisoned by the English, did business with Rashid al Mansur for all the years he was Spain's agent here in England. Each time Rashid was ready to return to Algiers, Tonio would arrange to find a little yellow-haired, blue-eyed girl to send with him. Some London waif or another that no one would miss. When the sale was made Rashid would take his ten-percent commission, and the rest of the monies would be deposited via the Kira bank into Tonio's account either here in England or at home in Spain. The same thing can be done for ye. Rashid will let us off at dawn on the French coast. From there we will make our sway to Spain. The king will give ye yer lands, and when yer cousin has been sold in Algiers, the wealth she brings ye will be deposited through the Kira bank in Algiers to the Kira bank in Spain. Is that not simple enough?"

"What do ye think she'll bring?"

Miguel de Guaras looked at Aidan with a critical eye. "I'd have to see her naked, but from what I can see, I'd say several hundred pounds. It is not the wealth ye lost, but 'tis a fine amount, and the truth of the matter is, amigo, that ye'll be far better off than ye've ever been in yer entire life. Wealth, and lands, and with those the hope of a respectable wife. A wife who doesn't know, and can never learn of the sad accident of yer birth. Think well, amigo."

Aidan was horrified by what she had heard. This whole thing had been a mad plot to bring down Conn's family, but she didn't understand why, nor did it matter. What mattered was that she had to escape these two men who talked so casually of selling her into some kind of slavery. She stood up, and both men turned to her.

"I have no intention of standing by while ye kidnap me," she said bravely. "Cavan, if ye don't open that door I am going to start screaming. I will scream louder and longer than anyone ye've ever heard in yer entire life. I will not allow ye to be responsible for Conn's death! I love my husband! Whatever made ye think I could love ye? I despise ye! As a man yer a jest!"

He hit her a blow that sent Aidan reeling, her hand to her face. "Bitch! I only wanted ye for yer money!" he said cruelly.

"Amigo," cautioned de Guaras, "do not damage yer merchandise lest ye drive the price down."

"She's an overproud bitch," said FitzGerald. "Neither her father, nor that pretty husband of hers ever beat her. She needs it!"

"There is no time, amigo," said de Guaras. "Let whoever buys her see to her discipline. Yer angry now, and ye could hurt her, and ye would, I promise ye, regret it. She is valuable merchandise." He smiled toothily at Aidan. "Ye have not finished yer wine, madonna," he said in a silky voice. "Let me freshen it for ye." He took the goblet from the table, and without any pretense emptied some powder into it from one of his rings. Then he added additional liquid, and handing it to her he ordered her: "Drink!"

Aidan stared down into the cup horrified. She could see nothing but the reddish wine. Whatever he had put so boldly into the goblet had instantly dissolved. "What did ye put into it?" she demanded, her voice slightly shaky.

"It will not kill ye," he responded without answering her query. "*Drink!*"

"Never!" Aidan shouted, and she attempted to stand up once again.

Miguel de Guaras was of no mind to argue. He had but one interest now. To leave England. With surprising strength for so slight a man he pushed her back into the chair, barking an order to Cavan at the same time. "Hold her down, amigo. I will see she drinks," and as Cavan went behind Aidan and pinioned her arms so she might not prevent him,

190

Miguel de Guaras pinched Aidan's nose shut with two fingers, and when she was finally forced to open her mouth to gasp for breath, he forced the potion down her throat.

Aidan gagged, and choked in an attempt to spit the wine out before she swallowed it, but releasing his grip on her nose de Guaras used his two hands to close her jaws, thereby impelling her to swallow. With a burst of superhuman strength Aidan tore one of her arms free, and struck him a hard blow. The Spaniard grunted, surprised, and staggered slightly while Aidan opened her mouth and began to scream at the top of her lungs. Cavan FitzGerald released his grip upon his cousin, and leaping around the chair hit her on the chin. With a look of total surprise on her face, Aidan slumped, unconscious.

"Do ye think anyone heard her?" Cavan said.

Miguel de Guaras shook his head. "These rooms are at the back of the building. The window was closed, and the dining room is full right now. No one heard her over the din of all those voices, the eating, and the serving people. Now, amigo, go and tell the lady's coachman that ye'll personally escort yer lady cousin back to her home after she has taken the evening meal with ye."

"What if he insists upon waiting?" Cavan was becoming nervous. He suddenly realized the implications of what he had done, of what he was doing, should he be caught.

"He will not question ye at all. English servants are such an independent lot that he will be delighted for an evening off. Tell him that her ladyship says he may have the evening off. That will do it, I guarantee it."

Cavan hurried from the room, and Miguel de Guaras smiled. The Irishman was a fool, he thought, and then he shrugged. If it were up to him he would eliminate him, but the king had been most specific. Cavan FitzGerald was to be brought to Spain where he would continue to be of use to Philip. He would indeed be given his land, and a wife would be found for him, to help bind him even more to Spain; and then just when he was feeling comfortable and safe, he would be brought to the king to learn the real price of all his newfound wealth. Spain needed men like Cavan FitzGerald to foment trouble in Ireland, to prepare for the eventual uprising against England that Spain would finance.

At least, thought Miguel de Guaras, he had saved his king the monies he had intended to bestow upon Cavan. Selling off the Irishman's cousin in Algiers had been a stroke of genius on his part. He moved to the chair where she was slumped, and tipped her head back. Pretty, he thought to himself again, but no great beauty. Still in all the hair, the eyes, and the skin more than made up for it. It really would have been too much had she been beautiful as well. His gaze moved downward as he remembered Cavan saying she had plump tits. He pulled the lace from her bodice for a better look, and a creamy flesh swelled provocatively. Very nice, he thought to himself. They would get a better look at the woman once safely aboard al Mansur's vessel later tonight, but for now it appeared as if she would bring a pretty penny to FitzGerald.

The door opened readmitting the Irishman. "Her coachman's gone, de Guaras. Now when can we get out of here?"

"Immediately," said the Spaniard. "Rashid al Mansur is expecting us although our little bit of extra baggage will come as a surprise to him. A pleasant one, however. Let us depart through the window and go out through the back courtyard so no one will see us. It being the dinner hour all will be engaged. The bill is paid through today so the landlord will have no cause for complaint, but it is best no one know when we went, nor see us with the lady." He picked up Aidan's cloak which he had taken from her as she entered earlier, and with Cavan's aid managed to get it around the unconscious woman.

"Put the hood up about her face," said de Guaras. "If we meet anyone in the street we don't want them remembering her red hair."

Neither man had much baggage, just a few changes of linen, and they were willing to leave that behind in their flight. Cavan opened the window, and climbed out. The Spaniard half-lifting, half-dragging Aidan managed to get her over to the window where Cavan pulled her through. Miguel de Guaras followed, and carefully drew the window closed behind him. Balancing the woman between them they moved carefully across the inner courtyard and out the alley behind the Swan. A dark shadow scuttled across their path, too large for a rat, either a small dog, or a cat. The two men crossed themselves, and continued on down the alley which led to the river. Above them they heard the sound of a window opening, and quickly flattened themselves and their burden against the wall of the house as both the contents of a slop jar, and the words "Guardez 'low!" emerged from the building at the same time.

The alley was very dark, and here and there slippery with the slime of garbage of all descriptions. It had been a warm day, and the air in the alley was fetid and stunk with a thousand unpleasant odors, not the least of which was the mud flats of the low tide from the river ahead. Reaching it they could only stand helpless and wait for a werryman with a large enough boat to come by, and they worried about finding one for already a fog was beginning to arise from the Thames. Then just as Cavan was thinking he would have to begin walking downriver to find a vessel for them one came rowing out of the fog, and they eagerly hailed it. To their relief the boatman pulled for the shore, and took them on.

"Is the laidy all right then?" he asked helping to drag Aidan aboard. "It ain't plague, is it?"

"Nay, man," laughed Cavan lightly. "My wife is young, and not used to good wine. She is drunk!"

The werryman poled into the middle of the river, nodding. "My old woman is just like that. Some just don't have a head for it. Wine is a rich man's drink." Then he asked, "Where will ye be going, sir?"

"To the *Gazelle* in London pool," said Miguel de Guaras.

"The *Gazelle* it is, sirs," said the werryman, and he began to row downriver.

Chapter 8

⸙

The *Gazelle*, having taken on its passengers, weighed anchor and slipped easily down the Thames with the outgoing tide. Its captain waited until his vessel had safely nosed out into the stretch of water that the English liked to call the English Channel before he joined his old friend Miguel de Guaras and his Irish companion. Settling themselves comfortably in Rashid al Mansur's cabin they shared a bottle of dark, red, wine, served to them by a silent black slave.

"Yer not so much a Muslim, Rashid, that ye still don't enjoy a fine bottle," Miguel de Guaras chided.

Rashid al Mansur laughed. "Old habits, especially bad habits, die hard, Miguelito. This will be the last bottle I enjoy until I return to Europe, however. In Algiers I keep strictly to the law of the Prophet."

"So yer a renegade," said Cavan bluntly. "I've heard of men like ye, but until now I'd never met one."

Miguel de Guaras winced delicately, and Rashid al Mansur turned cold eyes on Cavan. "I owe ye no explanations, Master FitzGerald, but I would suggest ye never use the word *renegade* in the presence of a man like me again. Have ye ever been a slave? Let me tell ye about slavery in Barbary. A slave is a thing without a soul. A slave is subject to its master's every whim. If a man chooses to destroy one of his slaves for no reason he can do it. Every breath a slave takes is dependent upon its master's goodwill. A slave has no rights, can own nothing, is nothing.

"Worst of all is the lot of a Christian slave who can receive brutal treatment for no other reason than his beliefs. Miguel has, I am certain, told ye that he, his brother, and I grew up together. Actually we are cousins. When I was sixteen I was caught in a slave raid, captured, and brought to Algiers to be sold. My fate was carefully outlined to me by the slavemaster in the state-controlled bagnio which is a combination clearinghouse, prison, and slave market. If I became a Muslim, he told me, my lot would be infinitely better for whoever bought me would eventually free me for my belief in Islam. I was fortunate for I was bought by an elderly sea captain to work in his gardens.

"Within a short time I converted to the faith of Islam to my master's delight. He freed me, and as he and his wife were childless they adopted me. He taught me his old trade, and I am pleased to say I became a kapitan reis before his death which made him very proud. My adoptive father left me a rich man. I am feared and respected by my peers. I might have clung to the faith of my homeland, but had I, I would now be dead after several unpleasant years in the quarries, or in the galleys.

"Tell me, Master FitzGerald, what would ye have done in my place?" and then Rashid al Mansur laughed for he knew the answer to that question. "Your scruples cannot be so great else ye would not be selling your own flesh and blood into bondage simply for gold," he noted dryly.

"I apologize for bringing aboard an extra passenger," said Miguel de Guaras.

"Our voyage is not that long, and we have plenty of food and water," replied Rashid al Mansur. "Actually I have several maidens aboard this trip by a stroke of good fortune."

"Several?" said Miguel de Guaras. "How did ye manage that?"

"Pure luck, amigo! Pure luck! I came across two young sisters whose mother had just died, and they were being dispossessed from their slum by an irate landlord to whom they owed money. He was ready to place those two delicate flowers in a local brothel. I paid him what he was owed plus a little extra, and took the girls with me back to the ship. They are eleven and ten, and both blond virgins! A third girl, another blond virgin, I bought from a friend of mine who has a brothel, and keeps an eye out for me when I am in London. He used to work for your brother, Tonio. This girl, however, is older. Thirteen, I believe she told me. I will clear a nice profit with those three plus my commission on the woman you brought me. Is she a virgin, too? She looks a bit old for it."

"She is in her early twenties," said Cavan, "and she is with child, or so she says. She is a prime piece of goods, a noblewoman of impeccable breeding with hair like polished copper, fair skin, and light eyes of silvery gray."

Rashid al Mansur looked over to his bed where the caped figure of a woman lay. The Irishman certainly knew how to pander his merchandise, but he had yet to see that merchandise, and so he would reserve judgment. "What did ye give her?" he asked Miguel.

"Just a drop of sleeping powder," replied the Spaniard. "She'll doze several hours."

"Then let's strip her now and see what we've got," said the captain. "It'll be easier with her unconscious. Highborn wenches always carry on so, and ye end up having to tear the clothing from them. Her garments are expensive, and will bring a nice penny, too, if they are kept in decent condition."

The three set to work removing Aidan's garments. They were careful, indeed almost gentle, but when Cavan went to remove the necklace from his cousin's neck Rashid al Mansur stayed his hand.

"Leave it, Irishman! Naked upon the block such adornment will add interest to her." He signaled to his slave. "Take the woman's clothing, and put it away for sale. All but the chemise. She will need that while we are at sea."

The slave gathered up Aidan's clothes, and began to go through them looking for the undergarment he had been ordered to leave. Finding it he put it aside, and departed the room. The three men stared in awed silence down on the nude, sleeping woman.

"Madre de Dios," breathed the Spaniard, "she is perfection!" and he felt himself hardening, but he could not look away.

Cavan FitzGerald was speechless with surprise. He had not expected such a beautiful body on Aidan, but she was totally incredible with her long legs and torso, and her beautiful breasts. He, too, felt desire bolting through him. Maybe he shouldn't sell her. Maybe he should keep her for himself.

Rashid al Mansur correctly divined his thoughts. "Don't be a fool, Irishman," he said. "In the light of day there are few women who would bring you on the block of Algiers what this woman is going to bring you."

Cavan shook his head to clear it, and took a deep breath. "Yer right," he said, "but by God I'd have liked to have fucked her once!"

They put her chemise back on, and then Rashid al Mansur called his slave to him, and had him carry the unconscious Aidan into the cabin next door where the other three girls were being kept. The slave gently placed her upon a straw pallet covered in a red cotton, and not once did she stir until morning colored the skies to the east over France.

Her head ached, and her mouth felt dry and unpleasant. Her belly cramped uncomfortably, and she thought hazily that her line with the moon must be broken and upon her. As that idea penetrated her brain Aidan gave a cry, and sat up. How could that be? She was with child! She felt a stickiness between her legs, saw the blood upon her chemise, and then she began to scream in earnest startling the three young girls sharing the little cabin with her into terror so that they began to shriek also.

The door to the cabin was opened, and a large black man hurried into the room. Aidan cried louder, totally confused, and frightened, and very much aware that she was losing her baby, *Conn's baby*. A hard pain tore into her, and she retched up a yellow bile. The black man took one look, and shouted some unintelligible words into the room behind him. Rashid al Mansur pushed by the slave, and went directly to Aidan.

"Stop screaming!" he said in a firm, no-nonsense voice, and surprised she did. "Tell me what the matter is, copper-haired woman." He spoke in English although his words were heavily accented.

"I am losing my child," she said, and she began to sob.

"It is God's will then," he answered her. "How far gone are ye?"

"Two months, perhaps a little more."

He nodded. "Lie down while I call for the physician."

She obeyed him, but asked as she did so, "Where am I?"

"In time, copper-haired woman. For now let us concentrate upon your difficulties." He turned to the black slave, and said, "Send for the physician."

The slave ran from the room, returning in a very few minutes with a small, white-robed elderly gentleman.

"The woman believes she is losing her child," Rashid al Mansur said to the doctor. "She is two months gone."

The physician nodded, and kneeling down examined Aidan with gentle hands, sighing, and shaking his head sadly. Finally he looked up. "The deed is already done, my lord kapitan reis, but she is young and will undoubtedly live to bear many fine sons. I will clean her up, and attend to her birth canal so that there will be no infection. She will be all right in a few days, and certainly by the time we reach home."

Rashid al Mansur looked to Aidan, and spoke in as kindly a fashion as he might considering what he had to tell her. "Achmet says you have indeed lost your baby, but that ye will live to bear many fine sons. He will take care of ye so that there is no infection. I am going to put ye in my own cabin for yer comfort."

"Who are ye?" she asked him.

"My name is Rashid al Mansur, and I am a kapitan reis out of the city of Algiers."

"Is that where we are going?"

"Aye."

"So ye may sell me into slavery?"

"Yes."

"Where is my cousin, Master FitzGerald?"

"He and his companion were put ashore on the French coast just before dawn," said Rashid al Mansur.

"I am a very wealthy woman, captain. Turn back to England, and I will see ye well rewarded, far in excess of whatever commission ye might get from my cousin."

"I know your story, copper-haired woman," said Rashid al Mansur. "You have no monies."

"But I do!" Aidan insisted, and the tears began to pour down her face. "Telling my cousin I didn't was merely a ploy on the part of Lord Burghley to smoke out Cavan and his accomplice. Turn back, I beg ye!"

"Desperate women tell desperate lies," said Rashid al Mansur. "It could be that you are speaking the truth, copper-haired woman, but what if you are not? I could be arrested by your people, and thrown into prison, and easily lose everything that I have spent my life building. On the other hand if I go on to Algiers, you will bring your cousin a fine price on the slave block, and I will have a nice commission for my troubles. Tell me what you would do, copper-haired woman?"

"I know what ye are saying to me, captain," said Aidan, trying to keep the hysteria from her voice. "Ye are telling me that ye will not jeopardize all ye have for my sake, but I am not appealing to yer sense of greed, I swear it. Lord Burghley suspected that my cousin was involved in some plot against the queen. He knew that my husband was not, but they did not know if the plot was political, or if Cavan was simply attempting to rid me of Conn so he might marry me and have my wealth for himself. Telling Cavan I was now penniless was the means by which Lord Burghley hoped to smoke out my cousin.

"I am not lying when I tell ye that I am a rich woman! We do not speak of my husband's wealth, but mine! Turn back to England, and I swear ye will not be arrested, nor imprisoned. I will pay ye whatever ye desire if ye will free me!"

Rashid al Mansur had lived in Barbary for twenty-five years, but never had he forgotten his fear when he had been first captured by slavers. He knew that the copper-haired woman was even now experiencing the same thing, and since he was not an unkind man by nature he was genuinely sympathetic. Therefore he deigned to attempt an explanation to this woman.

Kneeling by her side so that their faces met he said, "Listen to me, copper-haired woman, attempt to understand. You appear to be intelligent for a female, and so I will try to explain this to you. You are now technically the property of the Dey of Algiers, whose gracious overlord is Sultan Murad III, Defender of the Faith, and master of the Ottoman Empire. I could not return you to England if I wanted to because you do not belong to me, and I am an honorable man. You will be sold in the state-owned slave market. Your cousin will be given a share of your profit, as will I, but the dey will also profit, and I have not the right to steal from him. Do you understand?"

Aidan looked at him a moment, and then she turned her head away, but not before he had caught a glimpse of the tears that had sprung into her eyes.

"Can you give her a potion to make her sleep, Achmet?" Rashid al Mansur asked his physician. "I have just explained to her her fate, and with the loss of her child to add to her woes she might consider the unthinkable."

"Of course, my lord," was the reply.

"How is she physically?"

"She is a strong, healthy woman by nature. I cannot say if she would have lost the child without the distress of her situation, but I doubt it. She needs rest, freedom from worry, and good food now to recover. She should be quite well by the time we reach Algiers, but it would not hurt to cosset her somewhat. Tomorrow let the other girls of her race come to keep her company. It will prevent her from going into herself."

Rashid al Mansur nodded, and then said to Aidan, "My physician will see that you are well cared for, copper-haired woman. No one will harm you, and you have only to get well again."

Aidan would not even look at him when he spoke to her, but the kapitan reis understood. Quietly he departed the room leaving Achmet, the physician, to cope with his patient. Achmet had completed his examination of Aidan, and he had skillfully attended to her body which was yet in pain. Her chemise had been soaked in blood, and so it had been removed, and finished with her he covered her with a light coverlet. Then reaching into his medical pouch he took out a round, gilded pill, and pushed it between her lips. It never occurred to Aidan to refuse him. She accepted the goblet he next handed her, and swallowed the medication. He stayed with her the few minutes it took for her to fall asleep again, and then the physician left the cabin.

The next time she awoke the moon was streaming in through the cabin's windows. Aidan lay quietly beneath the coverlet, barely breathing as she sought for answers to the questions that popped into her head at a rapid pace. Where was she? A ship! Was she alone? Aye. There seemed to be no one else in the cabin. Where was Conn? *Conn was in the Tower!* And with that knowledge she remembered all. She was a prisoner aboard a ship of the Barbary fleet. She was being taken to Algiers to be sold into slavery. She had lost Conn's child, and she was never to see her husband again! Aidan began to cry.

She wept softly for some time, and her eyes burned with the salt from her tears. If this was a nightmare, and she prayed that it was, then why couldn't she awaken? She pinched herself cruelly, but nothing changed. She still lay naked beneath a soft coverlet on a strange bed in a strange place, and she suddenly felt empty, as hollow as a drum with the loss of her child. There at least, she thought, God had been merciful. She would not have wanted her baby born into slavery.

The door to the cabin opened, and she could see in the light from the passageway the little doctor entering. He smiled and nodded at her, and handed her the cup again. Then into his pouch his fingers dipped, and removing another of the gilded pills he once again pushed it between her lips. Why not, she thought wearily, and dutifully swallowed the medication which quickly tumbled her back into sleep. The next time she awoke it was day. This time her memory did not fail her.

For a few brief moments she considered slipping from the cabin, and throwing herself over the ship's rail to drown, but she quickly decided that she wanted to live and return home to her beloved England. She knew what she contemplated would be considered impossible, but if she gave up all hope she would die of despair. Surely whoever bought her could be tempted by a fat ransom even if Rashid al Mansur could not. She would offer enough gold to buy a dozen beautiful women, and certainly a normal man could be tempted by that. That was exactly what she would do, and having decided it Aidan realized she was hungry. *Very hungry.*

How did one go about getting food on this ship? She could hardly go to the door of the cabin, and call. Her state of undress would provoke a riot. She would have to wait for them to come to her. Wrapping the coverlet about her she stood up, and just as quickly sat down again. She had been immediately overcome by a spell of dizziness. She tried again, and this time rising she stood there for a moment until the giddiness had passed. Then she moved slowly across the room toward a table that held a decanter, and several goblets. She was very thirsty, and still felt pain. She stumbled as the door opened, and Rashid al Mansur entered the cabin.

Quickly he moved across the room, and put a steadying arm about her. "Easy, copper-haired woman. You are weak."

"I am also thirsty," she said.

He helped her back to his bed. "I will fetch you a drink. How are you feeling today?"

"I am yet in pain, but it is better," she answered him honestly.

"Good! I knew you were strong. Are you hungry?"

"Ravenous!"

He chuckled. "I will have Sa'id bring you something. I am going to give you some company today. In the little cabin next to this where you were your first night there are three young English girls who are also going to Algiers to be sold. You will keep each other amused."

He spoke, Aidan thought, as if they were on a pleasure cruise. He fetched her a goblet of watered wine as he had promised, and then ignoring her he went about the business of washing himself, and changing his clothing for clean garments. Finally without another word he left her to herself. Shortly after his departure Sa'id appeared with a tray of food for her. There was a steaming bowl of a cereal-like mixture that had chunks of lamb and vegetables in it; a soft flat bread which she assumed was to aid her to eat what was in the bowl since she was given no utensils; and a smaller blue-and-white bowl with fresh orange sections in it.

Aidan took the tray, and ate every morsel upon it. While she did, the slave, Sa'id, sat patiently at her feet, and when she had finished he fetched her a soft cloth and a basin of fragrant water to wash the grease from her hands and face. Since she could not speak his language, she smiled and nodded her thanks to the black man who seemed gratified that she had noticed. With a blinding grin he went to the door of the little cabin adjoining Rashid al Mansur's quarters, and opened it. Then taking the tray up he left her.

Aidan stood up, and this time there was no dizziness at all. Walking across the cabin she peered into the next room. There in a corner huddled three young girls. Aidan's heart went out to them immediately. "I won't hurt ye," she said. "I'm in the same position as ye are. Come, and share my day with me."

"Who are ye, my lady?" asked the eldest of the girls.

"My name is Aidan St. Michael. I am Lady Bliss."

"Coo!" said one of the two smaller girls. "Laidy no less! And does ye know Bessie Tudor herself?"

Aidan smiled at the London accent of the child, as well as her disbelief. In her world the lords and ladies of the court were safe from the kind of harm that could happen to an ordinary mortal. "Indeed I do know her majesty," she said nonetheless. "In fact I was even one of the queen's maids of honor."

"Ye never was!" said the child disbelievingly.

Aidan laughed. "Yes, I was," she said, "and yet here I am in just as difficult a position as ye are. Even worse for I don't have any clothing!"

The older girl arose, and came toward Aidan. "My name is Margaret Browne," she said. "I come from Kent. My stepmother sent me to London to be apprenticed to a dressmaker, but instead I was sold into a brothel by her brother. The brothel keeper sold me to this ship's captain. Do ye know what is to happen to us, my lady? Where are we going?" She was a pretty girl with a sweet face, long pale gold hair like thistledown, and eyes of deep blue.

"We are going to Algiers. The ship's captain, Rashid al Mansur, says we are to be sold into slavery."

"I should sooner be dead!" cried Margaret Browne.

"How old are you?" Aidan asked the girl.

"I am thirteen," came the reply.

"Are you a virgin? Answer me honestly, lass!"

"Yes, my lady. I was only in the brothel keeper's charge a few hours before the captain bought me. I think she was expecting him for I neither was abused nor badly treated."

"Who are the little girls?" Aidan said.

"We can speak for ourselves," said the elder of the sisters as they came from their corner. Reassured by Margaret Browne's contact with Aidan, they now felt bolder. "I am Rosamund, and this is my little sister, Pipere. If we had another name we don't remember it."

"How old are you?" asked Aidan.

"I'm eleven, her's ten," came the answer.

"Tell me how ye both ended up on this ship," Aidan queried them.

"Our mum died, and the landlord put her body in the garbage heap cuz we didn't have no money to pay the gravediggers. Then he took what little we had, even the bedding, for back rent, he says the barstid! We was out in the street cuz he wouldn't let us back into the house, and we was yelling back an forth when along come this fellow down the street, and he stops, and looks at Pipere and me, and then he says to the landlord, 'How much will ye take for these two?' and the landlord gets this gleam in his eye, and says, 'They're both virgins, as pure as the driven snow, me lord. Young, and in prime condition they've got to be worth at least five pieces of gold.' Well the captain laughs, and he says, 'I'll give ye three, and a silver penny to see their mother is buried properly,' so here we are."

Aidan looked at the two little sisters. They were both extremely pretty, and looked enough alike to be taken for twins. They had corn-colored blond hair and sky-blue eyes. "Ye heard what I told Margaret?" said Aidan. "We are to be sold into slavery. We shall all undoubtedly end up in harems."

Margaret Browne began to weep bitterly. "Never, never," she sobbed. "I should sooner be dead than held in carnal bondage by an infidel!"

"Wot's the matter wiv her?" demanded Rosamund. "Is her crazy or somfin? Listen, girl, all women end up under a man. If we was bought by a rich man we could spend the rest of our lives at ease! Wot's wrong wiv that I'd likes to know? Our ma was a whore, and her always wanted better for Pipere and me. Why does ye think we still got our cherries? She always said, 'I'll not let ye two go cheap, Rosy. I'll find ye a good man to takes care of ye, and ye'll not have to open yer legs to every Tom, Dick, and Harry up from the country for a good time!' Our ma was a good woman, her was," finished Rosamund with a sentimental sniff.

Margaret Browne looked horrified at Rosamund's words, but Aidan rather admired the little Londoner. She was a tiny tough sparrow of a survivor. With luck she would prosper. The Kentish girl put her face in her hands and began to weep again. Rosamund looked so totally out of patience with her that Aidan almost laughed.

"What does Pipere say to all of this?" she asked Rosamund.

"Her does what I say, right, Pipere?"

"Right, Rosy," came the perky reply from the littlest girl.

"The captain says that ye may join me in this cabin," Aidan said, and she led them into Rashid al Mansur's quarters.

"Coo-ee," said Rosamund looking admiringly about the large and beautifully furnished cabin with its fine window seat beneath mullioned windows in the stern of the vessel. "Are ye the captain's doxy for this voyage, laidy?"

"Nay," said Aidan, "I most certainly am not!"

"Then how come ye gets such fancy treatment? No one gives anyfing for nuffin in this world."

"I miscarried my baby last night," said Aidan softly, "and the captain being a good businessman did not wish me uncomfortable for he believes I will bring him a great deal of money in Algiers."

"Why? Ye ain't no beauty. Ye ain't ugly, but ye ain't no beauty," said Rosamund bluntly.

"Women with fair skin, light eyes, and light hair are highly prized in Barbary, Rosamund. Women, however, with fair skin, light eyes, and red hair are the rarest creatures of all, and I am told they bring a fortune. Hence my value."

"How can ye speak so calmly about it?" said Margaret Browne in a voice that Aidan could hear was laced with near-hysteria.

Aidan sat Margaret down, and put an arm about her. "I have been kidnapped from my husband," she said. "I have lost my first child because of it. I am as frightened as ye are, but if I give into those feelings I will lose control of myself, and then others can control me totally. That I will not do! I am alive, and as long as it is God's will that I live, then there is hope. Do ye understand me, Meg, for I suspect that is what ye were called."

"My father called me Meg," said the Kentish girl.

"Do ye understand what I have said to ye, Meg?"

"Aye," said the girl.

"And ye will no longer be afraid?"

"I will try, my lady."

"Stupid cow," grumbled Rosamund. "Don't she know how much worse it could be?"

"Aye, Rosy," said Pipere. "It could be worse."

Aidan didn't know how it could be much worse, but the two little Londoners kept her cheered during the voyage to Algiers which was made in just under two weeks. She in turn kept up the spirits of the Kentish girl who now became her shadow. She learned that Meg had been the cosseted only child of a fairly prosperous farmer. Poor child, Aidan thought. At least I learned a little about the world during my stay at court. This poor girl is totally and completely innocent.

They reached their destination late one afternoon as the sun dappled the gleaming white walls surrounding the city, and its buildings which seemed to march straight up the hillsides. It was a very impressive sight as approached from the sea, the harbor, and the long mole built by the Spanish, framed by the city itself. In contrast to its outer beauty, however, was the stench of the city which was carried on a warm wind that blew across the city from the desert beyond.

"It is too late to parade you four to the jenina," said Rashid al Mansur. "I will notify the dey of our arrival, and then in the morning we will go. I will have fresh water brought aboard so that you may wash yourselves and your hair. I want you to show to your best advantage."

"What is the jenina?" asked Aidan.

"A literal translation would be 'the king's house,'" said Rashid al Mansur. "It is where the dey comes to assess his legal rights over a percentage of the captives. Usually his servants do it, but in the case of such rare merchandise as yourselves I suspect he will come himself."

"The dey is the ruler of Algiers?" said Aidan.

"The dey is appointed by the sultan to govern Algiers in his name," was the answer.

Rashid al Mansur was gone but a short time when Sa'id arrived to herd them all into the little cabin next to the captain's. Leaving he closed the door behind him, and then they could hear a great deal of trekking back and forth in the room next to them. Finally after some minutes Sa'id opened the door between the two cabins, and waved them back into the larger room. There four steaming tubs awaited them. Aidan gave a cry of delight for she had not been able to bathe properly since they had sailed from England. Sa'id signaled them to enter the tubs, and they shooed him from the room laughing.

Joyously the four females washed themselves, enjoying every minute of the treat for the water was fragrant with sweet, flower-scented oils that pampered their skins. There was even a bar of soap that lathered lavishly, and which they passed around amongst each other. They washed their hair first, and then their bodies. Aidan had been cleaner than her three companions for the physician had seen to it lest she court an infection. She had bled for several days following her miscarriage, and then the flow had stopped as it had come. Rashid al Mansur had told her that Achmet worried for she should have flowed longer, but that he thought her emotional state might have something to do with it.

"He says that the mind can do powerful things," said the kapitan reis with a shrug.

They had finished bathing, and stepping from their tubs looked for something to dry themselves with, and for their chemises; in Aidan's case, her coverlet; but these things had disappeared. They stood very uncomfortable in their nudity, looking horrified at one another as the door to the cabin began to open. They turned to flee to the smaller room, but found its door barred to them now. Huddling together they looked distinctly uncomfortable as Rashid al Mansur, and Achmet the physician came into the room.

"Kapitan, where are our garments?" Aidan demanded bravely.

"You won't need them any longer," was the reply. "You are clean now, and tomorrow you will be paraded naked to the jenina as is our custom, and afterward to the bagnio. It helps to drum up interest in your sale, and bring in the buyers. Stand apart now for I want to see you, and gauge your value. Achmet will examine each of you so I may honestly attest to your health."

"Sweet, holy Mary," moaned Margaret Browne, and Aidan was inclined to agree with her, but Rosamund and Pipere flung the Kentish girl a look of impatience that was so obvious that it caused both the captain and the physician to give a chuckle.

"Courage, Meg," said Aidan in a kindly voice, and she moved away from her companions.

Rashid al Mansur walked slowly around her with admiring eyes. "My eyes did not fail me that first night," he said to Achmet. "The woman is pure perfection of form." He took a handful of Aidan's coppery hair, and rubbed it between his thumb and forefinger. "It's heavy, and like silk," he remarked. His hand ran over her buttocks, and she winced, her teeth sinking into her lip as he squeezed the flesh lightly. "The skin tone is good, Achmet." He moved around to face her, and cupped one of her breasts in his palm. "The breasts are firm as well," he said, and then concluded, "She's going to bring us a fortune! Her cousin will be a rich man."

He moved away from Aidan, and began a similar examination of Margaret who although she stood still, wept bitterly as she was inspected.

"They're treating m-me l-like one of m-my father's m-mares," sobbed Meg.

"A woman ain't nuffin but a piece of meat," said Rosamund. "Sooner ye gets that inter yer head, the better off ye'll be, Mistress Fancy."

"Rosamund," said Aidan, gentle reproof in her voice. "Yer mother had a hard life, and she taught ye to be realistic, but Meg's world was a little bit gentler. Don't frighten her any more than she already is. This is not easy for any of us."

"Yer a high-and-mighty laidy, and yet yer managing to hold yerself together," said the child. "Meg is just too soft! Listen to me, Mistress Meg. If yer too soft in this life people takes advantage of ye. Remember that! If ye wants to survive, then ye've got to be strong!"

God's nightshirt! thought Aidan. Out of the mouth of this child comes a wisdom that even I should heed. If I show weakness for even a moment, I will be destroyed.

"Check for the truth of their virginity," said Rashid al Mansur, and even the feisty child-woman, Rosamund, looked askance, for he had spoken in English that they be warned of the physician's intent. Then he quickly gave the order in Arabic as well.

The physician, who had inspected each girl for her general health and blemishes now led each of the three blonds to the captain's bed where he laid them down in a row preparatory to examining them.

"Don't struggle!" Aidan quickly warned the girls. "He will not disturb your virgin state, he only wishes to attest to it. Don't be frightened, Meg," she added as the girl began to whimper.

"You are quick-witted, copper-haired woman," said Rashid al Mansur approvingly. "You are fit to be a sultan's consort."

"I have a husband," said Aidan, "and he would ransom me if ye would but contact him."

"Your husband is by now probably dead, and your wealth is gone, copper-haired woman. There is ransom for men of position and power and wealth, but for lovely women, whatever their rank, there is no ransom. Do not be afraid. You will be bought only by someone of great wealth for none else could afford you. You will be cherished, and loved by your master. Allah may even grant you children of your own. A wonderful life awaits you, copper-haired woman. Do not fight so hard against your fate."

Aidan turned away from him. His words unnerved her. They took away her hope, and that frightened her. I will tell the man who buys me the whole story, she thought, and he will contact Conn, and my husband will ransom me. It is going to be as I have planned. *It is!*

When Achmet had finished examining the three younger girls, and had assured his master, Kapitan Reis Rashid al Mansur, of their pure state, the two men left the cabin. They were fed a particularly good supper that evening for now that they were in port fresh food was available to them again. There were slices of baby lamb that had been roasted with tiny white onions, and green peppers; and a small capon for them to share, and a bowl of saffroned rice. There was a platter of fresh fruits, already sliced, and swimming in a tasty mixture of their juices. Aidan didn't recognize all of the fruits, but they were certainly delicious. To drink there was something that Sa'id called lemon sherbet. It was tart and yet sweet. Wine, Rashid al Mansur had told Aidan, was forbidden in Muslim countries. She did not question him about the wine she had drunk on his ship earlier.

They slept fitfully that night, all together upon the captain's large bed, but the noise of the port, and their own nerves combined to make them restless, even the usually tough Rosamund and her little sister, Pipere. For a brief time between the darkest hour of the night, and the dawn, the city grew still, and they slept their only peaceful sleep of the night. Then the sun burst over the horizon, and the city as quickly burst to life again, the sound of the muezzin's voice calling the faithful to prayer, and then the sounds of commerce beginning as the prayers ended and the day began in earnest.

Sa'id came and brought them rosewater with which to freshen their mouths, and then they were fed that peculiar flat bread they had first seen upon this ship, briny olives dripping oil, and goat's cheese. Afterward more rosewater was brought for them to bathe their hands and faces, and to once more purify their breaths. Then the black slave motioned them out the door of the cabin.

For a long moment they stood and stared at the open door, and then Meg voiced their thoughts. "I can't go out there . . . *naked!*" she whispered.

Aidan took a deep breath. Meg was going to have to fend for herself now. She, herself, could barely keep from shaking. *Naked.* They were being asked to walk naked out onto the deck of this ship, down its gangway, and onto the streets of this city. It was a terrifying thought, and

Aidan wasn't certain that she could do it, but she knew if she didn't then the others wouldn't. Somehow it was better, she reasoned, to go under her own steam than to be carried kicking and screaming from this ship.

Gritting her teeth she walked through the open door, and followed Sa'id down the narrow ship's passageway onto the deck. She was stark naked but for a necklace of gold and large pearls that she had been wearing the day she was kidnapped. Her long red-gold hair hung to her hips like a shining silken mantle, and from her ears bobbed fat baroque pearls. At the entry to the open deck she hesitated a moment as she saw the bright blue sky and the sun above.

I can't do it, she thought. *I just can't!* Then behind her young Rosamund hissed, "Ye've got us this far, yer laidyship, don't fail us now. That silly Meg is hanging on to Pipere so hard that she'll strangle her sure unless ye keeps moving." Aidan looked quickly behind her, and saw that what the child had said was true. She also saw that Rosamund for all her bravado was frightened.

Drawing another deep breath she gave the girl's hand a hard squeeze, and stepped out onto the deck where Sa'id handed her a pair of sandals, Rashid al Mansur's one concession to his captive women. Sandals were given to the other three, and they barely had time to get them onto their feet when Rashid al Mansur was saying, "Hurry, for I have been sent word that the dey himself will be at the jenina for just this hour. I will be the most envied man in Algiers tonight for having brought in such fine captives! Follow me, all of you!" and he strode across the deck, the four women hurrying behind him.

For a moment all was silent, and then the air erupted with whistles, and shouting and catcalls in every tongue imaginable. A large smile split the face of Rashid al Mansur at the cacophony of voices. The voices were those of slaves working the waterfront for their masters, galley slaves on their benches, porters, sailors from the various ships, and vendors of all sorts. By the time he walked his captives the short distance to the jenina the word would be racing like wildfire about the city with regard to his captives' beauty and worth. The auction for them would be packed, and frantic.

"*Etes-vous francais?*" called a voice, and other voices that Aidan comprehended cried out in their languages also. "Venice? Are you from Venice?" "I am Jean-Paul Thierry from Marseilles! Are you from Marseilles?" "Are you from Napoli?" "Genoa?" "San Lorenzo?" "Beaumont de Jaspre?" "Amsterdam?" "Paris?" "London?"

London? Had he said London? She stopped and her head swiveled about seeking the face to match the voice. "Who said London?" she demanded.

"I am Aidan St. Michael, Lady Bliss. My husband is Conn O'Malley of Innisfana Island! Tell him where I am, I beg ye!"

Rashid al Mansur grasped Aidan's arm, and dragged her forward. "Do you want to start a riot, copper-haired woman? Whenever new captives are unloaded from the ships the slaves in the harbor attempt to elicit information as to who they are, and where they're from. It doesn't mean that they themselves are from those places. Hurry now! The jenina is just up ahead."

"How could any of those poor creatures tell yer husband anyfing?" said Rosamund. "If they ain't chained to some oar, they got manacles around their feet. I thought ye was a practical woman."

Aidan said nothing, but her hand itched to smack Rosamund. The child was far too bold for her own good. Rashid al Mansur led them through an archway, and into the tiled courtyard of a low white building.

"Take off your sandals," he ordered them.

The tiles felt deliciously cool beneath her feet, and Aidan followed the captain across the courtyard which had a lovely bubbling fountain in its center, and into a small square room.

"Wait here," he commanded them, and hurried out.

"Sweet Jesu," wept Meg, "in my wildest dreams I could never have imagined what just happened to us!"

"Nuffing happened to us," snapped Rosamund. "At least not yet. All we did was walk the short distance from the ship to here."

"Naked!" sobbed Meg. "Naked, with men shouting and calling to us! God only knows what they said!"

"They said nothing that would have distressed ye had ye been able to understand them," said Aidan with more calm than she was feeling. "They were simply poor captives like ourselves, calling out their names, and where they came from because they were curious as to where we came from, Meg."

"What is going to happen to us now?"

Aidan turned surprised for the question had come from little Pipere. She stroked the child's head, and said, "I am not certain, Pipere, but I believe that the governor of this place is allowed the first pick of the captives. Then we are sold in the market."

"Will Rosamund and me be separated, me laidy?"

"I don't honestly know, Pipere, but I would expect so."

Rashid al Mansur reentered the room. "Come!" he commanded them. "The dey has arrived, and wishes to see you."

They followed him into a large room with arched windows that looked out over the harbor. The building, Aidan realized, was built on a hillside.

At one end of the room there was a dais, and two men sat upon the pillows of the dais. One was an elderly man with a snow-white beard, and sharp, brown eyes. He was dressed in an embroidered robe of black with red and gold roses upon it. The other man was garbed simply in a white robe.

"The old man is the dey," hissed Rashid al Mansur. "The other man is his friend, the famous astrologer, Osman Bey." Then the kapitan reis prostrated himself before the dey. "Hail, my gracious lord! Representative of he who is the Shadow of Allah upon this earth!"

"Rise, Rashid al Mansur," came the reedy voice of the dey. "As I came from my palace the city was already abuzz with word of the fine merchandise you have brought us. It will be a pleasure to view your captives. The city is yet awash with a surfeit of Portuguese captives from our recent victories, and not a beautiful woman among them. The price of slaves has been driven to an all-time low, and they are not even worth the little we must feed them. Your females are a welcome delight."

"They are English, my lord. The three younger ones are virgins, attested to by my own physician. They are ten, eleven and thirteen respectively." He prodded Meg, Rosamund and Pipere forward hissing, "Display yourselves for the dey and his guest!"

"Blonds," sighed the elderly dey. "They will bring a fortune on the open market, Rashid al Mansur. Certainly Allah has smiled upon you!"

"My lord has the right of first choice," said the kapitan reis.

The dey sighed again, this time loudly. "Alas I am an honorable man, and the price of these exquisite virgins will be far too much for my purse. Who is the other woman?"

Rashid al Mansur drew Aidan forward, and said with flourish, "This, my lord dey, is an English noblewoman. She is now widowed so alas I cannot claim virginity for her, but look at the color of her hair, her skin, and her eyes! Is she not fit for a king? When have you ever seen such hair? It is the color of burnished copper! And her skin! Like mare's milk! Look into her eyes, my lord dey! They are silvery in color. Behold her form, my lord dey! Is it not the most perfect body you have ever seen?" He had embellished his speech by touching Aidan's hair as he spoke of it, her breasts, her face, and it had taken every ounce of her courage not to scream, and slap his hands away.

The dey leaned forward, and his tongue ran quickly around his lips. "Osman Bey, what think you? She is indeed lovely, and a rarity."

"She is certainly fair," said Osman Bey, "and only once before have I seen a form to rival hers."

The elderly dey arose from his pillows, and came down from his dais for a closer look at Aidan. Into her nostrils poured the scent of sandalwood for his clothing and body reeked of it. Slowly he walked around her. His hand came up to stroke her hair, and he said, "It is like the finest silk, Rashid al Mansur." The dey took Aidan's hand. "Tell her to place her hands behind her head," he said to the kapitan reis, and Rashid al Mansur translated the command to Aidan who reluctantly obeyed. The dey's hands reached up to fondle Aidan's breasts, and tears sprang to her eyes, but he did not notice them. "The skin is most firm, and yet soft. This is a slave of the first rank." He looked at Rashid al Mansur. "What value do you put on this woman, kapitan reis?"

"She is yours by right if you so choose, my lord dey," said the kapitan reis.

"I know that," replied the old man, "but even I have a conscience. Taking a share of a thousand seamen who have been captured in battle, and selling them does not cause me to turn one hair; but this is different. This slave is of great value, and I want her not for myself, but to send as a gift to the sultan. To send my master a gift for which I have paid nothing is to send him nothing. Therefore I would buy this woman from you for a fair market value."

"My lord dey, I do not know what value to place upon the woman for it is not my business to price slaves. Why not call from the bagnio the chief slavemaster, and have him put a price upon the copper-haired woman. I will abide by whatever decision he makes."

The elderly dey agreed, and sent immediately for the chief slavemaster who came quickly, his eyes lighting at the sight of the four women. He had already heard of them for he had spies who waited and watched upon the docks to inform him of the choicest captives being brought for sale.

He prostrated himself before the dey, and only when bidden to arise did he dare to speak. "How may I serve you, my lord dey?"

"Give me a fair market value on the red-haired woman," said the dey. "I would send her to our master, Sultan Murad. Such a valuable and rare female will please him, and do Algiers honor."

The dey's words told the chief slavemaster that he actually did desire a fair-value price on the slavegirl for to send the sultan a woman of insignificance would be an insult. Walking over to where the four stood he pulled Aidan from the group, and looked her over with a careful and trained eye. "Is she a virgin?"

"No."

The chief slavemaster knelt, and put his hand between Aidan's legs. It was too much. She could bear no more of this! She twisted away, pressing her legs tightly together. The chief slavemaster said nothing. He simply signaled to two of the dey's men-at-arms who coming over, pinioned

Aidan tightly between them so that she could not struggle, and the chief slavemaster resumed his examination of her most intimate parts.

"Her body is fresh and clean, my lord," he said matter-of-factly, and, he thrust a finger within Aidan, who at that simply swooned away. "Her passage is tight. She has not been used greatly," he said.

The two men-at-arms held the half-fainting woman between them as the chief slavemaster continued. With expert hands he ran his fingers over her breasts, nodding with satisfaction as the nipples puckered beneath his light touch. He slid his hands over her torso, and around to feel her buttocks. His knowledgeable hands explored her legs, and her feet, and then he stood again. Aidan was conscious now, but she wished she weren't. The slavemaster peered into her eyes, and then to her surprise pried open her mouth to view her teeth. Lastly he felt the weight and texture of her hair, and nodding satisfied said to the dey, "This is definitely a slave of the first ranking, my lord. She will be a very expensive gift for Sultan Murad, but one that he will undoubtedly gain much pleasure from, and therefore remember with kindness the giver. She is worth ten thousand pieces of gold, even without her virginity."

The dey winced, but nodded. "Very well," he agreed, and turned to Rashid al Mansur. "So be it, kapitan reis. I will purchase the woman from you."

Rashid al Mansur was jubilant. Normally the dey would have deducted ten to twelve percent of the purchase price as his due, but he would not do that in this case because the copper-haired woman was to be a gift for the sultan. That percentage along with his own percentage would be his! He turned to Aidan. "You have brought me luck, copper-haired woman. The dey has just purchased you for ten thousand pieces of gold, and he is sending you as a gift to the sultan! If you are clever, your fortune is made!"

"I don't want to be a gift to anyone!" Aidan shouted. She was suddenly very, very angry. She had been poked, and prodded, and invaded as if she were a prize heifer. "I am Aidan St. Michael, Lady Bliss. I am a wealthy woman of rank, and I will be no one's slave! *No one's!*"

"Ahh," smiled the dey, "she has spirit. So much the better. Phlegmatic beauties can be a bore." Then he turned to his men-at-arms. "Take her to my harem for safekeeping, and remember, she is a gift for Sultan Murad. If she tells me you have touched so much as a hair on her head it is your heads that will roll in the dust. Do you understand?"

The men-at-arms nodded. "We hear and obey," they chorused, and then they dragged Aidan, struggling, and shrieking, from the room.

"My treasurer will see that you are paid, Rashid al Mansur. Go to him after noontime prayers."

"Thank you, my lord dey," said the kapitan reis, and bowing he turned to leave with his other captives.

"A moment, Rashid al Mansur."

The sea captain stopped, and turned back to the dais. "My lord?" It was the powerful Osman, the famous astrologer, who had spoken to him.

"I am curious, Rashid al Mansur, as to where you have obtained a high-born Englishwoman. Did you capture her vessel?"

"No, my lord Osman. I am a merchant, not a man of war. I trade frequently in London, bringing the English oranges, and moroccon leather goods, sometimes cods of musk for perfume making. I return with their fine wool, and tinware, and raw tin. As you may know I began my life in Spain. My cousins are agents for the Spanish king there, and often the opportunity to obtain a blond English virgin comes my way."

"I had heard," remarked Osman, "that you frequently brought back fair maidens, but this woman is slightly older, and not the sort of female that I imagine you would come in contact with."

"You are correct, my lord. This was a rare opportunity. The lady in question is indeed a noblewoman. Her husband's family had given offense to the Spanish king, and he contrived to make it appear as if they were involved in a plot against the English queen. The lady's cousin was involved in the plot, and planned when her husband was killed to marry the lady and thereby gain her wealth. What he did not expect was that the English queen would confiscate the lady's wealth as part punishment for the alleged crime of her husband's family. So this gentleman decided to sell his cousin to me to gain some of the monies he lost by the queen's action.

"She, however, claims that her husband has not been executed, and that the English suspected a false plot, and told her to tell her cousin that she was penniless so they might catch him, and his accomplices. She is a very quick-witted female, and she is fighting hard against her fate."

"They are always like that at first," said the dey. "European women can be very stubborn."

"The husband's family must have given great offense to the Spanish king that he would bother to involve himself in so byzantine a plot," noted Osman, the astrologer. "What was their name? Do ye know?"

"They were Irish," said Rashid al Mansur. "I don't think she ever mentioned their name . . . wait, this morning as we came here a captive called out that he was from London, and she called back that her husband was Conn O'Malley. That is all that I can tell ye except that her cousin's name was FitzGerald."

"Thank you, Rashid al Mansur," said Osman calmly, but he felt anything but calm. *O'Malley!* Allah! Was it a coincidence, or was the woman related to his friend Skye O'Malley? What could he do to help her! He couldn't! His friend, the dey, had just paid ten thousand pieces of gold for this woman, and she would be on her way to the sultan in Istanbul in a very short time. There was simply no way he could prevent it, but he might at least be certain of who she was. He smiled at the dey. "Will you allow me to visit the slavewoman you have purchased for the sultan, my old friend? I shall do her chart for you so you may be certain she will bring good fortune to the sultan."

"An excellent idea, Osman! Why did I not think of it, but what if her chart is not in sympathy with his majesty? I have paid a fortune for her!" The dey's forehead puckered with worry.

"If her stars should prove to be wrong you can always sell her for even more than you paid for her," said Osman soothingly, "but I sincerely doubt you will have to resort to such tactics. It is very unlikely she will prove to be the wrong woman for him."

"You are right, Osman, as you always are. Yes, yes! You may come to the palace this afternoon, and see the woman, but how will you converse with her?"

"It has been my experience that European noblewomen speak several languages other than their own, at least French, and I am as you know, quite conversant in French."

"Your wife, of course! How is she?"

"Well, and the children also."

"You will give my greeting to the lady Alima."

"She will be honored, my lord."

The two men departed the jenina, the dey returning in his litter to his palace, and Osman Bey in his litter to his home high above the city. The dey was delighted with his purchase for he knew the sultan's capacity for beautiful women. It was said that his eunuchs were kept constantly busy scouring the slave markets of Istanbul for new and lovely women to fill his harem. This woman, the dey thought with satisfaction, was a rare creature with her red hair. It was said that his favorite, a woman named Safiye, had red hair as did the sultan himself. This slender highborn beauty with her milky skin, her gorgeous hair, and her fine breasts would catch his eye easily. The dey felt satisfaction coursing through his tired old veins. Undoubtedly the sultan would show his pleasure with his loyal servant, who knew what form that reward might take. The dey smiled to himself within the privacy of his litter. He had been generous with his master. Why should he not be as generous with himself? He would send his chief eunuch to the state bagnio to purchase the eldest of the three blonds Rashid al Mansur had for sale. It was true she would cost a fortune, but he was an old man, and how many years did he have left?

Aidan seeing Meg brought into the harem of the dey's palace late that morning ran to her young friend, and put her arms about her. Meg was trembling violently, and she burst into tears as Aidan's embrace tightened about her. Aidan let her cry, and when she had finally wept for some minutes her sobs gradually died, and she looked up into Aidan's face saying, "It was awful, my lady! It was awful!"

"I know," Aidan answered her realizing from her own experience of this morning just what the gentle girl must have gone through, "but it's all over now, and you are safe."

"Rashid al Mansur was almost beside himself with delight," Meg said. "He told me that the dey himself purchased me. That I am to be the concubine of that old man! I cannot bear it!"

"It could be worse, Meg. The dey appears to be a kindly gentleman. I do not think he will hurt you, and the plain truth of the matter is that you don't have any choice now. What if you had been sold into a brothel, Meg? But tell me, what of Rosamund and Pipere? Do you know what happened to them?"

"Yes," came the reply. "They were purchased by the same man for the slavemaster sold them together as twins. The man who bought them is said to be one of the wealthiest men in the city, but he is a gross, fat creature with eyes like a pig. Rosamund laughed when the sale was made final. She said once she learned the ways of this place she'd have her fat master under her thumb if he wanted her under his bulk. She wasn't one bit afraid, my lady."

"No," said Aidan, "she wouldn't be. I have no doubt that she'll do exactly what she says she'll do."

"What will happen to us, my lady?" Meg asked tremulously.

"Your future is settled, Meg. You belong to the dey, and you will become his mistress. Mine is not so simple. I am being sent to Istanbul to the Turkish sultan as a gift from the dey."

"I will kill myself!" said Meg beginning to sob again.

"What would that solve?" Aidan demanded.

"At least I should not have to submit to the shame of being the dey's kept woman!"

"That seems to be the normal thing here, Meg," said Aidan. "This place we are in now is called a harem. It is the women's quarters of the palace. I have already learned that the dey has two wives, and over a hundred concubines!"

"How did you learn all that?" Meg was astounded.

"I speak French," said Aidan, "and French seems to be the universal language here whatever a lady's native tongue. Even the eunuchs speak it. They are the men you see guarding us. They are gelded so they are considered safe to be around the dey's women. That is another custom of the place."

Meg was incredulous. "Gelded men! What a terrible custom! This is a frightening place. Did you see the heads in the wall niches where you enter into the palace? Some of them were still bloody, and there were flies all over them."

"I saw them," said Aidan quietly. "They were slaves who rebelled against their masters. They were caught and punished. That, too, is the way here. Justice, it seems, is swift."

"I am so afraid," said Meg.

"You don't have to be, Meg. The women here tell me that the dey is a good master, and a kindly one. You can be very comfortable here if you will just not fight it." Aidan was amazed with herself. What was she telling this poor child? But then what chance did poor Meg have of ever returning to England, and if she did what did she have to return to? Better she convince her to make her peace with her fate so that she could get on with her life. "The women here tell me that the dey is very generous to his ladies. They have beautiful clothing, and jewelry, the finest foods, and even a little allowance with which to purchase trinkets from the market women who come here to sell their wares."

"I am used to living on a farm," said Meg. "I miss my animals."

"I am sure that if you make the dey happy he will allow you to have a cat. Many of the women do. They are considered sacred to the Prophet."

"Will they force us to renounce our Christian faith, my lady? I could not bear to be tortured!"

"Then agree to whatever they ask you, Meg. God knows what is in your heart, and who is to know if you pray to our Lord Jesus in secret?"

A young eunuch came up to them, and said in soft French, "My ladies, I have been ordered to escort you to the baths. Please to follow me."

"We are to go to the baths," said Aidan to Meg, and taking the girl's hand she followed the eunuch from the little room where they had been kept.

The baths in the dey's harem were spacious, and cool. The walls were pale gold marble, and the floors were blocks of green and gold marble. The room was crowded with women of all sizes, shapes, and colors, all nude, and all being bathed or otherwise cared for by an army of slave-women. Their arrival was greeted with curiosity for there was not a great deal to do in the dey's harem. A lovely older woman with dark hair, just beginning to silver, came up to them, and Aidan bowed saying to Meg, "This is the lady Zada, the dey's first wife. My lady, this is the maiden who was with me on my voyage. Alas, she does not understand any language but our own, but I will attempt to teach her in my time here."

The dey's eldest wife smiled at Meg. "She is lovely. Tell her we welcome her to our house. Now you will wish to bathe the filth of your long journey from your bodies so I will not keep you. The slaves have been ordered to give you the best of care, especially to you, my lady, for you are going to our master, the sultan." The lady Zada touched Meg's cheek gently, and then passed on her way out of the baths.

"The dey's wife welcomes you," said Aidan.

"That was his wife?"

"His first wife. His second wife is that young woman with the long dark hair over there." Aidan pointed discreetly. "The one with the little girl. The child is their daughter."

Meg said nothing more, but Aidan could tell that she was considering her position. None of the women surrounding them looked unhappy or abused. There were several small children with their mothers in the bath, and there seemed to be no distinction between wives and concubines or their children.

They were bathed carefully, and a pink paste smelling of roses was smeared over their body hair. When it was washed off some time later they found themselves totally smooth-skinned. Aidan didn't bother translating the rather ribald remarks she overheard in the baths. The dey, it seemed, enjoyed his ladies, and was considered quite potent a man. It had been some time since he had acquired a female for himself, and the women of his household speculated on the chances of Meg's finding favor with him. If she did her life would be a joy, but if she did not one of two things could happen. She would be left alone and ignored for the rest of her days, or she would be quickly resold. That much, Aidan thought, she would warn poor Meg about. The girl was timid by nature, and would therefore want to stay where she was rather than face another unknown future.

When they were once again in their little room Aidan explained this to Meg. The young Kentish girl looked distressed.

"But how shall I go about pleasing the dey so that he will not sell me again? I know nothing of men."

"Surely you've seen the animals mate on your father's farm," said Aidan.

"Is it like *that*?" Meg seemed shocked.

"Well not quite," Aidan admitted. Lord, she had to help this poor girl to understand. After all, hadn't Skye helped her? She drew a deep breath, and explained the procedure of passion between men and women as far as she knew it. "There may be some pain the first time," she warned Meg, "but it's not severe, and it goes away quickly. I can only tell you from my own experiences for a year ago I was as innocent as you are now. You should like it. I do."

"Why?" said Meg disconcertingly.

"Why?" Aidan laughed. "Because it makes you feel so wonderful, so incredibly marvelous; so like nothing you have ever felt before, and don't ask me to explain that for I can't. No woman can. There are no words to really describe what it is like between a man and a woman, Meg. It simply is."

Late in the afternoon they were served a meal, their first since they had entered the dey's palace. There was a small chicken for them to share, and saffroned rice with bits of fruit in it, and the ever-present flat bread, and a bowl of both green and ripe olives in oil, and a bowl of figs. They were given water flavored with some sort of fruit that reminded Aidan of oranges, but wasn't. When they had eaten, and bathed their faces and hands, the young eunuch assigned to them told them that they should rest.

"It is rumored that our lord will call the blond virgin to him tonight, but I have not yet been informed officially," he said.

"Are we to be given any clothing?" Aidan demanded boldly.

"When the blond virgin finds favor with our master she will be rewarded suitably. As for you, copper-haired woman, a wardrobe is even now being prepared for you to take to Istanbul with you. For now, however, you can remain as nature intended you."

Aidan passed all of this on to Meg who said with surprising insight, "It is obvious that everything depends upon the will of the master here, my lady. I can see I am really going to have to please him. When do you think he will ask for me?"

"Perhaps tonight," said Aidan, "and since we are both in the same position, Meg, I think it is now time that you called me by my given name, which is Aidan."

"Tonight!" said Meg. "It is so soon!"

"If you are still afraid then it is better to get it over with sooner than later," Aidan remarked wisely.

They came for Meg as the moon rose over the city of Algiers. She was garbed in pale pink pantaloons that were edged with silver at the ankles, and at the waist which actually fit low over her hipbones. A tiny bolero edged in silver and crystal beads was her only other garment, and it was extremely skimpy being sleeveless, and ending just below her breasts. The eunuch brushed her pretty silvery-blond hair, and darkened her eyes with kohl to make them stand out even more. Then he fastened a sheer piece of veiling across her face which fell from the bridge of her nose to just below her chin. Her feet were left bare, and they made a lovely little sound as they followed the eunuch off down the corridor.

Well, thought Aidan, there is nothing more I can do for her. Hopefully her innocence will please the old man, and he will be kind to her. It was her own situation she was going to have to worry about now. Having been considered just barely pretty her entire life she had never really taken to heart Rashid al Mansur's ravings about her value. She had expected to be purchased by some rich man who would welcome the opportunity of growing richer with her ransom. A ransom that would have brought him much in exchange for the tall, rather plain girl that she considered herself. She was more than startled to find herself considered a rare beauty by these people, and more than distressed to learn that she was to be sent even further east than she already was. Did she dare to offer the dey a ransom for her person, but on reflection she knew she couldn't. It wasn't money the dey wanted, it was favor with his own overlord, the sultan. What was she going to do?

"Lady."

She started for she had not even heard the young eunuch come into the room. "What is it?" she asked, looking up at him.

He handed her a garment. "Please to put it on, lady. You have a guest. The great astrologer, Osman, has come to plot your stars so the dey may be certain that your future is with the Shadow of Allah upon this earth."

Here was a possibility, thought Aidan. With luck this astrologer would find her incompatible. She arose, and slid the shapeless garment over her. It was really quite lovely, of a pale green silk embroidered in darker green and gold threads about the neck, and on a wide band that encircled the sleeves. She smiled wryly at herself in the mirror that the eunuch held up for her so she might see herself.

The eunuch smiled himself. "Properly garbed," he said, "you are even more beautiful, lady."

Aidan chuckled. "I don't think anyone has ever called me beautiful in my whole life," she said.

"Are the men of your land blind then, lady? I cannot understand that. You have a delicacy of features that is rare, and in your face is strength, another rarity. You will be a great woman one day."

He left her for a moment, and she awaited his return with the astrologer he called Osman. She didn't know what it was that she had expected, but the man who came through the door was not it. He was a man of medium height and build with a totally bald pate and a round moon face. She had expected a large and blustering charlatan, not this kindly looking man with warm golden-brown eyes.

"Good evening, my lady," he said in a quiet, yet surprisingly commanding voice. "I am Osman the astrologer. Here in the city of Algiers I have some small fame, and the dey has asked me to consider your nativity in the stars with relation to our gracious lord, Sultan Murad, the third of that name."

"Is it proper to ask you to be seated, Master Osman?" said Aidan.

"It is, and if you will instruct this young eunuch, he will bring us coffee, and perhaps even some sweets."

Aidan looked at the eunuch. "Let it be as he says," she ordered, and then as the eunuch left the room she said, "How is it that you speak French, Master Osman?"

"Many here in Algiers do, my lady, but in my case, my wife is French. She was a captive many years ago. She was given to me on the occasion of the marriage of two of my dear friends. They wished to celebrate their happiness with their guests." Then Osman arose, and going quickly to the door, opened it, and looked outside. Seeing nothing he closed it again. "There is no time for me to be subtle, my lady. Tell me quickly before the eunuch returns. Why did you shout the name of O'Malley this morning on your way to the jenina?"

"My husband was born Conn O'Malley," said Aidan, and her heart began to pound. Why was he asking her this thing?

"Does your husband have a sister named Skye?"

"Yes!" breathed Aidan. "Oh, Osman, how is it you know this? Have you consulted the stars in my behalf already?"

"Skye O'Malley is an old and dear friend of mine. Now tell me swiftly how it is you came to be here."

The words tumbling frantically over one another Aidan told Osman her tale, and when she had finished the astrologer groaned. "What a coil! What a coil!"

"Please, Master Osman, can you help me? I will pay the dey any ransom he so desires!"

Osman shook his head. "There is rarely ransom for women from Barbary, and in your case the dey plans to send you to his master in Istanbul. There is no amount of ransom that could assuage his disappointment should he be denied his desire."

"Can you not tell the dey that my stars are not compatible with those of the sultan?" Aidan begged.

Osman smiled a small smile at her hopeful tone. "No, my child, I cannot, for I am an honorable man, and the dey trusts me. You must go to Istanbul as I suspect it is your fate, but I will promise you that I will inform Skye of where you are. She is not without power, and I believe that your queen is even now seeking to establish formal relations with the Sublime Porte as the Sultan's government is known. If anyone can work the miracle that you need it is Skye O'Malley. Now, tell me your name, my child."

"I am Aidan St. Michael, Lady Bliss. My husband, Conn, took my name upon our marriage for my father had no sons."

Osman nodded. "I understand," he said. "Now, Aidan, we must do what I promised the dey I would do, and that is chart your stars. Tell me your birthdate, my child."

"I was born on the nineteenth of August in the year of Our Lord fifteen hundred and fifty-four."

"Do you know what time you were born, my child? By that I mean the hour."

"Yes, Master Osman, I do. I was born at dawn, just a few minutes before five o'clock in the morning, at *Pearroc Royal*, which is just a few miles west of Worcester. My mother always told me that she remembered pushing me forth from her body, and seeing the sun crawl above the horizon at the same moment. She said that she was watching the sky for it helped to take her mind from the pain of childbirth."

"Excellent!" said Osman. "Knowing the moment of your birth helps me to make a more exact chart of your stars for you. I can be far more accurate this way, and there is less chance for error. By chance do you know when your husband was born?"

"Why do you want Conn's birthdate, Master Osman?"

"For comparison, my child," he answered her without hesitation, but in truth Osman sought to learn if Aidan and Conn were meant to be reunited, and hopefully a comparison of their natal charts would tell him this.

"My husband is a year younger than I am," said Aidan. "He was born on Innisfana Island, just after ten o'clock in the evening on the twenty-third of June, fifteen hundred and fifty-five."

At that moment the eunuch chose to return with tiny cups of boiling hot coffee in thin eggshell cups, and a plate that held tiny gazelle pastries which were confections of ground nuts, sesame seeds, and honey. Osman showed Aidan how to drink the coffee, adding small chips of ice to it to cool it should she not like it hot, and adding sugar to it to sweeten its sharp, bitter taste. Aidan had never tasted coffee, and she wasn't certain that she liked it. Osman, however, gulped his little cup down after lacing it liberally with sugar. When he had finished he arose, and said with grave courtesy, "Now that I have the proper information I can prepare your natal chart, my lady Aidan. Should it be favorable then you will indeed be the most fortunate of women." His words were for the benefit of the attending eunuch. His golden-brown eyes said another thing. It was almost as if she could hear his calm voice reassuring her; easing her fears.

"Thank you, Master Osman," she said softly.

"I will not fail you," he said, and then he was gone through the door of the small chamber.

"Do you know how fortunate you are?" said the eunuch excitedly. "He is the most famous astrologer in all the East. Kings come from beyond the great southern desert to gain his wisdom! The dey will not make a serious decision without the advice of Osman, yet for all his influence he is a modest and well-liked man. When the sultan learns that you come to him with not only fine clothes and jewels, but a natal chart prepared by Osman himself, your value will increase even more!"

"He seems a kind man," said Aidan, not knowing what else she should say.

The eunuch's eyes rolled up in his head for a moment. He was a coffee-colored man and his whole face expressed its astonishment at her apparent stupidity. Then with a mild snort of derision he went about the business of preparing the room for Aidan to sleep. From a cubicle built into the wall he drew forth a mattress, and unrolled it. Next came a coverlet of medium weight for the night could be cool. On a tiny low table next to the mattress he placed a goblet of fruit juice and a small plate of sticky, sweet candy of a gummy consistency. "You will be comfortable now, lady," the eunuch said. "I will awaken you in the morning. Do not be tempted to stir from the room in the night for the dey looses his hunting cats within the harem at midnight, and they are trained to attack whatever moves in the darkness." With a bow he left her.

It had not occurred to her to leave her small cubicle, but she was glad that the eunuch had imparted that little piece of information. How clever, she thought, of the dey to use his animals as guards, and far more effective. They could not be bribed or cajoled like humans could be, and even if one attempted to lure them with meat one would have to find them first. It was more likely you could be attacked before that happened. It was obvious that Meg would not be returned that night, and so there was nothing else to do but settle down and go to sleep.

Lying down Aidan thought back over the last few weeks. How could she and Conn have been so entangled in such a plot? She should have refused Lord Burghley's request that she tell Cavan she was penniless. She should have obeyed her husband, and not seen the wretch again. She should have gone home to *Pearroc Royal*, but then Lord Burghley's request had seemed such a simple one, and who could have imagined Cavan FitzGerald would have acted as he had. Certainly not Aidan.

She sighed deeply. Surely with her disappearance they would have realized that Cavan FitzGerald had indeed involved Conn even as Lord Burghley had suspected. Had they released her husband, and was he all right? Osman had said he would not prevent her being sent to the sultan, but he had also promised to tell Skye where she was. Would he keep that promise, or on reflection would he decide not to for whatever reason? She had never heard Skye mention him, but then there was much she didn't know about her beautiful sister-in-law. Aidan fell into a troubled sleep.

Chapter 9

*C*onn St. Michael had learned of his wife's disappearance from her faithful tiring woman. When Aidan had not come home to Greenwood that evening Mag had wasted no time in hurrying back to the Tower of London, and demanding to see her master. The guards were not wont to allow her in at this late hour for she was no one of importance, but Mag with a boldness that surprised even herself had said, "If ye'll not let me see Lord Bliss, I want to see the governor of this place, and ye'd better step lively, my lads, for the information I bring is of vital importance to her majesty's safety!"

The captain of the guard was called, and Mag calmly repeated her speech to him. The captain leaned over and smelt her breath, but there was no wine or ale upon it, and so he reasoned that she must be sober. "If yer wasting my time, woman, I'll see yer put in the stocks for a month!" he threatened. "I'll not be made a fool of before Sir John."

"Then take me to Lord Bliss," said Mag, "and let him decide the importance of my information."

Thinking it over the captain of the guard decided that this was the better course to follow for if the woman was lying her master would have her punished, and the captain would not look silly before his superior. "Very well," he grudgingly allowed, "ye can see yer master," and he ordered one of his men to escort Mag to Conn's cell.

They found Conn dicing with his guards who were delighted for the interruption for they were losing, much to their discomfort. "What is it, Mag?" said Conn arising from the floor where he had been seated.

"Her ladyship ain't come home, my lord. She went to the Swan, and she ain't come back since."

"The Swan!" Conn was instantly alert. "Why did she go to the Swan, Mag? Surely she didn't go to see Master FitzGerald? Why did you let her do such a foolish thing?"

"It weren't me, yer lordship, 'twas that man of the queen's, Lord Burghley. 'Twas he who sent my lady to Master FitzGerald, and now she's not come home!" Mag began to sob, covering her face with her worn hands.

Conn gritted his teeth in frustration. He had to be patient for Mag's story at this point made absolutely no sense whatsoever. "Get Mag a chair, Cluny," he snapped at his serving man, and when Cluny had complied, he gently seated Aidan's tiring woman, and said in what he hoped passed for a calm voice, "Now, Mag. I want ye to tell me exactly what happened when ye left here this afternoon. Begin at the beginning, and leave nothing out."

Mag snuffled a bit, and then she slowly, as if she were very carefully remembering, began to speak.

The clever old fox, thought Conn, as Mag concluded her story. Basically it was a sound plan, but it had been a dangerous thing to do with his wife, something, of course, that William Cecil would not have deeply considered. Lord Burghley's main interest was the queen's welfare. "How did Aidan get to the Swan?" he asked Mag.

"Lord Burghley sent her in his own coach. It was supposed to wait, and bring her safely back to Greenwood, but she never came home." Mag began to blubber again. "She never came home, my lord!"

"Bring me parchment, pen, and ink, Cluny," said Conn. "When I have sent a message to Lord Burghley ye will deliver it, and then take Mag safely back to Greenwood before returning here." He turned to Mag to offer her some small comfort. "We'll find her, Mag, and don't you fret. Master FitzGerald wouldn't harm her. He's a greedy bugger, but I don't believe there is any serious malice in him."

Lord Burghley had been settling down for the night when Conn's message was brought to him. With a sigh he called for his coachman to be sent for, and Lady Burghley with a knowing smile departed for her own bed. "I told ye to wait for Lady Bliss," said William Cecil without any preamble as his coachman entered his study.

"A gentleman comes out of the inn, and says to me that her ladyship was staying to have supper with her cousin, and that I was to have the evening free. I thought that was a funny thing to say to me as the lady weren't my mistress, but I just thanks the gentleman, and comes home, my lord."

"Did this gentleman's speech sound of Ireland?"

"Yes, my lord."

"God's nightshirt!" swore Lord Burghley using a favorite oath of the queen's. What had the villain done? "Yer dismissed," he said to the coachman with a wave of his hand.

"I hopes I didn't do wrong, my lord," said the coachman.

"Nay, Jeffers, ye but did as ye were told which is the best trait in a good servant."

The coachman left the room, and Lord Burghley was shouting for his secretary, an overworked little man who hurried into the room. "Send some men-at-arms to the Swan, by the river, and find out if Master Cavan FitzGerald is still there. If he isn't then find out who was with him, and if there was a lady with them. Hurry!"

The men wearing Lord Burghley's badge were respectfully greeted by the landlord at the Swan. "Yes, indeed! Master FitzGerald is indeed a guest of this establishment. He and his friend have rooms on this very floor, in the rear, for they wished quiet. Aye, a lady came calling earlier, and they are still here." The landlord led Lord Burghley's men down the narrow corridor to the rooms that Cavan had taken, and he knocked upon the door, but there was no answer. After a moment or two the door was opened to reveal the empty rooms. Lord Burghley's men departed back to their master, there to tell him that Cavan FitzGerald, and another gentleman, a foreigner who claimed to be French although the landlord thought he had the look of Spain about him, had disappeared from the Swan along with Lady Bliss.

Lord Burghley was puzzled. What had happened to Lady Bliss? Men-at-arms were dispatched back to the Swan, and its surrounding neighborhood. No one had seen the three, or at least remembered seeing the three. An alley went from the rear courtyard of the inn down to the river, and it was concluded that this had been their route of exit from the Swan. From the muddy riverbank they had probably hailed a passing werryman, but where had they gone from there? Lord Burghley's men spread out, questioning every boatman that they could find upon the river, but there were so many of them. It would take a miracle to find the one who had picked up three passengers at that exact spot, and taken to who knows where.

William Cecil, Lord Burghley, was certain of one thing now. Lord Bliss had not been involved in any plot against the queen. In fact he was certain there had been no real plot at all for other than the butcher and his two sons, Walsingham's agents had found no one else involved, nor had there even been the hint of a Spanish plot against Elizabeth. One interesting thing had turned up, however. The ex-Spanish agent, now imprisoned in the Tower, had been sent a tun of wine. As he had received nothing since the day of his imprisonment the tun had been examined, and a note found within a small earthenware ball that floated within the keg. It read:

Rejoice, brother! I will shortly remove the tarnish ye placed upon our name, and we may hold our heads up once more before our king. Another message will soon follow. Be watchful!

Your brother,
Miguel

It did not make a great deal of sense to Lord Burghley, but Walsingham informed him that obviously Antonio de Guaras had a brother, who was now in England. It appeared that this Miguel de Guaras might be involved with Cavan FitzGerald, but what the real purpose behind their actions might be he would not know until he had them both within his custody. An arrest warrant had already been issued for Cavan FitzGerald. Now a second warrant was signed to seek out the Spaniard. Conn was released from the Tower, and returned to Greenwood to find that Skye and Adam had arrived from *Queen's Malvern*.

"I know that I'm forbidden London and the court," said Skye to her brother when he questioned her presence, "but the court is with the queen on her progress, and Chiswick is not London. I want to speak to Lord Burghley. You and Adam fetch him to me."

"Fetch William Cecil to ye?" Conn was angry and incredulous all at once. "Just like that, Skye? Bring me William Cecil! I never want to see that man again! It is thanks to him that I have lost my wife! My darling Aidan who was the best thing that ever happened to me! My wife, and my expected child! They are both gone!"

Skye's face puckered with sympathy for her youngest brother. She had never seen him look so vulnerable in his entire life. Poor Conn, she thought. The Handsomest Man at Court had fallen in love, and now that love had been taken from him, and his world was crashing about him. She caught his big hands in her slender ones. "Listen to me, Conn! No one in this family can deal better with Lord Burghley than I can. I cannot go to London, nor can I chase after him if he leaves to rejoin the queen which he will undoubtedly do very shortly. His presence here will not ensure Aidan's return, and ye know which way his loyalties lie. He may not have even told ye all the truth of this matter, but he will tell me!"

He looked at her. She was his beautiful and incredibly wise and competent big sister. There had never been a woman like Skye in this world. His handsome face crumbled, and he wept unashamedly. "Help me, Skye! Help me find my Aidan!"

Skye cradled her brother against her bosom, and stroked his hair all the while making soothing noises to him as if he had been a child. "There,

Conn, my sweet baby brother! There, my love. We'll find yer Aidan, I promise ye. We'll find her."

Strangely William Cecil was not surprised to find Skye so close to London as Chiswick-on-the-Strand. At Conn and Adam's request he came readily, grumbling. "Not that I can tell Lady de Marisco anything more than I have already told ye, my lord Bliss. However I know yer sister well, and she will worry this matter like a terrier unless I speak with her."

Arriving at Greenwood, Skye's London house, he noted that country living was obviously agreeing with her. She had put on just the faintest bit of weight, but it was enormously becoming to her. Like his mistress, the queen, Lady de Marisco, was always slender to the point of emaciation in his estimation. A woman should have some meat on her bones. With a courtly bow he took her hand up, and kissed it. It was not something he did for all women for Frenchified manners did not appeal to him, but her hands, like the queen's, were so beautiful. She was wearing a deep blue silk gown trimmed in dainty, handmade lace, and her haunting damask rose fragrance brought back memories of other encounters. "Madame, ye look well. It is obvious that the queen made the right choice for ye in sending ye to *Queen's Malvern*."

"I miss the sea," Skye said which was not so much truth, but she enjoyed being arbitrary in this instance. "Will ye be seated, my lord?" He sat. "Wine? The day is quite warm."

He accepted the wine, and then before she could attack, he did. "Just what is it ye want of me, Lady de Marisco? Ye come dangerously close to disobedience to the queen's will coming so near to London."

"I would have come into London proper if I thought it might help, sir! I have heard from my brother, but now I would hear from you just what ye did to involve my sister-in-law in some plot that has resulted in her disappearance."

"There is no great mystery about it, madame. I asked Lady Bliss to go to Master FitzGerald, and pretend that her wealth was about to be confiscated by the crown for her husband's alleged treasons. My theory was quite simple. I sought to learn if there really was a plot against the queen's life, or if this Cavan FitzGerald was in fact merely attempting to rid himself of yer brother so he might marry his widow, and thereby inherit wealth. There was no danger."

"There must have been," snapped Skye, "for is Aidan not gone off the face of the earth, my lord? Where is Master FitzGerald? Has he turned up?"

"None of the three have been seen since the night that Lady Bliss disappeared," said William Cecil.

"Three? There was a third person? Who was he?"

"The innkeeper at the Swan said he claimed to be a Frenchman, but that he had the dark look of Spain about him. Our agents have only discovered that the ex-Spanish agent, Antonio de Guaras, has a brother, Miguel, now in England. We believe that he and Master FitzGerald are involved, and warrants have been issued for both."

"But why this elaborate charade of a plot?" fussed Skye. "The Spanish would not help the bastard get of an Irish priest simply out of the kindness of their hearts. I wonder . . ." She stopped for a long moment considering, and Lord Burghley smiled to himself. He could almost see her facile mind working. "My O'Malley half-brothers," Skye began again, "have harried Spain hard in the new world. They have captured more of the dons' rich galleons, and brought more treasure to England than Drake and Hawkins combined. It is possible this plot was devised in order to stop them? If England had executed Conn, would his brothers have been willing to enrich England's queen?"

"You make a good point, madame," William Cecil answered her, "and it is entirely possible, but I am satisfied that there was no plot against the queen, and that yer brother is quite innocent of any wrongdoing. That is the only thing that matters to me. If the Spanish have a grudge against ye and yers, Lady de Marisco, that is yer problem, and not the queen's."

"While that is comforting, my lord," said Skye, her voice edged in sarcasm, "it does not tell us what happened to Lady Bliss. Have any bodies washed up from the river that could not be identified?"

"No, Lady de Marisco," came the answer.

"What ships sailed that night from the London pool?" asked Skye.

"Ships? Why I do not know, madame. Do ye think that Master Fitz-Gerald might have kidnapped Lady Bliss? What on earth for? She told him that she was penniless."

"I don't know what for, my lord, but Aidan seems to have disappeared. No trace whatsoever can be found of her here. Therefore the possibility exists that we cannot find her because she isn't here. Ye've checked the werrymen up and down the river?"

"It is impossible to talk with all of them although we are trying, madame."

"Have ye offered a reward, my lord?"

"A *reward?*" Lord Burghley looked startled.

"It is the only sensible thing to do, my lord. Ye cannot go to all the werrymen, but offer a reward for information, and more than likely the werryman who took the three will come to us."

"Madame, I can no longer have anything to do with this matter personally. I must rejoin the queen at Long Medford where she is meeting with the French delegation with an eye toward marriage to the Duc d'Alençon. Yer family, however, will have the total cooperation of her majesty in yer search, and ye, madame, I will give leave to enter London if ye must, provided that her majesty is not there. Once this matter is resolved, however, yer banishment is restored until the queen lifts it."

"Ye are too kind, my lord Burghley," Skye said with a sweet smile that did not fool William Cecil for a moment. "We shall indeed deepen and intensify our search. So the queen seeks a French alliance again? The little duc is but half her age, but a charming boy." Skye smiled again.

"Of all who know her, madame, myself excluded, I think ye know her better than any," said William Cecil.

"There will be no marriage," said Skye. "She seeks but a summer's diversion. She is growing old as we all are, and she is momentarily frightened. She longs for her youth. What good would a marriage do at her age, my lord? Certainly she is not capable of bearing children?"

"The physicians assure us she can," said Lord Burghley, "and I am not so certain this time that she is not serious about marrying. A legitimate heir of her body would end all these intrigues."

"I look to be amazed," said Skye dryly.

The faintest of smiles touched Lord Burghley's lips, and then was gone so quickly that neither Skye, nor Adam, nor Conn was certain it had ever really been there. William Cecil took his leave of them, and they knew that whatever had happened to Aidan, it was now up to them to find her. They would not be hindered, but neither would they really be helped in any way.

Several criers were hired, and they paraded up and down the riverside offering a reward for any werryman who could tell them whether he had taken three passengers to a ship in the London pool on the night in late June. Adam had already contacted the portmaster, and obtained the information that five ships had left the London pool the night of the twenty-fourth. Several weeks went by, weeks in which no information at all was obtained, and Conn began to lose weight with his worry. Each day the criers repeated their offer, and each day the reward was sought by several werrymen, but none had the right combination of passengers, or the correct day, or had actually taken passengers meeting the correct descriptions to any ship. Skye was beginning to wonder whether her quarry had left London at all, or if they had left it by land rather than by sea, to depart from another English port.

Finally one day when a month had gone by a werryman came to the door at Greenwood, and claiming to have the information they sought was admitted. Hat in hand he had knelt before Skye, but she had urged him up.

"Did ye listen carefully to the crier, man? Do ye know what it is we seek?"

"Aye, m'lady. I took a lady and two gentlemen to a ship in the London pool on the night of June twenty-fourth, and strange I thought it was at the time, but a man like me don't question his betters. One gentleman, he had a quick tongue he did, was Irish, I believe. The other, he didn't talk loud enough for me to really tell, but he was a foreigner, of that I'm certain."

"What of the lady?" said Skye.

"I couldn't really see her, but she was unconscious. Her husband, the Irish fellow, said that she was unused to fine wine, and had gotten drunk. When they took her aboard the ship her hood fell back, and I could see that she had red hair."

"It's Aidan!" said Conn excitedly.

"What ship?" asked Skye.

"It was called the *Gazelle*, my lady."

"It's on the list," said Adam. "It's a merchant vessel out of Algiers."

"Algiers?" both Skye and her brother exclaimed together.

"Do I get the reward, my lady?" the werryman asked hopefully.

"Aye," said Skye, "ye do for ye've earned it," and reaching into a casket upon the library table she drew out a purse, and handed it to him. "Have ye got a family?" she asked.

"Aye, m'lady."

"Then give yer wife half of this before ye go out and get drunk," she ordered him with a smile.

His eyes widened slightly at the weight of the purse in his palm, and with a bob of his head he thanked her, and was gone.

"Why would Cavan take Aidan aboard a ship bound for Algiers?" said Conn.

"It is possible that the ship was putting into several ports before it reached Algiers, Conn," said Adam. "We must find out where the *Gazelle* was going before she reached Algiers, or if she was sailing straight for home."

"Why take Aidan at all?" wondered Skye aloud. "And who was the other man in Cavan FitzGerald's company? These are all questions that need to be answered. First let us find out if the *Gazelle* normally puts into London, and if it does perhaps we can learn something about its master."

They were not, of course, happy with what they learned. The *Gazelle* normally traveled between her home port of Algiers and London with no ports of call in between. Although she brought fruit and morocco leather goods and plain leather to England, and carried away wool and tin, it was rumored that her master, a renegade Spaniard named Rashid al Mansur, also traded in young and fair girls. It could not be proved, but innuendo was there. Further digging brought them the name of a brothel keeper who when visited was at first reluctant, but upon the payment of gold coin, admitted that she had sold several blond virgins to Rashid al Mansur, one just several weeks ago before he sailed.

"I don't understand," said Conn when they returned to Greenwood. "Aidan is neither blond, nor a virgin, nor very young, nor a beauty. Why did Cavan FitzGerald take her aboard a vessel bound for Algiers?"

They had no answers, and then a clerk from the trading warehouse owned by Skye and her business partner, Sir Robert Small, arrived at Greenwood one afternoon, asking to see Lady de Marisco. He was shown into her presence, and given leave to speak said,

"One of the pigeons ye use as messengers arrived in the cote just a short while ago. It is not one of our usual birds, my lady, but when we removed its message we found it was addressed to ye. I was sent directly. Shall I await a reply?"

A prickle of excitement went through Skye, and she said, "Tell me, what color was the bird?"

"Brown and white, my lady."

" 'Tis one of the birds Robbie and Khalid el Bey kept when they were in partnership so that they might never be out of touch with one another. The birds had a cote at our house which is now Osman's. What can Osman have to say to me? My ties are totally cut with Algiers now." She opened the message, and unfolded it carefully, smoothing the parchment free of its creases. Slowly her eyes traversed the writing upon the page, and then looking up she said to the waiting clerk, "There is no answer now, but keep the bird that brought this message in readiness. It is to be well fed, watered, and rested."

"Yes, m'lady," said the clerk, and he backed from the room.

"What is it?" demanded Adam de Marisco of his wife.

"Aidan is in Algiers. She was brought in by our friend, Rashid al Mansur, and sold to the dey. He has sent her to Istanbul as a gift to the sultan. What a fool I am! Fair-haired and fair-skinned virgins are indeed prized in the East, but so too are women with fair skin, and red hair! But where are Cavan FitzGerald and his friend in all of this? We will have to go to Algiers!"

"Conn will have to go to Algiers," said Adam quietly. "Ye cannot go, Skye, and ye know it."

"Of course, I must go, Adam. I know Osman Bey, and I know the East."

"Ye are forbidden from leaving England right now, Skye, and I will not allow ye to jeopardize our entire family by running off again. Remember our daughter, Velvet, and what of the promise ye made to yer daughter Deirdre never to leave her again? Conn must go to Algiers to learn more of this, and he can go with Robbie who will be returning from Devon tomorrow. Robbie knows Algiers as well as ye do, and he also knows Osman. Yer brother is a man, and this is his problem. Yer no longer the O'Malley, little girl. Yer first responsibility now is to yer immediate family."

She bit her lip in vexation. "But, Adam, I want to help Conn!"

"Adam's right," said Conn speaking for the first time since his sister had read the message from Osman. "This isn't yer battle, Skye. It is mine. Aidan is my wife, and I am going to have to go to Algiers, and learn what this is all about, and then if she is gone I will go to Istanbul, or wherever, but I will find my wife, and I will bring her home. Our child, too."

Skye looked at her younger brother. "Sit down," she said. "We must talk. We must talk about the East, and how it treats its women, and the fact that Aidan may be forced by another man. How will ye feel, Conn, should ye find yer wife in the sultan's harem? Find Aidan the sultan's newest plaything? Will ye still love her? Will ye still want to bring her home?"

"For God's sake, Skye, what kind of thing is that to ask me?" he demanded.

"It is an honest thing, brother. By the time ye reach Aidan she will have been gone from ye many months. She wasn't a virgin. What if Rashid al Mansur, the sea captain, availed himself of her? It could have happened. The fact that she was newly with child would not have deterred him should he have desired her. What if she catches the sultan's fancy? What will ye do? How will ye feel?"

"I love Aidan," he answered her. "If other men have used her I know it will not have been with her consent. How can I hold her responsible, Skye? I'd rather she'd submit than kill herself in shame. I want my wife back! I'll go where I have to go; do what I have to do; but I will bring Aidan back home, I swear it!"

It was enough, thought Skye to herself. What could Conn know of how a woman really felt, or how she would react under duress, or passion? He could not know what went on in her mind, but it was enough that he wanted Aidan returned to him no matter what had happened to her. From her own experience in the East she believed the sea captain who transported Aidan would have valued her much too highly to have vio-

233

lated her despite what she had said to her brother. The dey would not have touched her since he was sending her as a gift to the Sultan of Istanbul. As for the sultan, there were so many women in his seraglio that there was probably a very good chance he would not see her for months despite her status as a gift from the dey. It was entirely possible that they would manage to retrieve Aidan unscathed. On the darker side was the possibility that they would not.

Elizabeth Tudor might keep Skye O'Malley from the sea, but the very nature of Skye's business ensured that she would be fully informed on the politics of the countries in which her ships traded. The O'Malley-Small fleet had been trading in the Levant, and in Istanbul for years. They had discreetly kept an agent in the capital of the Ottoman Empire for several years, and just three years ago they had been joined by two agents, Sir Edward Osborne and Master Richard Staper, London merchant princes who had decided, having seen the cargoes brought in by Skye and Robbie's ships over the last several years, that perhaps revival of trade with the Levant might indeed be a good thing. The presence of the Osborne-Staper agents along with the O'Malley-Small agent had won a safe conduct for Sir Edward's factor, William Harborne, allowing him free access to the sultan's domains. Master Harborne would be sailing soon for Istanbul.

Skye was aware of all this. Her information was fresher, and usually quicker than the queen's. She knew that the current sultan, Murad III, was a young man ruled by twin vices: his unquenchable lust, and towering avarice. While she could hope that he would never see Aidan, and be attracted to her, there was also the chance that he would. These thoughts, however, she retained to herself. It was easy to get Conn to Istanbul. The seemingly impossible problem was going to be extracting Aidan from the middle of the very sticky web in which she was entangled.

Skye looked at her brother. "I can get ye to Istanbul, and I can do it quickly. First, however, ye must go to Algiers, and speak with my old friend, Osman; but even before that we must consider how to regain Aidan. Ye cannot simply go to Istanbul and tell the sultan ye want yer wife back. In Islam it is not the custom to take the wife of a living man for one's own wife or concubine, but only the most scrupulous of men practice this rule. Although the sultan is called the Defender of the Faith he may well argue that since ye are not a Muslim the rule does not necessarily apply. Actually ye cannot decide what to do until ye have discovered the position in which Aidan is situated."

"I don't understand," Conn said to her.

"Osman writes that the dey is sending her to the sultan as a gift. His harem is, by tradition, large. It is entirely possible he won't ever see her.

On the other hand Sultan Murad is known for his rather large appetite for women. It is said of him that his lust has driven up the price of lovely slavewomen, and that his eunuchs keep the Istanbul bazaars emptied. Therefore she could be presented to him relatively quickly, particularly due to her status as a present from the Dey of Algiers. There is another possibility. The sultan might give her to someone he wished to honor either in Istanbul or elsewhere. The final possibility, of course, is that harshest of all. Aidan could be dead."

"Dead?" He looked horrified.

"She could die in childbirth, Conn. She could resist her fate, and be executed. She could simply not survive the voyage to Istanbul. We must think of all of these things. Osman Bey has the means of communicating with Istanbul for he has many friends there, and is well known through the sultan's empire. In a few days I will release the pigeon he sent with a message to Osman. I will ask him that he learn if Aidan reached Istanbul in safety, and if she still lives. Hopefully that information will await ye on yer arrival in Algiers. Then should all be well, ye must make the voyage to Istanbul. Ye cannot delay for come autumn the seas will not be pleasant as they are now."

"And ye remember, don't ye, my sister, how my stomach detests the sea." He smiled.

"I remember 'tis a wee bit delicate, Conn."

"Delicate?" He roared with laughter. "Aye, 'tis a good word for my belly at sea. *Delicate!* How I remember Brian railing at me for my seasickness when I was a boy. He couldn't understand how I could be sick in all the wonderful excitement of a howling gale from the northeast!"

"Brian," said Skye of her eldest half-brother who was Conn's elder by several years, "doesn't know the meaning of the word, delicate. He is a throwback to some Viking raider who passed through the family at one point. He is blunt, and forthright, and has all the tact of a rampaging bull. Nonetheless he's a good man to have at yer back in a fight. I'm going to send for him, and Shane and Shamus, too, to go with ye to Istanbul."

"He'll not like being under Robbie's command," said Conn knowingly.

"No, he won't. None of them will, but I shall make it worth their while to help ye. Privateering has given them a taste for profit," she noted wisely. "There is no sentiment in our brothers."

"I will furnish them with their profit, Skye. Yer kind to offer, but I am a wealthy man in my own right, and Aidan is my wife."

She was about to debate with him when she remembered Adam's words *Yer no longer the O'Malley.* Swallowing her arguments she said, "Yer right, Conn," and Adam's eyes beamed with approval of her decision.

Conn's elder brothers were sent for, and they came from Ireland, grumbling and complaining. They sailed straight into the London pool where they were met by their sister's barge which took them to Greenwood. She watched them as they came ambling up her lawns from the house's quay.

They were as big as their father had been. Great, shaggy men with bushy black beards, and full heads of thick, black hair. Of course Conn was handsomer by far than his brothers were in their dark plaid trews and sleeveless doeskin jerkins. Wide leather belts with ornate silver buckles girded their waists, and Brian and Shamus each wore a gold earring in their right ear while Shane had rings on every finger of both his hands. Born to the sea they respected her and loved her even more than the women to whom they were wed, crooning or cursing the wild waves they sailed in their Irish Gaelic tongue; or sometimes railing at the waters in a queer mixture of Gaelic and English that the Irish used more and more these days.

"God's toenail," said Conn softly. "Was it so short a time ago I was like them?"

"Four years," replied Skye. "Do ye regret yer decisions?"

"Nay!" he said with such heartfelt expression that she almost laughed.

The brothers each in their turn embraced Skye in a bear hug, and then turned to look at their youngest sibling with something almost akin to admiration, but then Brian, the eldest, said sneeringly,

"Is this perfumed English dandy actually our brother?" Next to him Shane and Shamus grinned foolishly, ever the perfect ciphers of Brian O'Malley.

Conn drew himself up to his full height which was a good inch over the others, and looking down his elegant nose drawled lazily in his best court manner, "Conn St. Michael, Lord Bliss. Do ye think, dearest sister, that these three shaggy beasts are actually capable of following me into Barbary? Better ye let me take them to the bear gardens to fight with the dogs for they surely look like animals, and I could probably win a fortune running them."

"Ye've a quick tongue for a man who's called for our aid, little brother," said Brian in rather good English.

"So ye actually understood me, Brian. Did the others? I'm amazed that ye finally speak and comprehend an intelligible English. Why have ye bothered after all these years I wonder."

"Ye can't run with the English on the Spanish Main, and not learn to speak their accursed tongue," said Brian. "We even have a smattering of French and Spanish. Besides, having spent the last few years fighting with the English rather than against them, I have gained rather a grudging admiration of the bastards." He eyed Conn. "They seem to have done well by ye, little brother."

"Let us go into the house," said Skye. "There is a great deal to discuss, and it looks like rain."

They followed her inside, and into the library of Greenwood. There Adam de Marisco awaited them, and Brian, Shane, and Shamus O'Malley greeted him enthusiastically for he was the one Englishman whom they liked and admired. He settled them comfortably, placing goblets of rich burgundy wine from his mother's vineyards in France in their big paws. A good fire burned in the large fireplace, taking the chill from the room on this damp August day. Skye had been correct, and drops of rain were already beginning to fling themselves against the windowpanes. They drank deeply, and in unison, and then Brian, the leader, looked up, and asked,

"Why are we here? We should be on our way back across the Atlantic at this very minute."

"It's a bad time of year to sail where ye were going," Skye said dryly. "Conn needs yer help, and 'twill take ye into smoother waters for now."

Brian swallowed another draft, and looked at Conn. "Well?" he demanded.

"As I'm certain ye know, for I wrote mother about it last winter, I was married on St. Valentine's Day to Aidan St. Michael. Her mother was Bevin FitzGerald, the daughter of a man named Rogan FitzGerald, a cousin of Elizabeth FitzGerald, the great heiress from Kildare. Aidan's mother died years ago, and her father last year. He left her in the queen's care, and the queen matched us, and saw us wed. In May a man named Cavan FitzGerald, claiming to be her cousin, arrived in England. In late June my wife was kidnapped by this man."

"Sweet Jesu!" exclaimed Brian O'Malley. This was high drama in which his brother was involved. "Let me guess," he said. "He's whisked the lass back home to Ireland, and is holding her for ransom. Ye want us to rescue yer bride, and hang that little FitzGerald sneak from our yardarms. 'Tis done, Conn! Ye may call yerself St. Michael now, but yer still an O'Malley to us."

"I'm grateful for yer attitude, brother," said Conn quietly, "but, 'tis not quite the way it happened. Cavan FitzGerald has taken my wife to Algiers, and sold her into slavery." Then as his three elder brothers stared silent, surprised, and openmouthed, he explained what had happened, ending with "I'll be going first to Algiers, and then on to Istanbul to rescue Aidan. I need the best men I can find to go with me, and who's better than the sons of Dubhdara O'Malley? I'll make it worth yer while financially, and best of all, brothers, ye'll have more than enough adventure to last ye a lifetime. 'Twill be a nice change from the Spanish, I'm thinking."

For several long minutes Brian O'Malley and his shaggy brothers sat mutely, and then Brian said, "We'll take not a pennypiece from ye, Conn, in this venture. If we should pick up a little profit along the way then so much the better, but yer wife is our kin, and we can't take reward from ye for aiding our own sister."

"I'd rather ye accepted my offer of payment," said Conn. "Ye can't raise hell in Turkish waters, Brian. It could endanger Skye's trading company with the sultan. I can't do that."

"Och, man, don't ye worry yer head," said Brian with a grin. "We'll just take a few fat Barbary merchants from the Turks off Gibraltar on our way home. 'Twill pay us for our time, and nothing more."

Skye laughed. "Why, Brian," she said, "I can see ye've developed a sophisticated sense of humor these last years. One thing, however, and I know 'twill chafe ye a bit, but Sir Robert Small must be in charge of this expedition. It isn't that he's a better seaman for he isn't, but he has traded back and forth in the Levant for years, and knows their ways and customs. I hope that ye understand."

"Of course, I understand, Skye," said Brian goodnaturedly. "What the hell do we know of Barbary, or the Turks? Yer Robbie will be invaluable to us, and I promise we'll follow his lead in all matters even if we are better sailors than that little Englishman. When do we leave?"

"I'll want yer ships turned out, scrubbed down, repaired, and provisioned at Conn's expense," said Skye. "With luck we can be ready within ten days to sail. I'll put my people aboard to do the work. Let your men spend the time raising all the hell they want for once ye sail ye must impose tight discipline on them."

Brian nodded. "I'll not disagree with any of that, Skye."

"Ye'll all stay here at Greenwood," she said. "There's no plague in London despite the summer's heat."

"Do ye think we might get to see the queen?" asked Shane O'Malley. "They say she is the fairest woman in Christendom."

"The queen is never in London during this time of year," said Skye to her disappointed brother. "She spends the summer months on progress visiting other parts of her realm. Her people enjoy seeing her."

He looked disapppointed. "I didn't ever expect to put my foot on the soil of this land, but since I'm here I had at least hoped to get a glimpse of the witch's daughter," Shane said.

Skye looked at Adam and both repressed their laughter. Then Skye said, "Elizabeth Tudor's mother wasn't a witch, Shane. She was simply a rather determined woman as is her daughter."

"Well then," he answered her, "what is there to do in this stinking city?"

"I think ye'd enjoy the bear gardens that Conn mentioned earlier. In the summer there are many outdoor entertainments in and around the city. There are archery contests which I think might be of interest to ye; there are fairs and some of the best inns in the world are here in London. Both Conn and Adam can show ye about during yer stay."

The three O'Malley brothers nodded, and Brian said, "Are there women to be had, Skye? We've heard that London whores are buxom and bonnie."

Adam chuckled. "Aye, our lasses have a reputation for being very friendly, Brian. Of course, 'tis been many a year since I've found it necessary, or even desirable to avail myself of such company." He looked to Conn. "Yer experience is surely more recent than mine."

Conn couldn't help but grin. "Aye," he admitted without any reluctance, "it is, and I'll be glad to steer my big brothers in the right direction. One thing, however, Brian. A good whore is an expensive whore. You must understand that. I'll have no embarrassing haggling about the price particularly after ye've partaken of the merchandise."

"In other words," said Brian dryly, "ye don't want us acting like the country bumpkins ye consider us to be."

Conn never batted an eye. "Aye," he said, and Brian laughed.

The O'Malley brothers set about enjoying the vices of London with a good will. Although Adam and Conn had promised to chaperon them, neither man was much for whoring or drinking, and so they merely pointed the three brothers in the correct direction, and in some cases gave them entry into some of the city's better brothels. Washed and barbered, Brian, Shane, and Shamus O'Malley were handsome, presentable men. The gold in their pockets made them even more welcome, and so Skye saw little of them during their stay in London.

Sir Robert Small, Skye's business partner, had arrived from his home, Wren Court, in Devon. He had been away at sea the previous winter when Conn and Aidan had been married, but upon his return he had come to *Queen's Malvern* to see his sister, and had met the bride. He had fully approved of Aidan, and he had said so in no uncertain terms much to the de Mariscos' amusement. In stature he was a small man, his ginger-colored hair was fading, but his bright blue eyes were as sharp as they had ever been.

Looking up at Conn he had said, "Well, the queen has once more done well by ye, Conn, my lad. Yer pretty lass is, to my mind, too good for ye, but I can see she loves ye. Be good to her or ye'll answer to me."

Aidan had blushed becomingly, and Robbie's sister, Dame Cecily, had said, "Everyone who has met Aidan has loved her, Robbie."

Robbie was devastated by the news of what had happened to Aidan. Next to Skye he was the only one who understood the true seriousness of the problem facing them. Conn was beginning to, but as for his elder brothers, it would just be another rollicking adventure. "How the hell are we going to get her out of the sultan's seraglio, Skye?" Robbie demanded one evening just before they sailed. They were seated about the table of Greenwood's family dining room. "Once a woman is incarcerated there, it's impossible to get her out. The Ottoman sultan doesn't ransom slaves. Hell! All the women in his personal harem are captives! I've never heard of any woman once she entered the sultan's harem getting out unless she is sent as a gift to someone the sultan wants to honor, or unless she dies."

"There has to be a way, Robbie," said Conn. "If Aidan lives to reach Istanbul we have got to find a way to rescue her, and my child."

Robert Small pursed his lips, and his brow furrowed in honest thought. Finally he said, "Well, if there's a way, my lad, I cannot for the life of me think of it now, but before we get to Istanbul we had better know."

"Ye'll need a source of ready credit at yer disposal," said Adam.

"Our bankers here in London are a family of Jews called Kira. They have people, usually their family members, in almost every important city in Europe. I am certain they must have someone in Istanbul who can aid us," said Skye. "I will send for them to come to Greenwood, and we will talk to them."

A footman was dispatched almost immediately to the city, and to the surprise of everyone Master Eli Kira returned with him that evening. He was a tall spare man with gray locks and serious dark eyes that nonetheless could twinkle with humor on occasion. He was dressed in a long, fur-trimmed gown of black velvet. Upon his head was a flat velvet cap which was generally worn by all professional city gentlemen, and about his neck was a heavy gold chain of the finest workmanship.

"Having seen the ships docked by yer warehouses being prepared for a voyage," he said, "I had to assume that ye needed to see me before they departed, and I leave myself for France in another day. My brother died in Paris last week, and I must go there to decide which of his twin sons is the more capable of running our business. How may I serve ye, madame?"

"My brother must go to Istanbul, Master Kira, and we need to know if there are any of yer family there from whom we may obtain credit based on our deposits with ye here in London."

"Istanbul? Istanbul, madame, is the center of my family's banking business. Our great-uncle had a small business there many years ago, but it is actually thanks to my aunt, Esther, that our family's business has thrived, and is one of the most important banking houses in the world today. Esther Kira, blessed be her name, still rules the family in Istanbul in this, her eighty-eighth year! Of course, it is her son, Solomon, who is known as the head of the family, but it is really my aunt who controls all. If ye go to Istanbul we can most assuredly be of service to ye."

Skye was curious. "How is it," she asked Eli Kira, "that yer aunt is such a woman of power and means?"

"Aunt Esther and her brother, my father, Joseph, blessed be his memory, were orphaned at an early age. They were raised by an uncle in Istanbul, but as her own father had been a poor younger brother, she had no dowry, and so at the age of twelve she was selling hard-to-find goods to the harem ladies of the rich. She was so successful that her reputation spread, and at the age of sixteen she was allowed entry into the imperial harem. At twenty she met and became close friend of the favorite wife of Sultan Selim, whose son, Suleiman, was to be the next sultan. That lady was the great Cyra Hafise, and her friendship brought incredible fortune to my family. Within the Ottoman Empire we are exempted from paying taxes because of a secret service my aunt rendered to the sultan's family. My aunt named her eldest son, Solomon, after the eldest son of Cyra Hafise, the great ruler, Suleiman the Magnificent. For many years my aunt has not needed to ply her trade among the ladies of the imperial harem, but yet she still does so for I suspect she would be bored sitting in the courtyard of her house telling tales to her great-grandchildren. As she was the friend of the lady Cyra Hafise, so was she friend to Suleiman's favorite, the lady Khurrem and to the favorite of Sultan Selim II, Nur-U-Banu, and to Safiye, who is favorite of the current sultan, Murad III."

Conn felt a prickle of excitement run up his spine. "Then," he said, "perhaps yer aunt will be able to aid me in a rather delicate problem that faces me when I reach Istanbul."

"Conn," warned Skye nervously. "I do not know if it is wise to burden Master Kira with our problems."

"If I'm to have the help of his aunt I'm going to have to confide in him," said Conn.

"No, my lord," said Eli Kira, "yer sister is correct. Do not confide in me. Since I am not going to be in Istanbul, it is not necessary that I know yer problems there. I will send along with yer letter of credit a letter to my aunt saying that ye can be trusted, and that the family should aid ye if they can without endangering themselves. It is better that I know nothing of yer business. If it is a dangerous business then the fewer people who know the better off ye will be."

The matter settled, Eli Kira took his leave of them. He would see that the necessary information and documents be dispatched first thing in the morning. There would be three messengers sent. The first would be a pigeon who would make its way to Paris where its message would be removed, and affixed to another bird who would continue on to the next destination where here it, too, would be replaced by yet another bird and another until the last bird reached Istanbul. The other two messengers would be human. Both would begin their journey by sea, but only the man traveling the southern route through the Mediterranean would go all the way by ship. The other man would go only as far as Hamburg by sea, and from there on he would continue on by horse down through the German states, and into the Ottoman Empire's northernmost reaches and from there on to Istanbul. It was very likely that all three of Eli Kira's messengers would arrive safely in their own time in Istanbul, but three were nonetheless dispatched for safety's sake. There would be no doubt of who Conn O'Malley was when he reached the capital of the Ottoman Empire. The Kiras were totally reliable.

They hadn't seen the three older O'Malley brothers in several days' time, but three days later when they sailed from the pool of London Brian, and Shane, and Shamus were each aboard their own ship as were their loyal crews. It was true that most on that first day were quite the worse for wear, but they were there, and from experience Conn knew that he would rather sail with O'Malley-trained and dependable crews than with any other sailors alive.

Conn had bid his sister and her husband farewell at Greenwood. There had been tears in Skye's blue-green eyes as she had kissed him. He brushed her tears away with his own hand, and said with a wry grin,

"The only danger I'm going to be in, Skye, is from seasickness."

She laughed softly. "Ye were always the worst sailor of us all, and ye a son of Dubhdara O'Malley!"

"The old man's seed was obviously running weak when I was conceived, Skye. I received all the charm God forgot to give my brothers, but a weak stomach in return."

"Take no chances, Conn. Yer no good to Aidan dead, and I know that she is alive. I feel it! Be sure ye give my message to Osman, and tell him I am sorry that I could not come myself, but that I am trying not to struggle against my fate. He will understand." She hugged him hard, kissed him on both cheeks, and said, "Godspeed, my brother, and the Blessed Mother bring ye home with Aidan quickly."

"Don't worry, Skye," he promised her, "I shall return, and with Aidan, I promise ye. It won't be like Niall for I know that is what troubles ye." Hugging her hard he then turned to his brother-in-law, and the two men clasped hands.

"She's said it all," Adam said with a smile, "but then she usually does. Godspeed, lad! Ye'll both be back to us soon, I know it!"

The Greenwood coach took him to the London pool where he was rowed out to Robbie's ship, which was a fairly new vessel that the Devon captain had taken on a shakedown cruise just this winter past. The vessel was called the *Bon Adventure*, and Robbie was full of praise for her speed and maneuverability. Conn would be sharing the captain's quarters on their voyage out with Robbie.

Looking about the spacious cabin Cluny smiled satisfied. "Aye, we'll be comfortable here, m'lord, and 'tis good to feel a deck beneath me feet once again."

Conn said nothing. His stomach seemed to be coping so far, but it did no good to tempt fate. He could feel the motion of the ship as it edged its way among the moored vessels, and swung out into the Thames. "I think I'll go on deck, Cluny," he said. He didn't see Cluny's grin for Cluny knew of the O'Malley shame as Conn's stomach had always been referred to by the people of Innisfana Island. Outside he still felt well with the smell of the river in his nostrils, and secretly hoped that he had really outgrown his embarrassing malaise.

The day was sunny and cool although there was nothing of the autumn to come. A light breeze filled the sails, and the ship moved with a slow and stately gait down the Thames toward the open sea. They passed by the Strand and there upon the lush green lawns of Greenwood stood his sister, her husband, and the entire staff waving their final good-byes, and calling Godspeeds and Good Fortune to him and to his fleet of four ships. He waved back to them, his eyes wet with emotion, and he stood watching them until he could no longer see them for the river curved, and they were suddenly gone.

A little farther on they passed Greenwich, empty now and silent with the court's absence. It was the queen's favorite place, and he understood why as he viewed it from his vantage aboard ship. He felt a small tightness in his chest remembering that it was here that he had first seen Aidan. It was here that they had been wed, and it was from here that they had departed on their journey home to Aidan's much-loved *Pearroc Royal*. He wanted his beloved wife! He wanted her back safely again, and he was going to find her no matter what stood in his path. Had he not once told her that theirs was a love for all time? He prayed that she would hold onto that thought wherever she was.

The landscape ahead was flat and he could see Southend on his left. Beyond that Conn knew was Margate, and then that arm of the open sea called the English Channel. *Bon Adventure* swept out of the Thames with the grace of a dancing maiden and feeling the familiar roll of the seaborne vessel, Conn's heart hammered with the certain knowledge that the greatest adventure he was ever likely to have had finally begun.

Part Three

THE GIFT FROM THE SEA

Chapter 10

~❦~

The warm autumn air caressed her cheek as the ship carrying Aidan to Istanbul neared the great city of Constantine. Although the vessel upon which she traveled had stopped several times to take on fresh water as it had woven itself through the Greek isles, she had not been allowed the privilege of going ashore, and walking about for she was considered too valuable a piece of property to lose to bandits. It had been many weeks since she had put her foot upon firm land, and she was anxious to do so again. Not that her trip had been an uncomfortable one for it hadn't. Indeed everything had been done to ensure her comfort. Still in her entire lifetime she had never felt so confined.

Her every move had been monitored since her purchase by the dey. Her boundaries had been limited in Algiers, and they had certainly been curbed even more aboard this ship which had been her prison since she left Algiers. She had been at the dey's palace for a full week before she had been taken in a closed litter back to the harbor, and put aboard this vessel. Shortly after dawn on her second day in Algiers the door to her room had opened suddenly as she sat up startled, and Meg had reentered the room.

Aidan scrambled to her feet. "Are ye all right, Meg?"

Margaret Browne looked at her friend through somewhat glazed eyes. "I am fine," she said. "Perhaps, tired, but I am fine otherwise."

Aidan had to ask. "Did the dey . . ." she began, but Meg cut her short.

"I am no longer a virgin," Meg said softly. "He is not a young man, Aidan, but he is assuredly a potent one, and he was not unkind."

Aidan took the girl into her arms, and hugged her gently. "If there is anything I can do for ye, or explain to ye, Meg, ye have but to ask. I would have done so last night, but they came so quickly for ye."

"I am fine," the blond girl repeated for a third time, "and I am resigned to spending the rest of my days here with my lord and master. I shall not

247

see Kent ever again in this life. It is not the worst thing that could happen to me, Aidan. I might even have a child. The dey's favorites are still producing children, and a child would mean the world to me. It would be something of my own, my family."

Then Meg had curled up upon the mattress that Aidan had only recently vacated, and fallen asleep. When she awoke late in the day she seemed clearer-headed, and her blue eyes were no longer glazed, but her attitude had not changed. She had made up her mind to accept her captivity, and having done so was now content. "Ye must no longer call me Meg," she said to Aidan later that afternoon. "Meg Browne no longer exists. The dey has said that my name is to be Sadira. It means the Dreamy One, and my lord says I am like a dream come true to him for I have brought back the feelings of his youth."

It was one of the last things that the English girl said to Aidan for shortly afterward the head eunuch came for her to take her to her own apartment, for he said to Aidan pompously, "She has found great favor with her lord and master. May ye do the same with yours." Aidan never saw Meg again.

The young eunuch who had been assigned to her was named Jinji and it was through him that her scant information came. He was a brown-skinned man with classical features, liquid dark eyes, and closely cropped black hair. He was far different looking than anyone Aidan had ever known but she thought him quite handsome. He had been gelded when he had been only three years old, he told her proudly, for the operation that took away his complete manhood was very dangerous, and over half the boys subjected to it died of it. Nevertheless it had rendered him twice as valuable as he would have been by merely having his seed sack removed. Then Jinji went on to show Aidan the beautifully carved tube through which he passed his water. It had been a gift from his former master who had been forced to sell him when he had come upon hard times.

Aidan was astounded, and she had to refrain from laughing for the whole situation was simply ludicrous. Barely less than a year ago she had been Lord Bliss' sheltered daughter. She had thought that her stay at court before her marriage to Conn had opened her eyes to the world, but now she was finding that there were many things that she didn't know, had not even dreamed of, had never even imagined existed. Oh, what wonderful tales she would have to tell when she returned home again, she thought, for she would not give up the hope of going back to England.

"We leave for Istanbul in the morning," Jinji told her on the morning of her sixth day in Algiers, "and I am to go with you!" He was very excited for he had in effect received a promotion within the ranks of his hierarchy.

"What of the star chart that the famous astrologer, Osman, was doing to see if I was to be a fortuitous gift for the sultan?" she demanded of him.

"Oh," Jinji said offhandedly, "it has been done, and Osman will be here this very afternoon to interpret it to you so you may understand your fate more clearly."

"Am I to greet him as I am," she said, "or have the promised clothes finally been made for me? Surely I am not to go to the sultan as I am?"

"Patience, copper-haired woman," he counseled her. "Your new garments will arrive this very day, even before the great Osman has left his house."

"How many times must I tell you that my name is Aidan, Jinji?" They conversed in French which was the only language that they knew in common.

"That name is what you are called in your old world, but when you reach Istanbul you will be named by the sultan or his agha kislar. It is a waste of my time to learn a name you will not use when you are to be given a new name shortly," and nothing she could do would convince him otherwise.

When Osman arrived that afternoon Aidan greeted him garbed in a caftan of peacock-blue silk, which was one of her favorite colors. The sleeves of the garment were embroidered with four-inch bands of gold thread, tiny seed pearls, and crystal beads. There was a matching band about the hem of the caftan and about the rounded neckline before it opened to plunge between her lovely breasts. Upon her feet she wore heel-less sandals of gold kid. Jinji was a skilled hairdresser among other things, and he had brushed Aidan's heavy hair back from her face, and woven it with gold ribbons and pearls into a long, sleek braid which hung down her neck.

"How lovely you look, my child," he greeted her, and plumped himself comfortably amongst the cushions. Looking at Jinji who was busying himself in the hopes of hearing what Osman had to say, the astrologer said, "Get thee gone, eunuch, and do not bother to listen at the door. What I have to say is for this lady alone, and I will know if you have disobeyed me."

Jinji reluctantly bowed to Osman, and hurriedly left the room. With someone else he might have ignored the warning, and placed his ear to the door, but the astrologer was known to have a second sight, and the eunuch would take no chances at turning away the good luck that had so recently begun to shine upon him.

Aidan looked anxiously at Osman. "Jinji says we are to leave tomorrow, Master Osman. Am I indeed to go to Istanbul? Will I not return to England?"

"You are indeed to go to Istanbul, my child, but do not fear for I see in your chart no prolonged contact with Sultan Murad."

"What a pity I must go there at all," Aidan remarked lightly, "if I am not to stay there."

"I did not say that, my child. I said that you would not become involved deeply with the sultan, but there is someone else I see entering your life, a man, not your husband, but someone who will nonetheless have a strong hold upon you. For a time you will have no choice but to yield to this man, but beware him for he is the scorpion, and the scorpion can force the lioness to his will. I am not certain that you can overcome him. There is confusion in your chart, and something else I do not understand. There is rebirth."

"What does it mean, Master Osman? Do you see Conn in my chart?"

"Yes, the Gemini is indeed there, but in the end, my child, it is you who must overcome your barriers. Your fate is in your hands, and yours alone. Others can only be of aid to you, but in the end *you* must gain the final victory."

"Victory over what?" she asked him.

"I do not know, my child, but perhaps it is yourself."

"Master Osman, you frighten me, and I looked to you for reassurance."

"My child," he said, and leaning across the small round table that separated them he patted her head, "the greatest truth I can tell you is that there is only one person in this world upon whom you may rely with complete confidence, and that person is yourself. You hold your fate in the palm of your hand. The stars can only tell so much, but each choice we face offers us two paths which we may follow. The path we walk determines our course. You have been very sheltered in your lifetime to not know that."

"Yes," she answered him, "I have been most sheltered." For a few minutes they sat in companionable silence, and then Aidan asked, "Have you sent word to my sister-in-law, Master Osman?"

"I have," he told her.

"Then Conn will come for me. Wherever I am he will find me, and we will be reunited."

"You must hold that thought, my child," Osman told her. "Remember what I have said. You are the helmsman of your fate, and you alone."

She had relived that conversation over a hundred times in the days that had followed, but now as she focused her silvery eyes upon the domes and spires of the city of Istanbul she was afraid. From the sea she found the city a strange and beautiful place, yet it was foreign to her, and she wondered what fate it held for her.

"My lady." Jinji was at her elbow.

"Yes?"

"My lady, you must come with me to your quarters so I may prepare you to go ashore."

Without another word Aidan turned and followed the young eunuch back to her cabin. The ship upon which they had traveled was a large commercial galley that the dey had hired to transport his tribute to his master. Its chief power was the wind that filled its sails, but it also carried a crew of oarsmen to row should it be necessary, though it had not been this trip. These oarsmen were not slaves, but rather sailors who earned their living on the rowing bench, and the owner of the galley preferred them to slaves for they worked of their own free will, and therefore there was no chance of his losing a cargo through rebellion.

The entire ship had been booked by the dey to transport his gifts to his master. Below, and carefully secured, were a full dozen perfect Arabian mares and a magnificent golden Arabian stallion. There were also two pairs of lion-hunting dogs from south of the great desert, and two pairs of long-haired salukis, the graceful and swift hunting dogs of the Arabs. There was a marvelous clock from France made of pure gold, and inlaid with precious stones that the dey had commissioned for the sultan whose hobbies were painting and clockmaking. There was a saddle tooled of the best moroccon leather with a matching bridle for the stallion. The bridle had a solid gold bit, and was decorated with semiprecious stones. The saddle was worked with gold leaf, and the stirrups, like the bit, were of pure gold. There were a full hundred healthy, strong young male slaves, all Portuguese; two perfectly matched pigeon's-blood rubies the size of small lemons; three identical female dwarfs; a pair of black panthers; a bag of perfectly matched pink pearls each one the size of a cherry; and Aidan. A full dozen gifts in all.

Aidan had grown quite used to the comfortable and beautiful garments that were worn by the upper-class Turkish woman. These consisted of baggy trousers which were tight at the ankle, a sheer blouse over which was worn a slash-skirted dress with long sleeves and a low-cut neckline beneath which the delicate fabric of the blouse showed, and tied about her hips a lovely embroidered shawl. Jinji had told Aidan that when she found favor with the sultan she would probably be given gifts of jeweled belts that she would wear instead. Now as they prepared to leave the ship Jinji helped his mistress into a garment that he called a feridje. It was made of pale lavender silk lined with pale mauve silk, and it covered her from her head to her feet. Carefully Jinji fastened a veil across the bridge of her nose successfully muffling Aidan to all who might dare to gaze upon a chosen woman. Only her eyes were visible to the bold.

She could hear upon the deck the sounds of the sailors making the galley fast to the dock; the thump of the gangway as it was lowered from the ship's deck to the land. Jinji tugged at her sleeve.

"Come, my lady. You are to be the first ashore before the animals and the dwarfs. There will be a litter from the palace awaiting you on the shore."

Taking a final look about the cabin which had been her shelter these last few weeks, Aidan followed Jinji from the room, and back out onto the deck. There she found the captain awaiting them. He bowed low to her.

"My lady," he said in accented French, "I hope your voyage has been a comfortable one, and that you will remember us kindly."

"Thank you," she replied. "It has been most pleasant." Pleasant, she thought, considering that I am entering slavery.

"May Allah guard you, and guide you along your path," the captain said, and then he moved away to direct the unloading of the horses.

"Look! Look! Did I not tell you?" Jinji exclaimed excitedly. "There is an imperial litter upon the dock!" He helped Aidan down the gangway, and hurried her over to it. There were four bearers seated on the ground awaiting their passenger, and a rather bored-looking eunuch who arose to his feet at their approach.

"I am Omar," said the eunuch. He spoke in Turkish, and that much Aidan understood for Jinji had been tutoring her these last weeks. "Is this the slavewoman from the Dey of Algiers?"

"This is she," said Jinji, "and I am her eunuch, Jinji."

"You are not to be returned?"

"No, I am to remain with my lady."

"What is her name?"

"She has not been named yet. The dey thought that the sultan would enjoy naming her."

"The sultan has more important things to do than to name a slavegirl. I expect that Ilban Bey will do that."

"Who is Ilban Bey?"

"You do not know who the illustrious Ilban Bey is? You really are from the ends of the earth," said Omar scornfully. "Ilban Bey is the agha kislar of Sultan Murad's household. It is he who will decide if this woman sent by the dey is even worthy of being entered into our master's harem, but we must not stand here talking. Help your mistress into the litter."

As Jinji did so he said to Aidan, "How much of that did you understand, my lady?"

"Enough," she replied in French, "to know that Omar is an insufferable little slug."

Jinji smiled broadly. "My lady is wise," he replied, and he fluffed the pillows behind her back. "Remember what I have told you, copper-haired woman. There is a hierarchy within the harem, and you are on the lowest level of that hierarchy. Be deferential, and modest, and I will be able to advance you once I have learned the lay of this land." He drew the gauze draperies shut on the litter.

A moment later she felt the vehicle raised, and the four black slaves with their heavy gold collars which were studded with pearls and semiprecious stones, began the journey back to the royal palace which was called the Yeni Serai. She had noticed that other than their collars, and their baggy red silk trousers they wore no other clothing or shoes. She could hear the thick slap, slap, of their feet upon the ground, and she thought that the soles of those feet must be like leather itself.

Aidan longed to peep between the curtains, and see where she was going. She could hear the sounds of the city all about her, but the gauze was heavy enough to blur the sights without. There was a variety of smells beginning with the waterfront which reeked of the sea and of the strong odor of fish. These scents lessened, and as they moved farther away from the docks, others began to take their place. There was the smell of cooking oil, and ripening fruits, of leather being tanned, and flowers. The sound of voices was a cacophonous blend of unintelligible noise, but gradually as they entered the area near the Yeni Serai the noise lessened. Then suddenly the litter was placed firmly upon the ground, the draperies were drawn open, and Jinji reached in to hand Aidan out.

"Follow me," said Omar, and he hurried off across the courtyard without even looking to see if they were behind him. He simply assumed that they were. Aidan barely had time to look around her, but Jinji did manage to whisper to her before they entered the building, "Do you see the gardeners there, my lady? Innocent-looking aren't they, but they are really the sultan's executioners."

Aidan shivered. Executioners! It was a frightening thought. She increased her speed behind Jinji and Omar as they entered a two-storied building, and moved down a cool dim corridor. They came to a carved door before which stood two tall, muscled black men with rather fierce-looking curved swords. Omar moved past them, opening the door, and then stepping back to allow Aidan entry into the room beyond. As her eyes became used to the darkened room she saw sitting before her on a low dais a small spare old man. He motioned her forward impatiently.

"Do you understand Turkish?" he demanded in a high and reedy voice.

"I am learning, my lord," she said slowly. "If you do not speak too quickly I think that I can understand you. I speak French."

"Then so will I for now," said the man. He was richly dressed in a heavy brocaded gown of red and black trimmed in dark fur, and upon his head he wore a turban of cloth of gold with a ruby. "Remove your feridje. Help her, Omar. Do not stand there basking in your own self-importance."

Omar hurried to do the man's bidding, quickly removing her veil, and then undoing the long enveloping cape, and carrying it away.

"I am Ilban Bey," said the little man. "I am the agha kislar of the Sultan Murad's household. Among my duties is the care of the women who live here. You speak French. Are you French?"

"No, my lord, I am English."

"The English! An interesting people ruled by a woman of all things! We are only beginning to deal formally with the English."

"I am an intimate of the queen's," said Aidan, stretching the truth slightly. "I was one of her maids of honor. I am a married woman who was stolen from her home and husband. My family can and will pay a large ransom for me."

"So," said Ilban Bey, "you are of the noble class? That is good. We have women from all lands and of all classes from the highest to the lowest. I like noblewomen, however, for I find them more intelligent. They comprehend a situation more clearly." His sharp dark eyes peered out of his brown face, looking her over carefully. "Now," he said, "remove your clothing for me so I may see just how greatly the dey has honored my master."

Aidan gasped. "Remove my clothing?"

He nodded. "Would you like your eunuch to help you?" His hand signaled to Jinji.

He scampered forward, his expressive eyes pleading with Aidan not to cause a scene. She shrugged, and sighed softly. What good would it do her to complain and struggle? Ilban Bey wanted to see her without her clothes, and so he would. She nodded to Jinji to begin, holding out her arms so he might more easily remove the slash-skirted dress while she removed the shawl that was tied artfully about her hips. Jinji worked swiftly, and Aidan quickly stood nude before the agha kislar of Sultan Murad's household. The eunuch undid the heavy braid of her hair, and fluffing it with his hands spread her copper-colored tresses over her shoulders. Then falling to his knees he touched his head to the floor saying, "It is done, my lord."

A faint smile touched the lips of Ilban Bey. If there was one thing he recognized it was ambition. Then he brought his thoughts back to the woman who stood before him. She was big for a woman, taller than most women and even some men, yet she was nicely proportioned. Rising he came off his dais to look more closely. His hand smoothed over her skin as if he were examining a high-strung mare. She shivered when he cupped one of her breasts impersonally, and fingered the nipple which to her intense embarrassment puckered slightly. A flush spread across her cheeks, but Ilban Bey fixed her with a look, and said,

"Your breasts are the most beautiful that I have ever seen, and they are quite sensitive I can see. That is a marvelous thing in a woman. What are you called?"

"I am Aidan St. Michael, Lady Bliss," she said in a level voice. It was amazing, her mind reasoned, what a woman could bear under the most trying of circumstances.

"No," he said quietly. "You are Marjallah, which means 'A Gift from the Sea'; and you will answer from now on to the name of Marjallah. Is that understood?"

"Yes, my lord," she said low.

He could see the distress and the confusion in her eyes. She was obviously a woman of spirit, but in this very different situation for her she was not certain just what to do. She chose to be obedient under the circumstances, until she might consider her position. It was the wise choice, but it disturbed him. She was a lovely woman with her flawless body, and her gorgeous hair, but if there was one thing that the sultan did not need at this time it was another woman influencing him. There were already four women doing that, and it was causing difficulty. This was not the time for the dey to have sent an intelligent woman to the sultan. Intelligent women were ambitious women as a rule. Ilban Bey wished that they might indeed ransom this beauty back to her family. Alas, however, the dey could not be insulted, and besides it was not his decision. He must consult the sultan valideh, Nur-U-Banu, the sultan's mother, on this matter.

"Dress yourself, Marjallah," he said to her, and then to Omar, "The lady Marjallah is to be housed in the oda of the lady Sayeste for the time being." Then to Aidan again, "Lady Sayeste speaks the tongue of the Franks, and she will help you to adjust to your new life, Marjallah. She is kind, and you may trust her."

Dressed again Aidan was led with Jinji from the room. The agha kislar waited but a few minutes, and then he left his quarters, and walking through the palace gardens followed a path that led to the small, separate palace of the sultan valideh, Nur-U-Banu, which was located amid beautiful gardens near the seraglio point. Murad's mother preferred her own home to the women's quarters of the Yeni Serai.

He found her seated by a pool of water lilies watching the goldfish swimming back and forth. She was a beautiful woman, a Circassian by birth and of medium height. Her golden hair was yet bright, but her figure was somewhat fuller than it had been in her youth when she was the favorite of the late sultan, Selim II. She raised her blue eyes to him as he approached, but remained seated.

"Good afternoon, Ilban Bey," she said in a slightly deeper voice than one might have expected from so delicate-looking a woman.

"Good afternoon, gracious lady. I come to lay a problem at your dainty feet."

"Then be seated, Ilban Bey. You have my permission to speak."

He settled himself next to her on the edge of the pool. "The Dey of Algiers sent a shipload of gifts to his majesty which arrived just today."

"I know," she said. "I understand that there are two pairs of salukis amongst the tribute. I should so like a pair of those dogs, but then so does my son's favorite, Safiye Kadin."

"Did you know that among these gifts was also a woman, my lady valideh?"

"Murad is always being sent women," said Nur-U-Banu.

"Beautiful women, fluffy kittens of girls, wide-eyed virgins are what usually pass through the gates of the harem, but this is different. The dey has sent the sultan an Englishwoman, stolen from her family. She has the most perfect form I have ever seen on any woman, and hair like polished copper. Her face is pretty, although she is certainly no great beauty, but she is intelligent, my lady valideh. Far too intelligent to remain merely a plaything of your son should he favor her, and I do not believe he can see her, and not desire her. She is truly lovely."

"What you are saying to me, Ilban Bey, is that we must rid ourselves of this female."

"Yes, my gracious lady."

"You do not think we could use her against Safiye Kadin?"

"You could use her, gracious lady, but although I believe she would attract the sultan, I do not believe she would give her loyalty to anyone but Murad. Safiye would fight with her, and she would defend herself. She would resent you if you tried to influence her, and then she, too, would be an enemy. Better we used mindless beauties to thwart Safiye Kadin, and this woman is not stupid."

"Then we must remove her from the harem, Ilban Bey. Let me think this through. Surely we can find a use for her. We cannot return her to her family for the dey would be mightily offended. We need to find a way that will make use of her without involving her with my son, and at the same time doing honor to the dey who sent her to Murad." Her smooth brow furrowed in thought for several minutes during which time Ilban Bey sat quietly by the sultan valideh's side, and waited for her decision in the matter. Finally Nur-U-Banu said, "We shall make a gift of her to someone whom my son wishes to honor, but who, Ilban Bey? Who?"

"Prince Javid Khan, my gracious lady. He is the perfect choice."

The sultan valideh clapped her hands. "Of course, Ilban Bey! Of course! It is the perfect choice. My son is giving a reception tonight to welcome Javid Khan, and he can present the woman to him then as a token of his esteem. Where did you place the woman?"

"With the lady Sayeste's oda."

"Very good! There is no chance of Murad's seeing her by chance before tonight. I will, however, suggest to my son that such a gift be readied for the prince, and I shall offer to choose the woman myself."

Ilban Bey arose. "I shall see that Marjallah is prepared carefully tonight."

The sultan valideh was pleased. "Marjallah? Is that her name?"

"I took the liberty of naming her as the dey had not."

"*A Gift from the Sea.* How clever of you, Ilban Bey, but then that is why you are my son's agha kislar, because you are clever."

"And loyal to my gracious mistress," Ilban Bey said.

Nur-U-Banu laughed. "But first clever, my old friend. First and foremost, clever."

"Who is clever, dear mother Nur-U-Banu?"

Ilban Bey and the sultan valideh turned to see Murad's bas kadin, Safiye, with a group of her handmaidens.

Nur-U-Banu smiled coolly. "How quietly you move, Safiye. Like a cat, I think. How is my grandson?"

"He is well," came the short answer. The bas kadin was mother of Sultan Murad's only son, and heir, Prince Memhet. "Now tell me who is clever?" Safiye would not be denied her curiosity.

"Ilban Bey is clever," said the valideh.

"Because he has run to you with news of another potential rival for me, dear mother Nur-U-Banu? Perhaps the dey's red-haired slavewoman will hold my Murad's interest for a short time, but when will you admit to yourself that he will never forsake me? It is me that your son loves! *Me!*"

The sultan valideh looked coldly at the bas kadin. "You are mistaken, Safiye, as you frequently are," she said. "Since I do not want you feeding on your groundless fears all day, however, let me assure you that your supposition is incorrect. Ilban Bey has come to inform me that he thought the dey's gift would make an excellent gift for my son to give to Prince Javid Khan tonight. I am just on my way to see the girl. Will you come with me? I think it would be refreshing for my son to see his mother, and his favorite at one accord for a change, don't you?"

Safiye was somewhat taken aback. "You are giving this woman away?"

"She is not mine to give away, Safiye, she is my son's. I am going to suggest, however, that as his harem is full to overflowing that perhaps this lady would make a charming present for our new ambassador from the Khanate of the Crimea. Don't you agree?"

Surprised as she was Safiye's wits were not so muddled that she didn't see the advantage of ridding herself of a potential rival. Every woman who entered the harem was a personal threat to her, and to her influence. As it was she had to share Murad's attention with three serious rivals: his mother; his sister, Fahrusha Sultan; and the woman, Janfeda, who although she did not share his bed, nonetheless had considerable influence with him for they were of all things, *friends*! "I think that a gift of that nature would be perfect for Prince Javid Khan," Safiye agreed with her mother-in-law. "Yes, I should very much like to go with you, and see her."

The sultan valideh smiled, but there was no warmth in the gesture. "Come along then, Safiye, but send your maidens away for I do not want the entire harem apprised of our business."

The two women in the company of Ilban Bey found their way back into the Yeni Serai, and moving along a dark corridor came to a small room which they entered. Ilban Bey removed three plugs from a wall, and then he and his companions each putting an eye to the little openings looked through into the next room. Inside it there were seven women, one older, and obviously the leader, the other six in her charge. The older woman, a handsome creature with dark hair, and white, white skin, was richly garbed in cherry-pink trousers, a light pink gauze blouse, and a slash-skirted dress of pink and silver brocade. She was seated upon a divan, and even now was speaking, although they could not hear her, to a young woman who stood before her.

The valideh scrutinized Aidan carefully. She obviously liked what she saw for a small smile flitted across her face, and she said, "The prince should be quite pleased, and impressed with such a gift. She is not beautiful in a classical sense, but she is a lovely woman, and the fact she is not virgin is a good thing for I am told that Javid Khan is a man of sophisticated tastes." She looked at Safiye, and said wickedly, "You are fortunate, my daughter, that I have not chosen to use Marjallah against you, for I truly believe that she might be the one woman who could take my son from you permanently." Then Nur-U-Banu laughed.

Safiye flushed angrily, but she did not dare to oppose the sultan's mother who was the most powerful woman in the entire empire.

Seeing her discomfort the valideh laughed again, and then said to Ilban Bey, "Spare nothing to prepare Marjallah for her presentation tonight to Javid Khan. I want him grateful to Murad, and when she is ready, bring Marjallah to me so I may instruct her in her deportment."

"It will be done, gracious lady," said the agha kislar, and he escorted the sultan valideh from the room.

For a brief moment Safiye remained behind to look once again at the woman who might have been her rival. She did not like what she saw for she knew that Nur-U-Banu was correct in her estimation of the female Marjallah. She would have been a serious threat, and Safiye wondered why the valideh had not used such a threat. With a final glance and a sigh of relief she left the spy chamber, and returned to her own spacious apartments to rest before this evening's entertainment.

She was a beautiful woman, a Venetian of the noble family of Baffo. Her father had been made governor of the island of Corfu, and she had been on her way to join him when her vessel had been seized by pirates. She had been brought to Istanbul to be sold in the slave market of the Great Bazaar. There she had been purchased by the agha kislar's agents, and brought to the Yeni Serai. At thirteen she had been presented to Murad who had been enchanted by her fair skin and her red hair. Red-gold hair not too unlike the hair of the slave Marjallah.

They had fallen in love, and she had borne him his only son, Prince Memhet. For several years she had kept him close to her side, and he had not looked, not even dreamed of another woman, but his mother had grown jealous of Safiye's power over Murad. It was Nur-U-Banu, the *Lady of Light*, who had insisted that her son take other maidens to his bed. Oh, she had claimed it was all for the sake of the succession as Murad had but one child, but Safiye, whose name meant *Purity*, believed otherwise.

She had found an old recipe that had been used it was said by the sultan valideh Cyra Hafise, and her three best friends who were also kadins of Sultan Selim I, to prevent their rivals in the harem from conceiving. Together with several of her women she had brewed the concoction and seen that it was introduced into the sherbets that were drunk by her rivals, and they had indeed not conceived. Then the sultan valideh had found out, and her women were executed as a warning to her, a warning she had taken.

The sultan discovered that after several years of being faithful to one woman, he was actually quite polygamous. He enjoyed beautiful women, and he found that his appetite for them was quite prodigious. Suddenly slavegirls were bringing incredible prices on the open market in Istanbul, and the more beautiful the girl, the richer her owner became. The reputation grew as stories filtered out from the harem telling of how Murad often took two and three girls in a single night. Although he had not fathered any more sons to date he did have a houseful of little daughters. Still despite his lust for women, he had remained faithful, at least in his heart, to Safiye which was a small consolation to her.

At ease in her own apartments she lay back upon a divan, and wondered why it was that Nur-U-Banu really wanted to give Marjallah to the ambassador from the Khanate of the Crimea. Why it was she was not going to use this woman to steal Murad from her? It was not enough that she would be safe from Marjallah. She needed to know the reasoning behind the sultan valideh's thinking. Restless she arose, and began to pace back and forth. Her handmaidens looked nervously at one another, and finally she sent them away in annoyance. What was Nur-U-Banu up to? Safiye wondered.

Finally she could bear it no longer, and so leaving her apartment she hurried to the oda of the lady Sayeste. She would not be denied entrance to such an unimportant oda. Indeed it would be deemed an honor that she deigned to visit it.

"Safiye Kadin!" Sayeste almost fell over her feet as she came forward to greet the sultan's bas kadin. Sayeste was a Syrian of faded prettiness who had once attracted the late sultan. For some reason that Safiye could never fathom, Nur-U-Banu liked Sayeste, and when Selim II had died, Nur-U-Banu had chosen Sayeste to rule an oda of maidens who would belong to her son. Although she owed her place to Nur-U-Banu, she was painfully aware that if the valideh died it would be Safiye, the bas kadin, who would then be in charge of the harem. Not unmindful of her tenuous position she greeted Safiye warmly. "How may I be of service to you, my lady?"

Safiye looked around the room where six girls were expected to live, and she remembered her early days in the harem in an oda quite similar. "Where is the new slave, Marjallah?" she asked.

"She has been taken to the baths, my lady. Although she has not been told yet, she is to be given to the ambassador from the Khanate of the Crimea tonight at the sultan's reception."

"Who is she?"

"It is hard for me to speak with her, my lady. Her Turkish is very slight, and I know no other language. However she does have her own eunuch,

Jinji, who can speak to her in the language of the Franks. He is quite talk-ative. Shall I call him?"

"Yes," said Safrye. "Bring him to me, and then see that we are not dis-turbed. Do you understand, lady Sayeste?"

"Yes, my lady Safiye."

Sayeste scurried out to find Jinji, and hurried him back into the room. He had not been far, down the dark corridor gossiping with others of his kind, attempting to gather what information he might while his mistress was at the baths.

"Hurry," said Sayeste breathlessly. "The bas kadin would speak with you, worthless spawn of a slave mother!" She pushed him through the door to the room, and then pulling the door shut stood guard herself outside.

Jinji fell to his knees, and touched his head to the floor before the beautiful woman. "My lady," he mumbled afraid to say anything else for he had not really been given permission to speak, and to offer his services to her would have been presumptuous on his part. It could ruin his mis-tress' chance in this place.

"Tell me of your mistress, Jinji," the bas kadin commanded, but she did not give him permission to rise. Let him speak from a position beneath her. She had learned that trick from Murad. It kept the person speaking to you at a disadvantage.

Jinji settled back upon his heels, and looked up at Safiye. "There is lit-tle that I can tell you, my lady. She arrived in Algiers in the charge of a kapitan reis named Rashid al Mansur. Brought to the jenina she was pur-chased by the dey for the great sum of ten thousand gold pieces to be the chief jewel in the diadem of gifts that the dey intended to present to our mighty lord, Murad, the third of that name, may Allah bless him and may he live a thousand years!"

Safiye's lips twitched at the eunuch's flowery speech, but she managed not to laugh outright. "But what of the woman? Who is she?"

"I can only tell you, gracious lady, that she is a woman of high rank in her land. It is all I know. She is not very open with me yet although I have pledged my devotion to her."

Yes, thought the sultan's bas kadin, he most certainly would have pledged his devotion to his new mistress with an eye toward getting ahead within the hierarchy of the harem. In that sense he was like her own Tahsin who had been with her almost since the beginning, and that she thought was not a bad thing. It was good for a woman entering the strange world of the harem to have a defender and a protector. Safiye re-membered all too well the frightening early days of her career. She fixed the eunuch with a sharp gaze. "Do you think that you can find the apartments of the bas kadin, Jinji? When your mistress has returned from the baths you are to bring her to me. Do you understand?"

"Yes, my lady kadin," he answered nervously.

Safiye smiled slightly, and walking past the kneeling eunuch left the room. Jinji was just scrambling to his feet when Sayeste hurried back into the room, her curiosity high.

"What did she want?" demanded the oda mistress.

"To see my mistress when she returns from the baths." He looked concerned. "Is it safe for me to take Marjallah, my lady Sayeste? How can I not obey the sultan's favorite, yet I fear for my lady."

"You need not," replied Sayeste dryly. "Your mistress is to be no threat to the bas kadin for it has been decided that Marjallah is to be given tonight to the ambassador from the Khanate of the Crimea. The harem is invited to a reception and entertainment in his honor, and the sultan wishes to give Prince Javid Khan a token of welcome. That token is Marjallah. You will, of course, accompany your mistress into the household of the prince. It will be quite a step up for you, Jinji, for I am told that the prince left his women behind when he came to Istanbul. Knowing of our justly famous slave markets he intended to begin afresh here. With no need for any other than his personal servants you will find yourself the only eunuch in the prince's household at present. This is a great opportunity for such a young eunuch, but if you behave correctly and with wisdom you could find yourself Prince Javid Khan's chief eunuch here in Istanbul. Not only that, if your mistress manages to attract him your fortune will be doubly made." She smiled toothily at him.

Jinji's mind reeled at the oda mistress' words. This was incredible good fortune indeed! Sayeste was perfectly right. He had the opportunity to be the head eunuch in a prince's harem! His lovely mistress had the singular opportunity to become the prince's favorite without any competition, at least until the prince desired other women, which with luck would be shortly, and it would be he who would go to the slave markets to pick out exquisite beauties with which to tempt his new master.

"Is the prince a young man?" he asked, suddenly aware that if he wasn't, then all his hopes were for naught. What if this prince were a tired old graybeard?

"He is not a youth," said Sayeste, "rather he is said to be in the prime of his life."

The eunuch nodded satisfied. Good! he thought. A man in his full vigor, and hopefully a man with a good appetite for the sweet flesh of the female of the species. "This is fine news," he said with great understatement to the oda mistress, "and I thank you for sharing it with me. Tell me, my lady Sayeste, does my mistress know of her fate yet?"

"I do not believe that she has been told," said Sayeste, "but I have not been informed that she should not be told so perhaps you will tell her of her fate before you take her to see the bas kadin. I wonder what the lady Safiye wants with her."

"Should I take her then?" fretted the eunuch.

"I see no reason why not," came the reply, but even as she spoke Sayeste was planning to send a message to the sultan valideh about this turn of events. She focused on the eunuch. "What did the lady Safiye want with you, Jinji?"

"She wanted to know about my mistress, but I could tell her little," said the eunuch. "The lady Marjallah keeps very much to herself."

"She is still frightened," said the oda mistress wisely. "New captives usually react this way. Poor dear. She has certainly been hustled from pillar to post these last months. Well, once she is comfortably settled in the prince's palace she will bloom I am certain." She gave him a friendly, almost conspiratorial smile. "Why don't you go to the baths, Jinji, and tell your mistress of your combined good fortunes. Then go directly to the bas kadin's apartments from there."

He bowed politely. "Yes, my lady Sayeste," he said, and tried not to show how eager he was to impart his news to Marjallah by not hurrying, at least within her sight, but once out of it Jinji almost ran, racing down the staircase from the second story of the women's quarters where the oda of Lady Sayeste was located, and along the roofed portico that opened onto the open courtyard of the women. By the time he had reached the bath he had to pause to catch his breath so that he might regain his dignity before the others. Entering the large and steamy room he stopped an attendant and politely asked, "Do you know where I may find my mistress, the slave Marjallah, who is being prepared as a gift for Prince Javid Khan? She has copper-colored hair."

"She is being massaged at the moment," said the attendant. "You will find her over there by the blue-tiled fountains."

Following the direction of her pointing finger Jinji moved across the room to where he found Aidan, prone upon a marble bench, being quite skillfully massaged by a young black girl with long, supple fingers. Kneeling the eunuch whispered softly, "My lady Marjallah, I bring wonderful news!"

She turned her head, and looking at him said, "What is it, Jinji?" She did not, however, really sound very interested.

"By the greatest stroke of good fortune we are not to remain here even one night, my lady Marjallah! You will be presented tonight to Prince Javid Khan at a reception that his majesty is giving for him. That great prince is the new ambassador from the Khanate of the Crimea! He has not brought his harem to Istanbul as knowing of its famous slave markets he intended to build himself a new harem here. You are to be the first woman for that harem! Is that not wonderful news?"

Her silvery eyes widened in shock and distress, and Aidan's hand flew to her mouth to stifle the cry that arose in her throat. Good news? Dear God, no! At least here amongst all these hundreds of women she had hoped to remain anonymous until a ransom could be arranged for her for she refused to believe that such a thing was not possible despite what everyone told her. Of course she could be ransomed, and she would be! In the meantime, however, she wanted nothing more than to remain nameless and faceless among the many women of the sultan's harem. She had been so encouraged earlier when she had realized how large an establishment this royal palace really was. Her hopes had soared greatly when Omar had boasted as he led her and Jinji to the chamber of the lady Sayeste that Sultan Murad's harem housed over a thousand beauties who only lived to be called to their master's bed. She had almost shouted her relief at that juicy tidbit of information for it indicated to her she should be able to hide herself among the others until Conn could ransom her which would surely be soon.

Now she realized that she was in great danger if the sultan planned to give her away to another, and here was Jinji so delighted that she was to be the first woman into the new harem of this prince! Her heart began to hammer, and for a moment her breath failed her. Then she considered the possibility that the man might be elderly, or perhaps he would be able to be reasoned with and she could explain to him that her family would pay a great ransom for her safe return. A ransom that would buy him women who were willing and anxious to gain his favor as she was not. He had to listen to her! He had to listen to reason! How could she yield herself to another man? She was Conn's wife, and her husband loved her even as she loved him. How could she return to him with the sin of adultery standing between them? But if she was forced was it adultery? She didn't know. She simply didn't know.

Jinji was still babbling on, unaware of her distress. "And my lady, the sultan's bas kadin has requested that you come to see her when you have finished in the baths. This is a great honor, and the only greater one you might receive is if the sultan's mother wanted to speak with you, but of course, such a thing is not possible. Still in all we are most fortunate, you and I. I do believe that you have been born beneath a very fortuitous star.

Did the great Osman say anything to you about this? You told me little of your natal chart."

Do not panic, she told herself. Do not be fearful of this situation. If you lose control then all will be lost. Answer his questions calmly, and do not let him see your fear. Fear can be a weapon used against you, Aidan reminded herself. "Osman did say," she replied coolly, "that I should not remain long in the sultan's house."

"Aiii! He knew! He saw! Tell me, my lady, what else he saw. Will you become the prince's favorite?"

"That he did not tell me," she replied unable to help smiling even in the midst of her fear. Jinji was so openly ambitious.

"You will capture the prince's heart, I know it," said the young eunuch. "I can feel it in my bones! Our fortune is made, my dearest mistress! Our fortune is made!"

Aidan thought it better to say nothing further to Jinji for he was obviously devoted to his advancement, and to share with him the hopes of her ransom from this captivity would be foolish. He would, of course, do anything in his power to prevent her release. When she had made her arrangements with the prince she would temper the faithful eunuch's disappointment with the suggestion that he would have several new beauties from which to mold a favorite for the prince. She suspected that he would, upon reflection, enjoy that.

The masseuse had finished her work, and she whispered in a musical voice to Aidan, "You are ready, my lady, to be dressed."

"I will take care of my mistress," said Jinji, self-importantly.

"Of course," said the masseuse politely. "Fresh clothing has been brought for the lady, and if you will both follow me I shall show you." She led them from the baths into another room where several women, and their various attendants were dressing. Opening a cabinet that was built into the wall she extracted from it a pair of pale blue silk trousers, a matching gauze blouse, and a little sleeveless bolero of deep blue silk embroidered with red and gold threads, and edged in gold fringe. There was also a narrow belt of polished brass links that looked like gold from which hung bits of ruby-colored glass beads, a small cap made from cloth of gold, and a pair of matching slippers. These she handed to Jinji, and then with a polite bow she returned to the baths.

"I doubt," said Jinji somewhat scornfully, "that these are the garments that you are expected to wear tonight. They are not nearly grand enough for a sultan's reception."

"What of the clothing that was made for me in Algiers?" asked Aidan.

"It is pretty enough," came the reply, "and it is certainly of the best materials for the dey would not have dared send you with garments that were not the finest. But it is mostly caftans, the dey wishing to display you in the costume of his province. He fully expected that you would be clothed properly by the sultan's household once you gained the sultan's favor. Although you will be garbed beautifully I do not think you will be given a wardrobe other than what you have with you." He lowered his voice. "Sultan Murad is said to love to collect gold, but not to disburse it. He is not a miser, but he is known for his avarice as well as for his lust." As he spoke he reached into the pocket of his voluminous trousers, and drew forth a small brush with which he succeeded in untangling Aidan's wet and tangled hair. "There," he said as he finished, "now we may go before the bas kadin with pride," and he was off with Aidan behind him.

She had absolutely no idea where they were, but Jinji certainly seemed to know exactly where he was going. She followed him from the baths into a large tiled corridor, and as quickly into another wide, tiled hallway through a doorway and into a series of narrower passages, the last of which he told her was called the Corridor of the Kadins. There Jinji stopped before a large carved door, and knocked deferentially. The guards on either side of the door ignored him. A pretty slavegirl opened the door, and Jinji said to her, "The lady Marjallah has been asked to attend upon the bas kadin."

The slavegirl stepped back to allow them admittance to the apartments of the bas kadin, and moving into the room Aidan was amazed. Both in Algiers, and here today in the Yeni Serai all she had seen of a harem had been the baths and the tiny room where she had been kept. She had wondered to herself if this was all that there was to a harem, simply baths and tiny cubicles where its inhabitants were kept. Now she knew she had been greatly mistaken. Perhaps women of no importance were kept in those little rooms, but here was an apartment of spacious size, and gracious decor. Large windows looked out upon a planted garden from one wall, allowing in the afternoon sunshine. The room's walls were of decorated wooden panels, each one painted with a stylized tree in a gilded pot, and surrounded by colorful flowers of rainbow hues. The ceiling was composed of yellow and blue Italian tiles, and on one wall was a tiled fireplace with a tall conical hood of beaten copper. Upon the wooden floors were fine wool rugs woven in hues of soft rose, dark blue, and cream.

The furniture consisted of low tables of ebony and mother of pearl inlaid together to form elegant geometric designs, comfortable seating of low upholstered pieces, and silken pillows. The lamps, hanging, standing, and those that simply sat upon tables were of polished silver, copper, or ruby glass. There were arrangements of flowers everywhere, and to

Aidan's surprise there were also several cats, one of which wound itself about her legs in a friendly fashion. She bent down, and patted the silky creature which had long white fur, and was of a breed she had never seen.

"Arslan likes you," said a musical voice, and Aidan stood to face a beautiful woman. She bowed politely for this was obviously a woman of rank, and there was no need for rudeness. The woman, who was petite with a full bosom, slowly looked Aidan over, and with such careful scrutiny that it brought a flush to Aidan's cheeks. The woman laughed softly seeing it, and reaching out patted Aidan's hand in a gesture of conciliation. "Forgive me for staring so hard," she said, "but I still cannot decide why it is the valideh is having my lord Murad give you to Prince Javid Khan. You really are lovely, but how unmannerly of me. I have not introduced myself. I am Safiye Kadin, the mother of Prince Memhet, the sultan's heir." She spoke accented French.

Aidan curtsied, although she felt the gesture awkward in her trousers.

"How prettily you do that," said Safiye. "I have not seen a curtsy since I was a child in Venice. I am a Venetian, you know. Come let us seat ourselves, and you will tell me how you came to be here. Besma, fetch us refreshments," she ordered a hovering slavegirl, and then drew Aidan over to sit down upon a pillow-strewn divan. "I know that they call you Marjallah, but what was your other name? Mine was Giulietta Lucrezia Fiora Maria Baffo. I actually think that I like Safiye better. It is simpler." She smiled in a friendly fashion at Aidan.

"I am Aidan St. Michael, and I am English. Until my marriage I served the queen as a maid of honor." Her silvery eyes filled with tears. "I want to go home," she said, and despite her best efforts several tears rolled down her face, but she quickly brushed them away.

"I felt the same way when I first came here," said Safiye, "but then I gained the great love of my lord Murad, and it no longer mattered."

"I want to go home," Aidan repeated. "I want to go back to my husband, madame. If you love your lord then surely you must understand how I feel! I was stolen from my family by a wicked relation, who when he failed in his attempt to have my husband murdered so he might marry me and steal my wealth, kidnapped me, and saw me sold into slavery for his own profit! I should not be here!"

"But nevertheless you are," said Safrye, "and it will be so much easier for you if you simply accept what has happened, and begin your life anew. You have no other choice, Marjallah."

"There is death," said Aidan softly. "If I cannot return to my husband, Conn, then I should rather be dead!"

The bas kadin was only four years Aidan's senior, but she had lived in the harem for more than half her life. There were indeed women who chose suicide over enslavement, but it was not necessarily the brave choice. "It takes more courage to live, Marjallah," she said, "and I have always heard that the English were a brave people."

"But to become a plaything of an infidel," Aidan protested, and Safiye was unable to contain her laughter.

"Infidel?" she said. "Oh, Marjallah! That is so typical of the European Christian, yet I have heard even they now disagree amongst themselves, and your England is one of the chief culprits warring against the pope. The Muslims worship but one diety. Christians call him God. Muslims call him Allah, and the Jews, according to my friend, Esther Kira, call him Yahweh. Muslims are very moral people, Marjallah. They are allowed four legal wives because they believe it unfair that one poor woman be burdened with responsibilities of a household, and bearing all the children that a man usually wants. Not all Muslims take four wives, but the choice is there. Muslims often keep concubines for they feel it unfair that a man confine himself to a single woman. Is that not more honest than your European gentleman who has but one wife, and keeps a mistress or two, and then not satisfied lifts the skirt of any maiden who is willing, or who simply takes his fancy? You do not appear to me to be unintelligent, my dear. The Muslim may have different customs, but he is certainly not an infidel."

"I beg your pardon, madame," said Aidan, chastened, "but I would still go home. My husband lives, and can pay a very generous ransom for my return. Please help me!"

Safiye's beautiful face puckered with genuine sympathy. "I truly wish I might," she said, "and if you were simply a captive who had shown up in the slave markets of the Great Bazaar, I could, but you are not. You are a gift to my lord Murad from an important official of his empire. To return you to your people would be to scorn the dey's gift, and we cannot, of course, do that. Accept your fate, Marjallah. I understand that Prince Javid Khan is a very attractive man, and he is only a few years older than my lord Murad. You are a very fortunate girl! If you make the prince happy then my lord Murad's gift will be considered lucky for the prince, and I shall be your friend. Since you are not to remain here in the Yeni Serai we will not become rivals, and therefore I can be your friend. A woman in my position has few friends."

Aidan sighed deeply. This was a strange sort of nightmare in which she found herself. She felt like a bug caught within an empty spider's web. For now there was no spider to hurt her, and yet she was still caught, and unable to escape. "Will it be like that for me, too?" she asked Safiye.

"Probably," came the honest answer. "There are always women attempting to steal your lord's heart from you. Your only advantage is to bear him sons before the others; and in the end should you lose him to another at least you will have his children, and if you are lucky you will have his friendship and his respect. It is the most that any woman can hope for, Marjallah." She smiled. "At least you will not have the problem I have, his mother! Here in the harem the two most powerful women are the sultan's mother, the sultan valideh; and the mother of his heir, the bas kadin. They are usually at odds as are Nur-U-Banu and myself. For many years I held my lord's sole attention, but Nur-U-Banu was jealous of Murad's love for me, and sought to replace me in her son's affections. She has succeeded to a certain extent. That problem you will not have with Prince Javid Khan. He has come to Istanbul alone but for a few trusted servants."

At this point Besma interrupted in order to serve them with the refreshments that the bas kadin had ordered. There were exquisite goblets of delicate crystal that had been filled with a chilled, thick, sweet drink that tasted of peaches. Safiye called it sherbet. And there was a silver plate of dainty flaky pastries filled with chopped nuts, and raisins, and honey. As distressed as she was Aidan found that her appetite was totally intact, and Safiye smiled seeing her enjoyment. The bas kadin found that much to her surprise she liked the English girl, and she was very relieved to know that the sultan valideh's only purpose in seeing that Murad give Marjallah to Prince Javid Khan was to put the Crimean ambassador in the sultan's debt. It was important therefore that the English girl cooperate. To that end Safiye tried to reassure her.

"Life here is not so terrible," she said. "When I first came to Istanbul I was absolutely terrified, but then I was only twelve at the time. How old are you?"

"I had my twenty-fourth birthday on the ship as we sailed from Algiers to Istanbul," came the soft reply.

Interesting, thought Safiye, she does not look that old, and then she said, "Then you are twice the age I was when I was stolen from my family. Still fright is fright no matter your age. You will be, however, more sophisticated than I was when I came here."

Aidan laughed, and it was a sound of genuine, if rueful amusement. "Would you be surprised, my lady Safiye, if I told you that a year ago at this time I was practically as innocent as the twelve-year-old maid you once were? My mother and sisters died when I was only ten, and from that time on my father kept me close to his side. We lived in the country, and my father never went to court. Then suddenly he was dead, and I found that he had entrusted the queen with not only my care, but with the task of finding me a husband as well which was something that he had neglected to do. I had not minded for I enjoyed being with my father, and found him the most interesting of men.

"But he was gone, and the queen, who is a wonderful woman, took me under her wing, and made a place for me amongst her maids of honor. It was she who matched me with my husband."

"And you grew to love him," said Safiye. "How fortunate that was for you, but now, Marjallah, that life is over. You are in the same position that I was sixteen years ago. Believe me when I tell you that to your husband you are now dead. It is what happens when a Christian woman is taken into the empire. To her family she is a dead woman. You cannot go back, and so it is best to face that, and make a new life with Prince Javid Khan."

"It would not be that way with Conn and me," Aidan protested. "It wouldn't! Our love is a special love; a love that will always be."

"Of course it will!" agreed Safiye, "but that love is finished, Marjallah. Think of it as you would a new year.

"Oh, my new friend, tonight you will be given to an attractive, and virile man. When he sees how lovely you are he will waste no time in taking you to his bed. If you loved your husband then you enjoyed the sweetness that two people make between them. Will you deny yourself that sweetness with the prince? By now your family has given you up for lost, and who knows that your husband is not already consoling himself with a new wife. You were not wed long, and men must have sons! That is a woman's reality. Your husband has already made his new start. Now you must make yours. If you returned to your old world you would not be welcomed. You would be considered declassed. You would be called whore, or worse. If he loved you as you say he did, then your husband would want you to be happy as he is now undoubtedly happy."

Aidan was devastated by the bas kadin's words because she had understood exactly what the beautiful Venetian was saying to her. She felt drained of all emotion as she realized that Safiye was probably totally correct. *Never to see Conn again? Never to feel his touch, his kiss?* The thought pained her and her hand flew to her mouth, but not before a sharp moan escaped her lips. Dear sweet Jesu! How could she go on living? How could she even *be* without Conn? She had never truly known what happiness was until she had become his wife. Tears of anguish slid down her pale cheeks, and her entire being ached with the helpless reality of this new knowledge.

In a tender gesture Safiye Kadin put her arms about Aidan, and said, "I know, Marjallah, I know just how you feel. Weep, my new friend. Purge your sorrow now so that tonight when the prince sees you he will fall instantly in love with you, and you will receive him in joy!"

For several minutes Aidan sobbed her sorrow against the ample bosom of the bas kadin, but then as her tears began to abate she questioned herself. Slowly she was coming to accept the unpleasant reality of what everyone was telling her. Yet why did she still believe she could not survive without Conn? She had survived quite nicely her entire life until seven months ago without Conn. She loved him. She had loved him from the first moment that she had laid eyes upon him, but she was never going to see him again, and she had not a doubt that he would live on into a ripe old age. Why should not she?

He would mourn her, for she did not even now doubt the intensity of his love and devotion for her, but Safiye Kadin was right. Men must have sons. If anyone understood that Aidan certainly did based upon the history of her own family. At least the St. Michaels would go on, she thought with some satisfaction. Through Conn her family would survive, and her father's dying wish would be granted although perhaps not in the way that he had wanted. She must resign herself to what was, and not what had been, or what might be.

Raising her head up she wiped her cheeks with the back of her hand, and then said in a tremulous voice, "Tell me what you know of Javid Khan, my lady Safiye."

Safiye heaved a mental sigh of relief. The crisis was over, and the Englishwoman would accept her fate. She would be grateful to the sultan's bas kadin, and now that the empire was beginning to open its doors seriously to the English she would be a valuable friend to have. "He is said to be a handsome man, and a good one or else he would not have been sent as the ambassador from the Khanate of the Crimea. He is a Tartar, but I understand that his mother was a slave from Western Europe although I do not know where. You will find out soon enough. He will be a wonderful lord for you to have, Marjallah!"

There was actually little that Safiye could tell Aidan about Javid Khan, but the fact that his reputation appeared to be more good than bad was of some comfort to her. At least she had made a friend of the sultan's favorite, and she already suspected that Safiye's friendship could be important to her. Despite being confined within the walls of their harem, women here seemed to have a certain amount of power. She began to relax a little, enjoying the chatter of the bas kadin, the sweets they nibbled on as they talked, and Arslan, the large, long-haired white cat who had now settled himself quite comfortably in Aidan's lap, and was purring contentedly as she stroked him.

It was this picture, the two young women, their heads together, giggling, that greeted the sultan valideh as she entered the favorite's apartments. She had already learned from Sayeste of Safiye's visit. What was the bas kadin up to? Nur-U-Banu wondered. Why did she want to interview Marjallah? Gliding into the room she smiled sweetly, and said, "What a pretty picture you make, my daughters. Ahh, Marjallah, you like cats. They are the beloved animal of the Prophet. My own Peri has just recently had a litter of three adorable kittens whose father, I suspect, is Safiye's naughty, wandering Arslan. Would you like one? They are of an age to be separated from their mother. No! You shall have them all for Prince Javid's palace will have no cats yet, and they are an excellent deterrent to the mice and rats."

"Thank you, madame," said Aidan softly. "I do love cats, and am most grateful to you for the gift."

"I shall have to take Marjallah from you now, Safiye. We must choose just the right garments for her to wear tonight."

"No, no, dear mother! There is no need for Marjallah to bother with the mistress of the wardrobe. We are of the same coloring, and I have recently had some lovely new garments made."

"How generous of you, Safrye," said the sultan valideh, "but alas, Marjallah is much taller than you are. I'm afraid that only the mistress of the wardrobe can properly outfit her."

"Then I shall come with you, dear mother."

Aidan's head swiveled back and forth between the two women. Why on earth were they fighting over her like this? she wondered. It was all so damned silly.

"I shall value your exquisite taste," said Nur-U-Banu silkily. "Come along, my dears," and turning she swept from the room while they scrambled up quickly to follow exactly as the sultan valideh had intended.

The mistress of the wardrobe was most deferential to both the sultan's mother, and the sultan's kadin. She looked Aidan over with a critical eye, and then said, "Her coloring is so very like Safiye Kadin's, that I would suggest greens."

"No," replied Nur-U-Banu. "I do not disagree, Latife, that green is a marvelous color for her, but for tonight let us choose something that will make her stand out even more when she is presented to the ambassador. Find me garments in shades of purple."

Latife nodded. "You have the eye, madame!" she said admiringly and she hurried off to find the requested garments. Within a very few minutes she was back, her arms filled with a jumble of silks and satins. Laying the fabrics out across a divan she held up the first item for inspection, full silk gauze pantaloons in a wide stripe of deep lavender and cloth of gold. The ankle bands of the pantaloons were wide strips of cloth of gold embroidered in tiny seed pearls and pink crystals. The valideh nodded her approval. The second item presented was a short, sleeveless bodice of a lighter lavender silk edged in deep purple silk threads which were embroidered with seed pearls, pink crystals, and pieces of purple jade. Again the valideh nodded her approval, and so the final item, a pelisse, was held up for their inspection. It was of royal purple satin lined in lavender silk, and edged identically as the bodice. It had a frog closure of lavender-colored carved jade in the shape of a flower.

"Well, Safiye, what do you think?" Nur-U-Banu inquired.

"I would not have thought of it myself," Safrye admitted admiringly. "You are right, my mother, it is perfect."

The sultan valideh smiled, well-satisfied. There were still a few tricks she could teach her son's bas kadin. She had no doubt that Safiye would soon be appearing before her lord and master in shades of purple. Then she looked at the English girl who had been silent through all of the exchange. "Do you like my choice, Marjallah? It is important that you be comfortable in your clothing tonight. First impressions are always so critical with men. Be truthful with me, my daughter. If you prefer the greens then you shall have them." Her tone with Aidan was kindly.

"No, madame, I am satisfied to rely on your wisdom," said Aidan, knowing that despite the valideh's solicitous tone that she preferred to be agreed with. She, too, would be a useful friend, and then Aidan suddenly realized that she was beginning to think like these women. It was somewhat of a shock.

"Very well, Latife. See a slave brings these garments to the oda of Sayeste within the hour. You will also include a cap, slippers, and a girdle of gold."

The mistress of the wardrobe bowed respectfully to the sultan's mother, and without another word Nur-U-Banu turned, and left the room. To Aidan's surprise Jinji was by her side.

"You are to return to the oda of Sayeste and rest before this evening, my lady," he said.

Safiye gave Aidan a little hug. "Remember what I have told you, dear Marjallah, and do not be afraid. After all, Javid Khan is only a man." And then she laughed mischievously. "I will come to see you when you are settled, my friend," she said, and then she too turned, and hurried away.

Jinji led Aidan back through the winding corridors of the Yeni Serai to the oda of the lady Sayeste. I could never find my way around this vast palace, Aidan thought to herself. Arriving at the oda she was greeted by Sayeste, given a mattress, and shown where to place it upon the floor.

There were already five other girls in the room resting, but none of them paid any attention to Aidan. They were not interested in being friendly.

"You must rest," said Sayeste, "and then we will have our supper. There is time to sleep if you so wish."

Aidan did want to sleep for if she didn't then she would begin to think, and she knew that thinking of what had happened to her, thinking of her handsome Conn, thinking of what Safiye had said to her, would only make her want to weep again. She had led such a sheltered life, she thought, not quite able yet to turn off her mind. Were women like her, enslaved in Barbary, really considered lost by their families? If she told her tale to the prince, and he returned her to England, would Conn indeed repudiate her? Would he really believe that she had escaped her apparent fate, unscathed? Given the reputation, deserved or otherwise, of the Turks, would she believe such a thing if it happened to one of her friends? She wasn't certain, and that doubt began to convince her that perhaps Safiye Kadin was correct. She was as good as dead to Conn, and their family.

It was a frightening and serious thought, and if it were true then her entire life up until this day was gone. She would be like a baby, ignorant, unsure, and learning everything anew. Yet she could not quite relinquish her memories no matter what they said. *Conn!* She called out to him in her mind. *I am not dead! I'm not!* She shifted restlessly upon her pallet. I am going to get hysterical again if I do not stop this, she thought. She drew a deep breath, and then several others. Gradually she began to feel in control of herself once more. Safiye is right, she decided. I am here, and I must make the best of this situation. Tired now, for it had been such a long day, she allowed her heavy eyelids to close, and within minutes she had fallen into a deep and healing sleep.

Chapter 11

he sultan's reception to welcome Prince Javid Khan, the ambassador from the Khanate of the Crimea, was held that evening in the sultan's private garden which opened directly off his quarters. Although it was night, the large garden was well lit by torches and lanterns that had been strung across the fountains and paths, and in the trees. The garden was carefully and beautifully landscaped, its paths of pristine white marble chips raked smooth. At the end of the garden nearest the palace there was an open lawn where a large baldachin had been fashioned from wood, carved and gilded to look like the canopy was actually pure gold. Beneath it was a large divan of crimson satin embroidered with golden stars upon which sat Sultan Murad and his honored guest.

Nur-U-Banu's son was in his middle thirties. He was slender, and of medium height with languid dark eyes, and pale skin. His hair, and his close-cropped beard were of a golden-red color. He was every inch the Oriental monarch in his robe of red velvet tulips which were set upon a heavy gold brocade edged in lustrous dark fur. Upon his head he wore a cloth-of-gold turban which was hung with a rope of fiery rubies, and sported a golden aigrette which sprouted forth from a square of pure gold in its center.

To his left sat his mother, resplendent in her midnight blue tunic dress which was embroidered in gold threads, pearls, and diamonds. Upon her blond head Nur-U-Banu wore a veil of gold gauze shot through with sparkling, metallic threads. Her jewelry, an incredible rope of diamonds and baroque pearls, was magnificent. Because of her position as the sultan's mother she wore no covering over her face, although for that matter none of the sultan's women did this night for Murad enjoyed showing this new ambassador from the Crimea the fabled beauties of his harem. Normally he would not have done such a thing, but he was in the privacy of his own apartments, and other than himself, Prince Javid Khan was the only real man in the garden.

Below the divan seated upon an array of brightly colored velvet cushions sat his beautiful kadin, Safiye, and some half-dozen other of his favorites, women who pleased him in his bed, called ikbals. Some of these women had even borne him daughters. They had positioned themselves like so many dazzling, colored butterflies, Safiye being seated closest to him with her head resting against his knee. The bas kadin had arrayed herself in greens and gold tonight.

Among the rose beds there had been placed tall cages of singing birds for the night was warm. The women of the harem, all arrayed in their very best garments, strolled arm in arm along the paths, admiring the September flowers, and enjoying the delicious fruit-flavored sherbets, and tasty pastries. It was an extremely pleasing picture, and no one appreciated it more than Prince Javid Khan.

"I would wish," he said to the sultan, "that all my nights in Istanbul could be as pleasant as this, but then how can someone like myself possibly hope to equal perfection, my lord?"

Murad smiled. He was no fool, but he enjoyed the courtly flattery. "I am going to make your night even more perfect, Javid Khan," he said. "I understand that you came to Istanbul without your women. Is this rumor correct?"

For the briefest moment Javid Khan's mouth tightened, and then he said, "The rumor is correct, my lord."

"So," chuckled Murad. "The gossip is true, Javid Khan. You really do wish to avail yourself of our famous slave markets. The Great Bazaar offers more beauty, and more variety than any slave market in the world. The women are incredible! Everything from virgins of twelve to women of more experience. There is something for every taste. Sometimes I go there in disguise not just to buy, but to gaze upon the lovelies displayed there."

"I have never known you not to come back with at least one purchase to your credit," chuckled the valideh. "My son is a connoisseur, and a collector of beauty. Is it not so, my lion?"

He smiled a smile of great and genuine affection at her, looking somewhat like a boy who has been caught stealing fruit from the orchard. "Alas, Javid Khan, my mother will allow me no illusions. She is right."

"Your reputation precedes you, my lord. My father is kept busy seeking the most perfect maidens to send you in tribute each year," the prince answered.

"When we learned that you had come alone to us but for your servants," said the sultan, "we decided that we would help you to build a new collection of beauties. Just today a ship arrived from the Dey of Algiers and among the gifts he sent me was a lovely woman whom I am going to present to you." Murad looked up at the agha kislar who was stationed just behind the throne. "Have the woman brought in now, Ilban Bey," he ordered. "She is a rare creature," he said turning back to the prince; "an English noblewoman, captured by the Barbary fleet. Because of my love for my bas kadin I am always being sent women with red hair who are a rarity here in our empire. Of course it is done to please me, but no one can possibly replace my perfect pearl of purity," he finished, stroking Safiye's hair.

Javid Khan smiled, and with warm words thanked the sultan, but he was thinking that right now a woman was the very thing he did not need, or even want. Nonetheless he could not refuse her under the circumstances.

"Do not thank me until after you have seen her," said the sultan with a broad smile, "but then thank me you will, and when she gives you a son, you will thank me even more. The English are said to be a hardy, beautiful, and intelligent race. Some of them have been coming to the Levant to trade for years now, but I will shortly be allowing their first ambassador to come. Did you know that they are ruled by a virgin queen? Is that not odd? Yet they seem very much like you and me."

"I know little about the English," answered Javid Khan. "They do not come to the Crimea."

Suddenly the sultan's crier began shouting to the assembled guests, "Silence! Silence! Our lord, Sultan Murad III, the Defender of the Faith, and the Shadow of Allah upon this earth, would present to the new ambassador from the Khanate of the Crimea, Prince Javid Khan, son of the Great Khan Devlet, ruler of the Crimea, a token of his esteem. All be silent! Look and admire the generosity of our great Sultan Murad III. Let the gift be brought forth."

"Let the gift be brought forth," echoed the entire harem.

From the darkened far end of the garden, down the center path between a row of Flame of Persia roses came the sound of thick-soled feet crunching upon the gravel. Then in the first dim light, and finally into the brightness of the lanterns that lit the lawn came four exceptionally tall, and very proud, elegant black slaves wearing white pantaloons and leopard skins slung across one shoulder, and bearing an enclosed litter of pure silver about which fluttered pale gold draperies of metallic silk gauze. Padding up before the divan where the sultan and his guest awaited they stopped, and carefully set the divan upon the ground in front of their lord and master. As if from nowhere Ilban Bey appeared like a genie, and slowly walked over to the litter he extended a birdlike talon of a hand, and drew the curtains back from one side of the litter.

There was an expectant hush over the garden as the agha kislar reached into the litter, and drew forth from it the heavily veiled form of a female. Bringing her forward so that she stood directly before both the sultan, and the prince he allowed them a moment to look upon her before he drew away the sheer golden veil covering her face, and the matching veil that covered her glorious hair. Next the chief eunuch removed Aïdan's long pelisse, and finally her little short bodice to bare her breasts. Then he stepped back.

"Well, my friend," said the sultan, "is she not everything I promised you she would be?" There was a smile upon his lips, and his voice was jovial to the assembled, but both the valideh, and the bas kadin heard something the others did not. Murad was not pleased. Casting a quick look at her son Nur-U-Banu saw his eyes but briefly skim over Marjallah lustfully. He obviously regretted the loss of the lovely Englishwoman, but there was little he could do about it now.

Javid Khan looked but briefly at Aidan. "She is very fair, my lord, and you are most generous in your gift," he said.

"You will take her to your palace with you this evening, my friend," said the sultan. "She is not a virgin, I am told, and so you may enjoy her without delay." He waved his hand to Ilban Bey. "See she is ready to travel," he commanded the eunuch.

The agha kislar bowed, and refitting Aidan with her bolero he signaled a slave to pick up the other garments, and hurried her away. Once they were out of hearing of the guests he said to her, "You will travel with the prince in his caïque. His palace is located on the sea outside of the city to the north. Jinji has already been dispatched with your things. I will leave you in charge of Omar," he said waving to his shadow, "for I must hurry to find a special maid to share my lord Murad's bed tonight. He was most put out by his loss of you. In that the valideh and I have made a small miscalculation. You would have found favor with the sultan quite quickly. Perhaps it is because you are so statuesque, Marjallah. Good fortune to you with Prince Javid Khan, and remember that you are a gift from the sultan. If the prince is content with you then you will find you have powerful friends among the harem. Do you understand what it is I am saying to you?"

"Yes, my lord agha, I understand," Aidan replied.

To her surprise Ilban Bey patted her hand, and then he hurried off. "He is a good friend to have," said the eunuch Omar.

"And, I think, a dangerous enemy," she replied.

Omar nodded. "You are not unintelligent, my lady Marjallah," he said, and then he helped her into her pelisse, replacing the long gold gauze veil that covered her hair, and refastened the veil across her face. Leading her through a maze of darkened gardens, a little white page boy lighting their way with a large, blazing torch that was almost as big as he was, he brought her to the royal boat basin where the prince's vessel awaited him. "You will be safe here," said Omar, helping her down into the boat. "Good fortune to you!" Then he turned away from her, and spoke sharply to the prince's boatmen, and she caught the phrases, *prince's woman*, and *guard her well*, and *the sultan's wrath*. Then Omar was gone, hurrying back up the sloping, hilly gardens to the palace.

To all intents and purposes she was now alone. The boatmen did not even cast surreptitious glances at her for she was their master's property, and as such not meant for their eyes. There was nothing to do but sit back and wait for Prince Javid Khan, the arbiter of her fate. She had not gotten a particularly good look at him for she had been warned by both Nur-U-Banu and Safiye to keep her eyes modestly lowered when she was presented to the men for Murad was a fanatic about good manners, and in the Ottoman world a woman of breeding kept her eyes lowered in such a situation. From beneath her lashes, however, Aidan had stolen a look at the prince, but her only impression was that he was neither old nor ugly.

She gazed about the vessel in which she was seated. The torches from the marble quay at which it was moored gave her some visibility. She hadn't gotten a good look at the outside of the caïque but from what she could see it appeared to be painted in a dark lacquer, its decorative carvings overlaid in gold leaf. The oarlocks of the boat were silver, as were the handgrips of the oars. Looking up she saw that the canopy was striped in a light blue, a midnight blue, silver and gold. The low divan within was upholstered in deep blue silk, and strewn with pillows in the same colors as the canopy. Aidan sighed, and wondered how long she would have to sit here waiting for Javid Khan. Unawares she was soon lulled to sleep by the gentle rocking of the boat.

Javid Khan stared down at the woman who slept so peacefully in his caïque. The dark silk of the divan showed her fair skin to perfection. A smile crossed his usually stern features. How untroubled her sleep was, but then she could not possibly have the cruel memories that haunted his dreams. He stepped down into the vessel, and said quietly to his galley slaves, "Let us go." Expertly the boatmen maneuvered the caïque out into the main channel of the waterway called Bosporus. Then with a smooth and rhythmic stroke they began to row north toward the end of the Bosporus where it emptied into the Black Sea. It was there on a point of land that Prince Javid Khan had his palace, facing toward his homeland of the Crimea.

He looked down on Aidan, and reaching out fingered one of her curls. Hair like molten copper, and it was soft to the touch. He hadn't seen the color of her eyes, but the sultan's mother had assured him that they were light. Not the sky blue of his own, but nonetheless of a light hue. Fair skin, red hair, and light eyes. He had never seen a woman like her before although he had certainly seen plenty of blonds. His own mother had been one, but hair the color of this slavegirl's was truly unique.

He liked her face, he decided. She was not a great beauty like the valideh Nur-U-Banu, or the bas kadin Safiye. She had not the pouting, childlike prettiness of many young women. No, her face was much more interesting with its high cheekbones, and dimpled chin. She was a tall woman although not big-boned. He wondered what her voice was like, or if she even spoke a language that he understood. A new woman was like anything else new; full of unknowns and interesting to explore. It was a pity, he thought, that at this point in his life he was not interested. He wished he could have told the sultan so, but one did not refuse the gift of the greatest monarch in the world, especially when it had been obvious to him that once Murad saw her he was loath to part with her.

Poor Murad. He chuckled, a deep sound, and Aidan awoke with a start, sitting up suddenly, her cheeks flushed, her generous mouth an O of surprise. Javid Khan reached out, and undid the sheer little scrap of fabric that barely shielded her features. He cupped her face in his hand for a moment, his fingers smoothing over the soft flesh, his thumb running over her lips. Wide-eyed she watched him, and he saw now that her eyes were a silver-gray. "Do you speak Turkish?" he asked her quietly.

"I am learning," she answered him slowly.

"Tell me what language you do speak."

"I speak several. My own which is English, French . . ."

"I am conversant in French," he said switching to that tongue. "My mother was a Frenchwoman."

"Then that is why your eyes are blue!"

Javid Khan felt his face breaking into another smile. "That is why my eyes are blue," he agreed.

"Where are we going, my lord?" Aidan had suddenly remembered her manners.

"Your new home is a palace on a point of land at the end of the Bosporus. You will be able to see the Black Sea, too, from it."

"All of it is strange to me," she said quietly.

"Have you a servant? You will be the first woman in my house here."

"The Dey of Algiers sent me to Istanbul with a eunuch called Jinji. If I might, my lord, I should like some women about me. I find it strange to be dressed, undressed, and bathed by one who looks like a man even if he isn't."

"We shall send this Jinji to the slave markets tomorrow to buy you some handmaidens," Javid Khan answered.

"My lord? Would it be possible for me to go to Istanbul also? It is not that I don't trust Jinji, but if these women are to be my companions, I should prefer to choose them myself. Jinji does not know me well enough to do that."

"I see no harm in it," he answered her, "as long as you are properly chaperoned. What kind of women would you choose?"

"I am not certain, but perhaps women who like myself are new to slavery, and frightened."

Her words gave him pause for thought. He was rather charmed by her soft heart. "Are you frightened of me?" His blue eyes searched her face curiously.

"Yes," she admitted honestly.

"You have no need to be, but tell me, why are you afraid?"

"I do not know what is expected of me, my lord. A year ago at this time I was a virgin daughter mourning the death of my father who was my only surviving parent. Seven months ago my queen had me married to my husband. Less than three months ago I was kidnapped and sold into slavery. Everything has happened so quickly for me in the last year. Before that my days were calm and orderly. Now I find myself seated in a boat next to a strange man who I am told is to be my *master*. I am afraid, my lord. Can you understand why?"

"You need not fear me, Marjallah. I will be quite frank with you when I say that had you not been a gift of my liege lord that I would not have accepted you. As it is I did not have the choice. You will live in my house, and I will try to see that you are as happy and as comfortable as you can be under these circumstances."

The words slipped out before she could think. "Do you not like women, my lord?" She had heard of men like that.

Rather than being offended Javid Khan was amused. "Are you asking me if I prefer the Temple of Sodom to the Temple of Venus? The answer is no, I do not. I very much enjoy women."

"Oh." Aidan's face fell. He didn't want her. Here was the final humiliation. Once again she was a loser in this game of life. It seemed that only Cavan FitzGerald, damn his black soul to hell, had been a winner. Then she had a brighter thought as the hurt of his rejection began to fade. "If you do not want me, my lord, would you consider applying to my family for a ransom? We are very wealthy, and my husband would pay well for my return." It mattered not what Safiye Kadin had said earlier. She would rather face the shame of her captivity in England than chance being sold from Javid Khan's household because he did not want her.

"To sell the sultan's gift to me, even back into her own land, would be considered an appalling breach of etiquette, Marjallah." The tone of his voice indicated that the matter was closed. He sat staring straight ahead, and did not touch her, or speak to her again until they had reached his palace. Then he escorted her from the caïque through darkened gardens into the building where Jinji was waiting.

As the eunuch bustled forward, brimming over with his own self-importance, the prince tipped her face up to his, and said in a quiet voice, "Good night, Marjallah. I hope you will sleep well."

Watching him disappear down a hallway she felt a tiny pang of regret. What kind of man was he? What did he really want of her? If he did not want her then why did he insist upon keeping her? Would the sultan be *that* offended if Javid Khan ransomed her to her family? Would such a great monarch even know, or care about such a trifling matter as a slave-girl?

"Why are you not to go to him? Have you angered him already?" Jinji fumed about her. "You cannot offend a great prince."

"Be silent!" she ordered the startled eunuch, speaking sharply, and showing spirit for the first time since her capture. "The prince does not want me tonight. Perhaps he is courteous enough to want me to get some rest after my long voyage."

"Of course, my lady Marjallah, of course! Why did I not think of that in the first place myself." He was all smiles again.

"Why indeed, Jinji? Now where are my rooms? Why are you making me stand here like a beggar at the gates?" She almost laughed aloud as he tumbled over himself to escort her to her rooms. If she had learned one thing today it was that in the strange world of the harem the woman must be in charge else the eunuch overrule her. She had watched both Safiye and Nur-U-Banu today with their servants, and they had both kept the upper hand. "Tomorrow," she continued, "my lord Javid Khan has said that you and I may travel to the slave markets in the city and obtain a bevy of maidens to serve me, and to keep me company. This household is naught but men. Take this heavy pelisse from me, and give me my sleeping garments. Did you bring the kittens that the valideh promised me? I would see them before I sleep."

He scurried about like a small bug, desperately trying to keep up with her. Removing her clothing he passed her a comfortable caftan, exclaiming at the marks that the heavy golden girdle with its baroque pearl decoration had left upon her hips. "The valideh's chief eunuch said that the kittens would be sent to you within a few days, my lady, and not a moment too soon, I say. This palace has been closed up for many years, and I have seen mice."

"Not in my apartment, I should hope." She moved quickly through the haremlik of the palace exploring the space that had been set aside for the women of the household. There was a very large salon with a center fountain off which were a dozen, windowed cubicles. There was a good-sized tiled bath, as well as the small tiled bath that was attached to her private apartment within the harem which consisted of a small salon, her bedroom, and several small servants' rooms. Since it was night she could not tell what was outside of the windows in the harem but when morning came she discovered that her salon windows faced both onto the sea, and onto a private garden. It was much too big a space for one woman, she thought, but perhaps the prince would eventually fill it.

They traveled the following morning to the city by water in a larger caïque than had been used the night before. The prince had not forgotten his promise to her, and had supplied Jinji with a more than generous purse.

"He said," the eunuch said excitedly, "that you were to purchase anything else you so desired. You have caught his eye, my lady Marjallah! I know you have!"

Their vessel was big enough to hold her litter as well as the four black slaves necessary to carry it, and once they had arrived in the city, she entered her transport, and was brought thusly to the slave markets of the Great Bazaar. They went to a market that dealt in women only, and there Aidan realized how truly fortunate she had been not to have been sold at public auction from the block. The entire place reeked of misery, but then how could anyone be content in the state of slavery? she thought. She was soon to learn that many slaves were precisely that: content. For many it was a perfectly acceptable way of life for they had been born to it. For others it was an escape from poverty, but there were enough captives, formerly free, and enough women being sold from situations in which they had been happy, to make for an air of discontent.

The women's slave market was mostly peopled by men although there were a few heavily veiled women like herself, carefully chaperoned by their servants. She concluded her business as quickly as possible for it disturbed her greatly to have to stand helplessly by and watch as other women were stripped naked, and minutely examined by their prospective buyers. She saw some tears upon the faces of these women, but saddest of all was the look of utter hopelessness in the eyes of too many.

By having Jinji obtain the ear of the owner of the slave market she was able to quietly voice her needs. She wanted, she explained, three servants, European if possible, for she sought to rescue in her own way at least a few of her sisters in captivity.

The bazaar owner smiled, showing yellowed teeth that somehow reminded Aidan of a dog's teeth. "Please tell your gracious mistress that I have exactly what she seeks," he said for Jinji. He would not speak to Aidan for she was only a woman, but she was also socially above him by virtue of belonging to Prince Javid Khan. The bazaar owner clapped his hands, and gave instructions to a slave who came running. "I have a mother, and her two daughters," he said to Jinji. "They do not speak Turkish, and they appear totally incapable of learning it. They are also extremely stupid, and although I had high hopes for the two daughters it has been impossible to separate them. Each time we have tried they have created the most terrible trouble. They have even tried suicide. I wish to Allah I had never laid eyes upon them, but perhaps your lady can do something with them. I have told you this openly because I am an honest merchant. Unless I can sell them together into a situation like this one, I might as well strangle them for they are costing me a fortune in food!"

Aidan held up her hand to Jinji when he went to repeat what the merchant had said. "I understood him," she said. "Let us see these three."

The trio who shuffled into the room were indeed a discouraging-looking lot. They were tall, big-boned women with dark blond hair that was now matted, and filthy. Sullen-looking creatures she could see the mutinous light in their eyes. It did not look very promising she thought.

"Do you speak French?" she asked them.

No answer.

"Are you German?"

No answer.

"Are you Venetian?"

"No, lady," said the elder of the three, "but we understand the tongue of the Venetians as they trade with our people. We are from a place near the city of Dubrovnik."

"You were not born slaves?"

"Never! We were free-born women! My husband was the owner of a factory that processed fish. We lived in a house with four rooms, and my daughters had respectable dowries, but business was bad last year. My husband could not pay his taxes to the sultan. Soldiers came, and took our daughters. When I protested they laughed, and said if I was so concerned about my girls I could come with them. That is how we came to be here."

"If I purchase you," said Aidan, "will you serve me faithfully? I cannot free you for I, myself, am no longer a free woman. I belong to Prince Javid Khan."

"What would you want us to do, my lady?"

"Be my servants."

"You will buy us all, my lady?"

"Yes," said Aidan. "I would not separate a mother and her children. How old are your daughters?"

"Eleven and thirteen, but they are hard workers, my lady."

Aidan turned to Jinji. "Pay the slave merchant for these three, and let us return home. This place depresses me."

Jinji looked her choice over critically. "They aren't very pretty," he said, and then smiled knowingly. "Of course, my lady Marjallah! How clever you are! The prince will not even see them! You would be foolish to bring rivals into your own house until you have secured the prince's total and undying affection." He chuckled, and set to work bargaining for the trio of females with the slave merchant who now having a buyer had decided that his merchandise was valuable.

"What are you called?" said Aidan turning back to the woman.

"Marta. My daughters are Iris and Fern."

"I am called Marjallah," said Aidan, and to her surprise the statement didn't seem strange to her, and she realized that she was beginning to accept the situation in which she found herself.

"The bargain is concluded, my lady Marjallah," said Jinji. "This robber who calls himself an honest man has been bested by my superiority."

Aidan laughed. "Jinji, Jinji!" she scolded him gently. "Have you no shame at all in your quest for high position?"

"None, my lady," he told her with an engaging grin. For the first time since he had been made her eunuch he was beginning to feel that the venture might be a successful one. She had just teased him, and to him it indicated that she was beginning to feel more comfortable in her position. "These females will need more suitable clothing," he said to Aidan. "Let us go to the Street of the Clothing Vendors, and purchase something more suitable for the servants of a prince's favorite. We will also visit the cloth merchants' quarter, and obtain material for other garments for both yourself and your women; but first let us take them to the Women's Hamam so they may be bathed. We cannot take them with us into the prince's caïque as they are. They are ridden with vermin, and I suspect it has been months since their hair was clean."

Looking closely at Marta and her daughters Aidan had to agree. They were absolutely filthy which she found rather interesting since the Turks seemed to pride themselves upon their cleanliness. Why they would allow healthy slaves to get into such a condition was curious. She shortly had her answer to the puzzle.

"I am going to find you clean and decent clothing," she said to Marta, "but first I will leave you and the girls at the women's baths. They will see that you are washed. You do not look as though you have had a bath in weeks, and your hair is a disgrace."

"A *bath?*" Marta looked uncomfortable. "We have been taught by our priests that bathing is ungodly, that only through mortification of the flesh can one truly find God. Please do not make us bathe, my lady."

God's toenail! thought Aidan. What incredible foolishness, but then she said to the woman bluntly, "Your priests are wrong, Marta, but I will not argue the point. You promised me if I purchased you and your daughters that you would serve me faithfully, and obeying me implicitly is part of that service. I am taking you to the baths where you will be thoroughly washed, and groomed. If you cannot obey this simple first command of mine, how will you obey me later on? The choice is yours, however. You may refuse, and I will see you returned to the market; or you may obey, and be happy and safe in my service. I will not tolerate disobedience amongst my servants, nor will I tolerate the sin of uncleanliness." She looked sternly at the woman, and Marta was thoroughly cowed.

"We will obey you, my lady, and go to the baths."

Aidan nodded, but said nothing more.

They left the woman and her daughters at the public baths set aside for women only. Jinji had gone into the building with them, and instructed the head bath attendant as to what was desired by his illustrious mistress, the beloved of Prince Javid Khan. Aidan would have laughed had she heard the tale that he spun to the not easily impressed bath attendants who were quite taken in by the eunuch. He exited the baths with an enormous grin upon his face, and said to Aidan,

"We may return for them in two hours' time. They will be in perfect order then, my lady Marjallah."

Then he moved proudly through the crowded streets, making room for Aidan's litter and her slaves to pass. They first went to the Bazaar of the Cloth Merchants where with Jinji's help she picked some pretty, but practical cottons, light wools, and linens for her new servants. She tried to find attractive colors for even if the three were servants, they had female souls, and it was such little trouble to help bind them to her. Having made her purchases they moved on to the shop of a merchant who sold only the finest fabrics, and Aidan chose for herself a turquoise-colored silk with little silver stars woven into the fabric, a grass-green silk with wide stripes of gold, and a pale gold silk gauze.

The merchant was eager to be of help for Jinji quickly informed him that this was the favorite of the Sublime Porte's new ambassador from the Khanate of the Crimea, and if her master, the very illustrious Prince Javid Khan was happy with her purchases, then the lady Marjallah would be returning. His fortune would be made for the prince could not be too generous when it came to his favorite.

Aidan understood enough of what her eunuch was saying to dissolve into laughter, but she did not embarrass her servant by reprimanding him before the merchant. Besides it amused her, and she was laughing more now than she had in months. However when they had exited the shop she said, "You are really quite wicked, Jinji. Be careful lest your galloping tongue lead you into a pit from which you cannot dig yourself out, my friend. It is only fortunate that the prince cannot hear you for I do not think he is the least bit interested in me at all right now, and if it continues where will we both be?"

"I learned something this morning, my lady, from the cook in the kitchen. Hammed says that the prince mourns his wife and his sons who are but recently dead. I was not able to learn anything more for I did not wish to pry lest I compromise your new position in the household. At least we know he is a real man, my lady. You will help him recover from his grief in time, and in the meantime, your position in his household will be secure from other women. We need that time, my lady Marjallah, so do not fret that the prince seems cool to you."

"Poor man," Aidan said. "I know just how he feels," and she remembered not only her father, but the deaths of her mother and little sisters as well.

By this time they had arrived at the Street of the Used Clothing Vendors, and Jinji, who seemed to have a great deal of knowledge for someone in Istanbul only one day, went directly to the stall of a Jew he appeared to know by reputation. There he successfully bargained for a total of six outfits for Aidan's slaves; baggy trousers, and blouses and boleros, as well as sashes, capes, and shoes. Everything was of good quality, and very clean. Having paid for his purchases they now began the return trip to the baths.

"How is it," Aidan's curiosity got the better of her, "that you seem to know this city so well?" she demanded of Jinji.

"My very first master lived here in Istanbul," the eunuch answered. "I know the city very well. It is my first memory, and is like home to me. I was made a eunuch, after all, when I was very young. I love this place, and I hope for nothing better than to end my days here."

Having reached the baths Jinji escorted his mistress into the reception room of the hamam for it would have been unthinkable for her to remain outside for any long period of time, and they could not be certain that Marta and her daughters were ready to return with them. The eunuch made inquiries, and was told it would be just a moment or two more before the three were ready. Jinji handed the bath attendant three sets of clothing with instructions that they were for his mistress' slavewomen.

"I told them to burn those vermin-ridden rags that they were wearing when we brought them into the baths," he said to Aidan.

She chuckled. "A very wise decision although I suspect that poor Marta will be most distressed to find the last remnant of her past life has been consigned to destruction."

"She will survive the tragedy," he said somewhat wryly. "What you have bought them will probably be the nicest things they have ever owned in their lives."

"She was no poor woman," said Aidan. "Her husband, she tells me, was a man of means."

"More than likely she was a fisherman's wife," Jinji sniffed, "but no matter. I only hope she is trainable. We should have no trouble with her daughters, but a woman of her years is most likely to be set in her ways, my lady Marjallah. I hope you were right in purchasing them. You have too kind a heart, I fear."

Then the bath attendants were leading before them three females, and both Aidan and Jinji gasped in surprise. Clean, Marta and her two daughters were handsome females with pretty brown eyes, and dark blond braids. Each was neatly dressed in light blue baggy trousers, rose-colored cotton blouses, and short boleros of a blue-and-rose-striped satin. They had pretty matching slippers upon their feet, blue-and-silver-patterned shawls tied about their hips, and little caps of cloth of silver upon their heads. They were a trio of most presentable handmaidens, and Aidan said so.

"How lovely you all look, and don't you feel better now?"

"Well," said Marta, "I must admit that bathing is not so bad, but all that nudity! Still we're none the worse for wear, my lady, and I thank you for our new clothing."

Aidan smiled. "That is but the first of many new things you have to learn. You are going to have to learn to speak Turkish, Marta, but come now. We must return to the prince's palace before he begins to wonder what has happened to us."

They returned to Javid Khan's palace, and seeing it in the late-afternoon light for the first time Aidan was enchanted with it. It was called the Jewel Serai, and indeed it was placed precisely as a fine gem might be within a precious setting. Javid Khan had said it sat upon a point of land between the Bosporus and the Black Sea which was not precisely so. Actually the Jewel Serai had been built upon a spit of land very near the mouth of the Bosporus where it emptied into the Black Sea, but it was most definitely on the Bosporus. It was possible, however, to see the Black Sea easily from the palace itself, and the property belonging to it widened as one moved back from the point itself and curved into the shore of the larger body of water.

The Jewel Serai had been built of white marble, and Aidan imagined that with the sunset or sunrise tinting it golden it would be absolutely gorgeous. It sat directly on the water, its gardens to its right side and to the rear of the building. A graceful dome rose over the center portion of the building, and a pillared, open portico ran along its entire length. The private section of the palace was in the right wing of the building, the left section was open to those who might come to deal officially with the ambassador from the Khanate of the Crimea.

The Great Khan had bought the palace for his son from the heirs of a wealthy merchant who did not want it. Its distance from the center of Istanbul made it undesirable to them, and to many others who preferred living nearer the city. In the years since the merchant's death the beautiful gardens had become overgrown, and neglected, wildflowers seeding themselves in the beds along with what had once been perfectly cultivated blooms. From the sea, however, the tangled growth was colorful and beautiful.

The eyes of Aidan's serving women widened as they gazed at the Jewel Serai. "Is that where we are to live, my lady?" asked Marta in a voice filled with awe. "Is the prince's harem a large one? Will there be many women?"

"The prince," said Aidan, "is but newly come to Istanbul, and I was only presented to him by the sultan yesterday. He has no other women although he assures me that he enjoys them." She blushed at that statement, and then continued on. "Jinji tells me that the prince mourns the loss of his wife which may account for his behavior."

The large caïque had nosed itself into the shore, and its passengers disembarked. Watching them from a window of the building Javid Khan saw that Marjallah had three other females with her. He smiled to himself. Here was his first fact about Marjallah. She was obviously not extravagant. His favorite wife, Zoe, had been like that, never wanting more than she needed. She had been a gentle girl, a quiet girl, a girl of peace to whom all other members of his harem had turned because they trusted Zoe to solve their disputes fairly. She had been a lovely woman, mother of two of his sons, and a daughter.

Yet he had been equally attracted to the woman he had made his second wife, the mercurial Ayesha. What a marvelous contradiction Ayesha had been. One moment she would be purring like a kitten, and the next minute she would be flaming like a volcano. Her moods had both fascinated and infuriated him, but her very differences when compared with Zoe had intrigued him, kept him always coming back to her couch. Her saving grace had been that Ayesha had never held a grudge in her entire life. Her anger might flare quickly, but it was over and done with just as quickly. She also had given him two sons.

His sons. He felt a pang of anguish ripping through him as it did each time he remembered his children. He had fathered six sons and two daughters. His eldest, Devlet, named for his own father, would have been fourteen this year. The youngest of his sons had been a chubby toddler of only two. As for his daughters, and now he felt tears pricking at the back of his eyelids, the eldest of all his children had been the daughter that he and Zoe had first created. Her name had been Oma, and she had been her mother's image. This would have been her sixteenth year, and she had been betrothed to the heir of a neighboring khan. His youngest daughter was seven, and had been a mischievous imp called Leila.

Gone. They were all gone now. His strong, healthy sons; his beautiful daughters, his women. It was as if they had never existed. Not a trace of them remained except in his memory, but the memories were too painful right now. He didn't want to remember. Even a strong man could bear only so much. He focused his eyes again toward the quay, but Marjallah and her attendants had already entered the building.

He would go to the harem, and see them, and if she pleased him today he would allow her to eat the evening meal with him. He was sad, and he was lonely. He had not been happy when the sultan had so jovially presented him with Marjallah last night, but now he was beginning to have second thoughts. All the mourning in the world would not bring back his women and his children. His father had sent him to Istanbul to make a new start. To remove him from his sorrow, and although he could not entirely forget, nor should he ever, at least he could try to live again. He had never been a man for self-pity.

He strode purposefully from his apartment, and down the hall into the women's quarters. Her eunuch—what was the creature's name?—hurried forward to welcome him effusively. He was hard put not to smile for the eunuch was so damnably anxious to please.

"Welcome, my lord prince! Welcome!"

Aidan turned, and took her first really good look at the man who was called her master. She bowed prettily. "Welcome, my lord prince," and remembering both the hospitality of Safiye and Nur-U-Banu said, "Bring refreshments, Jinji." She then seated the prince where he might have a view of the sea. He was every bit as handsome as Conn, she thought, but in an entirely different way. Conn's good looks were almost pretty in their perfection, but Javid Khan's face was a stern one upon first glance although now as he smiled at her the severeness eased. His face was long rather than round, his chin gave the appearance of having been carved from stone so hard and determined was it. His cheekbones were very high and sculpted, and his eyes, although not narrowed as his pure Tartar ancestors had been, were almond-shaped although they were a startling sky blue in color. Bareheaded within the privacy of his own home, Javid Khan proved to have tawny gold hair.

"My lord, I am not certain if what I do is the correct thing," Aidan said quietly. "I fear my ignorance of customs in this land will shock and repel you, and so I pray you tell me if what I do is right, and when I am wrong."

"Are women not the same everywhere, Marjallah?" he asked her.

"From what I have seen here in Istanbul I do not believe so, my lord."

"Elucidate to me then," he replied.

"In my land we are ruled by a queen."

"And her husband?"

"She has none. She is a virgin queen, but if she took a spouse, he would not automatically become king. Only she could make him so. He would be her husband only."

Javid Khan was interested, and his face showed it. "Say on, Marjallah. Tell me more."

"Do your women ride upon horses?"

"Once they did," he said, "but no more. It is a woman's role to bear her children, sons preferably, and to care for her home, her children, and her lord. That is why there is a harem. It is a safe place where a woman may live without distractions."

"How dull for your women," Aidan said before she realized the words, but seeing his mouth quirk at the corners in a small smile she knew she had not offended him, and continued. "Our women are not cloistered. They ride upon horses, they eat with their husbands and families, they study, they even dance with men. You cannot tell me that women here do all of those things, my lord."

"Yet even in your land a man's word is supreme. That much I am certain of despite what you have told me."

"A man in my country, indeed in all the civilized lands of Europe, does certainly have more rights than a woman, but we are not powerless."

"Can women in your land own property and goods?"

"We can!"

"But a man manages those properties and goods."

"Not always," she said quickly. "My sister-in-law is one of the wealthiest women in Europe. She has made her own wealth, and she manages that wealth, too!"

"But," he said with a small smile, "did she not begin with a man's portion?"

Aidan laughed. "You are absolutely correct, my lord, she did; but she increased that portion!"

"And you, Marjallah, did you manage your own lands and wealth?"

"Since I was my father's only heir he thought it wise I know such things, but until he grew too ill to do things himself I only oversaw his work. I freely admit that he did it himself." She nodded to Marta who was holding a decanter of fruit sherbet, and anxiously wondering where to place it. "Here, Marta, upon the table. You may pour the prince a gobletful."

"Yes, my lady." Marta never raised her eyes to them as she set her tray down. Little Fern hurried up with a plate of almond cakes, and scampered away as quickly, but not before she had flashed a shy smile at the prince and Aidan.

"She is a pretty child," remarked the prince.

"I bought Marta and her two daughters this morning. You said I might have women to serve me." Aidan passed him a cake.

"I expected you to come back with a dozen giggling maidens, Marjallah. Are this woman and her daughters really enough to serve you?"

"To serve me personally? Of course, my lord. Why would more than three be necessary? If, however, you wanted me to obtain servants of a lower order to serve you, and to keep the palace in order you should have told me. I do not know what my duties are here yet."

He smiled a slow smile at her, and said, "Your duties are to please me in any way that I should so desire, Marjallah," and then he sat back to enjoy the slow blush that suffused her cheeks. He reached out, and gently touched her burning face. "I believe that you were given to me to be a houri, and not a prim little housekeeper." She was temporarily rendered speechless, and it amused him to have done so, not that he was angry at what she had said for he was enjoying her openness and her blunt speech, but he had not felt in command of the situation before, and now he did. A wife she might have been, but not, he suspected, an experienced one. He was going to enjoy finding out *everything* about her. "I came to ask you to have supper with me tonight, Marjallah. We will dine at seven." He drained his goblet, and popped the almond cake whole into his mouth. Then standing he left the room without another word.

She was stunned. Had she angered him? What was a houri? She looked to Jinji, her only guide in this strange new world of which she had become a part.

The young eunuch's features were filled with delight. "You have pleased him, my lady Marjallah! I did not think he would take you to his couch so quickly for his servants say that he mourned his family deeply."

"What happened to them?" she asked.

"I do not know," he said. "I do not feel it is important. What is of import is that the prince favors you, and now is your time, my lady Marjallah. You have no rivals, and it is possible to bind him to you before his attention wanders. You must have a son! If you bear his son, you will never lack for anything no matter how many women he may take to his couch."

A son, she thought. I wonder if Conn's baby was a son? She turned her head away from Jinji a moment so he might not see her tears. The reality was beginning to really seep into mind. Unless Conn walked through the door of the harem this minute, believed that she had been untouched so far in this adventure, and carried her off back home to *Pearroc Royal*, it was going to be indeed as Safiye had said. She would be dead to her husband. She sighed. She was dead to him. She simply had to face it. How could she escape? There was no way at all, and her common sense told her so. She had to make peace with herself, and this situation. If she displeased Javid Khan he could dispose of her. She did not think he would sell her for she had been a sultan's gift, but what use would she have in this house if she could not please him? She would be at the mercy of any other woman, or women who attracted him. Jealous, spiteful women who knew better than she did the ways of the harem. Suddenly she understood the not-so-subtle battle between Nur-U-Banu and Safiye for supremacy with Sultan Murad, and she was a little afraid.

"We have not much time," Jinji was chattering. "We must bathe and perfume you so that you will be a delight to the senses! Aiiii! I have so little with which to work. Why did I not think to buy musk and ambergris when we were in the city this morning? I must go back tomorrow. If we did not live at this distance from Istanbul then the bazaar women would come to us, but here!" He looked greatly aggrieved. "Here I must do everything myself."

"I like it better," said Aidan frankly. "It means that I can sometimes visit the city which I could not do if we lived there. I wouldn't like being cooped up all the time."

Jinji was not listening too attentively to her, however, for he was far too busy rumaging through her things, seeking bath oil, and soaps, and lotions with which to soften her already soft skin.

"What a way for a woman to have to live," said Marta expressing Aidan's own thoughts.

"But we are here," she answered, "and there is no help for it, Marta. I do not think I can change the prince's ways, do you?"

"No, my lady, I do not. It is easy to see that he is a strong man, and," she added, "a handsome one, too. Having seen some of the creatures who lurked about the slave markets I can tell you honestly that you are very well off. My daughters and I, too, for that matter."

Aidan submitted herself to the ritual of the bath although Jinji complained that without trained attendants, and the proper soaps and oils he wondered why he was lavishing his time and skills. He made Aidan laugh, and even Marta smiled at the eunuch's fussiness, while Fern and Iris giggled behind their hands, half-afraid that Jinji would see them for the two little sisters were very much in awe of the eunuch even if they did not understand him. Jinji took their teasing good-naturedly for he actually did have a good disposition, and he was, Aidan suspected, only imitating older and more experienced creatures of his kind for their inexperience in harem matters really made him their superiors.

"Never has a woman been so fortunate as you, my lady Marjallah! Do you know how rare it is for a woman to have such a chance as you do with a man of experience? Usually this opportunity only comes to some silly chit first chosen by a sultan, or a sultan's heir."

"You are telling me that I must go out of my way to both please and attract the prince tonight, Jinji, is that not it? But what if a companion at his supper is all he really wants of me? Will you then be disappointed?"

Jinji handed her a pair of beautiful midnight-blue trousers that had small metallic gold thread moths woven into them. "I do not believe at this moment in time that even the prince is aware of how he desires the evening to proceed. That, I suspect, will be up to you, my lady."

"Am I to seduce the prince then, Jinji?" Aidan drew the silk pantaloons on.

"Gracious, no!" the eunuch cried, his dark eyes rolling so far back in his head that only the whites showed for a moment. "That would be considered much too forward. The prince will lead you along the path that he wishes to, my lady. You have but to follow." He helped her into a sleeveless bolero of the same deep blue silk as her trousers. It was edged with delicate gold fringe. Kneeling he fastened about her hips a wide belt of gilt kid that was lavishly sewn with small pearls. Then while Marta knelt to fit Aidan's feet into matching kid slippers, Jinji sat his mistress upon a stool, and personally brushed out her long, soft hair. Carefully he braided her tresses, weaving into the one thick braid a small strand of fine seed pearls which were affixed to a ribbon of gold. "Please stand, my lady Marjallah," he said. Then hurrying to a chest he drew forth from it a leather case, and opening it displayed to her two ropes of pale pink pearls, and a pair of wonderful earbobs to match. "They are a gift from the valideh to you," said Jinji pridefully, and he bedecked her with the jewelry, adding some gold and silver bangles that were also in the case.

"The sultan's mother gave me these?" she was astounded. "Why?"

"Because she would be your friend. She is jealous of the lady Safiye's attempt to befriend you, and so she attempts to woo you away from her son's favorite."

"I think," said Aidan, "that I must tread a fine line between these two warring ladies. Both must be my friends. Is that not so, Jinji?"

The eunuch nodded. "Exactly! The favorite is likely to outlive the valideh, but one can never be too certain of these things. Life's path has a funny way of turning when you least expect it. You can gain another benefit by this tact. Stand between both of these great ladies, showing no favoritism, and causing no difficulty, and you will gain the sultan's favor, too. That would not be a bad thing, my lady Marjallah, and it would be of great advantage to the prince. Who knows what his needs will be with regard to his ambassadorship. That, too, can endear you to him."

Iris stood before her holding up a round polished silver mirror. She looked into it, and Aidan was quite surprised by her own appearance. For the first time in her entire life she felt beautiful. Perhaps she was not, but the lavishness and at the same time the simplicity of her Oriental garb, seemed to flatter her.

"You are pleased with what you see," said Jinji, "but wait for there is one last thing I must do. Sit down again." He turned to little Fern. "Bring the kohl and the brushes that I showed you earlier," he ordered her gently using the words as Aidan told him so the child would understand, and she ran to do his bidding. When she returned she held the small alabaster pot of kohl for the eunuch while he carefully made up Aidan's eyes. When he had finished he said, "Now, my lady, look!"

The transformation was amazing. She was exotic-looking, and she could barely believe it. Oh, she thought, if only Conn and those silly girls I served with at court could see me!

"Now," said Jinji proudly, "you are fit and ready to go to our master. Come! I will escort you."

To her surprise Marta gave her a quick hug before she left her apartments, saying, "God go with you, my lady!"

Jinji walked her the short distance from the harem quarters to the prince's apartments, and opening the door into those rooms ushered her inside while pulling the door closed back behind her.

"How formal your Jinji is," the prince said coming forward to greet her. "He might have simply brought you across the garden," and he gestured with a hand through the wide glass windows.

Aidan realized that the overgrown garden she saw from the harem was also shared with the master of the house which she thought made a great deal of sense. "I think Jinji feared we should get lost in the undergrowth," she said with a smile. "Do you think it would be possible to hire gardeners from the countryside to clear that tangle? I should very much like to see what is actually there."

"Do you like gardens?" He was seated at a low table wearing a comfortable, white robe that was embroidered about the deeply cut open neckline in gold threads, and Persian lapis that matched his eyes.

"I like gardens," she answered him softly.

He waved her forward. "Come and sit by me, Marjallah," and his eyes approved her dress. When she had seated herself next to him he reached out and touched her hair. "I almost expect it to be hot," he said with a half-smile. "It is a most wonderful color. My mother was a Frenchwoman, and she had hair like silvered gold. I always believed that no other color could match it, but now I see I was wrong."

"I know nothing about your land or your people," she said. "Where is the Crimea? What kind of people live there?"

"My land is north of here on the Black Sea, and its peoples migrated long ago out of Asia. We are called Tartars, and yet we are today as different from our brothers to the east as a black man is from a white man. Although our customs have not changed, the appearance of the Crimean Tartars was due to our intermarriage with the women of the region, and of course other women slaves, like my mother, who have come into our possession. Our people are proud, fierce, and loyal. We are herdsmen by both instinct and by our nature. When we settled in the Crimea, however, we began to become men of the cities, too." He slipped an arm about her slender waist. "Do you really want a lesson in the history of my people tonight, Marjallah? Perhaps one thing that you should know about them is that Tartar men are passionate and vigorous lovers." He dropped a kiss upon her shoulder.

Her first instinct was to pull away. She was a married woman, but then she forced herself to remain still for her old life was over, and this man was the key to her future. So far he had done nothing to incur either her distrust or dislike. "I have never had any lovers," she said softly.

"Was your husband not your lover?" His mouth lingered warm and teasing upon her skin.

"Yes," she said upon reflection, "he was, wasn't he?"

The prince turned her so that they were facing each other, and then he took her face between his two big hands. "Did he tell you that your eyes reminded him of storm clouds, and the flecks of black and gold within them are like leaves caught in the wind of that storm?"

For a very long moment Aidan thought that she would suffocate for it seemed that she was unable to draw a breath. He had the most incredible bright blue eyes she had ever seen, and he was gazing at her with those eyes. Gazing? No! It was the wrong word. He had caught her with his eyes, and she felt as if she was drowning in his look.

Releasing her face from his grasp he smoothed his hands beneath her bolero, brushing his palms across her breasts as he did so. "And," he continued, "you have skin that is the softest I have ever felt. It is like the finest Bursa silk, Marjallah, smooth, and cool, and flawless to the touch."

Aidan felt her nipples harden beneath the palms of his hands, and her cheeks grew pink and warm. She swallowed, and then was finally able to draw a breath which to her embarrassment only had the effect of rubbing the tips of her breasts against his hands. She bit her lip in confusion. God! She wasn't a maid, and yet he was making her feel like one. Her heart hammered in her ears, and for the briefest moment she thought she might faint. She could not escape his eyes which were now warm with amusement.

"I think," he said quietly, "that I am going to have to kiss you, my jewel," and then his mouth took complete and total possession of hers.

His lips were firm and warm, and to her great surprise she found her own lips responding to his masterful skill. Gently, but firmly he made his first penetration of her, running his tongue softly across her mouth, coaxing it open to plunge within. The touch of his tongue as it met hers caused a churning of tumultuous sensations to burst within her that reminded her of the strange and wonderful fireworks that she had seen at a court gala. She clung to him to keep from fainting for she felt even closer to it now.

His hands ran through the tangle of her hair, and releasing her head he looked down upon her. The bright blue eyes silently searched her face, asking, to her surprise, not demanding. There was a tenderness about this man, Aidan thought, which startled her. She had not expected it in him for Jinji had done nothing else but babble on about the fierceness of the Tartar men, and the prince himself had just teased her about his race being passionate and vigorous lovers. She wanted to please him for unless she did her future was very much in doubt. But then suddenly the image of Conn O'Malley rose up between them, and to her immense horror Aidan burst into tears.

Javid Khan responded instinctively, reaching out to draw her into his arms. Holding her close he allowed her to release the grief that had been pent up within her. Aidan clung to him, sobbing wildly while at the same time the thought drifted through her head that this was not the way to his heart, yet she could not help herself. When at last her misery had run its natural course, and her weeping quieted, she was too embarrassed to raise her head, and huddled against his chest despondently.

Sensing that her sorrow had finally abated Javid Khan said quietly, "I want the truth, Marjallah. For whom do you grieve?"

What difference did it make now? Aidan thought sadly. With a sigh she raised her head to meet his serious glance, and said, "I cry for my husband, my lord."

To her surprise he nodded. "Yes," he said softly to her. "I understand that, my jewel. You loved him, and so now that he is lost to you, you weep for what was. So do I, my jewel, so do I."

"My lord," she began, "I realize that I should be grateful for your kindness, and I am. I would truly please you, but at this moment it is so hard not to remember."

"I know that," he answered, "for my dreams both waking and sleeping are filled with things that no longer are, can no longer be." He stroked her long, soft hair. "Ahh, my jewel, I am probably the only man to whom the sultan could have given you who understands what you feel, for I feel the same thing. This is the first time since my great loss that I have reached out to a woman for comfort. I need comfort, Marjallah! Do you not need comfort, too?"

Shocked by his admission as much as by his vulnerability she could only answer with the truth. "Yes," she said, nodding as she met his glance. "Yes, my lord Javid, I, too, need that comfort."

Pulling her close he hugged her gently, and then said, "Let us eat the fine supper that Hammed has prepared for us. He has gone to great trouble to create delicacies that he hopes will encourage us to love. He has been with me for many years; and he, too, misses my family."

"What happened to your family, my lord?" she asked him looking up at him. "Was it an epidemic?"

"Would that it had been," he said, and a spasm of pain passed over his face. "No, Marjallah, it was not an epidemic that took my wives, my concubines, and my children from me, rather it was my twin brother, Temur. As I have told you, our mother was a Frenchwoman. She was captured by my father many years ago in his youth, when he went with a party of his friends, raiding deep into the heart of Europe. They wanted to reinforce their manhood with our people and so they traveled as far as the kingdom of Hungary one spring and summer. My mother, of noble lineage, was traveling with her family to her marriage with a prince of the country when my father and his men swept down upon their party, and captured them. He claimed her for himself. Her two sisters were taken by his second and third in command. Her father and mother were killed in the raid, only her brother escaped.

"At first, my father told me, she fought him like a tigress, but when she learned she was with child, she softened toward him, and when Temur and I were born they were quite reconciled. She went on to give him three additional sons, and four daughters. She was his favorite wife and so it pained them sorely that my brother Temur was so discontented even from the day of his birth.

"Temur is a throwback to the Tartars of old, although he has the height our people have gained through their centuries of intermarriage. Where I am blue-eyed and tawny like our mother, Temur has narrow black eyes, and black hair. He always prided himself on it, too, although I think it was just another reason for his discontent. Our parents never favored one of us over the other, and Temur is even my elder by several minutes, yet he has always been jealous of me, claiming that it is I our parents prefer.

"In our youth he constantly sought to outdo me, but he was always striving so hard that he invariably failed. His sullen disposition, his constant bullying and bragging ensured his isolation from the other boys our age, but for those malcontents like himself. I never deliberately sought to outdo him. To my sorrow he has always hated me. So it was we grew to manhood, and began to take women for our own.

"Over the years I took two women to wife. My beloved Zoe, a lovely creature with a nature so gentle that she could lure the wild birds from the trees to eat from her hand. There was no one who knew Zoe who did not love her. My second wife, Ayesha, was as mercurial of disposition as Zoe was sweet. I also possessed several concubines. We had six sons and two daughters.

"Regrettably my brother Temur, with his four wives, and his large harem could not produce anything but one son and a clutch of daughters. Here was another reason for his discontent, and his burning jealousy against me. Several months ago in a burst of madness he invaded the sanctity of my home with his men while I was away to slaughter my entire household. No one escaped. Not my women. Not my children. Not a single slave but for my cook, Hammed, who hid himself in an oven."

Aidan was horrified, and filled not only with pity for the victims of Temur's bestiality, but with compassion for the prince. "Oh, my lord prince," she said, and without realizing it she reached out to caress his cheek in a comforting manner, "how terrible it must have been for you. What happened to your brother?"

"No one knows," said Javid Khan. "Perhaps regaining his reason he realized the extent of his crime for he disappeared without a trace taking his men with him. My father ordered his wives and children bowstringed, but my mother and I begged for their lives. The women were innocent of Temur's crime as were his offspring. Actually his son is a sickly child who I do not believe will even live to reach manhood, and for the girls they are valuable to my father for the purposes of alliances. It would have been a shame to waste them. Besides my father has other sons who have sons, and so his line is safe.

"For weeks after the crime I grieved for my household. Finally my father decided that rather than send the yearly delegation of his sons to Istanbul with the sultan's tribute, he would send me as his ambassador for the sultan has long wanted us to send him an ambassador. It greatly adds to the prestige of the Sublime Porte."

"Does no one look for your brother Temur?" Aidan asked curiously.

"Several of our younger brothers seek him. He will not escape our vengeance. Eventually my family will wipe out the blot upon our honor, and Temur will be removed from the face of the earth. His name has already been stricken from our people's history. It is as if he never existed at all, and I, Marjallah, will speak no more on it."

"Yes, my lord," she said, and thought to herself how Conn would have laughed at her obedient tone. Conn whom she would never see again. For a moment she wanted to cry once more, but then she thought how much greater his loss was than hers. Javid Khan's wives and children were dead. Their lives were over and done with, but her husband lived. He would find happiness elsewhere, and father the dynasty that they had so proudly planned upon the body of another woman. For a moment she wondered if he would forget her. She would certainly never forget him, but now her life was with this man. This man who had suffered so greatly, and who so patiently sought her love. She wondered if she could ever really love him, but she would try. Oh yes, she would try!

He sensed the inner struggle that she had, and gave her time to reconcile herself. Clapping his hands he signaled the slaves who had waited discreetly and unseen. They came forth bringing with them a variety of dishes to please the most picky appetite, and set their offerings upon the low round table at which the prince and his slavewoman sat.

From the platters and bowls there arose an array of most appetizing smells. The tiny leg of baby lamb studded with rosemary and garlic cloves was placed before them along with a platter containing pigeons roasted golden brown, and a whole fish dressed with thin slices of lemon and capers. There were bowls of saffroned rice; pieces of pickled cucumbers; dark, ripened olives in a heavy, briny oil; and something he told her was called yogurt.

"May I serve you, my lord?" she asked him, and when he nodded she filled his plate high with everything, and set it before him. One of the slaves placed before the prince a goblet of rosewater.

The prince set about eating with a good appetite, and then noticing that Aidan had nothing upon her plate said, "When I ask you to dine with me that is just what you are to do. Eat, Marjallah! Hammed is a fine cook!"

"I was not certain it was allowed," she said, and gratefully heaped her own plate with everything upon the table.

Javid Khan smiled to see her appetite. It reminded him of his mother who had always had an excellent appetite, but who was also as slender as a girl. How his wives had envied his mother both her form, and her ability to eat whatever she chose.

When they had each helped themselves twice to the bounty before them so that little remained, the slaves brought silver ewers of warm, perfumed water and tiny towels so they might bathe the grease and oil from their hands and faces. Then the prince's coffeemaker appeared to grind his beans and brew the coffee while the other servants put upon the table plates of little gazelle-horn pastries and a bowl of fresh fruit. There were plump purple grapes, juicy pink-and-gold peaches, and fat, sweet brown figs. When the coffee was made, and placed before them with bowls of both chips of ice to cool the boiling liquid, and sugar to sweeten its bitterness, the prince warned, "Be careful not to drink the grounds for they linger at the bottom of the cup waiting for the unsuspecting enthusiast."

"I am not certain I can learn to like this coffee." She smiled at him.

"What do you like?" he asked, curious about her more than ever now.

"In England I loved to ride, and I loved my home, and I loved children and flowers, and I have a terrible sweet tooth," she answered him with another smile.

"You will have all these things here with me," he said.

"Even horses?"

"We will think about the horse," he replied.

"May I have the gardens for my own to restore?"

"Yes," he said wanting to see her smile again. He barely knew her, and yet he wanted her to be happy, to be content with him for there was something about this woman that bespoke a peace he needed to find once again. A tranquillity that he had never thought would be his again, and yet with her he believed he might regain some measure of his former happiness, even children. She was a big strong female who would undoubtedly bear him healthy sons to take the places of those that he had lost to his brother's madness.

The slaves came again with ewers of fresh water so they might perform their final ablutions before continuing on with the rest of the evening. Now she grew silent once more, and the prince knew that she was thinking again of what was to come. She had responded warmly to his tentative lovemaking before, and he thought that once he overcame her shyness that all would be well. He liked her reticence for it bespoke modesty on her part. He did not regret her lost virginity, but it pleased him that she lacked great experience. It would make their coming together far more interesting.

Finally the slaves had cleared away the last of their meal, the lamps had been trimmed so they would not smoke, and lowered so that they glowed softly. Then the slaves silently withdrew from the prince's apartments, and Aidan knew that they would remain alone. Standing, the prince reached out a hand to her, and drew her up.

"Come," he said. "Let us walk in the gardens for a bit."

They moved from the salon through a small door and outside into the evening. Considering her scanty garb it was fortunate that the night was warm, Aidan thought somewhat wryly. The garden was surrounded on three sides by the palace, but the fourth side opened into the larger gardens, and it was here that he chose to lead her. The night was very still, and overhead a huge moon rode full across a cloudless sky. Its light dappled the waters that surrounded them.

Silently they walked deep into the large garden, and there in the brightness of the moonlight Aidan got her first good look at the Black Sea. "It looks as vast as our ocean," she said.

"But it is not," he answered. "Still it is a power to be reckoned with, my jewel. The storms upon it can be fierce beyond belief. It has been a major waterway since the beginning of time. The great empire that controlled Istanbul before the Ottomen claimed it, and there are great cities built upon it that date back to ancient times."

"It looks so beautiful in the moonlight," she said.

"As do you," he answered quickly, and catching her to him looked down in her face saying softly, "I want you, Marjallah! It is not simply my need for a woman for since the death of my wives I have not felt that need; but there is something about you, my jewel, that intrigues me, and ensorcells me so that I must have you! How have you captivated me so completely and so quickly? Was it only last night that the sultan gave you to me? It cannot be for surely we have known each other since the beginning of time."

His words seemed almost like poetry to her, and Aidan's heart fluttered madly at these romantic utterances. "My lord," she whispered, "you attribute to me powers that I can never before remember having."

"You are so fair, Marjallah," he replied. "I can never again look upon the fullness of the moon without thinking of the fullness of your beauty."

"I am not beautiful," she said. "I am big and almost plain."

"You *are* beautiful, my jewel!" he insisted, "and it is your radiance that reflects upon the moon to light it!" He cupped her oval face in his hands, his thumbs smoothing across her cheekbones. "Your skin is like heavy cream washed with roses. Your stormy eyes and your burnished copper hair ravish me. I am," he continued, kissing the very tip of her nose, "going to fall in love with you."

Her eyes widened just slightly at his words, and she again was overcome with that breathless feeling that had assailed her earlier. She swayed, and put out a hand to steady herself. Loosing her face he wrapped his arms tightly about her drawing her hard against him so that he might feel the fullness of her breasts, so that she might feel the urgency of his need for her. Lowering his head he nibbled on her lips sending little shivers down her spine. Slowly her eyes closed, and she gave herself up to his kisses, returning the homage of his lips one for one. For a long time they stood there, their mouths hungrily exploring each other, their bodies pressed against each other.

She liked his kisses, Aidan decided. Although she felt him in complete control of the situation he also allowed her the freedom to express her budding passion. Her palms pressed against the silk of his robe and felt the hardness of his body beneath. Slowly she moved her hands up the smoothness to finally wrap about his neck. This had the effect of wedging her even more tightly against him, and Javid Khan groaned against her mouth breaking off their desperate embrace.

Startled Aidan asked, "Have I displeased you, my lord?"

"*Displeased me?* Nay, my jewel, you have not displeased me. You please me very much in fact. So much that did I not cease kissing you just then

I should have next taken you upon the very ground where we now stand. I do not want to do that, Marjallah. You are not a honeyed confection to be greedily gobbled up, and I am not a green boy unable to control his desires. Passion must be shared if it is to be savored to the fullest. Come! You are ready to be loved now. Let us return to my chamber where I may pay my full tribute to your exquisite loveliness." Taking her by the hand he led her back into his apartments. Once they had regained the salon he commanded her gently, "Remove your garments now, my love."

Her heart was hammering, and suddenly she felt shy of him again, but when she looked at him his bright blue eyes were warm, and filled with encouragement. Aidan slipped off the little sleeveless bolero, and laying it aside stood to meet his gaze. His eyes were filled with admiration as they swept over her round breasts. They were, he thought, probably the most perfect breasts he had ever seen. Zoe and Ayesha could certainly not match Marjallah's perfection of form which even without her removing the rest of her garments he could see. With great restraint he forced himself not to touch her. *Not yet.*

Undoing her belt Aidan let it drop to the floor, and pushed the full dark blue pantaloons over her hips so that they too slipped down about her feet. Undoing the tight anklebands she stepped from the trousers to stand nude before him, and it was precisely as he had anticipated. She was flawless. There was nothing, he considered as he walked slowly around her, that he would change. Reaching up he removed the ribbons from her hair, and then without a word he picked her up and carried her into his bedchamber to lay her gently upon his couch.

Now he stood before her, and raising the long embroidered robe he wore he drew it over his head, and tossed it aside. Curiously Aidan gazed upon the second naked man she had ever seen in her life, and found that although men like women were basically the same, each had his differences. Where Conn had had a great growth of dark hair covering his arms, his legs, and his chest and torso, Javid Khan's well-muscled and tanned body was smooth, and devoid of hair. He stood quietly for a long minute giving her the same privilege that he had so recently taken. The time to view him as he had viewed her. He was not as tall as Conn, nor as finely made, but he stood six feet, and was sturdily built. Where Conn had a bush of dark hair to encircle and pillow his manhood, Javid Khan's groin was as smooth as the rest of his body giving his manhood the appearance of being larger. It thrust straight out from his body, and she was somewhat taken aback to see that at its tip was a fiery knob that Conn had not possessed, but then she realized that he was circumcised which Conn had not been. How strange, she thought, and she almost giggled for it had been Skye who had told her the differences between the two types of manhood, but she had certainly never expected to see such a thing or encounter any other man but her husband.

"Do I please you?" he asked her as he lay down upon the bed next to her.

"You are very handsome, and very different from . . . . from Conn," she said softly.

He reached out and took her hand, giving it a squeeze, and then raising himself up he looked down into her face.

"You have little experience, I know, but I promise you that I shall be kind to you, my jewel." Then his lips brushed tenderly over her lips and her chin moving down her slender throat and around to the sensitive little hollow beneath her earlobe that Conn always liked to kiss. For a moment his warm mouth tickled her there, and then slipped downward to trail kisses over her graceful shoulders, and down a long arm. Taking her hand he turned it, and placed a hot kiss in the center of her palm. A hard shudder rocked her for it was as if a streak of lightning had pierced her vitals.

Javid Khan rested upon one elbow now, his head in his hand while his other hand touched her in earnest for the very first time. Tenderly his long fingers traced the shape of her breast following the swell and the curve of her flesh in a manner far more provocative than if he had simply fondled her. Teasingly he lingered about her sensitive nipple, encircling it slowly and in a deliberate manner several times until she squirmed ever so slightly under his ministrations. She could not help but watch him, but when he lowered his head to take her nipple within his mouth her eyes grew suddenly heavy, and closed. Now the hand that had so lately caressed her first breast moved to the second while his mouth greedily loved her nipple. She could feel both her breasts growing tight, and the nipples began to ache with what she knew was a longing for far more than the prince was now giving her.

He transferred his attentions to the second nipple, and when he had contented himself he raised his head to her saying, "Sweetness seems to pour from your beautiful breasts, my jewel. I can never remember a woman's breasts giving me such incredible pleasure. Tell me that I have given you pleasure, too?"

"Oh, yes!" The sound was breathless, and he smiled well satisfied.

His hand smoothed over her belly, and slipped downward to push between her soft thighs that his fingers might insinuate themselves between the tender folds of sensitive flesh to quest for the sentient little pearl of her womanhood. Finding what he sought he lowered his tawny head, and loved her with his mouth.

Aidan stiffened, and gasped with shock. What was he doing to her? Conn had never done such a thing! "No! No!" she cried even though her body was beginning to melt with sweet rapture.

He raised his head up, and looked at her. "Did your husband not do this?" he asked frankly.

"No! Never!"

"Then he deprived you of great pleasure, Marjallah, and I will not." The tawny head lowered itself again as his mouth found her once more.

For a moment she was simply stunned. He wasn't hurting her, yet she wondered about the rightness of what he was doing. Surely it couldn't be right, and yet . . . ? An ache was beginning to rise in her loins, and she could not help the little sob that slipped through her lips. She could feel his tongue teasing at her flesh, and unexpected heat raced through her veins to overwhelm her. He was making her fly with the wind as happened to her when Conn took her. She hadn't known that it could happen so strongly without having a man pulse within her, then he was to her dismay stopping, but before she could protest he was swinging over her, and thrusting himself totally within her.

Her arms, one above her head, the other at her side, raised themselves, and clasped him to her. Her rounded nails dug half-moons into the hard flesh of his shoulders, and she groaned aloud at his sudden entry. The walls of her hidden passage were being stretched to their capacity, and she realized that he had only been half-roused when he had disrobed himself. He was enormous, and she could actually feel his bigness within the tightness of her body.

He had almost shouted with exultation at his possession of her. She lay pinioned between his two strong arms, *his*, now totally his! Slowly he withdrew his great shaft almost to its tip, and then plunged back within her. She cried out, and the sound was one of utter passion. He repeated the motion over and over again, slowly delving within her honeyed flesh, pushing as deep as he could possibly go only to withdraw slowly and as tantalizingly. Soon, however, he began to tire of the game as his own passion began to boil, and so his movements became quicker and quicker as he moved back and forth within her tight passage.

Aidan was sobbing now with unconcealed pleasure as Javid Khan made tender love to her. Her body, passionate in its nature as Conn had quickly discovered, could not help but respond to the handsome prince; and yet her mind struggled against what she believed was a betrayal of everything her love for Conn O'Malley had been. She was enjoying his lovemaking, and yet how could she? She had given him her body without a struggle because she had believed she could not possibly enjoy the attentions of any man but her husband. She had had no real choice but to yield herself to him, but she had never expected to savor the prince's attentions, and yet she was. How could it be? she tried to question herself, but the rapture was much too great for her to do naught but obey its commands, and so she gave herself over to it, sliding helplessly into the maelstrom of white-hot desire that he had woven so tightly about them.

Aidan remembered nothing more until she awoke sometime later. Beside her Javid Khan slept, if not sated, at least contented for the time being. What had happened? She had obviously lost consciousness, and for a moment Aidan was filled with admiration for her lover. Gingerly she sat up, and turned to look at him. His strong features were only slightly softened in sleep, and she felt a sudden tenderness for him. He had been kind where perhaps another would not have been. She had seen the look that Sultan Murad had given her before he had lifted the prince with her. It had been a look so full of lust that it had taken all her willpower not to shiver openly. The sultan, she knew, would not have been kind. He would have ravished her without a thought or care for her body or her emotions. She now knew how very fortunate she was to have been given to Javid Khan.

Reaching out she gently caressed his face, and was startled when, eyes still closed, his voice said, "Oh, Moon of my Delight, I am fast learning to adore you!" And then his blue eyes opened, and he smiled up at her with love.

Chapter 12

❧

$\mathscr{A}$ night in Aidan's arms had told Javid Khan a great deal about the woman called Marjallah. He had never been a man to hide his feelings, nor had he been slow at making a decision. That single night had told him that although he could never be totally relieved of the pain of his household's slaughter, at least Allah had given him another woman he might love. She was as painfully vulnerable as he himself was, and it was that weakness that endeared her to him. They had each suffered a tragic loss, and now together they would build a new life.

To Jinji's delight he gifted her with exquisite jewelry that he traveled to Istanbul to personally purchase for her. Emeralds for constancy, he told her smiling down into her eyes, and when she smiled back the eunuch saw she was less guarded, and knew that his lady was also beginning to love again even if she didn't know it yet. He bought her gossamer fabrics of pale mauve, springtime lilac, apple green, tawny orange, and a carved silver belt studded with moonstones and lapis lazuli from Persia. There were a full dozen slaves (the market was simply flooded with Portuguese captives from the battle of Alcazarquivir) to tend to the gardens, and whose purchase Javid Khan smilingly explained by saying,

"We cannot be certain of the local farmers, my jewel. If it looks cloudy they will not come for fear of rain. If the day dawns fair they are just as likely to remain at home because of the heat. They will always put their own fields first. They are simply not reliable. These men belong to you, and must do your bidding whether it be hot or cold, rainy or dry."

"First they must be housed," she reminded him. "We have no place here in the palace for them for it is small."

"Let them sleep in the stables until they can build a place for themselves," he answered. "You need not be concerned with them. My wives never bothered with the servants. They are replaceable."

"My lord," she said patiently, "perhaps in your homeland you had a large establishment, and it was run very efficiently by a large staff of servants; but here, my lord, you have a small palace, and naught but Hammed to cook for us, and that scruffy troup of Tartars that you have brought with you to serve you. They are not house servants, and are, I see, far more adept at riding, and hunting than they are at being domestic. Therefore I must be, and I should like to spend my time being useful. I was trained for it. I always have. I cannot occupy my time simply bathing and perfuming myself to lie idly upon a couch awaiting your attentions! As your father's ambassador you must attend upon the sultan at his court most days. I will not just sit eager for your return!"

He chuckled at her outrage. "But I want you eagerly awaiting my return," he teased her. "After all, was not woman created merely for man's pleasure?"

"You will not find much pleasure in an empty belly, or dirty linens, my lord, and that is exactly what you shall have if you do not let me run your house," she threatened, but her gray eyes were laughing at him.

"Woman," he growled at her, and with a leap across the room he captured her. To his delight Aidan shrieked her surprise, "You presume far too much. First you wheedle the gardens from me, and now you desire the house. Will you never be satisfied?" He held her tightly within his embrace.

"Never," she giggled, rubbing her body against his until they both felt his rising desire, and she boldly drew his head down to kiss him passionately.

"Ah, my jewel, you are becoming so much a part of me," he admitted softly.

"Then give me the house," she murmured seductively against his mouth, and her hand caressed the nape of his neck with a sensuous touch.

"You must earn your privileges," he teased back, and then with a movement she certainly wasn't expecting he kicked her legs out from under her, and together they fell to the thick carpet. His hands pulled her pantaloons down, exposing her vulnerability, and Aidan shrieked again with surprise.

She was not helpless, however. Realizing that it was but a game he played with her she rolled quickly from beneath him, kicking out with a kid-shod foot. "Give me the house!" she cried.

His answer was to grasp at both her ankles, and yank her forward, pulling her legs over his shoulders as he did. Then his mouth fastened upon her flesh. He tongued her provocatively, seeking every hidden crevice, probing softly at the delicate flesh until she gave down her honey.

She writhed beneath him, both fire and ice filling her veins at the same time. "My lord! My lord!" she moaned desperately.

Javid Khan lifted his head. "Say please," he whispered.

It was enough of a respite from his delicious tortures. "Give me the house!" she managed to gasp.

He lowered his head to tease at her again for a few moments, and then pulling himself up so that their faces were level he kissed her deeply and passionately as he pushed his swollen shaft into her welcoming body.

She sighed with open relief, and smoothed her hands down his back to cup his tight buttocks to her as opening herself to him she wrapped her long legs about his body. He was, she thought, the most marvelous lover. As tender as her husband had been, but different, and she liked it. She thrust her body up to meet his downward movement for she was not a passive partner. She could already feel the tumult building in intensity, and she welcomed it. "Yes, my darling," she whispered with hot breath into his ear encouraging him, "oh, yes, my lord Javid! Oh, I am shameless! I cannot get enough of you, my lord! Please, please, do not stop!" She shuddered with passion. She could feel him pulsing and quivering within her soft body. She could feel him growing bigger with his hunger.

The prince gritted his teeth with his great desire for the woman beneath him. Allah! *She could not get enough of him?* If he spent the next thousand years in her arms like this he would never be satisfied! He could feel the great shaft of his manhood, engorged with his love for her, throbbing within her soft sheath. Over and over again he drove into her softness until unable to bear any more his love juices cascaded into her hidden garden, and in his own language, a language she could not understand, he groaned, "I love you, my jewel! I love you!" Then he fell across her breasts.

Instinctively she cradled him within the circle of her arms for she, too, was lost in paradise. Then as reason began to return she gently stroked his tawny head, and asked, "What did you say to me, my lord?"

"I said that the palace is yours, my jewel," he murmured in reply. It was not that he regretted his words for he did not, but he would not say them to her until she had learned to love him. She must not have any advantage over him. With women such a thing was dangerous. He rolled off her, and she put her head upon his shoulder.

"You are so good to me, my lord Javid," she said.

"I want you to be happy," he answered her, "but I fear that my father and brothers would chide me for I spoil you dreadfully."

"Ah," she teased him, "but do their women care for the house as I do? I am a very valuable slave, my lord."

"Yes," he said, tenderly kissing the top of her head, "you are a most valuable woman, my jewel. Now, however, I think we should get up from the floor. My poor Tartars would be shocked to find me so enslaved by my slave."

The master enslaved by his slave. This was hardly the picture that Conn O'Malley had of his wife's plight as he entered the house of Osman the astrologer in Algiers with his three brothers. A white-robed servant ushered them into the main salon of the house, and said in perfect French, "The master will be with you shortly, good sirs."

The O'Malley brothers gazed about the beautifully tiled room. In its center was a fountain in whose middle was a two-tiered basin from which water dripped into the main fountain. There were thick colorful wool rugs upon the floor, and the lamps were all of polished silver and ruby glass. There were several low overstuffed couches in red velvet and beautiful low brass tables set upon ebony bases. It was a lovely and very rich-looking room, and the brothers, escorted by Sir Robert Small, looked about goggle-eyed much to Robbie's amusement.

He was an old friend of long standing of Osman, and he knew this house almost as well as he knew his own for it had originally belonged to his first trading partner, the renegade Spaniard, Khalid el Bey, who had been Skye's second husband. Osman had bought the house from the widowed Skye when she had fled to England after her husband's death to escape the unwelcome attentions of the commander of the Kasbah fortress who had designs not only on her person, but her vast wealth as well.

"This was once your sister's house," he told the O'Malley brothers, and then fleshed out the tale.

They listened to him openmouthed for such incredible adventure was beyond belief to Brian, Shane and Shamus O'Malley who despite their privateering activities led very circumspect lives. Conn, however, knew the story, and noted that Robbie did not tell them that Khalid el Bey was the Great Whoremaster of Algiers at the time he was married to their sister. Robert Small, knowing the small minds of his audience, simply told the brothers of the Spanish merchant who was their eldest niece's father. It was enough to keep them interested until, as Robbie had known, Osman the astrologer viewed them secretly through his spy hole, and then made his entrance.

He entered the room quietly, and at first Conn thought that this gentle-looking man of medium height with his hairless pate and his bland, moon-round face was naught but a servant. Certainly his garb of plain white robes with its dark silk embroidery about the neck and the sleeves was not the impressive garment of the powerful man that Robbie had said that Osman was. Then, however, Conn looked into the eyes of the man, and he instantly knew that this was Osman. The golden-brown eyes were not simply intelligent, they were knowing, and Conn realized somewhat eerily, at least a thousand years old. How he knew this he did not understand. He just did.

"Robert!" Osman embraced the little Englishman. "As always you look not a day older. In anticipation of your visit I have found the most exquisite twin sisters. You have not lost your appetite for sweetmeats, I trust."

"I'll never lose that appetite, Osman, my friend," grinned Robert Small. "I may be going gray," and Robbie ruefully ran his hand through his fading ginger-colored locks, "but my cock's as randy a fellow as ever! Let's get to business, and then I'll partake of your expansive hospitality, man!"

Osman smiled warmly back at the Englishman. He was deeply fond of him for he was an honest man in a world where honesty, it seemed, counted for very little. Then before Robbie could make the introduction he turned to Conn, and said quietly, "You will be Lord Bliss. You look very much like your sister. Your eyes are a mirror of your soul. Do not be afraid for your wife, my lord. She is a very strong woman."

"You saw her?"

"Several times before she left for Istanbul. The dey is a friend of mine, and my position allowed me access to his harem where another man would certainly not be admitted."

"She is gone then?" Conn looked crestfallen.

"Several weeks ago, my lord. You could not possibly have reached her in time, and she is by now in Istanbul. She will be safe there."

"*Safe?* In bondage to some infidel? Fash, man! Ye don't know what it is ye say!" Brian O'Malley looked belligerently at Osman.

"I have neglected to introduce my brother to you, my lord Osman," said Conn with grave understatement, and the great astrologer's eyes twinkled. "This gentlemen with the quick tongue is Brian, the eldest, and next is Shane, and then Shamus."

Osman nodded politely to the three elder O'Malley brothers, and then he said quietly, "Are not all women in bondage to men? As for being an infidel," and he chuckled, "why is it that when we both worship the same God we each think the other an infidel?"

Brian had the good grace to flush uncomfortably, but before he might excuse his quick speech Osman spoke again.

"This being your first visit to Algiers, brothers of my dear friend Skye, I have planned what I hope will be a delightful diversion for you." He clapped his hands, and instantly a servant appeared. "If you will follow Ali, my three new friends, he will lead you to the baths where you will be refreshed after your journey. Captain Small and Lord Bliss will join you later when we have discussed our business for there has been a minor complication of sorts with which we must deal."

Somewhat surprised, but nonetheless intrigued, Brian, Shane, and Shamus departed the room trailing in the wake of Ali, who bowed low and grinned broadly at them before turning to lead them out with a chuckle. When the door had closed behind them Robbie began to smile.

"They will be happy men when they come from your baths, Osman."

Osman returned the smile. "But happier when they see the luscious companions I have chosen for them during their stay. Each one, my old friend Robert, is a veritable houri. It will be a delightful experience for them after the tavern wenches they have no doubt tumbled enthusiastically along the Spanish Main."

"We are not staying in Algiers, my lord Osman," said Corm. "We but came to learn what we could from you regarding my wife, Aidan."

"That, Lord Bliss, is the minor complication I am talking about. You are staying in Algiers for the present, and there is nothing that even I can do to expedite matters. On the fourth day of August the Portuguese met the forces of the sultan at Alcazarquivir. They were very badly defeated, and their young king, Sebastian, was killed. As a consequence the slave markets have been flooded with captives, most of them Portuguese, but as contingents from virtually every country in Europe were represented in the Portuguese army, there were Spanish, English, French, Flemish, Dutch, Germans, and Italians captured also.

"The sultan is extremely annoyed that countries who claim to want relations with him would send their forces into battle against his forces. He is therefore clamping down on trade and all ships of non-Muslim nations entering his ports, of which of course Algiers is one. The order came through just last week, and I could not inform you, and warn you not to come."

"Does that mean that our vessels are impounded?" asked Conn.

"No, no, nothing of that nature, my lord. It merely means that now that you have made port here the officials of the dey's government who control the harbor facilities will inspect your entire cargo minutely for contraband, and check amongst your crews for runaway slaves. I must warn you here that even though you do not carry contraband, nor have escaped slaves amongst your men, both will be found. That will mean that you will have to pay fines to the dey's government which is, of course, the sultan's government, and then you will have to buy back your men who are accused of being slaves. Do not fear for your men. I will see that no harm comes to them, and I will use my influence to see that you are not stung with regards to the price for them. The market is flooded right now with slaves, and so the prices are not high. It will mean, however, that you will be detained for a time before you are allowed to travel on to Istanbul. When the sultan has gotten his message over to the rulers of Christian Europe things will be normal once again. I am sorry."

"What of my wife, Osman? How will she bear this captivity? She will lose heart when I do not come."

"She does not know whether you will come or not, my lord," came the answer. "Although I promised her that I would send to my dear friend, your sister, the news of her predicament, I warned her that it might not be possible to gain her release. I know that you also have been warned of this eventuality."

"I want my wife back," Conn almost shouted, "and if I must storm the walls of your Sultan Murad's palace to regain her, then I will!"

"Inchallah," said Osman fatalistically.

"What the hell does that mean?"

"It will be as Allah wills," said Osman with a small smile. "How like your sister you are, my lord."

"You call my sister by her name," said Conn. "I would be more comfortable if you would call me by mine. It is Conn."

Osman smiled a little smile. "Then Conn you shall be, brother of my dear friend Skye, and now I will talk to you as I so often spoke to her. Your wife has been sent to the most powerful ruler upon the face of the earth as a gift from one of his officials. Understand right now that it will not be possible to ransom her for the sultan is not some common pirate. He will not give her back to you because you ask, and if you did he would most likely order your head removed from your shoulders."

"Then how am I supposed to retrieve her if I can't storm the sultan's palace, ransom her, or even ask for her back?" demanded Conn irritably.

"There I cannot help you," said Osman, "for I do not know Istanbul, or the particular situation that you will face when you get there. It is even possible that you may not be able to gain your wife's freedom, Conn, but unless you try you will not know, and if you turn back now, the question of whether you would have been successful or not will haunt you all your days."

Not get Aidan back? Of course he would get Aidan back! Or would he? Even now the doubt began to assail him, and Conn felt something that if it was not fear, was very akin to it. They were young, he and Aidan. They had a long and wonderful lifetime ahead of them. He could not imagine spending that lifetime without her. He did not want to spend that life-time without her! He knew better than to ask Osman for any more hope than the great astrologer had offered him. Had there been no hope at all, Osman would have told him that. The one thing Skye had emphasized to Conn was Osman's honesty.

With a deep sigh he asked, "How long do you think we will be detained in Algiers, my lord Osman?"

"It will be several weeks," said Osman honestly. "Here in the East things move more slowly than in your land."

"Government, no matter whose," remarked Sir Robert Small, "always hurries forward at a snail's pace, Osman, and ye know it."

Osman chuckled. "Yes," he said, "the great and those others in power seem to have a fascination with their own wonderfulness, and are might-ily impressed with the wisdom of the words they speak. We rarely really hear ourselves, Robbie."

"What am I to do for several weeks?" Conn wondered out loud.

"Algiers is a good place to wait," said Robbie with a grin.

"Ahh, but since Khalid el Bey there have been no houses of pleasure as fantastic as his. Algiers is not what it once was, my friend. You will have to see that the crews of your ships behave themselves for the Janissaries are more swaggeringly irritating than usual right now. Since Jamil's death there is no kapitan strong enough to keep them in check. He was a wicked man, but he had the knack of command."

For a moment both men were silent remembering their old enemy, but then Robbie demanded, "I want a visit to your baths, Osman, and then after ye've fed me one of yer fine meals that only yer wife, Alima, can oversee properly, I want those twins! I've a great appetite for everything tonight!"

Osman chuckled again, and arising from his comfortable seat said, "Come, gentlemen, and I will even join you myself, the hour being late, and the day hot."

Conn demurred. "I'll just go back to the ship," he said, but neither Robbie nor Osman would let him.

"Come on, lad," Robbie encouraged. "Ye've not had a real bath until ye've had a bath in Osman's house. Why, bless me, I think it's the only reason I ever come to this benighted city at all anymore! Come along! Don't be shy! I'll wager yer brothers are already addicted to the pleasures of Osman's baths."

And they were, although it had taken Brian, Shane, and Shamus quite by surprise when they had been ushered into the household baths to find themselves greeted by several very nubile ladies who were as naked as the day that each had been born. There were some half-dozen of them ranging in color from very fair to ebony, and they came forward giggling to draw the three startled men into the room, two girls quickly attaching themselves to each man. Before the surprised brothers realized what was happening they found themselves divested of more than half of their clothing.

"Here now, lass, stop that!" Brian O'Malley was a brave man, but he'd never had all his clothing off before a woman in his entire life. Not even his wife, Maggie! He slapped away the facile little hands that had just yanked his shirt over his head.

"Monsieur!" The brothers turned to look at a beautiful black woman who had just entered the room. "You must allow my girls to complete their task of disrobing you. How else can you be bathed? Our master, the lord Osman, would be very displeased." She moved to stand right before Brian O'Malley. "Surely you do not want us punished?"

Brian O'Malley looked down at the woman, and realized that she was one of the most beautiful creatures he had ever seen. Her skin was like polished mahogany, and she had the most elegant head he had ever seen on a woman. It was long, the hair tight curls cropped close to the scalp, the cheekbones high, the dark eyes oval, the nose amazingly classical, the lips wide and sensuous. She was very tall for a woman, at least six feet, and as slender as a reed but for her wonderful full big breasts. Brian felt his lust arising, and he wondered if he dared touch those magnificent tits.

The woman smiled at him knowingly for she had easily sensed just what was going through his head. Her eyes mocked his insecurity, and then she said, "Well, monsieur, will you allow the girls to finish or not?"

"Who are ye?" Brian croaked, his voice husky.

"I am Nigera, the lord Osman's bath mistress."

"Will ye bathe me?" Some of Brian's natural boldness was coming back now.

"I will oversee all, monsieur," she said, "and you may be certain that you will be well taken care of."

Brian nodded, bedazzled by the woman, while his two brothers watched openmouthed. They had, neither of them, ever seen their elder at a loss for either words or direction where a woman was concerned. Still, the black wench was a prime piece of goods, and they hadn't a doubt that Brian would eventually get her on her back.

When all three brothers had been totally divested of their garments, they were led, still somewhat embarrassed by their own nudity, into the baths themselves where they were first rinsed with warm water, and then scraped free of surface dirt before being most thoroughly bathed with sweet-smelling soft soap which the girls took up by the handful from alabaster pots, and smeared over their bodies. They grinned self-consciously at each other as the bath attendants impersonally cupped and rubbed at their genitalia which became aroused to their personal mortification, but the women bathing them seemed to either not notice, or not care. This might be something new to the O'Malley brothers, but to them it was simply a task that they performed for all their master's guests, male and female alike.

"God's good cock," chortled Shane O'Malley, "this is a nicety I wouldn't mind at home. I don't think I've ever been bathed by a woman before."

"Ye don't ever bathe at all," teased Shamus O'Malley. "A wee bit more to the left, darlin'," he instructed the plump little blond who was scrubbing his back with a large sea sponge. "Ahh, yes, darlin', that's exactly it." He turned to Brian. "Do ye think," he asked switching from French to his native Irish tongue, "do ye think, Brian, that we get to fuck them later? All this sweet flesh, and our little time at sea has made me as hot as a live coal."

"I'd have to ask Robbie," said Brian thoughtfully. "We wouldn't want to do anything to offend our host for he is Skye's good friend, and he is helping Conn."

They were being rinsed when Osman, Robbie, and Conn, now free of their own clothing, entered the baths. Like his brothers, Conn had been somewhat taken aback by the news that he was to be bathed by a group of pretty women, but far more sophisticated than his elder siblings he had thought little about it other than it was a new experience. Nigera hurried forward to greet her master, and his guests.

"Nigera, ye toothsome wench!" said Robbie smacking her fondly upon her plump bottom.

Nigera smiled broadly at him. "Welcome, kapitan! I have heard that you were here. It is good to see you once again, and in such obvious good health."

"I see," said Osman to the bath mistress, "that my three other guests are well taken care of, Nigera. You had no difficulties, I trust?"

"None, my lord."

"You have done well," said Osman, "and I would reward you. Do you fancy any of the three?"

"The biggest one seems to lust after me," she said. "It might prove amusing, my lord, if you would permit me."

"He is yours," came the reply.

Conn looked somewhat stunned by this exchange, and so Robbie explained to him as they were rinsed and scraped by two of the bath girls, the other O'Malley brothers now being massaged with a sandalwood-scented cream by three of the girls.

"Nigera has been with Osman for years. She was practically a child when he first bought her, and her sister, Africana. Osman has never had but one wife to whom he is faithful, but he is very fond of Nigera and Africana, and he spoils them. Nigera is in charge of the baths, and her sister is the housekeeper. They are normal, passionate women, and so when Osman has guests who appeal to either of them, he allows them the freedom to seduce his guests. Yer brother, Brian, has obviously taken Nigera's fancy. I've fucked the wench myself several times, and she'll give him a night that he'll never forget, I promise ye!" Robbie chuckled. "Aye, she's a rare one! Brian won't soon forget his stay in Algiers."

Soaped, scrubbed, and rinsed the three latecomers soon joined the earlier visitors to the baths on the marble massage benches. Conn found the supple hands of the bathgirl as she massaged him very relaxing, and he fell asleep. He was awakened from an hour's nap with a cool sherbet of fresh peaches. Embarrassed he sat up with a start, but found that the others had also slept. Finished with their drinks, the men were dressed in loose-fitting white robes, and comfortable sandals. Then their host escorted them to the dining room where they sat down upon large pillows about a long, low table where a fine meal was served.

The food was placed along the length of the table for them to help themselves, and the beautiful blue-and-white Fezware plates were soon heaped high from the bounty before them. There was a whole baby lamb upon a bed of greens; a sea bass that had been braised over a charcoal fire, and was now served surrounded by lemons that had been carved into floral shapes; several chickens that had been roasted golden, and were stuffed with rice and apricots; and a steaming crock that held what looked to the O'Malley brothers like a stew made of meat, and vegetables and cereal which Osman informed them was called couscous. There were artichokes in a dish of red-wine vinegar; and saffroned rice with bits of green and red pepper in it; and pickled cucumbers; and both purple and green olives swimming in their briny oil. There was fresh flat bread, and a pat of sweet butter, and mountain water flavored with lemon and mint to drink.

When the meal had been totally consumed, the coffeemaker came, and squatted beside the edge of the table. Carefully he selected his beans one by one, and grinding them he brewed each cup of the Turkish coffee individually. Robbie and Osman showed the O'Malleys how to sweeten the bitter brew, and quickly drink it down. Upon the table the slaves had placed plates of gazelle-horn pastries, sugared almonds, pistachio nuts, and bowls of green grapes, fat little golden apricots, and sticky sweet dates.

They sat back amid the pillows now utterly sated, and totally unbelieving as Osman apologized for the scantness of his table tonight, but alas, he had not been certain when to expect them; and in this climate food could not be kept easily, and thus they needed more time for a feast which would certainly be prepared tomorrow. Then he clapped his hands, and the women who had earlier bathed them ran into the room, and began to dance for them. They had not noticed the musicians enter the room, but there they were at its end madly playing upon their instruments. Slaves brought in water pipes, and again Osman and Robbie instructed the others in their use, and they sat comfortably watching the colorfully clad women whom Conn thought far more sensual in their sheer gauze garments than entirely naked.

The water pipe was enormously soothing, and then the lamps were dimmed, and Conn noticed that both Osman and Robbie were gone as were the musicians. The women were amid the cushions with the men, and Conn saw that the beautiful black woman, Nigera, was in complete command of his elder brother, Brian. Shane and Shamus were each entertaining two girls apiece. Conn struggled to arise from the cushions, but he was pushed gently back by two brown-skinned Berber girls who despite his vehement protests began to stimulate him.

Sinuously they entwined themselves about him, their little hands and their mouths playing with him. He didn't want them, he thought foggily, but his limbs felt like jelly right now, and he couldn't seem to make them understand. Slowly, with great care and skill, they aroused him until his great manhood stood up straight and hard upon his body. Then each took him in her turn, lowering herself upon his shaft to ride him. Yet he was not satisfied, and so each took him in her mouth again before riding him once more, and finally his lust burst, and more relaxed than he had been in weeks, he allowed the two girls to help him again to unbelieving heights for as skilled a lover as he was, they taught him things that Conn had never even considered possible. While one girl knelt, presenting her sleek flanks to him, her companion grasped Conn's shaft, and presented it to a place he had heard men used, but he certainly never had.

"Nay, wench, not there," he protested. "I could hurt her."

Both women laughed, and then the one in possession of his cock said, "No, you won't, my lord. This is the way of the men of our tribe in the desert. We are used to it, and we like it. I think you will, too, if you will but try."

"Please, my lord," begged the kneeling girl. "I need you to fill me full! Please!"

He was still drunk enough from the water pipe that they were able to persuade him, and so grasping the girl's hips in his hands Conn plunged forward. His first thrust met with resistance, but he persisted, and finally was able to lodge himself within the tightest passage that had ever enclasped his throbbing manhood. Slowly he began to pump her as if he were in the proper place, and she moaned with unfeigned pleasure, and came to a quick climax. He was stunned.

"Now, me!" the other girl begged him, and she then presented his still-hard and unrelieved shaft with her plumper bottom. Why didn't he refuse them? he wondered, but he didn't, but with each stroke he gave the girl he thought of his beloved Aidan. Aidan who might be forced to give herself to the sultan even as these two girls so willingly gave themselves to him. *Aidan! Aidan!* And with a groan his passion burst, and Conn fell into a stupor from which he did not awake until past noon the next day.

When he did awake, however, it with the full knowledge of what had passed between himself, and the two girls the night before. He was filled with a loathing for himself, but Osman seeing his distress, and realizing its cause took him aside to speak to him.

"It is not the nature of a man to remain long celibate, my friend," he said. "You have been without a woman for many weeks now, Conn. What passed between you and my slavegirls was healthy for you and quite natural."

"But I love my wife!" Conn protested.

"What has loving your wife got to do with the needs of your body? Your wife is not here to satisfy those needs, and they must be satisfied else you build up a store of bad humors within your body which could poison you. It is neither safe nor moral for a man to deny himself the comfort of a woman's body."

"But in my world," said Conn, "a man cleaves only to his wife."

"In your world," said Osman, "a man marries one woman, and plays with many others in secret. Here in Islam we make no secret about that which is normal."

"Yet you keep only to your wife, Osman."

The astrologer smiled. "My desire for women is not particularly great despite the large family I have fathered. The children were to keep Alima happy and busy so that she would not feel neglected because I spend most of my time at my work. Had I taken other wives or even concubines, I should not have had that luxury for they would have all been at me; but even I, my friend, have occasionally dipped my gourd in other wells when desire overtook me." He looked seriously at Conn. "Your wife will have known another man by the time you reach her. Will you condemn her for her conduct because you believe she should cleave only to you?"

Suddenly Conn realized that it was Osman who had seen to it that he had gotten drunk on the water pipe the previous evening. He had done it to make a point with Conn, and that point was that a body had needs that perhaps could not be overcome by the mind. As he had lain virtually helpless being seduced by the two Berber girls, so would Aidan be as sweetly seduced despite her love for him. In their own world Conn knew that his wife would have always been faithful to him just as he would have been faithful to her; but they were not in their own world now. This world was one in which a woman's value was judged by how many goats, or horses, or camels could be gotten for her, and it was, Conn suddenly realized, the same world over. A woman was considered chattel by most men although he did not feel that way about Aidan. Still females were judged by what they brought men in the way of valuables. He looked directly at Osman, and was bathed by the golden light that came from the astrologer's warm gaze.

"I love my wife," he said quietly, "but I understand what it is you are trying to teach me, Osman, and I thank you."

"But have you learned my lesson, Conn?"

"My heart comprehends what it is that you say to me, Osman, but it is so difficult for my mind to accept it. The thought of my wife in the possession of another man is maddening. It somehow does not seem as bad for a man to take another woman as it is for a woman to accept another man." He sighed deeply. "Yet I want her back."

"Be absolutely certain, brother of my beloved friend. Your wife has suffered greatly in the matter, far more than you ever possibly could. I had not told you, I did not want to tell you until you were perhaps a little more settled in your own mind about this matter, but your wife lost the child even before she reached Algiers."

"Then there is nothing to bind us together but our love," Conn said softly, and then he thought of how once he had so bravely proclaimed theirs a love for all time. Was that love strong enough to withstand the loss of their baby, and the knowledge that she had known other men? Yes! Yes, it was! Whatever their difficulties they were stronger together than they were apart. If he had to come to terms with what had happened then so did Aidan, too, and hers would be the harder battle. She needed him, and he needed her. He needed her now more than he had ever needed her for she was the only woman who could make him happy, had ever made him happy. He wanted her back!

Osman smiled at him, and Conn knew that he had understood what was going through his mind. "It will become easier, Conn, I promise you that each day it will become easier," the astrologer said.

"My sister Skye says that you see things that other people do not, Osman," Conn began. "Will I really be able to rescue my wife, and will we be happy again?"

"Each person's fate depends in great part upon they themselves," began Osman. "We are always offered several paths to follow, and how we go is our choice. Those things we have control of, Conn. Our fate, we call it *kismet*, controls other things. Illness, the loss of a child, the chance for wealth. Those things we have no control over. Because there are others involved of whom I know little I can tell you nothing beyond the fact that you will see Aidan again. That much is in both your stars, and I will not lie to you about anything else for I have not built my reputation upon hocus-pocus as some have. Your sister has, I know, told you that I am an honest man above all."

Conn nodded disappointed. Like a child he had wanted to be reassured that everything would work out perfectly. He had wanted to believe that he was fated for success, that nothing could go wrong, that he and Aidan would have a happily-ever-after as did the hero and the heroine in the children's tales that his mother had told his brothers and himself when they were little boys. "So," he said with as much good nature as he could muster, "you are telling me that I must sit patiently for the next few weeks until the dey, in his wisdom, has agreed to release my ships; and then I must sail on to Istanbul with only the slim belief that I will succeed. I must step into the unknown, Osman, and take my chances."

"Like any other mortal man, brother of my friend Skye," chuckled Osman. "Just like any other mortal."

"Then I shall do it, but for God's sake, Osman, speak to your friend the dey. If my brothers spend too many more nights being as debauched as I suspect they were last night, they shall be no good to me at all."

Osman chuckled again. "Fear not, Conn. I have some excellent restoratives that I shall share with them. They will, I promise you, when you sail from the city, be as new men."

"If your women don't kill them with kindness first," laughed Conn.

"They are young yet, Conn."

"They may not be when we leave Algiers, Osman!"

This time Osman laughed. "Trust me," he said. "I have taken care of Robbie all these years, and he is yet vigorous, is he not?"

"I haven't seen him yet this morning," Conn noted.

"You will not see him for several days," said Osman. "Our little friend has a great capacity for loving, and it will take the twins I had for him at least that long to slake his fires."

"God's nightshirt! This life is absolutely not for me any longer, Osman, although there was a time before I married my Aidan that I would have kept up with the best of them, but no longer. I want to go home to *Pearroc Royal* with Aidan, and lead the quiet life. I am not the adventurer that I once thought I was."

"Few are despite what they may think." Osman smiled. "You have simply learned earlier than most what you want. That is a blessing, Conn, my friend. A very rare blessing from Allah. Be grateful for it. You are fortunate enough to see your pathway. Many do not."

"The memory of what Aidan and I have shared shines in my heart like a bright beacon, Osman. It is that which lights my way, and makes it possible for me to see where my ultimate goal leads. The twists and turns of the path, however, cannot be seen, can they?"

"Nay, they cannot," came his answer, "but you will surmount them my friend. You will surmount them."

Chapter 13

***

$\mathcal{B}$oth the sultan valideh, Nur-U-Banu, and the bas kadin, Safiye, as well as Murad, the sultan himself, were taking credit for the sudden marriage of the ambassador from the Khanate of the Crimea, Prince Javid Khan. The prince had married the beautiful slavewoman that the sultan had presented him with just three weeks prior. He had also, it was rumored, legally freed the woman from the bonds of her slavery. It was a love story worthy of the famed tales of Scheherazade, and the gossips of Istanbul made the most of it crediting the woman with such rare and unique beauty that she had bewitched her husband. It was even suggested that she might be a peri or possibly a witch.

It had been a simple ceremony at the local country mosque, attended by the bridegroom, a few of his fellow ambassadors including William Harborne, the unofficial English ambassador whose formal appointment would soon be confirmed, and Sultan Murad. Afterward the gentlemen of the wedding party had made their way back to the prince's palace to partake of a celebration feast. At no time did they even glimpse the bride who remained within the women's quarters overseeing her own small celebration with the sultan's mother, Safiye, and her three women servants.

"You are very fortunate, young woman," said Nur-U-Banu, "to have been made the prince's wife. He must love you very much. I knew that there was something special about you when I first saw you, and decided that you should be my son's gift to Javid Khan."

"Is it true he has freed you legally?" asked Safiye.

Aidan nodded. "He went before a man he called the kadi, and I have the papers safely in that carved sandalwood box you so admired in my bedchamber. I really have much to thank you both for, my friends. My lord Javid is a good man."

"But you do not love him, do you?" said Nur-U-Banu.

"No. I will never love anyone but my beloved Conn," replied Aidan.

"I am, I suppose, a one-man woman, but that does not mean I shall not give all my attention and my caring, and my loyalty to my lord Javid, for I will."

Nur-U-Banu nodded. "You are very wise, my child, and who knows that in time you may learn to love the prince, especially if you should be fortunate enough to bear him children. That often changes a woman's heart. You did not, after all, bear your first husband any children."

"Did you love my lord Murad's father?" asked Safiye wickedly, for Sultan Selim II had been a notorious drunk, and weak ruler.

"Not at first," said the sultan valideh looking piercingly at Safiye. "We are not all so lucky as you were, my dear. My Selim was not a lovable man upon first acquaintance. It was only when I took the time to know him that I saw why he was as he was, and so I made the effort to care for him which in return brought me his love. It is harder to work at love, Safiye, but perhaps in the end it is more rewarding."

"Tell me of Sultan Selim," said Aidan, for she was curious about the man about whom Nur-U-Banu spoke with such tender affection.

"He was the son of the great sultan, Suleiman, whom we called the *lawgiver*, although in the West he was called the *magnificent*. His grandfather was Selim I, a brilliant general; his great-great-grandsire was Mohammed, the conqueror of Constantinople, now called Istanbul. As you can see, my Selim came from an illustrious line. Alas, however, his mother, Khurrem Kadin, was a wicked, wicked woman. He was her first child although she bore Sultan Suleiman two other sons, and a daughter. Sultan Suleiman had another son though by his bas kadin, Gulbehar, and it was this boy, Prince Mustafa, who was his heir. He was in his middle twenties when Khurrem turned his father against him, and had him murdered. His harem and his children were eliminated also. Khurrem then caused the death of her second son, Prince Bajazet, another able young man. Her third son was a cripple, and could not by law inherit due to his deformity. He died, some said, of a broken heart, for he had adored his half-brother, Prince Mustafa, who was always so kind to him, and his brother Bajazet.

"My Selim then became his father's only heir. From his birth his mother had doted upon him, and spoilt him. He was short whereas his brothers were tall. He was plump while they were slender. He was shortsighted whereas they had good vision, and as a youth he was spotty, a fact he later disguised with a beard but even here he was lacking for his beard was a thin and stringy one. In appearance my Selim very much resembled his great-uncle Ahmet, but in personality he was quite like another great-uncle, the scholarly Korkut. He was simply not cut out to be a ruler, a fact which Khurrem refused to acknowledge while she went about ruthlessly removing any possible competition to her eldest son.

"The plain truth is that my husband was ruined by his power-seeking mother. He was weak-willed and vacillating. He had no sense of majesty, but what was worse he was more cut out to be a simple man than a great one. His mother wanted it that way for she intended to rule through her son as she already half-ruled through her husband. She died, however, long before Selim inherited his royal mantle, and her inheritance to this empire was a son, unfit to rule; a spoilt, superstitious child in the guise of a man. It was a blessing to this land that his reign was a most mercifully short one, and that my son, Murad, is like his grandfather Suleiman, and his great-grandfather, Selim I, an able ruler.

"And that, Marjallah, is the official story of my husband's life and reign. History already knows him as Selim the Sot, a Muslim who went against his own holy law, and was a drunkard. For me, however, it was a different story. Like Safiye I was little more than a child when I was brought to the Yeni Serai. My parents were Circassian royalty, and I was sent, like you, as part of a tribute to Sultan Suleiman. I was trained as all girls who enter the harem are trained, and then I was assigned the task of bath attendant to Prince Selim. It was in his bath that he first noticed me. He was recovering from the effects of a night of too much forbidden wine, and it was I who kept changing the cool cloths upon his head.

"At his request I was made a guzdeh, which means I was *in his glance*. I was given my own little room, and a slave to wait upon me. It was not long before I was called to his bed, escorted there fearful and trembling despite all my instruction from the old women of the harem. When my Selim saw my fright he immediately set about to reassure me. He was the most gentle and considerate of lovers, and never was he in his cups when he called for me. I did grow to love him. Yes, even before I conceived my son who was my husband's firstborn son although he had fathered several daughters before Murad was born. I was given the title of bas kadin upon Murad's birth, and although my dear lord took others to his bed over his short life, I remained his favorite. He was not a bad man whatever history may say of him," she finished.

"It seems to me that you brought Sultan Selim II great happiness, my lady valideh," said Aidan.

Nur-U-Banu smiled, and patted Aidan's hand. "As I hope you will bring happiness to Prince Javid Khan, but you most obviously already have since he has married you this day. This is a fortunate thing for you, my dear Marjallah, for it will give you stature amongst his other wives and women when you return with him to the Crimea someday."

"There are no others, nor children either," said Aidan, and then she told the sultan valideh and Safiye the story of Javid Khan's great tragedy.

Nur-U-Banu nodded when she had finished. "It is indeed a terrible thing for the prince, but it is a wonderful piece of luck for you, Marjallah! He obviously loves you having made you his wife. Now bear him sons, and your fortune is made no matter how large a harem he rebuilds."

"Which you may be assured he will," said Safiye with a trace of bitterness in her voice.

"What do you care?" snapped Nur-U-Banu to Safiye. "It is your son, Memhet, who is his father's heir. You bore him no other children despite your exclusive hold upon my son all those years. One Ottoman prince was not enough! Besides it is not in the nature of a man to cleave to only one woman. When will you accept that?"

"I will never accept it!" cried Safiye. "Never!"

"Bah! You waste your life in bitterness, my daughter. Do not be a fool. Accept what Allah has given you, and be grateful for it. Do you know how many women would love to be in your position? Memhet, praise Allah, is a strong and healthy boy already looking at the slavegirls with a lustful eye. One day you will be in my slippers, Safiye. Love is a good thing, but power is a better one," and Nur-U-Banu laughed.

When the sultan's mother and his favorite departed in the early evening with the sultan, and the other guests, Aidan repeated this conversation to Javid Khan as they lay together upon his couch. He had positioned her between his long legs, her back against his chest, so he might avail himself of her beautiful breasts. Even now as they spoke he fondled those glorious orbs of milky flesh.

"Yes, they war against each other within the harem walls, it is said. They are two very strong women, but as long as Sultan Murad lives, or his mother, it is she who will rule the women, and her son's heart first above all others."

"Why does Safiye dislike Nur-U-Banu?" Aidan wondered. "She seems like a good woman to me. I like her."

"Do you like Safiye, too?"

"Of course. She is close to my age, and like a friend."

"Good, my jewel. Take no sides between them else you get caught in the crossfire. Safiye Kadin resents the valideh because it is Nur-U-Banu who insisted that her son take other women. For many years he confined his attentions in monogamous fashion to Safiye, but she only produced one child, Prince Memhet. The Ottoman dynasty could not be safe with just one heir, and as time went by it became obvious that Safiye could not produce any more children despite her as yet youthful age.

"Nur-U-Banu and the vizier finally convinced the sultan to favor other women; but when he at last agreed to their pleadings he found that he could not function with anyone but Safiye. It was then discovered by the valideh that Safiye had purchased charms and potions from one of the bazaar women to bind the sultan to her alone."

Aidan was fascinated. "How did the valideh find out?"

"The most famous bazaar woman in all of Istanbul is an old lady by the name of Esther Kira. She is so old that she was the favorite of Sultan Murad's great-grandmother, Cyra Hafise. She began coming to the harem of the sultan when she was just a girl, and she quickly became greatly in demand for the quality of her merchandise was the very best, and her prices more than fair. It is said that she did the legendary Cyra Hafise some great favor, and for that her family has been exempted forever from paying taxes. This allowed them, for they are Jews, to build a great banking house, and it is said that anywhere you may go in the civilized world today there is a Kira banker. There is even one in the Crimea," he laughed. "Actually the old lady keeps coming to the harem with her wares simply to amuse herself for she does not need the monies, but I digress.

"The bazaar woman who sold Safiye Kadin her charms and potions was a Jewess, and she could not resist bragging amongst the other women of her great service to the bas kadin, a service she said that might very well win her family the same tax exemption as old Esther Kira had won for hers in her youth. Of course this kind of talk was not long in coming to Esther's ears, and she informed the valideh, but at the same time she insisted to Nur-U-Banu that it was the bazaar woman who had initiated the sale of the charm and potions to a distraught Safiye, who she said she was certain would not have acted in such a fashion had not the temptation been placed in her path. That way the wily old woman saved the bas kadin her deserved punishment, and retained the friendship of both these powerful ladies for herself and her family." He chuckled. "As a friend of both Safiye and Nur-U-Banu, I expect you will eventually meet the fabled Esther, but my jewel, I do not want to spend our wedding night telling you tales as a father tells his child," said Javid Khan gently pinching her nipples. "I want to make love to you, my sweet wife, Marjallah. You have brought me much happiness in such a short time, beloved. I never expected to be happy again."

Aidan turned her body so that she might look up into his face. "You have made me happy also, my lord, and I, too, did not think to be content again." Reaching up she caressed his face, and then drawing his head to hers she kissed his mouth in a quick kiss, seeing in his beautiful sky-blue eyes a simple wish that she knew was in her power to grant him; a desire that he didn't even know he revealed. It did not matter, she thought, that she lied to him for the lie was one of the white variety, a harmless thing that would bring him happiness. He could never really know what was in her heart for no man ever really knows the secret heart of a woman. "I love you, my lord Javid," she said softly, and was rewarded by the joy that lit his whole face.

His arms instantly locked about her in a tight embrace, and he almost sobbed, "I love you, too, my jewel! I have from the first, and I feared that you could not love me so great was the love that you bore for your first husband. I thank Allah that he has given me you, my beloved wife, Marjallah!"

"Conn is lost to me," she said honestly, "as are Zoe and Ayesha lost to you. We go on, however, and if we could not love again, my lord, then we should dishonor the memories of those we loved before." I might even, in time, come to believe my own words, she silently decided.

He laid her upon the silken mattress that they shared, and loved her tenderly with both his hands, and his mouth, and his tongue. His delicate, yet sensuous touches sent ripples of sweet fire throughout her whole body; and when at last he believed her ready, he entered her whispering, "Let us make a son this night, my jewel. Let us make a son!"

With a soft cry she received him, and her nails raked wildly down his broad back, but at his words she trembled, which he took for passion, and her mind rebelled as she silently prayed, Oh not yet, dear God! Not yet, for then shall my beloved Conn truly be lost to me! Not yet!

And Javid Khan filled her womb with his potent seed, but Aidan's prayer was answered for she conceived not.

The autumn was warm and fair, and each day when the prince journeyed to the city to take part in the sultan's day as was his duty, Aidan ventured into the gardens to instruct her gardeners. Slowly, and with total patience the ground was cleared of its great overgrowth until the outline of the original beds was quite clear. They found one large fountain and several smaller ones beneath the tangle, and with her husband's permission Aidan sent to Istanbul for workmen to repair the waterworks, and replace the tiles that had been damaged by the neglect of so many years.

Knowing her background, and understanding her more as each day passed, Javid Khan gave his wife the unusual freedom to come and go as she pleased; and Aidan, understanding the cultural differences that separated them, realized the deep trust he had in her, and did not abuse that trust. Never did she leave the little palace without informing him beforehand of her destination, or whom she would be seeing. Her trips were usually to either the Yeni Serai to visit with the valideh and Safiye, or to the Great Bazaar to shop for rare plants for her new gardens.

One afternoon in early November Aidan arrived to visit Safiye, and ushered into the bas kadin's apartments she saw that her friend already had a visitor. Seated with Safiye was a small, plump woman with black, black hair and bright black eyes. She was beautifully dressed in crimson brocade tunic dress, and wore magnificent heavy gold earrings and bracelets. Upon her plump fingers was only one ring, but it was a diamond of such incredible size that Aidan could not help but stare for a moment before her manners caught up with her.

"Marjallah! Come and meet Esther Kira," said Safiye.

"Good afternoon, my lady," said Aidan politely, and then in response to Safiye's hand signal, she sat down with them.

"So," said Esther Kira in a voice that belied her years, for she was now eighty-eight, "this is the lady of whom the valideh has spoken so highly. Your lovely hair reminds me of my friend, Cyra Hafise, she of blessed memory. She was a great beauty, my lady Cyra."

"Which I most certainly am not," laughed Aidan. "My father used to say that I was just barely pretty, and then only if I worked at it."

The old woman cackled back her own laughter. "It is a good thing to know one's own shortcomings as well as one's strengths," she answered. "You are, I can tell, an intelligent woman who understands such things, but then if you were not the prince should not have married you. You have given us all something to talk about this rather dull autumn, my lady Marjallah. Istanbul is a city that thrives on gossip. Is that not so, my lady bas kadin?"

"Most assuredly so," said Safiye, and then she said to Aidan, "Have you been on one of your already famous shopping expeditions, dear Marjallah? Ahh now, there is sweet grist for the mills of chatter. Prince Javid Khan actually allows this wife of his the freedom to come and go as she pleases, Esther Kira. Is that not scandalous?"

"I would say that the prince is an intuitive man," remarked the old woman, and Aidan liked her in that moment.

"I cannot find anywhere in all of Istanbul," Aidan complained, "tulip bulbs, and I do so want a spring garden for my lord Javid. My Portuguese have spent these last weeks clearing the ground of all the overgrowth and weeds, and the fountains have been repaired and are operable, the flowerbeds have been raked and prepared, but nowhere can we find bulbs to plant. The merchants in the Great Bazaar claim that you must obtain them in the late spring after the gardens have bloomed. I am so very disappointed."

"Perhaps Esther can obtain the bulbs you need," suggested Safiye, and she looked at the old woman.

Esther Kira smiled. "It is just possible," she said nodding. "It is just possible that I can."

"Oh, if you only could," Aidan wished.

"Esther can always do the impossible, can't you, my old friend?" teased Safiye.

"Just sometimes, my lady bas kadin," and then she smiled at Aidan. "You see, my lady Marjallah, I, too, know my limits, but in this matter of tulip bulbs I am certain that I can be of help."

It was no surprise therefore to Aidan when she received a visit from Esther Kira several days later. The elderly lady arrived by her private, and quite luxurious caïque, and having been lifted ashore by one of her slaves she hurried up to the house, trailed by a large black eunuch clutching an enormous bundle.

Aidan greeted her warmly. "Why did you not tell me that you were coming, Esther Kira? You will think me a bad hostess. Marta! Make tea, and bring cakes." She settled the old lady by a brazier. "It is chilly out on the water," she scolded gently. "You will catch your death."

"You sound like my great-granddaughter Rachael," Esther chuckled. "My daughter, and daughters-in-law long ago gave up fretting over me. Rachael, however, is yet young and determined. She reminds me of myself at that age."

"I have the distinct feeling," said Aidan with a smile, "that you will live so many more years that you will finally fret even Rachael."

"Heh! Heh! Heh!" laughed the old lady, and she nodded quite vigorously. "May it be from your mouth to God's ear," she said.

Marta and her two daughters brought the refreshments, an earthenware pot with its own brazier in which they brewed the hot and refreshing drink that Javid Khan had taught her was called tea. He had brought from the Crimea two small chests, each containing several foil-wrapped bundles of leaves from which the drink was made. The red lacquered chest held packets of black tea, the green lacquered box held the green tea. It was his favorite beverage, even more than coffee, and he had showed her how to brew it.

Filling a handleless cup with the hot drink Aidan passed it to Esther Kira, who sipping at it, smacked her lips appreciatively. Aidan offered her almond cakes, and sticky, sweet Turkish paste candy which she knew from Safiye was Esther's favorite. The old woman settled back to let Esther tell her why she had come. She did not have long to wait.

"I have brought you a goodly selection of tulips including some very rare and unusual specimens from Persia which are not even in the sultan's gardens. They are my gift to you, Lady Marjallah."

"Oh, Esther Kira," protested Aidan, "they must be very valuable, and I cannot let you gift me like that. You must let me pay you!"

"No, no, child! I want to give them to you. For me it is such a little thing, and I did not purchase them for you. They are but extra bulbs from my own gardens, but I really want you to have them for I know how happy they will make you in the spring when they bloom. Your gardens will be a feast for the eyes, and your husband will be pleased. The sultan valideh will come to see them, and you will bring honor on your house. Perhaps someday you can do something for me." She smiled.

"You are so kind," Aidan said, and she felt the tears pricking at her eyelids although she did not know why.

"Are you happy, my child?" asked Esther Kira.

"I am not unhappy," Aidan answered. Then she sighed. "That kind of an answer must sound as if I am avoiding your question, and I am really not. Yes, I am happy in the sense that I am grateful to be the prince's wife. I am only beginning to realize what could have happened to me as a captive. I have had great fortune in this matter."

"But you do not love him," said Esther Kira.

"Not the way I love Conn," she said quietly, instinctively knowing that this wise old woman would not repeat their conversation. It felt good to have someone whom she could trust again. She did not have that feeling with Nur-U-Banu or Safiye although she was glad for their friendship.

Esther Kira nodded. "You are making peace with yourself, my child, and that is a good thing. In my long lifetime I have seen many women who were not born to this world enter into it from the western part of Europe. The ones who were the happiest were the ones who accepted their fates, and then got on with their lives. They were the women, like Safiye, who went on to power. You are young yet, but you will find that passion is a fleeting and nebulous commodity. Whatever you left behind is simply that. Behind you now. Did you have children?"

"No. We had not been wed that long."

"Then all you have left behind is a man, and they, you will find, my child, are quite replaceable. As replaceable as they seem to think we are although of course *that* is not really true." She chuckled wickedly. "Men believe that they run the world, but it is not so, is it? In my youth I remember my dear lady Cyra Hafise, and how she guided her beloved husband, Sultan Selim I, without his ever realizing that she was doing it. When her son inherited his father's throne she again, this time in her role as the sultan valideh, guided him also. She only made one mistake."

"What was that?" Aidan loved the garrulous old lady's reminiscences.

"Sultan Suleiman had but one favorite, Gulbehar, the Rose of Spring. She was a princess from the city of Baghdad. They had one child, a son, but my lady Cyra could not let well enough alone, and tempted her son with a Russian captive, Khurrem, the Laughing One. Khurrem had for Sultan Suleiman the same fascination that a moth has for a flame. He was intrigued by her, consumed by her, he could not get enough of her. It was the end for Gulbehar, and my lady Cyra regretted her meddling to her dying day for her son, the sultan, could not be wooed from Khurrem's side as he had been from Gulbehar's, and he chose no other favorites so in the end the sultan valideh had only exchanged one for the other."

"A situation similar to Nur-U-Banu and Safiye's," noted Aidan.

"Yes," agreed Esther Kira, "and yet not quite. It is true that Safiye held Sultan Murad's undivided attention for many years, but he is an abnormally sensual man, and his mother recognized it. I will not tell you that the valideh's intentions were all noble, for they were not, but she preferred to see him channel that particular energy in his harem rather than in a destructive fashion such as a useless war. The sultan, however, took his mother's suggestion a little too much to heart. Although he spends his mornings attending to the business of his government, and in the company of creatives and intellectuals; the rest of his time is now devoted to his harem. He is fathering children at an alarming rate. Hardly more than two or three months go by that one of his women does not give birth. It is most obvious now that it was Safiye who grew infertile after Prince Memhet's birth, and not the sultan. Still the bas kadin has no cause for complaint. The sultan loves and honors her above all women but for his mother. You will find as you learn more about the Ottoman sultan that there are four women he respects and admires. Here in Istanbul they are called the four pillars of the empire. One, of course, is Nur-U-Banu, his mother. Another, Safiye. The other two are his full sister, Fahrusha Sultan, and the mystic, Janfeda.

"Janfeda entered the harem during the time of Selim II. She and Nur-U-Banu became close friends, and each promised the other that if she became a favorite she would not forget the other. Of course it was Nur-U-Banu with her golden hair and pink-and-white complexion and her dark eyes whom Selim II noticed. Eventually at Nur-U-Banu's behest he favored Janfeda. Strangely she is more beautiful than the valideh, yet Selim could never see it, but it was just as well. Janfeda has a rare gift of seeing things that other people cannot. Sultan Murad is deeply fond of her, and values her advice."

"Listening to you, Esther Kira, is like being a little girl again, and hearing my mother tell me fairy stories," said Aidan.

"Except," said Esther Kira, "these tales of Arabian Nights that I spin for you are truth. Now, however, dear child, I must leave you if I am to be home in time to light my sabbath candles. I do not feel my years, but I know I am an old woman when I sit telling tales instead of minding the time." With Marta's help she arose to her feet. "I like you, my lady Marjallah, and I would be your friend. Remember that you may rely upon me." Then escorted by Jinji, who had been beside himself with delight that his mistress had received a visit from the great Esther Kira herself, the old woman departed the prince's palace to return to Istanbul.

"We shall have our spring garden!" Aidan told Javid Khan when he returned from the city that evening, and then she related her visit with Esther Kira.

"You," he said approvingly, "become more of an asset each day, my jewel. In your short time here you have become friends with the sultan's mother, his favorite of favorites, and now the matriarch of one of Europe's wealthiest banking families. If I but knew the name of the good genie who blessed me so I should thank him."

"Oh, I am so glad to have made you, happy," she said, "for you make me happy! In the spring when the gardens are at their peak we shall invite the sultan—that would be permissible, wouldn't it?—Nur-U-Banu, Safiye, Janfeda, and Fahrusha Sultan, and whoever else you think, to partake in a festival of flowers."

Her enthusiasm was a delight to him for it bespoke a zest for living. Taking her onto his lap he sat amid the fat pillows with her. "It would be very permissible to ask the sultan and his ladies to our home, and you are very clever to think of it. How did you learn of Janfeda and Fahrusha Sultan?" His hand slipped beneath her silken blouse to fondle her breasts.

"Esther Kira told me," she said snuggling against him with a sigh. "Listening to her is like living the history of this dynasty, my lord Javid."

"And she has indeed lived it herself, my jewel, and appears to show no signs of departing this life. I would not be surprised despite her great age to see her live on into the next reign." He shifted her so that she lay back against his arm, and dipping his head fastened his mouth upon one of her nipples, encircling the quickly rigid tip with his hot tongue so that she murmured with pleasure, her hand kneading strongly at the back of his neck. He played with both her glorious breasts for some minutes, squeezing them firmly, caressing them with gentle touches, licking and blowing on the nipples. Beneath him she wiggled with abandon out of her dark purple silk pantaloons, and discovering it he gave a growl of laughter.

"Shameless houri," he murmured, kissing her passionately, but she pulled away from him, and with eager hands began to disrobe him to his delight.

"I adore you without your clothes," she teased him audaciously, and he chuckled.

"You are bold as well as shameless," he teased her back. She was so unlike any woman he had ever known. She did not hide her emotions from him, but was open. It was a sort of honesty he had not expected to find in a woman, but he liked it. Once her initial shyness had worn off he discovered that she was daring enough to sometimes take the lead in their lovemaking, and he found that incredibly exciting for Javid Khan was used to passivity in his women.

"Tonight," he said as she yanked his pantaloons off his long frame, "I shall teach you how the women of my land sometimes love their lords."

"How?" She sat back on her haunches looking curiously at him.

No one, he thought looking at her, no one has the right to look so delectable. Letting his eyes slide slowly down her lush form he enjoyed the knowledge that she was his, and his alone. If the sultan had but guessed at the incredible beauty of her body he should not have given her away. If Murad had but suspected her delightful passionate nature, a nature that was only just beginning to reveal itself to Javid Khan, Marjallah would not be his. But she was!

His blue eyes caught her silvery-gray ones in thrall. "You know the special way in which I love you, my jewel? The way that sets your lovely body afire for me?" She nodded. "I want you to love me in that way," he said.

"I have never done that," she said slowly, and she looked down at his manhood which lay quietly against his body.

Javid Khan drew his wife against him, and kissed her mouth with a slow and sensuous kiss, his tongue sliding through her lips to dart daringly about her mouth. Then releasing her he gently pushed her head down to his manhood. "I will not force you," he said, "but I want you to try. Take me in your mouth, Marjallah, and love me as I love you."

Aidan shivered. She had never considered doing what it was that he now importuned her to do, and yet she had also never imagined that a man could love a woman in that way. It gave her great pleasure when he did. Was it possible that she could give him the same pleasure? If it was, then she wanted to do so. Reaching out with her tongue she touched but the tip of it to his shaft; then growing bolder ran it about the ruby head, a second shiver, this one of excitement when he groaned, "Ahh, my love!" Emboldened now she opened her mouth and took him between her lips, sucking upon him as upon a delicious morsel.

His voice tight he instructed her, and she carefully followed his bidding, quickly realizing from the fact he grew bigger and harder with every growing minute, and from the pleasured moans that escaped his lips, that he was indeed gaining a great deal of pleasure from her. Finally he cried out, "Cease my jewel! Now, before I spill my seed in a useless place," and she obeyed him, expecting him to order her upon her back, but to her surprise he said, "Now, my adorable wife, I want you to mount yourself upon me as you would upon the horses you tell me that you can ride." Surprised she stared at him, and he laughed as he lifted her up, and placed her upon his body. "Impale yourself, my jewel, upon my shaft. I want you to ride me!"

Aidan caught her lower lip between her teeth as for just a moment she considered what he was asking, but then a small smile turned up the corners of her mouth, and she gracefully mounted him, her breath catching sharply as his hardness filled her sheath. "Ohhh," she said in a soft surprised voice.

Javid Khan laughed, and reaching up began to handle her breasts with firm, but insistent touches. "Now, my fair huntress, ride me. Ride me hard!"

He was throbbing inside her! She could actually feel him pulsing, and it excited her terribly. She considered, perhaps just the tiniest bit shocked, that it was she who in this amorous bout of theirs had the upper hand. She controlled him this time! It was he who would writhe between her thighs this night! It was an incredible thought. The most thrilling she had ever experienced. An almost primitive look came into her silvery-gray eyes, and as she looked down upon him they narrowed. Leaning down over him she began a sensual movement with her hips, and his own hips pushed up to meet her thrusts.

She caught his head between her hands, and pressed her lips to his, pushing her tongue into his mouth to swirl around teasingly for just a minute. Then her tongue found his ear, and with the feathery movement of just the tip she licked that shell of flesh. Next her tongue licked the side of his face, and his neck while with her firm thighs gripping him she continued to plunge her lower body up and down upon his rigid manhood.

He watched her through half-closed eyes, very much enjoying her performance, and rather delighted by the way she had so easily taken him over, obviously liking this switch in their roles. He had had other women ride him before, but none of them had ever actually savored the encounter as Marjallah was doing. Now, however, he felt the need to reestablish his position as her husband and her master. He forced his upper body into a half-seated position effectively pushing her into a full seated pose. His arm wrapped itself tightly about her narrow waist while his other hand reached out, and grasping her breast in a firm grip he took the nipple into his mouth, sucking hard upon it as their bodies moved rhythmically.

The effect upon Aidan was incredible. Her body stiffened briefly, and then suddenly she began to moan wildly, her head starting to thrash. He was so big and hard within her. His mouth was so hot and insistent upon her sensitive nipple. She felt her body beginning to soar, but as it did she also felt a burst of fiery sweetness enveloping both her body and her brain. His thrusts came faster and faster, and suddenly she was falling backward, still impaled upon his mighty manhood as he now towered over her, pounding into her willing and eager body.

"Ahh, houri! Ahh! I can't stop with you! I don't want to stop with you! Ahhhhh, Mar-jallaaaah!" and he shuddered his release.

Beneath him Aidan didn't know if she was even still alive. Her heart was pounding violently, her entire body was drenched in wetness, and her mind had become a vast blur. All she knew was that the words he spoke to her were precisely how she herself felt. She couldn't stop the frantic movement of her hips. She didn't want to stop! She wanted him to go and on and on forever loving her, but when she felt his love juices flooding her secret garden it was suddenly perfect, and she wrapped her arms about him to cradle him against her breasts as he fell forward, exhausted with their passion.

Aidan suddenly began to weep. It had all been too much for her. Javid Khan reversed their position so it was he who was holding her against his chest. He felt the wet heat of her tears, but he said nothing. The sounds she made were of deep sorrow, and what could he possibly say to alleviate that sorrow? All his wife needed to know was that he loved her which he hoped his act of comfort indicated. Women were such wonderfully emotional creatures. Perhaps she might even be breeding. Whatever it was that had distressed her he knew from his experience with her sex would pass. As her sobs turned to sniffles he said quietly, "You know that I love you."

She raised her head to look up at him, and her sandy lashes were gathered in damp, spiky clumps. "I know," she whispered. "It's just that it was so wonderful!"

"Yes," he agreed with her. "It was wonderful! Ah, houri, may you and I always be able to make it that wonderful!" Then he stroked her coppery hair with a gentle hand.

During the remainder of the autumn Aidan worked with her Portuguese gardeners at preparing and planting the large garden of the palace. It was very irregular, Jinji told her somewhat disapprovingly, that a princess such as herself should stoop to even associating with such barbaric infidels. They were uncircumcised, and worse, they had not even been deprived of their functional abilities. It was scandalous that the prince had whole men working in his gardens while his precious wife and her women were about.

"But they are old men," Aidan protested. "They are toothless, old men, all of them! Most of them were impressed into their country's service, convinced that they were fighting a great holy crusade that would assure them a place in heaven, Jinji. It is a tragedy that these poor old men cannot spend their remaining days in their own villages with their wives, and their grandchildren. My lord Javid chose them for their ability to work the land, and from the kindness of his heart."

Jinji sniffed. He still did not approve either his mistress or his master's actions, but what could he do? He was but a slave himself. He had had such high hopes when he had been assigned to be the lady Marjallah's eunuch in Algiers. He had known from the beginning that they were coming to the sultan's seraglio, and had she remained there, he thought, what a miracle could he not have worked! She might have been a favorite, even a kadin! Still when she was presented to the prince his hopes had soared once more. She would become the prince's favorite, and he, Jinji, would rebuild Javid Khan's harem. In a smaller way he would be like the mighty agha kislar, Ilban Bey. Now even that, too, appeared unlikely.

Prince Javid Khan was in love with his princess Marjallah. He wanted no other woman. He would not even consider allowing Jinji to purchase a few beauties for him. The prince's palace had become like the house of a wealthy merchant. One wife, and boring little daily duties consumed their lives. There was no excitement. The prince and his wife were totally wrapped up in each other. Each day the prince went to the city. Marjallah, in good weather to her garden; on an inclement day she oversaw the running of the house which beneath her competent hand needed little care. They ate their evening meal together, and spent their evenings making love, playing chess, simply talking. If only Marjallah would conceive a child, the eunuch thought, then he might have an opportunity to enlarge the population of the harem.

The winter passed uneventfully, and spring slipped slowly into the gardens of the prince's little palace. Each day Aidan, in the company of Marta and her two daughters, walked lingeringly along the carefully raked marble chip paths inspecting each bed for the progress of the tiny green shoots which every day grew taller and bigger. As Aidan had had each plot of ground planted in a pattern, she now checked on each area to make certain that the patterns would be totally perfect. Outside the garden shed in a sunny space sat rows of pots, their green shoots awaiting the failure of any of their brothers in the patterns, that they might replace them.

During the winter Aidan had broken the routine of her days to frequently go into the city to visit with the sultan valideh and Safiye. She had learned from them during the course of her many conversations that Turks prized their gardens, even going as far as to write poetry to them. Each sultan was, by custom, taught a trade, and the conqueror of Istanbul had been a gardener as was Sultan Murad. It was very important to Aidan, therefore, that her gardens be as perfect as possible when the sultan came to see them. There must be symmetry, purity of design, and glorious color, all to please the eye of the beholder. It was to this end she worked, filling her days, blotting out her memories of her beloved Conn, and of her home in England.

Sometimes it was easy, especially when Javid Khan made such exquisite love to her. She had come to realize that what her body experienced in pleasure had nothing to do with the way her heart felt. She loved Conn. He was the only man she would ever love; but her fate was obviously with Javid Khan, who was a good and kind man. It was true that his look did not make her heart leap as had Conn's, but he loved her, and if only a child would come, she convinced herself, all would be well.

Toward the end of April Aidan could see that her gardens would, in two days' time, be at their peak. She consulted Miguel, the eldest of her gardeners, for he was an absolute marvel at knowing the weather. He stood before her, eyes lowered, for it was not right that he gaze directly upon the prince's wife. She was a great lady.

"What do your bones tell you, Miguel?" Aidan asked him. "I want to invite the sultan to come and enjoy the gardens in two days' time. Will the skies be fair? Will it be warm?"

"Answer carefully, infidel dog!" snarled Jinji. "If you are wrong I will personally flay the gristle from your miserable bones."

Miguel shot the eunuch a black look. He and his companions disliked Jinji, who was always bullying them when Aidan was not looking. "The weather, my lady princess, will be fair and quite warm for the next four days at least. You may have the sultan without any fear of rain."

"Thank you, Miguel," Aidan replied. "There will be wine for you all tonight. Just a little though for I would not offend my lord Javid."

The gardener nodded, and gave her a shy smile. He and his fellows all wished that they were safely home in Portugal, but it could have been a lot worse than it was. "Thank you, my lady princess. You are kind to us, and we bless you for it."

Aidan sent Jinji with a note to the sultan valideh inviting the sultan's mother, her son, Safiye, Fahrusha Sultan, Janfeda, and whatever ladies of the sultan's court she felt should come. It was politely and formally worded, and came as no surprise to Nur-U-Banu who had been expecting it. Aidan would not presume to direct her invitation to the sultan himself. It would have been considered an appalling breach of good manners.

On the morning of the visit Aidan arose early, and pulling a silken robe about herself hurried out to check on both the weather and the gardens. The morning was cloudless and quite warm. As she moved along the pathways Aidan was delighted to see that virtually every blossom was in bloom. She couldn't believe it, and she thought to herself that she must bring Esther Kira to see how her bulbs had fared. She would do it tomorrow before the weather changed, and before the flowers were past their peak.

Javid Khan was stirring when she reentered her chamber for he had spent the entire night with her. Pulling her down into the bed he slipped his hand between the halves of her silken garment, opening it, and buried his face between her fragrant breasts. She felt his warm tongue moving up the valley between the hills, and she laughed softly scolding him, "My lord! Fie! The sultan will be here, and we shall not be ready."

"I am already ready," he chuckled, and turning her onto her back he was quickly atop her. His hand was between her thighs teasing at her little pearl, and finding her responsive to his passion he said softly, breathing warmly into her ear, "Ahh, my jewel, you, too, are ready for love," and then he entered her in a smooth motion.

Aidan's laughter was low as she received him. He was a very skilled and persuasive lover, and he had never failed to bring her to that crisis that gives such extra pleasure to a husband and a wife. "You are a wicked man," she teased him, but he was not in the least fooled.

"You have a glow after I have loved you," he said. "I want the sultan to see that glow, and envy me! I want him to see how happy we both are!"

His words were so thrilling, she thought. He was an extremely different man from what she would have expected of a Tartar prince. Perhaps it was the influence of his French mother, but whatever it was it made him a kind and gentle man to live with. Reaching up she drew his head down so that their lips just barely touched. "I glow," she whispered against his mouth, "because you make me happy, my husband!" and then she kissed him passionately, her mouth fiercely pressing against his, her little teeth nibbling at his lips, her tongue running swiftly over his mouth.

Slowly, and with deliberately exaggerated motion he moved upon her body, pressing deeply into her tight sheath, withdrawing almost to the tip of his manhood before plunging back again. She had the power to arouse him as no woman in his memory had ever done, and this morning unable to satisfy his desire for her, he drew her legs over his shoulders so he might drive deeper into her.

Aidan cried out for she could never remember having been penetrated so deeply before. His large and lengthy shaft felt as if it were pushing into the very mouth of her womb itself. His ardor kindled within her an inferno of passion so great that Aidan believed that she was dying. She couldn't breathe. Her eyes would not focus. Her blood thundered like boiling liquid through her veins. Strangely she felt no fear for whatever was happening to her also left her with a feeling of total acceptance. She never even heard her own voice as she cried out, and then she sank into a warm velvet darkness.

Although she was certain she lay unconscious for hours it was only a few minutes, and as she regained her senses she became aware of the fact that he was raining kisses upon her face. She had never felt more wonderful in her entire life, and she didn't want to let go of the feeling. She had always enjoyed lovemaking from the first time Conn had taken her virginity. She had always floated away on a cloud of delight, but *never* had she experienced what had just happened to her now.

"Marjallah!" His voice sounded slightly frantic. "Oh, my beloved jewel, awake! Tell me I have not hurt you!"

Slowly, reluctantly, she opened her eyes to view his handsome anxious face. "I am all right, my lord Javid," she said.

"You are magnificent!" was his response.

"It . . . it was never like that before," she said puzzled. "What happened to me?"

"It is called *la petite morte*, the little death," he answered her, and then he said, "I love you, my darling wife. I can never forget what happened to my family, but each day that goes by I realize how fortunate I am to have you; to have the chance to begin anew, my jewel."

"Oh, Javid," she said, and her silvery eyes were bright with tears of joy, "we are both lucky!" I am, she thought, beginning to really care for this man. I am beginning to love again. Not the way I loved my Conn, but nonetheless what I feel for Javid is love. Then suddenly Aidan's practical nature took over, and with a gasp she cried, "My lord husband! The sultan will be here shortly, and we have neither broken our fast nor bathed! Arise quickly!" and she leapt from their bed.

"We will bathe together," he said, but she sent him an arch look.

"We most certainly will not! Do you not remember what happens each time we bathe together?"

"Yes," he said with a smile, "I do."

"You will bathe in your own bath," she scolded him with the bossy prerogative of a wife. "Jinji! Jinji! Where are you, you useless lump of a half-man?"

The eunuch came running into the bedchamber. "What is it, my lady princess?"

"Escort my lord to his bath, Jinji, and oversee the bathmen that they hurry. We are late, and the sultan will be arriving much too soon!"

With a grimace of defeat Javid Khan arose from his wife's bed, and followed the eunuch from the room. Aidan then called to Marta and her daughters to come and aid her while she bathed and prepared for the royal visit. To Aidan's delight she found her favorite fragrance, lavender, available here in Turkey. Javid Khan liked the scent on her for it reminded him of the open steppes of his homeland, and was not the usual heavy fragrance worn by women. Marta's daughter Fern poured bath oil into the bathing pool, and instantly the room became like a garden. Marta busily scrubbed her mistress down, and rinsed her with clear, warm water before Aidan finally entered the bath to relax for just a few precious minutes before she must once more hurry to greet the sultan and her other guests.

When she came from the bath she was enfolded in a large towel that Marta had warmed, and she sat down to eat her first meal of the day. Iris presented her mistress with a tray containing a small bowl of fresh yogurt, another bowl of newly peeled and seeded green grapes that had come from Syria, a small loaf of freshly baked bread, a little pat of butter, and a comb of honey, and lastly a small pot of delicate green tea. Aidan's appetite had never failed her, and she made short work of the food, rinsing her hands and face in a basin of warmed water afterward.

Her clothing had already been laid out, and when he saw his wife Javid Khan was immensely proud of her. Her wide harem trousers were of cloth of gold, the anklebands embroidered in black jets and small pearls. The transparent chemise that she wore was of a sheer silk fabric that had been shot through with metallic gold threads of such delicacy that they did not irritate her skin. Over these two garments she wore a long-sleeved, slash-skirted dress of black silk brocade that had been embroidered with a design of cloth-of-gold narcissis and tulips. About her hips was a gold belt encrusted with pearls, black jets, and golden beryls.

Since Aidan's hair was really her crowning glory she rarely wore it pulled back in a thick braid as did so many of the women of the sultan's harem. Instead she wore an embroidered gold ribbon sewn with golden beryls as a band above her forehead, and allowed her lovely hair to fall loosely. Having learned from his wife's women what she would be wearing, Javid Khan gifted Aidan with a necklace of creamy pearls and black jets strung upon very thin golden chains which had matching earbobs. Upon her arms she wore gold bangles, some plain, some wide and carved, some studded with bright stones which were echoed in the rings upon her slender fingers. Her slippers were of black velvet but had no heel lest Aidan stand higher than the sultan.

As Aidan had worn her black and gold, Javid Khan decided to complement her by wearing white and gold which suited his tawny good looks. His dress, however, was Persian with white trousers, and a simple white coat that closed with golden frogs. Upon his head he wore a cloth-of-gold turban from which a single white plume fluttered from the heart of a large ruby. Together they made an extremely handsome couple, a fact that was quite noticeable from the sultan's caïque.

"Was it really necessary to give Javid Khan such a treasure?" grumbled Murad to his mother as their caïques drew abreast of one another upon reaching the prince's dockage.

"She is no beauty, my son," said Nur-U-Banu. "You have at least fifty girls in your harem right now who have red hair not to mention Safiye. If Princess Marjallah looks lovely it is because she blooms with her husband's love."

"She might have bloomed with mine, mother."

"Do not be so greedy, elder brother," said Fahrusha Sultan, Murad's sister, who traveled with their mother in her caïque. She was a lovely woman with her mother's fair hair and skin, and wonderfully expressive black eyes.

The sultan chuckled at his sibling's remark. "I am as greedy for women as you are for gems, my sister. Greed seems to be an inherited trait where we are concerned. Where did we get it from, I wonder?"

"Be silent!" said the valideh. "Here are our host and his bride to greet us."

The sultan's caïque was the first of the little flotilla to bump the prince's quay, and it was immediately made fast. Only then did the sultan step out of his vessel onto the land. "Greetings, Javid Khan! It is a fine day you have conjured up for our visit."

The Tartar prince knelt respectfully until raised up by the Great Ottoman. "Welcome, my lord Murad. You do my house a great, and undeserved honor."

Murad smiled pleased at the flattery which had the ring of sincerity about it. Then he looked down to where the prince's wife knelt, her forehead pressed to his boot. Her glorious hair quite excited him. It was all well and good for his mother to say he had other women with red hair from which to choose in his harem, but none had hair the incredible coppery shade of Marjallah's, not even his wonderful Safiye. In his secret heart he lusted after Marjallah, and seeing her now at his feet, so submissive and fair, quite aroused him. Reaching out he raised her up, and gazed into her eyes. "And you, my princess, do you welcome me also?"

"Of course, my lord sultan, with all my heart. I can only hope my poor preparations will not displease you," Aidan said sweetly, but she saw the desire that lurked deep in his dark eyes, and it quite frightened her. She was glad she was Javid Khan's wife, and not at the mercy of this man.

"I do not believe that you could ever displease me, Marjallah," he said with double meaning.

Fortunately Nur-U-Banu's caïque followed by that of Safiye Kadin had now been made fast to their moorings, and Aidan could turn away from the sultan to dutifully greet his mother, his sister, his favorite wife, and Janfeda, who all expressed their delight at having been invited to the prince and princess' Festival of the Spring Flowers.

"You are radiant, my child," approved Nur-U-Banu. "I suspect that you have found great happiness with Prince Javid Khan."

"I have, dear madame," replied Aidan, "and I owe my joy to your great wisdom in seeing what others could not see." My God, thought Aidan, I am beginning to speak like them!

"Now," said the sultan valideh, "you need children to complete your happiness. We must pray that Allah will fill your womb soon."

"Indeed, children are a blessing and a comfort," replied Safiye. "I do not know what I would do without my dearest Memhet."

To Aidan's vast amusement both Janfeda and Fahrusha Sultan raised their eyes heavenward at this remark, but Nur-U-Banu chose to ignore it, instead drawing forth her pretty daughter, and then the lady Janfeda to meet Aidan for the first time. Aidan found the sultan's sister a charming woman, but it was Janfeda who fascinated her for this close friend of the sultan valideh was one of the most beautiful women she had ever seen.

The lady Janfeda was a tiny creature with a delicate bone structure. Her unlined skin was the color of white roses, her hair blue-black, and her eyes above which soared winglike dark brows were as black as the jets in Aidan's necklace. They were not, however, cold like stones, rather they were bright, and interested, and quite lively. She was at least Nur-U-Banu's age, and yet she resembled a girl in her appearance, and for some reason she reminded Aidan of Osman Bey.

"Dear child," she said in a voice as rich as heavy cream, a voice which was in distinct contrast to her dainty frame, "you are so kind to include me in this delightful party." Her eyes studied Aidan, and it was then that

Aidan realized why the woman reminded her of Osman Bey. She could see beyond the ordinary!

"How could I not include the lady Janfeda, who is called one of the Pillars of the Empire?"

Janfeda laughed. "I like to think," she said, "that such a thing is a compliment."

"I am certain that it is," replied Aidan.

Janfeda reached out, and touched Aidan's hand with a soft touch. "You are a sweet child," she said, "and I like you."

"Gracious," said Fahrusha Sultan, "you are greatly complimented, Princess Marjallah! My aunt Janfeda does not easily accept new people. She obviously sees in you things that the rest of us cannot."

"If she does, your highness, then I am grateful that whatever my lady Janfeda sees meets with her approval."

"Come," said the sultan who had been speaking with Javid Khan, "come, Princess Marjallah, and show me your gardens which even from this distance look lovely. As lovely as you, I will vow." He took her by the hand, and led her away.

Javid Khan then offered to escort the sultan valideh. Nur-U-Banu as head of all the women in the sultan's realm was supposed to set an example of womanly good behavior that was to be emulated by all females within her son's dominion. It was thus for the other women of the sultan's party, including some dozen maidens from the harem, to follow along behind him and the prince which they quite happily did.

The gardens were a riot of color with bulbs of every known kind. Aidan had cleverly had her gardeners plant flats of the earliest bulbs which were kept in the cool darkness of the garden shed until just a few days ago when they were brought out to be planted in the main gardens. Consequently the botanical display ran the entire gamut from snowdrops and crocuses to varieties of narcissi to tulips and hyacinths. Aidan led the sultan to the beginning of a pathway which led into the gardens. Here were beds of pure white snowdrops with round centers of dainty little starch lilies carrying dense heads of small blue, grape-shaped flowers.

Murad stopped to admire the symmetry of the display. He had never considered planting beds of snowdrops, let alone planting them with starch lilies. "Magnificent, my dear Marjallah! Absolutely magnificent!" he enthused. "How in the name of Allah did you manage to get your snowdrops to bloom so late?"

She explained, and then said, "I wanted the gardens to be awash with color for your majesty's visit, and the only way I could do it was to tamper with nature to a small extent. Come though for I have much more to show you," and she led him onward.

They next came upon several beds of colorful crocuses, arranged in wide strips of contrasting and complementary hues. These included a golden flower, whites and creams with lilac patterning, and old gold flushed with bronze, a deep buttercup yellow, a white streaked with gray-purple, a blue edged with silver with a golden throat, a deep purple, and a dark orange-suffused mahogany. There were also some larger-sized crocuses with colors ranging from blues and mauves, plain or striped, to white and deep mauve with orange throats. It was this last that caught the sultan's fancy, and Aidan promised, "When the bulbs are lifted, your majesty, I will see that you are sent some for naturalizing within the gardens of the Yeni Serai."

"How generous you are, fair Marjallah," said Murad, and he took her hand in his as they walked slowly on to the next display.

Javid Khan noted this with a rising irritation, but knowing his wife he felt no jealousy. Still in all he would be in Istanbul a year come late summer, and when his father's yearly tribute arrived he would take the opportunity to return home with his wife. Let the Great Khan send someone else as his ambassador to the Sublime Porte. Preferably an old man whose wife would not be a temptation to the Sultan Murad.

"Ahhh," breathed the Ottoman ruler as they came upon a rock garden filled with tiny narcissi. Waterworks had been cleverly disguised amid the rock to look like a small spring that bubbled from the top of the hillock to tumble down among the miniature crags into a pool below. Nearest the water grew little hoop petticoats of yellow with their skirt-shaped centers and their narrow little petals. Native to Spain they had been brought to Turkey by Moors fleeing the persecution of the Christian church. These were planted with several varieties of small, sweetly scented jonquils, bunches of blossoms in gold, clear yellow, and white on delicate stems with their rushlike, deep green leaves. The ladies of the harem chattered their delight at this particular display for it was from these jonquils that a rare oil, highly essential to the making of their perfume, was obtained. For contrast in the rock garden Aidan had planted Glory of the Snow, clusters of small funnel-shaped flowers of bright blue with a white base as well as deep blue; Puschkinia with its powder-blue flowers, a deep blue stripe upon each petal; and dainty Siberian Scilla whose blue flowers reminded Aidan of the bluebells in the woods about *Pearroc Royal*. They were, perhaps for this reason, her favorites.

Passing into the next section of the gardens the sultan and his party were treated to large beds bordered in deep blue hyacinths, and filled with large narcissi in yellows and whites. As she looked out over the beds it appeared to Aidan that there wasn't a bulb there that wasn't in bloom, and at the peak of perfection. It was an incredible panorama.

"Your head gardener is a genius to have planned this all," said Murad.

"But he did not," replied Aidan quietly. "I did. My slaves only work the soil. It is I who tell them what to do."

"And do you soil your beautiful hands with the dirt of this land, fair Marjallah?" He had stopped, and was now holding up her hands for his inspection. They were lovely hands, slender with long fingers, soft and white perfectly shaped nails. Casually he kissed her fingertips, and then lowering her hands moved on again.

"I enjoy working in my gardens, your majesty," she replied, deliberately forcing her voice to remain cool and totally impersonal. His bold action had both frightened her somewhat, and shocked her for she felt that by his actions the sultan was disloyal to Safiye. She would never get used to a world where a man took his pleasure of as many women as suited him.

They had passed through now into what Aidan considered the main part of the garden, and here was planted bed upon bed of tulips. Graceful goblets that swayed in the gentle breeze, their colors ranged from white and cream to pink, red, scarlet, crimson, gold, and deep blue-purple. There were exquisite water-lily tulips from Turkestan, and from the fabled city of Samarkand there were glorious brilliant scarlet blossoms. Planted in groups of both solid and contrasting colors they sprang from beds that were both round and rectangular in shape, some encircling the newly repaired fountains and pools some of which had pink water lilies just coming into bloom, and were now home to schools of large, fat goldfish. At the corner of some of the flowerbeds were yellow azaleas native to the region just across the Bosporus, and therefore quite comfortable in Aidan's garden.

There were other plants growing in the gardens, but none was yet in bloom. As the season progressed there would be roses of many varieties, bougainvillea, lilies, and sultan's balsam as well as two flowers of the night-blooming species, sweet nicotiana and moonflowers. There were, however, blooming even now with her bulbs almond and peach trees whose feathery blossoms stood in delicate contrast to the sturdy dark green pines and cypresses.

Aidan and the prince now led their guests to a pavilion that had been set up at the end of the garden. It offered both a view of the deep blue sea beyond, and of the glorious garden itself. An awning made of cloth of gold, and grass-green silk had been placed over the wooden pavilion to protect its inhabitants from the heat of the midday sun; and it was furnished with a thick wool carpet in soft blue and gold spread over the flooring of the platform upon which had been placed two divans, one for the sultan, and the other for his mother. Stools with red velvet pillows had been provided for Safiye, Fahrusha Sultan, and the lady Janfeda while the rest of the ladies were forced to make do, positioning themselves about the sultan's divan on plump silk cushions in jeweled colors.

The sultan invited Javid Khan to share his divan while inviting Aidan to sit upon a cushion on the rug between them. Refreshments were then served consisting of several different kinds of sherbets, some flavored with strawberries, lemon, or orange, others flavored with rose or violet. There was an abundance of fresh fruits, oranges already sectioned, and peeled free of their delicate white membrane; wild, sweet strawberries of dark red hue; green figs; early golden peaches and apricots as well as bunches of fat purple grapes that had been brought from the orchards of the Holy Land; and a golden platter upon which had been arranged plump dates, each stuffed with an almond. A selection of delightful pastries, flaky layers of dough filled with chopped nuts and honey, gazelle horns, treats made with sesame and honey, and delicate almond cakes, completed the repast.

When the sweet feast had been finished, and Aidan's slaves had passed around fragrant moist towels to all the guests so that they might wipe the stickiness from their hands and faces, the entertainment began. There was an amusing gypsy family with their troupe of performing dogs that had the sultan roaring with laughter. He so much enjoyed them that he took a large, virtually flawless diamond from his finger, and presented it to the patriarch of the family, a proud mustachioed man who accepted the tribute as graciously as it was given. Next came an elderly Indian who placing several deep, round baskets before the pavilion then seated himself behind them, and began to play upon a pipe. As the reedy tune filled the air there came from the baskets—one at a time—the tune changing ever so slightly as each basket's inhabitant took his cue—large, hooded snakes that Javid Khan told the assembled gathering were called cobras, and were native to the snake charmer's land. The rather frightening reptiles writhed and bobbed seemingly in time to their master's music. Aidan was not sorry to see the finish to the snake charmer's performance.

In the trees about the pavilion there had been placed silver and gold cages of singing birds who now went wild as a young girl appeared to entertain the assembled guests with a flock of doves and pigeons that she had trained to fly in various formations according to her whistled signals. The conclusion of her recital was a spectacular exhibition in which the birds first flew in a wide circle above the gardens, and then descended in a line to position themselves upon their mistress' outstretched arms. The spectators clapped wildly, and the sultan valideh rewarded the girl with a necklace of semiprecious gemstones.

The conclusion of the entertainment was provided by a troupe of very sensual and exotic dancing girls who traveled about the sultan's empire with their master, who was a Syrian. It was a great honor for them to dance before Murad, and they strove to give him their best performance. The sultan was enchanted enough to consider buying the troupe for his own amusement, but he was prevented from his folly by his mother who hissed at him, "Would you make yourself a laughingstock? You already have too many dancing girls, and if you want more then leave it to Ilban Bey to see to it. Do not lower yourself to bargain like a common merchant! You are the Grand Turk, my lion!"

Murad compressed his lips in a tight line, and nodded. "You are right, mother. I was but carried away by the moment, and the deep and great pleasure this day has given me." He turned to Javid Khan. "I do not know when I have enjoyed myself so much, my friend. Your hospitality and that of your lovely wife has warmed my heart." He sighed effusively. "It is rare that I can allow myself the privilege of behaving like an ordinary man. Today has meant much to me."

Similar thanks were forthcoming from Nur-U-Banu. "Dearest Marjallah, I am so relieved to see you happy and obviously content. I well remember the agony of first captivity, but then we are not really captives, are we? It is the way of nature that a woman be subservient to her lord. Thank you for a lovely day."

Safiye took Aidan's hands in her own. "I am so glad," she said softly, "that we are friends. You know my difficulties, but now I have you to rely upon, and you, Marjallah, have me. Remember that."

Fahrusha Sultan and the lady Janfeda took their leave of their hostess politely as did the other ladies of the harem who had accompanied their master to Javid Khan's palace. Then like a troupe of pastel-colored butterflies they fluttered across the lawn and down to the waiting caïques. The sultan, however, had remained behind, and now taking Aidan's hand in his once more he raised it to his lips, turning it to kiss her palm. His dark eyes locked hypnotically onto hers.

"You have pleased me, Marjallah," he said quietly. "Your perfect demeanor and your clever wit have brought honor upon my house because you were my gift to Javid Khan. I will think carefully of the best way to reward you for your behavior.

"I am already rewarded by your majesty's presence, and his gracious words," Aidan replied all the while stifling the urge to pull her hand back and wipe his kiss from her skin. Murad frightened her with his intensity.

"You are perfection," he said, "and in a few days' time I will send you a gift to match your spirit. Farewell, Marjallah!" Then he was gone, striding away down the quay, and only when he had gone did she shudder with repugnance.

Her husband's arm went tightly about her shoulders. He had seen the sultan's leave-taking of his wife, and Javid Khan's anger had burned hot that Marjallah must be forced to stand uncomplaining while Murad had salivated over her. "I agree with the sultan in one thing," he said. "You have a magnificent and incomparable spirit, my jewel. I will not, however, allow you to be insulted like that again. In a little over three months' time my father's tribute will arrive from the Crimea. I will write to my father to send a new ambassador to the Sublime Porte so that we may return home then."

"Oh, Javid, do you really want to? Will it not displease your father that you leave this post he has honored you with only after a year's time?" Her face was a mask of concern for him, and it didn't occur to Aidan that she wasn't even afraid of leaving Istanbul for a place that would be more distant from England.

His arm still about her as they walked back into the gardens, he said, "The Khanate of the Crimea has never before sent a resident ambassador to Istanbul. The Ottoman is our overlord, and each year we have sent our tribute to him in late summer, but Murad wanted an ambassador. My father chose to ignore his request, politely, of course, but nonetheless he ignored it. When my brother Temur murdered my family those long months ago, my melancholy was so great that my mother persuaded my father to honor the sultan's desire for an ambassador, and to send me. It was done to remove me from the scene of my greatest happiness, and my greatest sorrow. Now, however, I have found new and even greater happiness with you, my precious jewel. As long as we are together I shall lack for nothing.

"You will like my homeland! Although the upland plains that comprise most of our lands are cold and windy in the winter, and hot and dry in the summer season, my home is along the coast where it is mild and healthful. The lands along that southeast coastal strip are very fertile. The orchards and the vineyards are numerous. The variety of fruits in the marketplaces is amazing to behold. There are cherries, and peaches, figs, apricots, apples, pomegranates, pears, and grapes. I had an entire orchard of almond trees, and on the steppes I grazed a great herd of horses. Praise Allah that Temur was so busy indulging in his blood lust that he did not destroy my orchards although he burned my home and my stables, but not before he ran off my stock. He behaved exactly like our rather fierce ancestors. He always took great delight in the fact that he was named after the great Tartar warlord, Timur, descendant of the mighty Genghis Khan, grandson of the famed Kublai Khan."

"Why did you not revenge yourself upon him, my lord Javid? Why did you not kill him?" This was something that had been disturbing Aidan for some time now.

"I am a Muslim, Marjallah, and I like to think that if I am not a very devout man, at least I am a good Muslim. The Koran, our holy book, forbids the taking of a brother's life. Temur is not just my brother though, he is my twin. We shared the same womb at the same time. We were birthed together. Despite his bestiality I cannot kill him for to do so would be to kill off a part of me, a part of our mother who has suffered deeply the actions of one of her sons, our father who has always been a wise and fair man. Destroying Temur would have given me but momentary satisfaction. It would not, however, have brought back my wives and family.

"Temur and I seem to be like night and day. He has ever flouted our laws, our religion, our ways. Each day he lives he is punished now for his actions have cut him off from his own family, his people, and this for a Tartar is the worst punishment of all. His name has been struck from our history, and it is as if he never existed at all. It is a living death, Marjallah."

She nodded. "I understand," she said, "and now I even feel a little sorry for your brother. There is no way he can right the wrong that he has committed. He will never see his own wives and his son again. How terrible, my lord Javid! What devils have ever driven him that he would perpetrate such folly not only upon you, his twin, but upon himself?"

Javid Khan stopped, and tipped her face up to his. Looking down on her, his eyes brimming with love he said, "This is why I adore you, my wife. You have a heart that could understand the devil himself!"

Blushing prettily at his extravagant compliment Aidan hid her face against his shoulder. "You make me sound so good," she said, "and I am not! If I could get my hands upon your brother I should make him suffer for all the pain he has caused you!"

The prince laughed heartily. "Ahh," he said, "I think that you must have a little Tartar blood in your veins, my jewel! How very fierce you sound, and what is more I believe that you would do exactly as you threaten."

"I would!" She looked back up at him, her gray eyes stormy.

"We are going home to the Crimea," he said firmly. "I will send my father word, and I shall rebuild us a new palace, but not upon the site of the old one lest the ghosts of the slain trouble us. I will take you home, my darling wife, and we will become settled old married folk."

"Who shall raise almonds, and children," she teased him.

"Sons," he corrected her.

"And daughters, too," she insisted.

"Only," he said, "if they are pretty and as clever as their mother."

Aidan smiled up at Javid Khan. "I promise," she said solemnly.

Chapter 14

❧

$\mathcal{I}$n the hour before dawn Aidan was awakened by Marta, and she arose to dress for she was going to Istanbul to bring Esther Kira back for a visit. Normally she would have let the elderly lady come to her, but since the matriarch of the Kira family had given her the means of creating her beautiful gardens, she wanted to show her friend the courtesy of coming for her herself. She dressed warmly for although it was mid-spring, it was chilly out upon the water in the early morning, and the lined sleeveless robe of sky-blue silk that she put on over her other clothing was welcome.

Sipping a handleless cup of strong black tea she gave Marta her final instructions. "Be sure to wake my lord Javid shortly after I leave so that he may ride at dawn. Tell Hammed that he is to serve baby lamb for the meal today, but under no circumstances is he to serve any dairy product upon the table with the meat for it is against Esther Kira's religion for such things to be mixed, I am told. Be sure that the servants use the new dishes, the ones I had blessed by the Jewish priest so that Esther might eat with me. Do we have plenty of Turkish paste candy for Esther does love it?"

"Yes, my lady, yes, yes, yes!" laughed Marta. "Everything is in perfect readiness as you ordered. There is nothing to worry about, and I will oversee all in your absence. Now go, for if you do not then you will not reach the city in time, and then you and your guest will not be able to enjoy the sunrise from the water."

Aidan slipped back into her bedchamber, and leaning over the bed she kissed Javid Khan. Instantly he was awake, and rolling over he pulled her down into the bed atop him. "My lord! You will make me late," she protested.

His mouth found hers in a searing kiss, and then releasing his grip only slightly he said, "We have no time at all?" and his hand slipped skillfully through several layers of her clothing to tease at her nipples.

"Shameless one!" she laughed pulling his hand away. "Did you not sate yourself last night?"

"Ahh, my jewel, but that was last night. I am awake and hungry once again for your sweet body."

"Damn you, Javid," she muttered, "there really is no time."

"Then I can but await the departure of our guest who has not even arrived yet. Tonight, however, I shall exact a severe revenge from you for my disappointment of this morning." His sky-blue eyes twinkled at her. "Go now!"

"I shall eagerly await your rebuke, my lord husband," she teased him as she went out the door.

"I love you, Marjallah, my wife," he called after her, and Aidan smiled with genuine happiness.

Jinji, ever mindful of her appearance, would not allow her to travel alone the short distance to the city, and so he and Marta's daughters, Fern and Iris, were now awaiting her. Together the four of them hurried to the caïque where the oarsmen sleepily awaited them.

The water in the chill of the predawn was black and calm. Above them the sky was slate-colored, its flat surface broken here and there by clear, cold stars, some of which were blue-white in color, and others an icy red. There was absolutely no wind and no sound other than the slap-slap of the caïque's oars as they creased the water. The prince's vessel moved slowly from its mooring, and then guided by their helmsman who stood at the stern of the boat gripping his long oar, the oarsmen slipped out into the main channel of the Bosporus. Quickly finding their rhythm the oarsmen soon had the caïque moving swiftly through the mirror-still waters.

Aidan didn't bother drawing the curtains of the caïque, and looking out she could see the passing landscape although in the predawn darkness there was little to see. The hills on the Asian side of the Bosporus resembled nothing more than great lumps, and the island in midstream that was located halfway between Istanbul and Javid's palace was equally indistinguishable. Jinji for once was silent. He was not a morning person. Fern and Iris sat sleepily nodding against each other, and Aidan was frankly grateful for the quiet. Esther Kira was to meet them at the waterfront quay reserved for vessels belonging to ambassadors to the Sublime Porte. Rounding a point Aidan saw the towers, the domes, and the minarets of the city come into view. The sky was now a light gray, and the stars had almost all faded away but for bright Jupiter.

The caïque began to nose itself in toward the shore, steering a course between vessels that were anchored in the harbor. The city was beginning to awaken, but it was not yet noisy. Reaching their destination Aidan saw the ornate and comfortable litter of Esther Kira already waiting. Jinji leapt from the caïque as it touched the quay, and hurried over to escort the venerable old lady from her vehicle to the boat. For a moment he stopped to chatter with a eunuch of the Kira household who had accompanied his mistress, and then the two of them aided the matriarch from her litter, and helped her into the caïque of Javid Khan.

"Good morning, Esther Kira," said Aidan. "I believe that we are to have a beautiful day."

"Indeed, my child, I trust that you are correct." She turned back to her own servant. "Where is my shawl, Yakob? I am already cold."

The negligent Yakob hurried back to the litter, and returned bearing his lady's garment which he handed to a smirking Jinji, who entering the boat wrapped it about Esther Kira with great ceremony.

"Bring the brazier near the lady Esther's feet, Jinji," said Aidan, "and where is that soft woolen lap robe I asked you to bring?"

Jinji almost stumbled over himself to do Aidan's bidding, and very quickly everything was as she had ordered. Taking his seat he signaled to the helmsman and the oarsmen to get their craft under way once again.

"We shall return your lady at sunset, Yakob," Aidan called out as the caïque pulled away from its dockage. "I hope," she said turning back to her guest, "that you do not mind my coming for you so early, but I wanted us to have the entire day together for I owe you so much, Esther Kira. Yesterday the sultan, his mother, Safiye, and a party of ladies from the harem including Fahrusha Sultan, and the lady Janfeda came to celebrate our gardens with us. They were most pleased, and went away content. It cannot but help my husband in his position as ambassador from his homeland."

"It has ever been a woman's duty to aid her husband along his chosen pathway wherever she may, Marjallah. I am happy I have been able to be of service to you. It has been my life to be of service to others, and the lord God, whom we call Yahweh, blessed be his name forever, has rewarded me greatly by giving my family wealth and a power of sorts in this strange land which we inhabit."

"Have you lived here all your life, Esther Kira?" asked Aidan.

She loved the tales the old lady told, and she was eager to encourage her to further stories.

"Yes," said Esther Kira, "I was born here. My family was forced to leave the land of Israel, the homeland given to us so long ago that the date is lost in time, after the fall of the citadel of Masada, when the mighty Roman Empire ruled the world. You call Israel, Palestine, the Holy Land. My family wandered for many years until coming to the city of Constantinople in the days of the great Constantine himself. We have lived here ever since."

"Then your family has been here hundreds of years," noted Aidan.

"Yes," agreed Esther, "we have. We came when the people of the city were yet pagans, worshiping the old Roman gods, but Constantine, who was emperor of the Eastern Empire became a Christian, and we were persecuted for a time. Then in 1453 the Ottoman sultan, Mohammed, called the Conqueror, came from across the Bosporus, and took the city which was then called Constantinople. The old empire had been dying slowly for years, and the Turks even had a small foothold on this side of the water by virtue of a dowry settlement of Princess Theadora Cantacuzene who was married first to Sultan Orkhan, and then later to his son, the first Sultan Murad."

"She married her own son?" Aidan was shocked.

Esther Kira laughed. "Bless me, no, child! Princess Theadora was not the first Murad's mother. Murad was half-grown when the little princess was bartered into a loveless marriage with a man old enough to be her grandfather. In exchange the princess' father obtained military aid from the sultan. The story goes that the first Murad saw her in his father's house, and fell in love with her. When his father died he married her, and it is their great-great-grandson who was the eventual conqueror of Constantinople which is now called Istanbul. When the Turks came we were not persecuted, nor were the Christians. It is the way of the Ottoman Muslims to tax us for our slightly different beliefs, not only in money, but in sons for their corps of Janissaries, and beautiful daughters for their harems. It is a price we pay, and under the Ottoman rule we have prospered. Their government is a sound and a fair one although I fear the rule of the women that has been slowly overcoming the sultans recently, but enough of this chatter, dear child. Look! The dawn! Blessed be the Lord God! There is no artist like him. Behold, the sky!" and her plump, beringed hand pointed to the dark hills of Asia, now quite visible in the morning light.

The sky just above those hills was brightening, a thin band of molten gold widening quickly, and poured up to banish the dull gray of earlier. It was followed by an array of colors so breathtaking that Aidan caught her breath with delight. Like bolts of the finest China silk the colors—scarlet-orange, rose pink, pale mauves edged in royal purple, and lemon yellow—rolled across the sky until it shimmered and glowed with the ethereal light. Then the fiery ball of the crimson sun burst above the green hills, and the day had begun. A small breeze sprang up to ruffle gently the blue waters of the Bosporus as they drew abreast of the island Aidan considered the midway point in their journey.

"Is it not glorious?" said Esther Kira. "I will shortly be celebrating my eighty-ninth year, and no matter how many sunrises and sunsets I see, each one is different, each one a testimony to the greatness of God. It makes me feel quite unimportant in the scheme of things." She chuckled. "I believe I enjoy sunrises and sunsets because they have the ability to keep me humble and sensible. I tell my son, Solomon, and my grandsons, of this, but they, being superior beings, think I am naught but a foolish old woman."

"I do not believe for one moment that you think men superior beings, Esther Kira, no matter what they think," Aidan laughed.

"Men!" The matriarch smiled. "Men begin as helpless, crying infants who spring forth from women's bodies. They are nourished at a woman's breast, by a woman's milk, but for some reason the moment they begin to use their legs their brains tell them that they are superior to their mothers, and their sisters, and all other women. I find this an interesting phenomenon, don't you, Marjallah?"

"Indeed I do, but you have still not answered my question," replied Aidan.

Esther chuckled again. "You are an intelligent woman," she said, and then, "No, I do not necessarily consider men wiser than women in all cases, but that, as you well know, is a most radical viewpoint on my part. It is necessary for a wise woman to allow the men in her life their small illusions, is it not? They tell me that Prince Javid Khan loves you deeply, but you do not love him, I am certain, yet you give him the illusion of love, and he is satisfied."

Aidan flushed. "I do care for my lord Javid," she said, and then she sighed, "but you are right when you say I do not love him as he loves me. Perhaps in time I shall for he is such a kind and good man, and I do not want to cheat him of what should rightfully be his. Still, I cannot forget Conn, my true husband, Esther Kira. Pray God that in time I do."

"Again we are ruled by the infernal workings of the male mind," said the old lady. "You are given to the prince, and expected to wipe from your feeble female brain your entire past. It is a tribute to our stamina that women survive and cope so very well, Marjallah." She reached over, and patted Aidan's hand with her plump one. "Still you are happy, I can see, and I am glad. Now tell me of the gardens for we are almost there."

"Your bulbs are wonderful, Esther Kira! The sultan and his party were utterly enchanted, and I have promised to give the sultan some of the mauve crocuses with the orange throats. He was most taken by them." She went on to tell her friend of how she had arranged it so that all the bulbs were virtually at their peak, and Esther Kira nodded.

"You are a clever girl, Marjallah," she said. "Although the sultan's hobbies are clockmaking and painting, his trade is gardening. He is a very high-strung, intense man, and he enjoys the solitude that the gardens offer him. Working about the plants and flowers is very soothing to him."

"I can understand that," answered Aidan. "Plants ask only to be pruned and watered, nothing more. They do not talk back at you or argue with you over trifling matters."

Esther Kira laughed an amused chuckle which suddenly died in her throat. Her dark eyes widened, straining to see the shore, and she pointed with a finger toward the land.

"What is it?" Aidan followed the direction of Esther's finger, and a chill swept her body.

"Stop the vessel!" the old woman croaked in a surprisingly strong voice. "Do not go any farther!"

The helmsman nodded to the oarsmen who raised their dripping oars, and they all looked toward the palace which had just come into their view. Out over the water they could now hear shouting, and the sound of discord. Then without warning a spear of flame shot up from the palace itself to be followed by another, and another, and another.

"Oh, my God!" whispered Aidan. "It is my lord Javid's nightmare all over again. Quickly! To the shore! We must help them!"

"No!" The word was sharp, and they looked to Esther Kira. "Marjallah, be sensible. Do not allow your heart to rule you in this instance. Someone is attacking your palace. Three young women, an old lady, and a handful of slaves cannot help whatever is happening. We have no weapons. If we step ashore we shall all be killed. What purpose would that serve?" She looked to the helmsman. "Turn the caïque about," she said, "and row as swiftly as you can for the Yeni Serai!" Then as the vessel was being swung around she said to Aidan, "We will go to the sultan for aid. He will send his soldiers."

"Javid," said Aidan. "He was going to ride at dawn as he usually does. Marta is there."

Fern and Iris, ordinarily quiet girls, began to weep, sensing the disaster, and Aidan drawing her two little slavegirls to her put a comforting arm about both of them, but she said nothing for she didn't know what she could possibly say. The caïque sped over the water as if it were propelled by wings instead of oars. Aidan hadn't been aware that the vessel could move so quickly for under normal circumstances it moved at a stately pace. The city was soon in view, and they were once again wending their way through the harbor traffic, the noise, and the morning smells of the city calling out to them across the water. Across the mouth of the Golden

Horn they raced, and the caïque began edging itself in toward the shore as the Yeni Serai came into view. In a shorter time than she would have believed possible they were arriving at the palace, and the dockmen were making the vessel fast.

Esther Kira climbed out, and said, "We will go to the sultan valideh immediately. She will know what to do."

Aidan disembarked from the boat with Fern and Iris, and as they hurried through the gardens and the many courts that led to the valideh's apartments she worried, "It is so early. I doubt that the lady Nur-U-Banu will be up yet."

"Nur-U-Banu is always awake," said Esther Kira. "I cannot help but wonder when she sleeps although she assures me that she does. She is very involved in her son's government for she is a wise woman."

Arriving at the apartments of the sultan's mother they were ushered inside. Nur-U-Banu's well-trained slaves showed absolutely no surprise at such an early visit by Esther Kira and Princess Marjallah Khan. They were seated and offered tea and almond cakes which Aidan waved away although Esther Kira accepted.

"Please," said Aidan, "we must see the valideh! It is most urgent!"

"Her majesty is just coming from her bath," the eunuch said. "I shall see if she will receive you now."

"Tell her it is urgent!" Aidan repeated, and then sat nervously as she waited.

Several minutes—it seemed like hours to Aidan—the sultan valideh hurried into the room. She was wearing only a chamber robe, a beautiful quilted silk garment of rich lavender, and her fair hair was unbound. "Esther! Marjallah! What is it? The eunuch said you claim urgency."

Esther Kira gave Aidan no time to explain, instead launching into her own version of their tale. She was quick and to the point, and the valideh not even waiting to inform her son gave immediate orders that a full troop of Janissaries be dispatched to the palace of Prince Javid Khan at once. Then she sent a message to the sultan to attend her as quickly as he could.

"My dear Marjallah," Nur-U-Banu said as she sat herself next to Aidan, and put a motherly arm about her, "you must not worry. It is highly unusual for what appears to have happened to happen within the borders of my son's empire let alone so close to the city. Although the prince was not expecting to be attacked, he and his men have undoubtedly routed the invaders although not without damage to your home, and possibly even some casualties amongst your servants. With the arrival of our Janissaries your husband will have adequate reinforcements to thoroughly defeat these invaders. We will have a report as soon as it is possible, and in the meantime I want you to stay with me, dear child. You look fairly worn, and I can certainly see why. These last days have been utterly exhausting for you preparing your gardens for our visit yesterday, and then coming so early to the city to fetch our dear Esther. Kaspar!" she called to the eunuch. "Fetch a strawberry sherbet prepared my special way for the princess. Be quick!"

"Oh, I couldn't," said Aidan, for she was terribly distressed. Why had someone attacked her home? Where was Javid? Was poor Marta all right?

"Just a little something to drink, my dear," said the valideh persuasively. "I can understand you not being able to eat, but the sherbet will help you keep up your strength. Do it for me, my dear Marjallah."

Kaspar handed Aidan the sherbet, and because Nur-U-Banu was being so kind to her she knew that it would be churlish to refuse. Taking the goblet from the eunuch she sipped the sweet, slightly thick liquid down. Despite her anguish the strawberry-flavored drink did taste quite good. "I am so frightened," she said to no one in particular.

"There, dear child," the valideh soothed. "Everything will be all right, I am certain."

Aidan's head drooped onto Nur-U-Banu's shoulder, and she yawned. "Sleepy. Why am I sleepy?" and then she suddenly leaned heavily against the sultan's mother, unconscious.

"Take her into my bedchamber, and make her comfortable, Kaspar," said the valideh to the eunuch. Then she looked to Aidan's two little slavegirls, and the openmouthed Jinji. "You will stay with your mistress," she ordered them, and they obediently followed Kaspar. Then Nur-U-Banu said to Esther Kira, "I have lived long enough in the harem to see a fit of hysterics coming on, old friend. Our Marjallah will sleep long enough for us to ascertain what has happened. Stay with me, and help me keep this vigil. We will send word to your family so they know where you are and that you are safe."

Aidan awoke in the late afternoon, her memory of the morning instantly flooding back. Her eyes swept the valideh's luxurious bedchamber, and she saw her three servants dozing, Fern and Iris by the side of the great bed, Jinji at its foot. Someone had thoughtfully removed her sleeveless robe, her slash-skirted dress, her belt, and her slippers. She saw them placed carefully upon a chair, and arose quickly to don the last two items of her wardrobe. Then she slipped quietly out the door finding herself in a small corridor across which was another door she hoped led back into the valideh's salon. It did. Nur-U-Banu sat with Esther Kira, and several of the valideh's maidens. They looked up as she entered the room.

"What news?" she asked them.

"The Janissaries have only just returned to the Yeni Serai, Marjallah," said the valideh. "They will go to the sultan first, and then we will have word."

Aidan sat down on a stool, her face a study in despair. Javid Khan was dead. She sensed it. No, she *knew* it! How could it have happened? What would become of her now? What would become of all of them?

Nur-U-Banu, and Esther Kira were both too wise to speak now, or to attempt to comfort Aidan. They, too, suspected the worst had happened so why should they offer false hope to her? The minutes slipped by marked by the slow dripping of the valideh's water clock, and then suddenly the door to the salon flew open, and Murad entered into the room, and all eyes were upon him as they arose to make their obeisance.

He went immediately to Aidan, and seeing her at his feet he was assailed by that same heady feeling that attacked him yesterday. What was it about her that intrigued him so? Reaching down he raised her up. Her eyes met his, and the sultan said, "I am so sorry, Marjallah."

For a brief moment she closed her eyes, but quickly opened them again to ask, "Tell me what happened. I want to know it all. I am not afraid to learn the truth."

"They are all dead," said the sultan bluntly, "and the palace and its gardens totally destroyed. It was obviously a surprise attack. Javid Khan was cut down by the stables. He died instantly, Marjallah. At least he had no pain. It was Tartars, his renegade brother, I am certain. My Janissaries have already departed to hunt them down. They will find them, I swear it!"

"How do you know it was Tartars?" she demanded, her voice dull with her pain.

The sultan hesitated and then said quietly, "Because after they killed their victims, they decapitated them, and stacked their heads in two piles on either side of your palace gates. It is their custom."

Aidan felt the bile rise in her throat, but forcing it back she asked, "I had a serving woman. Is it possible she was taken captive?"

"I doubt it," said the sultan. "I suspect she was probably raped, and then killed along with the rest of them. The object of this attack seemed to be wanton destruction. Even your livestock and pets were slaughtered although my men did find this fellow wandering about the gardens." The sultan reached into his robes, and drew forth a half-grown cat with long orange-and-cream fur which he handed to her.

She took the squirming animal who immediately pressed himself against her, and looked up at Murad with a tearstained face and said, "It is Tulip. We called him that because of the orange blossom on the tip of his cream-colored tail. He likes to hunt at night in the fields about the

361

palace, and never comes home until after the sun is up. That is what saved him, my lord." Aidan buried her face into the cat's fur, and began to cry.

"Thank you, my son, for bringing us this news, tragic as it is," said Nur-U-Banu. "I will take care of Marjallah for now. Will you escort our dear Esther Kira to her litter which should even now be arriving in my courtyard?"

The sultan valideh was the only person in the entire empire who could thus dismiss the sultan, and obedient to her will he departed the room with Esther Kira. Aidan had sunk down onto a pillowed divan and was crying softly. Nur-U-Banu let her weep until finally she could weep no more, and she sat clutching her cat to her bosom, her fair face blotched unattractively. Finally she looked up at the sultan's mother, and the sadness in her eyes touched even the hardened heart of the sultan valideh.

"What will happen now?" she said softly to Nur-U-Banu.

"You will stay here in the palace, dear child, but you certainly cannot go back to the oda of our friend Lady Sayeste. You are the widow of a prince. You must have your own apartments. For now that is all we need worry about. There is time for us to decide your future later."

"What future can I possibly have?" said Aidan sadly.

Nur-U-Banu's eyes were wise. "Everyone has a future as they have a past."

"I seem to have nothing but pasts," said Aidan. "Each time I begin to care for a man either I am snatched from him, or he from me. First it was my father, then Conn, and now Javid Khan. Perhaps it is written that I am meant to live my life alone."

"No one is meant to live alone," said the valideh. "It is not natural. That is why Allah planned that there should be both men and women. You are in shock, my child. I shall call my good physician, a particularly clever Greek, to care for you. I have the utmost faith in him."

Aidan refrained from saying anything for there was nothing to say. Javid was dead. He had been taken from her as had Conn. She wasn't certain she even wanted to go on living. What was left? She was far from her native England, from *Pearroc Royal*, and just when she had been beginning to rebuild her life with Javid Khan, it was all gone as if some evil genie, jealous of her happiness, had stolen it from her.

The physician came, and mixing several powders into a cup of rosewater proclaimed that what she needed was rest. Aidan was strongly tempted to tell him that she had spent the day sleeping, but instead she gratefully drank down the contents of his brew. At least if she slept she would not have to remember. Sleep was, after all, just what she needed.

Nur-U-Banu herself escorted Aidan and her servants to a small two-room apartment right next to her own, and smilingly watched as she was put to bed. She was asleep before they had even finished with her.

The valideh returned to her own salon to find that her best friend, the lady Janfeda, had arrived. The two women kissed, and then settled themselves amid the colored and comfortable cushions of the divan.

"I have heard of your day," Janfeda began. "How is the princess Marjallah?"

"Grief-stricken. Frightened. Self-pitying. What you would expect, dear Janfeda. She presents, however, an unfortunate problem. You saw how Murad looked at her yesterday, and when he came to tell her the news tonight he could barely keep his eyes from her breasts which were visible beneath the silk of her blouse. With a harem full of incredible beauties my son is lusting after a barely pretty woman who has known two husbands already."

"Marry her off again," said Janfeda.

"Murad will never let her go this time," said Nur-U-Banu. "He is no fool, my son. He sees in Marjallah something more although I doubt he could tell you what it was if you asked him. He lusts to possess her, and I am afraid of what will happen if he does."

"What disturbs you about this woman?" Janfeda had never known her friend to deny her son's passions, indeed Nur-U-Banu encouraged them in order to keep Safiye's power at a minimum.

"Marjallah is no fluffy kitten of a female, nor is she eager for the sultan's favor; but if she gains it, if she conceives a child by him, and that child turned out to be a son, do you think an intelligent woman like Marjallah would be content then? I do not! She would want her child to be the next sultan! Of course she would! Would Safiye stand by and allow that, Janfeda? No, she would not! Oh, it is true that I keep the balance of power in the harem in my favor by seeing to it that Safiye no longer holds exclusive sway over my son, but the women that I have seen gain Murad's favor are vapid beauties with no more care than what jewels and toys they can wheedle out of the sultan by the clever use of their bodies. Marjallah is not this kind of a woman, Janfeda. What am I to do with her? If Murad insists on having her in his bed Safiye will instantly become her enemy, and there will be war in the harem. I cannot have it."

"Why must there be war in the harem, Nur-U-Banu? Did we not share the same sultan? We were not bitter enemies."

"No," said the valideh thoughtfully, "we were not, but then we were friends before we shared Selim."

"So are Safiye and Marjallah."

"But I never held such a hold on Selim as Safiye has held on my son. I understood the harem system, and I accepted it."

"Safiye understands it, too," said Janfeda.

"Oh, yes," agreed the valideh, "but she has never accepted it. She has bitterly resented the fact that I encouraged Murad to seek out other women, to take other kadins. How she has hated me for it, and how she has tried to undermine my authority at every turn. This business with Marjallah is the first time in several years that we have worked together for the good of my son.

"Safiye has always refused to understand that one son was not enough for the succession."

"Perhaps what she really objects to is the fratricide that follows a succession," Janfeda remarked.

"Fratricide is a necessity when a new sultan succeeds," said Nur-U-Banu coldly, "but before the succession many sons are necessary. Look at the first Selim. All those sons by his four kadins, and by the time he died only the eldest, Suleiman, remained. Some had died in battles, some of illnesses, but only one was left. What if there had only been one, and something had happened to him?"

Janfeda preferred not to argue the point with her friend. She privately thought the murder of a previous sultan's younger sons by his heir was an appalling thing. She was certain that another solution could be found if only they were willing to seek it out. "I am very grateful nonetheless," she said, "that I only have a daughter. I would have regretted losing your friendship, Nur-U-Banu."

The valideh pressed the other woman's hand warmly. "I do not know what I should do without you, Janfeda," she said. "Now help me to find a solution to this problem."

"Take Safiye into your confidence," said Janfeda. "Tell her that Murad lusts after Marjallah, and that he will probably claim her for his bed. Tell her although you *both* sought to avoid this that it now appears to be inevitable. Suggest to her that she continue her friendship with Marjallah despite it; that she and Marjallah be as you and I are. Be frank with her. Say what you have said to me. That Marjallah is not like the others; that she is intelligent; and that it cannot hurt to be her friend as it will allow her to know what Marjallah thinks and does. Safiye is no fool. Everyone needs a friend, even a bas kadin."

"Especially a bas kadin," said the valideh. "I think that you may be correct in this matter, Janfeda. It is certainly worth trying. If she intends to hate Marjallah she will hate her no worse for knowing now that Murad means to have her than knowing later. What other choice do I have?"

"I think none, my dear friend."

"That," said Nur-U-Banu, "is a masterpiece of understatement," and she laughed ruefully.

The main door to the sultan valideh's salon opened, and Murad entered the room. "You should be pleased, mother, that I have done your bidding without question. Esther Kira is safely returned to her own litter, and is at this very moment on her way home." He bent and kissed first Nur-U-Banu, and then Janfeda. "Good evening, aunt. You have heard the terrible news of Javid Khan's death?"

She nodded. "Is anything a secret for long in the harem, dear Murad?"

The sultan looked about the room. "Where is Marjallah?" he said.

"I have seen her put to bed," answered his mother. "She is totally worn out, and of course she is shocked by her husband's murder."

"Where did you place her? In your bedchamber? I certainly hope she is comfortable."

The sultan valideh sent Janfeda a quick look. "I have put Marjallah in the little apartment next to mine where your sister lived until her marriage. I think she will be perfectly content and safe there until we can decide her fate."

"It is already decided," said Murad.

"You cannot marry her off so quickly, my son, so I hope that is not what you are planning to do," said Nur-U-Banu.

"I want her myself," he said bluntly.

Janfeda laughed lightly. "What a greedy man you are, my dear nephew, but then you were a greedy boy. With a harem full of beautiful virgins you desire Marjallah who is surely in her middle twenties, is actually somewhat long in the tooth. Why not honor her as Prince Javid Khan's widow, and save her to eventually use in marriage with someone whom you wish to honor?"

"Because," he said, "I want her for myself. I owe neither you nor anyone else an explanation of my conduct. Remember that I am the sultan. However, I will tell you that she intrigues me, and fascinates me. I must have her! I will have her!"

Janfeda shrugged. "I cannot see it," she said, "but do as you please, dear boy."

"I always have," he said with a quick smile.

"You must allow Marjallah time to mourn," said the valideh.

"The longer she mourns Javid Khan," he said, "the more she will resist the idea of becoming mine. She is to come to me this Friday. I have already told Ilban Bey."

"*Murad!*" Nur-U-Banu looked shocked, and Janfeda even looked discomfited by his decision. "It is unthinkable! You cannot do such a thing! As Javid Khan's wife she technically belongs to his family. What if they want her sent to them?"

"Then we shall tell them that Javid Khan's bride died of her grief," the sultan answered promptly. "Understand me well, mother. I want this woman! No one shall prevent me from having her. *No one!*" Then turning from them he strode from the room.

"How can I tell Marjallah?" Nur-U-Banu looked genuinely distressed. "What do I say to her? This is impossible!"

"Instruct your people to say nothing, and keep her by your side. You must, of course, tell Safiye tonight," Janfeda counseled. "You and Safiye must then try over the next few days to persuade Marjallah of the great *honor* being done her by Murad. She does not know our ways. Tell her it is a custom if you must."

"Zeki!" the sultan valideh called to her personal eunuch.

"Yes, majesty?" The call was answered by a tall, spare white eunuch with silvery-gray hair.

"Go to the bas kadin, and tell her that though the hour is late that I would speak with her." The eunuch bowed, and hurried from the salon. "Serfiraz!" Nur-U-Banu spoke to her head woman servant. "I want refreshments immediately before the bas kadin arrives. Hurry your women!"

"Instantly, majesty," rejoined Serfiraz, and ran from the room to marshal her forces.

They did not have long to wait. Safiye returned with Zeki, her own personal eunuch, Tahsin, accompanying them. "You have sent for me, madame? How may I serve you?"

"Sit down, my dear Safiye," said the valideh smoothly, and the Venetian raised a curious eyebrow as she made herself comfortable.

Janfeda smiled across the low table of inlaid mother-of-pearl and ebony. "You look well, Safiye. How is Memhet?"

"Flourishing!" Safiye beamed for she liked nothing better than to speak about her only son.

"We have a problem," said the valideh.

"*We do?*" Safiye looked a trifle confused.

"We certainly do, dear Safiye. You will remember that we cajoled Murad into giving Marjallah to Javid Khan for we feared that such an intelligent woman could catch the sultan's fancy, and cause dissension in the harem. Well now Marjallah is back, and what you and I feared all along has happened. Murad has only just left me after telling me bluntly, and with a terrible lack of delicacy, that he intends to have Princess Marjallah brought to him this Friday!"

Safiye looked stunned. Then she said, "Can you do nothing, my mother valideh?"

"I have begged Murad not to do this thing! Janfeda has pleaded with him! Marjallah belongs to the Khan's family, but when I brought this very point up with Murad he said he should tell the Khan if he asked that the prince's bride died of grief! He is determined to have his way in this matter, Safiye. I cannot move him."

"Then why do you call me, my mother valideh? If you cannot change his mind, I certainly cannot."

"There is one thing that you can do, Safiye," said the sultan valideh.

"What?" Safiye looked dubious.

"Once I stood in your slippers, my daughter, as you will one day stand in mine by virtue of your son's inheritance. It is lonely being the bas kadin. It is lonely being the sultan valideh. Still I have Janfeda to comfort me. Were it not for my friend I hate to think what my life would be like. Do not desert your friend, Marjallah, because of something that is not her doing. She is not like the others in the harem. You need each other. Esther Kira has told me stories of how the kadins of the first Selim were all as close as sisters; fighting first for the family good, and then only for themselves and their children. One day I will not be here, and my responsibility will be yours. It will be good to have Marjallah by your side then."

"What if she has a son?" demanded Safiye. "How will she like me when Memhet inherits, and destroys her child? How can my lord Murad's favorites be friends? We cannot."

"She might have a daughter," said Janfeda. "I did. You might consider another way of protecting Memhet's succession than by murdering his brothers. Why could the other princes not be incarcerated in their own apartments with their attendants and sterile damsels to live out their lives in peace? What if Memhet could have no sons? The dynasty would die if his brothers were all dead, but at least the dynasty would be protected if the other princes lived in their comfortable captivity."

"No! Nothing must threaten Memhet's succession!" said Safiye. "Living heirs only tempt the malcontents. Still, you are right in one way. Marjallah might have a daughter. Most of my lord Murad's children are female. I don't want to lose my friend. She is the only real friend that I have, and I have been happy since she came."

Nur-U-Banu smiled. "You have grown wiser, Safiye, and I am pleased. Now, dear daughter, we must discuss how to tell Marjallah of the sultan's will. He insists that she come to him first this Friday which has, of course, shocked me greatly as I know it has you. I am certain that Marjallah will be of as delicate a nature as we are, and she is quite apt to resist the sultan. We must convince her otherwise. I know that she loved Javid Khan, but we both know that she will also learn to love Murad as well, will she not?"

"How can she not love him?" said Safiye softly. "He is the most wonderful of men! I loved him from the first moment that I laid eyes on him. He was my dream come true! Of course she cared for Javid Khan, but if she will but give herself the chance she will love Murad even more! She must! He cannot be hurt!"

"I will instruct Ilban Bey to silence any loose tongues," said the valideh, "and we will say nothing to Marjallah for a day or two, but in four days she must go to the sultan, and it is up to us to make her realize the honor, and the opportunity offered her.

"If she knows that we love her, and are happy for her," said Safiye, "I know that it will be easier for her."

The two older women smiled at the sultan's bas kadin, their eyes catching in a knowing glance which fortunately escaped Safiye. The valideh signaled to her servants, and they were instantly at the little table passing refreshments to the three women who now having solved their problem chatted quite companionably with each other. Finally Safiye arose and took her leave of the valideh, and Nur-U-Banu embraced her son's favorite with more warmth than she had in years. Janfeda smiled to herself. Nur-U-Banu was always the most amenable when getting her own way, she thought. Yet something distressed her, but she could not put her finger on it. She was anxious to depart for her own apartments so she might concentrate on what it was that was niggling at her. She always listened to the voice within.

Chapter 15

◦◦◦

$\mathcal{A}$idan had awakened the following morning, her memory of the previous day totally intact. She had a raging headache, and her mouth was dry. Unable to help it she wept herself into a frenzy, and Jinji, truly frightened, sent Iris for the valideh.

Nur-U-Banu, realizing that her actions could easily determine Aidan's cooperation, hurried to the little apartment next to her own. Enfolding the weeping woman into a motherly embrace she made soothing noises, and allowed Aidan to cry until she could cry no more. Finally when Aidan's sobs had subsided she said, "I know, dear child, what it is to lose a loved one. My second son, Ahmed, died when he was a little boy of two. Murad was his father's heir, but Ahmed was my baby. He even looked like me with his fair hair and dark eyes." She sighed. "I wept for days, but in the end it did me no good for I felt no better, and it did not bring him back to me."

Aidan looked up at the valideh. Her eyes were swollen almost half shut, and her nose was red. She was not a woman who looked appealing in grief, thought Nur-U-Banu. What a pity Murad could not see her this way, and save them all this difficulty. "I understand what it is you are saying to me, madame," said Aidan, "but it is so unfair! Javid Khan was a good man and he suffered deeply the loss of his family. For him to fall victim once again to some unknown raider is not right!"

"The raider is not unknown, dear child. Word came early this morning that my son's Janissaries had caught up late last night with those responsible for the death of Javid Khan and the destruction of his home and his chattels. They have been punished. Even as we speak, all are dead."

"Who?" demanded Aidan. "Who did this terrible thing?"

"It was your husband's twin brother, a savage called Temur. Did you not tell me he was the one responsible for the original attack on Javid Khan's home in the Crimea?"

"Yes," said Aidan, "but then he fled the justice of his father and his family. They could not find him although they searched. You must let me write to the Great Khan of the Crimea, and tell him what has happened."

"Do not trouble yourself, dear child," said the valideh. "The Great Khan will be informed, but by the sultan, his overlord. There is one happy thing I have to tell you, however. Your serving woman was found safe amongst the Tartars. She will be returned to you as soon as our Janissaries reach Istanbul."

A cry of joy burst forth from Iris and Fern who had been seated discreetly in the room awaiting their mistress' orders. "Thank God," said Aidan fervently.

"Praise Allah," corrected the valideh gently.

"What will now happen to my people and me?" Aidan asked.

Nur-U-Banu hesitated a moment, and then she said, "It is the custom of our country that as Javid Khan was an ambassador, and therefore here at the sultan's request, and consequently under imperial Ottoman protection, that the sultan take his widow into his harem as one of his wives."

"*No!*" Aidan's voice was sharp, and she looked horrified.

"Dear child, it is an honor that my son chooses you," said the valideh patiently.

"I do not wish it!" Aidan cried. "Please understand, dear madame. It is not that I am ungrateful, but as I am a free woman now, I should far prefer to return to my own homeland. There is no legal reason for me not to do so."

"My dear Marjallah, have we not discussed this before? You cannot possibly return to your homeland. You know how you would be received, and what if your husband has remarried? You have been gone almost a year. How awful for your poor first husband to have you appear upon his doorstep now. What if his new bride were with child? I know the Christian faith. He would be forced to reinstate you as his wife, but he would not want you, nor could he possibly bring himself to cohabit with you as a man and a wife. His new bride's child, his heir, would be considered a bastard babe. Could you really do that to a man you claim to have loved? Could you do that to some innocent girl, and her equally innocent child, your husband's only heir? I do not think you could.

"Dear Marjallah, I know how painful the death of your beloved Javid Khan, has been for you. I realize that his loss makes you remember the life you had before you came to us, but that life with Javid Khan is dead. You must begin anew, and my son, Murad, has admired you from the moment he saw you. Safiye and I rejoice to have you here with us. We all only want to make you happy."

"Safiye is not known for her love of her husband's other women," said Aidan bluntly. "I should rather be a servant in your house, or even be sold in the slave markets of the city than lose one of the few friends I have here."

"Safiye is delighted that in your sorrow there is a flame of hope, Marjallah. I swear to you that she will welcome you as a sister, and not an enemy." The valideh turned and said to Jinji, "Go to the bas kadin, and say that the sultan valideh wished to see her here in the apartment of the lady Marjallah." She turned back again to Aidan. "In the time of Sultan Selim I his four kadins were close friends who loved and supported one another. Safiye's attitude toward my son's other women is actually all Murad's fault. Both were quite young when they fell in love, and Murad would look at no other female but Safiye for too many years. Then when he finally realized the danger of having but one child, and began to take other women, have other children, she naturally became jealous. Certainly you can understand that?

"The other women of the harem then aligned themselves against Safiye for they were jealous of her position, and of her very healthy son, Memhet, who is his father's heir. It is, of course, entirely out of hand now, but what can I do? I cannot force them to like each other. You, however, are a different matter. You and Safiye have been friends since your arrival here. Nothing will change, I promise you, and Safiye will reassure you of that herself."

The words were scarcely out of the valideh's mouth when Safiye arrived. She looked particularly beautiful this morning, and Nur-U-Banu was again struck by the difference between the two women. There was a lushness about her son's favorite, a glow. Poor Marjallah on the other hand was pale and woebegone. Safiye instantly saw the differences, and was immediately sympathetic to her friend, and once again curious as to what it was about Marjallah that fascinated Murad so very much that he must possess her.

"Marjallah! Dear friend!" Safiye sat next to Aidan and put an arm about her. "I am so very sorry about Javid, but still that cruel tragedy has brought you back to us."

"The lady valideh tells me that as the sultan was responsible for the safety of his ambassadors, it is custom that he take me for one of his wives. Is it so?"

"Yes," said Safiye without hesitation, "and I am so happy that we will be sisters. You will be so good for my lord Murad, unlike those silly and foolish creatures he usually chooses. Is it really a wonder that I despise them? You, however, are a different matter. You are my friend, and I am glad we can continue to be so."

"I don't want this, Safiye. I really don't want this. Could not the sultan simply allow me his protection? Why must I be one of his women?"

"Oh, Marjallah! You must not be afraid of my lord Murad! Besides if he did not take you for one of his own, Javid Khan's family might insist you be sent to them. Surely you don't want to go to the Crimea? It is a terribly uncivilized place. Why until the last hundred years the Tartars roamed the steppes, and lived in tents! You cannot speak their language, and as Javid Khan's widow you would be under their control. They could marry you off to anyone they chose, even someone in a land more distant than theirs. Oh, Marjallah! You cannot leave me! You are the only *real* friend that I have!" wailed Safiye.

"Safiye, I don't want to forfeit our friendship, I truly don't, but I do not want to be one of the sultan's women. How can I go to his bed with my beloved Javid barely in his grave? I shudder to even contemplate it!"

Safiye misunderstood Aidan's reasoning, and thinking to comfort her friend she said, "Murad is the most marvelous lover any woman could have, Marjallah. He is so wonderfully masterful, and in his arms you will die a thousand sweet deaths!"

Aidan sighed. "Safiye, were you a virgin when you came to Sultan Murad's bed?" Safiye nodded. "You have never known any other man! I have, and am therefore in a better position to judge a man's prowess in passion. That, however, is not my objection. I simply do not want to be forced into another relationship so quickly. It is indecent!"

Her logic made both the valideh and the bas kadin uncomfortable for secretly both women agreed with her. Both knew that what Murad was doing was not only indecent, but insulting as well to the memory of Javid Khan, and to the honor of his wife. Still both knew that once Murad set his mind to something there was little that could deter him from his chosen whim. Safiye looked to Nur-U-Banu for help. It was, she thought, after all the valideh's obligation first.

"Dear child, dear child! How wonderfully delicate are your feminine sensibilities, but you are much too harsh. I would not call Murad's decision indecent, but rather proper devotion to custom. By making you his wife immediately he does the memory of Javid Khan honor for his actions say that he accepts the responsibility of what has happened, painful and as personally embarrassing as it may be to him, and to his government. For such a terrible event to occur in my son's empire, so close to his capital city, is deeply shameful. What must other governments think when they hear of it? Still his treatment of you, Javid Khan's widow, shows that he is an honorable man. Do not deny my son that, dear child, I beg of you!"

"When do I become the sultan's?" Aidan demanded irritably. Her head still hurt, and both Nur-U-Banu and Safiye were making her feel ungrateful for Murad's wonderful generosity simply because she did not want to be his new wife.

"It is tradition that a new woman go to him on Friday," said the valideh.

"*This Friday?*" Aidan looked positively horrified.

"I realize it is soon," said the valideh, "but there must be no delay in Murad's accepting you. You must understand that, dear child."

"Am I allowed no time to mourn the good man who loved me?" said Aidan.

"Of course you will mourn him, Marjallah. I suspect that you will mourn him for many weeks, but the prince would comprehend both your position, and the sultan's. He was a man who understood the stern obligations of one's duty."

My God, thought Aidan, she makes it all seem so correct, and I know that it is not! The sultan lusts after me, and I could see it when he came to our palace several days ago. She shuddered. I don't want to belong to him. I don't! I should rather be dead!

"Marjallah," Safiye said softly, "my lord Murad will understand your sorrow. He will be kind. I have never known him to be unkind to a woman."

Aidan looked up at Nur-U-Banu and at Safiye. They were both beautiful women. Extremely beautiful women. She couldn't remember seeing a female in this palace who wasn't lovely. Even the servant women were. She had never been a woman to hide from the truth. She was not beautiful. Pretty, perhaps. But not beautiful, and certainly not even pretty in grief. Although she had no mirror to see herself in she knew that her nose was red, and her face puffy with her crying. Neither the sultan valideh nor the bas kadin, Aidan wagered silently to herself, would ever look so unattractive in sorrow. They probably looked better! There were women like that.

She was not about to accept this fate meekly. Drawing a deep breath she said, "I do not understand why the sultan wants me, and please, I beg of you, do not prattle to me of his obligations. I am no beauty, and well I know it. There are several hundred women in this harem, and more gorgeous maidens arriving every day. I doubt the sultan has seen even half of the women who are brought here for his pleasure. Why must he have me? Can he not fulfill his duty simply by respecting my grief, and sheltering me until he finds another man whom he wishes to honor with a wife?"

Both Nur-U-Banu and Safiye were at a loss to refute Aidan's arguments for she spoke with logic, and neither woman was so stupid that she did not understand. Again Safiye looked to the valideh for it really was her place to handle this matter.

"I cannot disagree with what you say, Marjallah," said Nur-U-Banu. "Were you an ordinary wife what you suggest is probably just what my son would do. You, however, were a gift from the dey in Algiers. You were wife to one of his most useful and powerful allies. To pass you on to some other man as if you were merely a well-bred animal would be unthinkable. No, dear girl, Murad honors the memory of Javid Khan and his people by taking you for his own." She turned herself, and facing Aidan took her face between her hands. "That is the way it *must* be, Marjallah. I know that you understand me when I tell you that."

"Yes, madame, I understand you," Aidan replied, but she was unable to keep the mutinous tone from her voice. It was useless speaking with the sultan's mother and his favorite. They would, of course, take his side of the matter. Perhaps the sultan would understand better. After all the power was really with him. She could not ask to see him now for they would never allow such a thing, but on Friday night when she was brought to him she would tell him of her feelings, and perhaps if he were the sensitive man his women seemed to think he was, he would understand her position and her feelings, and release her. She was, after all, a free woman. Had not Javid gone to the kadi and had her papers of manumission drawn up? They all knew it for Javid Khan had spoken of it often. Tartars, he said, did not marry slaves. Their wives were free women.

Nur-U-Banu smiled at Aidan now. "It is settled then, my child. On Friday night you will go to my son, and I know you will find joy with him."

"Yes," said Safiye encouragingly, "and you and I shall be sisters together. It shall be with us as it is with Janfeda and our mother valideh."

Aidan wanted to scream. Javid Khan was barely gone, and the sultan was planning his seduction with a boldness that astounded her. It was obvious that he felt no shame in his actions. The idea of death flirted with her consciousness once again. Something within her did not quite believe Nur-U-Banu and Safiye when they said her road home to England was closed. She could not believe that Conn had replaced her in either his heart or his bed. Not yet. Conn was not a man who gave himself lightly. She was not a slave anymore. She was free to go home, wasn't she? If she could only get a message to the English ambassador, William Harborne, who had arrived in Turkey last summer. Perhaps Esther Kira would smuggle a message out for her. If she could not go home, she preferred death to belonging to the sultan.

During the next few days, however, she had no opportunity to speak with Esther. Her movements were kept restricted, and she was allowed no freedom but for her own and Nur-U-Banu's apartments, and the valideh's planted courtyard. Such confinement made her extremely edgy for she was not used to it. Her diet was a rich one, and the sultan's mother virtually stood over her to be certain that she ate every mouthful upon her plate.

"You are too thin," the valideh said with a smile. "We must put a bit more flesh upon your bones."

Aidan had no knowledge of the fact that her diet had been specifically tailored by the agha kislar, Ilban Bey, who was the sultan valideh's ally. Her meals were filled with foods believed to be conducive to increasing passion, and they were laced as well with herbs and drugs to increase her sensitivity and increase her awareness. She was also bathed twice daily and massaged with creams and lotions to refine her beautiful skin even more. It seemed to Aidan that she spent her entire time in either eating, sleeping, or washing. I can't live like this, she thought. I will go mad with the boredom!

Early Friday afternoon Aidan found herself taking part in the customary bridal bath, a tradition for those chosen to share the sultan's couch for the first time. Escorted by Nur-U-Banu and the bas kadin she led a procession consisting of every young woman in the harem to the baths. The sultan valideh and the kadins were attired in rich brocaded garments, but the rest of the women wore simple white silk robes, and each one carried a yellow tulip.

When they reached the baths Aidan was turned over to the head bath mistress by the valideh. The other women of the harem lined themselves about the room, standing against the walls, and sang a song that wished Aidan joy and good fortune in her chosen fate. At the conclusion of their melody the maidens of the harem flung their flowers at Aidan, and then turning as one they all trooped out. Nur-U-Banu kissed Aidan on the cheek, and then she and the kadins departed the room.

It seemed rather funny to Aidan that she was to be bathed again as if she had never been bathed at all over these last few days. There wasn't a single superfluous hair upon her body but for her head yet they smeared her with the almond-smelling pink paste that removed hair, and she was surprised to see a fine down wash away. Her hair was washed as it had been washed at least once a day since her return to the Yeni Serai, and then it was rinsed with lemon juice to encourage its fiery highlights. Her fingernails and her toenails were pared and shaped, the toes much shorter lest she offend the Shadow of Allah by inadvertently scratching him. She flushed as she had flushed twice daily in the baths as she was laid upon her back upon a marble massage bench, and her private parts delicately bathed first with warm water, then a mild mixture of soap and water, and finally with a gentle rinse of warmed water again.

She was massaged over her entire body with fragrant lotion, and not an inch of her skin was left untouched. The supple hands of the masseuse kneaded her arms and her legs, dug into the muscles of her back, smoothed over her torso, and skillfully manipulated her breasts until the nipples stood hard and throbbed. She knew that she should be used to it by now, but such treatment, however pleasant, embarrassed her.

At last she was deemed fit for the sultan, and she was wrapped in a white silk robe, placed in a litter, and returned to her apartments to await the evening when she would be escorted by Ilban Bey to Murad. The heat of the baths, and the hour spent beneath the hands of the masseuse had exhausted her. She felt weak and helpless and depressed.

Marta hurried forward to help her from the litter. The serving woman had been returned unharmed two days prior, and she told Aidan and the others of what had happened after her mistress had departed for the city to fetch Esther Kira back. She had seen that the prince arose, and fetched him light refreshment, and had then helped him to dress. He had left her to go to the stables, and that was the last she had seen of him. She had been going about her usual morning duties, seeing to the bed, when the Tartars had burst into the harem. At first she believed she would be raped, and murdered, but instead she had been carried off, the only survivor of the raid, thrown rudely across the saddle of one of her captors. She had seen the courtyard filled with the decapitated bodies of the other servants, seen the piles of heads by the gate; and then fainted. When she regained consciousness she found herself seated before her captor on his galloping horse, and they had ridden without stopping until well after dark. When they had finally stopped it was to fix a meal and see to their horses. She knew now that she had been carried off so that they might take their pleasure of her at their leisure, and she was frightened. Fortunately the sultan's Janissaries had ridden in to slay the Tartars before she might be harmed, and she had been rescued.

Both Aidan and Marta's daughters had welcomed her back warmly. She was not dear familiar Mag, thought Aidan, but she was a loyal servant. Even now she gently aided her mistress to her couch saying, "You need some food in your stomach, my lady. You missed the midday meal and you look positively pale."

Aidan said nothing. She knew that Marta was enormously relieved that they were safe in the Yeni Serai, and pleased that the sultan had chosen her mistress to grace his bed. Marta had liked the prince, but her practical peasant nature told her that Javid Khan was dead, and they had to live. "I could eat some fruit," Aidan told the serving woman to be amenable.

The lady Marjallah's wish was their command, and a platter of luscious fruits was instantly produced. Aidan ate an apricot, and then lay back, her eyes closed, feigning sleep so that they would not fuss at her to eat more. She was beginning to feel more and more like a prize brood animal, and it annoyed her. If only she had been enceinte with Javid Khan's child then perhaps she might have escaped the sultan.

It disturbed her that since the loss of her baby almost a year ago that she had not conceived again, but then she questioned herself, had she really wanted to have a child by someone other than Conn? She had been forced to accept the situation in which she found herself, but even Javid Khan's marriage with her had not, in her heart of hearts, been a real marriage. She had accepted it as she had accepted him, believing that she had no other choice for they were always telling her that she didn't. Aidan hadn't known what to expect for this whole world was foreign to her. The prince had been a good man, and because she knew that he had honored her by freeing her and making her his wife she had called him *husband*. He had said he loved her, and she had had no doubts that he did. The sultan, however, was a different matter.

She couldn't be certain if the story the sultan's mother told her about his obligations toward her was truth or simply a tale spun to gain her cooperation because Murad lusted after her. If it was truth then she wanted to free him of his obligation. The prince had made her a free woman, and come what may she wanted to return home. She did not want to remain in the Yeni Serai, a victim to the sultan's passions. Yet here she was, pampered and perfumed, and awaiting the evening when she was to be brought to Murad. She didn't know what to do other than tell him how she felt, and hope that he would release her. If he would not, Aidan thought, she would find a way to kill herself for she had no intention of remaining here the rest of her life. *Oh, Conn*, she thought, *I want to come home! I want to come home!*

"Home," Conn said quietly. "I want to bring my wife home. My sister's bankers in London told me that you could help me, madame. If you cannot, then I shall find someone who can."

Esther Kira sighed. "No one, my lord, can help you retrieve your wife. She is in the sultan's harem. My nephew in London had no right to tell you that I could aid you." Then her voice softened at the disappointment in his face, and she said, "If you had come just a few days ago, my lord, I might have considered helping you, but now I cannot. The success of my family is tightly entwined with that of the imperial Ottoman dynasty. To help you I should have to betray them, and I cannot do it, my lord. You English believe strongly in your honor, do you not? Well, I, too, have my honor."

"If you would have been willing to aid me a few days ago, madame, why not now?" he demanded.

Esther Kira seated herself comfortably upon her divan, and called to her servants for coffee and little honey-sesame cakes. Then she set about to explain to Conn his wife's history since her arrival in Istanbul. She finished by saying, "Now that the sultan desires her it is a different matter, but tell me, my lord. If you want your wife back why did you wait so long to come after her? She has been here for over eight months."

"And we have been caught in Algiers ever since last September," said Conn, and then he went on to explain to Esther Kira the sultan's punishment against the countries of Europe who had fought against him with the Portuguese.

"Aiiii," said the matriarch shaking her head, "it is as if the fates themselves have conspired against you. I am so sorry, my lord Bliss, but there is nothing I can do now to help you."

"I cannot leave without her," Conn said stubbornly. "I will not leave without her. She is the only woman that I have ever loved, will ever love!"

"It is strange," said Esther Kira, "but she has that effect upon men. Prince Javid Khan adored her, even going as far as to free her from slavery, and make her his wife. And the sultan, whose harem is filled to overflowing with beauteous virgins, has coveted her ever since he saw her, and would have had her these months past but that his mother had convinced him to give the dey's gift to Prince Javid Khan, sight unseen. When he saw her he greatly regretted it. It is strange for the lady Marjallah is not a beautiful woman, and the sultan is proud of the fact that his harem contains more beautiful women than any potentate's on this earth." She chuckled softly. "Beauty, however, fades, and if one has naught else to recommend oneself then what is left? Perhaps Sultan Murad is, at long last, growing sated with beauty, and seeks a woman of substance. Marjallah has great character."

"Twice you have used the name Marjallah," said Conn. "Who is Marjallah?"

"Marjallah is the name your wife was given when she arrived here. You could not expect they would call her by her English name. Marjallah means *A Gift from the Sea*, and she did indeed come across the sea to us."

"Esther Kira," said Conn, "have pity on me. I do not ask you to break faith with the sultan and his family for I do indeed understand your position; but Sultan Murad has a harem full of women, and I have but one wife. There must be some way in which you can help me."

The old woman pursed her lips, and he could see that she was considering his words. Thoughtfully she looked at him. He was the handsomest man she had ever seen, and she found it interesting that such an attractive man would be married to Marjallah. She had no doubt as to his sincerity for she had not survived so long in her world without the ability of being able to read a person's character correctly. She could see the pain in his green eyes, hear the sorrow in his voice. He obviously loved his wife, and really did want her back. It did not seem to disturb him that she had cohabited with another man, or was in danger of finding herself in the sultan's bed shortly. He wanted her back. "Perhaps," she said slowly, "perhaps there is a way, *but* I do not promise you, my lord. I only say perhaps. Do you understand me? It is but a slim chance, and only that."

"Tell me?" he begged her.

"No," she answered him, "I must first consider how to go about it, and I do not want to share my thoughts with anyone. Would you understand me if I told you my luck is in not revealing my plans on anything I undertake to anyone until I am certain those plans will work?"

"Yes," he said, "I understand that," and for the first time he smiled, and Esther Kira thought again that he was the most gorgeous man she had ever seen.

"Where are you staying, my lord?"

"You will be able to reach me at the palace of the English ambassador," he said. "My wife was a ward of her majesty before we were wed, and the queen is very fond of Aidan. As she has an interest in this matter, her embassy is open to me."

"If your queen is so concerned then why did she not approach the Sublime Porte herself?" demanded Esther Kira.

"I think you know the answer to that," replied Conn. "It is important that England build its trade with the Levant to counter Spain's hold over the new world. Trade is the lifeblood of my nation. As fond as Elizabeth Tudor is of Aidan she would not jeopardize the trading agreements of an entire nation for one person."

Esther Kira nodded. "Be certain," she warned him, "that both you, and those of your party are discreet in your dealing about the city. There is little that the sultan does not know about. There are spies everywhere. The sultan's spies, his mother's, those of his heir's mother, his other favorites, the vizier's, not to mention those of rival nations to your England. Trust no one, and draw no attention to yourselves lest the sultan learn the true nature of your business. I will contact you when I know if what I am considering is possible, or not possible. Perhaps you might even leave Istanbul for a short time to seek goods elsewhere. Sail across the Mamara, and go to Brusa for silk. It is not far, and it will look as if you have no real purpose here but that of trade. It will take me at least a week or more before I can know if my plans are workable."

"We shall do it," he agreed, for he thought that if he remained here in Istanbul he would be sorely tempted to storm the sultan's great palace, and rescue his wife, and that was a foolish notion.

"Good!" said Esther Kira. "You show common sense, yet I know it cannot be easy for you. Now should anyone ask why you came to see me you will tell them that your family banks with mine."

"Of course," he said, "and it is the truth, isn't it?"

She cackled a sharp bark of laughter. "So," she said, "you have learned that the best deception is the truth, my lord? You are, I think, a dangerous man."

"And you," he answered her with a smile, "are no better, Esther Kira. You hide behind the reputation for weakness of your sex, but you are a tough old spider who sits firmly in the center of a strong web. You are totally in control."

"I must be," she said, suddenly serious, "for I am that most despised of creatures, both a woman and a Jewess."

"Was not Jesus a Jew?" he said as he arose from the pillows.

She nodded slowly, and her eyes met his in a glance of total understanding. "You will hear from me, Lord Bliss," she said.

"Thank you, madame," he answered formally, "and farewell for now."

She watched him go from the room, and the door closed behind him. He was a strong man for one so very young, and she had no doubt that should her plan not be possible, that he would somehow find a way of retrieving his wife even if it meant turning the Ottoman dynasty upside down. She liked him, and she was beginning to see why Marjallah had mourned him in her heart all these months. Poor Marjallah. Although she had been kept from the girl the past several days she had seen Safiye in her apartments, and learned that Javid Khan's widow would be presented to the sultan for his pleasure this night. Would she yield, or would she fight her fate? Esther Kira was concerned for her young friend.

The door to her salon opened, and her great-granddaughter Rachael, a pretty maiden of fourteen entered the room. "Great-grandmother Esther," she said in her soft voice, "it is almost sunset, and time for you to light our candles. The family is waiting."

"Help me up, child. I must not be late and offend the Lord for I shall need his help in a small matter soon."

"Does it have to do with that beautiful gentleman who just left you?" asked Rachael aiding her great-grandmother to arise.

Esther Kira chuckled. "You must not ask me such questions, child, nor must you ever admit to having such sharp eyes. Keep your own counsel, Rachael. How many times have I told you that?"

"But if I do not ask questions, great-grandmother, then how am I to learn?" Rachael countered.

"There are questions, and there are questions," said Esther Kira. "Come now, child. The sunset is upon us!" and she hurried from the room with a surprisingly agile gait for one so old.

"Sunset," said Rachael, "and soon some lucky maiden will go to the sultan. If she is wise her fortune will be made, and if she is foolish she will be relegated to the old palace where the forgotten women live. If it were me I should be a wise virgin."

Esther Kira stopped, and turning looked at her great-granddaughter. "God forbid that it should be you, dear child!"

"But to become a kadin would be so fortunate!"

"Fortunate!" said the agha kislar. "You are the most fortunate of women, Marjallah." Then he handed her a small parcel that was wrapped in a square of cloth of gold, and bound with a rope of pink pearls. "These are the garments that are worn by a woman being presented to his majesty for the very first time. You are to dress now, and then I shall escort you to the sultan myself."

Aidan stared down at the little package in silent rebellion. She knew that she had to open it, and yet she had no curiosity as to what was within. It could not be a great deal, she thought. About her Jinji, Marta, and the girls watched her eagerly. With a deep sigh she undid the pearl tie, and unwrapped the cloth. Within were the traditional blue and silver garments worn by a woman attending her royal lord and master for the first time. She barely glanced at them, handing them to Marta.

"Usually," said Ilban Bey quietly, "that package is tied with a gilt ribbon. You have not even been in the sultan's bed yet, and he sends you gifts, Marjallah. How foolish you would be to scorn his attentions."

"I do not want those attentions," she said bluntly, and around her the others gasped.

Ilban Bey's eyes narrowed. "You do not appear to me to be mad, Marjallah. Perhaps it is your grief that affects you. Your conduct to date has been very good, and I do not believe you stupid as so many women are.

You have a wonderful life ahead of you. The sultan is already enamored of you, and both his mother and his favorite offer you their friendship. You need make only the slightest effort to make our lord Murad happy, and your fortune will be made."

Aidan did not answer him. She knew that whatever she said would be ignored for these people were dedicated to giving the sultan whatever he desired. It was their very reason for being. Her only hope was in an appeal to Murad. If he was truly enamored of her then perhaps he would grant her the right to go home to England.

"Prepare your mistress!" snapped Ilban Bey seeing that she had no intention of defending herself. He wanted to believe that she was considering his wise words, and would acquiesce to their plans for her.

The light silk robe that Aidan was wearing was removed and she stood nude before them. Iris and Fern presented their mother with a silver ewer that had been perfumed with oil of freesia, a heady fragrance distilled from the flower of the same name. Using a large sea sponge Marta squeezed the exotic-smelling water through it, and then sponged her mistress lavishly over her entire body. Aidan then scrubbed her teeth with a paste made from a mixture of pumice and mint leaves, rinsing her mouth with water flavored with mint. Next she was perfumed at all her pulse points with freesia scent.

Ilban Bey scrutinized her carefully, and then nodded to Jinji who quickly dressed his mistress in her garments of midnight-blue trousers of a sheer silk gauze, and a tiny sleeveless short jacket of blue and cloth of silver stripes edged in silver fringe. The rope of pink pearls was then added, but she was allowed no other jewelry this night lest it spoil the sultan's enjoyment of her body. Jinji then seated his mistress, and brushed out her luxuriant copper-colored hair with a brush that had been first dipped in oil of freesia. Then kneeling he slipped a pair of silver slippers upon her feet, and she stood up for their final inspection.

Ilban Bey nodded. "She needs no artifice," he said. "Her color is perfect. Not even kohl could make her eyes more beautiful, and her skin is like roses and cream. She is ready." He fixed Aidan with a stern look and held out his hand to her. "Come! The litter awaits you."

Before following him Aidan took little silk purses from the table, and presented to her servants the traditional baksheesh that Safiye had told her would be expected of her tonight. They murmured their thanks, and wished her good fortune. Aidan almost laughed aloud at that. The only good fortune she could have would be if Murad would allow her to go in peace.

In the hallway outside of her tiny apartment a golden litter awaited to carry her down the Golden Road to the sultan's apartments. Ilban Bey knocked discreetly at the sultan valideh's door, and Nur-U-Banu came out with Safiye to escort the guzdeh, as a woman first chosen by the sultan was known, to the door that opened into the Golden Road. When they had reached that point Nur-U-Banu came to the side of the litter, and embraced Aidan warmly.

"My son will make you happy, Marjallah, my daughter. Trust me in this. I wish you joy!" she said feelingly.

Then Safiye embraced her friend. "I envy you this night, dear Marjallah. I wish you joy!"

Immediately she stepped away from the litter, then the bearers were whisking it through the door, and suddenly all was dim and silent. It had been on the tip of Aidan's tongue to tell Safiye that if she truly envied her friend this night, her friend would exchange places with her, but she knew how rude and unkind that would have sounded. She was not after all angry with Safiye. At the end of the hallway the bearers stopped before the door of the sultan's rooms, and carefully placed the litter down. Immediately Ilban Bey was by her side helping her out, and the guards were opening the doors to the room.

The agha kislar escorted Aidan through a salon, and into the sultan's bedroom where he suddenly stopped and bowed low, hissing softly at Aidan as he did so. "On your knees, Marjallah! Do not forget your manners!"

Again rebellion rose up in her breast, but quickly realizing that offending the sultan was not the way to gain his favor, and her desire, Aidan slipped gracefully to her knees, and bending touched her head to the floor as Safiye had taught her.

"Arise, Marjallah," he said in his deep voice.

Ilban Bey was immediately there to help her, and by now, her eyes used to the dimness of the room which was only lit by a few lamps, she saw Murad clad in a loose white silk robe, lounging upon an enormous bed.

"Let me see her, Ilban Bey," he ordered the agha kislar.

Ilban Bey swiftly removed Aidan's little jacket, and before she could even protest he had loosened the narrow drawstring of her pantaloons, and was drawing them down to her ankles, where kneeling he slipped them over her feet, first removing her slippers. She was clad in naught but the strand of pink pearls.

"It is done, majesty," said the agha arising. Then turning he left the room.

With feline grace Murad slid off the bed, and walked toward her. Even at a short distance she could see his dark eyes were blazing with desire, and she shivered. She must speak now before he became intent upon his lust for her.

"My lord, I beg leave to speak!" she said, somewhat breathlessly for his intensity was overwhelming.

The ardor in his eyes was banked to be replaced by amusement. Murad realized that he had not deceived her in his rush to put her in his bed, and for that reason alone he said, "Speak, Marjallah." Let her get her pleading over with so he might spend the rest of the night kissing those adorable lips, teaching that beautiful mouth the various ways of pleasing him.

Aidan chose her words carefully. She suddenly knew that this man was a formidable opponent, and she would have but one chance with him. "My lord," she began, "I am not insensible of the honor that you are doing me; and I understand as the valideh has explained to me your wish to meet your obligations since my lord husband, the prince, was under your protection. I would free you of the obligation to take me as a wife. Javid Khan, as you know, freed me, going before the kadi to do so, and signing my papers of manumission. I wish nothing more than to return to my native land, and I beg you to allow me to do so."

"No." The word was crisp, and hung for a long minute in the space between them.

"I am not your slave!" Aidan protested.

"But you are," he said calmly.

"No! I am not, my lord! Prince Javid Khan made me a free woman, and as such I choose to return home. I do not want to be one of your women."

"You say," said the sultan mildly, "that the prince went before the kadi to free you, and even signed papers of manumission. Where are those papers, Marjallah? Show them to me. Although it will break my heart I will allow you to go from me now, and I will see you returned to your homeland. Show me the papers!"

"I do not have them," she answered him. "It was not necessary for me to carry them with me everywhere I went. They were in my jewelry box in my apartments at the prince's palace. I expect that they were destroyed in the fire that burnt our home to a shell."

"Then," said the sultan, a faint note of triumph in his voice, "you cannot prove the truth of your words, Marjallah. Without those papers you remain legally a slave. A slave sent to me by my friend, the Dey of Algiers. A slave given by me to the ambassador from the Khanate of the Crimea. A slave whose master is now deceased, and whose property therefore reverts to me. You are most certainly my slave, Marjallah." His dark eyes slid over her naked body.

She was astounded. He knew she spoke the truth. He had been a witness to her marriage! Forgetting the disadvantage that her natural state should have been to her, Aidan drew herself up to her full height. "My lord, you know that I speak the truth."

Allah! he thought as his eyes began to seriously consider the beauty of her form. She is beautiful! She is absolutely beautiful! Beneath his silken robe he felt his manhood take notice of her magnificent body, and begin to stir. Her breasts were wonderful. Big and full with their angrily thrusting nipples. His fingers itched to span the narrow waist at the end of the long torso; to fondle the softlooking flesh of her buttocks. "I never saw your papers of manumission, Marjallah. You cannot show them to me. Therefore as far as I am concerned they do not exist, and you, according to the law are mine to do with as I please."

"Then you had best kill me now, my lord," she said softly, "for I will not yield to you, I will give you nothing of myself, and I tell you truly that I prefer death to your embrace!"

Murad's dark eyes sparkled with anticipation. It had been a long time since any woman had fought him. The languid beauties usually presented to him each Friday night for the first time ordinarily swooned and sighed with delight when he made love to them. They had been trained to accept meekly the fate life had offered them. A fate most of them considered the best in the world. This, however, was a woman who until several months ago had lived her life as a free woman. *I will not yield*, she said. *I will give you nothing*, she had threatened. The sultan threw back his head and he laughed aloud.

"You need not give, Marjallah. It is my custom to take what I desire," and he reached out for her suddenly, catching her off her guard, drawing her into his arms to press his mouth wetly to hers.

Aidan had always been a strong girl, and as she had been quite unprepared to have the sultan capture her in his grasp, so was Murad surprised to have his prey twist from his embrace, and with perfectly pared fingernails scratch at his face above his red-gold beard.

With a howl of outrage he leapt back, touching his hand to his injured cheekbones, and seeing a faint stain of blood upon his fingertips. "Tigress!" he hissed at her. "I do not believe in destroying beauty such as yours. I will, however, tame you, and in time you will purr like a kitten beneath my touch."

"No, my lord," Aidan said grimly, "I will not! I will kill myself first. I am not like all those soft beauties that populate your harem. I descend from a race of warriors, and I do not fear death!"

He looked at her admiringly for a moment, and then with a faint smile upon his lips he said, "Bind her!" and from a darkened corner of the room two eunuchs of massive proportions stepped forward, and laid hold of her. Aidan did not capitulate easily. Her naked white body twisted and swiveled against the strong grasp of the two black eunuchs who nonetheless forced their captive over to the enormous bed, and then lifted her squirming onto it. First her arms were bound at the wrists to the pillars at the head of the bed, and then her legs were pulled apart, and bound at the ankles to the pillars at the foot of the bed. Their duty done the two eunuchs disappeared back into the shadows of the sultan's bedchamber.

Aidan could not believe what had just happened. No one had ever treated her in such a fashion, even the pirate, Rashid al Mansur, who had brought her to Algiers. Struggling, she tested her bonds, but the strong silk ropes held firm without cutting into her skin. Color flamed into her face as she realized that she was now spread open to his gaze, and helpless to whatever he wished to do. Her heart beginning to pound with fright she looked for him.

Murad, however, was not at this moment particularly interested in Aidan. She was secured, and would cause no further difficulty. He sat upon a chair while an elderly woman slave administered to his wounds, gently disinfecting the weals that Aidan had opened high upon his cheeks. The slave worked gently and carefully, and finished by delicately dabbing the injury with a clear lotion that removed the pain from it. The sultan smiled at the old woman, and politely thanked her. Aidan could not hear what she said in return to her master, but he laughed with genuine amusement, and then walked her to the door to usher her from the room.

Turning back he came directly to the bed where Aidan lay helpless and spread-eagled. "Old Ayse says that women with hair of fire, and peppery temperaments make the best lovers. I hope she is right, Marjallah." His eyes glowed warmly as they took her in, and he reached out to touch her.

Aidan managed to move away just enough to avoid his touch. He might have stretched his hand a little farther, but he did not. He simply laughed, a low intimate sound that sent a shiver of dread up her spine. She could not bear his look which was so possessive and passionate, and so she turned her head away from him. Seizing her chin in his hand he turned her head back to face him. "You will look at me," he said. Aidan closed her eyes in defiance.

Murad smiled at her disobedience. Her rebellion would only make his conquest sweeter. For several long moments, moments that grated upon Aidan's already edgy nerves, he sat by her side and debated how to begin. She really had the most incredible body. Now he knew why the dey had sent her to him. It was not just her copper-colored hair, it was her fabulous form. He must remember to send a letter to the dey telling him that Marjallah was back in his possession, and how delighted he was with her; so much so that he would not part with her this time.

Aidan's eyelids fluttered as she peeked from beneath her lashes at the sultan. What was he doing? What was he going to do? She was very frightened despite her show of boldness. Never had she felt so terribly lost as at this minute. Murad stood up, and loosening his robe removed it, and tossed it aside. Her heart hammered against her chest as he turned back to the bed. He was a slim man of medium height, his pale skin in great contrast to his gold-red beard and closely cropped hair.

Murad's languid, dark eyes once more viewed his helpless prey, and then without a word he slid his body between her legs, and lowering his head began to lick at her secret treasures. Aidan shrieked wildly at this totally unexpected first attack, and she attempted to twist herself away from him, but the ropes binding her to the carved posts of the sultan's bed would allow for only the smallest of movements, and she could not escape the warm, probing tongue that was slowly, and very thoroughly exploring her.

"Please don't," she gasped pleadingly, "oh, please don't do that to me!"

He ignored her as if she hadn't even spoken, his strong fingers firmly pulling her nether lips wide and holding the thick pink skin apart while the pointed tip of his tongue first caressed the ridge of flesh on either side with long, smooth strokes, and then touched delicately at the very core of her being. The scent of her, half female, half fragrant freesia, was the most intoxicating perfume he had ever known. His shaft was so rigid that the skin felt as if it was going to burst from around it. Flicking his tongue back and forth upon that sensitive little jewel of hers he worked with an inner rhythm learned so long ago in his history that he had actually forgotten the first time he had tasted a woman. It was a preference, however, that he had never grown tired of for each maiden was different.

Aidan was moaning, the sound a mixture of shame and pleasure. She was being ravished, and she hated it. Hated him for what he was doing, but yet her body was responding to the stimuli of his lovemaking. She didn't understand it, and again she considered the alternative of death. Somehow, she thought, somehow she would find a way to escape him, and this insidious degradation he was inflicting upon her. Murad plunged his tongue into her helpless body, swirling it about the pinkish passage, pressing his face into the most intimate part of her. Aidan struggled mentally to resist him, to deny him that final victory. Fiercely she pushed the pleasure away with so strong an effort that for a brief second she actually believed she would triumph over him, but then his lips fastened upon her little jewel, and he sucked hard upon her. It was too much, and an explosion of stars burst within her forcing her final surrender, and she sobbed as much with her pleasure as with her frustration at being beaten by him.

Murad pulled himself up level with Aidan, and reclining upon an elbow watched her. Helpless to her passion the lower half of her beautiful body writhed, straining against the silken ropes that bound her to the bed. He had always enjoyed watching a woman in the throes of desire, and he maintained the level of her craving for several long minutes by simply rubbing her sensitivity with his index finger every few moments.

Satisfied now that he had proven to her his superiority over her the sultan decided to inflict another salacious torture upon his victim as well as take the edge from his own lust. He called out to the two black eunuchs, and they, as ordered, hurried from the shadowy corner where they had been seated to place plump pillows behind Aidan's back propping her up. With no further foreplay Murad thrust himself into her readied sheath, and then, his shaft well lodged, he began to play with her breasts.

She had known that he had eventually planned to unite with her, and that bound as she was she had no choice but to accept him, but his entry was still so sudden and surprising. He filled her, his hardness pushing against the walls of her passage, but he made no other movement than to simply enter her. He was far more interested in her beautiful breasts which he handled as if they had been separate entities. He did not have large hands, and so her breasts overflowed his palms causing him to exclaim with delighted wonder.

His fingers fondled the flesh, leaving faint impressions on her fair skin. "I had my first woman when I was thirteen," he said quietly in a conversational tone that she somehow found embarrassing. "I have deflowered over a thousand virgins, and made love to over two thousand women in my lifetime, but never, exquisite Marjallah, have I seen such wonderful breasts on a woman. They are perfect in form, in texture, in color. You are perfect in form. The most perfect woman I have ever seen. I will not, however, be satisfied to simply possess your body. I must have all of you, and in time I will!" Leaning forward he began to suck upon her nipples.

A cry rose up in her throat, but she forced it back. What good would it do her to scream? Besides she could not allow him to have any more of a victory over her than he had already had. She hated him with an intensity that would have startled Murad had he but known it. Javid Khan had freed her, and the sultan knew it. Still he had forced her back into slavery to endure this shameful bondage. She had never known anything but tenderness and love from men. Now she was learning the darker side of passion. She was learning lust.

"Look at me, Marjallah!" he commanded.

She focused her gaze upon him, and he smiled cruelly seeing the truth of her feelings in her storm-gray eyes. "You will not always hate me, my exquisite one," he said self-confidently. "In time you will love me as they all love me. In time you will learn to hunger for my caresses, and there will even come a time, though you doubt it now, that you will beg for those caresses."

"I will be dead long before then, my lord," she hissed at him. "You can never really tame a free creature to your leash, and I was born free. Javid Khan understood that, and he freed me. You understand nothing of me, but be warned that I shall not flourish within the confines of your walled garden for I am not like the other flowers who bloom here. I shall wither, and I shall die, my lord, and you will never really possess me!"

Allah! How her defiance excited him! He could feel himself throbbing within the heat of her body, but he was not yet ready to take his release. Her words had stung him, and he felt the need to punish her, to humiliate her, to once again gain a mastery over her; and he knew precisely how he would do it. Abruptly he withdrew his swollen manhood from her body, and barked an order to the eunuchs again.

They hurried forth to pull the bolsters from behind her back, and to untie her. Have I beaten him? Aidan wondered, but she quickly found that she had not. Rather than releasing her the eunuchs turned her over upon her stomach, and rebound her once again. Two small, hard pillows were stuffed beneath her lower belly elevating her hips. She felt the sultan sliding his body lightly over her back, and then he pushed her hair aside so he might kiss her neck. The warmth of his lips sent a tingle down her spine.

His hands then moved her long tresses over her head, and onto the silken mattress above her head. His lips touched her ear in an erotic caress, and she felt his tongue licking the side of her face.

Then he whispered softly to her, "A woman has two maidenheads, Marjallah. I suspect that your second maidenhead has not been tampered with. Am I correct?"

"I . . . I do not know what you mean," she said puzzled. "A second maidenhead?"

He hovered over her prostrate form, and his hand smoothed over the bulb of her bottom, running along the division between the twin moons, a finger suddenly and boldly pushing between the halves to worm itself into her. "Here," he said, "is your second maidenhead, my exquisite Marjallah. Has any man ever penetrated this passage?"

"*Never!*" she gasped.

He gently worked his finger up to the knuckle.

Aidan panicked entirely. "Don't!" she begged him. "Please, don't." She tried to dislodge the offending finger, but she could not which only increased her sense of fear.

The finger was withdrawn, and she breathed a deep sigh of relief that she quickly discovered was very premature. She felt him lubricating the entry to her rear passage with some sort of ointment, and then he grasped her hips firmly. Some primitive instinct warned Aidan what was coming, and terrified, she shrieked wildly.

"In God's name, no! Have pity on me, my lord! *Doooooon't!*"

The sultan felt a strong surge of potency flooding him as he forced this woman to his will. Slowly, for he had no desire to harm her physically, he pressed the head of his manhood upon the puckered entry to her rear passage until at last it gave way, and he worked his way into her. Now he rested a moment having gained a bridgehead, and then he once again began to force himself forward, an inch at a time, until he was at last buried completely within her. Beneath him Aidan sobbed, broken in spirit at least for the moment.

Murad groaned against her ear. She was so wonderfully tight, and if he had throbbed within her frontal passage, he was throbbing twice as fiercely now. He had used women like this many times, but never had he had the feeling that she was now giving him. He wanted release. He needed it! Drawing himself almost completely out of her he plunged back in, and out, and in again and again and again while she wept uncontrollably beneath him. Finally the sultan shouted with exultation, and collapsed upon her, forcing the breath from her, and Aidan fainted.

When he finally rolled off her he found that they could not revive her. She lay insensible, and no amount of stimulants could arouse her. Disappointed Murad had her carried back to her chamber, and another maiden was sent for to entertain the sultan that night.

Aidan did not regain her senses until late the next afternoon. She awoke slowly to find the sultan valideh sitting by her bed, a very worried expression upon her face. Aidan's eyelids fluttered, and she finally opened her eyes.

"Dear child, praise Allah!" Nur-U-Banu exclaimed.

"Then I am still alive?" Aidan whispered. "I hoped that I had died."

"Say it not!" cried the sultan's mother.

"But it is true, and I mean it! Oh, madame, you have been so kind to me, and I realize I must seem ungrateful, but I do not want to be one of your son's wives. Why will no one listen to me? Javid Khan freed me, and I want to go back to England. Oh, I know you tell me that I cannot, but I could if you would but just free me! I know my husband, and he has not remarried as you suggest. He would want me back! I know he would! When I was wife to the prince I had no real choice in the matter, but I do now. I do!"

"What did my son do to you that put you in this state?" asked the valideh.

Slowly, and with flaming cheeks, Aidan told her. Nur-U-Banu snorted. "Among the men of Islam, this is a common practice, despite the Prophet's ban upon it. Murad's father forced me to it once, but when he learned I did not like such things he confined his urges for variation to those of his women who did, and believe me, Marjallah, there are those women. I will simply tell Murad that such practices are not to your taste, and he will not inflict it upon you again."

"I want to go home," Aidan said doggedly, but the valideh ignored her, and now convinced that she would be all right left her to rest. Aidan shook her head. They would not listen to her. There was therefore nothing left to her but death.

To her surprise, however, she found that Murad had taken her threats of suicide quite seriously. There was, she found, no means by which she could end her life, and she was rarely left alone. Her food was brought to her already cut up so there was no knife available to open her veins, or plunge into her heart. Her jewelry was locked away, and taken out only when she could be watched. She was, therefore, not able to swallow a piece of it, choking herself, thereby putting a quick end to her unhappy existence.

She was kept docile the next few days by means of drugs in her food for it was hoped that rest might cure her depression. Murad fretted irritably for his first experience with his exquisite Marjallah had only whetted his appetite to possess her entirely. Over the next several days a parade of women came to the sultan's bed, but after satisfying his physical urges he angrily sent them away for none of them really pleasured him anymore. None of them was the exquisite and unattainable Marjallah. *He had to have her!*

"He is obsessed with Marjallah," the valideh complained to Esther Kira. "No other woman will do now. At least it is not as bad as it was with Safiye for Marjallah despises the sultan. She will not use him so shamefully to her own ends as did the bas kadin use my son."

"Not now, perhaps," replied Esther Kira. "She has yet to accept my lord

Murad, but once she recovers from her depression, and realizes she has no other choice but to give herself body and soul to his majesty, what do you think will happen, my dear friend? I can tell you! She is intelligent, and she will strive to have a child, a son if possible. Having borne that son will she be satisfied to see him destroyed by any of his elder brothers? She will not! She will fight for her son as would any natural mother. She will buy and she will win allies against Safiye who is not particularly liked among the other women of the harem. She may even win Sultan Murad away from Safiye entirely which I know will not displease you, but think, my dear friend! Think of at what price!

"If Marjallah gains the sultan's love at Safiye's expense, she will influence him to choose her son over Safiye's. There will be war in the harem, war in the divan, and even war within the empire as these two princesses fight for possession of the mantle of Defender of the Faith. The Janissaries will become involved, and who knows which way they will swing. Both the black eunuchs and the white eunuchs will take sides, and we both know they never take the same side. Did not Javid Khan free Marjallah? What a pity the sultan does not simply let her return to her homeland."

Esther Kira's words gave Nur-U-Banu food for thought. The old woman had ever been a good friend of the royal family, and so the sultan valideh never even considered the possibility that she had a motive other than the Ottoman welfare. Nur-U-Banu thought of how she had discouraged Marjallah from even attempting to return to her homeland, and she felt guilty, but what else could she do? She loved her son, and Murad had been determined to have the woman. She sighed. For once she was at a loss to find a simple solution to a problem, and as each day passed Murad became more enamored of the woman who disdained him so.

She was now a raging fever in his blood. Murad had allowed Aidan four days to recover herself, and then he had called for her again. Learning from his first experience with her he had decided to change his tactics. Harshly forcing her to his will was not the answer. She was far too strong-willed a woman, and he knew that she really would die rather than give him too easy a victory. He intended to win her over, but at the same time he intended that she should understand that he was the master.

It was the sultan's habit to spend the morning attending to the business of his empire, and among the creative and intellectual men of his court. His afternoons, however, were always spent in the harem. Murad had given orders that the opiates being used to control the lady Marjallah be discontinued. He wanted her fully cognizant and clearheaded when they met, and he anxiously awaited her arrival, smiling welcomingly as she was escorted into the room by the agha kislar. She wore a beautiful gold embroidered caftan of peach-colored silk, and her marvelous hair was loose about her shoulders. There were faintly purple smudges of shadows about her gray eyes, and she was unsmiling.

The sultan took her hand saying, "I have missed you, my exquisite Marjallah. Each day without your sweet presence has been like a year. Each night without you, a century."

"The night I spent with you seemed more like a thousand years in hell, my lord," she answered him coldly.

Murad waved Ilban Bey from the room even as the agha opened his mouth to reprimand Marjallah. Then the sultan looked deeply into her eyes, and said, "I am going to say to you something I have rarely said to anyone in my lifetime, Marjallah. I am sorry, my exquisite one. I am not used to being defied by anyone, and you angered me very much the other night. Angered me so greatly that I foolishly sought to cruelly force you to my desires. In doing so I hurt and frightened you, and for that I am deeply sorry. I will say no more on it. We will begin anew, but one thing you must understand about me is that I am your master, and I will not abdicate that part of myself to any woman. You will obey me as do all my women. I will try, however, never to ask of you that which will hurt you. Do you understand me?"

"Yes, my lord," she answered him tonelessly.

"Good," he said, "and from now on, Marjallah, each time you enter this bedchamber you will remove your garments. I have already told you that you have the most flawless, and the most beautiful body I have ever seen on any woman. I want to enjoy that beauty whenever we are together like this."

Aidan unbuttoned the pearl buttons that fastened her caftan, and then drew the garment over her head, tossing the silk onto a chair. "As my lord wishes," she said.

He smiled. "Very good." Reaching into his pocket he drew forth a small pouch of black silk, and opening it poured into his hand two little silver balls. "Have you ever seen anything like these?" he asked her.

"No, my lord. What are they?"

"They're to give you pleasure, my exquisite one. They will give your passionate nature a fine edge whenever you are with me. The balls are hollow. Inside one is a tiny drop of mercury. Inside the other a minute little tongue of silver. Lie back upon the bed, and allow me to place them within your sweet passage. Then you will see what happens. "

Aidan was beyond caring. Normally she would have questioned such a thing, but now it didn't matter if she lived or died, and so she didn't care what he did to her. Obediently she lay upon the bed, opening her legs to him. Carefully Murad inserted the two little silver balls inside her, gently pushing them into position. Just touching her in so intimate a manner aroused him, but he successfully fought back his own lust, and drew her back up from her prone position. "Now," he said, "walk about the bed-chamber, and tell me what you feel."

She walked away from him, but scarcely had she gone a few steps than she began to feel as she did just before the marvelous melting feeling that always accompanied her passion with both Conn and Javid Khan. Star-tled she stopped, but then believing she had only imagined such a thing she then continued on across the large room. The feeling had not been imagined! Standing on her feet she found herself shuddering with passion.

"Oh God!" she exclaimed surprised, and then she turned to look at the sultan. "What have you done to me?"

"Only given you pleasure," he said softly, and then he said in an ordinary conversational tone, "Do you play chess, Marjallah?"

She nodded.

Murad called the ever-present black eunuchs, and the chess table was brought. Perhaps, thought Aidan, sitting down would ease the terrible, but wonderful feelings of desire which hinted of greater fulfillment with her every movement. They played, and Aidan played badly for she could not escape the building hunger within her. The sultan watched her, the amusement in his eyes veiled, for he did not want to offend her knowing as he did that he was far from winning her over.

Finally Aidan could stand no more, and unthinking she leapt from her chair. Her eyes were filled with tears. "Please," she pleaded with him, "please take them out! I am dying from desire!"

"Taking them out," he said "will not give you the surcease that you need. Only I can do that, Marjallah. If you will agree to yield to me will-ingly then I shall remove them. "

"And if I do not?" she whispered defiantly.

He smiled pleasantly. "Then they remain, my exquisite one. Shall we play another game? We seem to have reached an impasse with this one."

"Does it make no difference to you that I despise you?" she asked him. "What kind of man are you?" She felt suddenly very angry.

"I am a powerful man, and no, it makes no difference to me at all that you despise me. You will not always despise me. One day you will find that you are in love with me for love is the other side of hate." He stood up, and imperiously offered her a hand. "Come!" he said, and he led her across the room to the huge, canopied bed.

Each step they took was an agony to her. She had to get those damned little balls removed! She had to have relief! She could bear no more, and when they had reached the bed a whimper escaped her lips.

"Well," said the sultan. "The decision is yours, Marjallah, and whatever it is you decide I will abide by it, but remember that until you yield to me, the balls remain in the sweet darkness of your tight little passage."

"Take them out!" Her voice was almost a scream.

"You will give yourself to me willingly?"

"Yes!" She was beginning to tremble, her legs buckling beneath her. If those devilish little silver spheres banged together inside her helpless body one more time, she was going to go totally mad!

"Lie back, Marjallah, and I will remove them," he said to her.

Carefully, so as not to jostle the tiny instruments of her torture any further, Aidan lay back upon the bed, and opened her legs to him. The sultan knelt, but seeing her tempting pink flesh was unable to stop himself from leaning forward, and tonguing her with slow, sensuous strokes. Her body jerked in surprise, and she screamed as passion knifed her sharply. Realizing the cruelty he was inflicting upon her, Murad reached into her aching body with his slender fingers, and withdrew the tiny silver balls, one at a time. Then he kissed her swollen and throbbing little bud.

"Forgive me, exquisite one," he said raising his head from her. "I did not intend to cause you further pain, but I could not resist that which was so sweetly offered to me." The sultan stood up, and slowly drew off his own comfortable, loose chamber robe of plum-colored silk. Settling himself contentedly in the center of the huge bed he said to her, "It is the custom for a woman coming to me for the first time to enter my bed from the foot, and crawl up to me. You did not follow the custom the last time you were with me. It would please me if you would do so now. When you have shown me your new and properly pleasing obedience, Marjallah, then will I relieve your magnificent body of the excruciating agony it is now suffering. You will obtain no real relief from your distress until I give it." There was no menace in his words, no threatening or bullying tone. His bland voice merely offered her plain fact.

Aidan's pride warred with her aching body. In that moment she would have killed him had she the means, but her pain finally won the battle she fought, and sliding from her place on the edge of the great bed she stumbled to its foot, and facedown, upon her belly, crawled up the emerald-green silk coverlet to crouch at his feet.

The sultan purred with approval. "Verrrry good, exquisite one! Now I give you leave to come farther, and you may kiss my feet and my legs as you move forward."

One part of her was totally and utterly shocked by her easy acquiescence, but the other part of her reminded her that only when she had pleased him fully would he give her relief from the painful tension that racked her hapless body. The quicker she obeyed him, the sooner would she be free of her agony. Mindlessly Aidan straddled the sultan, and began kissing first his feet, and then she moved up his long, slim legs pressing feathery kisses alternately upon each limb. When she came abreast of his groin he reached down with a hand, and lifting his heavy, long manhood he held it out to her. Aidan shuddered, and raising her head looked pleadingly at him. Murad's eyes bore mercilessly into her silently commanding her. Tears spilling from her eyes down her cheeks she bowed her head, and took him in her mouth.

The sultan leaned back against the soft pile of pillows, and sighed with pleasure, his languid dark eyes partly closed in a half-ecstasy. Reaching out his hand he tangled his fingers in her thick, coppery hair, and kneading at her scalp encouraged her onward. "Use your tongue beneath the edge of the knob, Marjallah," he said, his voice thick. "Ahhh, Allah! Your mouth was made for such work!" he shuddered. "Enough, now, exquisite one, lest you unman me too soon. Come, and give me your lips."

She released her hold upon him, and he drew her up to take her mouth in a fiery kiss. He ran his lips along hers kissing and licking at them, and then he said, "Open your sweet mouth to receive my tongue, fair slave," and she obeyed him, sucking vigorously upon his tongue as she had only moments before performed upon his manhood. One arm about her waist, his other hand began to play with her large breasts. Squeezing them lovingly he then pinched the nipples hard, sending a bolt of desire into her very core where she already ached with more hunger than she had ever believed a woman could.

Tearing her head away from his she whimpered, "Please, my lord! Please give me relief!"

"How impatient you are, exquisite one," he scolded her gently. "Have I not warned you that I am the master? It is the master who decides the time, not the slave. What a hard lesson that seems to be for you to learn."

"Forgive me, my lord," she begged him. Dear God, why would he not give her release? Had he not promised it her? The burning, throbbing, aching pain seemed to grow within her vitals with each passing minute.

Murad could see the panic in her eyes, and realizing the total power he held over the object of his desire aroused him even more than she herself already had. "Of course I forgive you," he began soothingly, "but it would not be right if I did not punish you, Marjallah. It is most important that you learn perfect obedience. Do you understand?"

"Y-yes, my lord," she answered him, her voice shaking. What would he do to her now?

The sultan called one of the black eunuchs to him, and whispered something to the man while Aidan, having been put gently to one side sat downcast. The eunuch hurried out of the room, and they sat in silence, the sultan contemplating her beauty of form, Aidan now feeling ignored, and her pain building once more as he scorned to soothe her with his touch. She tried to focus her glance upon the room itself.

The last time she had been in it it had been night, and she had hardly been interested in the decor of the place. Now she tried to take her mind from her fear and her pain by concentrating on something else. They had come down the Golden Road into the Sultan's Hall where a door upon the far wall opened into the sultan's apartment. In her months in Turkey Aidan had gained a small knowledge of tiles having had to see to the repair of the fountains, and several other places in Javid Khan's palace. The walls of the sultan's bedchamber were lined with fine Iznik tiles done in a floral pattern. The lower range of tiles was all of the same coloring. Blues and reds upon a white background with borders in which the deep, rich red predominated. The upper and lower sections of the wall were divided by a frieze of dark blue tiles upon which were written in white lettering verses from the Koran. The most beautiful tiles in the room, however, were those above the fireplace surrounding the cone-shaped bronze chimneypiece. On that curvaceous panel were sprays of tiny plum blossoms stretching upward upon a deep blue background.

The ceiling of the room was domed and decorated with painted motifs in gold on a blue-green background. There was not a surface of the room that was not embellished, but the general effect of the chamber was lofty and lovely. There were two tiers of windows, the upper ones with small colored panes divided by plasterwork.

On one wall was a layered fountain with three projecting basins over which the water flowed, each basin having its own golden faucet in the shape of a lily to add to the flow of water. The fountain was framed in solid marble as were the doorways, and the doors themselves were inlaid in mother-of-pearl and had finely chiseled locks. On three sides, the square room looked out into gardens.

The sultan's hobby was clockmaking, and even now one ticked as they sat awaiting whatever it was that Murad had ordered of the black eunuch. Aidan studied the enormous bed upon which they sat. It was fashioned with four carved and twisted pillars and sat in a corner of the room, a large window of clear glass in the wall near its foot. Attached to the pillars was a beautiful carved and gilded wooden canopy. At the head of the bed were carved and gilded side rails. The mattress was firm, and upholstered in cloth of gold. Over it was an enormous second mattress of emerald-green silk filled with down. There were bolsters of ruby, and turquoise, and violet with matching pillows. Aidan hugged one of the violet silk pillows to her as the door to the bedchamber opened, and an exquisite girl entered the room.

She was one of the most beautiful creatures Aidan had ever seen, tiny and small-boned with huge blue eyes and silvery-blond hair. She was very, very young. Throwing off the pale pink silk robe she was wearing she fell to the floor in a gesture of total obedience.

The sultan smiled warmly. "Arise, Zora, and come to me."

The girl ran quickly to the bed, and climbed upon it, seating herself on the other side of the sultan, and holding up her lips to him to be kissed. He willingly obliged her, running his hands over her silken body as he did so, gently teasing her budding breasts.

"This is the lady Marjallah, Zora," he said, and then turned to Aidan. "Zora is one of my newest ikbals."

"I have heard of the lady Marjallah. She has caused a great stir within the harem for it is said, my lord, that you prefer her above us all, even Safiye Kadin."

Murad laughed. "I long ago learned the folly of confining myself to one woman, Zora, my pet. You may tell the ladies of my harem that although Marjallah pleased me greatly, and is very much in my favor, I shall not neglect them, nor shall any other woman ever take Safiye Kadin's place in my heart."

Zora hung her head, looking shamefaced. "I am rightfully rebuked, my lord," she said softly, and Murad kissed her again.

"You see," he said to Aidan, "what a charming model of docility Zora is, exquisite one? I have called her here so you may learn from her, but first open your legs to me again." Reaching beneath one of the bolsters he withdrew the black silk pouch, and poured the tiny silver spheres into his palm.

Aidan shuddered, but she now knew better than to protest. She was not certain the form her punishment would take, but it began with the reinsertion of those terrible little instruments of torture. Lying back she obeyed him, and felt the cold silver slipping into her, aided by his finger.

"Zora," said Murad, "show the lady Marjallah the movements of the Dance of the Veils. Marjallah, my exquisite one, you will follow what Zora does."

The dainty blond slid from the bed, and watched as Aidan, her teeth sinking into her lower lip, followed her. "It is really quite simple," said Zora, and she showed Aidan the movements involved.

"Now," said the sultan, "you do them." His dark eyes dared her to defy him, and once again Aidan wished she might kill him for what he was doing to her.

Trembling she repeated the movements, each change of position she forced her body into adding to her agony. Zora stood next to her, and the sultan commanded them to dance more quickly. A fine sheen of perspiration broke out over her entire body, and she could feel her heart hammering violently in her chest. For a moment she believed that she was going to die, and she welcomed the release that death would bring her, but then he commanded them to stop, and to return to the bed where he removed for a second time the silver rounds from her tortured body.

Murad motioned Zora to stimulate him further with her mouth, and the girl instantly obeyed her master. Then the sultan said, "Present your second maidenhead to me," and Zora turned herself about so that her bottom was to her lord, the upper half of her body resting upon her arms at a lower angle. Grasping her firmly by the hips he entered the girl's body in one thrust, and pumped against her for a short time completely overlooking Aidan who was wide-eyed at his performance. Then suddenly the sultan turned to her saying, "Kneel before Zora, my exquisite one," and when she had obeyed him he removed his hands from the blond girl's hips, and reaching out began to fondle Aidan's breasts while Zora pushed herself back and forth upon his shaft.

"You see, Marjallah, you see how flawless are Zora's manners. She is a perfect model of harem decorum, and eventually under my schooling you, too, will be a model of perfection. She does not find it difficult to obey me, and I am neither cruel nor unkind to her." His slender, but firm fingers dug into the creamy flesh of her breasts as he crushed the tender skin leaving red marks upon it. Taking one of her nipples between his thumb and his forefinger he pinched it hard, and tugged upon it. A soft whimper escaped her. The sultan smiled, and with a grunt released himself into his blond slave.

Zora fell forward for a moment lost in a little swoon, but then she revived, and slipping from the bed ran to the fountain where a silver basin sat stored in a wall niche. Filling it she then ran to the huge fireplace, and placed the basin upon a small grate above the coals for a short minute, and then gathering several soft cloths from another wall niche returned back to the bed. Murad stood, and allowed the blond girl to bathe his now limp part. When she had finished he thanked her, and patted the kneeling slavegirl upon her blond head.

All the while this whole tableau had taken place Aidan had died a thousand little deaths. When the sultan's manhood had grown long and hard she had desperately wanted him to plunge it into her fevered flesh. Instead she had been forced to watch him service the tiny Zora so vigorously that he had emptied himself, and now there was naught left to ease her pain. She wanted to shriek with her frustration and her outrage. Her tortured mind now added the blond Zora to her death list. Zora had taken what was rightfully hers! Aidan wished Zora dead!

Murad could tell that his proud Marjallah was close to the breaking point, and so he called to his black eunuchs to pour them some wine. He did not often indulge in alcohol as it was forbidden by the Prophet, and his drunken father had given him an example he most certainly did not wish to follow, but nonetheless it was occasionally a good restorative especially the decanter from which his black eunuchs now poured two drafts. The decanter had had added to it a strong opiate which acted as an aphrodisiac.

The wine was brought to the bed, and the sultan took one of the goblets and drank it down. "It is not for you, Zora," he warned, "but you, my Marjallah, may drink down but half the goblet. No more, however," he cautioned.

With trembling hand she reached out and brought the crystal goblet to her lips, tasting the first wine she had had in well over a year. It was hard not to gulp it, but she managed, replacing the goblet upon the tray held by the eunuch when she had taken the portion allowed her. The strong Cyprus wine slid into her stomach like boiling oil, and then flamed into her veins. Color began to return to her cheeks.

Murad could already feel the aphrodisiac beginning to work upon him, but he knew one thing that would restore him even more quickly. "Arise from the bed, both of you," he commanded, "and stand facing one another at its foot."

The two women obeyed, and Aidan wondered what new horror he had devised to torture her.

"Zora, my pet, I want you to take Marjallah into your arms and comfort her for she is in great pain."

Horrified at what he was suggesting Aidan stepped back a pace, her distaste quite evident upon her face.

"Are you disobeying me, exquisite one?" the sultan demanded. He rolled the little silver balls about in his open palm, displaying them threateningly, sliding them from one hand to the other.

Aidan shuddered hard. "No, my lord, I am not disobeying you," she whispered low, and she then submitted to the blond girl's soft embrace, kneeling so that they would be of a similar height.

She could not meet Zora's gaze, but strangely the ikbal was tender and gentle in her caresses. Murad watched them, his own ardor rising fast, as the two women's breasts met nipple to nipple, as they fondled each other's buttocks for Zora spoke low instructions to her reluctant partner, and in an odd, kindly way encouraged Aidan onward so that the sultan would be pleased.

"Don't be embarrassed," Zora whispered softly, her words not available to Murad.

"I hate him!" Aidan whispered back.

"So do I," came the startling reply.

"Then why do you submit?"

"Because what else is there for us if we do not?" said Zora.

"Come back to the bed," said the sultan, "and then, Zora, my pet, you will prepare her passage for my entry."

"Of course, my lord!"

Taking Aidan's hand Zora pulled her up, and led her back to the emerald-green coverlet. The two women climbed upon the bed, and then Zora told Aidan to lie back, and she firmly spread the older woman's legs.

"Ohhhh!" The small shriek escaped from between Aidan's lips as Zora's mouth and tongue began to tease and play against her badly overstimulated and sensitive flesh. Her eyes flew back in her head as she sought Murad fearing her cry had offended him, but instead the sultan leaned over her head, and kissed her lips tenderly while gently fondling her breasts.

"There, my exquisite one, is not Zora's mouth soothing?" He smiled warmly down at her. "When she deems you ready, my Marjallah, I will ease your discomfort entirely." He moved himself around so that he lay on his side next to her. "Come, my love," he said taking her hand, and placing it about his hard shaft. He nibbled at her lips. "Give me your tongue, sweet," and he sucked upon the morsel offered. "Work me with your hand, exquisite one," he told her, and kissed her eyelids.

"She is ready, my lord," came Zora's voice, and the blond girl arose from the bed.

Murad swung himself over Aidan saying, "You may go now, Zora, and as your reward Zaad will give you the replica of my manhood. You may keep it until the morning."

"Thank you, my lord," said Zora, and a black eunuch at her heels she hurried from the room.

Murad turned back to Aidan who lay trembling beneath him. She was like a finely tuned instrument, and very ready to play. "Tell me what you desire of me, my exquisite one?" he said softly as he sat astride her thighs, fondling his large weapon, moving it casually from one hand to another.

"I want you to make love to me," she said low.

"You want me to fill you with my shaft, and make you weep with pleasure?"

"Yes!"

"You desire this of your free will? I have not forced you to it?"

"Yes, I desire it of my free will!" she half-sobbed. "Please! Oh, please!" she begged him, beaten.

With a look of triumph that he was unable to keep from his dark eyes he slid into her passage with one smooth thrust, and she cried with relief as he began to move vigorously upon her. Clasped between his muscled thighs she felt blessed relief begin to pour through her entire body as he brought her to the first peak. Suddenly her brain was clear again, and in place of her previous helplessness came a white-hot anger at what he had done to her. To her amazement she was able to separate her mind from her body, and while he gave her orgasm after orgasm, releasing the terrible sexual agony he had inflicted upon her, her brain allowed Aidan to slip back into a secret place, and watch all that was happening to her body. Her body felt the release, but her soul did not. When once again her mind and body melded into one entity, she fainted from the excesses that had been visited upon her.

With a shout of victory Murad poured himself into her beautiful body, and exhausted fell to one side. Within a few minutes, however, the sultan had regained his senses, and he looked to his fair partner. He revived her with kisses, and as she awoke Aidan knew that she had gone about this the wrong way. She had wanted either her freedom or her death, and they had denied her both. Now she would make them give her the death she sought. She would convince the sultan that she had been won over, and when he trusted her, she would kill him! Then they would have no choice but to kill her. It was a foolproof plan, and she felt no remorse for the suffering she would cause to Nur-U-Banu, and Safiye. Neither, she decided, was really her friend. Well, perhaps Safiye was.

The valideh, however, had used her to keep her son's favor. She deserved to be brought down for pandering for her own son. As for Safiye she would hardly miss a man who hadn't paid any attention to her in years. She would, at Murad's death, have as the new sultan valideh, the power she sought in place of the love she had lost. At least Safiye had been kind, and welcomed her honestly. Safiye had been her real friend. Murad's death would free her as it was going to free Aidan, and the lovely Zora, and all the other poor women who were prey to the incredible lust of this wicked man!

"Have I given you pleasure, my exquisite one," he asked, "for you have certainly given me pleasure."

Raising her eyes to him she felt her cheeks grow pink which perfectly suited her purposes. She let her sandy lashes sweep back over her gray eyes. "Oh, my lord," she murmured, "I am ashamed to have resisted you! How could I have known? I did not, and I beg your pardon, sweet master." She twisted her body into a kneeling position upon the mattress, her coppery hair spreading across his thighs, a perfect picture of total submission.

"I understand," he said to her. "I understand perfectly, my exquisite one. I gave you no time to mourn your beloved Javid Khan, but my desire for you was, is so very, very great." He lifted her up, and kissed her passionately. "You are like a fever in my blood, Marjallah. Nothing is ever enough! For the last four days I have sat in the divan in the mornings, and it is your face that has been before me, the memory of your body that has tortured me beyond reason! Sinan, my architect, comes to me with plans for buildings we have been planning for months, and I cannot concentrate upon what he says. Perhaps now, my exquisite one, that you have yielded to me, at least some of my senses will be restored to me."

She smiled sweetly at him. "I would not cause you distress, my lord," she said, and slipping next to him she blew softly in his ear, then bit hard upon his lobe.

Murad chuckled, a pleased sound. He enjoyed getting his own way. "What a little tigress you are, Marjallah, and so full of surprises!"

"May I continue to surprise you, my lord," she said. "I should not want you to become bored with me."

Her dulcet tone inflamed him, and though it was but late afternoon, the sultan felt yet fresh. It was as if her acquiescence had renewed his vigor. "There is little chance of my becoming bored, my exquisite Marjallah." Arising from the bed he said, "I have a small surprise for you," and taking her by the hand he led her across the room, and touching a small floral panel on the tile he revealed a little door that swung easily open upon well-oiled hinges. Stepping through he drew Aidan with him, and she found that they were at the head of a narrow flight of stairs.

The walls of the inner passageway were covered in black and white tiles with just a touch of yellow. Holding tightly to the sultan's hand, Aidan followed him down the stairs, and through another door which opened into a large room which Aidan realized was directly beneath the sultan's bedchamber. It was domed, its marble arches supporting the sultan's rooms above. In the room was an amazingly lovely marble bathing pool which was entirely surrounded by a low, pierced marble balustrade which offered only one set of steps down into the pool at the far end. Directly in the center of the pool was a spurting fountain, and the marble columns had spouts from which water sprayed forth.

"Can you swim?" the sultan asked her.

"A little," she admitted. Would it be possible, she wondered, to drown him? No. Alas, she was not strong enough even if she was large for a woman.

He led her into the water, and they swam about for a few minutes. To amuse himself Murad lifted Aidan up so she might straddle the spurting fountain with her legs, and then he swam to the edge of the pool to observe her as the water sprayed between her long and shapely limbs. Sliding her hands up her torso she cupped her own breasts, and held them up as if she were offering them to him. He moved toward her, and she laughed aloud, taunting him when he commanded her to jump from the fountain back into the pool. She watched him where he stood just outside the range of the fountain's spray, and releasing one of her breasts she took a single finger, and rubbing against her little jewel then put the finger into her mouth to suck upon it. At no time did her eyes leave his.

With an animal bellow of pure lust Murad leapt toward the fountain, and in a burst of mocking laughter Aidan dove into the pool from the other side, and swam away from him. He was quickly after her, and catching her by her ankles he dragged her back into his embrace. She laughed up into his face, and furious Murad backed her against the side of the pool, and snarled at her, "Put your legs about my waist, slave!" and when she did he rammed forcefully into her, slamming her spine against the marble wall of the pool.

Her arms wrapped about his neck, and she kissed him passionately, and bit at his lips, and licked at him with her tongue. It was if she was possessed by some lewd devil, and the sultan was overcome by what he believed was her deep and growing ardor for him. Cupping her buttocks in his hands he used her fiercely until they were both overcome with their excesses, and Murad carried her from the pool and back up the stairs to his bedchamber where they slept until midevening.

With each day that passed now Murad grew more and more enamored of Aidan. He possessed her daily, and she no longer refused him. Indeed she entered most willingly into his passion, and yet there was something about her that he could not seem to possess try as he might. He showered her with gifts, but when he sought to move her from the little apartment next to his mother she begged he leave her there, and so he acquiesced. Quickly the impersonal little rooms took on a personality of their own, as the sultan gave to his exquisite Gift from the Sea rare pieces of furniture, made from fine woods, and inlaid with mother-of-pearl and semiprecious stones. The lamps in the apartment were all replaced with gold ones, and the simple rugs that had graced the floors had given way to thick wool carpets in dark jeweled tones from villages without names.

Her wardrobe expanded as Murad saw Aidan had her pick of the finest bolts of silks, and silk gauze, and cottons, and satins, and wools so delicate that they could be drawn through the band of a ring. The sultan could not gift her with enough jewelry for she had lost everything in the fire that had destroyed Javid Khan's palace. Ropes and more ropes of pearls were now hers, and emeralds and sapphires, and rubies from the East, and diamonds and all manner of precious and semiprecious stones set within red and pink gold, and some silver. She had refused his offer of more slaves telling him that she needed only Marta and her daughters along with the voluble Jinji to serve her.

She was neither aloof nor overly friendly with the other women of the harem, but she had rewarded Zora with jewelry and cloth for her kindness, and she was invariably good to frightened newcomers. She was befriended by the four most important women in the empire: Nur-U-Banu, Safiye, Janfeda, and Fahrusha Sultan; and so if she had any enemies amongst the harem women, they were not open enemies for fear of severe and cruel reprisals on the part of the powerful.

Esther Kira came often to the harem these days, and it was to her only that Aidan confided her misery. Esther was in a genuine quandary as to what to do. She liked Marjallah, and it was no secret that the sultan's vices and lusts were many, and sometimes perverted. Lord Bliss would be back any day now from his expedition to Brusa, and she did not know what to tell him. She had attempted to subtly set Nur-U-Banu against Marjallah so that she would aid her in leaving the Yeni Serai, and returning to her home, but with Marjallah openly content, and the sultan ecstatic with his new inamorata, Nur-U-Banu could not be persuaded of the possibility of future difficulty. Besides, the lady Marjallah had not conceived with Javid Khan, and had not yet conceived with Murad. It was entirely possible, the sultan valideh told Esther Kira, that Marjallah was sterile.

Only Esther Kira knew of Aidan's true misery, and she desperately wished she could aid the young woman in returning to her husband. She had not dared to tell Marjallah of his presence in Turkey. There was something about Marjallah these days that worried the old lady. She seemed the same, and yet she was not. Esther Kira could not betray the royal Ottoman to whom she owed so much despite her deep wish to help the lady Marjallah.

During her whole life Esther Kira had abided by the laws of her faith, and her faith had never failed her. Still she had tried not to disturb the mighty Yahweh with matters to which she could eventually find the solution herself. Now, however, Esther Kira prayed for a solution that would help her to resolve her divided loyalties.

When that solution appeared it was so sudden that she almost lost her opportunity. She had come to the palace with some especially fine examples of Brusa silk that Lord Bliss had brought to her from his expedition. The handsome Irishman had been very disappointed that she had not come up with a solution to his problem, but she had sent him back to his ship to await any further developments, developments she did not expect to be forthcoming.

Arriving at the palace she found that the sultan was entertaining the harem that afternoon, but because of her closeness with the valideh she was invited to join them. Murad was looking particularly handsome that day. He was wearing a beautiful cloth-of-gold robe lined in yellow satin and embroidered with red velvet plumes. Atop his head he wore a turban of white decorated with two small ropes of rubies, and a broad red plume. His golden-red beard had been recently trimmed, and was perfumed with sandalwood, and his dark eyes were bright with excitement.

It had not been an unusual fete. There had been the usual entertainments, and refreshments, and it had been a time for the women of Murad's harem, who numbered close to a thousand at this point, to don their finest clothing, and parade themselves before the sultan in hopes of catching his eye. Murad had been seated upon a pillowed dais beneath a carved wooden canopy with Safiye leaning against him on the right, and Marjallah leaning against his left shoulder. Each woman was garbed beautifully. Safiye, with her dark red hair, was wearing garments of forest green and gold while the lighter coppery-haired Marjallah had chosen turquoise and silver.

Murad had never felt more content in his entire life. He ruled a mighty empire, and in his harem were the most beautiful women in the entire world. On either side of him were his two favorites, each of whom was devoted to him, each of whom loved him. A servant bent low offering him a platter of perfect fruits. He turned to Marjallah, and smiling she reached out to the tray to take the fruit knife upon it, and plunged it into his chest. The room erupted into screaming pandemonium; and Esther Kira knew that her time had come as the black eunuchs surrounding Murad leapt forward to drag Marjallah off their master.

The sultan could not believe that she had attacked him despite the evidence of his own eyes. The knife was lodged within his flesh, and already blood was seeping out from around it. The black eunuchs were roughly dragging Aidan from the room. She was weeping wildly in her frustration at having failed to kill him, but at least now, she thought, they will give me what I want which is death.

"*No!*" Murad's voice was weak, but clear. "I want her here!"

The valideh nodded at the black eunuchs who stopped in their tracks, still clutching Aidan. The room was quickly cleared of all but Aidan and her captors, Safiye, the valideh, Esther Kira, Murad, and the sultan's doctor, a Greek with a fortunately cool head. Quickly the doctor examined the sultan, and then he said to them,

"I must take the knife out, my lord, and there will be some blood, but praise to Allah, the wound is not serious. Your assailant has missed your heart by a wide margin, and no other vital organ or artery has been cut. Have I your permission to remove the weapon?"

Murad nodded, and with no further delay the doctor drew the knife carefully from the sultan's chest. Almost at once the wound began to bleed, and the doctor's slave stanched the blood while the sultan was laid back, and the wound disinfected and stitched closed. Murad was then propped back up, and his eyes sought for, and found Aidan.

"Bring her here to me," he whispered for he was weak with shock, and blood loss.

A eunuch on either side of her Aidan was brought before the sultan.

"*Marjallah,*" he said softly, and when she raised her head to look at him he was astounded by the hatred in her eyes which reached out to him, and with icy fingers wrapped itself around his heart. "But I loved you, exquisite one."

"*Love?*" She burst into hysterical laughter.

She is mad, thought Esther Kira. That is what has been distressing me!

"Love," repeated Aidan bitterly. "You, my lord, do not know the first thing about love! Lust is your metier! If you truly understood about love you would have never put Safiye aside to sport among other women. If you understood love you would have had the decency to allow me a time to mourn Javid Khan, but no! You would allow me no time to weep for that good and gentle man. You could barely wait to bring me to your bed where you brutalized and humiliated me! I hate you! I hated it every time you touched me! My only regret is that I did not succeed in killing you, my lord! I chose both the wrong time, and the wrong weapon, and I had no time in which to kill myself! Now, however, you must kill me, and if you really feel anything for me then that will be my revenge upon you! You will go to your grave knowing that you were responsible for my death!" And Aidan burst out laughing, a chilling sound that sent a shiver down the spines of all in the room.

Murad groaned with agony at her words. Never had he been repudiated by a woman, and in such a fashion. "Confine her to her apartment," he ordered, and fell back exhausted with the effect his words had cost him. There were tears in his eyes as they took her from the Sultan's Hall.

A litter was brought, and Murad was carried to his bedchamber to be watched over by Safiye, and later on by his mother. Now, however, Nur-U-Banu needed a few minutes to herself for she was shocked at the turn of events of this afternoon. Esther Kira went with the valideh, and when they had reached her apartments, and Nur-U-Banu had been settled by her women she turned to Esther Kira and said, "Why did I not listen to you, Esther? Have you ever given me bad advice? Never! If my son had been killed I should have never forgiven myself!"

"But he is not dead, nor anywhere near it, Yahweh be praised!" She paused, and then asked, "What will happen to Marjallah?"

"She must die!" was the immediate answer.

"She is mad, you know," replied Esther, "and that madness was brought about, forgive me dear friend for saying it, by the sultan who could not wait for her to mourn Javid Khan."

"I know that," said Nur-U-Banu, "and in a way I blame myself for I might have discouraged Murad's passion long enough for Marjallah to recover from her grief, but I did not! I wanted my son to be happy, and he believed he could not be happy without Marjallah."

"He will have to be happy without her now," said Esther Kira. "Will it be done the usual way?"

"Yes. She will be placed in a weighted silk sack, and drowned off the Prince's Island in the Mamara."

"When?"

"It will be up to my son," said Nur-U-Banu.

"No, my dear lady," said Esther Kira boldly. "You must take the responsibility for this execution. The sultan is a man in love, and he will not want to see her killed, but it must be done. Not only did she attempt his death, but she said the most terrible things to him, and those words were heard by the physician and his assistant as well as the eunuchs and ourselves. The physician will be silent for he would not jeopardize his position, but the eunuchs will gossip, and by dawn the entire palace will know what Lady Marjallah said to the sultan, and it will not be an accurate version of her words, but rather a greatly embroidered tale.

"With every hour Marjallah continues to live the tale will grow, undermining the sultan's authority. Then there is her nationality. She is English, and the sultan is just beginning to enjoy his relationship with the English. Has not the English queen just sent him a boatload of fine gifts? If the English find out that Marjallah is one of them that budding diplomatic relationship could be destroyed. It should be done today. Before the sultan has the chance to even think about it, and it is you, my dear lady, who should make that decision. Let the judgment be swift!"

"You are right, Esther Kira," said Nur-U-Banu. "Murad will weaken, and forgive her, and she will continue to be trouble to us. If I had listened to you in the first place this would have never happened. I cannot forgive myself until Marjallah is dead!"

"You must show mercy in your judgment, my dear lady," counseled Esther Kira. "Marjallah's grief is what drove her to this act of madness, and we know that the mad are special to God. Let me go from you now, and I will return as quickly bringing with me a rare drug which will render her unconscious. You need not be unkind in carrying out her sentence of execution. The God we both worship does not abhor mercy."

The sultan valideh nodded. "Hurry, Esther Kira! I would do this before the day ends, and there are but two hours till the sunset."

When Esther Kira had gone the valideh's own personal doctor came to offer her a sedative, but Nur-U-Banu refused it, and sent him away. Her own servants knowing her well discreetly let her be. They were there should she want them, but for now they remained out of sight. The sultan valideh was saddened by what had happened, and she was equally saddened by what she must do, but she would do it. It was that sort of strength that separated a ruler from those meant to be ruled.

When Esther Kira returned the two women went to Marjallah's apartments. Two huge deaf-mute eunuchs guarded the doors. They were the fiercest of the palace eunuchs having been trained to kill without hesitation. Seeing the valideh they stepped aside, and unbarred the door to Aidan's apartment. Within Marta and her daughters huddled looking quite terrified. Jinji was ashen with anxiety, and almost fainted when he saw the sultan valideh.

"Where is your mistress?" she asked.

Jinji pointed toward Aidan's bedroom, and entering it they saw her sitting upon the bed, a vacant look in her eyes, her cat, Tulip, in her lap. Absently she stroked the beautiful beast, and his very loud purr was the only sound heard within the room.

"Fetch me a goblet," said the valideh, and Jinji scurried to obey her, almost dropping the silver vessel in his nervousness. Nur-U-Banu took it from him, and held it out to Esther Kira who poured what appeared to be a cherry sherbet into the goblet. The sultan's mother then held the beverage beneath Aidan's nose, saying, "Drink it, Marjallah, and your troubles will be over."

Without even the slightest protest Aidan took the silver goblet from Nur-U-Banu, and drained it down. Then she looked up and said, "Will you care for my servants, madame? I would not like to feel they suffered because of my actions. If it is possible I would free Marta and her daughters, and send them home. They were Javid's gift to me, and are therefore mine to dispose of as I wish."

"They shall be freed, and returned to their own land," replied the valideh. "What of Jinji?"

"I would give him to Safiye. She will know how to use him best."

The valideh nodded. "It will be done. Is there anything else?"

Aidan yawned. She was beginning to feel very sleepy. Her eyes were growing heavy, and it was becoming hard to form the words. "Tulip," she managed to say, and then she fell back onto the bed.

"Tulip?" said the valideh. "What did she mean, I wonder."

"Her cat is called Tulip," said Esther Kira. "Let me give the beast some of the potion, and it can be drowned with her."

Nur-U-Banu nodded, and called for a dish of chopped chicken which Jinji assured the sultan's mother was the cat's favorite food. The drug was mixed with the chicken, and sure enough the cat wolfed the treat down, falling quickly into a stupor upon the floor.

"It is a beautiful animal," remarked the valideh. "What a pity it must be destroyed."

"Its presence would only remind you of this incident," said Esther Kira. "Now there will be no loose ends to tie up."

The official executioners were called into Aidan's apartment, and she was put with her cat into a sack that had been fashioned of pale mauve silk. The sacque was then removed via the Harem Death Gate, and taken down the slope of the palace gardens to a tiny dock where waited the man responsible for the removal of bodies from the Yeni Serai. Receiving the sack he dumped it into the stern of his little boat, and accepted from the executioners the traditional baksheesh. Then as the executioners turned back to the palace the boatman began to row his craft away.

It was sunset, and the rays of the setting sun spread themselves lavishly over the waters of the harbor turning that arm of the sea that pushed up into the city, which was called the Golden Horn, molten with bright color. Rhythmically the boatman responsible for the disposal of bodies from the sultan's palace rowed on away from the city, and toward the deep water off the Prince's Island where he had for years, and had his father, and his grandfather before him, followed their trade of dumping bodies from the palace. Sometimes they were the bodies of women dead in child-birth, or some other natural cause. At other times they were the bodies of those women sentenced to be executed. Some were executed alive if the sultan chose to be particularly cruel, and the boatman on those trips blocked his ears with softened wax so that he did not hear their piteous cries for he was not a cruel man. At other times the women were either mercifully strangled or drugged as the body he now carried had obviously been.

For a brief time the little vessel was blocked from sight of the land as it was passed by a large ship outward bound for the Aegean, and possibly the Mediterranean beyond. As the last rays of the red-orange sun dipped below the horizon there floated across the water the high, wailing chant of Istanbul's chief muezzin, and his cohorts, all calling the faithful to prayer, and the small, bobbing boat was no more than a wisp of a shadow upon a darkling sea.

Part Four

LOVE LOST LOVE FOUND

Chapter 16

~❦~

$\mathcal{S}$ir Robert Small's vessel, the *Bon Adventure*, rocked gently at its berth on the Golden Horn in Istanbul's teeming harbor. It was late afternoon, but even here on the water the air was yet still and damply hot. In the main cabin of the ship Conn St. Michael sat with Robbie, and England's first ambassador to the Sublime Porte, William Harborne, about a heavy, rectangular oak table with fine carved legs. The rest of the room was as well furnished. The walls of the cabin were paneled, the span of dark linenfold hung here and there with silver sconces that had been hinged to move with the motion of the ship. Because of its location in the stern of the vessel the room had a fine large window as well as smaller windows on each side, but even with these ports open the cabin was stiflingly hot.

A window seat had been built into the stern window, and beneath it were several deep storage cabinets. Across from the main window was a large bed of heavy oak that had been fastened to the floor of the room upon whose wide and polished boards had been laid a fine Turkey rug of dark red with a black-and-gold design. The three elder O'Malley brothers threatened to wear a hole of serious proportions in that rug as they paced restlessly back and forth across the cabin; irritated by their inability to solve the thorny problem of their younger sibling's wife.

"The whole bloody thing is impossible," grumbled Brian O'Malley in his frustration.

"Impossible," replied Conn, "is a word that I refuse to accept in this instance, brother mine!"

Brave words, thought Robbie, looking at Conn who had grown noticeably thinner over the last few months, and whose purple-shadowed eyes were evidence enough of his lack of sleep.

"My lord," cut in William Harborne, "impossible is the only word that adequately describes yer wife's situation. There really is no hope, sir, short of the sultan's death, and I can assure ye that he is a robust gentleman, still in the first flush of his manhood."

"There's only one way then," said Brian O'Malley impatiently, "and God only knows we've got the firepower for it! We'll just have to bombard the infidel's palace from the sea where it is the most vulnerable. Then we'll be able to rescue our sister-in-law ourselves, and be off before they even realize she's gone! It is as good a plan as any."

" 'Tis the worst thing we could do!" snapped Robbie. "Are ye mad, man?"

"Well there seems to be naught else to do, little man," said Brian O'Malley surlily. "I haven't heard ye English come up with any ideas. All ye can seem to say is that 'tis impossible."

The English ambassador gritted his teeth, and hoped that when he spoke his voice would be a calm and reasonable one. "May I remind ye, Captain O'Malley, that this is not the Spanish Main. Yer swashbuckling tactics won't do here. Remember, sir, that yer sister, Sir Robert, Richard Staper, and my own master, Sir Edward Osborne, have spent years working to open a trading partnership with Turkey. I cannot, will not, allow ye to destroy everything that we have sought to gain for England. I represent her majesty's government, sir, and we must keep our relations with the Sublime Porte friendly relations. Turning yer cannons upon his majesty's home in order to conduct a raid upon his harem is hardly conducive to *friendly relations!*"

Brian O'Malley grinned a rather evil grin at William Harborne, and said, "But we're not English, man. When the dirty infidel complains, ye've but to tell him, and 'twill be the truth, that 'twas not the civilized English who came calling, but some wild Irishmen."

William Harborne's mouth tightened, and his hand slammed down hard upon the oaken table where he sat causing the pewter tankards upon it to jump suddenly. "Dammit, ye thick-headed bogtrotter! Get this into yer stubborn skull! The Sultan of Turkey is not some stupid fool of a man without a brain. Although I am certain that he would appreciate the subtlety ye've just offered me, and laugh heartily, he would still hold the English government responsible, and rightly so, for any breach of friendly relations." The ambassador turned to Conn. "Lord Bliss, surely you understand?"

"Ye keep telling me that I have no hope of regaining my wife, sir," said Conn quietly, "and right now I cannot accept such a thing, but neither do I propose to follow my brother's well-intentioned method either. There must be another way, and we have simply not thought about it yet."

"If there is, my lord," said the ambassador, "I cannot think of it."

"But, good sirs, I can," came a voice from the cabin doorway, and Esther Kira hobbled slowly into the room, aided by her small blackamoor page, and leaning upon a silver-headed cane. "Thank you, Yussef," she said to the boy, "now run back to the litter, and wait for me. You will find a bag of Turkish paste beneath my cushions for you, child."

With a bright grin, the lad ran from the room, greedily licking his lips in anticipation of the waiting treat.

Conn had leapt to his feet at her entry, and now he helped the old lady to a comfortable seat, asking as he settled her, "What has happened, Esther Kira? Are ye telling me that ye can now help us? *Why now?*"

The bright-eyed old woman accepted his aid, and settled herself into a chair. Quickly she explained the events of the past hour at the palace; and drawing a quick, deep breath so she might continue on with her tale, she explained that the boatman who disposed of bodies in the sea for the sultan was a Jew, currently in debt to the Kira family. He would aid them in rescuing Aidan, and his silence was guaranteed. When she had finished speaking Esther Kira reached into the voluminous folds of her brocaded gown, and drew forth a folded square of mauve silk which she handed to Conn. "Open it, and fill it with something heavy, my lord. Do you understand me?"

Conn's heart was hammering wildly. "Aye, Esther Kira, I do."

"You must get under way as soon as I leave your ship," she said. "If you have men still in the city then leave one of your vessels behind for them, and plan your rendezvous to meet up with them, but you must leave now! You will have but one chance, my lord, for Avram ben Yakob will not stop. This must be done while you are both in motion on the slightest chance that someone might see if you stopped to make the transfer. Put your own ship between the shore and Avram's so that your actions will not be visible to anyone on the palace side."

"How can I thank you, Esther Kira?" asked Conn taking the old lady's hands into his, and kissing them warmly.

"Do not thank me, Lord Bliss," she replied quietly, "for if fate had not interfered in this matter I know of no way that you could have obtained your wife's release for I certainly would not betray my friendship with the royal Ottoman family. I do so only now because of the events of the last few weeks, things which I must now tell you for not only your sake, but those of the lady Marjallah, who was my friend, and who I found to be a good and honest woman.

"When Javid Khan was murdered by his mad sibling the lady Marjallah went to the sultan for protection. Javid Khan had freed her legally when he had married her, but even knowing this the sultan took her for himself claiming that Marjallah's loss of the papers proving her freedom left her status in doubt. This was but a splitting of hairs for the sultan was there when Prince Javid Khan went before the kadi. He knew Marjallah's words to be the truth, but his lust was greater than his honor. There was nothing anyone could do to help Marjallah in her plight which was made worse by the sultan's eagerness to possess her. He gave her no time to mourn her loss for the lady Marjallah cared for the prince. Instead he forced her to his bed almost at once; and it is this that I believe rendered Marjallah slightly mad. Only a madwoman would have dared to stab the sultan with a fruit knife."

"*Mad?*" The men in the room spoke with one voice, and then Conn said, "Are you telling me, Esther Kira, that my wife has gone mad?"

"Yes, my lord, I am, but I have lived a long time, and I have seen many things. Your wife's ailment I believe is but temporary, brought on by her anger, and helplessness in her situation. Once she awakens from the sleep my potion puts her in, and sees you, I am certain that she will begin a complete recovery. Of course if you would rather not take the chance you can simply sail from Istanbul, and Marjallah will be drowned. She will feel no pain or fear as long as I give her the sleeping draft. You need have no remorse on that account."

"Perhaps it might be better, Conn," said Brian O'Malley. "For God's sake, man, if she's mad ye can't have children by her. It's over, Conn, and ye'd best face it."

Conn stood up slowly, and walking over to his elder brother calmly floored him with a single, powerful blow. Then leaning down he hauled Brian up to his feet again, and looking him straight in the eye said, "Aidan is my wife, Brian. I don't intend to allow her to be drowned in a sacque like an unwanted cat. For some reason I don't understand, I don't think that you've ever been in love. I don't doubt that if this had happened to your Maggie you'd have given her up for lost, and taken another wife. You would, Brian, *but I wouldn't!* Aidan is my life because she's the only woman I've ever loved, will ever love. D'ye understand me?"

"Aye," said Brian, loosing his younger brother's clenched fist from his shirtfront. Then he grinned. "Yer still a Celt for all yer English manners, Conn."

Esther Kira arose from her seat. "I can linger no longer, my lord," she said. "I am expected at the palace. May the Lord God favor your mission, and bring you safely home to your England."

"How do I thank you, Esther Kira?" asked Conn again, and his eyes were damp with his emotion.

"What payment can there be for a life, my lord?" she asked him seriously. "I know of none, and there is no value you would put upon your wife that would be great enough." Then taking the English ambassador's proffered arm she departed the room.

Having seen the elderly woman to her vehicle William Harborne returned briefly to the master's cabin. "If you would tell her majesty, Sir Robert, that all goes well here, and as we have planned. I block the French at every turn. She will be happy, I think, to hear that."

"Aye," said Robbie, "she will. My thanks, Master Harborne, for all the help you have been to us in this matter."

William Harborne shook his head. "I wish I could have helped, but your success is due to Esther Kira." He held out his hand to each of them in turn. "Godspeed to you all, and good fortune!" he said as he left them.

He was no sooner off the ship than the *Bon Adventure* prepared to set sail. It was decided that Shane O'Malley's vessel would remain behind to gather up the half-dozen crewmen from Robbie's ship who were yet ashore. Their counterparts from the O'Malley boat were put aboard the *Bon Adventure* so that it would not be shorthanded in case of an emergency. The gangway was drawn up, the heavy ropes that held the ship to the pier loosened, the anchor raised. *Bon Adventure's* sails were slowly unfurled, and the ship began to ease away from its mooring and out into the main channel of the harbor.

The sun was beginning its daily descent into the western skies, and had already begun to stain the narrow arm of the sea the molten gold that had given it its name. A light breeze caught the full sails of the ship, and swept it along the wine-dark surface of the Sea of Mamara. On the port side of the ship was Asia Minor, its hills touched with the brilliant sunset. On the starboard side the city of Istanbul, set upon its seven hills, sprawled untidily down to the sea. The Yeni Serai and its surrounding estate took up a large portion of the shoreline. Fascinated Conn looked at it. It was surrounded by a sea wall that was interspersed here and there with kiosks. He could see the lush gardens, the graceful domes, and soaring minarets of the palace and its Great Mosque that had once been the seat of Eastern Christianity. He wondered what it all looked like inside those walls.

The crew had been gathered once they had cleared the Golden Horn, and they had been told the plain and simple truth of their mission. All of them had sailed with Sir Robert Small for years, and they knew and liked both his business partner, Lady de Marisco, and her charming brother, Lord Bliss. To be able to rescue Lady Bliss from impending death was a chore their adventurous and brave English hearts relished. The substitute sacque was prepared, filled with the ship's garbage that they had not been able to dispose of because of their hasty departure. It was enough to weigh the sacque down so that it would sink.

"Vessel ahead, just off the port side," called the sailor who had been placed in the furthest part of the ship's bow to spot Avram ben Yakob.

"We're moving too fast," fretted Conn.

"Don't worry," Robbie reassured him, and then he called out, "Drag the sea anchor!" and Conn heard the splash as *Bon Adventure*'s captain was obeyed. "It will slow us down just enough so we may make the transfer easily," said Robbie.

Conn moved swiftly to the port side of the vessel where the boatswain's chair was being rigged. "I'll go over," he said.

"Nay, ye'll not," replied Robbie. "One look at all that water rushing by, and yer belly would be in revolt. We'd not only lose our chance with her ladyship, we'd lose ye as well. What the hell would I tell Skye?"

"Who then?"

"Young Michael, my cabin boy. He's strong, but light enough for the job, and he doesn't get seasick."

Conn grinned wryly, and protested, "I've done very well on this voyage."

"Aye, ye have, but I'll take no chances now, Conn. 'Tis my ship, and my decision."

A wide strap of leather was fastened about the cabin boy's waist to which was attached a heavy rope threaded through an iron loop that was embedded in the belt. Michael settled himself into the boatswain's chair, which was nothing more than a plain board fitted between two ropes. The chair was then raised up by means of a pulley, and swung out over the side of the ship. Normally the boatswain would have simply climbed onto his chair without the benefit of the leather safety belt, but as Michael was to be responsible for lifting the silken sacque from Avram ben Yakob's little boat he would need both his hands free, and should he lose his balance the result would be obvious.

With stately grace *Bon Adventure* skimmed along the silvered tops of the green waves. Avram ben Yakob could feel his heart hammering within the narrow cavity of his chest as he felt the great ship easing slowly by him. He lifted the mauve silk sacque, the muscles in his arms bowing with the weight of the stones used as ballast to sink the victim easily to the ocean floor. For a moment his tired brown eyes met the lively blue ones of a beardless boy as he transferred his burden to the lad who to his surprise hefted the sacque as if it were weightless, and was quickly whisked up the side of the ship. Avram ben Yakob saw the sacque pulled over the balustrade of the port side of the great vessel, and he could hear a cheer of victory on the wind. Then the boy was quickly lowered once more to deposit another mauve silk sacque into his little boat, and with a whish *Bon Adventure* was gone past him, and his craft rocked in its wake. Avram ben Yakob lowered his eyes, and continued rowing to his destination. It was not his business. The woman had been condemned. He had done a favor for Esther Kira, and she in turn had seen to it that his daughters would be well dowered, and that he and his Leah would be comfortable in their old age. No laws had been broken. His conscience was clear.

Ahead of the executioner's boatman the large ship sailed southwest down the Sea of Mamara toward the Dardenelles, and into the coming night. Upon *Bon Adventure*'s main deck the top of the sacque was untied, and Conn bestowed upon young Michael the gold ribbon sewn all over with pearls that had been used to enclose the silk. The sacque was then carried into the master cabin, and laid upon the bed. Gently Conn and Robbie rolled the mauve silk down to reveal an unconscious Aidan, and clasped within her arms where Nur-U-Banu had placed him, Tulip. Both men stared openmouthed at the long-haired orange-and-white cat who was gently snoring against his mistress' breasts.

"God's nightshirt!" Robbie swore. "They were going to drown her cat with her! Poor beastie!"

"Perhaps Esther Kira saw that it came with her," Conn said. "It is the sort of kindness I would expect from the old lady if she knew Aidan was fond of the animal." Gently he removed the cat from Aidan's arms, and placed it at the foot of the bed. Then he stared down at his wife. She didn't appear mad. "I wonder how long she'll sleep," he said.

"Best to leave her be until she awakes naturally," Robbie ventured. "Forcing her to consciousness could harm her."

The two men finished removing the sleeping woman from the silk sacque rolling it down until her feet were free, and the ballast stones were revealed. Then Robbie said, "I'll get rid of this. Ye stay with yer lady. I'll sleep tonight in the little cabin next door."

Conn nodded, barely hearing his friend, already settling himself into a chair by the side of the bed. Robbie made a mental note to send Michael with some food before the evening was finished not, he thought, that Conn would be hungry. He had what he wanted after all these months, and it would be enough for now. He tiptoed from the cabin. Conn heard the door latch click, but he didn't look up. All he wanted to do right now was feast his eyes upon his beloved wife. His love lost, his love found.

She looked so pale, and her breathing was shallow yet regular. She, like he, was thinner, and upon her face there were tearstains. It was his Aidan, and yet there was something about her that was exotic, and very foreign. Her eyelids were darkened with kohl, and the scent arising from her lush body was heavy with musk. Her clothing was very rich in appearance, if not a little shocking to him. He could see her slim, shapely legs through the thin silk of her long trousers; trousers whose anklebands were thick with embroidery and small sparkling gemstones. Cloth of silver and turquoise-blue silk. The colors were flattering against her fair skin.

He was glad he had not opened the sacque upon the deck for the skimpy little garment she wore on the upper half of her body left very little to the imagination. It was sleeveless, of a turquoise-blue silk that was edged in silver fringe, each piece of fringe tipped with a tiny aquamarine, and because it had no closures it revealed far more than it concealed. He could understand, he thought with a small smile, why a man would enjoy seeing his wife in such a garment especially if she was as perfect in form as was Aidan.

Reaching out he touched her glorious coppery hair. It was dressed in a fashion far different than he was used to seeing her wear it. Parted in the center it had been plaited into one long braid, the hair mixed with a silver ribbon that was sewn with pearls, and clear sea-blue aquamarines. It was quite lovely, but he longed to see her hair flowing free against her skin again.

Bending over Conn touched his wife's lips with his own, and whispered softly, "Ahh, Aidan, my love, how I have missed ye."

She stirred slightly, but she did not awaken, and at the bottom of the bed the long-haired cat stretched lazily with a small noise, and changed his position, but he, too, did not awaken.

The cabin door opened, and young Michael, Robbie's cabin boy, entered bearing a tray. With a triumphant grin he placed the tray upon the table. It contained half a chicken, some fresh bread, and a bowl of green figs. "Captain says yer lady won't waken till morning, my lord, and that ye'd best eat."

"Thank ye, lad," Conn replied. "I owe ye a great debt, ye know. Whatever ye want if it's in my power ye can have it! Name yer reward, Michael!"

"Well, my lord, I'm really a lucky fellow, I am. Ever since Sir Robert found me wandering in that alley, me head all bloody, and not remembering anything, I've had luck. Sir Robert gave me a last name. His. He taught me to read and to write, and I'm learning a trade. He says I'll be a captain someday if I continue to apply myself, and if I do, he'll give me a ship then. There's one thing, however, that I lack, and if yer lordship wouldn't think it too great a price, I would very much like to have it."

"No price is too great, lad, for what ye did this afternoon. 'Twas not easy to bring that sacque aboard *Bon Adventure* while she was moving, but ye did it! Tell me what you want."

"The only home I've got, my lord, is this ship. There's a small cottage outside Plymouth, overlooking the sea, that I know I could buy for the owner is dead, and the heirs don't need the place. It's been empty these last two years, and only needs a bit of work to make it right again. Once I've my own house, I can look for a wife to come home to in another year or so. Would that be too much to ask ye, my lord?"

"Nay, lad, 'tis a cheap price ye would have of me, and so I hope ye'll let me furnish yer house with all it will need to welcome a bride."

Young Michael smiled almost shyly at Conn. "Thank ye, my lord," he said. "I'm grateful for yer kindness." He bobbed a little bow to Lord Bliss, and was gone from the room.

Conn shook his head. *His kindness?* Without the boy's sure balance, and strong arms Aidan wouldn't be sleeping here upon this bed. Michael would have his cottage, repaired, and furnished, and a bit more into the bargain as well, thought Conn. He would deposit in Michael's name a nice sum of gold with the English Kiras. The boy would be a good match for some merchant's or well-to-do farmer's daughter. Pouring himself a goblet of Robbie's fine burgundy Conn nibbled on the chicken that had been brought to him, but he found he was suddenly too tired to eat. He drank his wine down, and drawing a coverlet over Aidan he lay down atop the bed, and was quickly asleep.

The *Bon Adventure* sailed serenely through the night on a light but steady breeze. It would take them several days before they reached the Aegean Sea, but they would be safe for they flew a pennant giving sure passage to all those who traded with Turkey. The night was lit with the glow of a waning moon, and as the sky began to turn from deep velvet black to ash gray Conn awoke, and arose from the bed. Aidan was still sleeping although she did not appear to be in as deep a sleep as she had the previous evening. He longed for, as well as feared her awakening. Was she really mad as Esther Kira had said? He heard the slight change in her breathing, and looked anxiously toward her.

Aidan was slowly rousing, but she did not open her eyes. As her brain began to function she remembered being handed the goblet of cherry sherbet which she had assumed was laced with poison, and indeed she had welcomed death. Better death than being bound to Murad for the rest of her natural days. Strange, she thought. She had not felt that way about Javid Khan, but then the prince had been the most tender and gentle of men. Death should have had no part of him for he was everything good about life.

She drew in a long, deep breath, and slowly let it out again. Where was she? Why had she been spared? Or had she? Perhaps the sherbet had just contained a sleeping potion to keep her quiet while some elegantly re-fined torture was devised prior to her execution. Murad, of course, would want to be involved in that. He occasionally enjoyed giving pain al-though at least she had been spared the worst of his nature on that ac-count. Safiye, however, had told her of how a slavegirl had once displeased him so greatly that he had personally beaten her to death. A shudder raced through her body, and Aidan opened her eyes.

A ship? Why was she in a ship's cabin? On the floor by the bed she saw a mauve silk sacque. Recalcitrant women were drowned! Had not Safiye told her that? She was going to be drowned alive! Frightened Aidan sat bolt upright, and shrieked, "*Noooooo!*"

Conn, across the room seated in the window seat staring out at their wake heard the animal-like sound that issued forth from her mouth, and leaping up he hurried across the room into her line of vision.

"Aidan! Aidan, my love!" His arms reached out to enfold her.

Terrified she scrambled back across the bed, her hand outstretched as if to fend him off. Her eyes were dull, unfocused, and filled with fear. "No!" she repeated. "No!"

"Aidan!" he persisted. "Look at me, sweeting! 'Tis Conn, yer husband. 'Tis Conn!"

Conn? What had she heard? Aidan attempted to gain control of the awful fear that was engulfing her. She forced herself to hear the voice. She forced her eyes to focus.

"Conn?" she said. "Conn! Oh, God! Is it really you? I don't understand! What has happened? Where am I?"

She seemed to be making sense, he thought. Perhaps she was not mad after all. "Yer on Robbie's vessel, *Bon Adventure*, sweeting. We're out of Istanbul bound for England. I've been seeking ye since last summer, but I only reached Istanbul several weeks ago. Yer attempt on the sultan's life yesterday made it possible for Esther Kira to help us to rescue ye. Had ye not done such a foolish thing, we would never have been able to get ye back short of storming the sultan's palace which, of course, my brothers were all for doing. I'm afraid ye've quite spoiled their fun, Aidan, my love." He tried to make his voice light.

"How did you rescue me?"

Conn quietly explained how Esther Kira had cleverly conceived the plan to rescue Aidan, and how young Michael Small had actually brought her aboard the vessel. He finished by telling her how they had opened the sacque to find not only Aidan, but her cat as well.

"Tulip? Tulip is here!" Aidan looked about the room, and then her eye lit upon the animal at the foot of the bed. "Ahh, this is Esther's doing,

God bless her!" Leaning over she reached out, and lifted the cat into her arms. The little beast's golden eyes opened, and seeing his mistress, he purred. A tear slipped down Aidan's cheek, and she said, "Javid loved him, too. He said Tulip was a perfect Tartar; unafraid, adventurous, and a great lover." She placed the cat back at the foot of the bed, and then looked up at Conn. "Javid Khan is dead, you know. His brother killed him, and destroyed everything that was his, but for me. I was not there."

"I know, sweeting," Conn said gently for he could see the pain and sorrow in her eyes. It amazed him that he could be so objective in the face of the fact that his wife had obviously cared for this prince.

"The sultan said I wasn't free," Aidan continued, *"but I was!* Javid Khan had freed me on our marriage, and when he was killed I wanted to come home to ye, Conn. They said ye wouldn't want me. They said ye had remarried another woman, and she would have yer children. They said without my papers I was not a free woman, and the sultan took me to his bed, and forced me to his will. I hated him! I wanted to kill him! *I wish I had!"*

"It's over, Aidan," he told her. "It's all over, and yer safe with me now."

"Ye haven't taken another wife?"

Conn laughed softly. "Lord, sweetheart, I never had the time to even think about it for I was far too busy chasing after ye. Besides, I don't want another wife. I have ye."

"How can ye want me now, Conn? I have known two other men. One I cared for, and in this land I was considered his lawful wife. In our land, however, I should be considered an adulteress and bigamous wife, a whore! Women taken in slavery by the infidel are supposed to resort to suicide and martyrdom rather than yield themselves willingly, yet the women I have known here desired only to live. Was I wrong in choosing life? It is a question I wish I did not have to ask myself."

"Let me answer it for ye then, Aidan. Ye were correct to choose life over death. I would not have had it any other way. I love ye, sweeting, even as I have always loved ye. I want ye, even as I have always wanted ye." Taking her into his arms he laid her back against the pillows, and kissed her passionately, his lips nibbling softly against hers, his firm mouth pressing firmly on hers. He covered her face with his kisses, and she shivered, but Conn pressed onward with his suit. He had to show her that he still wanted her, that he loved her, and he did it in the only way he knew how.

Drawing off her little sleeveless bolero he lowered his head to her beautiful, full breasts, and caressed them with his lips. His fingertips brushed over the satiny globes, relearning their contours. He gently teased at her nipples, and saw them pucker as her body began to respond to him. With surprising agility he removed the silk gauze trousers, and kissing her navel tenderly, he stopped to pull his own garments off, and then he laid himself atop her.

Taking her face in his hands he kissed her mouth again, and said, "I adore you, my lost love. *Ye must believe me, Aidan!*"

She felt his body on hers, and his hands and his lips that roved and roamed across her flesh. He said he loved her, and she wanted very much to believe him. This was Conn, her beloved Conn. Conn for whom she had mourned these many months of her captivity. This was her husband, *her true husband!* She felt him enter her with such incredible gentleness that she began to weep. Slowly he moved on her, attempting to aid her in gaining her pleasure, but she could not. It was as if her body had been frozen as cold as the snows that had been imported into the harem to cool the sherbets.

Finally Conn could contain himself no longer, and he poured his seed into her waiting womb knowing as he did that she had had no joy of their coupling, and he was deeply saddened by it. Rolling off her he drew her into his embrace, and tried to comfort her. "It's all right, sweeting, I love ye."

"Nay," she whispered, "it isn't all right, Conn, but ye must understand that I have been badly used these last few weeks. It is not something that I can put from me easily. Do not be angry with me nor impatient, I beg of ye. I am grateful that ye would want me back."

"Oh, Aidan, there was never a time when I didn't want ye back, my love! I would have come sooner, but that we were forced to remain in Algiers the winter," and Conn explained the predicament that had greeted them on their arrival in Algiers.

"I understand," she answered him, and she drew the coverlet over her naked body.

"Tell me of the cat," he said attempting to find a path that would be less painful for her. "Why is he called Tulip?"

A small smile touched her eyes. "When he awakens, and you can see his tail fully you will understand. The tip of it has the shape of a half-opened tulip bud, and its color is an orange in contrast to the rest of the tail which is creamy white. That is why he was given his name by Javid Khan."

"Can ye tell me of the prince?" he asked her curious.

She looked at him with haunted eyes. "Not yet," she said low. "Please don't make me speak of him. The wound is too fresh, Conn. I will tell ye this, though. He was a good man, and ye would have liked him."

He questioned her no more. Esther Kira had been correct. The daring that had enabled her to attack Sultan Murad with a fruit knife had been naught but a temporary madness. Aidan was sane. She was in pain from the terrors of the last few weeks of her life, but she was sane. Returned to her own world, however, she was having a difficult time coping with her own sudden feelings of guilt. At first she would allow no one else but Conn to enter the cabin where they were housed. Young Michael would bring them meals, and water; and leave them at the door.

Robert Small understood her anguish for he had spent many years of his life in trading with the Near East. The few women who managed to escape their captivity usually had a difficult time readjusting themselves to their old life; for everything they had learned in their youth in their native Christian lands told them that they committed a great wrong in surviving their shameful, carnal captivity let alone returning to their homes to take up their old lives again. Only his beloved trading partner, Skye, had come through her own captivity whole; but then Skye was a woman of enormously strong will. Still, Aidan must also be strong else she would not have survived herself, let alone attempting an attack on the sultan's life. Time, Robbie counseled Conn, was the great healer.

Time. They had enough of that, Conn thought, for it would take them eight to ten weeks to reach England. They had followed a Venetian trade route from Istanbul to Greece where they had made port in order to take on fresh water and food. Crossing the Gulf of Messenia they had slipped into a Genoese shipping lane that brought them to their second port of call in Sicily. Leaving Sicily they alternated back and forth through the Mediterranean between Venetian and Genoese routes stopping again in the Balearic Islands and at Gibraltar before entering the Atlantic for the last leg of their journey home. To avoid any run-ins with the Spanish *Bon Adventure* sailed well off her coast and across the Bay of Biscay around Brittany, and up into the English Channel. This was the longest leg of the voyage for they did not make port again between Gibraltar and London.

Aidan's uneasiness eased somewhat over the weeks to the point where she was able to finally greet Robbie, and meet Conn's three elder brothers who were, of course, anxious to see the lady whom they had spent so many months in rescuing. To Conn's surprise his usually self-confident wife was somewhat shy and reserved, but as Shane and Shamus were equally shy of this lady who had such an adventure, there was no offense taken on their part. Brian, however, blunt as always, was the one who strangely put Aidan at ease.

Enveloping his sister-in-law in a bear hug he growled at her, "Poor, little lass. Ye've been cruelly used, but we've got ye safe again. Welcome home, Aidan, and thank God for it, I say!"

Aidan burst into tears, but when Conn would scold his elder brother for his words she defended Brian O'Malley heatedly to them all. "He *really* makes me feel welcome," she said. "He makes me feel as if I have some hope of living a normal life again! Can ye not understand that?" Then she hugged Brian back. "Thank ye, my good brother," she said looking up at him. "Thank ye with all my heart!"

Brian blushed to his brothers' delight, and hoots of derision for they teased him about being softhearted over Aidan, and perhaps he was for Brian was a warrior at heart, and there was something in Aidan that spoke of her own personal strength and dignity that appealed to him. For a moment a familiar twinkle appeared in Aidan's eye, but it was quickly gone, and Conn mourned its loss even as he ached for the inner turmoil of conscience that racked his wife.

Beginning with the first morning he had attempted to resume their physical relationship as a means of proving to her his love and devotion. She had not denied him, and yet it was painfully obvious that she was not enjoying what had once been to her a joy. Finally he had found the courage to ask her to speak honestly to him on it for though he would not say it to her, making love to her had become very much like making love to a corpse.

"I love you," she said. "I never stopped loving you even though I gave up hope of ever seeing you, of being with you again. Do you understand me, Conn? I gave up hope for there was no hope. My friend, Safiye, was brought to the Yeni Serai when she was twelve years old. She was the daughter of the Venetian governor on Crete, but for women brought to the sultan there is no hope. Though my heart was, is yours, I made my peace with my situation, my *fate* as the Turks would call it. I made my peace, and I sought to make another life for myself with Javid Khan.

"He, too, was alone, and in pain for his wicked brother had murdered his two wives and his children. Like me, everything he had was gone. I have told you that he was a good man, and when we found ourselves thrown together by fate, we made peace with that fate, and we comforted each other. Between us it was good as it was between you and me.

"Esther Kira has told you what happened when Javid Khan was murdered. I cannot say that Murad is a bad man, but he is a lustful one. I cannot speak of what happened between us yet. Perhaps I shall never speak of it to you. I do not know, but I do know that whatever spark there is within my soul that caused me to respond with pleasure and with joy to you and to Javid Khan, that spark is now dormant, if indeed it even still exists.

"We have suffered in this past year, Conn. I would not cause ye further suffering, but if ye continue to seek my bed that is exactly what I shall do.

Perhaps once I am home again this will change. I need the green hills of Worcestershire, Conn. I need *Pearroc Royal!* These, I believe, will revive my soul. Can ye understand that? Can ye still love me?"

"Ye've not lost yer bluntness in our time apart," he said quietly.

"I am what I am, my lord, and there was a time when ye loved me for it," came her quick answer.

"I still love ye for it," he said smiling into her eyes, and for a brief moment she felt his warmth. He drew her into his embrace. "I don't just want half of ye back, Aidan. I want all of ye back, and so I shall wait until ye feel that ye can give me that part of yerself that is now lacking."

She laid her copper-colored head against his velvet-clad chest, and sighed softly, deeply. "Once," she said to him, "ye told me that ours was a love for all time. I believed then that I understood what that meant, but I think I am only just beginning to understand yer words, my lord husband. Understand them, and be grateful that even if I did not have full comprehension of those words, ye for all yer youth, did."

His chin touched the top of her head, and he stroked her hair with one hand. "We are only just beginning, Aidan, my love," he promised her. "Trust me as ye have always trusted me, and we will both come safely through this for the worst is over, sweetheart, and we have each other back again."

Chapter 17

〜❦〜

hey had landed in London, and Aidan and Conn had transferred from *Bon Adventure* to the large, comfortable Greenwood barge which was to take them up the Thames to Oxford. It was not the fastest way to travel, but it was the most comfortable. Aidan remembered the last time they had come this way, a far more innocent time of life for them both. The day of their arrival in England was August 19, and it was Aidan's twenty-fifth birthday, the first birthday she had ever spent with Conn.

There had been no time, of course, for him to purchase her a gift, but the barge was filled with flowers as was the room in the inn where they spent their first night home. At Oxford their large traveling coach was awaiting them, and Aidan faced the first of her retainers, but to her surprise Martin, the coachman, and his assistant, Tom, as well as the grooms merely welcomed her, she later noted to Conn, as if they had simply been on a visit to some mundane place.

"That is precisely what they do think," he informed her. "They believe that upon my release from the Tower we were sent to Skye's home in France, Belle Fleur, to cool our heels. It is the sort of thing that Bess would do."

"Then no one knows where I have really been?" There was just the faintest note of hope in her voice.

"Mag and Cluny, of course. My sister Skye and her husband, Adam, too."

Aidan nodded. She liked her sister-in-law, and she somehow thought that Skye would not condemn her for what had happened. Now if she could but make peace with herself, but that was a far harder task than any she had ever had before. She blamed herself for none of what had happened for Aidan was no fool, but what she could not erase from her memory was what she had gone through at the hands of Murad. It haunted her both waking and sleeping.

The countryside was lushly heavy with the late summer, and the fields were already being harvested of some of their crops. It had been a dry August, and the roads were dusty, but even so Aidan leaned from the coach windows as the landscape with each passing mile became more and more familiar. At last *Pearroc Royal* came into her view, and she wept unashamedly with joy for she had never thought to see her home again.

As they turned into the drive of the great estate Conn pulled his wife into the coach, and began wiping her cheeks with a damp handkerchief for her tears had mixed with the dust from the road, and her face was dirty. "Ye don't want to look like an urchin, sweeting," he said. "One of the grooms rode ahead this morning, and the whole staff will be awaiting us."

And they were. Beal and his wife, Erwina, Leoma, Rankin, Haig, Young Beal the steward, and his brother Harry the gamekeeper, and all their helpers right down to the potboy and the knife sharpener. Lined up in the order of their importance, and all smiling broadly as their master and their mistress descended their coach, they greeted them for the first time in well over a year. Aidan's eyes searched the crowd, and she found at last whom she sought. Mag, clinging to Cluny, and suddenly looking older than Aidan could ever remember her looking.

"Mag!" Aidan, smiling, and patting out at her retainers, moved through them to enfold her tiring woman into her arms. "Dearest Mag!"

"Thank God, my baby!" wept Mag. "Thank God yer safely home!"

"Now, Mag," said Aidan patiently, and she hugged her tiring woman, "France was not that far, and I promise ye that I shall not go away again!"

Mag was not so old that she did not still have her sharp wits about her, and so she hugged Aidan back, and said no more while about them the rest of the household staff smiled benignly upon their lord and their lady, happy to have them back. An estate without its master and mistress was never a whole thing.

"Lord and Lady de Marisco are awaiting ye in the house," Beal informed them when he was finally able to put in a word amid all the greetings.

Skye took one look at Aidan, and knew that there was something very wrong, but what it was would take time to ferret out. She had been in the Mid-East twice in her lifetime; the first experience being a wonderful one, the second a nightmare. She, however, had been more experienced than Aidan in matters of the flesh. She could see that Aidan was tired, and so after warmly greeting her sister-in-law, and welcoming her home, she and Adam departed.

As much as Aidan loved Skye she was relieved to see her go. She wanted to be alone, and she didn't want to have to make idle chatter. Waving her in-laws off she walked round the house to the gardens behind it, and slowly made her way along dearly familiar paths among the roses, the asters, the dainty sweet william, the many-colored gillyflowers, the baby's breath, and the Michaelmas daisies now in bloom. There were large fat yellow-and-black bumblebees drifting lazily with comfortable buzzings amidst the fragrant blossoms, and it was for a brief time as if she had never been away.

Returning to the house she walked through each room, reaching out to touch each piece of furniture, to finger the hangings, to rub her fingers over the well-remembered carvings on the chair backs. She breathed deeply the particular smell of the house; a mixture of old wood, and herbs, of Leoma's cooking, and of the flowers that filled the rooms. *Home!* She was really home!

Conn let her wander unrestrained. He knew better than most how dear *Pearroc Royal* was to his wife. *His wife.* His whole life he had roamed restlessly, never knowing exactly what it was he sought until Elizabeth Tudor had married him to Aidan. He was not a man for power. Wealth he had more than enough of, and his handsome face and quick wit had won him social acceptance with the queen and the court. Still it had not been enough. Nothing had until he had married Aidan, and discovered to his surprise that he was basically a simple man, a faithful man. With some delightfully beautiful fluff of a kitten he might not ever have discovered this surprising side of his nature; but Aidan with her sharp mind seemed to bring out the best in him. He was so very relieved to have her back, and whatever problems she had to overcome he would be there to help her for he loved her, and it was really as uncomplicated as that.

Those first few weeks passed easily enough, and Aidan seemed to be regaining her equilibrium. As the reality of her situation began to finally sink in he could see her old confidence beginning to renew itself. Although she could still not bring herself to give him her body, she was becoming more and more affectionate both in public and in private with him, and he hoped that in time all would be well between them again. Then one day all his hopes shattered when he arrived home from overseeing the last of the harvest to discover that Aidan had locked herself in their bedchamber, and refused to come out.

"She won't talk to me, my lord!" Mag sobbed.

"How long has she been in there?" he demanded of the near-hysterical tiring woman.

"She's not come out at all today, my lord. When I came to bring her

her breakfast the door was bolted, and she would not let me come in to her. Oh, what can be the matter?"

Ordering his servants to remain below Conn ascended the stairs and traversed the long hall to their bedchamber. Stopping outside the door he listened, but he could hear nothing. "Aidan?" he called to her. "Aidan, my love, what is it?" A deep silence greeted him. "Aidan, if ye do not answer me I shall have to break down the door to gain entry to the room. Ye have already frightened the servants half out of their wits for they cannot remember ever seeing ye this way. Do ye really want me to destroy a perfectly good door and lock as well as injure myself which I shall surely do?"

For a moment he thought she would not answer that plea either, but then her voice came through the door. "I want to talk to Skye."

"Very well, I shall send for her, but in the meantime will ye open the door to me?"

"No. Only to Skye."

"Very well, I shall ride to *Queen's Malvern* myself, Aidan, and fetch my sister back." Knowing she would say no more he turned, and hurried down the staircase to the Great Hall where the servants were clustered nervously. "There is naught to fear," he assured them. "Go back to yer tasks. I am riding over to fetch my sister for yer lady has requested to speak with her. It is undoubtedly some female whim that has set my wife into a sulk," and then chuckling false mirth he left the hall, leaving behind him a staff that was as much confused by his explanation as they were their lady's actions for Aidan was far too practical a woman to succumb to a fit of the sulks. At least she never had before.

Conn rode across the fields to his sister's house, and both Skye and Adam rode back with him. Adam came in reply to a look cast him by his wife for he had long since learned to read such looks. It was clear that Skye wanted him along if for no other reason than to keep Conn calm.

"She won't tell ye what's wrong?" Skye asked as they rode along. "There was no indication of anything amiss these past few days?"

"Nothing," replied Conn. "She's not felt well, but we both thought 'twas nothing but an early autumn flux. Basically she's a strong woman, but 'tis been a hard year for her."

They arrived back at *Pearroc Royal*, and leaving her husband and her brother in the Great Hall, Skye hurried up the staircase to Conn and Aidan's bedchamber. Knocking upon the door she called, "Aidan, 'tis Skye. Let me in."

"Yer alone?"

"Aye."

There was the sound of a key turning in the iron lock, and then Aidan swung the door wide. "Come in," she said ushering her sister-in-law into the chamber, and then she closed and locked the door behind Skye before turning to face her.

Looking at Aidan Skye was somewhat taken aback. She was wearing the simple silk nightrail she had obviously slept in, and her lovely copper-colored hair was loose and lank. There were deep purple shadows beneath her eyes which held a haunted look. She didn't even wait for Skye to question her, but rather looking directly at the beautiful woman she said in a dull, flat tone, "I am with child."

"But that is wonderful!" Skye answered her. "Why are you so cast down, Aidan?"

"I cannot be certain that it is Conn's child!" came the despairing cry.

Suddenly it was all clear to Skye, and she gathered Aidan into her arms saying, "Tell me about it."

The warm and sympathetic tone of her sister-in-law's voice was enough to cause Aidan to shed a few tears which acted to release some of her fear and tension. She cried softly for a moment or two against Skye's green silk shoulder, and then stopping as suddenly as she had started she pulled Skye down to sit upon the bed with her and began to speak.

"I lost Conn's child immediately after I was kidnapped, miscarrying it aboard the vessel that took me to Algiers. From that time my moon cycles have not been regular. I never knew when the link would be broken. That is why I cannot be certain whose child it is I carry. Within a relatively short period I was possessed by three men. Prince Javid Khan, the sultan, and Conn. I honestly do not know whose seed it is that now grows within my womb. How can I therefore be joyful about my state? What if it is not Conn's child?"

"If you cannot be certain, neither can Conn," said Skye. "I know my brother, and I believe that any child of yers he will consider a child of his."

"I should not mind if it were Javid Khan's child," said Aidan softly, and then she flushed embarrassed. "Ye must think me a terribly wanton creature for saying that, but in my way I cared for him, and he was a good man. I wish I could explain that to ye. Everything is so different in the East. I was considered the prince's wife for he married me in his own faith, and freed me as a wedding gift." She sighed. "How can anyone understand it?"

"I understand," said Skye quietly, "for you see, my dear Aidan, once I, too, was in a similar situation to yers. After the death of my first husband, Dom O'Flaherty, it was arranged that I wed with the man who had been my first love, Niall, Lord Burke. In those days I was already the mother of two sons, and at barely eighteen I was responsible for the entire well-being of my family. Despite the fact I had five brothers, they were all too young for the great responsibility of my father's office, and my elder sisters were not capable of it. So it was that my dying father appointed me the O'Malley of Innisfana. Conn was a little boy of three then." She smiled.

"During the period of my mourning for my father I built his ships into a respectable merchant fleet, and it was agreed that I should accompany my fleet to Algiers before my wedding. Niall, God rest him, had no love for the sea; but he came along with us. We were but several days out of Algiers when we were attacked by Barbary pirates. Our safe-conduct pennant had been blown ragged and away in a storm we encountered, and so the pirates who were out of Algiers did not know that we sailed under the protection of the man who was then the city's dey.

"In the battle that ensued I was captured, and I believed that I saw Niall Burke killed. The shock of it all took my memory from me, and when I finally regained my senses I found myself in the possession of a man called Khalid el Bey, a man known as the Great Whoremaster of Algiers. I could remember nothing of myself but my first name, Skye. He, however, called me publicly Muna el Khalid, which means Desire of Khalid, although in private he called me Skye.

"Khalid had meant to train me for his finest house of pleasure which was called the House of Felicity, but he fell in love with me instead, and I with him. He freed me when he married me as Prince Javid Khan freed ye when he married you according to the Muslim rite, I assume."

"Yes," said Aidan, and her eyes were wide with wonder at what Skye was telling her.

"We were very happy, Khalid and I," Skye continued. "Although it bothered me to a certain extent that I could not remember anything of my past but the fact that I was called Skye, I was content. It was during my first stay in Algiers that I met Robbie, who was Khalid's business partner in a trading venture that both had invested in, and it was then that I also met my good friend, Osman, the astrologer. The slavewoman who oversaw the operation of the House of Felicity, however, had been in love with Khalid for years, and she was painfully jealous when he married me. Khalid's best friend, Jamil Pasha, the kapitan commander of the Kasbah fortress, had seen me unveiled, and coveted me. Together these two plotted against us, and Jamil tricked poor Yasmin into believing that she was murdering me in my sleep, when it was really Khalid she killed. When Yasmin learned her mistake she confessed all to me, and then took her own life.

"Forewarned against the kapitan I was able to stave off the advances of Jamil Pasha for a thirty-day mourning period during which time with Robbie's aid I secretly moved Khalid's wealth from Algiers to England, and then escaped from Jamil. He was a very wicked man and my secretary's wife, Marie, sent him a plate of sweetmeats in my name just before we left. They were his favorites, and he ate them all; but Marie had added to the sweetmeats a drug which rendered Jamil impotent. It was a clever revenge."

"I wish I had been able to do that to Sultan Murad!" said Aidan with a vehemence that Skye had never believed her capable of. "God, how I hated him!" Her voice suddenly dropped, and she shivered as her eyes filled with loathing and memory. "The things he did to me, Skye! Terrible things he did to me!"

"Tell me," said Skye calmly.

"I cannot," Aidan whispered, her tone one of horror.

Skye leaned forward and took her sister-in-law's hands in hers. Her blue-green eyes were serene, yet as serious as her voice. "I returned to Algiers a second time many years after my first sojourn there, Aidan. By that time I had been married a third time to Geoffrey Southwood who had died along with our younger son, John, in an epidemic; and was now at last, my memory restored, the wife of Niall Burke. Our two children were born, but both were babies when Niall was captured, and sold into the galleys. It was there he was seen by a slave merchant who purchased him from the galleys because he knew that he could sell Niall to Princess Turkhan, a half-sister of your Sultan Murad, a lovely young widow who lived in the city of Fez in the kingdom of Morocco.

"The princess had a great taste for men, and kept a male harem of her own to the shock of all. No one, however, dared interfere with her for she was Sultan Selim's daughter; a fabulously wealthy royal Ottoman princess who gave so generously to the poor, and was so popular with the very people she cared for, yet shocking.

"When I learned where my husband was, Aidan, I sought to rescue him, but in order to reach Fez, which is a holy city, and therefore closed to foreigners and infidels, I had to be a member of a citizen of Fez's household. Osman had a nephew, Kedar, and pretending I was a slavegirl he had purchased in the bazaar he presented me to his nephew who came twice yearly to Algiers from Fez with his caravans, and always stayed with Osman.

"Kedar, my dear Aidan, was the most lustful man I have ever known. His appetite for women, for me, was insatiable. His sensuality knew no bounds. He enjoyed taking several women together, to seeing women perform acts upon each other. He invented sexual games in which all the women of his harem were required to participate. He resorted to lotions, and potions and he possessed several appalling ivory dildos fashioned exactly as he was fashioned which he used upon his women as either an instrument of pleasure, or one of torture as the mood suited him. There is nothing, Aidan, that ye can tell me that was done to ye by Sultan Murad that will shock me, but if ye are to relieve yerself of the unhappy memories ye possess, ye must face those memories bravely and squarely."

"Javid Khan," Aidan began hesitantly, "was a gentle lover. He taught me things that gave me pleasure. Things that Conn certainly never did to me."

Skye smiled. She could well imagine what Javid Khan had taught Aidan that gave her pleasure, that Conn had not done to her. Conn did not understand, having never been told, that there was really no great difference in making love to "good" women as opposed to making love to "bad" women. "I hope," she said, "that ye will tell Conn what it is that yer prince did that gave ye pleasure."

"Dare I?" Aidan was surprised by Skye's words.

"If ye do not tell him, then who will?" Skye demanded of her. "But go on with your story."

Aidan continued on with her story, her voice occasionally faltering, particularly when she described, or tried to describe the demeaning perversions that Sultan Murad had forced upon her. At that point she could go no further, and her eyes filled with tears.

Skye closed her eyes for a moment as her own dark memories assailed her. "It's all right, Aidan," she said comfortingly. "I know what it is ye are trying to say, and ye don't have to speak the words. What the sultan did to you is a particular unkind perversion favored by men who think by doing such a thing they prove their superiority over women."

"I hated it," Aidan said fiercely. "I felt so helpless, but that was only the beginning. Sometimes he liked having other women with us, and then there were the little silver balls with which he enjoyed torturing me."

Here was something new, thought Skye. She had never heard of this particular perversion. "Tell me about them," she said frankly curious, and Aidan obliged her. "God's nightshirt!" Lady de Marisco swore softly when Aidan had finished. "I thought I knew all, but I never encountered your little silver balls, Aidan."

"They were a gift to the sultan from the Emperor of China, I was told," replied Aidan. "Oh, Skye! It was so terrible! The sultan was never satisfied. There were nights when he kept me with him the whole night, and still had three or four others brought to him so he might use them while I watched. God, how I hated him, and how I pray that the child I carry is not his!"

"The child ye carry is yers, Aidan. Never stop thinking that! It is *yer* child who will bear *yer* name even as Conn bears yer name. Ye must tell my brother of yer honest fears. He will understand."

"How can he?" Aidan cried. "How can he be so accepting of such shame? Oh, we can pretend to the world that we have simply been in France these past months, waiting out a temporary exile meted out to Conn by the queen, but Skye, he and I know the truth of the matter. I have spent over a year away from my husband, enslaved in a carnal bondage by two other men! We cannot escape it, and now I am with child! A child whose paternal parentage I cannot be certain of, may God have mercy upon me! How do I wipe the shame of my child's possible bastardy from it, poor innocent?"

"Like ye, Aidan, I once had a Muslim husband. No child of ours would have been accepted in this society of ours, and yet my eldest daughter, Willow, is most respectable, is she not?"

"Willow is the daughter of Khalid el Bey?" Aidan was startled by Skye's admission.

"Aye," said Skye quietly, "and that secret I must insist ye keep to yerself, Aidan. Even Willow does not know that her papa was the Great Whoremaster of Algiers. For her peace of mind I gave her Khalid's European identity, with certain alterations, and both she and the world have been content with my explanations. Willow was born here in England, and despite an Irish mother and a Spanish father turned Algerian dey, she is the most English of all my children." Skye laughed. "Strangely it suits her though for the life of me I do not understand why." She gave Aidan's hands a squeeze. "Unless yer child is born looking exactly like its father, Aidan, there is simply no way for ye to know which of the three men involved has fathered it. Do not reject yer baby because ye fear Murad is its father. The child is not responsible for its parentage. As for Conn, he is, I think ye will agree, a kind man. He will understand that both ye and the child are innocent victims of circumstance, and besides there really is a very good chance that he is the bairn's father."

"Do ye really think so?" Aidan looked hopefully at Skye.

"Aye," Skye said, and seeing the look of relief upon Aidan's face she was glad she had answered in the affirmative for the truth of the matter was that she really didn't know herself what the odds were that her brother had fathered this child upon his wife.

"I've been so frightened," said Aidan. "It was only a few days ago that it dawned upon me that I might be with child. I haven't felt particularly well these last few mornings, and my nipples were suddenly sore. When I realized I was enceinte, and as quickly realized that I couldn't be certain of the baby's father, I became terrified."

"Understandable," said Skye dryly, "but I really think ye must speak with Conn now. Dear Lord, Aidan, I have never seen a man so in love with a woman as my brother is with ye. Ye have quite tamed the rogue. He will be simply delighted with yer news, and I will wager it never crosses his mind that he might not be the father of yer child."

"But I must still tell him," said Aidan. "I would rather die myself than hurt Conn, but if this child is a son, and not his, it is not fair to force it upon my husband as his heir. Conn must know the truth of the matter, and make the decision as to whether he wishes to acknowledge this baby as his own. If he does not, then I will go away, and bear it, and put it out with a decent family."

"He will reject neither ye, nor the child," said Skye with certainty. She knew her brother, and he was a softhearted man.

"Will ye fetch him in to me?" asked Aidan.

Skye nodded, and leaving the room hurried downstairs to find her brother, and bring him back to his wife. Aidan ran to the chest, and lifting out a fresh nightrail of creamy silk with soft pink ribbons, she replaced the wrinkled garment she was wearing with it. Then taking up her boar's-bristle brush she ran it vigorously through her tangled hair until it was smooth, and soft curls framed her serious face. She could hear Conn's familiar footstep upon the stairs, and grabbing for her scent bottle she dabbed her lavender water behind her ears, at her wrists, and in the hollow of her throat. She had only replaced the bottle down when the door opened, and whirling she turned to face her husband.

Conn stood awkwardly, unsure of whether he should take her in his arms or not, and Aidan was forced to smile slightly as the truth of Skye's words penetrated her brain. He really did love her, and that knowledge gave her the courage she needed to speak openly with him.

"I'm going to have a baby," she said quietly, and then waited to see what effect those six simple words would have upon him.

His handsome face lit with pleasure, but then it grew grave. "Are ye unhappy about it, sweeting? Is that why ye have been so out of sorts today?"

She had the incredible urge to giggle. *Out of sorts?* God's nightshirt! What understatement! Then she sobered. "I could never be unhappy about having yer baby, my darling husband. Ye cannot know how I regret the loss of our first child, a child barely conceived before it vanished, and yet thank God I did not have to bear that babe in slavery, Conn! Nay, my love, I am not sad about having yer child, it is just that I cannot be certain if it is yer child." She went on to explain to him her uncertainty, finishing by saying to him, "Ye do not have to accept this child, Conn. I can go away when my condition becomes obvious, we will make some reasonable excuse, and then the child can be put out to nurse as are other wealthy bastards."

"Is that what ye want, Aidan?" What did *he* want? he wondered. The reality of her words was beginning to penetrate his brain. *I cannot be certain if it is yer child*, she had said. If she could not be certain, could he? Was he really willing to raise the son of another man? Accept him as his heir? God help him! He loved her with all of his heart, but he wasn't sure.

"Nay, but I will not force this baby upon ye, Conn. What if it is a son? I cannot press another man's son upon ye as yer heir."

"Ye have said yerself, Aidan, that ye cannot be certain that this child is mine, but it could very well be, and frankly, my darling, I prefer to believe that it is. We will have no more nonsense about yer going away, or about farming out the child, Aidan. This child is our child. It will be born here at *Pearroc Royal* as it should be, and I will love it, and spoil it probably even more than ye will." Brave words, Conn, me lad, he thought, but then seeing the open relief in her eyes he forced his lips into a small, reassuring smile that broadened as she scolded him in her no-nonsense fashion.

"I will not have our children spoilt, Conn," she said sternly. "They must be strong in both mind and body, and learn to accept the responsibilities of their station in life."

"I intend to spoil them," he said, "even as I spoil ye," and then he closed the gap between them, and pulling her into his arms kissed her passionately, rendering her slightly dizzy and giddy with pleasure and happiness. "I love ye, Aidan. I shall always love ye, and I will keep saying it over and over again until ye are completely reassured, my darling. Now unless ye are feeling peaked, I want ye to dress yerself, and come downstairs to supper to celebrate with me the impending birth of our first child who will be born . . ." He stopped, and cocked his dark head to one side. "When?"

Aidan laughed for the first time in several days, and the sound was a happy one. "Late winter," she said. "Perhaps early March." She smiled shyly at him. "There is still time, my lord, for us to love each other," and she blushed softly.

His arms tightened about her, and he groaned with longing against her ear. "Aidan, my darling wife, are ye certain?"

She looked up at him, and he was startled to see a new light shining in her silvery-gray eyes. "Dearest Conn, in coming to terms with this child, I have realized that to continue to deny us the pleasure of each other because of the cruelty and perversion of one man is very foolish.

" 'Tis not ye, my husband who hurt me, and yet I have made ye suffer for what the sultan did to me.

"It will still not be easy for me, Conn, for I seem to no longer have any feelings, I don't understand it at all. It is as if the passion has frozen in my veins, but perhaps in time yer loving will thaw that passion again. I pray so, Conn for I love ye."

He held her close against his chest, breathing in the subtle perfume of her, feeling more certain now than he had in weeks that she was not mad. She was only his poor hurt Aidan, and it was up to him as her husband to make her whole again. He stroked her soft, thick hair gently for a long minute, and then he said, "Get dressed, and come to supper, my love. May I help ye?"

Looking up at him he saw genuine amusement in her eyes, and her mouth turned up in a smile as she said, "I'd rather have ye help me than dear, old Mag who will fuss and fret over me until I am ready to shriek; but can ye help me without being playful, Conn?" Stepping back from him she reached down and grasping the hem of her gown she pulled it over her head, and flung it aside. "Well?" she demanded.

Why was it, he thought, that each time he saw her she was more beautiful in form? He wanted to tell her to hell with their supper, and tumble her back into their bed to kiss and caress her to his heart's content. He wanted to call Mag, and send her down to the Great Hall to tell his sister, and his brother-in-law to go home!

"Well?" Aidan repeated.

With a sigh he opened the chest holding her petticoats, and chemises, and pulling out the necessary garments began to help her to dress. "Never let it be said," he chuckled as he regained his sense of humor, "that I am a man lacking in self-discipline, madame. 'Tis a great sacrifice I make in the name of propriety."

Aidan laughed. "Ye could tell Skye and Adam to go home," she teased him, "but 'twould really not be fair since it was I who took them from their own dinner table." She pulled on a pair of lightweight knitted silk stockings, deliberately giving him a fine view of her long and shapely legs. Handing him her silk garters she thrust out a limb.

Conn slowly slid the first garter up his wife's leg to her thigh, tying it firmly, but not too tightly there, and then mischievously pressing a warm kiss upon the soft flesh of the inside of that thigh. Hearing the surprised breath hiss through her lips he smiled, his head lowered as he diligently affixed the second garter to her other leg, so she could not see that smile. He saluted the second thigh as he had the first.

"Devil," she murmured, but there was no hint of rebuke in her voice. Then she moved away to choose a gown of warm cinnamon-colored silk which he helped her to fasten up. The dress had creamy lace set provocatively into the neckline, and more lace at the sleeves which hung over her hands just past the wrists.

Conn slipped his arm about her still-slender waist, and lowering his head pressed several ardent kisses upon the warm, scented flesh on the side of her throat. "I shall enjoy undressing ye far more, Aidan, than I have enjoyed dressing ye."

To her surprise she felt her mouth turning up in a smile at his words. "Yer a bold man," she scolded him. "Go, and tell yer sister that I shall be down shortly. I can see that yer easily tempted, my lord, and I would not have ye impugn the hospitality of our house."

With a grin he released her, and left her to fix her lovely hair, and choose her jewelry. Seeing him coming into the Great Hall the ghost of that grin still upon his face, Skye breathed a sigh of relief.

"Aidan has spoken to ye?" she asked him, wondering if her sister-in-law had told him all.

"Aye," he said, and then reaching Skye and Adam he lowered his voice so the bustling servants busy setting the table for the meal could not hear him, "but I am certain that the child is mine. Whatever has happened is not her fault, and what the hell else can I do? I love Aidan, and neither do I want her unhappy nor parted from me again." Skye felt her heart swell with a huge rush of love for her youngest brother, and her eyes misty she hugged him hard.

"What's that for?" he demanded.

"For being a real man, and the kind of brother that any sister would be proud to call her own, Conn," she answered him.

"I'm no saint," he reminded her. "I'm afraid, Skye. Afraid that it isn't my son. Afraid that it will be born with the stamp of another man upon its face, but what can I do? It might be my child, and I'll not have Aidan saddened any longer over something that was not her fault!"

Adam de Marisco nodded. "Yer wise. Aidan has suffered enough as it is. Poor lass. Only two years ago she was just come to court, the queen's little country mouse. What an innocent she was! Ah, well, Conn, 'tis all over now. Cavan FitzGerald is long gone, and thanks to God's luck ye've got yer wife back again."

"I'd like to get my hands upon the damned bastard," said Conn angrily.

"He deserves to be dead for what he did. What kind of a man would sell his own flesh and blood into slavery?"

"There might be a way," said Adam slowly. " 'Tis been confirmed that he was working with the Spanish. That ex-agent of Spain's, Antonio de Guaras, who has been imprisoned in the Tower since '77, was found to have been passing messages back and forth in the leathern bottles of malmsey wine that were regularly shipped in to the Tower governor. There was always one empty in the incoming shipment that one of the guards, a man with popish leanings, extracted and brought to de Guaras. It was even simpler to send out the messages in the empty bottles. De Guaras had worked out a cipher, but it was fairly simple for Walsingham's agents to break his code. That was how Cecil was so certain that ye were innocent.

"It seems that Antonio de Guaras' brother Miguel was the one involved with Cavan FitzGerald. The plot was to destroy the O'Malleys of Innisfana's credibility with the queen because not only have her brothers been wreaking havoc up and down the Spanish Main, but Skye and Robbie's trading company has been plucking some fat plums from the Spanish not only in the Levant, but in the East Indies as well. The Spanish and the Portuguese, of course, consider the East Indies their particular property. The plot had the heavy hand of Ambassador de Mendoza about it. God help the man for he lacks subtlety among other attributes. He is even worse than de Spes although I must say that his manners are a trifle better.

"Cecil and Walsingham learned from de Guaras' correspondence that Cavan FitzGerald fled with brother Miguel to Spain where the king was to reward him with his own land, and a wife. The monies that Cavan gained from Aidan's sale were to have financed our Master FitzGerald's new venture in Spain."

"Then he's in Spain," said Conn thoughtfully.

"Aye," said Adam.

"Where?"

"We don't know yet, but we could have our agents find out. Are ye interested?"

Conn nodded. "I want the bastard dead," he said grimly. "It is his fault Aidan suffered as she did. It is his fault that neither my wife nor I will ever know for certain if our eldest child is mine. Aye, I want the bastard dead! He's a man of no principles, and I see no reason for mercy in his case. He showed none to Aidan or to me. He would have seen me executed for a crime I didn't commit, and then he would have married my wife. When he found he couldn't do that, he dealt with Aidan in a ruthless and cruel fashion. Nay, I'll feel no regrets in destroying him. My only sorrow is that I can't do it myself."

"If ye had the opportunity," said Aidan coming to his side, "I should like the same opportunity. I think I could easily kill Cousin Cavan with my bare hands." She paused a moment as if in thought, and then she said to them, "My grandfather might know where Cavan is. If I were to write him, and if he were in contact with Cavan, how unnerving it would be for that bastard to learn that I am home again. It might bring him out of hiding. Of course we will not tell my grandfather the truth of my adventures, but I burn for vengeance more than even ye, my darling Conn. No matter how much ye may love me, ye cannot know what Cavan's actions really cost me. *How much he has cost us.*"

Conn looked at his wife thoughtfully. "One letter could do no harm," he said, "and there would be no danger to ye, my love. Cavan could not destroy our love for one another, but he has cost us time, and a child."

"Yet," said Skye wisely, "how much stronger is yer love for all yer problems. Do not waste yer time in futile hatred, my dears. Cavan FitzGerald will be punished in the end. It is preached that proper vengeance belongs to God."

"In this one instance," replied Aidan, "I could wish that God would allow me the vengeance."

"Be careful," teased Adam, "lest ye get yer wish. Fate can sometimes play us tricks. I do not think ye would want a man's death on yer conscience."

"Perhaps not," agreed Aidan, and then she smiled. "Let us speak no more of Cavan FitzGerald. It makes me unhappy, and I would not be unhappy now, Adam. Skye and Conn already know, but ye do not, dear brother. I am to have a baby! Is that not happy news?"

Adam de Marisco's deep blue eyes grew warm with approval. "A baby, is it?" he said. "Aye, Aidan lass, 'tis indeed happy news! Velvet and Dierdre will both be delighted to learn of their new cousin." Walking over to the high board where there was a decanter of wine, and some goblets, he poured the fragrant Archambault burgundy into four goblets, and passed them to the others. Then raising his hand he said, "A toast to the next generation of St. Michaels! Long life! Health, and good fortune to not only this child, but to all yer children!"

Conn slipped an arm about his wife, and looking down into her upturned face echoed a hearty, *"Amen!"*

Chapter 18

❦

The sky was a peculiar and flat gray-white in color. A misty, steady rain was falling, and there was a stiff breeze blowing off the sea which pushed the coastal freighter briskly along into the mouth of the River Shannon. Lifting his face to the sky Cavan FitzGerald said a rare prayer, and thanked God that he was home in Ireland again.

He had been enormously fortunate to have gotten passage upon the lumbering derelict which carried salted fish and hides to Spain, returning regularly with cargoes of wine filling its hold. Finding the vessel Cavan had paid his passage, and accepted the disgusting, vermin-ridden upper berth offered him in a cabin housing five other male passengers. He had not complained even when night after night they had blown evil-smelling farts and snored out their bad breath until the cabin was almost uninhabitable. He had paid for his water barrel in advance, and brought his own blankets and rations as had been expected of him. He did not so-cialize any more than was necessary, and it was quite unlikely that the captain of the *Mary Margaret* would even remember him, or be able to distinguish him from any other of the travelers who were forced to seek passage aboard his ship.

The vessel nosed its way up the river some miles, finally dropping an-chor opposite the river fortress of a once-powerful Irish earl which now belonged to an Englishman. Part of the cargo would be unloaded into the new lord's wine cellars, and Cavan FitzGerald went ashore with the first boat. From there it was but a short walk to a nearby village where he was able to purchase a somewhat bony nag to take him to his destination.

He wondered if old Rogan FitzGerald was still alive, or if his damned cousins had at last inherited. No, the old man was still alive. He could feel it in his bones. He was alive, and sitting dead center in the midst of it all just like a spider in his web. His eldest son, and heir, Eamon, would still be waiting for his inheritance if Cavan knew his uncle. And if he knew Rogan he knew, too, that he, Cavan, would have a great deal of explaining to do; but he suspected that he would be able to talk his way out of his predicament for he had ever been his uncle's favorite. He was more like Rogan FitzGerald than any of his sons.

He shivered as a blast of cold wind blew over him, and he pulled his cape tighter about him, kicking his horse into a faster pace. The time he had spent in Spain had taken the edge off his native-born hardiness, and for the first time in his life he felt the damp chill. If only Ireland could have some of Spain's sunshine. *Spain*. How he had hated the place! He had never even gotten to meet King Philip. His so-called reward had been handed over to him by some minor court functionary. A barren, broken-down estate on the hot and dusty plains of that cursed country that had failed in the first place by virtue of its very location. St. Patrick himself could not have made that worthless land given him fertile unless he had been able to place a river about it. It was no reward at all, and worse had been his marriage.

The king had generously saddled him with not an heiress of a respectable family, but the bastard daughter of one of his friends, Manuela María Gómez-Rivera. Short and plump and dark Manuela who was pious to a fault; and rarely if ever bathed. Making love to her had been like making love to a farmyard. Unable to escape this fate he had been quickly wed to Manuela by the king's own confessor who had afterward lectured the blushing bride and her new husband on their Christian duty which was to produce children.

Fortunately Manuela did not enjoy that particular duty of marriage, and so he was able to bed her twice a week and then be left free to dally with the many attractive peasant girls in the village that belonged to the estate. He dallied until his wife found out where he was spending his nights, and scolded him loudly in a shrieking voice. Still not satisfied she had complained to the village priest who had taken him sternly to task regarding his immorality, and his duty to his good and faithful wife.

Cavan, however, had had his subtle revenge. "But, padre," he said sadly, "Doña Manuela will not grant me my spouse's rights more than once or twice a week. How can I do my duty by her, and by the church under those circumstances? It is a man's duty to procreate according to God's law. The church expressly forbids the spilling of a man's seed upon the ground, and did I not copulate with the girls in the village I should break God's law because my wife refuses me." He bowed his head with apparent shame. "May the Blessed Mother forgive me, padre, but I am weak where the flesh is concerned, and were my wife willing, I should only cleave to her."

The priest nodded sagely. It was not unusual for a bride to be hesitant, particularly if she were a pious woman as was Doña Manuela. "My son," he said. "God has made man master over woman and the other beasts of the earth. It is your wife's duty to obey you in all things, and if she does not, then it is your duty to apply the rod of chastisement to her until she admits her faults, and abides by your wishes. Have you done this?"

"Alas," said Cavan who had never considered the possibility of beating his wife for he did not care enough, "I am a softhearted man, padre."

"A soft heart is a good thing, my son, but in your wife's case you do her no kindness by appearing to condone her willful behavior. She must be made to obey!" He put an arm about Cavan. "You Irish are a race of poets, and I know that your heart is good, my son, but Doña Manuela must not be allowed to wear the breeches in your family. It is a most unseemly thing when a woman takes upon herself the duties of a man. Look to England's bastard queen. Surely you cannot admire her manly behavior? Your wife must be beaten until she admits her faults, and promises never to disobey you again."

Cavan had gone back to his house, and with the church's blessing he had beaten Manuela until her screams for mercy rang throughout the whole village. Then he had raped her, and went off to the taverna to drink the evening away. No one thought the worse of him. Indeed he was lauded by his peasants for setting a fine example for Doña Manuela's behavior had only recently begun to be copied by some of the bolder women of the village.

From that time on Cavan FitzGerald had made his wife's life a hell, beating her on the least pretext, and the priest and the villagers had nodded and smiled their approval for a woman was supposed to be a docile and obedient creature. One day, however, Manuela in a frenzy of desperation had threatened to go to her father, the king's friend, with her complaints, and so Cavan FitzGerald had coolly killed his wife by strangling her, and buried her by himself beneath the dark of the moon, in a shallow grave, at the end of the house's parched and tangled garden. He was tired of her, and he was tired of Spain.

He explained Manuela's absence by claiming that his wife had run away, and his servants who had often heard the desperate Manuela threaten such action confirmed their master's story. Now, Cavan told the irate priest, he must go after his wayward wife, and bring her home. The priest had, of course, agreed, and Cavan FitzGerald had ridden off from the hot and dusty plain never to return again; heading for the coast to find a ship to return him to Ireland where the Spanish authorities would be unlikely to follow him should Manuela's body be discovered.

Wisely he left what remained of the gold he had received by selling his cousin Aidan into slavery, with a goldsmith who had a cousin in Dublin. His small wealth would be transferred to Ireland, and no one the wiser. Cavan gave a grimace of annoyance. Even there he had not profited by Aidan's sale, but after the Dey of Algiers had taken his percentage along with Rashid al Mansur, the Spanish king, and Miguel de Guaras, there was precious little left. What there was, however, would remain in Dublin, his secret, his hoard against the day his cousin Eamon came into his inheritance, and possibly removed him from his stewardship. That was if his uncle had not already replaced him.

The landmarks became more and more familiar as the day went on, and finally toward evening the tower keep of Rogan FitzGerald came into view. He pushed his tired mount onward, and as a stain of peach and yellow on the gray horizon to the west announced the sunset, Cavan FitzGerald came home. Dismounting in the stableyard he gave his horse into the keeping of a dirty-faced urchin who gaped at him as if he were back from the dead. With a surprisingly gentle gesture he ruffled the lad's head, and grinned down at him before turning to enter the keep. With almost eager steps he climbed to the Great Hall, and entered it, his eyes seeking out his uncle, and to his relief finding him, hale and hearty, a tankard in his hand.

"By God, look what the storm has blown in!" came the sneering voice of his cousin, Eamon.

Having learned long ago to give better than he got, he snarled back, "What, Eamon, no welcome home for yer cousin?"

"I thought ye'd gone back to hell from whence ye sprang, *cousin*," was the mocking reply.

"Where the hell *have* ye been?" demanded Rogan FitzGerald, glaring down from the high board. "Come closer, Cavan! I want to see yer face when ye feed me the pack of lies yer about to feed me. I know that ye and that Spanish weasel failed in yer mission for the O'Malleys of Innisfana still thrive, and good for them, say I! Still it would have been nice to have gotten our hands on my granddaughter's wealth for Ireland's coming battle with the English. My granddaughter writes me that she's expecting a baby soon. She writes me of her happiness with her husband even as my Bevin did long years ago."

"Ye've had letters from Aidan?" Cavan was beginning to feel as if he had entered a bedlam. "*When?*"

"Just last week. She and her husband were in France for almost a year, but they're back home again in England."

"She wrote in her own hand? Yer certain?"

"Of course I'm certain," snapped the old man. "I've not gone gaga yet, my lad, and I'll be a long time dead before I do!" Rogan FitzGerald's eyes narrowed with speculation. "So," he said, and there was a particularly vicious tone to his voice, "so ye've come crawling back to Ballycoille, have ye, nephew? Yer Spanish friends don't reward stupidity, do they? God knows 'twas a simple enough plan to bring down the O'Malleys, but ye couldn't do it, could ye, Cavan?

"Ye played in fast company, my lad, and ye've got nothing to show for it, have ye? Maybe now ye'll stay here where ye belong instead of trying to ape yer betters. Nothing will change the fact of yer birth." He peered down at Cavan. "I suppose ye'll be wanting yer place back? Well, yer a lucky bastard, nephew, for ye can have it! Eamon's lad has no talent for it, the young fool, and so it's yers for life, and yer sons after ye if ye'll ever settle down and have some, but ye'd best behave yerself, Cavan. Remember that ye owe me for yer very existence, and when I'm gone 'tis Eamon ye'll owe, if he'll put up with ye as I have, but then I've a soft place in me heart for ye, my lad, haven't I?"

Cavan FitzGerald nodded, stunned, and even somewhat grateful to have been so easily accepted back into the fold of his family once again. The old man must be growing soft in his dotage. Automatically he sat down in his old place, and a serving wench brought him a trencher filled with mutton, and bread, and winter vegetables. A tankard of ale was placed by his hand.

Aidan in England? How was it possible? He needed to know more, but it would take him time, and besides he had his money put aside at the goldsmith's in Dublin. He suffered no loss. Still there was Conn. Alive he might demand revenge, but then if he and Aidan were giving out to Rogan that they had been away in France, perhaps he would be safe because they would not want Aidan's sojourn in Algiers made public. Perhaps he might even benefit from that knowledge. Perhaps Lord Bliss would be willing to pay him to keep that knowledge to himself lest the paternity of his child be in doubt. It was an interesting thought, Cavan considered, but he needed to know more.

When the rest of the family had gone to bed he sat with his uncle as had always been his habit. The old man slept but three or four hours a night, and seemed to need no more rest than that. They had come down from the high board which was now cleared, and they sat together before the roaring fire, their tankards of ale in their hands.

" 'Tis good to have ye home again," muttered Rogan.

Cavan chuckled. "Yer children bore ye, uncle, admit it. There isn't one that's really like ye for yer an old rogue."

Rogan chuckled back. "Aye," he admitted, "I am, and ye, my bastard nephew are more like me than any of my own get." His eyes narrowed. "Tell me now where ye've been. On the run I've not a doubt."

Cavan debated a moment, and then he told his uncle the truth, making only slight modifications in the tale. His treatment of Rogan's granddaughter was to have brought Ireland a goodly fortune had not the damned Spanish and Arabs taken it all. Then they gave him that godforsaken estate, and Manuela, poor girl, who died in childbed, and so he had come home. He had intended to come eventually, but he was still so ashamed that his mismanagement had cost them Aidan's wealth.

Rogan nodded. "Well," he said philosophically, "at least yer safe home, lad, and glad I am to see ye. The stewardship of my lands belongs to yer family from now on. Let's find ye a nice lass, and settle ye down. 'Tis past time ye had yer own children."

Cavan took a deep breath, and then he said, "There might still be a way for us to obtain Aidan St. Michael's wealth for Ireland, uncle."

"How?" The word was sharp, and precise.

"I have a plan, uncle, and if ye don't mind killing off an O'Malley or two, we can profit quite handsomely."

"Go on then," replied Rogan nodding at his nephew.

"We must bring Aidan to Ireland, uncle. She must come of her own free will."

"And how do ye think yer going to manage that, my lad? My granddaughter is English-born, and English-bred."

"There must be something here in Ireland that she wants more than anything else in the world, uncle."

"And that would be?"

"Her child," came the devastating reply.

"Jesu, yer a bad one, Cavan FitzGerald!" swore the old man, "but what's even better, yer smart. I said ye were like yer mother, but by Jesu, yer not! Ye'd hold her bairn for ransom then?"

"I'd marry her, uncle."

"What? The lass is already wed. Has yer stay in the hot Spanish sun addled yer wits?"

"Aidan St. Michael was married by the English queen's own chaplain, and yet she was baptized, and raised in the Holy Mother Church. Therefore her marriage is no true marriage here in Ireland, or for that matter anywhere else but England, and a few of the German states. I, however, dear uncle, would marry her in the faith of her birth, the only true faith. Even the O'Malleys of Innisfana cannot deny the truth of that, and so when Master Conn O'Malley comes calling he will be alone, and I will kill him. Then there will be no doubt as to whose wife Aidan St. Michael really is, dear uncle. As my wife her wealth becomes mine. Simple, is it not?"

Rogan FitzGerald was openmouthed with astonishment. "By God, nephew, yer a bloody genius! 'Tis a perfect plan, and 'tis foolproof besides! I wish ye'd thought of it in the first place, and we could have dispensed with the damned Spanish. We've but to wait until she's been brought to childbed, and recovered."

"Did she write ye when the child was due?"

"Sometime in the late winter, or the early spring," came the reply.

"So come the summer, when the seas are smooth for travel, I'll go to England," said Cavan, "and bring ye back yer great-grandchild for a visit, uncle. I've not a doubt its mother will be right behind me," and he laughed. "Have ye written back to Aidan?"

"Nay."

"Then fetch the priest, and do so. Show our dear little Aidan how concerned ye are for her, and how happy ye are too."

Rogan FitzGerald sent for his second son, Barra, named after his brother, and like his brother, a priest. Rogan had given two other children to the church besides Barra. His second youngest son, Fearghal, was a monk; and his oldest daughter, Sorcha, was a cloistered nun. Of his three other living children, his sons, Ruisart, Dalach, and Carra, they had had the good instinct to find wives with small fortunes, and simple natures who were happy to marry with one of the handsome FitzGerald sons. All, however, including the two churchmen, were hard, sharp, and greedy men although they had not the subtle cleverness of their cousin, Cavan.

Informed of the plan to bring Aidan St. Michael to Ireland, Father Barra FitzGerald had said in a pious voice, "The church could hardly disagree with yer plans to make Aidan St. Michael an honest woman, cousin Cavan. Never fear for I shall marry ye myself. The banns will be posted and read even before she arrives so there will be no need for delay." Then he smiled coldly. "The church will expect a generous stipend for its cooperation, cousin."

"Ye'll have it," came the equally cold reply.

"Not too great a stipend," put in old Rogan FitzGerald. "Remember that my granddaughter's wealth is for Ireland. It is Aidan's gold that will help us to buy arms, and mercenaries to fight the English."

"Of course, uncle," soothed Cavan. "Of course."

So Barra FitzGerald wrote to his English niece on his father's behalf, and Aidan reading the letter was somewhat astounded by this sudden interest in her welfare shown by her mother's family who for years had ignored her very existence. True she had written to her grandfather telling him of her return to England, and her expected child, but she had only done so at the instigation of Conn and his family who hoped to smoke out the whereabouts of Cavan FitzGerald. She hadn't really expected to receive such a solicitous reply. Conn was suspicious for their past dealings with the FitzGeralds had made him wary of them. No mention, however, was made of Cavan's return to Ireland, and the agents of the O'Malley family searching for him in Spain had come to a dead end when reaching the village belonging to Cavan's holding, they learned that he was gone in search of his wayward wife, and neither of them had come back yet.

"I'm not surprised that she ran away from him," said Aidan. "Cavan FitzGerald was not, after all, a particularly nice fellow. She must be rich if he's chasing after her, or possibly," she continued with a small attempt at dark humor, "she is salable in the slave markets of Algiers."

"If she was smart enough to run from FitzGerald," remarked Conn, "she will no doubt be smart enough not to be caught by him again."

"Don't speak of my bastard cousin any longer, Conn. I don't want to think of him. Not ever! Particularly not today on our second wedding anniversary. Thanks to Cavan we did not get to celebrate our first anniversary, and I will not have him intruding now on such a happy occasion!"

They were comfortably ensconced in their bed on this cold and bright February morning, and now Conn leaned over, and caressed his wife's swollen belly. "Yer wish, madame, is absolutely my command. How can I dispute the mother of my son?"

"Daughter," she corrected him. "I know it is a daughter I carry, my lord, and ye cannot argue with me otherwise."

He chuckled. "How can ye be so certain?"

"I don't know," she replied, "but I am. I am absolutely positive that we will soon be the parents of a daughter."

"What shall we call our daughter, madame?" His lips found hers in a quick kiss. "Ummm," he said, "as always, yer delicious, my darling."

Aidan smiled. She was feeling more content and happy than she had felt in months. For a while until her body had become too bulky they had resumed their marital relationship, but as much as she loved him, that body refused to cooperate with her heart, and she continued to feel nothing of the sweet, hot passion that she had once felt with him, and with Javid Khan. It saddened her for she felt that she somehow was cheating him as well as she cheated herself; but Conn had brushed those concerns aside.

"Once the child is born," he promised her, "it will be again with us as it once was, Aidan, my love."

A small tear had slipped down her cheek, and she had asked him,

"How can ye be so certain, Conn? I am not," but he had dismissed her fears with soft words, gentle kisses, and tender caresses.

"And what do ye plan to call our daughter?" he repeated, bringing her back to the present.

"There is a Latin name, Valentinus, which comes from the verb, *valere*, meaning to be strong. I have learned that to survive in this world, Conn, a woman must be strong. I would therefore name our daughter, Valentina, the feminine of Valentinus. Perhaps the name will bring her luck."

"She is already lucky in having ye for her mother," said Conn gallantly, "and me for her father," he finished.

Aidan laughed, then growing serious caressed his cheek saying, "What a good man ye are, Conn."

He flushed. "Madame, what would all my fine friends at court think if they could hear ye praising me with such tender words? My reputation would be in tatters."

"Yer reputation," she teased him, "was in tatters years ago else the queen would not have wed ye to me!"

He began to tickle her in retaliation for her remark, and Aidan not to be bullied tickled him back until they both collapsed into gales of laughter, wheezing and gasping until the tears ran down their faces. Finally he regained control of himself, and leaning over her outstretched body he bent down to kiss her. His green eyes warm with the deep love he felt for her.

"Ohhh, I am so happy," Aidan declared with a deep sigh. "Is it wrong, Conn, to be so happy?"

"Nay, sweeting, it is never wrong to be happy."

"I love ye," she said simply.

"I know," he replied, "and I love ye," and then his big hand caressed her belly again, and he could feel the child stirring beneath his fingers, and it excited him. Would it indeed be the daughter Aidan insisted it was? What would she look like? Was it really his child that his wife carried, and would he be able to tell once the child was born who its father really was?

When Aidan was brought to bed on the twenty-first day of March in the year fifteen eighty, and delivered of the daughter she had said she would bear; Conn, looking into the baby's face could not for the life of him tell whether it was his own child or not, but it mattered not for he already loved her. Valentina St. Michael was a pink and white baby with the blue eyes of all newborns, and a faint fuzz of copper-colored hair upon her head. In the next few months those eyes became a wonderful violet shade, and she grew more hair which remained the copper color of her maternal parent.

"She looks like my mother," declared Aidan. "She is going to be far prettier than I ever was."

"Blurp," said Valentina St. Michael as she pushed her face into her mother's breast, and clamped her mouth around the nipple which was already seeping milk.

"She is absolutely thriving," remarked Skye who was sitting with her sister-in-law upon the camomile lawn that early July afternoon. "Ye've got rich milk, Aidan, and ye had such an easy confinement that I do believe yer meant to bear several more healthy babes before yer through. Considering yer age 'tis truly amazing."

"I'd like a lot more children!" said Aidan enthusiastically. "Look at me, Skye! For the first time in my life I've a bit of weight on my bones. I look at myself in the pier glass, and I am positively voluptuous. I can't believe it!"

"And do ye feel better now, Aidan? Is yer body responding once more to Conn?"

Here Aidan's face grew somber, and sighing she shook her head. "Nay, Skye. I still feel nothing, and I cannot understand it. I love Conn, and I thought surely when the child came my body would once more behave as it did before my cousin kidnapped me, and sold me into slavery; but alas, there is no change! I don't know why, but oh, how it saddens me. It is the one flaw in our happiness. Conn keeps saying that in time all will be well between us, but how long must we wait, Skye?"

"I don't know, Aidan, but one thing I learned in the East was that the human spirit is a strange thing. It is almost as if it possesses a secret life totally separate from what we can know and feel. Remember, my dear, that ye were really the most sheltered of girls yer whole life. Yer parents shielded ye, then the queen, and finally Conn. It wasn't until ye were faced with Cavan FitzGerald that ye truly learned what the face of evil looked like. That, and the year that followed must have been a terrible shock to yer poor soul."

"I think that ye are right," Aidan agreed slowly, and finishing nursing Valentina she handed the baby to its nursemaid, Wenda, "but how do I heal myself now?"

"I don't know," replied Skye, "how do ye? Think on it, Aidan. Something yet frightens ye. What is it?"

"Cavan FitzGerald," came the quick reply. "I keep dreaming that he is coming back to get me, Skye. I think it's not knowing where he is that frightens me most of all. There has been no trace of him since he disappeared from Spain. I keep thinking he might come to England. Foolish, isn't it? England is the one place Cavan FitzGerald dare not show his face for fear of arrest, and yet I cannot shake the feeling that he is near, is watching."

She turned her face to the nearby hills, and seeing her through his spyglass Cavan FitzGerald smiled cruelly, and shifted his cramped position. He had been watching *Pearroc Royal* for several days now in order to learn the routine of the family, and the servants. He had seen Conn going about his duties as the estate's master, and he smiled to himself. He intended doing exactly as he had told his uncle. He would kidnap the St. Michaels' child, and force her mother into following after them into Ireland. Conn would, of course, follow after his wife, and the trap would then be sprung. Once his rival was dead he would sell *Pearroc Royal*, and all its lands. The monies from that sale he would use to buy lands in Ireland. His estates would be far larger than his uncle's, and the old man would not be able to oppose him. Soon his sons, the sons that Aidan would give him, his sons and his daughters would overshadow the FitzGeralds of Ballycoille. And if anyone tried to stop him, he'd see them dead! As for Conn O'Malley's brat whether she lived or died was of no consequence to him. He needed her only to lure her mother to him, and after that . . .

He had already begun to effect his scheme by spying upon the estate. He knew when Conn was out; when Aidan spent time in her gardens; and most importantly, he knew when the nursemaid brought the baby out for airing, and which way she walked, carrying her charge into the clover fields near the house by the woods. Once in the fields she would spread a coverlet upon the ground, and placing the baby upon it she would play with the child in the sunshine until the baby fell asleep. Then the girl amused herself weaving daisy chains. She was not, Cavan had concluded, very bright, and she would be easy to frighten, and keep in line for he would need her to come along to care for the child.

He had not yet decided when to take the child, and then fate played into his hands. He had been having an ale at the local inn when the gamekeeper from *Pearroc Royal* had come in to refresh himself. Young Harry Beal was both known and liked, and the conversation flowed readily and openly. Nursing his ale Cavan was able to learn that Lord Bliss would be going to a horse fair in Hereford to purchase new stock, and would be gone for several days. This, Cavan knew, was the ideal time for him to put into operation his plan to kidnap Aidan's child. It would be several days before Conn would be able to return, and if Cavan knew Aidan as well as he believed he did, she would not wait for her husband to return before following after her child. He would have her, and the baby in his power before Conn could get to either of them which would allow him to lie in wait for his rival without distraction, making his kill an easy one.

He was going to enjoy killing Conn, he thought. Conn O'Malley who his whole life had had everything that Cavan FitzGerald had been denied. A loving father and mother, brothers and sisters, a family, a respectable place in society, a *name*. Why should Conn have had all those things, and not he? Why should Conn have been given a rich heiress, a title, and a great estate? Did he deserve it any more than Cavan did? By rights Aidan St. Michael should have been his wife in the first place, his twisted mind reasoned. She was *his* cousin, and it had been common practice since the beginning of time that families kept their wealth by intermarrying amongst each other. Conn had stolen what was rightfully his, and now he was going to get it back!

His arm clamped about the girl, and his knife pressed against her throat. "Do not scream, wench, or the baby is dead. Do ye understand me?" He rubbed the blade of his weapon threateningly over Wenda's neck.

"A-a-aye," she said, and her voice was shaking, her knees dissolving with fear beneath her. "Wh-wwh-what do y-ye w-w-want?"

"My man is in the underbrush, and he's a bow aimed at yer charge, so do not think to run when I release ye. Walk over to the baby, and wrap her up well. Then yer to come with me. Do you understand? Not a word, wench, or ye'll both be dead!"

Wenda nodded, too terrified now to even speak, and Cavan slowly releasing his grip on her, shoved her toward the spot where Valentina St. Michael lay dozing the warm summer's afternoon away. Cavan watched as the nursemaid wrapped her charge, and lifting her up carried her over to him. He had been correct in his assessment of the wench. She was not particularly intelligent, and she was used to obeying authority. This was a girl who would come with him without question for fear of both her life, and the child's for she was unquestioningly loyal to her mistress.

Lifting the blanket he looked down on Conn and Aidan's daughter, and for the briefest moment his hard gaze softened. The little one reminded him strongly of Bevin. Reaching out he gently stroked the rosy cheek, and he was amazed at its softness. This was no enemy. The little wench could be very useful in contracting a match with the son of an important family. Yes, better to keep her for she was really an asset.

It had been two days since he had overheard young Harry in the village inn. Conn had gone yesterday to Hereford. Aidan had ridden across this field this morning in the direction of *Queen's Malvern*. It would be nightfall before Wenda and her charge were found to be missing, and the first search the following day would concentrate in the area of *Pearroc Royal*. It would be several days before his note would be delivered to Aidan St. Michael, telling her where she might find her little daughter. It would be then she would send for Conn, but she would follow after him immediately.

His captive in tow Cavan FitzGerald headed south over the Malvern Hills to Cardiff. For some hours the child was quiet as they rode, but then she began to wail. For some minutes Cavan attempted to ignore the infant's howls, but finally he turned on Wenda, and snarled,

"What the hell is the matter with the bairn?"

"Sh-she's hungry, sir."

"Then give her yer tit, and shut her up," he snapped.

"I c-can't, sir!"

Cavan FitzGerald drew their mounts to a stop, and glaring at Wenda demanded, "Why not?"

"I'm not a wet nurse, sir! M-m'lady would allow n-no one b-but herself to f-feed the b-baby."

"*Jesu!*" The oath exploded from his mouth with such force that Wenda cringed, and the horses shied nervously. This was something that he had never even considered. He had assumed that a fine lady like Aidan would not nurse her own children. He had assumed that Wenda was the baby's wet nurse. What the hell good to him was the brat if she was dead before they reached Cardiff? He needed to think, and up ahead was a rather ramshackle-looking inn, but night was coming, and it would do.

Valentina St. Michael was now howling at the top of her little lungs. She was wet, and she was hungry, and she was chilled. Where was the warm, sweet-smelling breast with the milk that soothed her? She missed the soft voice that spoke so gently to her, and sang soft songs to her as she nursed. Something was not right in her world, and she knew it which caused her to cry all the louder.

The inn in which they sought shelter was surprisingly clean though it was plain and simple. There were some very good smells emanating from the regions of the kitchen in the rear of the building, and the innkeeper welcomed them with a smile which turned to a look of distress as he heard Valentina's cries.

"Here now, what's the matter with the little lass?" he said.

"Me wife died in childbirth," said Cavan quickly, "and I'm on my way to Cardiff for I've bought a shop there, and now here's the wet nurse gone dry on me. I pray me bairn won't die. She's all I've left of my Kate."

"Polly!" the innkeeper bawled at the top of his voice, and a large, fat woman hurried from the kitchen.

"What is it then, Harry?"

The innkeeper explained, and a smile wreathed the woman's face as he came to the quick end of the tale, and said, "Would ye be willing to help 'im, wife?"

"And me with milk enough for six? Here, girl, give me the bairn." The innkeeper's wife reached out, and took the screaming Valentina, and without another word opened her blouse right where she stood to heft out an enormous breast. Smelling the milk Valentina homed in on the nipple, ravenous, and not caring now that it wasn't her mother. "If yer staying the night," said Polly, "I'll keep the bairn with me, and see she's fed until ye leave. She's a hungry little wench, and maybe yer wet nurse just needs a day's rest. Yer too thin, girl," she said to Wenda. "No wonder yer having trouble with yer milk."

In the morning before they left the innkeeper's wife presented them with a stone bottle. "I've filled it with me milk, and a relief it is to have me tits empty for the first time in months. I had twins eight months past, but we lost one of the lads two weeks ago, and his mate couldn't take everything I was producing. I've always been a good producer." She turned to Cavan. "Ye'll have to sacrifice one of yer riding gloves, sir. If ye'll let me I'll poke a few holes in it with me needle. When the little lass is hungry just fill the finger with the milk, and use it like a tit. She'll last till ye get to Cardiff, and find another wet nurse."

Cavan thanked her, and pressed a piece of silver into Polly's hand to reinforce his gratitude. Polly's milk wouldn't last forever, but perhaps in Cardiff he could find a wet nurse who would come to Ireland with him, and he would send Wenda back to *Pearroc Royal* with his message to Aidan.

Cavan had been correct in his assessment of Wenda's intellect. She was not particularly bright, but she was deeply loyal to the St. Michael family. Her family had belonged to their family for several generations. It did not please her to leave her little mistress, but she was a practical country girl, and she knew that Valentina could not survive without food. She considered herself lucky to get off with her life. So clamping her legs tightly around the fat pony she had ridden from *Pearroc Royal* she began her return journey bearing with her a written message she was incapable of reading for Lady Aidan. The wicked man who had taken them had not harmed them, and he promised her he would not hurt little Mistress Valentina. He had even allowed her to choose the wet nurse for Wenda knew a diseased woman could pass on her weakness to the baby. Luck had been with her, and she had found a country girl who had come to the city to escape the shame of her stillborn bastard. The girl was clean, and healthy, and grateful for the opportunity offered even if it meant getting onto a sailing vessel, and sailing to Ireland.

Wenda drove her pony fiercely covering the distance between Cardiff and *Pearroc Royal* in two and a half days' time. As she suspected everyone was in an uproar over their disappearance although Lady Aidan had not yet sent for her husband. Her return was hailed with joy until it was discovered that Valentina was not with her. She would speak to no one until she had been ushered into her mistress' presence where she poured out her tale, ending it by handing Aidan the message that Cavan had entrusted her with.

Aidan had listened white-faced to the nursemaid's tale. She was in an agony of fear for her child, but she thanked God that Wenda's loyalty had preserved Valentina as far as Cardiff. Snatching the folded parchment from the girl she opened it up and read:

If ye wish yer daughter returned unharmed to ye, come to yer grandfather's home in Ireland. We have some unfinished business between us.

The signature was as she had expected it would be, had feared it would be. *Cavan FitzGerald!* She had instinctively known that he would come back to haunt her, but suddenly the fear she had felt all these months was gone, and in its place was a deep anger. What had she ever done to Cavan FitzGerald that he should seek to hurt her so? Why would he not leave her alone? Well he was going to leave her alone! she decided furiously. She was going to Ireland, and she was going to retrieve her child, and she was going to put that damned bastard upstart in his place, and if her mealymouthed old grandfather, Rogan FitzGerald, didn't help her, she'd put him in his place too.

Rogan FitzGerald had abandoned her mother when he had sent her to England to marry Payton St. Michael. Aidan had never met him in her entire life, and his sudden interest in her had rung false to both her and to Conn. Remembering some of the things her mother had said of Rogan FitzGerald Aidan realized with deep certainty that her grandfather was probably involved in whatever plot her cousin Cavan was attempting to hatch, using her child as bait. Well, they were going to regret it! Aidan thought to herself.

"Beal!" she shouted, and the butler came running.

"M'lady?"

"Send for young Beal. He is to carry a message to my husband this very afternoon. Then fetch me yer younger son, Harry." Aidan bent over her desk even as the butler hurried from the room to carry out her orders. She dipped her quill into ink and wrote her message to Conn upon the smooth parchment.

Cavan FitzGerald has stolen Valentina, and gone to my grandfather's home in Ireland. I am leaving this afternoon for Cardiff where I will take passage on one of yer sister's ships. Follow me as quickly as ye possibly can. We both need ye.

Yer loving wife, Aidan St. Michael,
Lady Bliss.

"Come in," she called to the knock upon the library door, and both younger Beals entered into the room, their caps in their hands. "Peter," she addressed the elder of the two who was known about the estate as young Beal since he bore his father's Christian name. "I want ye to take this message to his lordship at the Hereford Horse Fair with all possible speed. Don't stop until ye reach him. Take with ye a dozen armed men, and tell his lordship not to bother coming home, but to go directly to Cardiff to embark." She folded the parchment, dripped hot sealing wax upon it, and pressing her personal cipher into it handed the message to young Beal. "Godspeed," she said, and taking it from her young Beal turned and departed.

"Harry," she continued speaking to the youngest of the Beal sons, "yer coming with me to Ireland. Pick two other men to come with us. Good fighters, but clever as well. Do ye understand me?"

"Aye, m'lady," said Harry Beal with a grin.

"Then go," she ordered him. "We leave within the hour."

"Not without me, ye don't," snapped Cluny as he entered the library. "Ye ain't going nowheres unless I come with ye. Master Conn would never forgive me, and besides I know Ireland, and ye don't. Yer safe enough aboard one of Lady de Marisco's ships for every seaman in her employ is O'Malley loyal, but once we land in Ireland, 'tis a very different matter, m'lady. Each damned mile of the land is controlled by some chieftain or another, and not one of them really friendly to the others. Yer grandfather's holding is inland, and I'm not certain where we're to land so ye'd best be prepared, and I'm the man to prepare ye."

Aidan didn't argue. She knew that Cluny was right, and she was grateful for his help. "Can ye be ready in an hour?" she asked, and he grinned cockily at her.

"I'm ready now, m'lady!" he said.

Mag cried and fussed when Aidan told her of her plans.

"This is madness, my chick! Wait for his lordship," she begged her mistress.

"Nay, Mag. Every minute counts now. My baby needs me! Don't fret so.

His lordship will no doubt be in Cardiff ahead of me, and we'll embark together."

Mag sniffed, but Aidan's words reassured her. "What shall I pack for ye?" she worried. "How can ye carry trunks if yer riding? Is the baggage cart to go with ye?"

"Nay," Aidan replied. "I shall ride astride as Skye does, and wear one of those special skirts she gave me for doing so. We can make faster time if I do. Pack my saddlebag with an extra skirt, two shirts, and some stockings, the heavy kind I use when I wear boots. I'll need my hairbrush, and a warm cape with a hood. 'Twill do me quite nicely, dearest Mag."

"Ye can't go to visit yer grandsire in such clothing," protested Mag. "What will the old man think of ye."

" 'Tis not a friendly visit, Mag," said Aidan. "I believe that my grandfather may be involved in this matter."

"That wouldn't surprise me none," remarked Mag. "The old man was always a bit of a robber, even in his younger days, and well I remember it. Yer mother was fortunate to escape when she did, and I certainly never regretted coming with her. Ye be careful, Mistress Aidan. Rogan FitzGerald's an old devil, and he always was."

Aidan rode out across the fields for *Queen's Malvern*, her four men at her back. Reaching her sister-in-law's home she hurried to find Skye and Adam who were dining early that day. Seeing her dressed so, Skye immediately knew that Aidan was off to seek her daughter.

"Tell me," she said without any other preamble.

Aidan recounted Wenda's story, finishing with, "I've sent young Beal and twelve armed men off to Hereford to fetch Conn. I've told him to go directly to Cardiff. I'll not wait for him if he is not there when I get there. I want to get to Ireland as quickly as possible. What if those damned FitzGeralds mean my baby harm?"

"That isn't wise, Aidan," Adam put in. "The FitzGeralds aren't going to hurt Valentina. They're using her as bait to lure ye to them for some purpose or another. Wait for Conn to go with ye."

"I wouldn't wait for Christ himself!" Aidan declared vehemently. "My baby needs me, Adam!"

Adam threw up his hands in frustration, and looked to Skye.

"I understand how ye feel, Aidan," Skye told her, "but Adam is right. Wait for Conn."

"In all likelihood he'll be there ahead of me," Aidan said. "Will ye send one of yer pigeons to Cardiff to inform yer factor of our needs, and our arrival?"

"Aye," said Skye, "I will."

"Then I'm off," replied Aidan, and standing she blew them both a kiss, and strode purposefully from the room.

"Do ye think she'll wait?" Adam queried his wife.

"Aye. She's afraid of Cavan FitzGerald. She'll not want to face him alone," came the reply.

But Aidan wasn't afraid of her cousin any longer. A deep burning anger had replaced her equally deep fear, and with every mile she traveled that anger grew stronger, her fear weaker. She was no longer the sheltered creature she had been two years ago when Cavan had so cruelly sold her into slavery. She had seen more of the world now than even he had. She had learned by virtue of her sex that an inner strength was necessary for human survival. She now had that strength, and she felt confident, and unbeatable. With or without Conn she was going to Ireland to retrieve their daughter, and she would do it!

She was tired of Cavan FitzGerald, and the threat that he posed to her life. She had lived in fear of him since her return. That fear was, she suspected now, at the root of her inability to enjoy her marital relations with her beloved husband. What more could he do to her than he had already done? He had sold her into slavery, stolen her child, and made it impossible for her to enjoy her husband's loving! Enough was enough!

Aidan pushed both herself and her men to the limit. She knew now that in order to destroy the hold that Cavan FitzGerald had over her she had to beard him herself. She must face him alone, and in order for her to do that she had to reach Cardiff, and embark for Ireland before Conn got there. It was then that she understood something that Skye had recently said to her. She had openly admired her beautiful sister-in-law's obvious control over her own life, and Skye had said:

"Until I became my own person instead of merely the extension of some man, I had no control over myself, or my life."

"But how did ye gain that control?" Aidan asked her.

"By facing up to my fears honestly," said Skye.

She hadn't really understood Skye at the time, but now she did, and she was facing up to the one great fear she had. That Cavan FitzGerald would once again get her in his power. Well her odious cousin might believe by stealing Valentina that that was exactly what he was doing, and perhaps with the old Aidan it might have been so, but not now. This time she was going to face up to him, and she was going to fight him with every ounce of her strength, and she was going to win. Oh, yes! She was most certainly going to win!

Chapter 19

⁕

*A*idan St. Michael's first glimpse of her mother's homeland was a gray and misty one.

"A soft day," said Captain Bran Kelly of the light rain that was falling. He said it with a smile.

They had sailed from Cardiff out into the Bristol Channel and past Lundy Island, once the stronghold of the de Marisco family. The weather had held as they crossed the short sea distance between the two countries rounding the southern end of Ireland to sail effortlessly across first Bantry Bay and then Dingle Bay. There had been little sunshine. The days had been gray, the nights foggy, but the seas had been smooth and there had been just enough wind to move them at a goodly pace. Sailing into the mouth of the Shannon Aidan admired the velvety green of the land. It was very beautiful.

"The wind is freshening now," said Bran Kelly as he saw them and the horses that they had carried with them safely embarked upon a deserted beach. "I'll have a quick trip to Innisfana, m'lady, and I'll be back with a good strong contingent of O'Malley retainers to back ye up, never fear."

"Conn will appreciate the reinforcements when he arrives," said Aidan. "From what I can gather my grandfather is land rich, but lacking in the hard coin it takes to keep trained men-at-arms. I don't know what the FitzGeralds want with me, but I don't believe that they mean me any harm."

"I think yer probably right," agreed the ship's captain. "Yer grandfather's family have a reputation for knavery, but not murder." He flushed realizing how rude his blunt speech must have sounded to Aidan who was such a gentle soul. "Yer pardon, m'lady."

Aidan laughed. " 'Tis no insult, Bran Kelly, to tell me what my own mother told me. And Mag, too, I might add. My mother was happy to escape her family, and marry my father. If she continued to correspond with them it was out of a sense of filial duty. I owe the FitzGeralds no such duty. I've come to get my daughter back, that's all."

"Be careful," he warned her. " 'Tis said that St. Patrick drove the snakes from Ireland, but there are still a few at Ballycoille, m'lady."

"I've Cluny, and Harry Beal, and two of the lads to come with me, and protect me. We can hold that old devil who calls himself my loving grandfather at bay for a few days until Conn arrives. Ye fret too much, Bran Kelly. I'll take no chances, I promise ye."

Watching her ride off he was of a mind to worry despite her reassurances. She had always, according to Lady de Marisco, been so sheltered; yet she had seemed levelheaded and competent to him. He shook his head. He believed her when she said she could hold her own for a few days. Still the FitzGeralds of Ballycoille were a rough lot.

For Aidan, however, there was no doubt in her mind that she would accomplish her purpose in coming to Ireland. She pushed her mount, and her men hard to cover the distance between the Shannon River, and her grandfather's holding as quickly as possible. She was anxious to see her baby again. She hoped that Valentina was all right, but she quieted any fears she had on that account by reassuring herself that it was she the FitzGeralds wanted. Her child had only been a means to their end, and they would not harm her.

She was not surprised at the shabbiness of her grandfather's tower house when she first saw it. Her mother had spoken often of the great contrast between her childhood home in Ireland where she had run barefoot most of her life, and her beautiful and quickly beloved home, *Pearroc Royal* in England. The tower was an ancient one, and even at a distance it was quite obviously in need of repairs. Built of a harsh-looking dark gray stone it sat upon a hill which gave it an uncluttered view of the entire unforested countryside surrounding it. It would be a difficult place to approach undetected, or to escape from without being easily seen. It gave Aidan some pause for thought, but there was no going back now.

There were several outbuildings about the tower, and the entire group of structures was surrounded by a low stone wall. The heavy oak gates to the enclosure opened now, and a rider came forth, his dark cape fluttering wildly in the wind. She instantly recognized him, and her heart hardened even as her mouth curved up into a brief smile of amusement as Cavan FitzGerald hallooed across the distance separating them, and waved as if she'd been invited to a family celebration.

"Little Aidan," he said as he pulled even with her. "Yer as lovely as ever, cousin!" He smiled broadly at her.

"As lovely as when ye last laid eyes upon me, ye black-hearted bastard?" she demanded in a level voice, her gray eyes as flat as lead.

"Now, sweet cousin, let us let bygones be bygones," he began, but she cut him short.

"*Let bygones be bygones?* Jesu, yer not only mad, Cavan, yer stupid as well." Then in a move he had not at all anticipated she kicked her horse to shove past him setting him so badly off balance that he almost fell from his mount.

He was barely saved from that embarrassment by two of the men who accompanied her who slipped up on either side of him, preventing the accident as one of them reached out to lift him back into his saddle, and the other steadied his horse. As he attempted to move forward to catch up with her, however, one of them, a beefy, bearded ruffian, leaned over and relieved him of his reins thus preventing him from guiding his own horse.

The other whom he immediately recognized as Lord Bliss' personal servant smiled and said, "There now, Master FitzGerald, ye best mind yer manners, and let yer betters precede ye."

Cavan seethed with impotent rage. The little bastard would pay for that remark as soon as he took care of his master! Aidan, his better? A *woman* his better? She'd soon know who her better was. He'd quickly tame the English bitch, and have her running at his heels like a well-trained beast. He licked his lips in anticipation of the easy victory.

A small smile on her lips at her first little triumph over her cousin, Aidan rode boldly into her grandfather's keep. She was pleased to see through the open doors of the large stable building that it was well kept for the rest of the outbuildings were rather dilapidated. There were pigs rooting about in the courtyard in the garbage pile, and a number of barefoot, dirty-looking children in shapeless smocks tumbling with each other, and the large number of dogs who seemed to be vying avidly with the pigs for the bones and scraps of the garbage pile. A lump came to her throat. Had her mother once been as these children? Could her beautiful mother have sprung from the filth of this appalling pig wallow?

She slid from her mount giving orders as she did so. "Mark, ye and Jim stay with the horses. See they're properly stabled, cooled down, and then fed and watered. Check their hooves for any stones. 'Twas such a rocky trail up here. Cluny, ye and Harry Beal come with me." She turned and glared at Cavan who was just managing to get off his horse. "Well, *cousin*, will ye lead the way, or shall I find it myself?"

Somewhat off balance by her tone, and her manner, Cavan obeyed her sharp command, and hurried into the tower house. With a wink at her men Aidan followed him up the stairs, and into the hall where seated at the high board at the opposite end of the hall from its door was a tall, white-haired old man with bright blue eyes and harsh features. Aidan strode boldly the length of the room, and stopping directly in front of the old man said, her voice cold, and quite angry to his ear.

"Ye'll be Rogan FitzGerald, my grandsire. Where is my infant daughter, and how dare ye allow this bastard," her hand made a sweeping gesture in Cavan's direction, "to endanger Valentina in whatever madcap scheme he has up his sleeve now!"

There was a long silence as Rogan FitzGerald contemplated this virago who had just arrived into their midst. Then peering down his nose at her he said with some humor, "And welcome to Ballycoille, granddaughter of mine." Then his eyes narrowed, and he said in a sharper, more menacing tone, "I like neither yer tone nor yer stance, granddaughter. Remember that I am master here at Ballycoille. Ye'll respect me, lass, for yer no different in my sight than any other woman, and I'll give ye a beating such as ye've never had if ye can't remember yer manners when speaking with me."

"Where is my child?" Aidan repeated. Her heart hammered wildly within her chest as she realized she was actually bearding her grandfather and his entire household with only two men at her side. Should she have waited in Cardiff for Conn? Still she would not let the old man know she was fearful, and so she glared at him boldly.

Rogan FitzGerald looked to one of his servants, a rather slatternly-looking woman, and snapped, "Fetch the brat and her wet nurse!"

There was an even larger silence as they waited, Aidan standing firmly before him, her legs apart, her rather outlandish garb rather attractive to his eye, and certainly practical for riding astride, he thought. She was, however, no simple and sweet-natured woman who would be easily led as Cavan had suggested. Still, she was his granddaughter, and she would eventually see reason, he was certain. There was no warmth in her eyes right now, however, and the two men who accompanied her both looked as if they meant business. Family retainers obviously. Loyal and tough. He nodded to himself absently. His nephew would have no easy time of it, but together they could make her obey them he was certain. She'd not be an easy mare to force to the bit, but he was sure they would prevail. Finally the wet nurse, and the child entered the hall, and Aidan showed the first touch of softness Rogan could see in her, and he smiled to himself. The bairn was her weakness as it would be with any loving mother. Seeing the girl carefully coming down the staircase into the hall Aidan ran to the foot, and held out her arms for the child. Valentina was, she could easily see, clean, well-fed, and content. As the wet nurse placed the baby in her mother's arms Aidan said to the girl, "What is yer name?"

"I'm Nan, the smith's daughter, m'lady. Lord Cavan hired me in Cardiff to care for the little miss. I've done me best."

"I can see ye have," said Aidan kindly. The girl was almost too thin but for her breasts, she had several ugly bruises on her arms, and she looked absolutely terrified, her light blue eyes darting about her as if she were waiting to dodge the next blow. "I'll want ye to return to *Pearroc Royal* with me, Nan. When Valentina was *stolen* from her father and me by my great-uncle's *bastard*, who ye should know is but plain *Master* Cavan and no lord, I had to bind my own breasts, and now my milk is gone. Will ye come with me back to England? Ye'll be well treated, I promise ye."

The light of hope sprang into the girl's eyes, and she nodded vigorously. "Thank ye, m'lady! Thank ye!"

"Will ye swear yer loyalty to me alone, Nan? Will ye swear on the name of Jesus himself?"

Nan never hesitated a moment. "I will, m'lady! I swear on Jesu's name."

"Then ye need have nothing further to fear. Now, how did ye get those awful bruises?"

The girl flushed scarlet, and her eyes went to Cavan FitzGerald, but she said nothing, and Aidan knew she was afraid.

"Has Master FitzGerald raped ye?" she asked in a low voice.

"Aye, m'lady. He threatened to kill the bairn if I would not yield to him."

"He will not touch ye again," said Aidan quietly, and then she walked back across the room to where Cavan FitzGerald stood speaking to her grandfather who yet sat in his place. She pierced the old man with such a fierce look that he immediately noticed her, and without meaning to acknowledged her. "If," said Aidan in a hard voice, "this miserable offspring of yer brother ever touches my daughter's wet nurse again, I'll cut his throat, I swear it!" She then looked scornfully at Cavan. "Oh, 'tis a brave gallant ye are, Cavan FitzGerald, selling helpless, innocent women into slavery, and forcing yerself upon a poor, frightened girl. Ye make me want to puke!" Then turning her back upon him she demanded of Rogan FitzGerald, "Where am I to sleep? 'Tis too late for me to set out again for the coast tonight."

"Would ye go before I've had the chance to offer ye my hospitality?" whined the old man.

"Aye, I would, if I had the light, but this damned twilight of yers is not good enough for strangers, and the path here is steep. I'd not endanger my child, my people, or my animals. The morning will be time enough, *grandfather*. I trust we will be safe in yer house this one night."

"There, girl, there is no need to be insulting," he complained.

"Swear on the name of the crucified Christ, and my mother's memory!" she said coldly to him.

"I swear," he snapped at her, and the look he gave her was a baleful one for her scorn was obvious.

"Where do I sleep then?" she demanded.

"Ye can go in with the wet nurse, and the child at the top of the tower. There's just the one room up there. Yer men can bed down in the stable."

"I've already two men in the stable minding the horses," she said. "Cluny and Harry will be outside my door to discourage any visitors."

"It's insulting ye are," Rogan FitzGerald grumbled. "As I remember yer mother was a sweet-natured and biddable lass. Yer nothing like her in either yer manner, nor yer face. I see only English."

"Good!" she answered him with a quick smile, "but ye'd best beware of my Irish, grandfather. That's the part ye can't see, and my experience with the FitzGeralds had led me to be wary of them."

Rogan FitzGerald suddenly chuckled. He had decided that he liked this granddaughter of his. He was going to enjoy having her live here with him. She had his Ceara's spirit in her, and several of her mannerisms reminded him of his wife in her youth. "Come, and sit by me, Aidan St. Michael," he said. "Ye must be hungry after yer ride."

The tension began to ease in the hall now that the young woman and the old man seemed to have settled their differences. Aidan sat next to her grandfather, and signaled to Cluny and Harry to find themselves places which they did, their backs to the stone wall of the room. The rest of the family living in the tower house began to make their appearances now that the dinner hour was approaching. There was Rogan's eldest son, his heir, Eamon, and his wife, Moire, and their several noisy children. Rogan's other married sons lived in their own homes thanks to their wives. Father Barra, the priest, was there, a heavyset man with cold and dead-looking brown eyes, and a narrow mouth that bespoke cruelty. He had been a total puzzle to his mother, the long-dead Ceara, who had never understood that Barra's bitterness stemmed from not having been born first. The two eldest sons of Eamon and Moire were married, and also lived in the tower house. It was not a comfortable situation.

The meal was not a particularly appetizing one. There was mutton, somewhat stringy and tough; a sea bass that had suffered slightly from its trip inland, and was, Aidan decided, somewhat past its prime. The capon, however, was freshly killed, and roasted nicely. There were no vegetables other than a turnip that was obviously the last of the past autumn's harvest, but there was freshly baked bread, and sweet butter, and a sharp, hard cheese. Wine was a luxury that Rogan FitzGerald rarely wasted on his family, and certainly not on his retainers. Ale was the drink served.

Aidan concentrated upon the capon, the bread, butter, and cheese. When Cluny and Harry had finished eating she sent them to the stables with food for Mark and Jim for she knew if she didn't send her own people the two men with the horses would starve. Her grandfather's hospitality was hardly the gracious bounty that hers had been. When she finished eating, and her two men had returned she arose, and abruptly bidding the assembled FitzGeralds good night, she stamped up the staircase to the small room at the tower top, passing as she went the other chambers for the other members of the family. Entering into the room she threw the bar across the door while outside Cluny and Harry prepared to stand watch.

Nan was already there with Valentina, and Aidan saw that the girl had tried to make the small stone chamber welcoming. There was but one narrow bed in the room with a trundle beneath it, but the coverlets were fluffed and neatly arranged, and there was a small fire in the little fireplace to help take the evening's chill off the room. Quietly Aidan sat down, and when Nan had finished nursing the baby she handed her to her new mistress. There had been little time earlier to ascertain that Valentina was all right. Now Aidan examined the child carefully, and satisfied that her daughter was in good health, she cuddled her close, and said, "Ye've been a brave girl, Nan, and ye've taken good care of Valentina. It is very possible that we will have to leave Ballycoille rather quickly. Can ye be ready on a moment's notice, and will ye not be frightened no matter what happens?"

"I'd follow ye into hell, m'lady, to get out of here. I've never been more frightened in me life. Having me baby in a ditch in an alley in Cardiff weren't half as frightening as being in this place has been. I can barely understand these people, and Master Cavan is a mean one, he is."

"Aye," Aidan agreed with the girl, "and those are the kindest words I've ever heard to describe Cavan. Don't worry, my girl, I promised ye that I'd protect ye, and I will. We leave here tomorrow for the coast where I've a vessel waiting, and then it's back to England. Ye'll like *Pearroc Royal*. It's a good place."

"How can I thank ye, m'lady?" said Nan, her voice shaky, her eyes teary.

"How can I thank ye, Nan? Ye saved my baby's life with yer milk, and ye've a home at *Pearroc Royal* as long as ye want it, and a yearly wage to be paid each Michaelmas. I want more than one baby, and Valentina's nursemaid won't be able to handle two babies. I need ye, lass."

It had been a long day, and the two women were tired so they lay down to rest, Nan placing Valentina in her cradle, which old Rogan FitzGerald told her earlier had once housed Aidan's mother, Bevin. On the other side of the chamber door, Cluny and Harry diced to keep themselves amused while below in the hall Cavan FitzGerald fumed at having been temporarily thwarted in his plan to marry Aidan.

"There's time, nephew," soothed Rogan FitzGerald.

"Time? With her planning to leave tomorrow? She's changed, she has. I'm not so certain that I want to marry her now."

"But ye will," said Rogan harshly. "How else can we get our hands on her wealth? Don't fret, Cavan, my lad. There's a storm coming, and by morning the rain will be so heavy that 'twill be impossible for Aidan St. Michael to leave us; at least until the storm is over which I suspect will not be for at least two days. By then we'll have ye a married man, and ye'll bed the wench firmly. She's a high-strung filly, I'll grant ye, but they're the kind that breed the best foals. She but needs a firm hand on the bridle to tell her who her master is."

"We'll never get near her as long as her watchdogs are at her heels," said Cavan referring to Cluny and Harry Beal. "The smaller of the two is Conn O'Malley's personal servant."

"Then we will have to remove them," said Rogan FitzGerald.

"Let me kill them!"

"Cavan, my lad, yer too impetuous. There's no need to spill anyone's blood. They'll go to take food to their companions in the stable come morning; and when they do, we'll simply bar the tower door so they cannot reenter. Ye'd best get some rest, my lad, for we'll celebrate yer wedding on the morrow, and tomorrow night ye'll get no rest at all!" and he laughed loudly, and poked his nephew playfully.

By morning a particularly wet and windy storm was lashing the southwest section of Ireland making travel, as Rogan FitzGerald had predicted, virtually impossible. Awakening early Aidan had heard the rain, and arising she had gone to the narrow window to look out. Dismayed she gazed out at the rain which was falling in a steady, gray sheet.

"Damn!" she swore mildly, and then she hurried to the door and opened it saying as she did to Cluny and Harry Beal, "It's pouring. I don't think we can travel today, but take some food out to the stables to Mark and Jim and see what they think."

"If it were just us," said Cluny, "I think I'd want to get out of here as soon as I could, but with the bairn, and her wet nurse, m'lady, I think they will agree we must wait for better weather. We passed no inn on the road here so there's nowhere else where we may shelter."

"Maybe it's not as bad as it looks," said Aidan hopefully.

"And maybe 'tis worse," chuckled Cluny teasingly. "Come on, Harry," he said. "I don't know about ye, lad, but I could use some food, and a tankard of ale right now. We'll not be too long, m'lady. Will ye be all right?"

She nodded. "I think my grandfather realizes now that I am not to be trifled with, but I will be interested to learn before I leave just why he wanted me here. Probably money. I suspect he could use some."

The two men disappeared off down the winding stone staircase, and Aidan reentered the room to discover that Nan and the baby were now awake. Taking a little bit of water she poured it into the basin, and washed her face. The water was cold, and Aidan thought of home, and how dear Mag always warmed the water before she put it in the basin. This was a whole new world, and one in which Aidan did not think she would enjoy living.

"Ye stay here," she ordered Nan. "Yer safe here. Bar the door, and I'll see the food is sent up to ye."

"If it pleases yer ladyship it would be better if I ran down now before the household is up. Valentina will want to eat shortly."

"Yer right," replied Aidan. "Go along now."

Nan slipped from the room, and Aidan sat down to study her daughter who was now playing with her toes. She was such a pretty baby with her violet eyes and her copper-colored hair. *My daughter without a doubt, but that she's far lovelier than I've ever been. Who is her father? I wonder.* Aidan looked hard at the baby who cooed and smiled back at her mother, bringing a smile to Aidan's own lips. *I see nothing of Conn, nor Javid Khan, nor Murad in her,* she thought. *Perhaps it is better that way. Ye'll know but one father, my dearest little one, and that is my darling Conn.* Reaching out she stroked Valentina's rose-petal cheek. "We're going home soon, my darling, if only the damned rain would stop!"

Nan came hurrying back into the chamber bearing a small loaf, a bowl of hot oat stirabout, and some ale. "Yer grandsire is already in the hall, m'lady, and he kindly asks that ye join him for morning prayer, and then the meal."

Aidan brushed her skirt off, and taking a clean shirt from her saddle-bags got dressed. Her long hair was unbraided, brushed out, and rebraided again. "Bar the door when I leave," said Aidan, "and don't open it to anyone but me whatever they tell ye. My men will be back shortly, and will be there to guard ye."

"Yes, m'lady," was the dutiful reply.

Aidan hurried from the room, and heard the thunk of the heavy wooden bar as Nan lowered it into place thus preventing entry into the tower room

471

by an unwanted guest. Making her way downstairs she joined her grandfather and his family who had already assembled in the hall for morning prayer as the tower house had no chapel. Her uncle Barra conducted the service in his cold, hard voice, and afterward joined them at the high board for the meal which was the same as Nan's. Aidan thought longingly of thick slices of pink ham, and eggs poached in sweet marsala; of honey and crisp fruity wine. Then with a grin at herself she settled down to eating what she had. She spoke little having little to say to her relations.

When the meal was finished, and the servants had cleared the table, Rogan FitzGerald said, "Ye won't be leaving today, of course, but 'tis just as well as we have certain unfinished business, Aidan St. Michael."

"Unfinished business? Ah, yes. The business of why yer nephew kidnapped my daughter, and forced me to chase after her to Ireland. Aye, grandfather, I should be most interested to learn the reasoning behind it all. Say on."

Rogan FitzGerald allowed a small smile to nudge the corners of his mouth. She was proud, this granddaughter of his, but very soon she'd yield to proper authority, and then her manner would not be so haughty. "It is time ye were married," he began.

"Married?" She looked at the old man as if he had lost his mind, and she was not certain he had not. "Grandfather, I am married."

"Not properly," he answered her firmly. "Not in the Holy Mother Church."

"I was married by the queen's own chaplain!" said Aidan hotly.

"We do not recognize Henry Tudor's bastard daughter, nor her chaplain! Heretics all! Ye were born, baptized, and raised in the Holy Mother Church. That which ye call a marriage is not according to its laws. Ye have been living in sin, Aidan St. Michael, but then ye had no family to guide ye properly. Yer father's people are gone, and so it is my duty as yer mother's father to see ye decently wed."

Aidan shook her head impatiently. This was totally ridiculous, but if it would make the old man happy, if this is what it had all been about, then when Conn arrived they would be married by a priest of the Holy Mother Church. "Very well, Rogan FitzGerald, when my husband arrives we will be remarried before ye by a priest of the Holy Mother Church. Will ye then be satisfied?"

"I do not fancy Conn O'Malley as a grandson," said Rogan quietly.

"The choice is not yers to make," she answered him.

"Ahh, granddaughter Aidan, but it is. I am yer eldest living male relation, and as such I am legally entitled to choose yer husband. I choose my nephew, Cavan FitzGerald."

"What?" She was astounded. She had been willing to go along with his foolishness because he was an old man, and she was bound to accept his hospitality; but for all her Irish mother, Aidan St. Michael was an Englishwoman, and to her mind her marriage to Conn O'Malley was a valid and a binding one. Her eyes blazed a strange golden light through the storm gray, and she said in a firm voice, "I am married to Conn O'Malley in the eyes of England's church, and England's queen. I would not marry Cavan FitzGerald if it were possible. 'Tis absolutely immoral for ye even to suggest it! Yer age is addling yer wits, Rogan FitzGerald!" She arose to leave the table.

Rogan FitzGerald's own eyes blazed back at his granddaughter, and his talonlike fingers closed about her arm, cruelly bruising the tender white skin. Then he stood, and even in his old age he towered over the tall young woman who dared to defy him. "Ye will do as I say, Aidan St. Michael!" he thundered at her. Then he released her arm, and his hand flashed out to make firm contact with her cheek. "Ye will marry Cavan FitzGerald this very day, and ye will remember that I warned ye last night about yer manners." He slapped her hard, two blows in quick succession that stunned her.

Furious now Aidan continued to oppose her grandfather. How dare he strike her! *"Never!"* Her eyes quickly swept the hall for Cluny and Harry Beal, and he saw it, and guessed at what she sought.

"The tower door is locked, and yer men without, Aidan St. Michael. There is no one left to protect ye. Ye will do as I tell ye!" The old man was working himself into one of his rages, and all who knew him saw it coming, but Aidan was unaware of how hard a man her grandfather actually was. Looking toward Cavan and his son Eamon, Rogan commanded, "Put her across the table!"

Uncomprehending Aidan was shocked to find herself caught by her arms, and dragged forward to be bent forward across the high board by Cavan and her uncle Eamon. When Cavan reached around her to unfasten her belt, and unloosen her waistband, she struggled futilely. Outraged and embarrassed she shrieked as her riding skirt was pulled down about her ankles baring her to the assembled company. "What are ye doing?" she screamed angrily. "How dare ye treat me so!"

"I warned ye," snarled the voice of her grandfather in her ear. "I warned ye if ye did not mind yer manners that ye'd get a beating, lass. I'll not have ye defying me before my entire household, Aidan. 'Tis I, Rogan FitzGerald, who am the master here at Ballycoille. 'Tis I who make the laws that this family must abide by. Yer a part of this family, lass, and by God, ye'll obey me, or I'll kill ye and yer bastard spawn!" He turned away from her, and she heard him say, "Fetch my leather tawse, and be quick about it, lad, or ye'll be tasting its sting, too!"

Aidan's heart began to thunder within her chest, but she was not so much afraid for herself as she was for Valentina. She had not believed, indeed everyone had assured her that the FitzGeralds would not harm her child. Were they right, or would that wicked old man she called her grandfather seriously threaten her daughter?

Cavan, his grip upon her arm still tight, leaned forward and whispered in her ear. "Do ye know what a tawse is, sweet coz? 'Tis a leather strap some three inches in width which has been cut into thongs. Ye've never felt its bite, I'll wager, but the old man is a master at wielding it." He blew softly into her ear, and as she shuddered with distaste he ran his tongue around the shell-like hollow of the ear, then continued low. "Yer bottom is plumper than I would have guessed, sweet coz, and shortly it will ache with yer grandsire's tender discipline. I think, perhaps I shall have a tawse made for my own use. Regular beatings are good for a woman."

"If ye ever lay a hand on me, Cavan," she hissed at him, "ye'd best not ever turn yer back on me, for I'll kill ye given the chance."

He laughed low. "We'll see how brave ye are after a good whipping, sweet coz, for here is yer first taste."

Before she might reply Aidan heard a faint swish of air, and then as the many thongs of the leather made contact with her skin she cried out surprised. Although it was the custom of parents in her age to physically punish their children and men to beat their wives, she had never been subject to such abuse by either her father or Conn. The tawse did not hurt her so much as it stung her, not just in one spot, but over a wide area of her flesh as the narrow fingers of the leather spread themselves out and bit into her tender skin. She gritted her teeth as the second blow came to be followed with rhythmic regularity by several others, and she realized that her grandfather despite his great age was not only used to such exercise, but skilled in it as well. As blow followed blow, and he seemed not to tire of the punishment; as her flesh began to ache and burn uncomfortably with his brutal ministrations; she was finally unable to continue to swallow back her cries, and she screamed. To her shock her admission of pain seemed to inspire him to further cruelty, and the blows came faster, and harder.

"Ye'll obey me lass," she heard his voice thundering over her shrieks of pain. "Ye'll accept my choice of a husband!"

Then slowly the blows stopped, her garments were yanked over her red and smarting body, and she was spun around to face the old man. His face was flushed, and perspiring with his exertions. His white hair was tumbled. "Ye'll marry Cavan FitzGerald, Aidan! Do ye understand me, lass? This small beating was just a taste of what ye'll get if ye continue to disobey me."

"There is no way ye can make me commit bigamy with *that creature*," snapped Aidan angrily. She impatiently wiped the tears from her cheeks with the back of her hand. "Do ye think I am afraid that ye have locked yer tower door, and keep my men without? Yer tower door will not keep out my husband when he arrives! He will batter down this crumbling structure of a tower about yer ears, Rogan FitzGerald, and then what will ye and yer brood do?"

The old man flushed angrily at her brave and defiant words, but he was not yet beaten, or deterred in his purpose. "Ye'll do as I say, Aidan St. Michael, or yer bastard get by Conn O' Malley will suffer the consequences."

"Are ye an eagle, Rogan FitzGerald, that ye can get into my tower-top room? The door is barred, and Nan will not open it for anyone but me."

"Break the door in," the old man snarled, and his son, his grandsons, and Cavan rushed to do his will.

She could hear the pounding of the ancient battering ram they used. Hear it beating and beating and beating against the old oak door at the top of the tower, and then she heard the splintering of the wood, and a scream from poor, hapless Nan as the men gained entry. Aidan sighed. She would have sworn that the door could hold, but it had probably given way at a weak point, and there was no help for it now. She couldn't believe, however, that her grandfather meant to harm her daughter, his own great-grandchild. It was a notion soon to be disabused as the men entered the hall with Nan and Valentina who was howling in fright.

Rogan FitzGeraid reached out and took the child into the curve of an arm. Then reaching down he drew forth his dirk, and laid it against the infant's stomach, and the old man's cold blue eyes looked directly into the now frightened ones of his granddaughter. A tiny movement of the knife, and a minuscule pearl of bright red blood shone against the silver dagger's tip. Valentina whimpered, and Nan gasped in terror.

"Ye old bastard," Aidan hissed at Rogan FitzGerald. "She is yer own flesh and blood. She's my child! An innocent!"

The old man smiled coldly. "Ye know the price of her safety, Aidan St. Michael."

"Old man, yer totally mad! Ye have no right of control over me. I am a free-born Englishwoman; a loyal and true subject to her majesty. I am a married woman in the sight of God and the laws of my country!"

"Ye will obey me, daughter of my favorite child. Ye will obey me, or the bairn will suffer."

"Kill Valentina, Rogan FitzGerald," said Aidan boldly, "and ye have no further hold on me. I do not believe ye would do that."

"Nay, lass, yer wrong. This bastard brat is but another mouth to feed, and food is hard to come by now. Yer child is of no more use to me for I have ye now within my power. I'd as lief toss her from the windows, or into the fire for fuel. If I let her live 'twill be because I loved yer mother, and yer yer mother's daughter, and ye will do my bidding as yer sweet and obedient mother did my bidding. Whether ye will or no ye'll marry Cavan FitzGerald, but whether the brat lives is up to ye. I trust that ye fully understand me, Aidan St. Michael. Do ye?"

Aidan looked at her baby's frightened little face, and knew she could not let Valentina be harmed any further. The old man had to be mad, but she had no doubt now that he meant every word he said. Slowly she nodded her head in agreement, but she was not beaten by any means. The whole situation was terrifying, but she could see no way out. When Conn came it would be a different matter. For now, however, she had no other choice open to her. She made one last effort to dissuade him. " 'Tis bigamy yer having me commit, Rogan FitzGerald. No English court will ever uphold a marriage between Cavan and myself when I'm already married to Conn."

"Yer not going back to England," Rogan FitzGerald said, "but if it will ease yer delicate female sensibilities, Aidan, my girl, Conn O'Malley will soon be dead for when he comes to fetch ye, and his little bastard, we'll kill him! As for yer alleged marriage by that fraudulent cleric who serves the usurper now sitting upon England's throne, 'tis not valid in the eyes of the true church as my son Father Barra will attest."

"And my dear uncle will undoubtedly marry us in the *true* faith once the banns are posted," said Aidan sarcastically. At least Conn would get here before she was forced into this travesty. She had no fears for his safety from this bumbling crew of fools for he would have a large contingent of retainers to overcome the FitzGeralds and their motley servants.

"The wedding will take place today, granddaughter," said Rogan FitzGerald with a smug smile. "The banns were posted in their proper order several weeks ago. I'd like to see ye in decent women's clothing for yer nuptials, however."

"What a pity then that I have only these clothes," she replied feeling rather pleased to annoy him, small victory though it might be.

"I'm sure," he said, "that we can find something for ye to wear, Aidan St. Michael, that will be more suitable."

He sent the slatternly woman servant she had seen yesterday off to rummage in the trunks that had once belonged to her aunt Sorcha, for he explained, "She was a big lass like ye." Bridget, the servant, returned shortly with a dark green velvet skirt.

" 'Twas the only thing that weren't mildewed or eaten by the moths, me lord." She held it up against Aidan. " 'Tis long enough, and with a clean shirt, and her belt, and some flowers, she'll make a nice enough bride."

"Cavan, my lad, escort yer bride-to-be to her room," Rogan FitzGerald ordered his nephew. "When yer clothes are ready," he told Aidan, "the wedding will begin."

"Keep that animal away from me," said Aidan icily. "I'll get to my chamber without his help. Force him on me now, and I'll be tempted to shove him down yer fine staircase."

"I can see," said Cavan attempting to show some hold over her, "that yer ripe for another beating, Aidan, and I'd not be averse to seeing that ye get one."

Aidan snorted softly. "Ye've a short memory, Cavan. Remember that I've warned ye not to touch me, or I'll kill ye, and I will. Perhaps ye can have me held down, and beaten as did my grandfather; but sooner or later ye'll have to be alone with me, and then . . ." She let the words trail off meaningfully as he laughed weakly; but his laughter had a hollow sound to it, and he did not meet her cold gaze. Aidan took Valentina from her grandfather's arms, and with a sharp, "Come, Nan," she stamped up the stairs to her tower, the wet nurse scuttling quickly behind her.

It was the old bar locks, she discovered, that had given way, and so it was possible to close the door of the chamber which she did. Going to the window she looked out. The rain was still pouring down, harder, if possible, than it had before. The day was very gray, and the weather showed no signs of letting up. Then a movement by the stables caught her eye, and she flung the tower window open, and called down over the rising wind, "Cluny! Up here, man!"

Cluny, the rain drenching him thoroughly, hurried over to the base of the tower. "M'lady, they've locked the door against us!"

"I know," she called back. "They say my marriage to Conn isn't a valid one, and they are forcing me into marriage with Cavan FitzGerald! They plan to kill Conn when he arrives, and keep me from returning home. Send young Jim back along the road to seek for my lord."

Cluny nodded. "Ye've got to escape, m'lady."

"There's no way out but the tower door, Cluny."

"If ye had some kind of rope," came the reply, "ye could come out the window, and down the side of the tower. "

" 'Tis possible! Good for ye, Cluny! One of ye stay by the tower at all times, and either I, or young Nan will communicate with ye. I'd best go back now lest they hear us."

"Not to worry, m'lady. They won't hear anything in this storm. In case ye can't get back to us, try tonight. We'll be waiting for ye whenever yer able." He slipped back into the shadows of the stables.

Aidan closed the window, and turned to Nan to explain her conversation to the girl. "It will take courage to do this," she said, "but I will go last so ye need not be afraid."

"But how can we transport the baby?" asked Nan.

"What if we tied two ropes about the cradle, and lowered her that way," Aidan suggested.

Nan nodded. "The baby must go first, m'lady, for if, God forbid, we're caught at it, one of us can hold them off while the other lowers the bairn safely."

"I'll need a weapon, and where are we going to get enough rope?" Aidan wondered.

"There is rope in the stables, m'lady. If yer man could bring it to the base of the tower just below our window we could make a length from the sheets upon the bed, and they could attach the rope to it for us to pull up!"

"Nan, yer a very clever girl!" Aidan praised the wet nurse. "Now where can I get a weapon?"

"I have one," came the surprising reply.

"Ye do? Then why didn't ye use it?"

"I was afeared, m'lady. I'm only a serving girl." She moved across the small room, and feeling along the wall pulled a stone loose to reveal a deep recess in the tower wall. Reaching in Nan pulled forth a dagger with a good six-inch blade on it. It was silver, and the handle had been enameled over the silver in a Celtic design of black, and yellow, and red. She handed it to Aidan.

"Where did ye get this?" Aidan asked the girl.

"Lord Eamon was drunk one night, and fell asleep at the high board. I saw him there in the very early morning, and there before him on the table was the dagger. I stole it. I thought, perhaps, that I might use it against Master Cavan, but I had not the nerve. What will ye do with it?"

"Kill Cavan FitzGerald," said Aidan quietly, and the young wet nurse sucked in her breath sharply, her eyes widening at Aidan's bold words. "I have no choice," Aidan continued. "They have schemed to marry me to him today, and there is no way in which I can escape it; but I'll be damned if I'll let him lie with me! We'll escape tonight, Nan, after I've killed the bastard, and everyone is celebrating my grandfather's apparent cleverness in forcing me to his will. I have an old score to settle with Cavan FitzGerald," and then Aidan told the servant of everything that had happened since her father's death almost three years ago. Nan goggled and gaped as Aidan unfolded her tale for never in her wildest dreams had she ever imagined the things that Aidan now spoke of to her.

When she had finished her story she said to Nan, "Ye must learn for me which room is to be the bridal chamber, and then when they are feasting before the bedding, place the dagger beneath the pillows for me. Do not do it sooner lest someone else find it. Did not Eamon miss his blade, Nan?"

"Aye, and a great fuss he made about it, but his wife said he probably lost it as he was always losing everything. They did not consider for a moment that any servant would have taken it for the poor souls here are as frightened of their masters as I have been; and they certainly never considered that I took it." She gave a little smile. "I wish I had been brave enough to stick it into him, and then, m'lady, ye'd not have all this trouble."

Aidan smiled back, and she patted the girl's hand in friendly fashion. She spoke coolly enough of killing Cavan FitzGerald, but it frightened her more than being forced to wed with her cousin. It was a terrible sin that she was contemplating, and yet she could think of no other way to escape him. She had no herbs with which to drug him into a deep sleep, and she knew that she would never, could never, yield herself bodily to him. The mere thought revolted her. She thought of the misery that Cavan FitzGerald had caused her and Conn. His cruel actions had been responsible for the loss of her first child, and her enslavement in Turkey, her brutal treatment at the hands of the Sultan Murad. Worst of all, however, was her own state, her inability to enjoy the passion that she had once shared with her darling Conn. Cavan FitzGerald's death might not restore her to the innocent she once was, but he would never endanger her, or those about her again. He must be killed! She hardened herself to the harsh fact, and prayed that God would forgive her, but if he did not she accepted the responsibility of what she was going to do this night.

A cursory knock sounded upon the door, and before she might give permission for those without to enter, Bridget came in carrying the dark green velvet skirt which she had managed to restore to some semblance of order. "Get a fresh shirt on," she said brusquely, "for they're ready to begin in the hall. The old skinflint, yer grandsire, has even opened his wine cellar tonight to the entire household. For that rare treat, I thank ye."

"Maybe I can get drunk," said Aidan with a chuckle, "and rob the bastard of his wedding night."

Bridget cackled, showing blackened and rotting teeth. "At least 'twill dull yer senses, lady, but ye'll not rob Master Cavan of his prize, I'll vow. I've never seen a bridegroom so eager to fuck his bride."

"And where is the bridal chamber in this pile of moldering stones?" Aidan demanded haughtily.

"The old man is giving ye his own chamber!" she reported with a perverse pride. " 'Tis just above the hall, and I've changed the sheets meself for ye. If that is all, lady, I'll tell them yer coming."

Aidan nodded. "Nan, in the saddlebag, a clean shirt."

Bridget shuffled from the room, and Nan handed Aidan the clean shirt. A fragrant, dried sprig of lavender fell from the silk as it was unfolded, and bending Nan picked it up.

"I'll put this on the pillow in the bridal chamber so's ye'll know that I've placed the dagger successfully, m'lady. Then I'll see that little Mistress Valentina is well fed so's she'll sleep tight for her escape. She's a predictable little 'un. If ye fill her belly good, there ain't nothing that'll wake her until morning when she's hungry again. She's a good baby, she is."

Aidan smiled. "Remember to tell Cluny where the rope is," she said as she put on the velvet skirt, and belted it with her own belt. The fresh scent of her shirt cheered her as she buttoned it to the neck, but then on second thought she undid the first three buttons. She could put Cavan well off his guard by offering him a good view of her charms. That, the wine she intended plying him with, and his own lecherous thoughts of the night to come would all serve to aid her in her plan to commit murder. She shivered briefly at her own thoughts, and with an encouraging smile at Nan she left the tower room, and walked down the winding staircase to the hall.

From the noise she could tell that the celebration was well under way. She stopped a moment, and steadied herself against the stone wall of the tower. Drawing several deep breaths she calmed her thumping heart, and shaking knees. Then she saw Conn's ring upon her finger, and she drew it off lest they steal it from her, placing it in the safety of her skirt pocket. Then continuing the short distance left to the hall she entered the room.

"The bride! The bride!" screeched Eamon's wife, a gaunt woman with a sly look about her. She hurried forward saying to Aidan, "Unbind yer hair, niece."

"Why?" Aidan demanded. "I am no maid, and Cavan well knows it."

Moire FitzGerald ignored her, and with bony, clumsy fingers undid the heavy braid of Aidan's hair, and running her fingers through it fluffed the bride's beautiful tresses into a more pleasing appearance. "There," she said satisfied, "now ye almost look beautiful."

Aidan laughed at her. "My wealth is beautiful, and it is that that this family seeks to possess and control. I could look like a frog, and Cavan would wed and bed me."

To her surprise her aunt lowered her voice saying, "Guard yer tongue, girl! Ye know FitzGeralds aren't afraid to beat their women, and most of them are mean bastards when in their cups." Then taking her niece by the arm she led her over to the high board which had been converted into a temporary altar for the ceremony.

Aidan's glance swept about the hall. It was not a big room, and it was filled now with family and servants. Most, she noted, were men; the only women being her aunt, Eamon's two daughters-in-law, his half-grown daughter, Maeve, and two other older serving women. They'd all overindulged on wine, she decided, and the men were already on their way to being drunk. She wondered if the cold-eyed priest would allow himself the luxury of overindulging. Right now he was the only one in the entire hall with the exception of herself who could lay claim to being sober.

"Let us begin," said Father Barra FitzGerald in a stony voice.

Aidan and Cavan were brought before him, and the ceremony began, but Aidan paid little heed to what was being said. It was the only way she could maintain her calm for if she seriously considered what was happening to her now she would have panicked entirely. They had placed her hand in Cavan's at the beginning of the ceremony, and he squeezed her fingers cruelly when she was required to speak. Finally the rite concluded they were pronounced man and wife.

A cheer went up from the assembled FitzGeralds and their servants and grabbing at his bride Cavan glued his mouth to hers in a hard, wet kiss. Angrily Aidan pulled away from him, her hand flashing out to make contact with his cheek. Stunned his own hand reached up to finger his injured face, and a dull flush crept over his visage.

"The money, Cavan," she hissed at him, "the money is what ye want!"

"Nay, bitch, I want it all!" he snarled back. "I want the wealth, aye, but I want ye also. I have from the moment I first laid my eyes on ye! Tonight I'll take some of the fight out of ye, ye may be certain!" He touched his cheek again. "Ye'll pay for this, *wife*." Then clamping his hand cruelly about her wrist he dragged her up to the highboard where the servants had already cleared away the trappings of religion to replace them with a wedding banquet of sorts.

There was a side of beef that had been roasted over an open fire, and several capons that tonight had a sweetish sauce upon them, and several meat pies, rabbit, Aidan guessed, and wonder of wonders a bowl of little onions and lettuce that had been braised in wine. There was plenty of fresh bread, butter, and cheese, and of course, wine from Rogan FitzGerald's carefully hoarded supply. There was no bridal cake for there had been no time to make one; and besides it was beyond the meager talents of the household women.

Aidan ate carefully, choosing beef and the vegetables and some bread. She also when no one was looking managed to slip a small loaf and some cheese into the pocket of her skirt, feeling Conn's ring as she did so. It gave her courage for what was to come.

Cavan FitzGerald could barely keep his eyes off the woman he claimed as his wife. Her fine silk shirt was open three pearl buttons, and he had an excellent view of her magnificent tits. He didn't dare to touch her again in public lest she attack him, and shame him before his relations once more. Soon she would be in his power, and then he intended availing himself of her wonderful body, and exercising his husband's rights to the fullest. He wanted to know every bit of her for before he killed Conn O'Malley he would enjoy describing to Conn just how he had fucked Aidan, and how she had responded. He had no doubt of the response for he had been sending women into swooning fits with his lovemaking since he was barely thirteen. It was a very satisfying talent to possess.

Several hours passed, and Cavan realized that if he drank much more wine he would be unfit to consummate his marriage this night, and that was a pleasure he had long awaited. He had eaten everything that he could, and had listened contentedly to his cousin Eamon's third son who was a bit of a bard, and now he was ready for his bed. Clamping a hard arm about Aidan he whispered in her ear, "Get ye to the bridal chamber, and prepare yerself for my coming. I'll not be long, bitch, so do not dally!" Then leaning over to Eamon's wife he said, "Get her ready, Moire. I'm not of a mind to wait any longer."

With a scornful glance at him which he didn't miss Aidan arose and walked from the hall and up the stairs, Moire and her two daughters-in-law and her daughter in her wake. When they reached Rogan's chamber on the floor above she was relieved to see a sprig of lavender on the pillow as she entered the room.

"Well, lass, off with yer clothes," said Moire FitzGerald briskly. "Yer no maid to be shy now." She reached out, and undid the belt, and waistband that held the velvet skirt in place.

Aidan calmly stepped out of it, and undid her shirt as her aunt pulled down her petticoats. "Give me my nightrail," she said as she sat down so they might pull her boots off.

Moire FitzGerald snatched up the nightrail that her daughter was holding out. "Ye'll not need that, Aidan my girl! He'll only tear it off ye, and 'tis a pity to ruin a perfectly good garment. Into bed with ye now!"

The protest died on her lips. What did it matter? she thought. Better to get this over with, and let them go back to their drinking. She certainly had enough experience at this point to hold Cavan FitzGerald off long enough to slay him. Without a word she climbed into the large bed, but when her aunt reached out to fluff the pillows she stayed her hand saying, "Nay, aunt, I hear the men coming now. They're fine as they are."

"Yer right," the woman replied, and then tossing Aidan's clothing carelessly on a nearby chair, she herded the other three females from the room before Cavan could arrive to find them there.

Quickly Aidan felt beneath the pillow, and the blade of the dagger pricked her finger. "God's nightshirt!" she swore softly, but the relief in her voice was evident. She sucked her finger to relieve the sting, and examining it was satisfied that there was no telltale blood to give Cavan cause for suspicion. She looked about the room. In the dim light from the fire, and the candle by the bed it appeared to be the best furnished chamber in the entire place which surprised her. Rogan didn't seem a man to be involved with personal comforts, but perhaps the room had been the result of her late grandmother's efforts.

Then she heard the sound of drunken laughter, and stamping in the passageway outside, and the door flew open to admit Cavan, and the other men of the family.

"There!" said Rogan FitzGerald triumphantly. "There she waits like a good and dutiful wife, Cavan. Ahh, yer a lucky man, my lad. A lucky man!"

Cavan stumbled across the floor, and yanking the bedclothes back said, "Stand up, Aidan! Stand up, and show the men of this family what fine big tits ye have," and he pulled her into a standing position to her intense mortification. Cavan's arm clamped about her waist quite successfully imprisoning her, and with his other hand he hefted one of her breasts displaying it to the others. "Look! Look at these beauties, and envy me! At last I've come into me own!"

There was a long painful silence for Aidan as she was forced to stand there on display before these virtual strangers. It took every ounce of her willpower not to turn on the drunken boor who now called himself her husband, and knock him to the ground. Instead she stared directly at

Rogan FitzGerald, and was finally satisfied to see him look away, saying as he did so, " 'Tis a lucky man, our Cavan is, but now let us leave him to enjoy the rewards of his wedding night," and the old man shepherded the others out, closing the door firmly behind him as he went.

Pulling her against him now Cavan FitzGerald pressed his mouth against Aidan's stopping her half-choked protests with a smothering kiss. She almost gagged in revulsion as he pushed his tongue into her mouth, but with a supreme effort of will she managed to retain her calm. His hands clamped about her buttocks forcing her into even closer proximity with his body which he now rubbed suggestively against hers.

"Jesu," he muttered against her mouth, "yer a real beauty with yer clothes off, Aidan. I never expected it, but yer more of a prize than I thought." Releasing her buttocks he slid an arm about her waist again, and began to fondle a breast with his fingers. Then his free hand grasped at her hand, and he forced her down so that she was forced to touch him. "Feel me," he groaned at her. "I'm hard as a stone, Aidan, and hot to give ye a good fucking, woman."

"And do ye usually fuck in yer clothing, Cavan?" she murmured at him. "Ye've a wife now, and a bed, and since ye've had a good look at me without my clothes, I'd like a good look at ye." She compelled her mouth into a suggestive smile, and gently loosing his grip on her she sprawled open-legged and temptingly upon her back upon the bed.

Stunned, he looked at her. "I thought ye loved Conn O'Malley," he said suspiciously.

"Oh, aye, and I do," she answered, "but Conn and I were really not wed according to the rites of the Holy Mother Church, were we? You and I, however, are, and there's nothing I can do about it, Cavan. I'm a practical woman, ye see, and besides my stay in Turkey gave me a taste for variety in my men."

"Play me false with another," he threatened, "and I'll beat ye within an inch of yer life, Aidan. Make no mistake about it. I'll not be made a cuckold."

"Ye won't be if yer man enough, Cavan, and I somehow think ye are," she purred at him. "Now, off with yer clothes, man, and let me see yer goods!" Casually reaching down with a hand she stroked herself lewdly, and smiled up at him. "Women get hot to fuck, too, Cavan."

He tore off his clothes, flinging them heedless of where they fell, and then naked he sat upon the bed's edge, and yanked off his boots. Then standing again he displayed himself to her proudly. "I doubt ye've ever seen better," he bragged grinning down at her.

Aidan almost laughed for Cavan FitzGerald was a man of but average size to her way of thinking, but instead she reached out and caressed his manhood with clever fingers. Her hand smoothed back and forth along his length several times, and then surprised him by slipping beneath his rod to cup and fondle his pouch. For a brief moment his eyes closed, and he groaned softly. "Ye've all the instincts of a wanton bitch," he said.

"Would ye rather I cry and make ye force me? I'll wager yer Spanish wife said her rosary when ye were atop her. I'll not say my rosary," she taunted him. "I'll tell ye instead all the ways I know to please a man. Secret things that I learned in the harem, Cavan; and I'll tell ye what pleases me. Ye want to know those things, don't ye, Cavan?" and she held out her arms to him.

With a hoarse cry he flung himself upon her, fumbling with himself as he sought to find his way. Aidan shuddered, unable to help herself, but she knew he would assume her reaction only passion. She wanted to shriek, and push him off her. Her dinner roiled unpleasantly in her stomach, and she was near to vomiting; but she forced herself to remember what it was she must do. She could feel him rubbing his hardness against the opening to her passage, and for a moment she felt panic. With a simulated groan of passion she wrapped her legs about him, one hand about his neck as with closed eyes she kissed him with what she hoped was great conviction. Slowly her other hand reached back to slip beneath the pillows, and she stealthily felt about for the blade she knew was there. Her heart was hammering wildly for she realized she had but one chance.

With a bellow of lust Cavan FitzGerald thrust his hardness into Aidan, and he ordered her thickly, "Work yer hips, ye wanton bitch! Work yer hips!"

Aidan's hand made contact with the dagger handle, and she breathed a sigh of relief as her fingers closed about it. Then she thrust herself up to meet his downward motions as slowly she drew her weapon from its hiding place. "Ohh, Cavan! Ohh, Cavan!" she moaned at him, knowing that he expected some reaction to his frantic thrusts.

He pumped at her hard and fast groaning as he did so, "Tell me no one's ever fucked ye better, wanton! *Tell me!*"

She had managed to bring her arm out and around into striking range. Opening her eyes she checked her position while he slobbered wet kisses against her neck, and humped her with ever-increasing urgency.

"*Tell me, bitch!*" he begged her.

"Yer the worst lover I've ever had, ye bastard!" she said with devastating frankness, and then she drove her dagger downward to plunge into his back, and make immediate contact with his heart.

Cavan FitzGerald raised his head in surprise, and he opened his mouth to speak, but there was no sound. With a supreme effort he lifted himself up, and his manhood, still hard, slipped from her body to Aidan's great relief for she had been afraid he would in his death throes release his seed into her, but he had not. Together in the heavy silence they watched as his firm shaft became naught but a small and flaccid white worm. His look was one of total disbelief, and shock. Then the life fled from his eyes, and Cavan fell dead across Aidan's naked body.

With a speed that surprised even her Aidan pushed his body off her. Backing into the farthest corner of the bed she put her hands over her face, and began to weep softly. For some minutes she couldn't control her shaking. She wanted Conn. She wanted her husband to come and put his warm arms about her, and tell her that everything was going to be all right. Then as the shock began to gradually wear off her, Aidan rose from the bed, and going over to the fireplace took the earthenware pitcher from the hot ashes in the corner and poured the warm water into the basin on the hearth. Adding a few pieces of peat to the fire to build it up a bit, she began to scrub at herself with a small scrap of cloth. She wanted to get his smell off her for even now it clogged her nostrils reminding her of the ordeal she had just undergone. Every now and then she glanced over to the bed to look at his sprawling body, to check again to be certain that he was dead, but he was much to her relief.

Opening the carved chest at the foot of the bed she found her split-legged skirt, another shirt, and her underclothing where Nan had promised to put it. With fumbling fingers she dressed herself, and then finding her stockings and her boots where the women left them, she drew them on. She started for the door, but then a thought took her, and going back over to the bed she rolled the corpse over, and withdrew the dagger from his body, wiping the blood off on the bedcovers. She might need that weapon again, she thought, and stuck it in her belt. Then creeping to the door she listened for a moment, but hearing no one, she opened it, and slipping out hurried up the winding staircase of the tower house to the topmost room where Nan and the baby were waiting.

Nan was awake, dressed and awaiting her. She had Aidan's cloak. "I thought ye weren't able to get away, m'lady," she said. "Is he really dead?"

Aidan nodded. "Aye, speak no more of it, Nan. It makes me sick to think of what I've done. Are my men below?"

The girl nodded. "All we need do is let down the sheets, and they'll send the rope back up to us. I don't mind telling ye, m'lady, that I'm frightened to death. 'Tis a fearful drop, it is."

For a moment Aidan thought, and then she said, "Nan, my grandfather's windows are the only ones below this one, aren't they?"

"Aye," said the girl slowly, and then she smiled broadly. "We can go out there, can't we!"

"If the sight of *his* dead body won't make ye faint, girl, and we can't take the cradle. We'll have to lower Valentina without any protection."

"I can swaddle her, m'lady, and we'll tie the ropes about her middle, and her ankles to lower her. I let her nurse extra long tonight, and she'll not wake, even with the rain."

Together the two women, Nan clutching the baby to her bosom, crept back down the winding staircase to Rogan FitzGerald's bedchamber which had been the bridal suite for tonight. As the door closed softly behind them Aidan turned the ancient iron key in the lock, and the baby put upon the bed, away from Cavan's body, together Aidan and Nan quietly moved a chair beneath the door handle, and the large carved chest against the whole thing. Then they set to work to strip the bed of its sheets which they lowered out the open window to where Aidan's four servants awaited. Quickly Cluny tied two thick ropes onto the sheets, and signaled for them to be pulled back up.

Looking out of the window as this transaction was undertaken, Aidan was glad that she had decided to escape from here rather than from the top of the tower. The drop from here was steep enough. In this room, however, there was little likelihood of their being disturbed as no one would invade the sanctity of the bridal chamber.

Working silently the two women tied one end of each rope tightly to individual bedposts. It would take more than their light weight on the bed to move it for the bed was an enormous creation of solid oak. While Aidan tested the knots for safety, Nan swaddled Valentina even more carefully than she had been, carefully covering the baby's little face with a light cloth to protect it from the rain. Then together they fastened the ropes about the child, and with great care began to lower her from the window, moving slowly until she had cleared the window entirely, and then letting the ropes down swiftly before the howling wind could catch at the little bundle, and slam the helpless baby against the stone tower. Aidan heaved a sigh of relief as her daughter reached the bottom, and unfastened, was taken into young Jim's arms.

Now it was Nan's turn, and as Aidan tied the heavy rope about the girl she warned her, "Now, no shrieking no matter how frightened ye get. I don't care how loudly the wind is howling, I don't want to take the chance of them hearing us even in this storm. Ye can't fall with the rope about yer waist. Just hold on, and brace yer feet against the side of the tower as ye go down. Ye'll be all right."

White-faced, Nan nonetheless gave her a brave nod, and without even a protest she climbed out on the sill, and pushed off, clutching desperately to the ropes as she swung out. Aidan watched her swift descent, relieved as Cluny and Mark reached up to help her the final few feet, and then quickly released her. Aidan pulled the ropes back up, and tossing her cloak down to the waiting men, she fastened the ropes tightly about her own waist. With a quick last glance about the room, and a silent prayer for Cavan FitzGerald, Aidan leapt out into the raging storm and gloomy summer twilight.

She was quickly at the bottom, and Cluny was undoing the ropes from about her, grumbling as he did so. "And if ye had waited for himself, yer husband, none of this would have happened. What did ye do with FitzGerald? Get him drunk?"

"Nay, I killed him, Cluny. If I had waited for Conn we would have walked into a trap that would have seen *him* killed. My dear FitzGerald relations were going to kill Conn, ye dolt! That would have settled the matter for good and all, wouldn't it?" His mouth fell open in surprise at her words, but he as quickly recovered himself as she hissed at him, "Where are the horses?"

"Locked in the stable," came the reply. "The old robber, yer grandsire, and his servants chased us from our shelter several hours ago with the admonition to seek our master out for ye did not need us anymore. We were lucky that we had already stowed the ropes away out here. We can come back for the horses, m'lady, but my advice is for us to go now. Even in this storm they're bound to hear us if we batter the stables in, and besides there are at least half a dozen servants sleeping there. This way we go now, and none the wiser until morning when they finally wonder why the happy couple haven't arisen, and decide to investigate."

"They'll have some fun getting into the bridal chamber," she chuckled. "Nan and I barricaded the door." Then she became serious. "Can we escape them on foot?"

" 'Tis but a few miles to the coast, m'lady, and we've got at least nine hours before they get curious. If we don't meet Lord Bliss on our way, there is a castle there on the coast, owned by Lord Glin, and he's loyal to the queen. We can shelter there."

"How did ye learn that?" she asked, him, once again amazed by Cluny's resourcefulness.

"One of the stable lads liked to talk," said Cluny offhandedly. "Come along now, m'lady, take yer cloak. We'd best be going." He wrapped the garment about Aidan, and drew the hood up to shelter her now wet hair.

"Give me Valentina," said Aidan to Nan. "I can shelter her beneath my cape, and ye have none. I'd have given ye mine, but I am so much taller than ye."

"Wait, m'lady," said Nan. "If I take this sheet, I can make a harness for ye to tuck the bairn into, and then yer hands will be free, and ye'll need them free on this path." Aidan nodded, and Nan swiftly fashioned the harness, and tucked the baby safely inside next to her mother's warm body, and away from the wind and rain.

Then Cluny and Mark leading the way, the two women between them, set off toward the coast along the rocky track that served as a road for the region. The storm had not abated one bit, and now seemed to Aidan, to be growing even stronger. The rain came down in sheets, making it almost impossible to see more than a few inches ahead of them; and the strong wind blew so hard that they had a difficult time keeping on their feet. Had the gale been any stronger they would not have been able to make any headway at all. They walked in a perpetual gloom that was neither quite night or day it being midsummer when there was only a short period of dark.

Aidan had no fears of their losing their way for as long as they kept to the path they were safe. After they had walked in silence for some time she moved up next to Cluny, and said, "Who is this Lord Glin?"

"His mother was the heiress to Glinshannon. She ran away with some English milord when she was fifteen, and her father disinherited her, but when the old man died it was discovered he had left everything to his daughter's eldest son, the catch being that the lad had to come and live in Ireland. Well, to everyone's surprise he did, turning over his future inheritance from his father to his next brother."

"How old a man is he?"

"Not too old, not too young I was told."

Aidan laughed. "That tells me little," she said.

"I know no more than ye, m'lady, but for this. Though he took his Irish inheritance, Lord Glin is a queen's man to his fingertips."

"Well, if we must seek shelter with him, I'd as soon he were a queen's man," Aidan said frankly. "I hope, however, that we can meet up with Conn before I must throw myself upon anyone else's mercy. The FitzGeralds want my wealth, Cluny, and my killing Cavan FitzGerald is not apt to deter them in their quest. Only Conn can do that, I believe."

"Then we had best pray that he get here soon, hadn't we, m'lady? When that old robber, yer grandsire, learns what ye've done to his nephew, there'll be hell to pay, and that's for certain. There's only one place ye can seek shelter in this region, and he'll be coming after ye at Glinshannon castle by midmorning tomorrow. Still if Lord Glin is a queen's man, it is not likely that he will turn ye over to the old man without a fair hearing."

"Conn will get here," she said, and despite the seriousness of their situation he heard laughter in her voice. "Does he not always rescue me, Cluny? Conn will get here, I know!"

Chapter 20

❦

$\mathcal{H}$enry Sturminster, Lord Glin, looked with curious eyes upon the party of six who sought refuge in his castle. There were four men, servants his trained eye told him. Two women, one again of the servant class; and a tall, bedraggled woman with fine features, and an air of command who intrigued him.

"I am Aidan St. Michael, Lady Bliss," she told him. "I need shelter for my servants, my child and myself."

"Ye came on foot I am told," Lord Glin drawled. "Where are yer horses?"

"At Ballycoille," said Aidan honestly.

"*Ballycoille?* Rogan FitzGerald's Ballycoille? What the hell were ye doing with that old devil?"

"The old devil is, to my mortification, my grandsire," she answered him, "and before I launch into this tale of mine I need to know if ye will shelter us from not only the storm, *but* from the FitzGeralds? If not, my lord, we will go. My husband is on his way from England right now to aid me."

Lord Glin was a handsome man with soft blond hair that had the habit of falling over his forehead, and amber-brown eyes. He now looked closely at Aidan, and for some reason that he himself could not fathom he decided to offer his protection. "I will be delighted to tender ye my hospitality, madame, and ye may rest safe that I would put nothing willingly into Rogan FitzGerald's hand, least of all a gentlewoman and her party." He signaled his servants. "Take Lady Bliss, and her people to their rooms," he said. Then taking Aidan's hand up, he kissed it gallantly. "When ye are more comfortable, madame, we will discuss yer predicament."

Aidan saw her men led off in the direction of what she suspected was the kitchens while she and Nan followed a serving wench up a broad staircase, down a wide hallway and into a gracious apartment. They were quickly surrounded by a bevy of serving women who taking the baby from

491

its mother then set about to make the two women comfortable. A hot bath was brought for Aidan, and she almost cried with joy at its sight. It had been some days since she had been able to bathe. When she finished she was offered a comfortable and warm dark blue velvet dressing gown which she gratefully put on, surprised at its fit which was a good one. Nan had been treated equally well, and she and the baby were nicely settled in a small room with a blazing fire just off the main chamber of the apartment.

The castle's housekeeper, a dour-looking woman garbed entirely in proper black came to Aidan and said, "His lordship would like to know if ye would allow him to take the morning meal with ye, m'lady."

"Please tell Lord Glin that I should be delighted to receive him," Aidan returned. She was feeling so much better now that she was warm and dry, and particularly now that there were several miles, and a strong stone castle between her and the FitzGeralds.

The castle's staff hurried about the salon of the guest apartment, and within a very short time the table was laid, and set for two. Aidan admired the heavy damask cloth that covered the oak board as well as the beautiful silver candlesticks with their pure beeswax tapers that burned with virtually no smoke at all. She raised her eyebrows somewhat in surprise as the servants placed gold plates, eating utensils, and exquisite gold goblets studded with green agate upon the table. It had not occurred to her that in such an isolated place as Glinshannon she would find such elegance. Not after her grandfather's paltry board which was little better than a peasant's.

She was halted in her thoughts by the arrival of Lord Glin, and taking a really good look at her host, Aidan thought that he was quite attractive. Although his face was a long oval, there was a sweetness of expression about it that gave him an almost vulnerable look. Still she noticed that his servants treated him with a deep respect that she knew had to come from a genuine liking of the man. The people here showed no signs of fear as had her grandfather's servants.

"Ye've been well taken care of?" he inquired of her as he took her hand and kissed it once more.

"As well as if I had been the queen herself," Aidan replied with a smile.

Why she is pretty, thought Henry Sturminster, surprised as the smile lit Aidan's whole features; and that halo of copper hair is simply breathtaking! "If ye are well enough now," he said, "I should like to hear the tale of how ye came to be seeking shelter from this storm, and why ye left yer horses at Ballycoille. Ye must admit that the situation is unusual, and quite frankly my curiosity is piqued." He led her over to a comfortable settle by the fire, and they sat down together.

"I will tell ye the entire truth of the matter, my lord," Aidan said, "but first I must have yer solemn word, yer oath really, that what I reveal to ye, ye will not reveal to anyone else. Parts of my tale are so shocking as to be almost unbelievable, but I swear to ye, sir, that all is true."

Lord Glin ordered his servants from the room with the stern admonition that they were not to return unless called. Then taking one of Aidan's hands in his he said, "I swear to ye upon the souls of my parents, may God assoil them, that I will reveal nothing ye tell me, Lady Bliss." His kind brown eyes looked deeply into hers. "Will that do?"

Her gray eyes twinkled, and she smiled a tiny smile. "Thank ye, my lord. 'Twill do quite nicely, and so I will begin. When my father died three years ago it was written in his will that I should become the queen's ward, and be wed at her discretion to a man who would in return for me and my vast fortune take my father's name so that his family might live on through us. Thus it was that I was wed to Master Conn O'Malley, the youngest son of Dubhdara O'Malley of Innisfana. My husband had been in England for several years, was a member of the queen's own personal guard, the Gentlemen Pensioners, and greatly in her majesty's favor. We were wed by the queen's own chaplain in her majesty's presence in her chapel two years ago this St. Valentine's Day past.

"On the queen's orders we returned to my estates in Worcestershire which, by coincidence, border the estates of my husband's sister and her husband, Lord de Marisco. In the months that followed Conn and I grew to love one another deeply. We were expecting a child. It was then that disaster, in the guise of a cousin, arrived from Ireland. His name was Cavan FitzGerald, and he came bearing tidings from my mother's father, Rogan FitzGerald. Since my grandsire had never bothered to communicate with my mother since she had wed with my father, I found it unusual. Still it would have been inhospitable for us to refuse Cavan FitzGerald our hospitality."

"I know the man," said Lord Glin. "I can imagine he was wearing his best face, and showing his best manners, but I know for a fact that he is indeed the bastard he was born. I hope I do not offend ye with such blunt speech, madame, but ye do not appear to me to be a woman of vapors and false prudery."

"Nay," she said quietly, "I am not, but let me continue for this is a longish tale, and I am certain that ye are growing as hungry as I am."

Henry Sturminster laughed, and nodded his agreement. "I also have a chef who comes to me from France, and is somewhat of a martinet given to tantrums. When he is ready, we must eat or risk offending him so that he will sulk for a full week during which time all my meals will be either burnt or undercooked!"

"God's nightshirt, my lord, I should feel very guilty to subject so kind a host to such a fate!" and so she continued on with her story.

As her astounding narrative continued he realized fully her demand for his oath of silence. The entire account was as fantastic, as filled with drama, as if she had made it up. He was amazed that any gentlewoman could undergo such trauma, and survive. He was not even sure he would have believed her epic but for the fact her eyes never wavered from his own as she spoke. No one, Henry Sturminster decided, could lie that convincingly, and so he believed her although that belief was shaken somewhat when Aidan explained how she had killed Cavan FitzGerald. Nonetheless her obvious embarrassment again confirmed his trust in her as she spoke of the travesty of her *wedding* night.

"Good lord, madame," he said when she had finished. "If I read such a tale I should be hard put to believe it, and yet I do believe ye. Still, their plans having been foiled, do ye really think that yer relations will come chasing after ye? The bird had flown their cage, and ye have certainly proven yerself a formidable opponent. If it were me, I do not believe I should want to tangle with ye again!"

Aidan shook her head. "Rogan FitzGerald seems determined to have my fortune although I do not understand why," she said.

"I do," said Lord Glin. "The old man has ever been mixed up in one plot or another to overthrow the queen's own government. He sees himself as a savior of Ireland which I admit to finding rather amusing as he's never been more than twenty miles from his holding in his entire life. If ye took him, and dropped him into the middle of the Kildare FitzGerald's holdings he would be as foreign to them as they would be to him."

Aidan laughed. "He's cousin to the Countess of Lincoln, although I know for a fact he's never met her. When my mother was a girl he petitioned her to find a place for his daughter in her service as my mother was his favorite child. Instead the countess made the match between my parents."

Lord Glin suddenly found himself impressed by the woman sitting by his side. "Ye actually know the Countess of Lincoln?"

Aidan nodded.

"And the queen?"

"I was one of her maids of honor," Aidan replied. "Have ye never been to court, my lord?"

He shook his head. "My mother," he said, "was the heiress to Glinshannon. Her father envisioned a great marriage for her to a great Irish name. In preparation for such an event he sent her to a convent school in France. It was at the home of a French friend that she met my father who was also studying in France at the time. For them it was love at first sight, and at the first opportunity they ran away, and were married." He shrugged fatalistically. "My father's English family were no more thrilled by the match than was my Irish grandfather, but by that time my mother was with child—me—and the marriage vows were undisputedly attested to by reliable witnesses, and so both families were forced to accept the union as a hard fact.

"My mother, however, had great strength of character, and having lost her own father who refused to communicate with her although at the time he had not disinherited her, she set out to win over her husband's relations which she did. My birth was quickly followed by that of my next two brothers, our two sisters, and a final brother. Although my family was comfortable we were not rich, nor were we influential, and so we were all fortunate enough to grow up at home in Dorset.

"When I was twelve my maternal grandfather informed my father that he would make me the heir to Glinshannon, and to his wealth, on one condition, I must come to Ireland immediately to live with him, and I must renounce my claim to my father's estates and title. The choice was to be mine alone, but once made could not be rescinded. My grandfather sent along as a present to me the most magnificent stallion I had ever seen. I had one month from the receipt of my grandfather's letter which was personally delivered by one of his servants to make up my mind. At the end of that time the servant would return to Ireland with or without me. There was no room for bargaining."

"And so ye came to Ireland," said Aidan. "Was it a hard choice to make, my lord? I do not think that I could give up *Pearroc Royal* easily for anything."

Henry Sturminster smiled. "My father was terribly upset, and wanted me to refuse my grandfather, but my mother rejoiced, and begged me to accept. She said that it was only fair my grandfather was given me as his heir as my father had taken my grandfather's heiress from him when my father and mother married. My mother said that my father had three other sons, and now at least one of the others would be settled, and then when my grandfather died, and I inherited his wealth, I could settle something upon my two youngest brothers thereby allowing them to find suitable wives. It was then that my father saw reason, and agreed to let me go if I so desired it."

"Which ye obviously did," remarked Aidan.

"Oh, I wanted to stay in England," said Henry Sturminster, "but I kept thinking about what my mother had said. How my future wealth could help provide opportunities for my two youngest brothers who without it would have little, not to mention my sisters whose dowries I increased thereby ensuring them of *very* good matches. At twelve, however, it seemed too great a responsibility for my shoulders, but I nonetheless for love of my mother took it upon myself. Do not, however, Lady Bliss, feel sorrow for me for I have never once regretted my decision. I fell in love with Glinshannon the moment I laid eyes on it, and my grandfather and I were great friends until he died when I was nineteen."

"And is there a Lady Glin?" Aidan inquired curiously.

The handsome man smiled now. "Ye sound like my mother," he chuckled. "I am scarcely thirty."

"My husband is yer junior, and we already have one living child," she scolded him.

"Now ye really do sound like my mother!" and this time he laughed, "but as by this time my mother is rejoicing in England at the news, let me share it with ye, Lady Bliss. I will be wed on Michaelmas to Maire O'Hara."

"Marriage is good for a man," said Aidan primly, but her eyes were alight with laughter.

"As I have already noted, Lady Bliss, yer a formidable opponent. However I shall no longer do battle with ye for I hear my servants in the passageway outside which means that our meal is here, and so if we are not to enrage Monsieur Paul, then we must now eat."

"I accept yer gracious surrender, my lord," she told him in bland tones, and Henry Sturminster laughed as he gave his staff leave to reenter the apartment.

They came in an orderly parade, each bearing some dish or other which was presented to the diners, now seated at the table. There were two egg dishes offered; fluffy pale golden eggs scrambled with heavy cream, tiny green onions and bits of chipped ham, as well as a silver platter with perfectly poached eggs in a sauce of cream and rich marsala wine. There was another platter that held a tender pink ham which the servant holding it sliced the thickness desired by the hungry diner. There were delicate little individual loaves of crusty bread served with sweet butter, and a choice of fresh wildflower honey from the castle hives, or an outrageously rich plum jam. There was a small wheel of delicious cheese with a sharp, biting taste to it that Aidan found excellent, particularly when eaten with a marvelous fruity golden wine that was served.

Hungry, she filled her plate twice, and finished it all to the amazement of Lord Glin who had never seen a female eat with so healthy an appetite. He was glad now that Monsieur Paul had done the two egg dishes for she had single-handedly finished the scrambled eggs herself, as well as cleaning up the entire supply of bread save for his first small loaf.

Satisfied now she sat back in her chair, her look one of a large, well-fed feline. "How," she said with genuine awe in her tones, "how do ye keep such a treasure in yer kitchens in this godforsaken place, Lord Glin?"

Henry Sturminster laughed. "By paying him too much," he answered, "and allowing him the outrageous concession of returning to France for two months every two years. Unheard of, isn't it, but I am afraid my father accustomed me to good food due to his own stay in France years ago. My grandfather, God assoil him, had an old woman who cooked for him for years. I gratefully retired her to her own cottage with a fat pension upon coming into my inheritance. The woman boiled everything, mutton, vegetables, puddings, and all in the same pot!"

Aidan laughed. "Well yer Monsieur Paul is an artiste," she agreed.

Lord Glin arose. "Ye must be very tired," he said, "having walked all the night, and in this weather. Rest now. I will set a watch on the castle heights for both yer husband, and the FitzGeralds. I give ye my word that ye are perfectly safe here. No one can enter Glinshannon without my consent. It is virtually impregnable."

Aidan was grateful for his reassurance, and the truth was that she was exhausted. Checking on Nan and the baby she found them sleeping soundly, the remains of a good meal on a tiny table in their chamber. She knew that it would not be necessary to ask after her four men for they had undoubtedly been taken care of as well. Henry Sturminster was a gracious host. Going into the spacious bedchamber with its beautiful rose velvet draperies and bedhangings she removed her chamber robe, and slipped beneath the lavender-scented sheets to fall quickly asleep.

How long she slept she did not know, but as she lay cradled in the wonderful comfort of the large bed she became gradually aware of a delicious warm languor, a feeling she had never thought to experience ever again, beginning to ooze slowly through her body.

"Aidan," she heard her name breathed softly into her ear. "Aidan, my love."

Slowly, ever so slowly, she opened her eyes to meet the gaze of her husband. "Conn!"

His mouth descended upon hers in a blazing kiss that left her feeling happily breathless. "Can ye never stay put where I leave ye, sweetheart?" he teased her as he feathered gentle kisses across her brow. Then his lips traveled lightly across her eyelids, her nose, and her mouth again, easily parting her lips again to plunge his tongue within the delicious cavern.

Aidan shivered hard, and their glances met surprised. Slowly he rolled over onto his side, and reaching out fondled one of her beautiful breasts, finding it already firm, the nipple rigid with desire. She watched him with big eyes, a sudden dawning realization insinuating itself into her consciousness. "Conn," she whispered, "Conn, I think it is again as it once was with us!"

"Indeed, I believe it is, sweetheart." He smoothed his big hand down her body.

"How did ye find me?" she sighed happily.

"Lord Glin signaled the ship," he said, "and when I came into the chamber ye looked so delicious sleeping there I could not help but take off my own clothes, and join ye."

"Conn!" she exclaimed half-shocked, yet thrilled by his bold actions, "what will Lord Glin think of us?"

"Far more than if I had simply bowed, and kissed yer hand, sweetheart. Ye've far more interesting parts I should rather kiss, my darling!"

"Oh, yes!" she cried, and lowering his head Conn began a delicate and delightful exploration of his wife's superb body with his lips. He didn't understand it, but she was suddenly blooming beneath his touch as she once had in the early days of their union before Cavan FitzGerald had almost destroyed their happiness. His mouth wandered across her smooth torso, and down her faintly rounded belly. Her skin was so silky and sweet that the very touch of it on his lips excited him unbearably. Brushing his mouth lightly across her lower belly he began to move upward again, but suddenly Aidan was gently pushing his head lower.

"Please, Conn," he heard her say to his great surprise, "love me *there*! I like it when I am loved there." Oh, God! she thought. I hope that Skye was right, and that husbands do not mind being told of what a woman likes.

For a moment he was shocked. He had loved other women in that tender, and tempting spot, but never had he touched his wife in such a manner. Wives were different, were they not? Then it came to him, and he almost laughed at himself. Wives were women like all women. Why had he not realized that before? Then another, darker thought intruded into his consciousness. He had not loved her *there*. Then who had? Then once again his common sense raised its head. What did it matter now what had happened in that year in which they were apart? They were together again, and she seemed to be whole once more.

Conn lowered his dark head, and gently began to love his wife in that most secret of places hidden upon a woman's body. Her soft cry of pleasure filled him with satisfaction, and he felt his own eyes tearing at the thought that she once again could feel the heavenly pleasure that she always offered to him.

Unbeknownst to herself Aidan was weeping also though the sounds she made were only those of happiness. She had never understood why the pleasure feeling that is between a man and a woman had left her when she had been returned to Conn, but that it had returned, of that there was no doubt now in her mind. Skillful little fingers of pure fire enveloped her body as the pleasure overwhelmed her, and she slid into that wonderful half-conscious floating state that passion had always evoked in her.

She was totally aware of everything he was doing, and yet she felt for the moment as if her limbs were paralyzed. She felt him leave that sensitive little jewel of hers, and move up again to play with her lovely breasts. Gently he fondled her full flesh, but when he dipped his head to suck upon her nipples Aidan felt as if she had been struck by a bolt of pure lightning. His lips tugged upon the sensitive tips of her breasts, sending a corresponding jolt of feeling to the place between her legs.

"I love ye, my darling wife," he said softly as he slid his large body over her. "I love ye, Aidan," he whispered as with one smooth movement he filled her passage with his great shaft. "I love ye, sweetheart," he murmured as he began to move upon her, and suddenly all the terrible memories that had filled her soul began to fade away as Conn's deep and abiding love for Aidan began to make new memories for her to dwell upon.

And afterward as they lay contented, and happy in each other's arms she told him of what had happened at Ballycoille, and he was once more amazed by her fortitude and her bravery. But he was also unhappy that she should have been put in such a position so soon after her ordeal in Turkey. Still she was none the worse for her adventure, and she had overcome whatever it was that had prevented her from enjoying their passion.

"Yer certain ye killed Cavan FitzGerald?" he asked her.

"His body was cold before we even made our escape," she assured him. Then suddenly she was aware of something. "The storm is gone!" she said. "Jesu! The FitzGeralds will be upon us if they're not already here! Get up, Conn! We may yet have time to make our escape!"

"Nay, sweetheart, we will remain here, and face them down."

"Conn, are ye mad?"

"Nay, Aidan, I'm not mad, but unless we can disabuse that damned old man, yer grandsire, of his wild notions, God knows what he'll try next to get his hands on yer wealth."

"Conn, don't ye understand? He's ready to kill ye!"

"Well, we'll have to convince the old man otherwise, won't we?"

She didn't know how that could be done, and she decided that he was mad for even trying, and she was madder yet for listening to him, but she knew better than to change his mind, and so laughing ruefully Aidan said, "I think we can convince him better if we have our clothing on, Conn, my husband!"

With a chuckle he was up, and dressing. Her own clothing she found laid out, clean and dried, upon a chair, and following his lead she quickly restored order to her person.

"Leave yer hair loose," he said softly, and with a smile she nodded. He had always liked her hair free and flowing about her shoulders. Conn reached out and stroking his hand down her tresses he tenderly fingered a lock. "It's a mixture of molten gold and orange fire, sweetheart. No one has hair like yers."

"Valentina will," she said. "Have ye seen her yet? I did manage to rescue our daughter."

" 'Twas the second thing I did after I assured myself that ye were all right. Who's the little lass with the baby?"

"The wet nurse Cavan found in Cardiff. 'Tis a long and sad story, Conn, but I'm bringing Nan back with us to *Pearroc Royal*. For one thing I need her to nurse Valentina because I had to dry my own milk up, and now Wenda's nose will be very much out of joint so I'm afraid we'll have to have another baby very quickly so we may give our faithful Wenda her own charge to care for again. Besides Nan is a good girl as I'll explain later."

"Another bairn so soon? Are ye certain yer ready for another baby, Aidan?"

She laughed, and the sound was pure happiness. "Conn," she said, "my father raised me as he would have raised a son had he had one. I can read, and I can write, and I can keep books. I know all about my family's London business, and if I must I will continue to control it, but it is not what I want."

"What do ye want then?" he asked her.

"I want to be yer wife, and have lots of babies, and run my estates, Conn. *That* is my life, and *that* is what I want. It makes me happier than anything else in this entire world. I want to go home, Conn, and be free from fear of ever being taken away from ye or from *Pearroc Royal* again! Whatever we have to do to face down that old man who is my grandsire, let us do, and then let us go home to England!"

"By God, Aidan St. Michael!" he said feelingly to her, "I bless the day that Elizabeth Tudor ever decided that ye were the woman for me, for ye surely are! Yer a woman who knows her own mind, and I love ye for it."

"I'm glad," she said deciding that now was the time for total honesty. "I'm glad that ye like a woman who knows her own mind, my husband, because the truth of the matter is that the queen couldn't think of who to marry ye to until I suggested that she marry ye to me!"

Conn's jaw dropped, and then he began to laugh. "Aidan," he said, "there is no one like ye in this entire world. Yer an original, and yer mine!" Then he gave her a quick kiss.

Before she could say another word there was a knock upon the door which sobered them both, and a servant entered to tell them that Lord Glin was awaiting them in the Great Hall with Rogan FitzGerald and his son Eamon. Without a word Conn and Aidan joined hands, and walked from their haven. Together they were invincible, and they felt it.

The sight of them, hand in hand, as they entered the Great Hall of Glinshannon Castle enraged Rogan FitzGerald so badly that for a moment he could not speak. His stern face darkened with his outrage as the blood rushed to his head, and he opened and closed his mouth several times like a fish gasping for water before he was finally able to say a word, but then he shouted at her, "*Murderess!* Ye killed my nephew in cold blood, ye damned English bitch! I regret yer any kin of mine!"

"No more than I regret it, ye old devil," Aidan shouted back. "Yer damned bastard nephew would be alive today if ye'd not forced me into a bigamous marriage! Did ye really think I'd allow ye to do that to me? Did ye really think I'd allow ye to kill my Conn? If ye did then ye've little opinion of my English antecedents, and less of yer own!"

He was stunned into temporary silence by her equal anger, but Eamon FitzGerald, cold and calculating, and now considering Aidan's wealth for himself said, "Lord Glin, as the queen's magistrate for this region, I demand the queen's justice. This woman, my niece, has coldly, and deliberately murdered her lawful husband in order to be with *that* man, Conn O'Malley. They are both responsible for the death of my cousin Cavan FitzGerald and should be punished to the full extent of the law."

Henry Sturminster, Lord Glin, considered the situation for a long moment, and then he said, "We have a problem that I cannot solve, my lords, and my lady. The question is to whom was Aidan St. Michael really wed? If she was indeed truly wed to Conn O'Malley, then ye gentlemen of Ballycoille committed a crime by forcing her into a bigamous match; and her act against Cavan FitzGerald was but a defense of her honor. On the other hand if her marriage to Master O'Malley was indeed invalid, then her wedding to Cavan FitzGerald was a legal one, and she is guilty of killing the man. There are other legalities to be considered, too. Aidan St. Michael is English, and as such she is subject to England's laws, and England's church, and most of all to the queen's will for she is the queen's own loyal subject; but gentlemen, before any of the legalities can be even considered I must straighten out the ecclesiasticalities of the matter, don't ye agree?"

Rogan FitzGerald was now fully recovered, and ready to do battle. "What the hell does all that mean?" he demanded. "What the hell does all that mean?" he demanded.

"It means," said Conn with a grin on his face, "that he needs a church decision on whom Aidan was married to before he can decide anything else."

"Aidan was married to Cavan FitzGerald in Holy Mother Church! It is the only true faith, and therefore no other marriage can be lawful and valid," the old man snapped.

"As the queen's loyal subject I cannot agree with ye, Rogan FitzGerald," said Lord Glin. "Our late sovereign, Henry VIII, parted us not from the Catholic faith, but rather from Rome's rule. The English will not suffer a foreign prince to hold sway over them."

" 'Tis a pity the English aren't as scrupulous of Irish feelings as they are of their own," said the old man.

Conn O'Malley chuckled. "There, Rogan FitzGerald, I agree with ye."

"If ye agree with me then why do ye live in England, son of the great Dubhdara O'Malley, may God assoil his soul?"

"Because unlike ye, Rogan FitzGerald, I am a realist. Yer a dreamer. The Irish will never be free until they can come together as one people as it once was in the ancient times. A time when a man was judged for himself be he a believer in the old gods, a Christian, or a Jew. A time when women were respected and considered equal in their rights. A time we lived, and fought, and died as *One People!* Those times are gone, old man, and we have become a splintered race where each man claims his descent from the old kings, and no man trusts another. That weakness allowed the English to overcome us. I do not see the changing in my time, Rogan FitzGerald, and so I prefer to live in England with my English wife raising my children in safety. It is but a father's wish that his bairns be safe, and I am no less Irish for it, old man!"

A servant had entered the Great Hall while they were speaking, and now Lord Glin said, "This will not solve the problem that faces us, gentlemen, but I believe we are about to gain the beginnings of our solution." He turned to the servant, and spoke something to him. Then as the man hurried out Lord Glin said, "The Bishop of Mid-Connaught has just arrived, and I believe that he will be able to untangle the churchly matter of this thorny situation."

"The Bishop of Mid-Connaught is an O'Malley!" protested Eamon FitzGerald.

"An O'Malley?" Aidan looked to Conn.

"My eldest brother," he whispered back to her, "actually my half-brother. He was the last child of my father's first wife, and the only live son she produced. Skye was the youngest of her daughters."

"I object!" shouted Rogan FitzGerald. "How can we get a fair hearing from an O'Malley?"

A tall handsome man strode into the room, his purple robes swinging vigorously about his long legs, and Aidan thought seeing him for the first time that she would have known him anywhere. There was no doubt that he was an O'Malley. "Are ye saying that I can't do my duty by the church, Rogan FitzGerald?" the bishop demanded in a stern voice.

"Yet from Connaught! This is Munster! I'll only be judged by the Bishop of Munster!" Rogan FitzGerald said.

"Then ye'll be waiting a long time, sir, for the Bishop of Munster died two days ago, and 'twill be one hell of a long time before the word reaches Rome, and the Holy Father gets around to appointing us another bishop for Munster. Ireland is not particularly important in the church's scheme of things, Rogan FitzGerald, so ye'll be judged by me, and if ye don't like my judgment then yer free to appeal to Rome." He looked at Conn. "Yer looking prosperous, little brother."

"Michael, this is my wife, Aidan."

"That remains to be seen!" yelled Rogan FitzGerald.

"Sit down, and shut up!" roared Michael O'Malley.

"My lord bishop, will ye have some wine?" asked Lord Glin.

. Michael O'Malley grinned engagingly, and answered, " 'Tis the first civilized thing's been said to me since I entered Glinshannon. Aye, my lord, I will have some wine, and thank ye."

Lord Glin settled the bishop at the high board, and together they spoke in low tones while servants bustled about them offering wine and cakes to the cleric.

"He looks like ye, and yet he doesn't," said Aidan.

"He looks more like my father every day. I barely remember Da, but there's a large portrait of him at Innisfana. Skye and I look more a mixture of Da and our mothers. He's a good man, and he'll render us a fair judgment."

"But what if he finds for the FitzGeralds? Then I'm guilty of murder."

"Don't worry, sweetheart," he soothed her. "Yer no murderess. Ye were but protecting yer honor from that bastard. We're married, Aidan!"

When Michael O'Malley had finished refreshing himself he gave orders that the hearing should begin, and he began by clearing the Great Hall of Glinshannon of everyone but those directly involved. He wanted no altercations breaking out between the O'Malley retainers who had traveled with him from Innisfana, and the rather motley crew who had accompanied the FitzGeralds from Ballycoille.

When no one but the complainants and the defendants and Lord Glin remained Michael O'Malley said, "All right, Rogan FitzGerald, let us hear yer side of this matter first."

"Aidan St. Michael is the only surviving child of my dear departed daughter Bevin. She has no family but me, and as the eldest male member of her family it is my duty to see that she is properly wed. I chose my nephew, Cavan FitzGerald, to be her mate, and they were wed yesterday by my own son Father Barra FitzGerald. They were wed in the faith of our family, a faith in which my granddaughter was born and baptized. Last night after we had put the newlyweds to bed that coldhearted bitch murdered her husband! Then she came running back to *that* man, her lover! I demand justice, my lord bishop!"

Michael O'Malley looked down at Aidan. "Is what he says true, Aidan St. Michael?"

"No!"

"Liar!"

"Be silent!" the bishop commanded. "Ye deny ye were wed yesterday to Cavan FitzGerald?"

"I deny that he was my husband, my lord bishop," said Aidan. "That I was coerced into making a mockery of the sacrament by being forced into a bigamous union, that I will not deny."

"Ye say ye were forced? How were ye forced?"

"Our infant daughter, mine and Conn's, was stolen from our home in England in order that I might come willingly to my grandsire's home. That wicked old man put his dagger to my child's helpless body! He drew blood, causing my baby to cry out with pain! That is how he forced me, my lord bishop! He said he would not kill Valentina, but rather he would see that she suffered constant pain unless I agreed to his terrible scheme. Until I could make good our escape from Ballycoille I had no choice but to go along with the FitzGeralds."

"These are serious charges, Rogan FitzGerald," said the bishop.

"There was no mockery of the sacrament," Rogan protested. "Her alleged marriage in England was not a valid one as it was not performed by a legitimate priest of the church! How then could there be a bigamy committed?" He looked triumphantly at Michael O'Malley for he knew that no matter how the bishop might feel personally, he must render his judgment based on religious convictions only.

"Ye old devil," Aidan shouted at him, furious, "I accept no law be it civil or religious unless it be English law!"

"Tell me of yer marriage to Conn," Michael said in a soothing tone. "When was it performed, and by whom?"

"We were married in the queen's own chapel at Greenwich Palace, on the fourteenth of February in the year of our lord fifteen hundred and seventy-eight. The ceremony was performed by one of the queen's own chaplains, in her presence, and that of our nephew the Earl of Southwood, my tiring woman, Mag, and Conn's man, Cluny."

"It is a consecrated chapel," said Michael O'Malley.

"But an unconsecrated priest!" protested Rogan FitzGerald.

"Do ye remember which of the queen's chaplains married ye?"

Here was the sticking point, thought the bishop. There were some who still served Elizabeth Tudor who had not yet been excommunicated for accepting the queen's rule over the church in England as opposed to the papal rule of England's church. The old faith was still the majority faith although the English now separated their faith from their patriotic loyalties.

"We were wed by Father Bede," said Aidan quietly.

"The marriage is legal and lawful in the eyes of the church," said O'Malley.

"*What?*" Rogan FitzGerald and his son Eamon were both totally outraged as they saw Aidan's wealth slipping from their grasp. They were not, however, going to give up without a fight. "I knew that we couldn't trust an O'Malley to render a fair judgment where another O'Malley was concerned! I protest yer decision, my lord bishop! I shall take my case to Rome itself if I have to in order to obtain true justice!"

"Listen to me, Rogan FitzGerald," said the bishop patiently. "Father Matthew Bede is still considered by Rome a priest of our faith. There are several who yet serve the queen with Rome's silent blessing for they seek reconciliation, and a return of England to the papal fold. Ye have no case. Indeed if Lady Bliss wished to file charges against ye for forcing her into a bigamous union she could do so. Yer an old man, Rogan FitzGerald, and ye'll soon be facing yer maker. Ye've much on yer soul, man, but as a good son of the church, ye have the chance to be shriven when yer hour comes. If ye were excommunicated, and cut off from Holy Mother Church, ye would have no chance, and yer soul would be flung into the fiery pit to burn forever. Yer at a serious crossroads, Rogan FitzGerald, and the choice is yers. Which path will ye take?"

He seemed to shrivel before their very eyes, and for the briefest moment Michael O'Malley felt pity for the old man, but then he remembered all the misery Rogan FitzGerald and his nephew, Cavan, had caused his youngest brother, and Aidan, and the bishop's heart hardened. Eamon FitzGerald, more practical than his father, saw that they had lost, and shrugged. The wealth had been his father's dream, and Cavan's dream. Only for a short time had he considered what he might have done with his niece's gold to restore and improve Ballycoille. He had been a fool to even consider such a possibility. Dreams were for children, and those imbeciles stupid enough to believe in them.

"Come, father," he said. "The day is waning, and we've a bit of a ride home." Taking the old man by the arm he began to lead him off.

"I want my horses," Aidan called after them, and her uncle turned.

"We brought them with us, but if I give them back to ye now some of our men will have to walk all the way back to Ballycoille."

"If I can walk it, uncle, then yer men can. Leave my animals in Lord Glin's stables."

"Yer a hard woman, Aidan St. Michael," he said.

" 'Tis the Irish in me, uncle," she answered him, and then she watched coldly as he led her grandfather from the Great Hall of Glinshannon. Rogan FitzGerald's shoulders were slumped, and his head was low.

"Farewell, *grandfather*," she called after him, but though he hesitated a moment, he did not turn instead disappearing through the doors of the hall, and out of her sight.

With the FitzGeralds went the tension that had filled the half. Henry Sturminster, Lord Glin, smiled at his guests, and said, "Ye'll all stay the night, of course."

They nodded.

"Lord Glin's chef is a great man," Aidan said reverently. "Having had one meal at his hands, my mouth waters for the next."

"I do not understand how ye can be hungry again after that large meal ye put away this morning," said Lord Glin admiringly.

"Aidan has a most prodigious appetite," said her husband with a proud smile, "and she never gains a pound."

The servants had now reentered the hall, and were bustling about in preparation for the evening meal. Large goblets of wine were passed to them, and as they stood by the fire warming themselves, for the summer's day was chilled now that the storm had passed, Lord Glin said, "How fortunate, my lord bishop, that ye knew that Father Bede is still a recognized priest of the church."

"I don't know," said Michael O'Malley quietly, and his bright blue eyes were twinkling mischievously in his ruddy face.

Lord Glin's jaw dropped open in surprise, and he gasped, "But ye said . . ."

"I know precisely what I said, and I shall give myself a most severe penance for the falsehood, I assure ye, my lord. However, my apparent knowledge did serve to solve our problem, didn't it? Rogan and Eamon FitzGerald are, with their men, on their way back to Ballycoille, and out of my brother and Aidan's life forever. When my brother went to England with my sister six years ago he made his choice with regards to his loyalties, and to how he would live his life. As our father's youngest child there was nothing for him here in Ireland, and I cannot disagree with his choices.

"For now Elizabeth Tudor is sovereign of England, Ireland, and Wales. Conn has given her his devotion, and having done so will not waver in his allegiance. He served her in her personal guard, he accepted her choice of a wife. Conn O'Malley, yer pardon, brother, Conn St. Michael, Lord Bliss, is a staunch queen's man, and his English-born wife is equally loyal to their queen. Their marriage in that queen's presence by her own cleric in her consecrated chapel is valid to them, and to all of the queen's loyal subjects. It would take months to straighten out this damn thing, and so I have taken the solution upon myself.

"I know, however, that Conn's mother as well as myself would be greatly relieved in our own minds if my brother and his wife would consent to have me remarry them in the faith into which they were born. There could never be any doubts then, could there?"

"We are married, Michael," said Conn stubbornly.

"I know that," returned his elder brother, "and in all probability that marriage is indeed valid in the eyes of Holy Mother Church, Conn, but so there can be no doubts ever again cast upon the union between ye and Aidan, indulge me in this small request, brother."

"Why not, Conn?" said Aidan laughingly. "After all we have only just made a new beginning of sorts, haven't we?"

"I consider our marriage at Greenwich valid," he said. "I have never once considered that it might not be."

"Nor I, my love, but what harm can this do, Conn?"

He took her oval face in his hands, and looked deep into her silvery eyes. "It would please ye?"

"It would please yer mother," she answered him with a smile, "and since we are so near to Innisfana, Conn, it seems a shame to me not to bring Valentina to see her grandmother. I want yer mother content with us, Conn. If this will do it, then I am for it. I do not doubt our marriage those two and a half years past, but I want no slur cast upon our union again by anyone. The future of our sons depends upon it."

He touched her lips lightly with his own, and then looking at Michael he said, "All right, but do it now, here before the fire!"

"Before all the servants who will wonder what it is about, and gossip," said Michael O'Malley. "I think not, Conn. Surely ye don't want to compromise my position as a churchman?"

"Come with me," said Lord Glin before another word could be said by the brothers.

They followed him from the Great Hall of the castle, and down a broad corridor to its end. Opening the double doors before him Lord Glin led them into a small chapel. Before them was a carved and gilded wooden altar with an exquisitely embroidered linen cloth upon it. Lord Glin moved up to the altar, and lit the golden candelabra with a taper he had dipped into the vigil light. The beeswax candles cast a soft glow over the room which was already lit with the light of the setting sun which came through the crimson, sapphire-blue, gold, emerald-green, and amethyst colored stained-glass windows behind and on either side of the altar.

Michael O'Malley knelt before the altar to pray. Then arising he turned to face his brother, and Aidan. Lord Glin remained as witness to the sacrament. Taking a deep breath the bishop began in his musical voice, "Dearly beloved, we are gathered here in the sight of God, and in the face of this company, to join together this Man, and this Woman in Holy Matrimony. . . ."

Epilogue

APRIL

1581

"If they don't stop all that banging and hammering soon," said Aidan St. Michael irritably, "I shall scream."

"The house needed to be enlarged," said Skye. "None of those bedchambers is really fit to house children. Valentina is already so adventurous at a year that I live in terror that she will fall down the staircase. She is always escaping Nan's vigilance."

"Only because of Nan's interest in Harry Beal," chuckled Aidan. "I saw that coming before we even left Innisfana. The rumor is that they are hoping to marry at Michaelmas if they can obtain our permission, and God knows I am willing enough. Nan deserves a bit of happiness."

"I like my servants married," said Skye. "It settles them."

"It settles all of us," said Aidan with a laugh, "and some of us more than others," she concluded patting her very swollen belly. "Oh, Skye, do ye think the new wing will be done before the baby is born?"

"Ye've another month or so to go," said Skye comfortingly.

"I don't know," said Aidan. "Look at me! I'm simply enormous with this baby, and I feel as if I'm going to burst at any minute. There is no getting comfortable anymore. I wasn't this way with Valentina. I am most relieved that yer sister Eibhlin has come early from Ireland to be with me."

"Ye birthed Valentina easily enough without her," Skye soothed.

"This is different," said Aidan firmly. "This is very different."

"Ye knew that Valentina was a girl," said Skye trying to lighten her sister-in-law's mood. "Can ye tell about this babe?"

"That's another odd thing," said Aidan. "I don't really know this time. Sometimes I see a boy, and other times 'tis another lass." She attempted to gingerly shift her position, but her bulk made it almost impossible, and with a sound of irritation she flung the tiny shirt she had been sewing aside, and pulled herself into a standing position. "I am going to go and lie down, Skye," she said. " 'Tis the only time now that I can get half comfortable!"

"Go along," said Skye sympathetically. She had borne eight children of her own, and she knew how difficult these last weeks of a confinement could be. She watched Aidan waddle from the room, and for a moment she almost envied her brother's wife. Her youngest child, Velvet de Marisco, would be eight years old in just two weeks; and seeing Aidan so full with life, so wonderfully fertile, Skye longed for just one more child. If only she might have given Adam a son, but Velvet's birth had been an incredible miracle for them, and she knew she could ask God for no more. This marriage was the happiest, the most peaceful, the most contented match she had had, and she knew that she and Adam would live on together until death parted them; but no. Death would only be a temporary parting for them. They would always be together even into eternity.

"Yer deep in thought," said Eibhlin O'Malley as she came into the cheerful hall, her black robes swirling about her. " 'Tis a lovely day, and Aidan's gardens are wonderful."

"I was thinking I wished I could have another child," said Skye honestly.

"*What?* At yer age? Yer forty!"

"I don't need to be reminded of my age, Eibhlin," laughed Skye, "and besides 'tis impossible anyhow. Still, I cannot help but envy Aidan the coming child."

Eibhlin plunked herself into the chair that Aidan had so recently vacated, and said, "For a woman with a head for business, ye've a soft heart for children, Skye. Ye've done well by them all too for all yer not a conventional mother."

" 'Tis only what Da drummed into me all those years ago, Eibhlin. Family first! Family always! I've lived my life by that creed for all my *adventures*." She chuckled. "They haven't turned out so badly either, have they, my seven babies with their five fathers?"

Eibhlin smiled at her younger sister, and the smile relieved the severity of her dark religious habit. "Out of all Da's bairns we four, ye, and me, and Michael and Conn were the odd ones. Michael insisting upon the priesthood despite being Da's eldest son and heir. Me with my doctoring, and ye and Conn with yer adventuring. I wonder what the next generation will turn out to be like. I hope that I'll be here to see it."

"I think we'll all live to ripe old ages," said Skye. "One reason we were never like the others was that we were always questioning, always seeking, and Eibhlin, I believe we still are. As for the next generation, children never really turn out to be like their parents. They have their own fates to find and to follow."

"How did ye get so wise, sister mine?" Eibhlin smiled.

"By living life to the fullest," came the reply.

"Excuse me, m'lady." Mag was suddenly by Skye's side.

"Yes, Mag?"

"Mistress Aidan isn't feeling very well. I can't be certain, but I think she may be getting ready to have the baby."

Eibhlin frowned. " 'Tis a bit too early yet," she said, and then she stood up. "Come along, Skye, and let us see what it is that is troubling Aidan."

The two women followed Mag from the hall and up the stairs to the master chamber. There Aidan, her pretty face beaded with moisture, lay upon her bed, looking very uncomfortable. Eibhlin hurried over to her patient, and did a cursory examination.

"How do ye feel?" she demanded of her sister-in-law.

"Like I felt before I went into labor with Valentina," came the nervous reply. "It's too soon, Eibhlin, isn't it? This baby is not due for several more weeks."

"Babies come when they choose to come, Aidan, not when we say that they should," chuckled Eibhlin. "If the bairn decides to be born now, 'tis a bit early, but it should be all right. It might be a bit smaller, but if its lungs are good then we'll have no problems. Besides, did ye and Conn ever consider that ye might have miscalculated? Get up now, and walk about a bit. The whole problem might simply be that ye've a cramp from lying in one position." She helped Aidan to her feet, and together they walked about the room.

Aidan, however, sensed that her hour had come, and that instinct was shortly borne out when without warning her water broke, and gushed down her legs to the carpet. "God's nightshirt!" she swore. "Mag, get the girls to mop the rug lest it be ruined." She turned to Eibhlin and Skye. "I think I'm going to have a baby," she said wryly. "Mag, send for my lord."

At Eibhlin's suggestion Aidan preferred to move about the room for the time being. She felt no pain at all at this time, and her cheerful attitude allowed Eibhlin to prepare for the imminent birth. A large, rectangular oak table was brought into the room to be set up as a birthing table. On Eibhlin's instructions it was padded with cotton quilts. The windows were opened to allow fresh air into the room on this bright and warm spring day, for unlike so many others, Eibhlin did not believe in delivering her patients in a gloomy atmosphere. A fire was carefully tended in the fireplace, and kettles of water hung from the iron arm over the flames. On another nearby table Eibhlin laid out clean cloths, and her medical instruments should she have need of them.

Conn came in from the fields where he had been supervising the planting of the estate farm, and gave his wife a hug. Eibhlin could have blessed his discretion for he made no mention of the fact the child was coming a little early. Instead he said, "I'll be in the library doing a bit of paperwork. When ye want me I'll come right up, sweetheart."

"Ye've already done yer part, and done it very well," she teased him. "If I let ye come in for the birthing, promise me that ye'll not get giddy at the sight of my blood the way ye did last time."

Conn flushed, and then laughed ruefully. "Well ye must admit it was quite a shock for me to see how a baby is born, and ye said some very unkind things to me in the midst of yer labor."

"I'll probably say even worse to ye today," she needled back, and then she winced. "First pain," she told Eibhlin.

Conn departed for his paperwork, and Aidan began the painful, yet joyful business of bringing another life into the world. She continued to move about her chamber, alternately walking and sitting awkwardly as the hours slipped by. By sunset, however, she was experiencing hard labor, and Eibhlin and Skye along with Mag, helped Aidan onto the birthing table.

The pains continued, coming now with greater duration, and less time between the pains for Aidan to catch her breath. Eibhlin sent for Conn to come into the room if he was to be present at the birth of the child. As Aidan had delivered Valentina in her bed, Conn was very surprised to see his wife propped up upon the birthing table, her legs up and parted.

"Sit by her head," Eibhlin ordered her brother. "Ye can be of help to Aidan if ye will but encourage her in her travail." She looked directly at her patient. "The baby is so anxious to enter this world that it would come feet first. I am going to reach into yer birth canal, and turn the babe around, Aidan, so ye must not push for a moment."

The room was silent, and for several minutes no one dared speak, and Aidan realized suddenly that she was actually holding her breath. Then Eibhlin looked up and smiled, and Aidan knew that she had been successful, and she relaxed.

"Now," said Eibhlin, "I want ye to push, and push again with all yer might. That's it, Aidan! Bear down hard!"

Aidan grunted and groaned with the effort, and when her eyes met the worried ones of her husband she was tempted to laugh for she remembered in this instant her threat to call him evil names in her labor. Instead, however, she concentrated upon the business at hand, and was rewarded several minutes later when Eibhlin cried out, "That's my girl! Here it comes! Oh, aye, here it comes!"

Aidan panted fiercely, and bore down again. Her eyes were squeezed tightly shut with her effort, and so she was very relieved to hear Conn say,

" 'Tis born, sweetheart! The baby is born!" And then she heard a cry, and the infant began to howl loudly. She opened her eyes then, and looked to Eibhlin questioningly.

" 'Tis a lass," said Eibhlin, "and a prettier, more perfect little girl I've never seen."

Aidan smiled, but then looking ruefully at Conn she opened her mouth to speak, but instead she gasped, and then she cried out sharply. "Eibhlin! The pains are back! God's nightshirt! 'Tis worse than before!"

Eibhlin bent down to examine her patient, and then she looked up with a huge grin upon her usually serene face. "There's another bairn yet to be born," she said. "Ye've twins, Aidan! Trust ye, Conn, to do the unusual! This will drive Brian, Shane, and Shamus wild with envy!"

They couldn't help but laugh at Eibhlin's comment, even Aidan chortled in the midst of her labor. Several more minutes passed during which Aidan worked to bring forth the second child in her womb. Finally with a mighty groan, and a fierce pain that she was certain had split her in two, the second of the twins slipped forth from her body and into Eibhlin's waiting hands. It was already crying as it came, filling its tiny lungs with great gasps of air, and waving its tiny fists in outrage at having been forced from the warm and safe shelter of its mother's body.

"A boy!" said Skye with a cry of delight. "Aidan, ye've birthed both a son and a daughter!"

Aidan felt the tears filling her eyes. She had so very much wanted to give Conn his son. Not that he was not happy with Valentina, but the shadow of her parentage would always be there no matter how much he might love her. With the twins there was no doubt, and now the boy was come they had an heir for Pearroc Royal! Aidan could not help but think how happy her father would have been about it.

While Mag and Skye cleaned the twins up, and then swaddled them in soft cloth, Eibhlin saw to the afterbirths, and Aidan and Conn glowed at one another speaking in soft tones. Finally Conn was chased from the chamber, and he descended into the hall of the house to inform first his elder daughter, Valentina, and then the servants, of the successful and safe birth of his first son, and his second daughter. Wine was brought, and a health drunk to the two new St. Michaels born this eighteenth day of April, in the twenty-third year of the reign of Elizabeth Tudor, this year of Our Lord fifteen hundred and eighty-one.

When afterward and at long last the house had quieted down, and Skye had ridden home across the fields to Queen's Malvern, and Eibhlin was abed with the rest of the household; Conn and Aidan settled down in their bed, the twins in their cradles, to talk.

"Since," said Aidan, "I named Valentina, 'tis only fair that ye get to name the twins." She snuggled down against his shoulder.

"I'd like to name the boy after my father," he said.

Aidan was somewhat taken aback. "Ye'd name our son, Dubhdara? 'Twill be a hard name for an English boy to bear, Conn."

He laughed. "Dubhdara was but a nickname, it means *Black Oak*. My father loved the black oaks, and insisted that all the prows of his ships be built of it. That's where the name came from, Aidan. He was O'Malley of the Black Oak. His Christian name, however, was Coilin, which in the English is Colin. I'd like our son to be called Colin St. Michael, if ye don't object. The lass I'd call Anne after my mother, and as Valentina's second name is Elizabeth after Bess, I'd give Annie the same second name, too. Anne Elizabeth St. Michael. We owe the queen far more than we can ever repay her for. We owe her for our love," and propping himself upon an elbow Conn looked down into his wife's dear face, and then he kissed her gently.

Aidan felt her heart swell with the unbearable weight of her happiness, and for a moment she wondered if it were wrong to be so content. She had the *Handsomest Man at Court* for a husband. She had two lovely daughters and a fine son. No, she decided. It was not wrong to be content; to be grateful for what they had was only saying thank you to God. In her darkest hour she had never given up because she had received the greatest gift of all; and it had always, would always, sustain her in the hardest of times. She had been given love. How had Conn once put it? For a moment her brow furrowed itself in thought, and then a smile lit her features. *Yes! That was it!* With another smile she looked into his eyes, and answered him.

"Aye, we owe the queen a mighty debt, Conn, but how shall we ever repay her for gifting us with a love for all time?"

A NOTE FROM THE AUTHOR

I hope that all of you who have read this book have enjoyed it, and if those of you who have read all the O'Malley Saga to date were a bit confused, allow me to explain.

Conn O'Malley first appeared as a grown man in *All the Sweet Tomorrows*. When he popped out of my head, and onto the pages of my manuscript I thought, now here's a fellow I can do something with in the future, and then put him out of my mind. *This Heart of Mine* was already into the publisher when the mail on *All the Sweet Tomorrows* began pouring in, and a good deal of it said in brief, "WE WANT CONN!"

I knew then that his appearance as a settled husband and father in *This Heart of Mine* was not enough, and I began to ask myself just how such a rogue ended up with a wealthy wife, a large estate, and a houseful of children. *A Love for All Time* is the answer. Conn and Aidan's story, however, could only fit in somewhere within the twelve-year time span between *All the Sweet Tomorrows* and *This Heart o f Mine*. So instead of going forward in time with the O'Malley Saga, we have gone backwards.

If that's all clear to you I hope you will take a minute of your time to sit down, and write to me at *P.O. BOX 765, Southhold, New York 11971* or at BertriceSmall@hotmail.com. I like hearing from my readers, but most important I like your input because it's you for whom I am writing. Good Reading, and love from,

Bertrice Small

*M*y dear Readers:

I know how you have waited for the reissue of *A Love for All Time*, which is Book III in the O'Malley Saga, and I hope you have enjoyed it. In 2002, however, I am going to bring you the first book in a brand-new series. The book is titled *Rosamund*, and the series is called The Friarsgate Inheritance.

The time is the late fifteenth and the early sixteenth centuries. The place is England and the border country of England and Scotland. At the age of three, Rosamund Bolton is orphaned. The heiress to a large land holding and several great flocks of sheep, she is taken into custody by her paternal uncle, Henry Bolton, who marries her off to his own five-year-old son. Two years later the children are infected with measles, and Rosamund's husband perishes. Desperate to keep his control of the Friarsgate inheritance, Henry Bolton makes a second marriage for his niece, this time to an elderly relation on his wife's side who is beholden to him.

But the groom, Hugh Cabot, is not as helpless or as doddering as he would seem. He treats his child bride like the daughter he never had, educating her and teaching her about her heritage and her responsibilities as the owner of Friarsgate. As Rosamund grows up, her uncle is not pleased to see the independence she is exhibiting. He realizes that it is Hugh who is thwarting his plans to eventually control Friarsgate. Hugh, too, has seen Henry Bolton's desire for the great estate. He applies to King Henry VII to take the wardship of his young wife should Hugh die; and indeed he perishes shortly thereafter under mysterious circumstances.

When Henry Bolton moves to take control once more of his niece, he discovers that he cannot. The king brings his new ward to court, putting her into the care of his queen, Elizabeth of York. The queen is grieving for the loss of her son Prince Arthur, but it is in her household that

Rosamund meets Katherine of Aragon and young Prince Henry, who will eventually become Henry VIII. When the queen dies in childbed, Rosamund's wardship is given to the king's mother, Lady Margaret Beaufort, the Countess of Richmond.

Rosamund is married off at the age of fifteen to her third husband, Sir Owain Meredith, a knight in Lady Margaret's household. Although he is some years his wife's senior, a happy marriage ensues. Children are born, and they all live together quite contentedly at Friarsgate until an accident takes Owain from his family. Widowed and distraught, Rosamund accepts the invitation of her old friend Queen Katherine to come to court. Henry VIII is now king and has married his brother's widow.

But upon seeing Rosamund again, Henry is unable to help himself. He seduces her. An affair takes place during the queen's pregnancy. Rosamund falls in love with Henry but, realizing that the affair can go nowhere, decides to leave court. When the queen miscarries a son, Rosamund blames herself because she believes the queen may have learned of Rosamund's betrayal.

Returning home to Friarsgate, Rosamund finds the Scots raiding and stealing her flocks. Furious, she takes up arms and successfully beats them back, attracting in the process the Lord of Claven's Carn. And that's all I'm going to tell you! Please look for *Rosamund* in 2002.

God bless, and much good reading from your most faithful author,

Bertrice Small